OTHER WORLDS

WORLDS

—OF—

ISAAC
ASIMOV

OTHER WORLDS

— OF —

ISAAC ASIMOV

Edited by Martin H. Greenberg

AVENEL BOOKS
New York

Manufactured in the United States of America

Book design by Madge Schultz

Library of Congress Cataloging-in-Publication Data
Asimov, Isaac, 1920–
Other worlds of Isaac Asimov.
1. Science fiction, American. I. Greenberg, Martin
Harry. II. Title.
PS3551.S5A6   1987   813′.54   87-1153
ISBN 0-517-64375-8
h g f e d c b a

ACKNOWLEDGMENTS

The Gods Themselves copyright © 1972 by Isaac Asimov.

"C-Chute" copyright 1951 by Galaxy Publishing Corp., © renewed 1979 by Isaac Asimov, "Hostess" copyright 1951 by World Editions, Inc., © renewed 1979 by Isaac Asimov, "Nightfall" copyright 1941 by Street & Smith Publications, Inc., © renewed 1969 by Isaac Asimov, and "'In a Good Cause—'" copyright 1951 by Henry Holt & Company, Inc., © renewed 1979 by Isaac Asimov. All rights reserved. All from the book *Nightfall and Other Stories*.

"The Martian Way" copyright 1955 by Isaac Asimov, © renewed 1983 by Isaac Asimov, "Sucker Bait" copyright 1954 by Conde Nast Publications, Inc., © renewed 1982 by Isaac Asimov, and "Youth" copyright 1955 by Isaac Asimov, © renewed 1983 by Isaac Asimov. All rights reserved. All from *The Martian Way*.

"Profession" copyright © 1957 by Street & Smith Publications, Inc., © renewed 1985 by Isaac Asimov, and "The Ugly Little Boy" copyright © 1958 by Galaxy Publishing Corp., © renewed 1986 by Isaac Asimov. All rights reserved. Both from *Nine Tomorrows*.

"The Dead Past" copyright © 1956 by Street & Smith Publications, Inc., © renewed 1984 by Isaac Asimov. All rights reserved. From *Earth Is Room Enough*.

"The Key" copyright © 1966 by Mercury Press, Inc. All rights reserved. From *Asimov's Mysteries*.

"Lest We Remember" copyright © 1982 by Davis Publications, Inc. All rights reserved. From *The Winds of Change*.

The End of Eternity copyright 1955 by Issaac Asimov, © renewed 1983 by Isaac Asimov.

All reprinted by permission of Doubleday & Company, Inc.

CONTENTS

THE OTHER TALES

If you look hard you can find trouble anywhere.

For instance, since 1982 I have written two novels concerning the Foundation, adding them to the three "Foundation novels" that were written in the 1940s. I have also written two novels concerning Lije Baley and his robot partner, R. Daneel, adding them to the two "Robot novels" that were written in the 1950s.

The original volumes, written decades ago, were successful on the scale that science fiction success was measured in the '40s and '50s. The new volumes were successful on the much grander scale granted to science fiction in the 1980s. In fact, not to dig my toe into the ground too much, all four of these recent novels were best sellers in the straightforward sense that they appeared on the various best-seller lists.

It doesn't sound like much trouble there, so far.

What's more, it has fallen into my peculiar head to tie the four Robot novels that now exist to all the Robot shorter pieces I have written over the last half century. I am also tying the Foundation novels to the three "Empire novels" I wrote in the 1950s. And to top it off, I am tying the Foundation novels to the Robot novels to create a so-far thirteen-volume, 1,250,000-word, self-consistent history of the next twenty thousand years of humanity, with more volumes planned. And this is proving successful, too—or at least I am receiving a great many approving letters as a result.

It still doesn't sound as though I'm having trouble, does it?

Well, I am.

It so happens that I have written some fiction that is not part of either the Foundation series or the Robot series and, what's more , can't be made part of it no matter how ingeniously I try to squeeze them in.

And the trouble is—ah, *here's* the trouble—that people talk so much about my Foundation series and my Robot series that my nonseries books tend to be forgotten. What makes this troublesome is that I don't *want* them to be forgotten. I *like* them. They happen to be among my favorites.

For instance, one of them is *The End of Eternity*. It is a time-travel novel, and it is one of the very few times that I have immersed myself in that favorite corner of the science fiction field. I think I did a good job at it. I deliberately threw in every single time-travel paradox I could think of and tried to make the novel plausible anyway.

Another one is *The Gods Themselves*, which is actually my favorite science fiction novel. In the first place, I think it's very good—and it won the Hugo *and* the Nebula in 1973, so I'm not alone in my opinion. Second, it was written at a time when I wasn't writing much science fiction and I honestly thought the field had passed me by. The result flabbergasted me, but delighted me even more.

Then, too, I have been in the field now for just about half a century. During the first decade of my career there were no science fiction novels of consequence published, and in the second decade, only a few were. For those twenty years, the major part of my output consisted of stories of sub-novel length intended for the magazines. Many of them had nothing to do with either the Foundation novels or the Robot novels, and I worry about them being forgotten, also.

Let's face it. I don't want *anything* I've written to be forgotten.

Consequently, when Martin H. Greenberg, my wonderful friend and my frequent coeditor of anthologies (in that order of importance, please), suggested that he edit a large book of my other tales—the ones that were not part of my overshadowing series—I all but wept with delight.

"Great, Marty," I said. "The very thing, Marty. Argue some publisher into doing it." (That's his specialty. He can argue almost any publisher into doing almost anything. For that matter, you should see the beautiful girl he argued into marrying him.)

And here is the book. It contains both *The End of Eternity* and *The Gods Themselves* and an even dozen fairly long stories. And since none of the items are connected with any of the others, but stand each by themselves, you have fourteen different worlds (so to speak) that I have created. You're bound to like some of them. With luck, you might even like all of them.

Don't get me wrong. There's a great deal to be said about items that can be built into series. You have vast stretches of words through which you can erect an intricate world and fill in all the details. Each book in a series can support the others, so that the whole series may be more interesting than any of the component books.

Then, too, readers who have enjoyed the series so far wait impatiently for another volume and are prepared, to begin with, to buy it the moment it is published, to read it, and to love it. This inevitably means that each book in the series is going to earn money, even quite a lot of it, and this is *not* something I find unpleasant.

In that case, why can't I force myself to be pleased with my series success and shrug off my non-series items? Well, one does get tired of the same world sometimes. I got tired of the Foundation once and wouldn't write another for thirty-two years, till my publisher began to make wild threats and to wave enormous checks at me. (Enormous by *my* modest standards, anyway.)

There's something exciting about starting from scratch and constructing something you've never quite handled before. And, as a matter of fact, I'm doing it now. My last four novels were Foundation, Robot, Robot, Foundation, but my next one (now in press) is *Fantastic Voyage II*.

I had written *Fantastic Voyage* back in 1966, but that was only the novelization of a screenplay. This new one, *Fantastic Voyage II*, is not exactly a sequel, I assure you. It was what the first book would have been if I hadn't had a movie script to follow and had been working entirely on my own. It was not easy to write, but it was a delight just the same. So if you like this book, try *Fantastic Voyage II*. And, by the way, I don't mind your reading the Foundation and Robot novels also, if you want to.

—*Isaac Asimov*

THE GODS THEMSELVES

A NOVEL

NOTE

The story starts with section 6. This is not a mistake. I have my own subtle reasoning. So just read and, I hope, enjoy.

I
AGAINST STUPIDITY

— 6 —

"NO GOOD!" said Lamont, sharply. "I didn't get anywhere." He had a brooding look about him that went with his deep-set eyes and the slight asymmetry of his long chin. There was a brooding look about him at the best of times, and this was not the best of times. His second formal interview with Hallam had been a greater fiasco than the first.

"Don't be dramatic," said Myron Bronowski, placidly. "You didn't expect to. You told me that." He was tossing peanuts into the air and catching them in his plump-lipped mouth as they came down. He never missed. He was not very tall, not very thin.

"That doesn't make it pleasant. But you're right, it doesn't matter. There are other things I can do and intend to do and, besides that, I depend on you. If you could only find out—"

"Don't finish, Pete. I've heard it all before. All I have to do is decipher the thinking of a non-human intelligence."

"A *better*-than-human intelligence. Those creatures from the para-Universe are *trying* to make themselves understood."

"That may be," sighed Bronowski, "but they're trying to do it through *my* intelligence, which is better than human I sometimes think, but not much. Sometimes, in the dark of the night, I lie awake and wonder if different intelligences can communicate at all; or, if I've had a particularly bad day, whether the phrase 'different intelligences' has meaning at all."

"It does," said Lamont savagely, his hands clearly balling into fists within his lab coat pockets. "It means Hallam and me. It means that fool-hero, Dr. Frederick Hallam and me. We're different intelligences because when I talk to him he doesn't understand. His idiot face gets redder and his eyes bulge and his ears block. I'd say his mind stops functioning, but I lack the proof of any other state from which it might stop."

Bronowski murmured, "What a way to speak of the Father of the Electron Pump."

"That's it. Reputed Father of the Electron Pump. A bastard birth, if ever there was one. His contribution was least in substance. I *know*."

"I know, too. You've told me often," and Bronowski tossed another peanut into the air. He didn't miss.

— 1 —

IT HAD happened thirty years before. Frederick Hallam was a radiochemist, with the print on his doctoral dissertation still wet and with no sign whatever of being a world-shaker.

What began the shaking of the world was the fact that a dusty reagent bottle marked "Tungsten Metal" stood on his desk. It wasn't his; he had never used it. It was a legacy from some dim day when some past inhabitant of the office had wanted tungsten for some long-forgotten reason. It wasn't even really tungsten any more. It consisted of small pellets of what was now heavily layered with oxide—gray and dusty. No use to anyone.

And one day Hallam entered the laboratory (well, it was October 3, 2070, to be exact), got to work, stopped shortly before 10 a.m., stared transfixed at the bottle, and lifted it. It was as dusty as ever, the label as faded, but he called out, "God damn it; who the *hell* has been tampering with this?"

That, at least, was the account of Denison, who overheard the remark and who told it to Lamont a generation later. The official tale of the discovery, as reported in the books, leaves out the phraseology. One gets the impression of a keen-eyed chemist, aware of change and instantly drawing deep-seated deductions.

No so. Hallam had no use for the tungsten; it was of no earthly value to him and any tampering with it could be of no possible importance to him. However, he hated any interference with his desk (as so many do) and he suspected others of possessing keen desires to engage in such interference out of sheer malice.

No one at the time admitted to knowing anything about the matter. Benjamin Allan Denison, who overheard the initial remark, had an office immediately across the corridor and both doors were open. He looked up and met Hallam's accusatory eye.

He didn't particularly like Hallam (no one particularly did) and he had slept badly the night before. He was, as it happened and as he later recalled, rather pleased to have someone on whom to vent his spleen, and Hallam made the perfect candidate.

When Hallam held the bottle up to his face, Denison pulled back with clear distaste. "Why the devil should I be interested in your tungsten?" he demanded. "Why should anyone? If you'll look at the bottle, you'll see that the thing hasn't been opened for twenty years; and if you hadn't put your own grubby paws on it, you would have seen no one had touched it."

Hallam flushed a slow, angry red. He said, tightly, "Listen, Denison, someone has changed the contents. That's not the tungsten."

Denison allowed himself a small, but distinct sniff. "How would *you* know?"

Of such things, petty annoyance and aimless thrusts, is history made.

It would have been an unfortunate remark in any case. Denison's scholastic record, as fresh as Hallam's, was far more impressive and he was the bright-young-man of the department. Hallam knew this and, what was worse, Denison knew it too, and made no secret of it. Denison's "How would *you* know?" with the clear and unmistakable emphasis on the "you," was ample motivation for all that followed. Without it, Hallam would never have become the greatest and most revered scientist in history, to use the exact phrase Denison later used in his interview with Lamont.

Officially, Hallam had come in on that fateful morning, noticed the dusty gray pellets gone—not even the dust on the inside surface remaining—and clear iron-gray metal in their place. Naturally, he investigated—

But place the official version to one side. It was Denison. Had he confined himself to a simple negative, or a shrug, the chances are that Hallam would have asked others, then eventually wearied of the unexplained event, put the bottle to one side, and let subsequent tragedy, whether subtle or drastic (depending on how long the ultimate discovery was delayed), guide the future. In any event, it would not have been Hallam who rode the whirlwind to the heights.

With the "How would *you* know?" cutting him down, however, Hallam could only retort wildly, "I'll *show* you that I know."

And after that, nothing could prevent him from going to extremes. The analysis of the metal in the old container became his number-one priority, and his prime goal was to wipe the haughtiness from Denison's thin-nosed face and the perpetual trace of a sneer from his pale lips.

Denison never forgot that moment for it was his own remark that drove Hallam to the Nobel Prize and himself to oblivion.

He had no way of knowing (or if he knew he would not then have cared) that there was an overwhelming stubbornness in Hallam, the mediocrity's frightened need to safeguard his pride, that would carry the day at that time more than all Denison's native brilliance would have.

Hallam moved at once and directly. He carried his metal to the mass spectrography department. As a radiation chemist it was a natural move. He knew the technicians there, he had worked with them, and he was forceful. He was forceful to such an effect, indeed, that the job was placed ahead of projects of much greater pith and moment.

The mass spectrographer said eventually, "Well, it isn't tungsten."

Hallam's broad and humorless face wrinkled into a harsh smile. "All right. We'll tell that to Bright-boy Denison. I want a report and—"

"But wait awhile, Dr. Hallam. I'm telling you it's not tungsten, but that doesn't mean I know what it is."

"What do you mean you don't know what it is."

"I mean the results are ridiculous." The technician thought a while. "Impossible, actually. The charge-mass ratio is all wrong."

"All wrong in what way?"

"Too high. It just can't be."

"Well, then," said Hallam and, regardless of the motive that was driving him, his next remark set him on the road to the Nobel Prize and, it might even be argued, a deserved one, "get the frequence of its characteristic x-radiation and figure out the charge. Don't just sit around and talk about something being impossible."

It was a troubled technician who came into Hallam's office a few days later. Hallam ignored the trouble on the other's face—he was never sensitive—and said, "Did you find—" He then cast a troubled look of his own at Denison, sitting at the desk in his own lab and shut the door. "Did you find the nuclear charge?"

"Yes, but it's wrong."

"All right, Tracy. Do it over."

"I did it over a dozen times. It's wrong."

"If you made the measurement, that's it. Don't argue with the facts."

Tracy rubbed his ear and said, "I've got to, Doc. If I take the measurements seriously, then what you've given me is plutonium-186."

"Plutonium-186? *Plutonium-186?*"

"The charge is +94. The mass is 186."

"But that's impossible. There's no such isotope. There can't be."

"That's what I'm saying to you. But those are the measurements."

"But a situation like that leaves the nucleus over fifty neutrons short. You can't have plutonium-186. You couldn't squeeze ninety-four protons into one nucleus with only ninety-two neutrons and expect it to hang together for even a trillion-trillionth of a second."

"That's what I'm telling you, Doc," said Tracy, patiently.

And then Hallam stopped to think. It was tungsten he was missing and one of its isotopes, tungsten-186, was stable. Tungsten-186 had 74 protons and 112 neutrons in its nucleus. Could something have turned twenty neutrons into twenty protons? Surely that was impossible.

"Are there any signs of radioactivity?" asked Hallam, groping somehow for a road out of the maze.

"I thought of that," said the technician. "It's stable. Absolutely stable."

"Then it can't be plutonium-186."

"I keep telling you, Doc."

Hallam said, hopelessly, "Well, give me the stuff."

Alone once more, he sat and looked at the bottle in stupefaction. The most nearly stable isotope of plutonium was plutonium-240, where 146 neutrons were needed to make the 94 protons stick together with some semblance of partial stability.

What could he do now? It was beyond him and he was sorry he had started. After all, he had real work begging to be done, and this thing—this mystery—had nothing to do with him. Tracy had made some stupid mistake or the mass spectrometer was out of whack, or—

Well, what of it? Forget the whole thing!

Except that Hallam couldn't do that. Sooner or later, Denison would be bound to stop by and, with that irritating half-smile of his, ask after the tungsten. Then what could Hallam say? Could he say, "It isn't tungsten, just as I told you."

Surely Denison would ask, "Oh, and what is it, then?" and nothing imaginable could have made Hallam expose himself to the kind of derision that would follow any claim that it was plutonium-186. He had to find out what it was, and he had to do it himself. Clearly, he couldn't trust anyone.

So about two weeks later he entered Tracy's laboratory in what can fairly be described as a first-class fury.

"Hey, didn't you tell me that stuff was non-radioactive?"

"What stuff?" said Tracy automatically, before he remembered.

"That stuff you called plutonium-186," said Hallam.

"Oh, well it *was* stable."

"About as stable as your mental state. If you call this non-radioactive, you belong in a plumber's shop."

Tracy frowned. "Okay, Doc. Pass it over and let's try." And then he said, "Beats me! It *is* radioactive. Not much, but it is. I don't see how I could have missed that."

"And how far can I trust your crap about plutonium-186?"

The matter had Hallam by the throat now. The mystery had become so exasperating as to be a personal affront. Whoever had switched bottles, or switched contents, must either have switched again or have devised a metal for the specific purpose of making a fool of him. In either case, he was ready to pull the world apart to solve the matter if he had to—and if he could.

He had his stubbornness, and an intensity that could not easily be brushed aside, and he went straight to G. C. Kantrowitsch, who was then in the final year of his own rather remarkable career. Kantrowitsch's aid was difficult to enlist but, once enlisted, it quickly caught fire.

Two days later, in fact, he was storming into Hallam's office in a blaze of excitement. "Have you been handling this thing with your hands?"

"Not much," said Hallam.

"Well, don't. If you've got any more, don't. It's emitting positrons."

"Oh?"

"The most energetic positrons I've ever seen. . . . And your figures on its radioactivity are too low."

"Too low?"

"Distinctly. And what bothers me is that every measurement I take is just a trifle higher than the one before."

— 6 —
CONTINUED

BRONOWSKI CAME across an apple in the capacious pocket of his jacket and bit into it. "Okay, you've seen Hallam and been kicked out as expected. What next?"

"I haven't quite decided. But whatever it is, it's going to dump him on his fat behind. I saw him once before, you know; years ago, when I first came here; when I thought he was a great man. A great man—He's the greatest villain in the history of science. He's rewritten the history of the Pump, you know, rewritten it here—" Lamont tapped his temple. "He believes his own fantasy and fights for it with a diseased fury. He's a pygmy with only one talent, the ability to convince others he's a giant."

Lamont looked up at Bronowski's wide and placid face, wreathed now in amusement, and forced a laugh. "Oh, well, *that* doesn't do any good, and I've told it all to you before anyway."

"Many times," agreed Bronowski.

"But it just gravels me to have the whole world—"

PETER LAMONT had been two years old when Hallam had picked up his altered tungsten for the first time. When he was twenty-five, he joined Pump Station One with the print on his own doctoral dissertation still fresh and accepted a simultaneous appointment on the Physics faculty of the university.

It was a remarkably satisfactory achievement for the young man. Pump Station One was lacking in the glisten of the later stations but it was the granddaddy of them all, of the entire chain that girdled the planet now even though the entire technology was only a couple of decades old. No major technological advance had ever caught hold so rapidly and so entirely and why not? It meant free energy without limit and without problems. It was the Santa Claus and the Aladdin's lamp of the whole world.

Lamont had taken the job in order to deal with problems of the highest theoretical abstraction and yet he found himself interested in the amazing story of the development of the Electron Pump. It had never been written up in its entirety by someone who truly understood the theoretical principles (in so far as they could be understood) and who had some ability in translating the complexities for the general public. To be sure, Hallam himself had written a number of articles for the popular media, but these did not represent a connected, reasoned history—something Lamont yearned to supply.

He used Hallam's articles to begin with, other reminiscences in published form—the official documents so to speak—carrying them through to Hallam's world-shaking remark, the Great Insight, as it was often called (invariably with capital letters).

Afterward, of course, when Lamont had experienced his disillusionment, he began digging deeper, and the question arose in his mind as to whether Hallam's great remark had really been Hallam's. It had been advanced at the seminar which marked the true beginning of the Electron Pump and yet, as it turned out, it was extraordinarily difficult to get the details of that seminar and quite impossible to get the voice recordings.

Eventually, Lamont began to suspect that the dimness of the footprints left on the sands of time by that seminar was not entirely accidental. Putting several items ingeniously together, it began to seem that there was a reasonable chance that John F. X. McFarland had said something very nearly like the crucial statement Hallam had made—and had done so before Hallam.

He went to see McFarland, who was featured not at all in the official accounts, and who was now doing upper-atmosphere research, with particular reference to the Solar wind. It was not a top-echelon job, but it had its perquisites, and it had more than a little to do with Pump effects. McFarland had clearly avoided suffering the fate of oblivion that had overtaken Denison.

He was polite enough to Lamont and willing to talk on any subject except the events of that seminar. That he simply didn't remember.

Lamont insisted, quoted the evidence he had gathered.

McFarland took out a pipe, filled it, inspected its contents thoroughly, and said, with a queer intentness. "I don't choose to remember, because it doesn't matter; it really doesn't. Suppose I laid claim to having said something. No one would believe it. I would look like an idiot and a megalomaniac one."

"And Hallam would see to it that you were retired?"

"I'm not saying that, but I don't see that it would do me any good. What's the difference, anyway?"

"A matter of historical truth!" said Lamont.

"Oh, bull. The historical truth is that Hallam never let go. He drove everyone into investigating, whether they wanted to or not. Without him, that tungsten would eventually have exploded with I don't know how many casualties. There might never have been another sample, and we might never have had the Pump. Hallam deserves the credit for it, even if he doesn't deserve the credit, and if that doesn't make sense, I can't help it, because history doesn't make sense."

Lamont wasn't satisfied with that, but he had to make it do, for McFarland would simply say no more.

Historical truth!

One piece of historical truth that seemed beyond question was that it was the radioactivity that pulled "Hallam's tungsten" (this is what it was called as a matter of historical custom) into the big time. It didn't matter whether it was or was not tungsten; whether it had or had not been tampered with; even whether it was or was not an impossible isotope. Everything was swallowed up in the amazement of something, anything, which showed a constantly increasing intensity of radioactivity under circumstances that ruled out the existence of any type of radioactive breakdown, in any number of steps, then known.

After a while, Kantrowitsch muttered, "We'd better spread it out. If we keep it in sizable lumps it will vaporize or explode or both and contaminate half the city."

So it was powdered and scattered, and mixed with ordinary tungsten at first and then, when the tungsten grew radioactive in its turn, it was mixed with graphite, which had a lower cross-section to the radiation.

Less than two months after Hallam had noticed the change in the bottle's contents, Kantrowitsch, in a communication to the editor of *Nuclear Reviews,* with Hallam's name appended as co-author, announced the existence of plutonium-186. Tracy's original determination was thus vindicated but his name was not mentioned, either then or later. With that Hallam's tungsten began to take on an epic scale and Denison began to note the changes that ended by making him a non-person.

The existence of plutonium-186 was bad enough. To have been stable at the start and to display a curiously increasing radioactivity was much worse.

A seminar to handle the problem was organized. Kantrowitsch was in the chair, which was an interesting historical note, for it was the last time in the history of the Electron Pump that a major meeting was held in connection with it that was chaired by anyone but Hallem. As a matter of fact, Kantrowitsch died five months later and the only personality with sufficient prestige to keep Hallam in the shade was removed.

The meeting was extraordinarily fruitless until Hallam announced his Great Insight, but in the version as reconstructed by Lamont, the real turning point came during the luncheon break. At that time, McFarland, who is not credited with any remarks in the official records, although he was listed as an attendee, said "You know, what we need is a little bit of fantasy here. Suppose—"

He was speaking to Diderick van Klemens, and Van Klemens reported it sketchily in a kind of personal shorthand in his own notes. Long before Lamont had suceeded in tracking that down, Van Klemens was dead, and though his notes convinced Lamont himself, he had to admit they would not make a convincing story without further corroboration. What's more, there was no way of proving that Hallam had overheard the remark. Lamont would have been willing to bet a fortune that Hallam was within earshot, but that willingness was not satisfactory proof either.

And then, suppose Lamont could prove it. It might hurt Hallam's egregious pride, but it couldn't really shake his position. It would be argued that to McFarland, the remark was only fantasy. It was Hallam who accepted it as something more. It was Hallam who was willing to stand up in front of the group and say it officially and risk the derision that might be his. McFarland would surely never have dreamed of placing himself on official record with his "little bit of fantasy."

Lamont might have counter-argued that McFarland was a well-known nuclear physicist with a reputation to lose, while Hallam was a young radiochemist who could say anything he pleased in nuclear physics and, as an outsider, get away with it.

In any case, this is what Hallam said, according to the official transcript:

"Gentlemen, we are getting nowhere. I am therefore going to make a suggestion, not because it necessarily makes sense, but because it represents less nonsense than anything else I've heard. . . . We are faced with a substance, plutonium-186, that cannot exist at all, let alone as an even momentarily stable substance, if the natural laws of the Universe have any validity at all. It follows, then, that since it does indubitably exist and did exist as a stable substance to begin with, it must have existed, at least to begin with, in a place or a time or under circumstances where the natural laws of the Universe were other than they are. To put it bluntly, the substance we are studying did not originate in our Universe at all, but in another—an alternate Universe—a parallel Universe. Call it what you want.

"Once here—and I don't pretend to know how it got across—it was stable still and I suggest that this was because it carried the laws of its own Universe with it. The fact that it slowly became radioactive and then ever more radioactive may mean that the laws of our own Universe slowly soaked into its substance, if you know what I mean.

"I point out that at the same time that the plutonium-186 appeared, a sample of tungsten, made up of several stable isotopes, including tungsten-186, disappeared. It may have slipped over into the parallel Universe. After all, it is logical to suppose that it is simpler for an exchange of mass to take place than for a one-way transfer to do so. In the parallel Universe, tungsten-186 may be as anomalous as plutonium-186 is here. It may begin as a stable substance and slowly become increasingly radioactive. It may serve as an energy source there just as plutonium-186 would here."

The audience must have been listening with considerable astonishment for there is no record of interruption, at least until the sentence last recorded above, at which time Hallam seemed to have paused to catch his breath and perhaps to wonder at his own temerity.

Someone from the audience (presumably Antoine-Jerome Lapin, though the record is not clear) asked if Professor Hallam were suggesting that an intelligent agent in the para-Universe had deliberately made the exchange in order to obtain an energy source. The expression "para-Universe," inspired apparently as an abbreviation of "parallel-Universe," thus entered the language. This question contained the first recorded use of the expression.

There was a pause and then Hallam, more daring than ever, said—and this was the nub of the Great Insight—''Yes, I think so, and I think that the energy source cannot be made practical unless Universe and para-Universe work together, each at one half of a pump, pushing energy from them to us and from us to them, taking advantage of the difference in the natural laws of the two Universes.''

Hallam had adopted the word ''para-Universe'' and made it his own at this point. Furthermore, he became the first to use the word ''pump'' (since invariably capitalized) in connection with the matter.

There is a tendency in the official account to give the impression that Hallam's suggestion caught fire at once, but it did not. Those who were willing to discuss it at all would commit themselves no farther than to say it was an amusing speculation. Kantrowitsch, in particular, did not say a word. This was crucial to Hallam's career.

Hallam could scarcely carry through the theoretical and practical implications of his own suggestion all by himself. A team was required and it was built up. But none of the team, until it was too late, would associate himself openly with the suggestion. By the time success was unmistakable, the public had grown to think of it as Hallam's and Hallam's alone. It was Hallam, to all the word, and Hallam alone, who had first discovered the substance, who had conceived and transmitted the Great Insight; and it was therefore Hallam who was the Father of the Electron Pump.

Thus, in various laboratories, pellets of tungsten metal were laid out temptingly. In one out of ten the transfer was made and new supplies of plutonium-186 were produced. Other elements were offered as bait and refused. . . . But wherever the plutonium-186 appeared and whoever it was that brought the supply to the central research organization working on the problem, to the public it was an additional quantity of ''Hallam's-tungsten.''

It was Hallam again who presented some aspects of the theory to the public most successfully. To his own surprise (as he later said) he found himself to be a facile writer, and he enjoyed popularizing. Besides success has its own inertia, and the public would accept information on the project from no one but Hallam.

In a since famous article in the *North American Sunday Tele-Times Weekly,* he wrote, ''We cannot say in how many different ways the laws of the para-Universe differ from our own, but we can guess with some assurance that the strong nuclear interaction, which is the strongest known force in our Universe, is even stronger in the para-Universe; perhaps a hundred times stronger. This means that protons are more easily held together against their own electrostatic attraction and that a nucleus requires fewer neutrons to produce stability.

''Plutonium-186, stable in their Universe, contains far too many protons, or too few neutrons, to be stable in ours with its less effective nuclear interaction. The plutonium-186, once in our Universe, begins to radiate positrons, releasing energy as it does so, and with each positron emitted, a proton within a nucleus is converted to a neutron. Eventually, twenty protons per nucleus have been converted to neutrons and plutonium-186 has become tungsten-186, which is stable by the laws of our own Universe. In the process, twenty positrons per nucleus have been eliminated. These meet, combine with, and annihilate twenty electrons, releasing further energy, so that for every plutonium-186 nucleus sent to us, our Universe ends up with twenty fewer electrons.

''Meanwhile, the tungsten-186 that enters the para-Universe is unstable there for the opposite reason. By the laws of the para-Universe it has too many neutrons, or too few protons. The tungsten-186 nuclei begin to emit electrons, releasing energy steadily while doing so, and with each emitted electron a neutron changes to a proton until, in the end, it is plutonium-186 again. With each tungsten-186 nucleus sent into the para-Universe, twenty more electrons are added to it.

"The plutonium/tungsten can make its cycle endlessly back and forth between Universe and para-Universe, yielding energy first in one and then in another, with the net effect being a transfer of twenty electrons from our Universe to theirs per each nucleus cycled. Both sides can gain energy from what is, in effect, an Inter-Universe Electron Pump.

The conversion of this notion into reality and the actual establishment of the Electron Pump as an effective energy source proceeded with amazing speed, and every stage of its success enhanced Hallam's prestige.

— 3 —

LAMONT HAD no reason to doubt the basis of that prestige and it was with a certain hero-worshipfulness (the memory of which embarrassed him later and which he strove—with some success—to eliminate from his mind) that he first applied for a chance to interview Hallam at some length in connection with the history he was planning.

Hallam seemed amenable. In thirty years, his position in public esteem had become so lofty one might wonder why his nose did not bleed. Physically, he had aged impressively, if not gracefully. There was a ponderousness to his body that gave him the appearance of circumstantial weightiness and if his face were gross in its features he seemed able to give them the air of a kind of intellectual repose. He still reddened quickly and the easily bruised nature of his self-esteem was a byword.

Hallam had undergone some quick briefing before Lamont's entrance. He said, "You are Dr. Peter Lamont and you've done good work, I'm told, on para-theory. I recall your paper. On para-fusion, wasn't it?"

"Yes, sir."

"Well, refresh my memory. Tell me about it. Informally, of course, as though you were talking to a layman. After all," and he chuckled here, "in a way, I am a layman. I'm just a radiochemist, you know; and no great theoretician, unless you want to count a few concepts now and then."

Lamont accepted this, at the time, as a straightforward statement, and, indeed, the speech may not have been as obscenely condescending as he later insisted on remembering it to have been. It was typical, though, as Lamont later found out, or at least maintained, of Hallam's method of grasping the essentials of the work done by others. He could talk briskly about the subject thereafter without being overparticular, or particular at all, in assigning credit.

But the younger Lamont of the time was rather flattered, and he began at once with that voluble eagerness one experiences in explaining one's own discoveries. "I can't say I did much, Dr. Hallam. Deducing the laws of nature of the para-Universe—the para-laws—is a tricky business. We have so little to go on.

I started from what little we know and assumed no new departures that we had no evidence for. With a stronger nuclear interaction, it seems obvious that the fusion of small nuclei would take place more readily."

"Para-fusion," said Hallam.

"Yes, sir. The trick was simple to work out what the details might be. The mathematics involved was somewhat subtle but once a few transformations were made, the difficulties tended to melt away. It turns out, for instance, that lithium hydride can be made to undergo catastrophic fusion at temperatures four orders of magnitude lower there than here. It takes fission-bomb temperatures to explode lithium hydride here, but a mere dynamite charge, so to speak, would turn the trick in the para-Universe. Just possibly lithium hydride in the para-Universe could be ignited with a match, but that's not very likely. We've offered them lithium hydride, you know, since fusion power might be natural for them, but they won't touch it."

"Yes, I know that."

"It would clearly be too risky for them; like using nitroglycerine in ton-lots in rocket engines—only worse."

"Very good. And you are also writing a history of the Pump."

"An informal one, sir. When the manuscript is ready I will ask you to read it, if I may, so that I might have the benefit of your intimate knowledge of events. In fact, I would like to take advantage of some of that knowledge right now if you have a little time."

"I can make some. What is it you want to know?" Hallam was smiling. It was the last time he ever smiled in Lamont's presence.

"The development of an effective and practical Pump, Professor Hallam, took place with extraordinary speed," began Lamont, "Once the Pump Project—"

"The Inter-Universe Electron Pump Project," corrected Hallam, still smiling.

"Yes, of course," said Lamont, clearing his throat. "I was merely using the popular name. Once the project started, the engineering details were developed with great rapidity and with little waste motion."

"That is true," said Hallam, with a touch of complacence. "People have tried to tell me that the credit was mine for vigorous and imaginative direction, but I wouldn't care to have you overstress that in your book. The fact is that we had an enormous fund of talent in the project, and I wouldn't want the brilliance of individual members to be dimmed by any exaggeration of my role."

Lamont shook his head with a little annoyance. He found the remark irrelevant. He said, "I don't mean that at all. I mean the intelligence at the other end—the para-men, to use the popular phrase. They started it. We discovered them after the first transfer to plutonium for tungsten; but they discovered us first in order to make the transfer, working on pure theory without the benefit of the hint they gave us. And there's the iron-foil they sent across—"

Hallam's smile had now disappeared, and permanently. He was frowning and he said loudly, "The symbols were never understood. Nothing about them—"

"The geometric figures were understood, sir. I've looked into it and it's quite clear that they were directing the geometry of the Pump. It seems to me that—"

Hallam's chair shoved back with an angry scrape. He said, "Let's not have any of that, young man. We did the work, not they."

"Yes—but isn't it true that they—"

"That they *what?*"

Lamont became aware now of the storm of emotion he had raised, but he couldn't understand its cause. Uncertainly, he said, "That they are more intelligent than we—that they did the real work. Is there any doubt of that, sir?"

Hallam, red-faced, had heaved himself to his feet. "There is every doubt," he shouted. "I will not have mysticism here. There is too much of that. See here, young man," he advanced on the still seated and thoroughly astonished Lamont and shook a thick finger at him, "if your history is going to take the attitude that we were puppets in the hands of the para-men, it will not be published from this institution; or at all, if I have my way. I will not have mankind and its intelligence downgraded and I won't have para-men cast in the role of gods."

Lamont could only leave, a puzzled man, utterly upset at having created harsh feeling where he had wanted only to have good will.

And then he found that his historical sources were suddenly drying up. Those who had been loquacious enough a week earlier now remembered nothing and had no time for further interviews.

Lamont was irritated at first and then a slow anger began to build within him. He looked at what he had from a new viewpoint, and now he began to squeeze and insist where earlier he had merely asked. When he met Hallam at department functions, Hallam frowned and looked through him and Lamont began to look scornful in his turn.

The net result was that Lamont found his prime career as para-theoretician beginning to abort and turned more firmly than ever toward his secondary career as science-historian.

— 6 —
CONTINUED

"*THAT DAMNED FOOL,*" muttered Lamont, reminiscently. "You had to be there, Mike, to see him go into panic at any suggestion that it was the other side that was the moving force. I look back on it and I wonder—how was it possible to meet him, however casually, and not know he would react that way. Just be grateful you never had to work with him."

"I am," said Bronowski, indifferently, "though there are times you're no angel."

"Don't complain. With your sort of work you have no problems."

"Also no interest. Who cares about my sort of work except myself and five others in the world. Maybe six others—if you remember."

Lamont remembered. "Oh, well," he said.

— 4 —

BRONOWSKI'S PLACID exterior never fooled anyone who grew to know him even moderately well. He was sharp and he worried a problem till he had the solution or till he had it in such tatters that he *knew* no solution was possible.

Consider the Etruscan inscriptions on which he had built his reputation. The language had been a living one till the first century A.D., but the cultural imperialism of the Romans had left nothing behind and it had vanished almost completely. What inscriptions survived the carnage of Roman hostility and—worse—indifference were written in Greek letters so that they could be pronounced, but nothing more. Etruscan seemed to have no relationship to any of the surrounding languages; it seemed very archaic, it seemed not even to be Indo-European.

Bronowski therefore passed on to another language that seemed to have no relationship to any of the surrounding languages; that seemed very archaic; that seemed not even to be Indo-European—but which was very much alive and which was spoken in a region not so very far from where once the Etruscans had lived.

What of the Basque language? Bronowski wondered. And he used Basque as his guide. Others had tried this before him and given up. Bronowski did not.

It was hard work, for Basque, an extraordinarily difficult language in itself, was only the loosest of helps. Bronowski found more and more reason, as he went on, to suspect some cultural connection between the inhabitants of early northern Italy and early northern Spain. He could even make out a strong case for a broad swatch of pre-Celts filling western Europe with a language of which Etruscan and Basque were dimly-related survivors. In two thousand years, however, Basque had evolved and had become more than a little contaminated with Spanish. To try, first, to reason out its structure in Roman times and then relate it to Etruscan was an intellectual feat of surpassing difficulty and Bronowski utterly astonished the world's philologists when he triumphed.

The Etruscan translations themselves were marvels of dullness and had no significance whatever; routine funerary inscriptions for the most part. The fact of the translation, however, was stunning and, as it turned out, it proved of the greatest importance to Lamont.

—Not at first. To be perfectly truthful about it, the translations had been a fact for nearly five years before Lamont had as much as heard that there were such people, once, as the Etruscans. But then Bronowski came to the university to give one of the annual Fellowship Lectures and Lamont, who usually shirked the duty of attending which fell on the faculty members, did not shirk this one.

It was not because he recognized its importance or felt any interest in it whatever. It was because he was dating a graduate student in the Department of Romance Languages and it was either that or a music festival he particularly wanted to avoid hearing. The social connection was a feeble one, scarcely satisfactory from Lamont's point of view and only temporary, but it did get him to the talk.

He rather enjoyed it, as it happened. The dim Etruscan civilization entered his consciousness for the first time as a matter of distant interest, and the problem of solving an undeciphered language struck him as fascinating. When young, he had enjoyed solving cryptograms, but had put them away with other childish things in favor of the much grander cryptograms posed by nature, so that he ended in para-theory.

Yet Bronowski's talk took him back to the youthful joys of making slow sense of what seemed a random collection of symbols, and combined it with sufficient difficulty to add great honor to the task. Bronowski was a cryptogrammist on the grandest scale, and it was the description of the steady encroachment of reason upon the unknown that Lamont enjoyed.

All would yet have gone for nothing—the triple coincidence of Bronowski's appearance at campus, Lamont's youthful cryptogrammic enthusiasm, the social pressure of an attractive young lady—were it not for the fact that it was the next day that Lamont saw Hallam and placed himself firmly and, as he eventually found, permanently, in the doghouse.

Within an hour of the conclusion of that interview, Lamont determined to see Bronowski. The issue at hand was the very one that had seemed so obvious to himself and that had so offended Hallam. Because it brought down censure on him, Lamont felt bound to strike back—and in connection with the point of censure specifically. The para-men *were* more intelligent than man. Lamont had believed it before in a casual sort of way as something more obvious than vital. Now it had become vital. It must be proved and the fact of it forced down the throat of Hallam; sideways, if possible, and with all the sharp corners exposed.

Already Lamont found himself so far removed from his so-recent hero worship that he relished the prospect.

Bronowski was still on campus and Lamont tracked him down and insisted on seeing him.

Bronowski was blandly courteous when finally cornered.

Lamont acknowledged the courtesies brusquely, introduced himself with clear impatience, and said, "Dr. Bronowski, I'm delighted to have caught you before you left. I hope that I will persuade you to stay here even longer."

Bronowski said, "That may not be hard. I have been offered a position on the university faculty."

"And you will accept the position?"

"I am considering it. I think I may."

"You must. You will, when you hear what I have to say. Dr. Bronowski, what is there for you to do now that you've solved the Etruscan inscriptions?"

"That is not my only task, young man." (He was five years older than Lamont.) "I'm an archaeologist, and there is more to Etruscan culture than its inscriptions and more to pre-classical Italic culture than the Etruscans."

"But surely nothing as exciting for you, and as challenging, as the Etruscan inscriptions."

"I grant you that."

"So you would welcome something even more exciting, even more challenging, and something a trillion times as significant as those inscriptions."

"What have you in mind, Dr.—Lamont?"

"We have inscriptions that are not part of a dead culture, or part of anything on Earth, or part of anything in the Universe. We have something called para-symbols."

"I've heard of them. For that matter, I've seen them."

"Surely, then, you have the urge to tackle the problem, Dr. Bronowski? You have had the desire to work out what they say?"

"No desire at all, Dr. Lamont, because there's no problem."

Lamont stared at him suspiciously, "You mean you can read them?"

Bronowski shook his head. "You mistake me. I mean I can't possibly read them, nor can anyone else. There's no base. In the case of Earthly languages, however dead, there is always the chance of finding a living language, or a dead language already deciphered, that bears some relationship to it, however faint. Failing that, there is at least the fact that any Earthly language was written by human beings with human ways of thought. That makes a starting point, however feeble. None of this is the case with the para-symbols, so that they constitute a problem that clearly has no solution. An insolubility is not a problem.''

Lamont had kept himself from interrupting only with difficulty, and now he burst out, ''You are wrong, Dr. Bronowski. I don't want to seem to be teaching you your profession but you don't know some of the facts that my own profession has uncovered. We are dealing with para-men, concerning whom we know almost nothing. We don't know what they are like, how they think, what kind of world they live on; almost nothing, however basic and fundamental. So far, you are right.''

''But it's only *almost* nothing that you know, is that it?'' Bronowski did not seem impressed. He took out a package of dried figs from his pocket, opened them and began to eat. He offered it to Lamont, who shook his head.

Lamont said, ''Right. We do know one thing of crucial importance. They are more intelligent than we are. Item one: They can make the exchange across the inter-Universe gap, while we can play only a passive role.''

He interrupted himself here to ask, ''Do you know anything about the Inter-Universe Electron Pump?''

''A little,'' said Bronowski. ''Enough to follow you, Doctor, if you don't get technical.''

Lamont hastened on. ''Item two: They sent us instructions as to how to set up our part of the Pump. We couldn't understand it but we could make out the diagrams just sufficiently well to give us the necessary hints. Item Three: They can somehow sense us. At least they can become aware of our leaving tungsten for them to pick up, for instance. They know where it is and can act upon it. We can do nothing comparable. There are other points but this is enough to show the para-men to be clearly more intelligent than we are.''

Bronowski said, ''I imagine, though, that you are in the minority here. Surely your colleagues don't accept this.''

''They don't. But what makes you come to that conclusion?''

''Because you're clearly wrong, it seems to me.''

''My facts are correct. And since they are, how can I be wrong?''

''You are merely proving the technology of the para-men is more advanced than ours. What has that to do with intelligence? See here''—Bronowski rose to take off his jacket and then sat down in a half-reclining position, the soft rotundity of his body seeming to relax and crease in great comfort as though physical ease helped him think—''about two and a half centuries ago, the American naval commander Matthew Perry led a flotilla into Tokyo harbor. The Japanese, till then isolated, found themselves faced with a technology considerably beyond their own and decided it was unwise to risk resistance. An entire warlike nation of millions was helpless in the face of a few ships from across the sea. Did that prove that Americans were more intelligent than the Japanese were, or merely that Western culture had taken a different turning? Clearly the latter, for within half a century, the Japanese had successfully imitated Western technology and within another half a century were a major industrial power despite the fact that they were disastrously beaten in one of the wars of the time.''

Lamont listened gravely, and said, ''I've thought that, too, Dr. Bronowski, though I didn't know about the Japanese—I wish I had the time to read history. Yet the analogy is wrong. It's more than technical superiority; it's a matter of difference in degree of intelligence.''

''How can you tell, aside from guessing?''

"Because of the mere fact that they sent us directions. They were eager for us to set up our part of the Pump; they *had* to have us do it. They could not physically cross over; even their thin foils of iron on which their messages were incised (the substance most nearly stable in either world) slowly grew too radioactive to keep in one piece, though, of course, not before we had made permanent copies on our own materials." He paused for breath, feeling himself to be too excited, too eager. He mustn't oversell his case.

Bronowski regarded him curiously. "All right, they sent us messages. What are you trying to deduce from that?"

"That they expected us to understand. Could they be such fools as to send us rather intricate messages, in some cases quite lengthy, if they knew we would not understand? . . . If it hadn't been for their diagrams, we would have ended nowhere. Now if they *had* expected us to understand, it could only be because they felt that any creatures like ourselves with a technology roughly as advanced as their own (and they must have been able to estimate that somehow—another point in favor of my belief) must also be roughly as intelligent as themselves and would experience little difficulty in working out something from the symbols."

"That might also be just their naïveté," said Bronowski, unimpressed.

"You mean they think there is only one language, spoken and written, and that another intelligence in another Universe speaks and writes as they do? Come on!"

Bronowski said, "Even if I were to grant your point, what do you want me to do? I've looked at the para-symbols; I suppose every archaeologist and philologist on Earth has. I don't see what I can do; neither, I'm sure, does anyone else. In over twenty years, no progress has been made."

Lamont said, intensely, "What's true is that in twenty years, there has been no desire for progress. The Pump Authority does not want to solve the symbols."

"Why shouldn't they want to?"

"Because of the annoying possibility that communication with the para-men *will* show them to be distinctly more intelligent. Because that would show human beings to be the puppet-partners in connection with the Pump to the hurt of their ego. And, specifically," (and Lamont strove to keep venom out of his voice) "because Hallam would lose the credit for being the Father of the Electron Pump."

"Suppose they *did* want to make progress. What could be done? The will is not the deed, you know."

"They could get the para-men to cooperate. They could send messages to the para-Universe. This has never been done, but it could be. A message on metal foil might be placed under a pellet of tungsten."

"Oh? Are they still looking for new samples of tungsten, even with Pumps in operation?"

"No, but they'll notice the tungsten and they'll assume we're trying to use it to attract their attention. We might even place the message on tungsten foil itself. If they take the message and make any sense of it at all, even the slightest, they'll send back one of their own, incorporating their findings. They might set up an equivalence table of their words and ours, or they might use a mixture of their words and ours. It will be a kind of alternate push, first on their side, then on ours, then on theirs, and so on."

"With their side," said Bronowski, "doing most of the work."

"Yes."

Bronowski shook his head. "No fun in that, is there? It doesn't appeal to me."

Lamont looked at him with flaring anger. "Why not? Don't you think there'll be enough credit in it for you? Not enough fame? What are you, a connoisseur of fame? What kind of fame did you get out of the Etruscan inscriptions, damn it. You beat out five others in the world. Maybe six. With them you're a household word and a success and they hate you. What else? You go about lecturing on the subject before audiences amounting to a few dozen and they forget your name the day after. Is that what you're really after?"

"Don't be dramatic."

"All right. I won't be. I'll get someone else. It may take longer but, as you say, the para-men will do most of the work anyway. If necessary, I'll do it myself."

"Have you been assigned this project?"

"No, I haven't. What of it? Or is that another reason you don't want to get involved. Disciplinary problems? There is no law against attempting translation and I can always place tungsten on my desk. I will not choose to report any messages I get in place of the tungsten and to that extent I will be breaking the research-code. Once the translation is made, who will complain? Would you work with me if I guaranteed your safety and kept your part in it secret? You would lose your fame but you may value your security more. Oh, well," Lamont shrugged. "If I do it myself, there's the advantage of not having to worry about someone else's security."

He rose to go. Both men were angry and bore themselves with that stiff-legged courtesy one assumes when addressing someone who is hostile, but still mannerly. "I presume," said Lamont, "you will at least treat this conversation as confidential."

Bronowski was on his feet, too. "Of that you may be assured," he said coldly, and the two shook hands briefly.

Lamont did not expect to hear from Bronowski again. He then began the process of talking himself into believing it would be better to handle the translation effort on his own.

Two days later, however, Bronowski was at Lamont's laboratory. He said, rather brusquely, "I'm leaving the city now, but I'll be back in September. I'm taking the position here and, if you're still interested, I'll see what I can do about the translation problem you mentioned."

Lamont had barely time for a surprised expression of thanks when Bronowski stalked off, apparently angrier at having given in, than at having resisted.

They became friends in time; and, in time, Lamont learned what had brought Bronowski around. The day after their discussion, Bronowski had had lunch at the Faculty Club with a group of the higher officials of the university, including, of course, the president. Bronowski had announced that he would accept the position and send in a formal letter to that effect in due time and all had expressed gratification.

The president had said, "It will be quite a feather in our cap to have the renowned translator of the Itascan Inscriptions at the university. We are honored."

The malapropism had gone uncorrected, of course, and Bronowski's smile, though strained, did not actually waver. Afterward, the head of the Department of Ancient History explained the president to be more of a Minnesotan than a classical scholar and since Lake Itasca was the point of origin of the mighty Mississippi, the slip of the tongue was a natural one.

But, in combination with Lamont's sneer at the extent of his fame, Bronowski found the expression rankling.

When Lamont finally heard the story, he was amused. "Don't go on," he said. "I've been down that road, too. You said to yourself, 'By God, I'll do something even *that* knot-head will have to get straight.' "

"A little like that," said Bronowski.

— 5 —

A YEAR'S work, however, had netted them very little. Messages had finally come across; messages had come back. Nothing.

"Just guess!" Lamont had said feverishly to Bronowski. "Any wild guess at all. Try it out on them."

"It's exactly what I'm doing, Pete. What are you so jumpy about? I spent twelve years on the Etruscan Inscriptions. Do you expect this job to take less time?"

"Good God, Mike. We can't take twelve years."

"Why not? Look, Pete, it hasn't escaped me that there's been a change in your attitude. You've been impossible this last month or so. I thought we had it clear at the start that this work can't go quickly, and that we've got to be patient. I thought you understood that I had my regular duties at the university, too. Look, I've been asking you this several times, now. Let me ask again. Why are you in such a hurry now?"

"Because I'm in a hurry," said Lamont abruptly. "Because I want to get on with it."

"Congratulations," said Bronowski, dryly, "so do I. Listen, you're not expecting an early death, are you? Your doctor hasn't told you you're hiding a fatal cancer?"

"No, no," groaned Lamont.

"Well, then?"

"Never mind," said Lamont, and he walked away hurriedly.

When he had first tried to get Bronowski to join forces with him, Lamont's grievance had concerned only Hallam's mean-minded obstinancy concerning the suggestion that the para-men were the more intelligent. It was in that respect and that respect only that Lamont was striving for a breakthrough. He intended nothing beyond that—at first.

But in the course of the following months, he had been subjected to endless exasperation. His requests for equipment, for technical assistance, for computer time were delayed; his request for travel funds snubbed; his views at interdepartmental meetings invariably overlooked.

The breaking point came when Henry Garrison, junior to himself in point of service and definitely so in point of ability, received an advisory appointment, rich in prestige, that, by all rights, should have gone to Lamont. It was then that Lamont's resentment built up to the point where merely proving himself right was no longer sufficient. He yearned to smash Hallam, destroy him utterly.

The feeling was reinforced every day, almost every hour, by the unmistakable attitude of everyone else at the Pump Station. Lamont's abrasive personality didn't collect sympathy, but some existed nevertheless.

Garrison himself was embarrassed. He was a quiet-spoken, amiable young man who clearly wanted no trouble and who now stood in the doorway of Lamont's lab with an expression that had more than a small component of apprehension in it.

He said, "Hey, Pete, can I have a few words with you?"

"As many as you like," said Lamont, frowning and avoiding a direct eye-to-eye glance.

Garrison came in and sat down. "Pete," he said, "I can't turn down the appointment but I want you to know I didn't push for it. It came as a surprise."

"Who's asking you to turn it down? I don't give a damn."

"Pete. It's Hallam. If I turned it down, it would go to someone else, not you. What have you done to the old man?"

Lamont rounded on the other. "What do *you* think of Hallam? What kind of man is he, in your opinion?"

Garrison was caught by surprise. He pursed his lips and rubbed his nose. "Well—" he said, and let the sound fade off.

"Great man? Brilliant scientist? Inspiring leader?"

"Well—"

"Let me tell you. The man's a phony! He's fraud! He's got this reputation and this position of his and he's sitting on it in a panic. He knows that I see through him and that's what he has against me."

Garrison gave out a small, uneasy laugh, "You haven't gone up to him and said—"

"No, I haven't said anything directly to him," said Lamont, morosely. "Some day I will. But he can tell. He knows I'm one person he isn't fooling even if I don't say anything."

"But, Pete, where's the point in letting him know it? I don't say *I* think he's the world's greatest, either, but where's the sense in broadcasting it? Butter him up a little. He's got your career in his hands."

"Has he? I've got his reputation in mine. I'm going to show him up. I'm going to strip him."

"How?"

"My business!" muttered Lamont, who at the moment had not the slightest idea as to how.

"But that's ridiculous," said Garrison. "You can't win. He'll just destroy you. Even if he isn't an Einstein or an Oppenheimer really, he's more than either to the world in general. He *is* the Father of the Electron Pump to Earth's two-billion population and nothing you can possibly do will affect them as long as the Electron Pump is the key to human paradise. While that's true, Hallam can't be touched and you're crazy if you think he can. What the hell, Pete, tell him he's great and eat crow. Don't be another Denison!"

"I tell you what, Henry," said Lamont, in sudden fury. "Why not mind your own business?"

Garrison rose suddenly and left without a word. Lamont had made another enemy; or, at least, lost another friend. The price, however, was right, he finally decided, for one remark of Garrison had set the ball rolling in another direction.

Garrison had said, in essence, ". . . as long as the Electron Pump is the key to human paradise . . . Hallam can't be touched."

With that clanging in his mind, Lamont for the first time turned his attention away from Hallam and placed it on the Electron Pump.

Was the Electron Pump the key to human paradise? Or was there, by Heaven, a catch?

Everything in history had had a catch. What was the catch to the Electron Pump?

Lamont knew enough of the history of para-theory to know that the matter of "a catch" had not gone unexplored. When it was first announced that the basic over-all change in the Electron Pump was the Pumping of electrons from the Universe to the para-Universe, there had not been wanting those who said immediately, "But what will happen when all the electrons have been Pumped?"

This was easily answered. At the largest reasonable rate of Pumping, the electron supply would last for at least a trillion trillion years—and the entire Universe, together, presumably, with the para-Universe, wouldn't last a tiny fraction of that time.

The next objection was more sophisticated. There was no possibility of Pumping *all* the electrons across. As the electrons were Pumped, the para-Universe would gain a net negative charge, and the Universe a net positive charge. With each year, as this difference in charge grew, it would become more difficult to Pump further electrons against the force of the opposed charge-difference. It was, of course neutral atoms that were actually Pumped but the distortion of the orbital electrons in the process created an effective charge which increased immensely with the radioactive changes that followed.

If the charge-concentration remained at the points of Pumping, the effect on the orbit-distorted atoms being Pumped would stop the entire process almost at once, but of course, there was diffusion to take into account. The charge-concentration diffused outward over the Earth, and the effect on the Pumping process had been calculated with that in mind.

The increased positive charge of the Earth generally forced the positively charged Solar wind to avoid the planet at a greater distance, and the magnetosphere was enlarged. Thanks to the work of McFarland (the real originator of the Great Insight according to Lamont) it could be shown that a definite equilibrium point was reached as the Solar wind swept away more and more of the accumulating positive particles that were repelled from Earth's surface and driven higher into the exosphere. With each increase in Pumping intensity; with each additional Pumping Station constructed, the next positive charge on Earth increased slightly, and the magnetosphere expanded by a few miles. The change, however, was minor, and the positive charge was, in the end, swept away by the Solar wind and spread through the outer reaches of the Solar system.

Even so—even allowing for the most rapid possible diffusion of the charge, the time would come when the local charge-difference between Universe and para-Universe at the points of Pumping would grow large enough to end the process, and that would be a small fraction of the time it would take really to use up all the electrons; roughly, a trillion-trillionth of the time.

But that still meant the Pumping would remain possible for a trillion years. Only a *single* trillion years, but that was enough; it would suffice. A trillion years was far longer than man would last, or the Solar system either. And if man somehow did last that long (or some creature that was man's successor and supplanter) then no doubt something would be devised to correct the situation. A great deal could be done in a trillion years.

Lamont had to agree to that.

But then he thought of something else, another line of thought that he well remembered Hallam himself had dealt with in one of the articles he had written for popular consumption. With some distaste, he dug out the article. It was important to see what Hallam had said before he carried the matter further.

The article said, in part, "Because of the ever-present gravitational force, we have come to associate the phrase 'downhill' with the kind of inevitable change we can use to produce energy of the sort we can change into useful work. It is the water running downhill that, in past centuries, turned wheels which in turn powered machinery such as pumps and generators. But what happens when all the water has run downhill?

"There can then be no further work possible till the water has been returned uphill—and that takes work. In fact, it takes more work to force the water uphill than we can collect by then allowing it to flow downhill. We work at an energy-loss. Fortunately, the Sun does the work for us. It evaporates the oceans so that water vapor climbs high in the atmosphere, forms clouds, and eventually falls again as rain or snow. This soaks the ground at all levels, fills the springs and streams, and keeps the water forever running downhill.

"But not quite forever. The Sun can raise the water vapor, but only because, in a nuclear sense, it is running downhill, too. It is running downhill at rate immensely greater than any Earthly river can manage, and when all of it has run downhill there will be nothing we know of to pull it uphill again.

"All sources of energy in our Universe run down. We can't help that. Everything is downhill in just one direction, and we can force a temporary uphill, backward, only by taking advantage of some greater downhill in the vicinity. If we want useful energy forever, we need a road that is downhill both ways. That is a paradox in our Universe; it stands to reason that whatever is downhill one way is uphill going back.

"But need we confine ourselves to our Universe alone? Think of the para-Universe. It has roads, too, that are downhill in one direction and uphill in the other. Those roads, however, don't fit in with our roads. It is possible to take a road from the para-Universe to our Universe that is downhill, but which, when we follow it back from the Universe to the para-Universe, is downhill again—because the Universes have different laws of behavior.

"The Electron Pump takes advantage of a road that is downhill both ways. The Electron Pump—"

Lamont looked back at the title of the piece again. It was "The Road that is Downhill Both Ways."

He began thinking. The concept was, of course, a familiar one to him, as was its thermodynamic consequences. But why not examine the assumptions? That had to be the weak point in any theory. What if the assumptions, assumed to be right by definition, were wrong? What would be the consequences if one started with other assumptions? Contradictory ones?

He started blindly but within a month he had that feeling that every scientist recognizes—the endless click-click as unexpected pieces fall into place, as annoying anomalies become anomalous no more— It was the feel of Truth.

It was from that moment on that he began to put additional pressure on Bronowski.

And one day he said, "I'm going to see Hallam again."

Bronowski's eyebrows lifted. "What for?"

"To have him turn me down."

"Yes, that's about your speed, Pete. You're unhappy if your troubles die down a bit."

"You don't understand. It's important to have him refuse to listen to me. I can't have it said afterward that I by-passed him; that he was ignorant of it."

"Of what? Of the translation of the para-symbols? There isn't any yet. Don't jump the gun, Pete."

"No, no, not that," and he would say no more.

Hallam did not make it easy for Lamont; it was some weeks before he could find time to see the younger man. Nor did Lamont intend to make it easy for Hallam. He stalked in with every invisible bristle on edge and sharply pointed. Hallam waited for him frozen-faced, with sullen eyes.

Hallan said abruptly, "What's this crisis you're talking about?"

"Something's turned up, sir," said Lamont, tonelessly, "inspired by one of your articles."

"Oh?" Then, quickly, "Which one?"

" 'The Road that is Downhill Both Ways.' The one you programmed for *Teen-age Life*, sir."

"And what about it?"

"I believe the Electron Pump is not downhill both ways, if I may use your metaphor, which is not, as it happens, a completely accurate way of describing the Second Law of Thermodynamics."

Hallam frowned. "What have you got in mind?"

"I can explain it best, sir, by setting up the Field Equations for the two Universes, sir, and demonstrating an interaction that till now has not been considered—unfortunately so, in my opinion."

With that, Lamont moved directly to the thixo-board and quickly fingered the equations, talking rapidly as he did so.

Lamont knew that Hallam would be humiliated and irritated by such a procedure since he would not follow the mathematics. Lamont counted on that.

Hallam growled, "See here, young man, I have no time now to engage in a full discussion of any aspect of para-theory. You send me a complete report and, for now, if you have some brief statement as to what you're getting at, you may make it."

Lamont walked away from the thixo-board, with an unmistakable expression of contempt on his face. He said, "All right. The Second Law of Thermodynamics describes a process that inevitably chops off extremes. Water doesn't run downhill; what really happens is that extremes of gravitational potential are equalized. Water will just as easily bubble uphill if trapped underground. You can get work out of the juxtaposition of two different temperature levels, but the end result is that the temperature is equalized at an intermediate level; the hot body cools down and the cold body warms up. Both cooling and warming are equal aspects of the Second Law and, under, the proper circumstances, equally spontaneous."

"Don't teach me elementary thermodynamics, young man. What is it you want? I have very little time."

Lamont said, with no change of expression, no sense of being hurried. "Work is obtained out of the Electron Pump by an equalization of extremes. In this case, the extremes are the physical laws of the two Universes. The conditions that make those laws possible, whatever those conditions may be, are being bled from one Universe into the other and the end result of the entire process will be two Universes in which the laws of nature will be identical—and intermediate as compared with the situation now. Since this will produce uncertain but undoubtedly large changes in this Universe, it would seem that serious consideration must be given to stopping the Pumps and shutting down the whole operation permanently.''

It was at this point that Lamont expected Hallam to explode, cutting off any chance of further explanation. Hallam did not fail that expectation. He sprang out of his chair, which fell over. He kicked the chair away and took the two steps that separated him from Lamont.

Warily, Lamont pushed his own chair hastily backward and stood up.

"You idiot!" shouted Hallam, almost stammering in his anger. "Don't you suppose everyone at the station understands about the equalization of natural law. Are you wasting my time telling me something I knew when you were learning to read? Get out of here, and any time you want to offer me your resignation, consider it accepted.''

Lamont left, having obtained exactly what he wanted, and yet he felt himself to be furious over Hallam's treatment of him.

— 6 —
CONTINUED

''*ANYWAY,'' SAID* Lamont, "it clears the ground. I've tried to tell him. He wouldn't listen. So I take the next step.''

"And what is that?" said Bronowski.

"I'm going to see Senator Burt.''

"You mean the head of the Committee on Technology and the Environment?''

"The same. You've heard of him, then.''

"Who hasn't. But where's the point, Pete. What have you got that would interest him? It's not the translation. Pete, I'm asking you once again. What have you got on your mind?''

"I can't explain. You don't know para-theory.''

"Does Senator Burt?''

"More than you, I think.''

Bronowski pointed his finger. "Pete, let's not kid around. Maybe I know things you don't. We can't work together if we work against each other. Either I'm a member of this little two-man corporation or I'm not. You tell me what's on your mind, and I'll tell you something in exchange. Otherwise, let's stop this altogether.''

Lamont shrugged. "All right. If you want it, I'll give it to you. Now that I've got it past Hallam, maybe it's just as well. The point is that the Electron Pump is transferring natural law. In the para-Universe, the strong interaction is a hundred times stronger than it is here, which means that nuclear fission is much more likely here than there, and nuclear fusion is much more likely there than here. If the Electron Pump keeps on long enough, there will be a final equilibrium in which the strong nuclear interaction will be equally strong in both

Universes, and be at a figure about ten times what it is here now and one-tenth what it is there now.''

"Didn't anyone know this?"

"Oh, sure, everyone knew it. It was obvious almost from the start. Even Hallam can see it. That's what got the bastard so excited. I started telling him this in detail as though I didn't think he had ever heard it before and he blew up.''

"But what's the point then? Is there danger in the interaction becoming intermediate?"

"Of course. What do you think?"

"I don't think anything. When will it become intermediate?"

"At the present rate, 10^{30} years or so.''

"How long is that?"

"Long enough for a trillion trillion Universes like this one to be born, live, grow old, and die, one after the other.''

"Oh blazes, Pete. What odds does it make then?''

"Because to reach that figure,'' said Lamont, slowly and carefully, ''which is the official one, certain assumptions were made which I think were wrong. And if certain other assumptions are made, which I think are *right* we're in trouble *now*.''

"What kind of trouble?"

"Suppose the Earth turned into a whiff of gas in a period of about five minutes. Would you consider that trouble?''

"Because of the Pumping?"

"Because of the Pumping!''

"And how about the world of the para-men? Would they be in danger, too?''

"I'm sure of it. A different danger, but danger.''

Bronowski stood up and began pacing. He wore his brown hair thick and long in what had once been called a Buster Brown. Now he was clutching at it. He said, "If the para-men are more intelligent than we are, would they be running the Pump? Surely they would know it was dangerous, before we did.''

"I've thought of that,'' said Lamont. "What I guess is that they've started Pumping for the first time and they, like us, got the process started for the apparent good it would bring and worried about consequences later.''

"But you say you know the consequences now. Would they be slower than you were?''

"It depends on if and when they look for those consequences. The Pump is too attractive to try to spoil. I wouldn't have looked myself if I hadn't— But what's on *your* mind, Mike?''

Bronowski stopped his pacing, looked full at Lamont, and said, "I think we've got something.''

Lamont looked at him wildly, then leaped forward to seize the other's sleeve. "With the para-symbols? Tell me, Mike?''

"It was while you were with Hallam. While you were actually with Hallam. I haven't known exactly what to do about it, because I wasn't sure what was going on. And now—''

"And now?"

"I'm still not sure. One of the foils came through, with four symbols . . .''

"Oh?"

". . . in the Latin alphabet. And it can be pronounced.''

"What?"

"Here it is."

Bronowski produced the foil with the air of a conjurer. Incised on it, quite different from the delicate and intricate spirals and differential glistenings, of the para-symbols, were four broad, childlike letters: F-E-E-R.

"What do you suppose that means?" asked Lamont, blankly.

"So far all I've been able to think of is that it's F-E-A-R misspelled."

"Is that why you were cross-examining me? You thought someone on the other side was experiencing fear?"

"And I thought it might have some connection with your own obviously increasing excitement over the last month. Frankly, Pete, I didn't like being kept in the dark."

"Okay. Now let's not jump to conclusions. You're the one with experience with fragmentary messages. Wouldn't you say that the para-men were beginning to experience fear concerning the Electron Pump?"

"Not necessarily at all," said Bronowski. "I don't know how much they can sense of this Universe. If they can sense the tungsten we lay out for them; if they can sense our presence; perhaps they are sensing our state of mind. Perhaps they are trying to reassure us; telling us there is no reason to fear."

"Then why don't they say N-O F-E-E-R."

"Because they don't know our language that well yet."

"Hmm. Then I can't take it to Burt."

"I wouldn't. It's ambiguous. In fact, I wouldn't go to Burt till we get something more from the other side. Who knows what they're trying to say."

"No, I can't wait, Mike. I *know* I'm right, and we have no time."

"All right, but if you see Burt you'll be burning your bridges. Your colleagues will never forgive you. Have you thought of talking to the physicists here? You can't put pressure on Hallam on your own, but a whole group of you—"

Lamont shook his head vigorously, "Not at all. The men at this station survive by virtue of their jellyfish quality. There isn't one who would stand against him. Trying to rally the others to put pressure on Hallam would be like asking strands of cooked spaghetti to come to attention."

Bronowski's soft face looked unwontedly grim. "You may be right."

"I know I'm right," said Lamont, just as grimly.

— 7 —

IT HAD taken time to pin the senator down; time that Lamont had resented losing; the more so since nothing further in Latin letters had come from the para-men. No message of any kind, though Bronowski had sent across half a dozen, each with a carefully selected combination of para-symbols and each incorporating both F-E-E-R and F-E-A-R.

Lamont wasn't sure of the significance of the half-dozen variations but Bronowski had seemed hopeful.

Yet nothing had happened and now Lamont was at last in to see Burt.

The senator was thin-faced, sharp-eyed, and elderly. He had been the head of the Committee on Technology and the Environment for a generation. He took his job seriously and had proved that a dozen times.

He fiddled, now, with the old-fashioned necktie that he affected (and that had become his trademark) and said, "I can only give you half an hour, son." He looked at his wristwatch.

Lamont was not worried. He expected to interest Senator Burt enough to make him forget about time limits. Nor did he attempt to begin at the beginning; his intentions here were quite different from those in connection with Hallam.

He said, "I won't bother with the mathematics, Senator, but I will assume you realize that through Pumping, the natural laws of the two Universes are being mixed."

"Stirred together," said the senator, calmly, "with equilibrium coming in about 10^{30} years. Is that the figure?" His eyebrows in repose arched up and then down, giving his lined face a permanent air of surprise.

"It is," said Lamont, "but it is arrived at by assuming that the alien laws seeping into our Universe and theirs spread outward from the point of entry at the speed of light. That is just an assumption and I believe it to be wrong."

"Why?"

"The only measured rate of mixing is within the plutonium-186 sent into this Universe. That rate of mixing is extremely slow at first, presumably because matter is dense, and increases with time. If the plutonium is mixed with less dense matter, the rate of mixing increases more rapidly. From a few measurements of this sort is has been calculated that the permeation rate would increase to the speed of light in a vacuum. It would take some time for the alien laws to work their way into the atmosphere, far less time to work their way to the top of the atmosphere and then off through space in every direction at 300,000 kilometers per second, thinning into harmlessness in no time."

Lamont paused a moment to consider how best to go on, and the senator picked it up at once. "However—" he urged, with the manner of a man not willing to waste time.

"It's a convenient assumption that seems to make sense and seems to make no trouble, but what if it is not matter that offers resistance to the permeation of the alien laws, but the basic fabric of the Universe itself."

"What is the basic fabric?"

"I can't put it in words. There is a mathematical expression which I think represents it, but I can't put it into words. The basic fabric of the Universe is that which dictates the laws of nature. It is the basic fabric of our Universe that makes it necessary for energy to be conserved. It is the basic fabric of the para-Universe, with a weave, so to speak, somewhat different from ours, that makes their nuclear interaction a hundred times stronger than ours."

"And so?"

"If it is the basic fabric that is being penetrated, sir, then the presence of matter, dense or not, can have only a secondary influence. The rate of penetration is greater in a vacuum than in dense mass, but not very much greater. The rate of penetration in outer space may be great in Earthly terms but it is only a small fraction of the speed of light."

"Which means?"

"That the alien fabric is not dissipating as quickly as we think, but is piling up, so to speak, within the Solar system to a much greater concentration then we have been assuming."

"I see," said the senator, nodding his head. "And how long then will it be before the space within the Solar system is brought to equilibrium? Less than 10^{30} years, I imagine."

"Far less, sir. Less than 10^{10} years, I think. Perhaps fifty billion years, give or take a couple of billion."

"Not much in comparison, but enough, eh? No immediate cause for alarm, eh?"

"But I'm afraid that *is* immediate cause for alarm, sir. Damage will be done long before equilibrium is reached. Because of the Pumping, the strong nuclear interaction is growing steadily stronger in our Universe at every moment."

"Enough stronger to measure?"

"Perhaps not, sir."

"Not even after twenty years of pumping?"

"Perhaps not, sir."

"Then why worry?"

"Because, sir, upon the strength of the strong nuclear interaction rests the rate at which hydrogen fuses to helium in the core of the Sun. If the interaction strengthens even unnoticeably, the rate of hydrogen fusion in the Sun will increase markedly. The Sun maintains the balance between radiation and gravitation with great delicacy and to upset that balance in favor of radiation, as we are now doing—"

"Yes?"

"—will cause an enormous explosion. Under our laws of nature, it is impossible for a star as small as the Sun to become a supernova. Under the altered laws, it may not be. I doubt that we would have warning. The Sun would build up to a vast explosion and in eight minutes after that you and I will be dead and the Earth will quickly vaporize into an expanding puff of vapor."

"And nothing can be done?"

"If it is too late to avoid upsetting the equilibrium, nothing. If it is not yet too late, then we must stop Pumping."

The senator cleared his throat. "Before I agreed to see you, young man, I inquired as to your background since you were not personally known to me. Among those I queried was Dr. Hallam. You know him, I suppose?"

"Yes sir." A corner of Lamont's mouth twitched but his voice held even. "I know him well."

"He tells me," said the senator, glancing at a paper on his desk, "that you are a troublemaking idiot of doubtful sanity and he demands that I refuse to see you."

Lamont said in a voice he strove to keep calm. "Are those his words, sir?"

"His exact words."

"Then why have you agreed to see me, sir?"

"Ordinarily, if I received something like this from Hallam, I wouldn't have seen you. My time is valuable and heaven knows I see more troublemaking idiots of doubtful sanity than bears thinking of, even among those who come to me with the highest recommendations. In this one case, though, I didn't like Hallam's 'demand.' You don't make demands of a senator and Hallam had better learn that."

"Then you will help me, sir?"

"Help you do what?"

"Why—arrange to have the Pumping halted."

"That? Not at all. Quite impossible."

"Why not?" demanded Lamont. "You are the head of the Committee on Technology and the Environment and it is precisely your task to stop the Pumping, or any technological procedure that threatens irreversible harm to the environment. There can be no greater, no more irreversible harm than threatened by Pumping."

"Certainly. Certainly. *If* you are right. But it seems that what your story amounts to is that your assumptions are different from the accepted ones. Who's to say which set of assumptions is right?"

"Sir, the structure I have built explains several things that are left doubtful in the accepted view."

"Well, then, your colleagues ought to accept your modification and in that case you would scarcely have to come to me, I imagine."

"Sir, my colleagues will not believe. Their self-interest stands in the way."

"As your self-interest stands in the way of your believing you might be wrong. . . . Young man, my powers, on paper, are enormous, but I can only succeed when the public is willing to let me. Let me give you a lesson in practical politics."

He looked at his wristwatch, leaned back and smiled. His offer was not characteristic of him, but an editorial in the *Terrestrial Post* that morning had referred to him as "a consummate politician, the most skilled in the International Congress" and the glow that that had roused within him still lingered.

"It is a mistake," he said, "to suppose that the public wants the environment protected or their lives saved and that they will be grateful to any idealist who will fight for such ends. What the public wants is their own individual comfort. We know that well enough from our experience in the environmental crisis of the twentieth century. Once it was well known that cigarettes increased the incidence of lung cancer, the obvious remedy was to stop smoking, but the desired remedy was a cigarette that did not encourage cancer. When it became clear that the internal-combustion engine was polluting the atmosphere dangerously, the obvious remedy was to abandon such engines, and the desired remedy was to develop non-polluting engines.

"Now then, young man, don't ask me to stop the Pumping. The economy and comfort of the entire planet depend on it. Tell me, instead, how to keep the Pumping from exploding the Sun."

Lamont said, "There is no way, Senator. We are dealing with something here that is so basic, we can't play with it. We must stop it."

"Ah, and you can suggest only that we go back to matters as they were before Pumping."

"We must."

"In that case, you will need hard and fast proof that you are right."

"The best proof," said Lamont, stiffly, "is to have the Sun explode. I suppose you don't want me to go that far."

"Not necessary, perhaps. Why can't you get Hallam to back you up?"

"Because he is a small man who finds himself the Father of the Electron Pump. How can he admit his child will destroy the Earth?"

"I see what you mean, but he is still the Father of the Electron Pump to the whole world, and only his word would carry sufficient weight in this respect."

Lamont shook his head. "He would never give in. He would rather see the Sun explode."

The senator said, "Then force his hand. You have a theory but a theory by itself is meaningless. Surely there must be some way of checking it. The rate of radioactive breakdown of, say, uranium depends on the interactions within the nucleus. Has that rate been changing in a fashion predicted by your theory but not the standard one?"

Again, Lamont shook his head. "Ordinary radioactivity depends on the weak nuclear interaction, and unfortunately, experiments of that sort will yield only borderline evidence. By the time it showed sufficiently to be unmistakable, it would be too late."

"What else, then?"

"There are pion interactions of a specific sort that might yield unmistakable data now. Better still there are quark-quark combinations that have produced puzzling results recently that I am sure I can explain—"

"Well, there you are."

"Yes, but in order to obtain that data, I must make use of a large proton synchrotron on the Moon, sir, and no time on that will be available for years—I've checked—unless someone pulls the strings."

"Meaning me?"

"Meaning you, Senator."

"Not as long as Dr. Hallam says this about you, son." And Senator Burt's gnarled finger tapped the piece of paper in front of him. "I can't get out on that limb."

"But the existence of the world—"

"*Prove* it."

"Override Hallam and I'll prove it."

"Prove it and I'll override Hallam."

Lamont drew a deep breath, "Senator! Suppose there's just a trifling chance I'm right. Isn't even that trifling chance worth fighting for? It means everything; all mankind, the entire planet—"

"You want me to fight the good fight? I'd like to. There's a certain drama in going down in a good cause. Any decent politician is masochistic enough to dream now and then of going down in flames while the angels sing. But, Dr. Lamont, to do that one has to have a fighting chance. One has to have something to fight for that may—just *may*—win out. If I back you, I'll accomplish nothing with your word alone against the infinite desirability of Pumping. Shall I demand every man give up the personal comfort and affluence he has learned to get used to, thanks to the Pump, just because one man cries 'Doom' while all the other scientists stand against him, and the revered Hallam calls him an idiot? No, sir, I will not go down in flames for *nothing*."

Lamont said, "Then just help me find my proof. You needn't appear in the open if you fear—"

"I'm not afraid," said Burt, abruptly. "I'm being practical. Dr. Lamont, your half-hour is rather more than gone."

Lamont stared for a moment in frustration but Burt's expression was a clearly intransigent one now. Lamont left.

Senator Burt did not see his next visitor immediately. Minutes passed while he stared uneasily at the closed door and fiddled with his tie. Could the man have been right? Could he have had the smallest chance of being right?

He had to admit it would be a pleasure to trip Hallam and push his face into the mud and sit on him till he choked—but it would not happen. Hallam was untouchable. He had had only one set-to with Hallam nearly ten years ago. He had been right, dead right, and Hallam had been egregiously wrong, and events had since proved it to be so. And yet, at the time, Burt had been humiliated and he had almost lost reelection as result.

Burt shook his head in admonition to himself. He might risk reelection in a good cause, but he could not risk humiliation again. He signaled for the next visitor and his face was calm and bland as he rose to greet him.

— 8 —

IF BY this time, Lamont had still felt he had something to lose, professionally, he might have hesitated. Joshua Chen was universally unpopular and anyone who dealt with him was in bad odor at once with almost every corner of the Establishment. Chen was a one-man revolutionary whose single voice could somehow always be heard because he brought to his causes an intensity that was utterly overpowering, and because he had built an organization that was more tightly knit than any ordinary political team in the world (as more than one politician was ready to swear.)

He had been one of the important factors accounting for the speed with which the Pump had taken over the planet's energy needs. The Pump's virtues were clear and obvious, as clear as non-pollution and as obvious as for-free, yet there might have been a longer rear-guard fight by those who wanted nuclear energy, not because it was better but because it had been the friend of their childhood.

Yet when Chen beat his drum, the world listened just a little harder.

Now he sat there, his broad cheekbones and round face bearing evidence of the approximately three-quarter admixture of Chinese ancestry.

He said, "Let me get this straight. You're speaking only for yourself?"

"Yes," said Lamont tightly. "Hallam doesn't back me. In fact, Hallam says I'm mad. Do you have to have Hallam's approval before you can move?"

"I need no one's approval," said Chen with predictable arrogance, then he lapsed back into thoughtful consideration. "You say the para-men are farther advanced in technology than we are?"

Lamont had gone that far in the direction of compromise. He had avoided saying they were more intelligent. "Farther advanced in technology" was less offensive, but just as true.

"That is clear," said Lamont, "if only because they can send material across the gap between the Universes and we can't."

"Then why did they start the Pump if it is dangerous? Why are they continuing it?"

Lamont was learning to compromise in more than one direction. He might have said that Chen was not the first to ask this, but it would have sounded condescending, perhaps impatient, and he chose not to do so.

Lamont said, "They were anxious to get started with something that was so apparently desirable as a source of energy, just as we were. I have reason to think they're as disturbed about it now as I am."

"That's still your word. You have no definite evidence about their state of mind."

"None that I can present at this moment."

"Then it's not enough."

"Can we afford to risk—"

"It's not enough, Professor. There's no evidence. I haven't built my reputation by shooting down targets at random. My missiles have sped true to the mark every time because I knew what I was doing."

"But when I get the evidence—"

"Then I'll back you. If the evidence satisfies me, I assure you neither Hallam nor the Congress will be able to resist the tide. So get the evidence and come see me again."

"But by then it will be too late."

Chen shrugged. "Perhaps. Much more likely, you will find that you were wrong and no evidence is to be had."

"I'm *not* wrong." Lamont took a deep breath, and said in a confidential tone, "Mr. Chen. There are very likely trillions upon trillions of inhabited planets in the Universe, and among them there may be billions with intelligent life and highly developed technologies. The same is probably true of the para-Universe. It must be that in the history of the two Universes there have been many pairs of worlds that came into contact and began Pumping. There may be dozens or even hundreds of Pumps scattered across junction points of the two Universes."

"Pure speculation. But if so?"

"Then it may be that in dozens or hundreds of cases, the mixture of natural law advanced locally to an extent sufficient to explode a planet's Sun. The effect might have spread outward. The energy of a supernova added to the changing natural law may have set off explosions among neighboring stars, which in turn set off others. In time perhaps an entire core of a galaxy or of a galactic arm will explode."

"But that is only imagination, of course."

"Is it? There are hundreds of quasars in the Universe; tiny bodies the size of several Solar systems but shining with the light of a hundred full-size ordinary galaxies."

"You're telling me that the quasars are what are left of Pumping planets."

"I'm suggesting that. In the century and a half since they were discovered, astronomers have *still* failed to account for their sources of energy. Nothing in this Universe will account for it; nothing. Doesn't it follow then—"

"What about the para-Universe? Is it full of quasars, too?"

"I wouldn't think so. Conditions are different there. Para-theory makes it seem quite definite that fusion takes place much more easily over there, so the stars must be considerably smaller than ours on the average. It would take a much smaller supply of easily-fusing hydrogen to produce the energy our Sun does. A supply as large as that of our Sun would explode spontaneously. If our laws permeate the para-Universe, hydrogen becomes a little more difficult to fuse; the para-stars begin to cool down."

"Well, that's not so bad," said Chen. "They can use Pumping to supply themselves with the necessary energy. By your speculations, they're in fine shape."

"Not really," said Lamont. Until now, he hadn't thought the para-situation through. "Once our end explodes, the Pumping stops. They can't keep it up without us, and that means they'll face a cooling star without Pump-energy. They might be worse off than we; we'd go out in a painless flash while their agony would be long-drawn-out."

"You have a good imagination, Professor," said Chen, "but I'm not buying it. I don't see any chance of giving up Pumping on nothing more than your imagination. Do you know what the Pump means to mankind? It's not just the free, clean, and copious energy. Look beyond that. What it means is that mankind no longer has to work for a living. It means that for the first time in history, mankind can turn its collective brains to the more important problem of developing its true potential.

"For instance, not all the medical advances of two and a half centuries have succeeded in advancing man's full life-span much past a hundred years. We've been told by gerontologists over and over that there is nothing, in theory, to stand in the way of human immortality, but so far not enough attention has been concentrated on this."

Lamont said angrily, "Immortality! You're talking pipe dreams."

"Perhaps you're a judge of pipe dreams, Professor," said Chen, "but I intend to see that research into immortality begins. It won't begin if Pumping ends. Then we are back to expensive energy, scarce energy, dirty energy. Earth's two billions will have to go back to work for a living and the pipe dream of immortality will remain a pipe dream."

"It will anyway. No one is going to be immortal. No one is even going to live out a normal lifetime."

"Ah, but that is your theory, only."

Lamont weighed the possibilities and decided to gamble. "Mr. Chen, a while ago I said I was not willing to explain my knowledge of the state of mind of the para-men. Well, let met try. We have been receiving messages."

"Yes, but can you interpret them?"

"We received an English word."

Chen frowned slightly. He suddenly put his hands in his pockets, stretched his short legs before him, and leaned back in his chair. "And what was the English word?"

"Fear!" Lamont did not feel it necessary to mention the misspelling.

"Fear," repeated Chen; "and what do you think it means?"

"Isn't it clear that they're afraid of the Pumping phenomenon?"

"Not at all. If they were afraid, they would stop it. I think they're afraid, all right, but they're afraid that our side will stop it. You've gotten across your intention to them and if we stop it, as you want us to do, they've got to stop also. You said yourself they can't continue without us; it's a two-ended proposition. I don't blame them for being afraid."

Lamont sat silent.

"I see," said Chen, "that you haven't thought of that. Well, then, we'll push for immortality. I think that will be the more popular cause."

"Oh, popular causes," said Lamont slowly. "I didn't understand what you found important. How old are you, Mr. Chen?"

For a moment, Chen blinked rapidly, then he turned away. He left the room, walking rapidly, with his hands clenched.

Lamont looked up his biography later. Chen was sixty and his father had died at sixty-two. But it didn't matter.

"*YOU DON'T* look as though you had any luck at all," said Bronowski.

Lamont was sitting in his laboratory, staring at the toes of his shoes and noting idly that they seemed unusually scuffed. He shook his head. "No."

"Even the great Chen failed you?"

"He would do nothing. He wants evidence, too. They all want evidence, but anything you offer them is rejected. What they really want is their damned Pump, or their reputation, or their place in history. Chen wants immortality."

"What do you want, Pete?" asked Bronowski, softly.

"Mankind's safety," said Lamont. He looked at the other's quizzical eyes. "You don't believe me?"

"Oh, I believe you. But what do you *really* want?"

"Well, then, by God," and Lamont brought his hand down flat on the desk before him in a loud slap. "I want to be *right,* and that I have, for I *am* right."

"You are sure?"

"I am sure! And there's nothing I am worried about, because I intend to win. You know when I left Chen, I came near to despising myself."

"You?"

"Yes, I. Why not? I kept thinking: At every turn Hallam stops me. As long as Hallam refutes me everyone has an excuse not to believe me. While Hallam stands like a rock against me, I must fail. Why, then, didn't I work through him; why didn't I butter him up, indeed; why didn't I maneuver him into supporting me instead of needling him into fighting me?"

"Do you think you could have?"

"No, never. But in my despair, I thought—well, all sorts of things. That I might go to the Moon, perhaps. Of course, when I first turned him aginst me there was as yet no question of Earth's doom, but I took care to make it worse when that question arose. But, as you imply, nothing could have turned him against the Pump."

"But you don't seem to despise yourself now."

"No. Because my conversation with Chen brought a dividend. It showed me I was wasting time."

"So it would seem."

"Yes, but needlessly. It is not here on Earth that the solution lies. I told Chen that our Sun might blow up but that the para-Sun would not, yet that would not save the para-men, for when our Sun blew up and our end of the Pump halted, so would theirs. They cannot continue without us, do you see?"

"Yes, of course I see."

"Then why don't we think in the reverse. We can't continue without them. In which case, who cares whether we stop the Pump or not. Let's get the para-men to stop."

"Ah, but will they?"

"They said F-E-E-R. And it means they're afraid. Chen said they feared us; they feared we would stop the Pump; but I don't believe that for a moment. *They're* afraid. I sat silent when Chen make his suggestion. He thought he had me. He was quite wrong. I was only thinking at that moment that we had to get the para-men to stop. And we've got to. Mike, I abandon everything, except you. You're the hope of the world. Get through to them somehow."

Bronowski laughed, and there was almost a childlike glee in it. "Pete," he said, "You're a genius."

"Aha. You've noticed."

"No, I mean it. You guess what I want to say before I can say it. I've been sending message after message, using their symbols in a way that I guessed might signify the Pump and using our word as well. And I did my best to gather what information I've scrabbled together over many months to use their symbols in a way signifying disapproval, and using an English word again. I had no idea whether I was getting through or was a mile off base and from the fact that I never got an answer, I had little hope."

"You didn't tell me that's what you were trying to do."

"Well, this part of the problem is my baby. You take your sweet time explaining para-theory to me."

"So what happened?"

"So yesterday, I sent off exactly two words, our language. I scrawled: P-U-M-P B-A-D."

"And?"

"And this morning I picked up a return message at last and it was simple enough, and straightforward, too. It went Y-E-S P-U-M-P B-A-D B-A-D B-A-D. Here look at it."

Lamont's hand trembled as it held the foil. "There's no mistaking that, is there? That's confirmation, isn't it?"

"It seems so to me. Who will you take this to?"

"To no one," said Lamont decisively. "I argue no more. They will tell me I faked the message and there's no point in sitting still for that. Let the para-men stop the Pump and it will stop on our side too and nothing we can do unilaterally will start it up again. The entire Station will then be on fire to prove that I was right and the Pump is dangerous."

"How do you figure that?"

"Because that would be the only way they could keep themselves from being torn apart by a mob demanding the Pump and infuriated at not getting it. . . . Don't you think so?"

"Well, maybe. But one thing bothers me."

"What's that?"

"If the para-men are so convinced that the Pump is dangerous, why haven't they stopped it already? I took occasion to check awhile ago and the Pump is working swimmingly."

Lamont frowned. "Perhaps they don't want a unilateral stoppage. They consider us their partners and they want a mutual agreement to stop. Don't you suppose that might be so?"

"It might. But it might also be that communication is less than perfect; that they don't quite understand the significance of the words, B-A-D. From what I said to them via their symbols, which I might well have twisted utterly, they may think that B-A-D means what we consider G-O-O-D."

"Oh, no."

"Well, that's your hope, but there's no pay-off on hopes."

"Mike, just keep on sending messages. Use as many of the words they use as possible and keep ringing the changes. You're the expert and it's in your hands. Eventually, they'll know enough words to say something clear and unmistakable and then we'll explain that we're willing to have the Pump stopped."

"We lack the authority to make any such statement."

"Yes, but they won't know, and in the end we'll be mankind's heroes."

"Even if they execute us first?"

"Even so. . . . It's in your hands, Mike, and I'm sure it won't take much longer."

— 10 —

AND YET it did. Two weeks passed without another message and the strain grew worse.

Bronowski showed it. The momentary lightness of heart had dissipated, and he entered Lamont's laboratory in glum silence.

They stared at each other and finally Bronowski said, "It's all over the place that you've received your show-cause."

Lamont had clearly not shaved that morning. His laboratory had a forlorn look about it, a not-quite-definable packing-up look. He shrugged. "So what? It doesn't bother me. What does bother me is that *Physical Reviews* rejected my paper."

"You said you were expecting that."

"Yes, but I thought they might give me reasons. They might point out what they thought were fallacies, errors, unwarranted assumptions. Something I could argue about."

"And they didn't?"

"Not a word. Their referees did not consider the paper suitable for publication. Quote, unquote. They just won't touch it. . . . It's really disheartening, the universal stupidity. I think that I wouldn't grieve at mankind's suicide through sheer evilness of heart, or through mere recklessness. There's something so damned undignified at going to destruction through sheer thickheaded stupidity. What's the use of being men if that's how you have to die."

"Stupidity," muttered Bronowski.

"What else do you call it? And they want me to show-cause why I ought not to be fired for the great crime of being right."

"Everyone seems to know that you consulted Chen."

"Yes!" Lamont put his fingers to the bridge of his nose and wearily rubbed his eyes. "I apparently got him annoyed enough to go to Hallam with tales, and now the accusation is that I have been trying to sabotage the Pump project by unwarranted and unsupported fright tactics in an unprofessional manner and that this makes me unsuitable for employment on the Station."

"They can prove that easily, Pete."

"I suppose they can. It doesn't matter."

"What are you going to do?"

"Nothing," said Lamont indignantly. "Let them do their worst. I'll rely on red tape. Every step of this thing will take weeks, months, and meanwhile you keep working. We'll hear from the para-men yet."

Bronowski looked miserable. "Pete, suppose we don't. Maybe it's time you think about this again."

Lamont looked up sharply. "What are you talking about?"

"Tell them you're wrong. Do penance. Beat your breast. Give up."

"Never! By God, Mike, we're playing a game in which the stakes are all the world and every living creature on it."

"Yes, but what's that to you? You're not married. You have no children. I know your father is dead. You never mention your mother or any siblings. I doubt if there is any human being on earth to whom you are emotionally attached as an individual. So go your way and the hell with it all."

"And you?"

"I'll do the same. I'm divorced, and I have no children. I have a young lady with whom I'm close and that relationship will continue while it can. Live! Enjoy!"

"And tomorrow!"

"Will take care of itself. Death when it comes will be quick."

"I can't live with that philosophy. . . . Mike, *Mike!* What is all this? Are you trying to tell me that we're not going to get through? Are you giving up on the para-men?"

Bronowski looked away. He said, "Pete, I did get an answer. Last night. I thought I'd wait for today and think about it, but why think? . . . Here it is."

Lamont's eyes were staring questions. He took the foil and looked at it. There was no punctuation:

PUMP NOT STOP NOT STOP WE NOT STOP PUMP WE NOT HEAR DANGER NOT HEAR NOT HEAR YOU STOP PLEASE STOP YOU STOP SO WE STOP PLEASE YOU STOP DANGER DANGER DANGER STOP STOP YOU STOP PUMP

"By God," muttered Bronowski, "they sound desperate."

Lamont was still staring. He said nothing.

Bronowski said, "I gather that somewhere on the other side is someone like you—a para-Lamont. And he can't get his para-Hallams to stop, either. And while we're begging them to save us, he's begging us to save them."

Lamont said, "But if we show this—"

"They'll say you're lying; that it's a hoax you've concocted to save your psychotically-conceived nightmare."

"They can say that of me, maybe; but they can't say it of you. You'll back me, Mike. You'll testify that you received this and how."

Bronowski reddened. "What good would that do? They'll say that somewhere in the para-Universe there is a nut like yourself and that two crackpots got together. They'll say that the message proves that the constituted authorities in the para-Universe are convinced there's no danger."

"Mike, fight this through with me."

"There's no use, Pete. You said yourself, stupidity! Those para-men may be more advanced than ourselves, even more intelligent, as you insist, but it's plain to see that they're just as stupid as we are and that ends it. Schiller pointed that out and I believe him."

"Who?"

"Schiller. A German dramatist of three centuries ago. In a play about Joan of Arc, he said, 'Against stupidity, the gods themselves contend in vain.' I'm no god and I'll contend no longer. Let it go, Pete, and go your way. Maybe the world will last our time and, if not, there's nothing that can be done anyway. I'm sorry, Pete. You fought the good fight, but you lost, and I'm through."

He was gone and Lamont was alone. He sat in his chair, fingers aimlessly drumming, drumming. Somewhere in the Sun, protons were clinging together with just a trifling additional avidity and with each moment that avidity grew and at some moment the delicate balance would break down . . .

"And no one on Earth will live to know I was right." cried out Lamont, and blinked and blinked to keep back the tears.

II
...THE GODS THEMSELVES...

— 1a —

DUA DID not have much trouble leaving the others. She always expected trouble, but somehow it never came. Never real trouble.

But then why should it? Odeen objected in his lofty way. "Stay put," he would say. "You know you annoy Tritt." He never spoke of his own annoyance; Rationals didn't grow annoyed over trifles. Still, he hovered over Tritt almost as persistently as Tritt hovered over the children.

But then Odeen always let her have her way if she were persistent enough, and would even intercede with Tritt. Sometimes he even admitted he was proud of her ability, of her independence. . . . He wasn't a bad left-ling, she thought with absent-minded affection.

Tritt was harder to handle and he had a sour way of looking at her when she was—well, when she was as she wished to be. But then right-lings were like that. He was a right-ling to her, but a Parental to the children and the latter took precedence always. . . . Which was good because she could always count on one child or the other taking him away just as things grew uncomfortable.

Still, Dua didn't mind Tritt very much. Except for melting, she tended to ignore him. Odeen was another thing. He had been exciting at first; just his presence had made her outlines shimmer and fade. And the fact that he was a Rational made him all the more exciting somehow. She didn't understand her reaction to that; it was part of her queerness. She had grown used to her queerness—almost.

Dua sighed.

When she was a child, when she still thought of herself as an individual, a single being, and not as part of a triad, she was much more aware of that queerness. She was much more made aware of it by the others. As little a thing as the surface at evening—

She had loved that surface at evening. The other Emotionals had called it cold and gloomy and had quivered and coalesced when she described it for them. They were ready enough to emerge in the warmth of midday and stretch and feed, but that was exactly what made the midday dull. She didn't like to be around the twittering lot of them.

She had to eat, of course, but she liked it much better in the evening when there was very little food, but everything was dim, deep red, and she was alone. Of course, she described it as colder and more wistful than it was when she talked to the others in order to watch them grow hard-edged as they imagined the chill—or as hard-edged as young Emotionals could. After a while, they would whisper and laugh at her—and leave her alone.

The small sun was at the horizon now, with the secret ruddiness that she alone was there to see. She spread herself out laterally and thickened dorso-ventrally, absorbing the traces of thin warmth. She munched at it idly, savoring the slightly sour, substanceless taste of the long wave lengths. (She had never met another Emotional who would admit to liking it. But she could never explain that she associated it with freedom; freedom from the others, when she could be alone.)

Even now the loneliness, the chill, and the deep, deep red, brought back those old days before the triad; and even more, quite sharply, her own Parental, who would come lumbering after her, forever fearful that she would hurt herself.

He had been carefully devoted to her, as Parentals always were; to their little-mids more than to the other two, as always. It had annoyed her and she would dream of the day when he would leave her. Parentals always did eventually; and how she had missed him, when one day, he finally did.

He had come to tell her, just as carefully as he could, despite the difficulty Parentals had in putting their feelings into words. She had run from him that day; not in malice; not because she suspected what he had to tell her; but only out of joy. She had managed to find a special place at midday and had gorged herself in unexpected isolation and had been filled with a queer, itching sensation that demanded motion and activity. She had slithered over the rocks and had let her edges overlap theirs. It was something she knew to be a grossly improper action for anyone but a baby and yet it was something at once exciting and soothing.

And her Parental caught her at last and had stood before her, silent for a long time, making his eyes small and dense as though to stop every bit of light reflected from her; to see as much as he could of her; and for as long as possible.

At first, she just stared back with the confused thought that he had seen her rub through the rocks and was ashamed of her. But she caught no shame-aura and finally she said, very subdued, "What is it, Daddy?"

"Why, Dua, it's the time. I've been expecting it. Surely you have."

"What time?" Now that it was here, Dua stubbornly would not let herself know. If she refused to know, there would be nothing to know. (She never quite got out of that habit. Odeen said all Emotionals were like that, in the lofty voice he used sometimes when he was particularly overcome with the importance of being a Rational.)

Her Parental had said, "I must pass on. I will not be with you any more." Then he just stood and looked at her, and she couldn't say anything.

He said, "You will tell the others."

"Why?" Dua turned away rebelliously, her outlines vague and growing vaguer, trying to dissipate. She *wanted* to dissipate altogether and of course she couldn't. After a while, it hurt and cramped and she hardened again. Her Parental didn't even bother to scold her and tell her that it would be shameful if anyone saw her stretched out so.

She said, "*They* won't care," and immediately felt sorrowful that her Parental would be hurt at that. *He* still called them "little-left" and "little-right," but little-left was all involved with his studies and little-right kept talking about forming a triad. Dua was the only one of the three who still felt—Well, she was the youngest. Emotionals always were and with them it was different.

Her Parental only said, "You will tell them anyway." And they stood looking at each other.

She didn't want to tell them. They weren't close any more. It had been different when they were all little. They could hardly tell themselves apart in those days; left-brother from right-brother from mid-sister. They were all wispy and would tangle with each other and roll through each other and hide in the walls.

No one ever minded that when they were little; none of the grown-ups. But then the brothers grew thick and sober and drew away. And when she complained to her Parental, he would only say gently, "You are too old to thin, Dua."

She tried not to listen, but left-brother kept drawing away and would say, "Don't snuggle; I have no time for you." And right-brother began to stay quite hard all the time and became glum and silent. She didn't understand it quite then and Daddy had not been able to make it clear. He would say every once in a while as though it were a lesson he had once learned—"Lefts are Rationals, Dua. Rights are Parentals. They grow up their own way."

She didn't like their way. They were no longer children and she still was, so she flocked with the other Emotionals. They all had the same complaints about their brothers. They all talked of coming triads. They all spread in the Sun and fed. They all grew more and more the same and every day the same things were said.

And she grew to detest them and went off by herself whenever she could, so that they left and called her "Left-Em." (It had been a long time now since she had heard that call, but she never thought of that phrase without remembering perfectly the thin ragged voices that kept it up after her with a kind of half-wit persistence because they knew it hurt.)

But her Parental retained his interest in her even when it must have seemed to him that everyone else laughed at her. He tried, in his clumsy way, to shield her from the others. He followed her to the surface sometimes, even though he hated it himself, in order to make sure she was safe.

She came upon him once, talking to a Hard One. It was hard for a Parental to talk to a Hard One; even though she was quite young, she knew that much. Hard Ones talked only to Rationals.

She was quite frightened and she wisped away but not before she had heard her Parental say, "I take good care of her, Hard-sir."

Could the Hard One have inquired about her? About her queerness, perhaps. But her Parental had not been apologetic. Even to the Hard One, he had spoken of his concern for her. Dua felt an obscure pride.

But now he was leaving and suddenly all the independence that Dua had been looking forward to lost its fine shape and hardened into the the pointed crag of loneliness. She said, "But *why* must you pass on?"

"I *must,* little mid-dear."

He must. She knew that. Everyone, sooner or later, must. The day would come when she would have to sigh and say, "I must."

"But what makes you know when you have to pass on? If you can choose your time, why don't you choose a different time and stay longer?"

He said, "Your left-father has decided. The triad must do as he says."

"*Why* must you do what he says?" She hardly ever saw her left-father or her mid-mother. They didn't count any more. Only her right-father, her Parental, her Daddy, who stood there squat and flat-surfaced. He wasn't all smooth-curved like a Rational or shuddery uneven like an Emotional, and she could always tell what he was going to say. Almost always.

She was sure he would say, "I can't explain to a little Emotional."

He said it.

Dua said in a burst of woe, "I'll miss you. I know you think I pay you no attention, and that I don't like you for always telling me not to do things. But I would rather not like you for telling me not to do things, than not have you around to tell me not to do things."

And Daddy just stood there. There was no way he could handle an outburst like that except to come closer and pinch out a hand. It cost him a visible effort, but he held it out trembling and its outlines were ever so slightly soft.

Dua said, "Oh, Daddy," and let her own hand flow about it so that his looked misty and shimmery through her substance; but she was careful not to touch it for that would have embarrassed him so.

Then he withdrew it and left her hand enclosing nothing and he said, "Remember the Hard Ones, Dua. They will help you. I—I will go now."

He went and she never saw him again.

Now she sat there, remembering in the sunset, and rebelliously aware that pretty soon Tritt would grow petulant over her absence and nag Odeen.

And then Odeen might lecture her on her duties.

She didn't care.

— 1b —

ODEEN WAS moderately aware that Dua was off on the surface. Without really thinking about it, he could judge her direction and even something of her distance. If he had stopped to think of it, he might have felt displeasure, for this inter-awareness sense had been steadily deadening for a long time now and, without really being certain why, he had a sense of gathering fulfillment about it. It was the way things were supposed to be; the sign of the continuing development of the body with age.

Tritt's inter-awareness sense did not decrease, but it shifted more and more toward the children. That was clearly the line of useful development, but then the role of the Parental was a simple one, in a manner of speaking, however important. The Rational was far more complex and Odeen took a bleak satisfaction in that thought.

Of course, it was Dua who was the real puzzle. She was so unlike all the other Emotionals. That puzzled and frustrated Tritt and reduced him to even more pronounced inarticulacy. It puzzled and frustrated Odeen at times, too, but he was also aware of Dua's infinite capacity to induce satisfaction with life and it did not seem likely that one was independent of the other. The occasional exasperation she produced was a small price to pay for the intense happiness.

And maybe Dua's odd way of life was part of what ought to be, too. The Hard Ones seemed interested in her and ordinarily they paid attention to Rationals. He felt pride in that; so much the better for the triad that even the Emotional was worth attention.

Things were as they were supposed to be. That was bedrock, and it was what he wanted most to feel, right down to the end. Someday he would even know when it was time to pass on and then he would want to. The Hard Ones assured him of that, as they assured all Rationals, but they also told him that it was his own inner consciousness that would mark the time unmistakably, and not any advice from outside.

"When *you* tell yourself," Losten had told him—in the clear, careful way in which a Hard One always talked to a Soft One, as though the Hard One were laboring to make himself understood, "that you know why you must pass on, then you will pass on, and your triad will pass on with you."

And Odeen had said, "I cannot say I wish to pass on now, Hard-sir. There is so much to learn."

"Of course, left-dear. You feel this because you are not yet ready."

Odeen thought: How could I ever feel ready when I would never feel there wasn't much to learn?

But he didn't say so. He was quite certain the time would come and he would then understand.

He looked down at himself, almost forgetting and thrusting out an eye to do so—there were always some childish impulses in even the most adult of the most Rational. He didn't have to, of course. He would sense quite well with his eye solidly in place, and he found himself satisfactorily solid; nice, sharp outline, smooth and curved into gracefully conjoined ovoids.

His body lacked the strangely attractive shimmer of Dua, and the comforting stockiness of Tritt. He loved them both, but he would not change his own body for either. And, of course, his own mind. He would never say so, of course, for he would not want to hurt their feelings, but he never ceased being thankful that he did not have Tritt's limited understanding or (even more) Dua's erratic one. He supposed they didn't mind for they knew nothing else.

He grew distantly aware of Dua again, and deliberately dulled the sense. At the moment, he felt no need for her. It was not that he wanted her less, but merely that he had increasing drives elsewhere. It was part of the growing maturity of a Rational to find more and more satisfaction in the exercise of a mind that could only be practiced alone, and with the Hard Ones.

He grew constantly more accustomed to the Hard Ones; constantly more attached to them. He felt that was right and proper, too, for he was a Rational and in a way the Hard Ones were super-Rationals. (He had once said that to Losten, the friendliest of the Hard Ones and, it seemed to Odeen in some vague way the youngest. Losten had radiated amusement but had said nothing. And that meant he had not denied it, however.)

Odeen's earliest memories were filled with Hard Ones. His Parental more and more concentrated his attention on the last child, the baby-Emotional. That was only natural. Tritt would do it, too, when the last child came, if it ever did. (Odeen had picked up that last qualification from Tritt, who used it constantly as a reproach to Dua.)

But so much the better. With his Parental busy so much of the time, Odeen could begin his education that much the earlier. He was losing his baby ways and he had learned a great deal even before he met Tritt.

That meeting, though, was surely something he would never forget. It might as well have been yesterday as more than half a lifetime ago. He had seen Parentals of his own generation, of course; young ones who, long before they incubated the children that made true Parentals of them, showed few signs of the stolidity to come. As a child he had played with his own right-brother and was scarcely aware of any intellectual difference between them (though, looking back on those days, he recognized that it was there, even then).

He knew also, vaguely, the role of a Parental in a triad. Even as child, he had whispered tales of melting.

When Tritt first appeared, when Odeen saw him first, everything changed. For the first time in his life, Odeen left an inner warmth and began to think that there was something he wanted that was utterly divorced from thought. Even now, he could remember the sense of embarrassment that had accompanied this.

Tritt was not embarrassed, of course. Parentals, were never embarrassed about the activities of the triad, and Emotionals were almost never embarrassed. Only Rationals had that problem.

"Too much thinking," a Hard One had said when Odeen had discussed the problem with him and that left Odeen dissatisfied. In what way could thinking be "too much"?

Tritt was young when they first met, of course. He was still so childish as to be uncertain in his blockishness so that his reaction to the meeting was embarrassingly clear. He grew almost translucent along his edges.

Odeen said, hesitantly, "I haven't seen you before, have I, right-fellow?" Tritt said, "I have never been here. I have been brought here."

They both knew exactly what had happened to them. The meeting had been arranged because someone (some Parental, Odeen had thought at the time, but later he knew it was some Hard One) thought they would suit each other, and the thought was correct.

There was no intellectual rapport between the two, of course. How could there be when Odeen wanted to learn with an intensity that superseded anything but the existence of the triad itself, and Tritt lacked the very concept of learning? What Tritt had to know, he knew beyond either learning or unlearning.

Odeen, out of the excitement of finding out about the world and its Sun; about the history and mechanism of life; about all the abouts in the Universe; sometimes (in those early days together) found himself spilling over to Tritt.

Tritt listened placidly, clearly understanding nothing, but content to be listening; while Odeen, transmitting nothing, was as clearly content to be lecturing.

It was Tritt who made the first move, driven by his special needs. Odeen was chattering about what he had learned that day after the brief midday meal. (Their thicker substance absorbed food so rapidly, they were satisfied with a simple walk in the Sun, while Emotionals basked for hours at a time, curling and thinning as though deliberately to lengthen the task.)

Odeen, who always ignored the Emotionals, was quite happy to be talking. Tritt, who stared wordlessly at them, day after day, was now visibly restless.

Abruptly, he came close to Odeen, formed an appendage so hastily as to clash most disagreeably on the other's form-sense. He placed in upon a portion of Odeen's upper ovoid where as light shimmer was allowing a welcome draft of warm air as dessert. Tritt's appendage thinned with a visible effort and sank into the superfices of Odeen's skin before the latter darted away, horribly embarrassed.

Odeen had done such things as a baby, of course, but never since his adolescence. "Don't do that, Tritt," he said sharply.

Tritt's appendage remained out, groping a little. "I want to."

Odeen held himself as compactly as he could, striving to harden the surface to bar entry. "I *don't* want to."

"Why not?" said Tritt, urgently. "There's nothing wrong."

Odeen said the first thing that came into his mind. "It hurt." (It didn't really. Not physically. But the Hard Ones always avoided the touch of the Soft Ones. A careless interpenetration hurt *them,* but they were constructed differently from Soft Ones, completely differently.)

Tritt was not fooled by that. His instinct could not possibly mislead him in this respect. He said, "It didn't hurt."

"Well, it isn't right this way. We need an Emotional."

And Tritt could only say, stubbornly, "I want to, anyway."

It was bound to continue happening, and Odeen was bound to give in. He always did; it was something that was sure to happen even to the most self-conscious Rational. As the old saying had it: Everyone either admitted doing it or lied about it.

Tritt was at him at each meeting after that; if not with an appendage, then rim to rim. And finally Odeen, seduced by the pleasure of it, began to help and tried to shine. He was better at that than Tritt was. Poor Tritt, infinitely more eager, huffed and strained, and could achieve only the barest shimmer here and there, patchily and raggedly.

Odeen, however, could turn translucent all over his surface, and fought down his embarrassment in order to let himself flow against Tritt. There was skin-deep penetration and Odeen could feel the pulsing of Tritt's hard surface under the skin. There was enjoyment, riddled with guilt.

Tritt, as often as not, was tired and vaguely angry when it was all over.

Odeen said, "Now, Tritt, I've told you we need an Emotional to do this properly. You can't be angry at something that just *is.*"

And Tritt said, "Let's get an Emotional."

Let's get an Emotinal! Tritt's simple drives never led him to anything but direct action. Odeen was not sure he could explain the complexities of life to the other. "It's not that easy, right-ling," he began gently.

Tritt said abruptly. "The Hard Ones can do it. You're friendly with them. Ask them."

Odeen was horrified. "I *can't* ask. The time," he continued, unconsciously falling into his lecturing voice, "is not yet come, or I would certainly know it. Until such time—"

Tritt was not listening. he said, *"I'll* ask."

"No," said Odeen, horrified. "You stay out of it. I tell you it's not time. I have an education to worry about. It's very easy to be a Parental and not to have to know anything but—"

He was sorry the instant he had said it and it was a lie anyway. He just didn't want to do anything at all that might offend the Hard Ones and impede his useful relationship with them. Tritt, however, showed no signs of minding and it occurred to Odeen that the other saw no point or merit in knowing anything he did not already know and would not consider the statement of the fact an insult.

The problem of the Emotional kept coming up, though. Occasionally, they tried interpenetration. In fact, the impulse grew stronger with time. It was never truly satisfying though it had its pleasure and each time Tritt would demand an Emotional. Each time, Odeen threw himself deeper into his studies, almost as a defense against the problem.

Yet at times, he was almost tempted to speak to Losten about it.

Losten was the Hard One he knew best; the one who took the greatest personal interest in him. There was a deadly sameness about the Hard Ones, because they did not change; they never changed; their form was fixed. Where there eyes were they always were, and always in the same place for all of them. Their skin was not exactly hard, but it was always opaque, never shimmered, never vague, never penetrable by another skin of its own type.

They were not larger in size, particularly, then the Soft Ones, but they were heavier. Their substance was much denser and they had to be careful about the yielding tissues of the Soft Ones.

Once when he had been little, really little and his body had flowed almost as freely as his sister's, he had been approached by a Hard One. He had never known which one it was, but he learned in later life that they were all of them curious about baby-Rationals. Odeen had reached up for the Hard One, out of nothing but curiosity. The Hard One had sprung backward and later Odeen's Parental had scolded him for offering to touch a Hard One.

The scolding had been harsh enough for Odeen never to forget. When he was older he learned that the close-packed atoms of the Hard One's tissues felt pain on the forcible penetration of others. Odeen wondered if the Soft One felt pain, too. Another young Rational once told him that he had stumbled against a Hard One and the Hard One had doubled up but that he himself had felt nothing—but Odeen wasn't sure this was not just a melodramatic boast.

There were other things he could not do. He liked rubbing against the walls of the cavern. There was a pleasant, warm feeling when he allowed himself to penetrate rock. Babies always did it, but it got harder to do as he grew older. Still, he could do it skin-deep and he liked it, but his Parental found him doing it and scolded him. He objected that his sister did it all the time; he had seen her.

"That's different, said the Parental. "She's an Emotional."

At another time, when Odeen was absorbing a recording—he was older then— he had idly formed a couple of projections and made the tips so thin, he could pass one through the other. He began to do it regularly when he listened. There was a pleasant tickling sensation that made it easier to listen and made him nicely sleepy afterward.

And his Parental caught him at that, too, and what he had said still made Odeen uncomfortable in remembering it.

No one really told him about melting in those days. They fed him knowledge and educated him about everything except what the triad was all about. Tritt had never been told, either, but he was a Parental so he knew without being told. Of course, when Dua came at last, all was clear, even though she seemed to know less about it even than Odeen.

But she didn't come to them because of anything Odeen did. It was Tritt who broached the matter; Tritt, who ordinarily feared the Hard Ones and avoided them mutely; Tritt, who lacked Odeen's self-assurance, in all but this respect; Tritt, who on this one subject was driven; Tritt—Tritt—Tritt—

Odeen signed. Tritt was invading his thoughts, because Tritt was coming. He could feel him, harsh, demanding, always demanding. Odeen had so little time to himself these days, just when he felt that he needed to think more than ever, to straighten out all the thoughts—

"Yes, Tritt," he said.

— 1c —

TRITT WAS conscious of his blockiness. He didn't think it ugly. He didn't think about it all. If he did, he would consider it beautiful. His body was designed for a purpose and designed well.

He said, "Odeen, where is Dua?"

"Outside somewhere," mumbled Odeen, almost as though he didn't care. It annoyed Tritt to have the triad made so little of. Dua was so difficult and Odeen didn't care.

"Why do you let her go?"

"How can I stop her. Tritt? And what harm does it do?"

"You know the harm. We have two babies. We need a third. It is so hard to make a little-mid these days. Dua must be well fed for it to be made. Now she is wandering about a Sunset again. How can she feed properly at Sunset?"

"She's just not a great feeder."

"And we just don't have a little-mid. Odeen," Tritt's voice was caressing, "how can I love you properly without Dua?"

"Now, then," mumbled Odeen, and Tritt felt himself once more puzzled by the other's clear embarrassment at the simplest statement of fact.

Tritt said, "Remember, I was the one who first got Dua." Did Odeen remember that? Did Odeen ever think of the triad and what it meant? Sometimes Tritt felt so frustrated he could—he could— Actually, he didn't know what to do, but he knew he felt frustrated. As in those old days when he wanted an Emotional and Odeen would do nothing.

Tritt knew he didn't have the trick of talking in big, elaborate sentences. But if Parentals didn't talk, they thought. They thought about important things. Odeen always talked about atoms and energy. Who cared about atoms and energy? Tritt thought about the triad and the babies.

Odeen had once told him that the numbers of Soft Ones were gradually growing fewer. Didn't he care? Didn't the Hard Ones care? Did anyone care but the Parentals?

Only two forms of life on all the world, the Soft Ones and the Hard Ones. And food shining down on them.

Odeen had once told him the Sun was cooling off. There was less food, he said, so there were less people. Tritt didn't believe it. The Sun felt no cooler than it had when he was a baby. It was just that people weren't worrying about the triads any more. Too many absorbed Rationals; too many silly Emotionals.

What the Soft Ones must do was concentrate on the important things of life. Tritt did. He tended to the business of the triad. Then baby-left came, then the baby-right. They were growing and flourishing. They had to have a baby-mid, though. That was the hardest to get started and without a baby-mid there would be no new triad.

What made Dua as she was? She had always been difficult, but she was growing worse.

Tritt felt an obscure anger against Odeen. Odeen always talked with all those hard words. And Dua listened. Odeen would talk to Dua endlessly till they were almost two Rationals. That was bad for the triad.

Odeen should know better.

It was always Tritt who had to care. It was always Tritt who had to do what had to be done. Odeen was the friend of the Hard Ones and yet he said nothing. They needed an Emotional and yet Odeen would say nothing. Odeen talked to them of energy and not of the needs of the triad.

It had been Tritt who had turned the scale. Tritt rememberd that proudly. He had seen Odeen talking to a Hard One and he had approached. Without a shake in his voice, he had interrupted and said, "We need an Emotional."

The Hard One turned to look at him. Tritt had never been so close to a Hard One. He was all of a piece. Every part of him had to turn when one part did. He had some projections that could move by themselves, but they never changed in shape. They never flowed and were irregular and unlovely. They didn't like to be touched.

The Hard One said, "Is this so, Odeen?" He did not talk to Tritt.

Odeen flattened. He flattened close to the ground; more flattened than Tritt had ever seen. He said, "My right-ling is over-zealous. My right-ling is—is—" He stuttered and puffed and could not speak.

Tritt could speak. He said, "We cannot melt without one."

Tritt knew that Odeen was embarrassed into speechlessness but he didn't care. It was time.

"Well, left-dear," said the Hard One to Odeen, "do you feel the same way about it?" Hard Ones spoke as the Soft Ones did, but more harshly and with fewer overtones. They were hard to listen to. Tritt found them hard, anyway, though Odeen seemed used to it.

"Yes," said Odeen, finally.

The Hard One turned at last to Tritt. "Remind me, young-right. How long have you and Odeen been together?"

"Long enough," said Tritt, "to deserve an Emotional." He kept his shape firmly at angles. He did not allow himself to be frightened. This was too important. He said, "And my name is Tritt."

The Hard One seemed amused. "Yes, the choice was good. You and Odeen go well together, but it makes the choice of an Emotional difficult. We have almost made up our minds. Or at least I have long since made up *my* mind, but the others must be convinced. Be patient, Tritt."

"I am tired of patience."

"I know, but be patient, anyway." He was amused again.

When he was quite gone, Odeen uplifted himself and tinned out angrily. He said, "How could you do that, Tritt? Do you know who he was?"

"He was a Hard One."

"He was Losten. He is my special teacher. I don't want him angry with me."

"Why should he be angry? I was polite."

"Well, never mind." Odeen was settling into normal shape. That meant he wasn't angry any more. (That relieved Tritt though he tried not to show it.) "It's very embarrassing to have my dumb-right come up and speak out to my Hard One."

"Why didn't you do it, then?"

"There's such a thing as the right time."

"But never's the right time to you."

But then they rubbed surfaces and stopped arguing and it wasn't long after that that Dua came.

It was Losten that brought her. Tritt didn't know that; he didn't look at the Hard One. Only at Dua. But Odeen told him afterward that it was Losten that brought her.

"You see?" said Tritt. "It was I who talked to him. That is why he brought her."

"No," said Odeen. "It was time. He would have brought her even if neither of us had talked to him."

Tritt didn't believe him. He was quite sure that it was entirely because of himself that Dua was with them.

Surely, there was never anyone like Dua in the world. Tritt had seen many Emotionals. They were all attractive. He would have accepted any one of them for proper melting. Once he saw Dua, he realized that none of the others would have suited. Only Dua. Only Dua.

And Dua knew exactly what to do. Exactly. No one had ever shown her how, she told them afterward. No one had ever talked to her about it. Even other Emotionals hadn't, for she avoided them.

Yet when all three were together, each knew what to do.

Dua thinned. She thinned more then Tritt had ever seen a person thin. She thinned more than Tritt would ever have thought possible. She became a kind of colored smoke that filled the room and dazzled him. He moved without knowing he was moving. He immersed himself in the air that was Dua.

There was no sensation of penetration, none at all. Tritt felt no resistance, no friction. There was just a floating inward and a rapid palpitation. He felt himself beginning to thin in sympathy, and without the tremendous effort that had always accompanied it. With Dua filling him, he could thin without effort into a thick smoke of his own. Thinning became like flowing, one enormous smooth flow.

Dimly, he could see Odeen approaching from the other side, from Dua's left. And he, too was thinning.

Then, like all the shocks of contact in all the world, he reached Odeen. But it wasn't a shock at all. Tritt felt without feeling, knew without knowing. He slid into Odeen and Odeen slid into him. He couldn't tell whether he was surrounding Odeen or being surrounded by him or both or neither.

It was only—pleasure.

The senses dimmed with the intensity of that pleasure and at the point where he thought he could stand no more, the senses failed altogether.

Eventually, they separated and stared at each other. They had melted for days. Of course, melting always took time. The better it was the longer it took, though when it was over all that time seemed as though it had been an instant and they did not remember it. In later life, it rarely took longer than that first time.

Odeen said, "That was wonderful."

Tritt only gazed at Dua, who had made it possible.

She was coalescing, swirling, moving tremulously. She seemed most affected of the three.

"We'll do it again," she said, hurriedly, "but later, later. Let me go now."

She had run off. They did not stop her. They were too overcome to stop her.

But that was always the way afterward. She was always gone after a melting. No matter how successful it was, she would go. There seemed something in her that needed to be alone.

It bothered Tritt. In point after point, she was different from other Emotionals. She shouldn't be.

Odeen felt differently. He would say on many occasions, "Why don't you leave her alone, Tritt? She's not like the others and that means she's better than the others. Melting wouldn't be as good if she were like the others. Do you want the benefits without paying the price?"

Tritt did not understand that clearly. He knew only that she ought to do what ought to be done. He said, "I want her to do what is right."

"I know, Tritt, I know. But leave her alone, anyway."

Odeen often scolded Dua himself for her queer ways but was always unwilling to let Tritt do so. "You lack tact, Tritt," he would say. Tritt didn't know what tact was exactly.

And now— It had been so long since the first melting and still the baby-Emotional was not born. How much longer? It was already much too long. And Dua, if anything, stayed by herself more and more as time went on.

Tritt said. "She doesn't eat enough."

"When it's time—" began Odeen.

"You always talk about it's being time or it's not being time. You never found it time to get Dua in the first place. Now you never find it time to have a baby-Emotional. Dua should—"

But Odeen turned away. He said, "She's out there, Tritt. If you want to go out and get her, as though you were her Parental instead of her right-ling, do so. But I say, leave her alone."

Tritt backed away. He had a great deal to say, but he didn't know how to say it.

— 2a —

D U A   W A S aware of the left-right agitation concerning her in a dim and faraway manner and her rebelliousness grew.

If one or the other, or both, came to get her, it would end in a melting and she raged against the thought. It was all Tritt knew, except for the children; all Tritt wanted, except for the third and last child; and it was all involved with the children and the still missing child. And when Tritt wanted a melting, he got it.

Tritt dominated the triad when he grew stubborn. He would hold on to some simple idea and never let go and in the end Odeen and Dua would have to give in. Yet now she wouldn't give in; she *wouldn't*—

She didn't feel disloyal at the thought, either. She never expected to feel for either Odeen or Tritt the sheer intensity of longing they felt for each other. She could melt alone; they could melt only through her mediation (so why didn't that make her the more regarded). She felt intense pleasure at the three-way melting; of course she did, it would be stupid to deny it; but it was a pleasure akin to that which she felt when she passed through a rock wall, as she sometimes secretly did. To Tritt and Odeen, the pleasure was like nothing else they had ever experienced or could ever experience.

No, wait. Odeen had the pleasure of learning, of what he called intellectual development. Dua felt some of that at times, enough to know what it might mean; and though it was different from melting, it might serve as a substitute, at least to the point where Odeen could do without melting sometimes.

But not so, Tritt. For him there was only melting and the children. Only. And when his small mind bent entirely upon that, Odeen would give in, and then Dua would have to.

Once she had rebelled. "But what happens when we melt? It's hours, days sometimes, before we come out of it. What happens all that time?"

Tritt had looked outraged at that. "It's always that way. It's *got* to be."

"I don't like anything that's *got* to be. I want to know why."

Odeen had looked embarrassed. He spent half his life being embarrassed. He said, "Now Dua, it does have to be. On account of—children." He seemed to pulse, as he said the word.

"Well, don't pulse," said Dua, sharply. "We're grown now and we've melted I don't know how many times and we all know it's so we can have children. You might as well say so. Why does it take so long, that's all?"

"Because it's a complicated process," said Odeen, still pulsing. "Because it takes energy. Dua, it takes a long time to get a child started and even when we take a long time, it doesn't always get started. And it's getting worse. . . . Not just with us," he added hastily.

"Worse?" said Tritt auxiously, but Odeen would say no more.

They had a child eventually, a baby-Rational, a left-let, that flitted and thinned so that all three were in raptures and even Odeen would hold it and let it change shape in his hands for as long as Tritt would allow him to. For it was Tritt, of course, who had actually incubated it through the long pre-forming; Tritt who had separated from it when it assumed independent existence; and Tritt who cared for it at all times.

After that, Tritt was often not with them and Dua was oddly pleased. Tritt's obsession annoyed her but Odeen's—oddly—pleased her. She became increasingly aware of his—importance. There was something to being a Rational that made it possible to answer questions, and somehow Dua had questions for him constantly. He was readier to answer when Tritt was not present.

"Why does it take as long, Odeen? I don't like to melt and then not know what's happening for days at a time."

"We're perfectly safe, Dua," said Odeen, earnestly. "Come, nothing has ever happened to us, has it? You've never heard of anything ever happening to any other triad, have you? Besides, you shouldn't ask questions."

"Because I'm an Emotional? Because other Emotionals don't ask questions?—I can't stand other Emotionals, if you want to know, and I *do* want to ask questions."

She was perfectly aware that Odeen was looking at her as though he had never seen anyone as attractive and that if Tritt had been present, melting would have taken place at once. She even let herself thin out; not much, but perceptibly, in deliberate coquettishness.

Odeen said, "But you might not understand the implications, Dua. It takes a great deal of energy to inititate a new spark of life."

"You've often mentioned energy. What is it? Exactly."

"Why, what we eat."

"Well, then, why don't you say food."

"Because food and energy aren't quite the same thing. Our food comes from the Sun and that's a kind of energy, but there are other kinds of energy that are not food. When we eat, we've got to spread out and absorb the light. It's hardest for Emotionals because they're much more transparent; that is, the light tends to pass through instead of being absorbed—"

It was wonderful to have it explained, Dua thought. What she was told, she really knew; but she didn't know the proper words; the long science-words that Odeen knew. And it made sharper and more meaningful everything that happened.

Occasionally now, in adult life, when she no longer feared that childish teasing; when she shared in the prestige of being part of the Odeen-triad; she tried to swarm with other Emotionals and to withstand the chatter and the crowding. After all, she did occasionally feel like a more substantial meal than she usually got and it did make for better melting. There was a joy—sometimes she almost caught the pleasure the others got out of it—in slithering and maneuvering for exposure to Sunlight; in the luxurious contraction and condensation to absorb the warmth through greater thickness with greater efficiency.

Yet for Dua a little of that went quite a way and the others never seemed to have enough. There was a kind of gluttonous wiggle about them that Dua could not duplicate and that, at length, she could not endure.

That was why Rationals and Parentals were so rarely on the surface. Their thickness made it possible for them to eat quickly and leave. Emotionals writhed in the Sun for hours, for though they ate more slowly, they actually needed more energy than the others—at least for melting.

The Emotional supplied the energy, Odeen had explained (pulsing so that his signals were barely understood), the Rational the seed, the Parental the incubator.

Once Dua understood that, a certain amusement began to blend with her disapproval when she watched the other Emotionals virtually slurp up the ruddy Sunlight. Since they never asked questions, she was sure they didn't know why they did it and couldn't understand that there was an obscene side to their quivering condensations, or to the way in which they went tittering down below eventually—on their way to a good melt, of course, with lots of energy to spare.

She could also stand Tritt's annoyance when she would come down without that swirling opacity that meant a good gorging. Yet why should they complain? The thinness she retained meant a defter melting. Not as sloppy and glutinous as the other triads managed, perhaps, but it was the ethereality that counted, she felt sure. And the little-left and little-right came eventually, didn't they?

Of course, it was the baby-Emotional, the little-mid, that was the crux. That took more energy than the other two and Dua never had enough.

Even Odeen was beginning to mention it. "You're not getting enough Sunlight, Dua."

"Yes I am," said Dua, hastily.

"Genia's triad," said Odeen, "has just initiated an Emotional."

Dua didn't like Genia. She never had. She was empty-headed even by Emotional standards. Dua said, loftily, "I suppose she's boasting about it. She has no delicacy. I suppose, she's saying, 'I shouldn't mention it, my dear, but you'll never guess what my left-ling and right-ling have gone and went and done—' " She imitated Genia's tremulous signaling with deadly accuracy and Odeen was amused.

But then he said, "Genia may be a dunder, but she *has* initiated an Emotional, and Tritt is upset about it. We've been at it for much longer than they have—"

Dua turned away. "I get all the Sun I can stand. I do it till I'm too full to move. I don't know what you want of me."

Odeen said, "Don't be angry. I promised Tritt I would talk to you. He thinks you listen to me—"

"Oh, Tritt just thinks it's odd that you explain science to me. He doesn't understand— Do you want a mid-ling like the others?"

"No," said Odeen, seriously. "You're not like the others, and I'm glad of it. And if you're interested in Rational-talk, then let me explain something. The Sun doesn't supply the food it used to in ancient times. The light-energy is less; and it takes longer exposures. The birth rate has been dropping for ages and the world's population is only a fraction of what it once was."

"I can't help it," said Dua, rebelliously.

"The Hard Ones may be able to. Their numbers have been decreasing, too—"

"Do they pass on?" Dua was suddenly interested. She always thought they were immortal somehow; that they weren't born; that they didn't die. Who had ever seen a baby Hard One, for instance? They didn't have babies. They didn't melt. They didn't eat.

Odeen said, thoughtfully, "I imagine they pass on. They never talk about themselves to me. I'm not even sure how they eat, but of course they must. And be born. There's a new one, for instance; I haven't seen him yet— But never mind that. The point is that they've been developing an artificial food—"

"I know," said Dua. "I've tasted it."

"You have? I didn't know that!"

"A bunch of the Emotionals talked about it. They said a Hard One was asking for volunteers to taste it and the sillies were all afraid. They said it would probably turn them permanently hard and they would never to able to melt again."

"That's foolish," said Odeen, vehemently.

"I know. So I volunteered. That shut them up. They are *so* hard to endure, Odeen."

"How was it?"

"Horrible," said Dua, vehemently. "Harsh and bitter. Of course I didn't tell the other Emotionals that."

Odeen said, "I tasted it. It wasn't *that* bad."

"Rationals and Parentals don't care what food tastes like."

But Odeen said, "It's still only experimental. They're working hard on improvements, the Hard Ones are. Especially Estwald—that's the one I mentioned before, the new one I haven't seen—he's working on it. Losten speaks of him now and then as though he's something special; a very great scientist."

"How is it you've never seen him?"

"I'm just a Soft One. You don't suppose they show me and tell me everything, do you? Someday I'll see him, I suppose. He's developed a new energy-source which may save us all yet—"

"I don't want artificial food," said Dua, and she had left Odeen abruptly.

That had been not so long ago, and Odeen had not mentioned this Estwald again, but she knew he would, and she brooded about it up here in the Sunset.

She had seen that artificial food that once; a glowing sphere of light, like a tiny Sun, in a special cavern set up by the Hard Ones. She could taste its bitterness yet.

Would they improve it? Would they make it taste better? Even delicious? And would she have to eat it then and fill herself with it till the full sensation gave her an almost uncontrollable desire to melt?

She feared that self-generating desire. It was different when the desire came through the hectic combined stimulation of left-ling and right-ling. It was the self-generation that meant she would be ripe to bring about the initiation of little-mid. And—and she didn't want to!

It was a long time before she would admit the truth to herself. She didn't want to initiate an Emotional! It was after the three children were all born that the time would inevitably come to pass on, and she didn't want to. She remembered the day her Parental had left her forever, and it was never going to be like that for her. Of that she was fiercely determined.

The other Emotionals didn't care because they were too empty to think about it, but she was different. She was queer Dua, the Left-Em; that was what they had called her; and she *would* be different. As long as she didn't have that third child, she would not pass on; she would continue to live.

So she wasn't going to have that third child. Never. *Never!*

But how was she going to stave it off? And how would she keep Odeen from finding out? What if Odeen found out?

— 2b —

ODEEN WAITED for Tritt to do something. He was reasonably sure that Tritt would not actually go up to the surface after Dua. It would mean leaving the children and that was always hard for Tritt to do. Tritt waited, without speaking for a while, and when he left, it was in the direction of the children's alcove.

Odeen was almost glad when Tritt left. Not quite, of course, for Tritt had been angry and withdrawn so that interpersonal contact had weakened and the barrier of displeasure had arisen. Odeen could not help but be melancholy at that. It was like the slowing of the life-pulse.

He sometimes wondered if Tritt felt it, too. . . . No, that was unfair. Tritt had the special relationship with the children.

And as for Dua, who could tell what Dua felt? Who could tell what any Emotional felt? They were so different they made left and right seem alike in everything but mind. But even allowing for the erratic way of Emotionals, who could tell what Dua—especially Dua—felt?

That was why Odeen managed to be almost glad when Tritt left, for Dua was the question. The delay in initiating the third child was indeed becoming too long and Dua was growing less amenable to persuasion, not more. There was a growing restlessness in Odeen himself, that he could not quite identify, and it was something he would have to discuss with Losten.

He made his way down to the Hard-caverns, hastening his movements into a continuous flow that was not nearly as undignified as the oddly exciting mixture of wavering and rushing that marked the Emotional curve-along, or as amusing as the stolid weight-shift of the Parental—

(He had the keen thought-image of Tritt clumping in pursuit of the baby-Rational, who, of course, was almost as slippery, at his age, as an Emotional, and of Dua having to block the baby and bring him back, and of Tritt cluckingly undecided whether to shake the small life-object or enfold him with his substance. From the start, Tritt could thin himself more effectively for the babies than for Odeen and when Odeen rallied him about that, Tritt answered gravely, for of course he had no humor about such things, "Ah, but the children need it more.")

Odeen was selfishly pleased with his own flow and thought it graceful and impressive. He had mentioned that once to Losten, to whom as his Hard-teacher, he confessed everything, and Losten had said, "But don't you think an Emotional or a Parental feels the same about his own flow-pattern? If each of you think differently and act differently, ought you not to be pleased differently? A triad doesn't preclude individuality, you know."

Odeen wasn't sure he understood about individuality. Did that mean being alone? A Hard One was alone, of course. There were no triads among them. How did they stand it?

Odeen had still been quite young when the matter had come up. His relationship with the Hard Ones had only been beginning, and it suddenly struck him that he wasn't sure that there were no triads among them. That fact was common legend among the Soft Ones, but how correct was the legend? Odeen thought about that and decided one must ask and not accept matters on faith.

Odeen had said, "Are you a left or a right, sir?" (In later times, Odeen pulsed at the memory of that question. How incredibly naïve to have asked it, and it was very little comfort that every Rational asked the question of a Hard One in some fashion, sooner or later—usually sooner.)

Losten answered quite calmly, "Neither, little-left. There are no lefts or rights among the Hard Ones."

"Or mid-l— Emotionals?"

"Or mid-lings?" And the Hard One changed the shape of his permanent sensory region in a fashion that Odeen eventually associated with amusement or pleasure. "No. No mid-lings either. Just Hard Ones of one kind."

Odeen had to ask. It came out involuntarily, quite against his desire. "But how do you stand it?"

"It is different with us, little-left. We are used to it."

Could Odeen be used to such a thing? There was the Parental triad that had filled his life so far and the sure knowledge that he would at some not-too-distant time form a triad of his own. What was life without that? He thought about it hard now and then. He thought about everything hard, as it came up. Sometimes he managed to catch a glimpse of what it might mean. That Hard Ones had only themselves; neither left-brother, nor right-brother, nor mid-sister, nor melting, nor children, nor Parentals. They had only the mind, only the inquiry into the Universe.

Perhaps that was enough for them. As Odeen grew older, he caught bits of understanding as to the joys of inquiry. They were almost enough—almost enough—and then he would think of Tritt and of Dua and decide that even all the Universe beside was not quite enough.

Unless— It was odd, but every once in a while it seemed that there might come a time, a situation, a condition, when— Then he would lose the momentary glimpse, or, rather, glimpse of a glimpse, and miss it all. Yet in time it would return and lately he thought it grew stronger and would remain almost long enough to be caught.

But none of that was what should involve him now. He had to see about Dua. He made his way along the well-known route, along which he had first been taken by his Parental (as Tritt would soon take their own young Rational, their own baby-left.)

And, of course, he was instantly lost in memory again.

It had been frightening, then. There had been other young Rationals, all pulsing and shimmering and changing shape, despite the Parental signals on every side to stay firm and smooth and not disgrace the triad. One small left, a playmate of Odeen, had, in fact, flattened thin, baby-fashion, and would not unflatten, despite all the efforts of his horribly embarrassed Parental. (He had since become a perfectly normal student. . . . Though no Odeen, as Odeen himself could not help realizing with considerable complacency.)

They met a number of Hard Ones on that first day of school. They stopped at each, in order that the young-Rational vibration pattern might be recorded in several specialized ways and for a decision to be reached as to whether to accept them for instruction then, or to wait another interval; and if then, for what kind of instruction.

Odeen, in a desperate effort, had drawn himself smooth as a Hard One approached, and held himself unwavering.

The Hard One said (and the first sound of the odd tones of his voice almost undid Odeen's determination to be grown-up), "This is quite a firm-held Rational. How do you represent yourself, left?"

It was the first time Odeen had ever been called "left" instead of in the form of some diminutive, and he felt firmer than ever as he managed to say, "Odeen, Hard-sir," using the polite address his Parental had carefully taught him.

Dimly, Odeen remembered being taken through the Hard-caverns, with their equipment, their machinery, their libraries, their meaningless, crowding sights and sounds. More than the actual sense perceptions, he remembered his inner feeling of despair. What would they do with him?

His Parental had told him that he would learn, but he didn't know what was really meant by "learn" and when he asked his Parental, it turned out that the older one didn't know either.

It took him a while to find out and the experience was pleasurable, so pleasurable, and yet not without its worrisome aspects.

The Hard One who had first called him "left" was his first teacher. The Hard One taught him to interpret the wave recordings so that after a while what seemed an incomprehensible code became words; words just as clear as those he could form with his own vibrations.

But then the first one didn't appear any more and another Hard One took over. It was a time before Odeen noticed. It was difficult in those early days to tell one Hard One from another, to differentiate among their voices. But then he grew certain. Little by little, he grew certain and he trembled at the change. He didn't understand its significance.

He gathered courage and finally asked. "Where is my teacher, Hard-sir?"
"Gamaldan? . . . He will no longer be with you, left."

Odeen was speechless for a moment. Then he said, "But Hard Ones don't
pass on—" He did not quite finish the phrase. It choked off.

The new Hard One was passive, and said nothing, volunteered nothing.

It was always to be like that, Odeen found out. They never talked about
themselves. On every other subject they discoursed freely. Concerning themselves—nothing.

From dozens of pieces of evidence, Odeen could not help but decide that Hard
Ones passed on; that they were not immortal (something so many Soft Ones took
for granted). Yet no Hard One ever said as much. Odeen and the other
student-Rationals sometimes discussed it, hesitantly, uneasily. Each brought in
some small item that pointed inexorably to mortality of the Hard Ones and
wondered and did not like to conclude the obvious, so they let it go.

The Hard Ones did not seem to mind that hints of mortality existed. They did
nothing to mask it. But they never mentioned it, either. And if the question was
asked directly (sometimes it was, inevitably) they never answered; neither
denying nor affirming.

And if they passed on, they had to be born also, yet they said nothing of that
and Odeen never saw a young Hard One.

Odeen believed that Hard Ones got their energy from rocks instead of from the
Sun—at least that they incorporated a powdered black rock into their bodies.
Some of the other students thought so, too. Others, rather vehemently, refused
to accept that. Nor could they come to a conclusion for no one ever saw them
feeding in any way and the Hard Ones never spoke of that either.

In the end, Odeen took their reticence for granted—as part of themselves.
Perhaps, he thought, it was their individuality, the fact that they formed no
triads. It built a shell about them.

And then, too, Odeen learned things of such grave import that questions
concerning the private life of the Hard Ones turned to trivia in any case. He
learned, for instance, that the whole world was shriveling—dwindling—

It was Losten, the new teacher, who told him that.

Odeen had asked about the unoccupied caverns that stretched so endlessly into
the bowels of the world and Losten had seemed pleased. "Are you afraid to ask
about that, Odeen?"

(He was Odeen now; not some general reference to his left-hood. It was
always a source of pride to hear a Hard One address him by personal name.
Many did so. Odeen was a prodigy of understanding and the use of his name
seemed a recognition of the fact. More than once Losten had expressed
satisfaction at having him as a pupil.)

Odeen was indeed afraid and, after some hesitation, said so. It was always
easier to confess shortcomings to the Hard Ones than to fellow-Rationals; much
easier than to confess them to Tritt, unthinkable to confess them to Tritt. . . .
Those were the days before Dua.

"Then why do you ask?"

Odeen hesitated again. Then he said slowly. "I'm afraid of the unoccupied
caverns because when I was young I was told they had all sorts of monstrous
things in them. But I know nothing of that directly; I only know what I have been
told by other young ones who couldn't have known directly either. I want to find
out the truth about them and the wanting has grown until there is more of
curiosity in me than fear."

Losten looked pleased. "Good! The curiosity is useful, the fear useless. Your inner development is excellent, Odeen, and remember it is only your inner development that counts in the important things. Our help to you is marginal. Since you want to know, it is easy to tell you that the unoccupied caverns are truly unoccupied. They are empty. There is nothing in them but the unimportant things left behind in times past."

"Left behind by whom, Hard-sir?" Odeen felt uneasily compelled to use the honorific whenever he was too obviously in the presence of knowledge he lacked that the other had.

"By those who occupied them in times past. There was a time thousands of cycles ago when there were many thousands of Hard Ones and millions of Soft Ones. There are fewer of us now than there were in the past, Odeen. Nowadays there are not quite three hundred Hard Ones and fewer than ten thousand Soft Ones."

"Why?" said Odeen, shocked. (Only three hundred Hard Ones left. This was surely an open admission that Hard Ones passed on, but this was not the time to think of that.)

"Because energy is diminishing. The Sun is cooling. It becomes harder in every cycle to give birth and to live."

(Well, then, did not that mean the Hard Ones gave birth, too? And did it mean that the Hard Ones depended on the Sun for food, too, and not on rocks? Odeen filed the thought away and dismissed it for now.)

"Will this continue?" Odeen asked.

"The Sun must dwindle to an end, Odeen, and someday give no food."

"Does that mean that all of us, the Hard Ones and the Soft Ones, too, will pass on?"

"What else can it mean?"

"We can't all pass on. If we need energy and the Sun is coming to an end, we must find other sources. Other stars."

"But, Odeen, all the stars are coming to an end. The Universe is coming to an end."

"If the stars come to an end, is there no food elsewhere? No other source of energy?"

"No, all the energy-sources in all the Universe are coming to an end."

Odeen considered that rebelliously, then said, "Then other Universes. We can't give up just because the Universe does." He was palpitating as he said it. He had expanded with quite unforgivable discourtesy until he had swelled translucently into a size distinctly larger than the Hard One.

But Losten merely expressed extreme pleasure. He said, "Wonderful, my left-dear. The others must hear of this."

Odeen had collapsed to normal size in mingled embarrassment and pleasure at hearing himself addressed as "left-dear," a phrase he had never heard anyone use to him—except Tritt, of course.

It had not been very long after that that Losten himself had brought them Dua. Odeen had wondered, idly, if there had been any connection, but after a while wonder burned itself out. Tritt had repeated so often that it was his own approach to Losten that had brought them Dua, that Odeen gave up thinking about it. It was too confusing.

But now he was coming to Losten again. A long time had passed since those earlier days when he first learned that the Universe was coming to an end and that (as it turned out) the Hard Ones were resolutely laboring to live on anyway. He himself had become adept in many fields and Losten confessed that in physics there was little he could any longer teach Odeen that a Soft One could profitably learn. And there were other young Rationals to take in hand, so he did not see Losten as frequently as he once did.

Odeen found Losten with two half-grown Rationals in the Radiation Chamber. Losten saw him at once through the glass and came out, closing the door carefully behind him.

"My left-dear," he said, holding out his limbs in a gesture of friendship (so that Odeen, as so often in the past, experienced a perverse desire to touch, but controlled it). "How are you?"

"I did not mean to interrupt, Losten-sir."

"Interrupt? Those two will get along perfectly well by themselves for a time. They are probably glad to see me go, for I am sure I weary them with over-much talk."

"Nonsense," said Odeen. "You always fascinated me and I'm sure you facinate them."

"Well, well. It is good of you to say so. I see you frequently in the library, and I hear from others that you do well in your advanced courses, and that makes me miss my best student. How is Tritt? Is he as Parentally stubborn in his ways as ever?"

"More stubborn every day. He gives strength to the triad."

"And Dua?"

"Dua? I have come— She is very unusual, you know."

Losten nodded, "Yes, I know that." His expression was one that Odeen had grown to associate with melancholy.

Odeen waited a moment, then decided to tackle the matter directly. He said, "Losten-sir, was she brought to us, to Tritt and myself, just because she was unusual?"

Losten said, "Would you be surprised? You are very unusual yourself, Odeen, and you have told me on a number of occasions that Tritt is."

"Yes," said Odeen, with conviction. "He is."

"Then oughtn't your triad include an unusual Emotional?"

"There are many ways of being unusual," said Odeen, thoughtfully. "In some ways, Dua's odds ways displease Tritt and worry me. May I consult you?"

"Always."

"She is not fond of—of melting."

Losten listened gravely; to all appearances unembarrassed.

Odeen went on. "She is fond of melting when we melt, that is, but it is not always easy to persuade her to do so."

Losten said, "How does Tritt feel about melting? I mean, aside from the immediate pleasure of the act? What does it mean to him besides pleasure?"

"The children, of course," said Odeen. "I like them and Dua likes them, too, but Tritt is the Parental. Do you understand that?" (It suddenly seemed to Odeen that Losten couldn't possibly understand all the subtleties of the triad.)

"I try to understand," said Losten. "It seems to me, then, that Tritt gets more out of melting than melting alone. And how about yourself? What do you get out of it besides the pleasure?"

Odeen considered. "I think you know that. A kind of mental stimulation."

"Yes, I know that, but I want to make sure *you* know. I want to make sure you haven't forgotten. You have told me often that when you come out of a period of melting, with its odd loss of time—during which I admit I sometimes didn't see you for rather long periods—that suddenly you found yourself understanding many things that had seemed obscure before."

"It was as though my mind remained active in the interval," said Odeen. "It was as though there was time which, even though I was unaware of its passing and unconscious of my existence, was necessary to me; during which I could think more deeply and intensely, without the distraction of the less intellectual side of life."

"Yes," agreed Losten, "and you'd come back with a quantum-jump in understanding. It is a common thing among you Rationals, though I must admit no one improved in such great jumps as you did. I honestly think no Rational in history did so."

"Really?" said Odeen, trying not to seem unduly elated.

"On the other hand, I may be wrong"—and Losten seemed slightly amused at the other's sudden loss of shimmer—"but never mind that. The point is that you, like Tritt, get something out of the melt besides the melt itself."

"Yes. Most certainly."

"And what does Dua get out of the melt besides the melt?"

There was a long pause. "I don't know," said Odeen.

"Have you never asked her?"

"Never."

"But then," said Losten, "if all she gets out of a melt is the melt, and if you and Tritt get out of it the melt plus something else, why should she be as eager for it as you two are?"

"Other Emotionals don't seem to require—" began Odeen, defensively.

"Other Emotionals aren't like Dua. You've told me that often enough and, I think, with satisfaction."

Odeen felt ashamed. "I had thought it might be something else."

"What might that be?"

"It's hard to explain. We know each other in the triad; we sense each other; in some ways, all three of us are part of a single individual. A misty individual that comes and goes. Mostly it's unconscious. If we think about it with too great a concentration, we lose it, so we can never get real detail. We—" Odeen stopped rather hopelessly. "It's hard to explain the triad to someone—"

"Nevertheless, I am trying to understand. You think you have caught a portion of Dua's inner mind; something she has tried to keep secret, is that it?"

"I'm not sure. It is the vaguest impression, sensed with a corner of my mind just now and then."

"Well?"

"I sometimes think Dua doesn't want to have a baby-Emotional."

Losten looked at him gravely. "You only have two children so far, I think. A little-left and a little-right."

"Yes, only two. The Emotional is difficult to initiate, you know."

"I know."

"And Dua will not trouble to absorb the necessary energy. Or even try to. She has any number of reasons but I can't believe any of them. It seems to me that for some reason, she just doesn't want an Emotional. For myself—if Dua really didn't want one for a while—well, I would let her have her way. But Tritt is a

Parental, and he wants one; he must have one; and somehow I can't disappoint Tritt, not even for Dua.''

"If Dua had some rational cause for not wanting to initiate an Emotional, would that make a difference with you?''

"With me, certainly, but not with Tritt. He doesn't understand such things.''

"But would you labor to keep him patient?''

"Yes, I would, for as long as I could.''

Losten said, "Has it occurred to you that hardly any Soft Ones''—here he hesitated as though searching for a word and then he used the customary Soft-One phrase—"ever pass on before the children are born—all three, with the baby-Emotional last.''

"Yes, I know.'' Odeen wondered how Losten could possibly think him ignorant of so elementary a bit of knowledge.

"Then the birth of a baby-Emotional is equivalent to the coming of time to pass on.''

"Usually, not till the Emotional is old enough—''

"But the time for passing on will be coming. Might it not be that Dua does not want to pass on?''

"How can that be, Losten? When the time comes to pass on, it is as when the time comes to melt. How can you not want to?'' (Hard Ones didn't melt; perhaps they didn't understand.)

"Suppose Dua simply wants never to pass on? What would you then say?''

"Why, that we *must* pass on eventually. If Dua merely wants to delay the last baby, I might humor her and even persuade Tritt to, perhaps. If she wants never to have it—that simply cannot be allowed.''

"Why so?''

Odeen paused to think it out. "I can't say, Losten-sir, but I know we must pass on. I know it more and feel it more with each cycle, and sometimes I almost think I understand why.''

"You are a philosopher, I sometimes think, Odeen,'' said Losten dryly. "Let's consider. By the time the third baby comes and grows, Tritt will have had all his children and can look forward to passing on after a fulfilled life. You yourself will have had the satisfaction of much learning and you, too, can pass on after a fulfilled life. But Dua?''

"I don't *know*,'' said Odeen, wretchedly. "Other Emotionals cling together all lifelong and seem to get some pleasure out of chattering with each other. Dua, however, will not do that.''

"Well, she is unusual. Is there nothing she likes?''

"She likes to listen to me talk about my work,'' mumbled Odeen.

Losten said, "Well, don't be ashamed of that, Odeen. Every Rational talks about his work to his right and his mid. You all pretend you don't, but you all do.''

Odeen said, "But Dua *listens,* Losten-sir.''

"I'm quite sure she does. Not like other Emotionals. And does it ever seem to you that she understands rather better after a melt?''

"Yes, I have noticed that at times. I didn't particularly pay any attention, though—''

"Because you are sure Emotionals can't really understand these things. But there seems to be considerable of the Rational in Dua.''

(Odeen looked up at Losten with sudden consternation. Once Dua had told him of her childhood unhappiness; only once; of the shrill calls of the other Emotionals; of the filthy name they had called her—Left-Em. Had Losten heard of that, somehow? . . . But he was only looking calmly at Odeen.)

Odeen said, "I have sometimes thought that, too." Then he burst out, "I am *proud* of her for that."

"Nothing wrong with that," said Losten. "Why not tell her so? And if she likes to pamper the Rationalness in herself, why not let her? Teach her what you know more intensively. Answer her questions. Will it disgrace your triad to do that?"

"I don't care if it does. . . . And why should it, anyway? Tritt will think it a waste of time, but I'll handle him."

"Explain to him that if Dua gets more out of life and a truer sense of fulfillment, she might not have the fear of passing on that she now has and might be more ready to have a baby-Emotional."

It was as though an enormous feeling of impending disaster had been lifted from Odeen. He said, hurriedly, "You're right. I feel you're right. Losten-sir, you understand so much. With you leading the Hard Ones, how can we fail to continue succeeding in the other-Universe project?"

"With me?" Losten was amused. "You forget it is Estwald who is guiding us now. He is the real hero of the project. It would be nowhere without him."

"Oh, yes," said Odeen, momentarily discomfited. He had never yet seen Estwald. In fact, he had not yet met a Soft One who had actually met him though some reported having seen him in the distance now and then. Estwald was a new Hard One; new, at least, in the sense that when Odeen had been young, he had never heard him mentioned. Didn't that mean that Estwald was a young Hard One, had been a child Hard One when Odeen had been a child Soft One?

But never mind that. Right now, Odeen wanted to get back home. He couldn't touch Losten in gratitude, but he could thank him again and then hasten away joyfully.

There was a selfish component to his joy. It was not just the distant prospect of the baby-Emotional and the thought of Tritt's pleasure. It was not even the thought of Dua's fulfillment. What counted with him at this very moment was the immediate gleeful prospect ahead. He was going to be able to teach. No other Rational could feel the pleasure of so doing, he was sure, for no other Rational could possibly have an Emotional like Dua as part of the triad.

It would be wonderful, if only Tritt could be made to understand the necessity. He would have to talk to Tritt, somehow persuade him to be patient.

— 2c —

TRITT HAD never felt less patient. He did not pretend to understand why Dua acted the way she did. He did not want to try. He did not care. He never knew why Emotionals did what they did. And Dua didn't even act like the other Emotionals.

She never thought about the important things. She would look at the Sun. But then she would thin out so that the light and food would just pass through her. Then she would say it was beautiful. That was not the important thing. The important thing was to eat. What was beautiful about eating? What was beautiful?

She always wanted to melt differently. Once she said, "Let's talk first. We never talk about it. We never think about it."

Odeen would always say, "Let her have her way about it, Tritt. It makes it better."

Odeen was always patient. He always thought things would be better when they waited. Or else he would want to think it out.

Tritt wasn't sure he knew what Odeen meant by "think it out." It seemed to him it just meant that Odeen did nothing.

Like getting Dua in the first place. Odeen would still be thinking it out. Tritt went right up and asked. That was the way to be.

Now Odeen wouldn't do anything about Dua. What about the baby-Emotional, which was what mattered. Well, Tritt would do something about it, if Odeen didn't.

In fact, he was doing something. He was edging down the long corridor even as all this was going through his mind. He was hardly aware he had come this far. Was this "thinking it out"? Well, he would not let himself be frightened. He would not back away.

Stolidly, he looked about him. This was the way to the Hard-caverns. He knew he would be going that way with his little-left before very long. He had been shown the way by Odeen once.

He did not know what he would do when he got there this time. Still, he felt no fright at all. He wanted a baby-Emotional. It was his right to have a baby-Emotional. *Nothing* was more important than that. The Hard Ones would see he got one. Hadn't they brought them Dua when he had asked?

But who would he ask? Could it be any Hard One? Dimly, he had made up his mind *not* any Hard One. There was the name of one he would ask for. Then he would talk to *him* about it.

He remembered the name. He even remembered when he had first heard the name. It was the time when the little-left had grown old enough to begin changing shape voluntarily. (What a great day! "Come, Odeen, quickly! Annis is all oval and hard. All by himself, too. Dua, look!" And they had rushed in. Annis was the only child then. They had had to wait so long for the second. So they rushed in and he was just plastered in the corner. He was curling at himself and flowing over his resting place like wet clay. Odeen had left because he was busy. But said, "Oh, he'll do it again, Tritt." They had watched for hours and he didn't.)

Tritt was hurt that Odeen hadn't waited. He would have scolded but Odeen looked so weary. There were definite wrinkles in his ovoid. And he made no effort to smooth them out.

Tritt said anxiously, "Is anything wrong, Odeen?"

"A hard day and I'm not sure I'm going to get differential equations before the next melting." (Tritt didn't remember the exact hard words. It was something like that. Odeen always used hard words.)

"Do you want to melt now?"

"Oh, no. I just saw Dua heading topside and you know how she is if we try to interrupt that. There's no rush, really. There's a new Hard One, too."

"A new Hard One?" said Tritt, with distinct lack of interest. Odeen found sharp interest in associating with Hard Ones, but Tritt wished the interest didn't exist. Odeen was more intent on what he called his education than any other Rational in the area. That was unfair. Odeen was too wrapped up in that. Dua was too wrapped up in roaming the surface alone. No one was properly interested in the triad but Tritt.

"He's called Estwald," said Odeen.

"Estwald?" Tritt *did* feel a twinge of interest. Perhaps it was because he was anxiously sensing Odeen's feelings.

"I've never seen him, but they all talk about him." Odeen's eyes had flattened out as they usually did when he turned introspective. "He's responsible for that new thing they've got."

"What new thing?"

"The Positron Pu— You wouldn't understand, Tritt. It's a new thing they have. It's going to revolutionize the whole world."

"What's revolutionize?"

"Make everything different."

Tritt was at once alarmed. "They mustn't make everything different."

"They'll make everything *better*. Different isn't always worse. Anyway, Estwald is responsible. He's very bright. I get the feeling."

"Then why don't you like him?"

"I didn't say I didn't like him."

"You *feel* as though you don't like him."

"Oh, nothing of the sort, Tritt. It's just that somehow—somehow—" Odeen laughed. "I'm jealous. Hard Ones are so intelligent that a Soft One is nothing in comparison, but I got used to that, because Losten was always telling me how bright I was—for a Soft One, I suppose. But now this Estwald comes along, and even Losten seems lost in admiration, and I'm *really* nothing."

Tritt bellied out his foreplane to have it just make contact with Odeen, who looked up and smiled. "But that's just stupidity on my part. Who cares how smart at Hard One is? Not one of them has a Tritt."

After that they both went looking for Dua after all. For a wonder, she had finished wandering about and was just heading down again. It was a very good melting though the time lapse was only a day or so. Tritt worried about meltings then. With Annis so small, even a short absence was risky, though there were always other Parentals who could take over.

After that, Odeen mentioned Estwald now and then. He always called him "the New One" even after considerable time had passed. He still had never seen him. "I think I avoid him," he said one time, when Dua was with them, "because he knows so much about the new device. I don't want to find out too soon. It's too much fun to learn."

"The Positron Pump?" Dua had asked.

—That was another funny thing about Dua. Tritt thought. It annoyed him. She could say the hard words almost as well as Odeen could. An Emotional shouldn't be like that.

So Tritt made up his mind to ask Estwald because Odeen had said he was smart. Besides, Odeen had never seen him. Estwald couldn't say, "I've talked to Odeen about it, Tritt, and you mustn't worry."

Everyone thought that if you talked to the Rational, you were talking to the triad. Nobody paid attention to the Parentals. But they would have to this time.

He was in the Hard-caverns and everything seemed different. There was nothing there that looked like anything Tritt could understand. It was all wrong and frightening. Still, he was too anxious to see Estwald to let himself really be frightened. He said to himself, "I want my little-mid." That made him feel firm enough to walk forward.

He saw a Hard One finally. There was just this one; doing something; bending over something; doing something. Odeen once told him that Hard Ones were always working at their—whatever it was. Tritt didn't remember and didn't care.

He moved smoothly up and stopped. "Hard-sir," he said.

The Hard One looked up at him and the air vibrated about him, the Odeen said it did when two Hard Ones talked to each other sometimes. Then the Hard One seemed really to see Tritt and said, "Why, it's a right. What is your business here? Do you have your little-left with you? Is today the start of a semester?"

Tritt ignored it all. He said, "Where can I find Estwald, sir?"

"Find whom?"

"Estwald."

The Hard One was silent for a long moment. Then he said, "What is your business with Estwald, right?"

Tritt felt stubborn. "It is important I speak to him. Are *you* Estwald, Hard-sir?"

"No, I am not. . . . What is your name, right?"

"Tritt, Hard-sir."

"I see. You're the right of Odeen's triad, aren't you?"

"Yes."

The Hard One's voice seemed to soften. "I'm afraid you can't see Estwald at the moment. He's not here. If anyone else can help you . . . ?"

Tritt didn't know what to say. He simply stood there.

The Hard One said, "You go home now. Talk to Odeen. He'll help you. Yes? Go home, right."

The Hard One turned away. He seemed very concerned in matters other than Tritt, and Tritt still stood there, uncertain. Then he moved into another section quietly, flowing noiselessly. The Hard One did not look up.

Tritt was not certain at first why he had moved in that particular direction. At first, he felt only that it was good to do so. Then it was clear. There was a thin warmth of food about him and he was nibbling at it.

He had not been conscious of hunger, yet now he was eating and enjoying.

The Sun was nowhere. Instinctively, he looked up, but of course he was in a cavern. Yet the food was better than he had ever found it to be on the surface. He looked about, wondering. He wondered, most of all, that he should be wondering.

He had sometimes been impatient with Odeen because Odeen wondered about so many things that didn't matter. Now he himself—Tritt!—was wondering. But what he was wondering about *did* matter. Suddenly, he saw that it *did* matter. With an almost blinding flash he realized that he wouldn't wonder unless something inside him told it *did* matter.

He acted quickly, marveling at his own bravery. After a while, he retraced his steps. He moved past the Hard One again, the one to whom he had earlier spoken. He said, "I am going home, Hard-sir."

The Hard One merely said something incoherent. He was still doing something, bending over something, doing silly things and not seeing the important thing.

If Hard Ones were so great and powerful and smart, Tritt thought, how could they be so stupid?

— 3a —

DUA FOUND herself drifting toward the Hard-caverns. Partly it was because it was something to do now that the Sun had set, something to keep her from returning home for an additional period of time, something to delay having to listen to the importunities of Tritt and the half-embarrassed, half-resigned suggestions of Odeen. Partly, too, it was the attraction they held for her in themselves.

She had felt that for a long time, ever since she was little in fact, and had given up trying to pretend it wasn't so. Emotionals weren't supposed to feel such attractions. Sometimes little Emotionals did—Dua was old enough and experienced enough to know that—but this quickly faded or they were quickly discouraged if it didn't fade quickly enough.

When she herself had been a child, though, she had continued stubbornly curious about the world, and the Sun, and the caverns, and—anything at all—till her Parental would say, "You're a queer one, Dua, dear. You're a funny little midling. What will become of you?"

She hadn't the vaguest notion at first of what was so queer and so funny about wanting to know. She found, quickly enough, that her Parental could not answer her questions. She once tried her left-father, but he showed none of her Parental's soft puzzlement. He snapped, "Why do you ask, Dua?" and his look seemed harshly inquiring.

She ran away, frightened, and did not ask him again.

But then one day another Emotional of her own age had shrieked "Left-Em" at her after she had said—she no longer remembered—it had been something that had seemed natural to her at the time. Dua had been abashed without knowing why and had asked her considerably older left-brother, what a Left-Em was. He had withdrawn, embarrassed—clearly embarrassed—mumbling, "I don't know," when it was obvious he did.

After some thought, she went to her Parental and said, "Am I a Left-Em, Daddy?"

And he had said, "Who called you that, Dua? You must not repeat such words."

She flowed herself about his near corner, thought about it awhile, and said, "Is it bad?"

He said, "You'll grow out of it," and let himself bulge a bit to make her swing outward and vibrate in the game she had always loved. She somehow didn't love it now, for it was quite clear that he hadn't answered her, really. She moved away thoughtfully. He had said, "You'll grow *out* of it," so she was *in* it now, but in *what*?

Even then, she had had few real friends among the other Emotionals. They liked to whisper and giggle together, but she preferred flowing over the crumbled rocks and enjoying the sensation of their roughness. There were, however, some mids who were more friendly than others and whom she found less provoking. There was Doral, who was as silly as the rest, really, but who would sometimes chatter amusingly. (Doral had grown up to join a triad with Dua's right-brother and a young left from another cavern complex, a left whom Dua did not particularly like. Doral had then gone on to initiate a baby-left, a baby-right, in rapid succession, and a baby-mid not too long after that. She had also grown so dense that the triad looked as though it had two Parentals and Dua wondered if they could still melt. . . . Just the same Tritt was always telling her, pointedly, what a good triad Doral helped make up.)

She and Doral had sat alone one day and Dua had whispered, "Doral, do you know what a Left-Em is?"

And Doral had tittered and compressed herself, as though to avoid being seen, and had said, "It's an Emotional that acts like a Rational; you know like a left. Get it! Left-Emotional—Left-Em! Get it!"

Of course Dua "got" the phrase. It was obvious once explained. She would have seen it for herself at once if she had been able to bring herself to imagine such a state of affairs.

Dua said, "How do you know?"

"The older girls told me." Doral's substance swirled and Dua found the motion unpleasant. "It's dirty," Doral said.

"Why?" asked Dua.

"Because it's *dirty*. Emotionals shouldn't act like Rationals."

Dua had never thought about the possibility, but now she did. She said, *"Why* shouldn't they?"

"Because! You want to know something else that's dirty?"

Dua couldn't help being intrigued. "What?"

Doral didn't say anything, but a portion of herself expanded suddenly and brushed against the unsuspecting Dua before the latter could concavize. Dua didn't like it. She shrank away and said, "Don't do that."

"You know what else is dirty? You can go into a rock."

"No, you can't," said Dua. It had been a silly thing to say for Dua had often moved through the outer surface of the rock and liked it. But now in the context of Doral's snickering, she felt revolted and denied the whole thing, even to herself.

"Yes, you can. It's called rock-rubbing. Emotionals can do it easy. Lefts and rights can only do it as babies. When they grow up, they do it with each other."

"I don't believe you. You're making it up."

"They do, I tell you. Do you know Dimit?"

"No."

"Sure you do. She's the girl with the thick corner from Cavern c."

"Is she the one who flows funny?"

"Yes. On account of the thick corner. That's the one. She got into a rock all the way once—except for the thick corner. She let her left-brother watch her do it and he told their Parental and what she got for *that*. She never did it again."

Dua left then, quite upset. She didn't talk to Doral again for a long time, and never really grew friendly again, and yet her curiosity had been aroused.

Her curiosity? Why not say her Left-Emmishness?

One day when she was quite sure her Parental wasn't in the vicinity, she let herself melt into a rock, slowly, just a little. It had been the first time she had tried it since she was quite young, and she didn't think she had ever dared go so deep. There was a warmness about the sensation, but when she emerged she felt as though everyone could tell, as though the rock had left a stain on her.

She tried it again now and then, more boldly, and let herself enjoy it more. She never sank in really deeply, of course.

Eventually, she was caught by her Parental, who clucked away in displeasure, and she was more careful after that. She was older now and knew for certain fact that despite Doral's snickering, it wasn't in the least uncommon. Practically every Emotional did it now and then and some quite openly admitted it.

It happened less frequently as they grew older and Dua didn't think that any Emotional she knew ever did it after joining a triad and beginning the proper meltings. It was one of her secrets (she never told anybody) that she had kept it up, and that once or twice she had tried it even after triad-formation. (Those few times she had thought: What if Tritt found out? . . . Somehow that seemed to present formidable consequences and rather spoiled the fun.)

Confusedly, she found excuses for this—to herself—in her ordeal with the others. The cry of "Left-Em" began to follow her everywhere in a kind of public humiliation. There was one period in her life when she had been driven into an almost hermit-like isolation to escape. If she had begun with a liking for aloneness, that had confirmed it. And being alone, she found consolation in the rocks. Rock-rubbing, whether it was dirty or not, was a solitary act, and they were forcing her to be solitary.

At least, so she told herself.

She had tried to strike back once. She had cried out, "You're a bunch of Right-Ems, a bunch of dirty Right-Ems," at the taunting mids.

They had only laughed and Dua had run away in confusion and frustration. They *were*. Almost every Emotional, when she was getting on to the age of triad-formation, became interested in babies, fluttering about them in Parental imitation which Dua had found repulsive. She herself had never felt such interest. Babies were only babies; they were for right-brothers to worry about.

The name-calling died as Dua grew older. It helped that she retained a girlishly rarefied structure and could flow with a smoky curl no other could duplicate. And when, increasingly, lefts and rights showed interest in her, the other Emotionals found it difficult to sneer.

And yet—and yet—now that no one ever dared speak disrespectfully to Dua (for it was well known through all the caverns that Odeen was the most prominent Rational of the generation and Dua was his mid-ling), she herself knew that she was a Left-Em past all redemption.

She didn't think it dirty—not really—but occasionally she caught herself wishing she were a Rational and then she was abashed. She wondered if other Emotionals did—ever—or just once in a while—and if that was why—partly— she didn't want a baby-Emotional—because she wasn't a real Emotional herself—and didn't fill her triad-role properly—

Odeen hadn't minded her being a Left-Em. He never called her that—but he liked her interest in his life—he liked her questions and he would explain and he liked the way she could understand. He even defended her when Tritt grew jealous—well, not jealous, really—but filled with a feeling that it was all unfit in his stubborn and limited outlook on the world.

Odeen had taken her to the Hard-caverns occasionally, eager to posture before

Dua, and openly pleased at the fact that Dua was impressed. And she *was* impressed, not so much with the fact of his knowledge and intelligence, but with the fact that he did not resent sharing it. (She remembered her left-father's harsh response that one time she had questioned him.) She never loved Odeen so much as when he let her share his life—and yet even that was part of her Left-Emmishness.

Perhaps (this had occurred to her over and over), by being Left-Emmish, she moved closer to Odeen and farther from Tritt, and this was another reason Tritt's importunities repelled her. Odeen had never hinted at anything like that, but perhaps Tritt felt it vaguely and was unable to grasp it completely but did so well enough to be unhappy over it without being able to explain why.

The first time she was in a Hard-cavern she had heard two Hard Ones talking together. She didn't know they were talking of course. There was air vibration, very rapid, very changing, that made an unpleasant buzz deep inside her. She had to rarefy and let it through.

Odeen had said, "They're talking." Then, hastily, anticipating the objection. "*Their* kind of talk. They understand each other."

Dua had managed to grasp the concept. It was all the more delightful to understand quickly because that pleased Odeen so. (He once said, "None of the other Rationals I've ever met have anything but an empty-head for an Emotional. I'm lucky." She had said, "But the other Rationals seem to like empty-heads. Why are you different from them, Odeen?" Odeen did not deny that the other Rationals liked empty-heads. He just said, "I've never figured it out and I don't think it's important that I do. I'm pleased with you and I'm pleased that I'm pleased.")

She said, "Can *you* understand Hard-One talk?"

"Not really," said Odeen. "I can't sense the changes fast enough. Sometimes I can get a feel for what they're saying, even without understanding, especially after we've melted. Just sometimes, though. Getting feels like that is really an Emotional trick, except even if an Emotional does it, she can never make real sense out of what she's feeling. *You* might, though."

Dua demurred. "I'd be afraid to. They might not like it."

"Oh, go on. I'm curious. See if you can tell what they're talking about."

"Shall I? Really?"

"Go ahead. If they catch you and are annoyed, I'll say I made you do it."

"Promise?"

"I promise."

Feeling rather fluttery, Dua let herself reach out to the Hard Ones, and adopted the total passivity that allowed the influx of feelings.

She said, "Excitement! They're excited. Someone new."

Odeen said, "Maybe that's Estwald."

It was the first time Dua had heard the name. She said, "That's funny."

"What's funny?"

"I have the feeling of a big sun. A really big sun."

Odeen looked thoughtful. "They might be talking about that."

"But how can that be?"

It was just at that time that the Hard Ones spied them. They approached in a friendly manner and greeted them in Soft-One fashion of speech. Dua was horribly embarrassed and wondered if they knew she had been sensing them. If they did, though, they said nothing.

(Odeen told her afterward that it was quite rare to come upon Hard Ones talking among themselves in their own fashion. They always deferred to the Soft Ones and seemed always to suspend their own work when Soft Ones were there. "They like us so much," said Odeen. "They are very kind.")

Once in awhile he would take her down to the Hard-caverns—usually when Tritt was entirely wrapped up in the children. Nor did Odeen go out of his way to tell Tritt that he had taken Dua down. It was sure to evoke some response to the effect that Odeen's coddling simply encouraged Dua's reluctance to sun herself and just made the melting that much more ineffective. . . . It was hard to talk to Tritt for more than five minutes without melting coming into the conversation.

She had even come down alone once or twice. It had always frightened her a little to do so, though the Hard Ones she met were always friendly, always "very kind," as Odeen said. But they did not seem to take her seriously. They were pleased, but somehow amused—she could feel that definitely—when she asked questions. And when they answered it was in a simple way that carried no information. "Just a machine, Dua," they would say. "Odeen might be able to tell you."

She wondered if she had met Estwald. She never quite dared ask the names of the Hard Ones she met (except Losten, to whom Odeen had introduced her, and of whom she heard a great deal). Sometimes it seemed to her that this Hard One or that might be he. Odeen talked about him with great awe and with some resentment.

She gathered that he was too engaged in work of the deepest importance to be in the caverns accessible to the Soft Ones.

She pieced together what Odeen told her and, little by little, discovered that the world needed food badly. Odeen hardly ever called it "food." He said "energy" instead, and said it was the Hard-One word for it.

The Sun was fading and dying but Estwald had discovered how to find energy far away, far beyond the Sun, far beyond the seven stars that shone in the dark, night-sky. (Odeen said the seven stars were seven suns that were very distant, and that there were many other stars that were even more distant and were too dim to be seen. Tritt had heard him say that and had asked of what use it was for stars to exist if they couldn't be seen and he didn't believe a word of it. Odeen had said, "Now, Tritt," in a patient way. Dua had been about to say something very like that which Tritt had said, but changed her mind after that.)

It looked, now, as though there would be plenty of energy forever; plenty of food—at least as soon as Estwald and the other Hard Ones learned to make the new energy taste right.

It had only been a few days ago when she had said to Odeen, "Do you remember, long ago, when you took me to the Hard-caverns and I sensed the Hard Ones and said I caught the feeling of a big sun?"

Odeen looked puzzled for a moment. "I'm not sure. But go ahead, Dua. What about it?"

"I've been thinking. Is the big Sun the source of the new energy?"

Odeen had said, happily, "That's good, Dua. It's not quite right, but that's such good intuition for an Emotional."

And now Dua had been moving slowly, rather moodily, during all this time of reveries. Without particularly noting the passage of either time or space she found herself in the Hard-caverns and was just beginning to wonder if she had really delayed all she safely could and whether she might not turn home now and face the inevitable annoyance of Tritt when—almost as though the thought of Tritt had brought it about—she sensed Tritt.

The sensation was so strong that there was only one confused moment in which she had thought that somehow she was picking up his feelings far away in the home cavern. *No!* He was here, down here in the Hard-caverns with her.

But what could he be doing here? Was he pursuing her? Was he going to quarrel with her *here?* Was he foolishly going to appeal to the Hard Ones? Dua didn't think she could endure that—

And then the feeling of cold horror left her and was replaced by astonishment. Tritt was not thinking of her at all. He had to be unaware of her presence. All she could sense about him was an overwhelming feeling of some sort of determination, mixed with fear and apprehension at something he would do.

Dua might have penetrated farther and found out something, at least, about what it was he had done, and why, but nothing was further from her thoughts. Since Tritt didn't know she was in the vicinity, she wanted to make sure of only one thing—that he continued not to know.

She did, then, almost in pure reflex, something that a moment before she would have sworn she would never dream of doing under any circumstances.

Perhaps it was (she later thought) because of her idle reminiscences of that little-girl talk with Doral, or her memories of her own experiments with rock-rubbing. (There was a complicated adult word for it but she found that word infinitely more embarrassing than the one all the children had used.)

In any case, without quite knowing what she was doing or, for a short while afterward, what she had done, she simply flowed hastily into the nearest wall.

Into it! Every bit of her!

The horror of what she had done was mitigated by the perfect manner in which it accomplished its purpose. Tritt passed by within almost touching distance and remained completely unaware that at one point he might have reached out and touched his mid-ling.

By that time, Dua had no room to wonder what Tritt might be doing in the Hard-caverns if he had not come in pursuit of her.

She forgot Tritt completely.

What filled her instead was pure astonishment at her position. Even in childhood she had never melted completely into rock or met anyone who admitted she had (though there were invariably tales of someone else who had). Certainly no adult Emotional ever had or *could.* Dua was unusually rarefied even for an Emotional (Odeen was fond of telling her that) and her avoidance of food accentuated this (as Tritt often said).

What she had just done indicated the extent of her rarefaction more than any amount of right-ling scolding and for a moment she was ashamed and sorry for Tritt.

And then she was swept by a deeper shame. What if she were caught? She, an adult—

If a Hard One passed and lingered— She could not possibly bring herself to emerge if anyone were watching but how long could she stay within and what if they discovered her *in* the rock?

And even as she thought that, she sensed the Hard Ones and then— somehow—realized they were far away.

She paused, strove to calm herself. The rock, permeating and surrounding her, lent a kind of grayness to her perception but didn't dim it. Instead, she sensed more sharply. She could still sense Tritt in his steady motion downward as sharply as though he were by her side, and she could sense the Hard Ones though they were a cavern complex away. She *saw* the Hard Ones, every single one of them, each in his place, and could sense their vibratory speech to the fullest detail, and even catch bits of what they were saying.

She was sensing as she never had before and never dreamed she could.

So, though she could now leave the rock, secure in the knowledge she was both alone and unobserved, she did not; partly out of amazement, partly out of the curious exultation she felt at understanding and her desire to experience it further.

Her sensitivity was such that she even knew *why* she was sensitive. Odeen had frequently remarked how well he understood something after a period of melting, even though he had not understood it at all before. There was something about the melted state that increased sensitivity incredibly; more was absorbed; more was used. It was because of the greater atomic density during melting, Odeen had said.

Even though Dua was not sure what "greater atomic density" meant, it came with melting and wasn't this present situation rather like melting? Hadn't Dua melted with rock?

When the triad melted, all the sensitivity went to Odeen's benefit. The Rational absorbed it, gained understanding, and retained that understanding after separation. But now Dua was the only consciousness in the melt. It was herself and the rock. There was "greater atomic density" (surely?) with only herself to benefit.

(Was this why rock-rubbing was considered a perversion? Was this why Emotionals were warned off? Or was it just Dua because she was so rarefied? Or because she was a Left-Em?)

And then Dua stopped all speculation and just sensed—in fascination. She was only mechanically aware of Tritt returning, moving past her, passing in the direction back from which he had come. She was only mechanically aware—scarcely feeling the vaguest surprise—that Odeen, too, was coming up from the Hard-caverns. It was the Hard Ones she was sensing, only they, trying to make more out of her perceptions, trying to make the most out of them.

It was a long time before she detached and flowed out of the rock. And when that time came, she was not concerned overmuch as to whether she would be observed. She was confident enough of her sensing ability to know she wouldn't be.

And she returned home deep in thought.

— 3b —

ODEEN HAD returned home to find Tritt waiting for him, but Dua still hadn't returned. Tritt did not seem disturbed at that. Or at least he seemed disturbed, but not at *that*. His emotions were strong enough so that Odeen could sense them clearly, but he let them go without probing. It was Dua's absence that made Odeen restless; to the extent that he found himself annoyed at Tritt's presence simply because Tritt was not Dua.

In this he surprised himself. He could not deny to himself that it was Tritt who, of the two, was the dearer to him. Ideally, all members of the triad were one, and any member should treat the other two exactly on a par—both with each other and with him (her) self. Yet Odeen had never met a triad in which this was so; least of all among those who loudly proclaimed their triad to be ideal in this respect. One of the three was always a little left out, and generally knew it, too.

It was rarely the Emotional, though. They supported each other cross-triad to an extent that Rationals and Parentals never did. The Rational had his teacher, the proverb went, and the Parental his children—but the Emotional had all the other Emotionals.

Emotionals compared notes and if one claimed neglect, or could be made to claim it, she was sent back with a thin patter of instructions to stand firm, to demand! And because melting depended so much on the Emotional and her attitude, she was usually pampered by both left and right.

But Dua was so non-Emotional an Emotional! She didn't seem to care that Odeen and Tritt were so close, and she had no close friendships among the Emotionals to make her care. Of course that was it; she was so non-Emotional an Emotional.

Odeen loved having her so interested in his work; loved having her so concerned and so amazingly ready of comprehension; but that was an intellectual love. The deeper feeling went to steady, stupid Tritt, who knew his place so well and who could offer so little other than exactly what counted—the security of assured routine.

But now Odeen felt petulant. He said, "Have you heard from Dua, Tritt?"

And Tritt did not answer directly. He said, "I am busy. I will see you later. I have been doing things."

"Where are the children? Have you been gone, too? There is a been-gone feel to you."

A note of annoyance made itself plain in Tritt's voice. "The children are well-trained. They know enough to place themselves in community-care. Really, Odeen, they are not babies." But he did not deny the "been-gone" aura that he faintly exuded.

"I'm sorry. I'm just anxious to see Dua."

"You should feel so more often," Tritt said. "You always tell me to leave her alone. You look for her." And he went on into the deeper recesses of the home cavern.

Odeen looked after his right-ling with some surprise. At almost any other occasion he would have followed in an attempt to probe the unusual uneasiness that was making itself quite evident through the ingrained stolidity of a Parental. What had Tritt done?

—But he was waiting for Dua, and growing more anxious by the moment, and he let Tritt go.

Anxiety keened Odeen's sensitivity. There was almost a perverse pride among Rationals in their relative poverty of perception. Such perception wasn't a thing of the mind; it was most characteristic of Emotionals. Odeen was a Rational of Rationals, proud of reasoning rather than feeling, yet now he flung out the imperfect net of his emotional perception as far as he could; and wished, for just a moment, that he were an Emotional so that he could send it out farther and better.

Yet it eventually served his purpose. He could detect Dua's approach, finally, at an unusual distance—for him—and he hastened out to meet her. And because he made her out at such a distance, he was more aware of her rarefaction than he ordinarily was. She was a delicate mist, no more.

—Tritt was right, Odeen thought with sudden, sharp concern. Dua *must* be made to eat and to melt. Her interest in life *must* be increased.

He was so intent on the necessity of this that when she flung herself flowingly toward him and virtually engulfed him, in utter disregard of the fact that they were not in private and might be observed, and said, "Odeen, I must know—I must know so much—" he accepted it as the completion of his own thought and did not even consider it strange.

Carefully, he slipped away, trying to adopt a more seemly union without making it seem he was repulsing her. "Come," he said, "I've been waiting for you. Tell me what you want to know. I will explain all I can."

They were moving quickly homeward now, with Odeen adapting himself eagerly to the characteristic waver of the Emotional flow.

Dua said, "Tell me about the other Universe. Why are they different? How are they different? Tell me all about it."

It did not occur to Dua she was asking too much. It *did* occur to Odeen. He felt rich with an astonishing quantity of knowledge and was on the point of asking. How do you come to know enough about the other Universe to grow so curious about it?

He repressed the question. Dua was coming from the direction of the Hard-caverns. Perhaps Losten had been talking to her, suspecting that despite everything Odeen would be too proud of his status to help his mid-ling.

Not so, thought Odeen gravely. And he would not ask. He would just explain.

Tritt bustled about them when they returned home. "If you two are going to talk, go into Dua's chamber. I will be busy out here. I must see to it that the children are cleaned and exercised. No time for melting now. No melting."

Neither Odeen nor Dua had any thought of melting, but there was no thought in either mind of disobeying the command. The Parental's home was his castle. The Rational had his Hard-caverns below and the Emotional her meeting places above. The Parental had only his home.

Odeen therefore said, "Yes, Tritt. We'll be out of you way."

And Dua extended a briefly loving part of herself and said, "It's good to see you, right-dear." (Odeen wondered if her gesture was part relief over the fact that there would be no pressure to melt. Tritt did tend to overdo that a bit; even more than Parentals generally.)

In her chamber, Dua stared at her private feeding-place. Ordinarily, she ignored it.

It had been Odeen's idea. He knew that such things did exist and, as he explained to Tritt, if Dua did not like to swarm with the other Emotionals, it was perfectly possible to lead Solar energy down into the cavern so that Dua might feed there.

Tritt had been horrified. It wasn't done. The others would laugh. The triad would be disgraced. Why didn't Dua behave as she should?

"Yes, Tritt," Odeen had said, "but she doesn't behave as she should, so why not accommodate her? Is it so terrible? She will eat privately, gain substance, make us happier, become happier herself, and maybe learn to swarm in the end.''

Tritt allowed it, and even Dua allowed it—after some argument—but insisted that it be a simple design. So there was nothing but the two rods that served as electrodes, powered by Solar energy, and with room for Dua in between.

Dua rarely used it, but this time she stared at it and said, ''Tritt has decorated it. . . . Unless you did, Odeen.''

''I? Of course not.''

A pattern of colored-clay designs was at the base of each electrode. ''I suppose it's his way of saying he wishes I would use it,'' Dua said, ''and I *am* hungry. Besides, if I'm eating, Tritt wouldn't dream of interrupting us, would he?''

''No'' said Odeen, gravely. ''Tritt would stop the world if he thought its motion might disturb you while you were eating.''

Dua said, ''Well—I *am* hungry.''

Odeen caught a trace of guilt in her. Guilt over Tritt? Over being hungry? Why should Dua feel guilty about being hungry? Or had she done something that had consumed energy and was she feeling—

He wrenched his mind away from that impatiently. There were times when a Rational could be *too* Rational, and chase down the tracks of every thought to the detriment of what was important. Right now, it was important to talk to Dua.

She seated herself between the electrodes and when she compressed herself to do so, her small size was only too painfully evident. Odeen was hungry himself; he could tell because the electrodes seemed brighter than they ordinarily did; and he would taste the food even at that distance and the savor was delicious. When one was hungry, one always tasted food more keenly than otherwise and at a greater distance. . . . But he would eat later.

Dua said, ''Don't just sit silently, left-dear. *Tell* me. I want to know.'' She had adopted (unconsciously?) the ovoid character of a Rational, as though to make it clearer that she wanted to be accepted as one.

Odeen said, ''I can't explain it all. All the science I mean, because you haven't had the background. I will try to make it simple and you just listen. Later, you tell me what you didn't understand and I'll try to explain further. You understand, first, that everything is made up of tiny particles called atoms and that these are made up of still tinier subatomic particles.''

''Yes, yes'' said Dua. ''That's why we can melt.''

''Exactly. Because actually we are mostly empty space. All the particles are far apart and your particles and mine and Tritt's can all melt together because each set fits into the empty spaces around the other set. The reason matter doesn't fly apart altogether is that the tiny particles do manage to cling together across the space that separates them. There are attractive forces holding them together, the strongest being one we call the nuclear-force. It holds the chief subatomic particles *very* tightly together in bunches that are spread widely apart and that are held together by weaker forces. Do you understand that?''

''Only a little bit,'' said Dua.

''Well never mind, we can go back later. . . . Matter can exist in different states. It can be especially spread out, as in Emotionals; as in you, Dua. It can be a little less spread out, as in Rationals and in Parentals. Or still less so, as in rock. It can be very compressed or thick, as in the Hard Ones. That's why they're hard. They are filled with particles.''

''You mean there's no empty space in them.''

"No, that's not quite what I mean," said Odeen, puzzled as to how to make matter clearer. "They still have a great deal of empty space, but not as much as we do. Particles need a certain amount of empty space and if all they have is that much, then other particles can't squeeze in. If particles are forced in, there is pain. That's why the Hard Ones don't like to be touched by us. We Soft Ones have *more* space between the particles than are actually needed, so other particles can fit in."

Dua didn't look at all certain about that.

Odeen hastened onward. "In the other Universe, the rules are different. The nuclear-force isn't as strong as in ours. That means the particles need more room."

"Why?"

Odeen shook his head, "Because—because—the particles spread out their wave-forms more. I can't explain better than that. With a weaker nuclear-force, the particles need more room and two pieces of matter can't melt together as easily as they can in our Universe."

"Can we see the other Universe?"

"Oh, no. That isn't possible. We can deduce its nature from its basic laws. The Hard Ones can do a great many things, though. We can send material across, and get material from them. We can study their material, you see. And we can set up the Positron Pump. You know about that, don't you?"

"Well, you've told me we get energy out of it. I didn't know there was a different Universe involved. . . . What is the other Universe like? Do they have stars and worlds the way we do?"

"That's an excellent question, Dua." Odeen was enjoying his role as teacher more intensely than usual now that he had official encouragement to speak. (Earlier he always had the feeling that there was a kind of sneaking perversion in trying to explain things to an Emotional.)

He said, "We can't see the other Universe, but we can calculate what it must be like from its laws. You see, what makes the stars shine is the gradual combination of simple particle-combinations into more complicated ones. We call it nuclear fusion."

"Do they have that in the other Universe?"

"Yes, but because the nuclear-force is weaker, fusion is much slower. This means that the stars must be much, much bigger in the other Universe otherwise not enough fusion would take place to make them shine. Stars of the other Universe that were no bigger than our Sun would be cold and dead. On the other hand, if stars in our Universe were bigger than they are, the amount of fusion would be so great it would blow them up. That means that in our Universe there must be thousands of times as many small stars as there are larger stars in theirs—"

"We only have seven—" began Dua. Then she said, "I forgot."

Odeen smiled indulgently. It was so easy to forget the uncounted stars that could not be seen except by special instruments. "That's all right. You don't mind my boring you with all this."

"You're not boring me," said Dua. "I *love* it. It even makes food taste so good." And she wavered between the electrodes with a kind of luxurious tremor.

Odeen, who had never before heard Dua say anything complimentary about food, was greatly heartened. He said, "Of course, our Universe doesn't last as long as theirs. Fusion goes so fast that all the particles are combined after a million lifetimes.''

''But there are so many other stars.''

''Ah, but you see they're all going at once. The whole Universe is dying down. In the other Universe, with so many fewer and larger stars, the fusion goes so slowly that the stars last thousands and millions of times as long as ours. It's hard to compare because it may be that time goes at different rates in the two Universes.'' He added, with some reluctance, ''I don't understand that part myself. That's part of the Estwald Theory and I haven't got to that very much so far.''

''Did Estwald work out all of this?''

''A great deal of it.''

Dua said, ''It's wonderful that we're getting the food from the other Universe then. I mean, it doesn't matter if our Sun dies out, then. We can get all the food we want from the other Universe.''

''That's right.''

''But does nothing bad happen? I have the—the feeling that something bad happens.''

''Well,'' said Odeen. ''We transfer matter back and forth to make the Positron Pump and that means the Universes mix together a little. Our nuclear-force gets a tiny bit weaker, so fusion in our Sun slows up a little and the Sun cools down a little faster. . . But just a little, and we don't need it any more anyway.''

''That's not the something-bad feeling I have. If the nuclear-force gets a tiny bit weaker, then the atoms take up more room—is that right?—and then what happens to melting?''

''That gets a tiny bit harder but it would take many millions of lifetimes before it would get noticeably harder to melt. Even if someday melting became impossible and Soft Ones died out, that would happen long, long after we would all have died out for lack of food if we weren't using the other Universe.''

''That's still not the something-bad—feeling—'' Dua's words were beginning to slur. She wriggled between her electrodes and to Odeen's gratified eyes she seemed noticeably larger and compacter. It was as though his words, as well as the food, were nourishing her.

Losten was right! Education made her more nearly satisfied with life; Odeen could sense a kind of sensual joy in Dua that he had scarcely ever felt before.

She said, ''It is so kind of you to explain, Odeen. You are a good left-ling.''

''Do you want me to go on?'' asked Odeen, flattered and more pleased than he could easily say. ''Is there anything else you want to ask?''

''A great deal, Odeen, but—but not now. Not now, Odeen. Oh, Odeen, do you know what I want to do?''

Odeen guessed at once, but was too cautious to say it openly. Dua's moments of erotic advance were too few to treat with anything but care. He hoped desperately that Tritt had not involved himself with the children to the point where they could not take advantage of this.

But Tritt was in the chamber already. Had he been outside the door, waiting? He did not care. There was no time to think.

Dua had flowed out from between the electrodes and Odeen's senses were filled with her beauty. She was between them, now, and through her Tritt shimmered, with his outlines flaming in incredible color.

It had never been like this. Never.

Odeen held himself back desperately, letting his own substance flow through Dua and into Tritt an atom at a time; holding away from the overpowering penetrance of Dua with every bit of strength; not giving himself up to the ecstasy, but letting it be wrenched from him; hanging on to his consciousness to the last possible moment; and then blanking out in one final transport so intense as to feel like an explosion echoing and reverberating endlessly within him.

Never in the lifetime of the triad had the period of melt-unconsciousness lasted so long.

— 3c —

TRITT WAS pleased. The melting had been so satisfactory. All previous occasions seemed skimpy and hollow in comparison. He was utterly delighted with what had happened. Yet he kept quiet. He felt it better not to speak.

Odeen and Dua were happy, too. Tritt could tell. Even the children seemed to be glowing.

But Tritt was happiest of all—naturally.

He listened to Odeen and Dua talk. He understood none of it, but that didn't matter. He didn't mind that they seemed so pleased with each other. He had his own pleasure and was content to listen.

Dua said, on one occasion. "And do they really try to communicate with us?"

(Tritt never got it quite clear who "they" might be. He gathered that "communicate" was a fancy word for "talk." So why didn't they say "talk"? Sometimes he wondered if he should interrupt. But if he asked questions, Odeen would only say, "Now, Tritt," and Dua would swirl impatiently.)

"Oh, yes," said Odeen. "The Hard Ones are quite sure of that. They have markings on the material that is sent us sometimes and they say that it is perfectly possible to communicate by such markings. Long ago, in fact, they used markings in reverse, when it was necessary to explain to the other-beings how to set up their part of the Positron Pump."

"I wonder what the other-beings look like. What do they look like, do you suppose?"

"From the laws we can work out the nature of the stars because that is simple. But how can we work out the nature of the being? We can never know."

"Couldn't they communicate what they look like?"

"If we understood what they communicated, perhaps we could make out something. But we don't understand."

Dua seemed aggrieved. "Don't the Hard Ones understand?"

"I don't know. If they do, they haven't told me so. Losten once told me it didn't matter what they were like, as long as the Positron Pump worked and was enlarged."

"Maybe he just didn't want you bothering him."

Odeen said, huffily. "I don't bother him."

"Oh, you know what I mean. He just didn't want to get into those details."

By that time Tritt could no longer listen. They went on arguing for quite awhile over whether the Hard Ones should let Dua look at the markings or not. Dua said that she could sense what they said, perhaps.

It made Tritt a little angry. After all, Dua was only a Soft One and not even a Rational. He began to wonder if Odeen was right to tell her all he did. It gave Dua funny ideas—

Dua could see it made Odeen angry, too. First he laughed. Then he said that an Emotional couldn't handle such complicated things. Then he refused to talk at all. Dua had to be very pleasant to him for a while till he came around.

On one occasion it was Dua who was angry—absolutely furious.

It began quietly. In fact, it was on one of the occasions when the two children were with them. Odeen was letting them play with him. He didn't even mind when little-right Torun pulled at him. In fact, he let himself go in most undignified fashion. He didn't seem to mind that he was all out of shape. It was a sure sign he was pleased. Tritt remained in a corner, resting, and was so satisfied with what was happening.

Dua laughed at Odeen's misshapenness. She let her own substance touch Odeen's knobbishness flirtatiously. She knew very well, Tritt knew, that the leftish surface was sensitive when out of ovoid.

Dua said, "I've been thinking, Odeen . . . If the other Universe gets its laws into ours just a bit through the Positron Pump, doesn't our Universe get its laws into theirs the same little bit?"

Odeen howled at Dua's touch and tried to avoid her without upsetting the little ones. He gasped, "I can't answer unless you stop, you mid-ling wretch."

She stopped, and he said, "That's a *very* good thought, Dua. You're an amazing creature. It's true, of course. The mixture goes both ways. . . . Tritt take out the little ones, will you?"

But they scurried off by themselves. They were not such little ones. They were quite grown. Annis would soon be starting his education and Torun was quite Parentally-blockish already.

Tritt stayed and thought Dua looked very beautiful when Odeen talked to her in this way.

Dua said, "If the other laws slow down our Sun and cool them down, don't our laws speed up their suns and heat them up?"

"Exactly right, Dua. A Rational couldn't do better."

"How hot do their suns get?"

"Oh, not much; just slightly hotter, very slightly."

Dua said, "But that's where I keep getting the something-bad feeling.

"Oh, well, the trouble is that their suns are so huge. If our little suns get a little cooler, it doesn't matter. Even if they turned off altogether, it wouldn't matter as long as we have the Positron Pump. With great, huge stars, though, getting even a little hotter is troublesome. There is so much material in one of those stars that turning up the nuclear fusion even a little way will make it explode."

"*Explode!* But then what happens to the people?"

"What people?"

"The people in the other Universe."

For a moment, Odeen looked blank, then he said, "I don't know."

"Well, what would happen if our own Sun exploded?"

"It couldn't explode."

(Tritt wondered what all the excitement was about. How could a Sun explode? Dua seemed angrier and Odeen looked confused.)

Dua said, "But if it *did?* Would it get very hot?"

"I suppose so."

"Wouldn't it kill us all?"

Odeen hesitated and then said in clear annoyance, "What difference does it make, Dua? Our Sun isn't exploding, and don't ask silly questions."

"You *told* me to ask questions, Odeen, and it *does* make a difference, because the Positron Pump works both ways. We need their end as much as ours."

Odeen stared at her. "I never told you that."

"I feel it."

Odeen said, "You feel a great many things. Dua—"

But Dua was shouting now. She was quite beside herself. Tritt had never seen her like that. She said, "Don't change the subject, Odeen. And don't withdraw and try to make me out a complete fool—just another Emotional. You said I was almost like a Rational and I'm enough like one to see that the Positron Pump won't work without the other-beings. If the people in the other Universe are destroyed, the Positron Pump will stop and our Sun will be colder than ever and we'll all starve. Don't you think that's important?"

Odeen was shouting too, now. "That shows what *you* know. We need their help because the energy supply is in low concentration and we have to switch matter. If the Sun in the other Universe explodes, there'll be an enormous flood of energy; a huge flood that will last for a million lifetimes. There will be so much energy, we could tap it directly without any matter-shift either way; so we *don't* need them, and it *doesn't* matter what happens—"

They were almost touching now. Tritt was horrified. He had better say something, make them get apart, talk to them. He couldn't think of anything to say. Then it turned out he didn't have to.

There was a Hard One just outside the cavern. No, three of them. They had been trying to talk and hadn't made themselves heard.

Tritt shrieked, "Odeen. Dua."

Then he remained quiet, trembling. He had a frightened notion of what the Hard Ones had come to talk about. He decided to leave.

But a Hard One put out one of his permanent, opaque appendages and said, "Don't go."

It sounded harsh, unfriendly. Tritt was more frightened than ever.

— 4a —

DUA WAS filled with anger; so filled she could scarcely sense the Hard Ones. She seemed stifled under the components of the anger, each one filling her to the brim, separately. There was a sense of wrongness that Odeen should try to lie to her. A sense of wrongness that a whole world of people should die. A sense of wrongness that it was so easy for her to learn and that she had never been allowed to.

Since that first time in the rock, she had gone twice more to the Hard-caverns. Twice more, unnoticed, she had buried herself in rock, and each time she sensed and *knew,* and each time when Odeen would explain matters to her, she knew in advance what it was he would explain.

Why couldn't they teach her, then, as they had taught Odeen? Why only the Rationals? Did she possess the capacity to learn only because she was a Left-Em, a perverted mid-ling? Then let them teach her, perversion and all. It was *wrong* to leave her ignorant.

Finally, the words of the Hard One were breaking through to her. Losten was there, but it was not he speaking. It was a strange Hard One, in front, who spoke. She did not know him, but she knew few of them.

The Hard One said, "Which of you have been in the lower caverns recently: the Hard caverns?"

Dua was defiant. They found out about her rock-rubbing and she didn't care. Let them tell everybody. She would do so herself. She said, "*I* have. Many times."

"Alone?" said the Hard One calmly.

"Alone. Many times," snapped Dua. It was only three times, but she didn't care.

Odeen muttered, "I have, of course, been to the lower caverns on occasion."

The Hard One seemed to ignore that. He turned to Tritt instead and said sharply. "And you, right?"

Tritt quavered, "Yes, Hard-sir."

"Alone?"

"Yes, Hard-sir."

"How often?"

"Once."

Dua was annoyed. Poor Tritt was in such a panic over nothing. It was she herself who had done it and she was ready for a confrontation. "Leave him alone," she said. "I'm the one you want."

The Hard One turned slowly toward her. "For what?" he said.

"For whatever it is." And faced with it directly, she couldn't bring herself to describe what she had done after all. Not in front of Odeen.

"Well, we'll get to you. First, the right. . . . Your name is Tritt, isn't it? Why did you go to the lower caverns alone?"

"To speak to Hard-One-Estwald, Hard-sir."

At which again Dua interrupted, eagerly, "Are *you* Estwald?"

The Hard One said briefly, "No."

Odeen looked annoyed, as though it embarrassed him that Dua didn't recognize the Hard One. Dua didn't care.

The Hard One said to Tritt, "What did you take from the lower caverns?"

Tritt was silent.

The Hard One said, without emotion, "We know you took something. We want to know if you know what it was. It could be very dangerous."

Tritt was still silent, and Losten interposed, saying more kindly, "Please tell us, Tritt. We know now it was you and we don't want to have to be harsh."

Tritt mumbled. "I took a food-ball."

"Ah." It was the first Hard One speaking. "What did you do with it?"

And Tritt burst out. "It was for Dua. She wouldn't eat. It was for Dua."

Dua jumped and coalesced in astonishment.

The Hard One turned on her at once. "You did not know about it?"

"No!"

"Nor you?"—to Odeen.

Odeen, so motionless as to seem frozen, said, "No, Hard-sir."

For a moment the air was full of unpleasant vibration as the Hard Ones spoke to each other, ignoring the triad.

Whether her sessions at rock-rubbing had made her more sensitive, or whether it was her recent storm of emotions, Dua couldn't tell, and wouldn't have dreamed of trying to analyze; she simply knew she was catching whiffs—not of words—but of understanding—

They had detected the loss some time ago. They had been searching quietly. They had turned to the Soft Ones as possible culprits with reluctance. They had investigated and then turned to Odeen's triad with even greater reluctance. (Why? Dua missed that.) They did not see how Odeen could have had the foolishness to take it, or Dua the inclination. They did not think of Tritt at all.

Then the Hard One who had so far not said a word to the Soft Ones recalled seeing Tritt in the Hard-caverns. (Of course, thought Dua. It was the day she had first entered the rock. She had sensed him then. She had forgotten.)

It had seemed unlikely in the extreme, but finally, with all else impossible and with the time lapse having grown intolerably dangerous, they came. They would have liked to consult Estwald, but by the time the possibility of Tritt arose, he was unavailable.

All this Dua sensed in a gasp and now she turned toward Tritt, with a feeling of mingled wonder and outrage.

Losten was anxiously vibrating that no harm had been done, that Dua looked well, that it was a useful experiment actually. The Hard One to whom Tritt had spoken was agreeing; the other still exuded concern.

Dua was not paying attention to them only. She was looking at Tritt.

The first Hard One said, "Where is the food-ball now, Tritt?"

Tritt showed them.

It was hidden effectively and the connections were clumsy but serviceable.

"The Hard One said, "Did you do this yourself, Tritt?"

"Yes, Hard-sir."

"How did you know how?"

"I looked at how it was done in the Hard-caverns. I did it exactly the way I saw it done there."

"Didn't you know you might have harmed your mid-mate?"

"I *didn't*. I *wouldn't*. I—" Tritt seemed unable to speak for a moment. Then he said, "It was not to hurt her. It was to feed her. I let it pour into her feeder and I decorated her feeder. I wanted her to try it and she did. She ate! For the first time in a long while she ate well. We melted." He paused, then said in a huge, tumultuous cry. "She had enough energy at last to initiate a baby-Emotional. She took Odeen's seed and passed it to me. I have it growing inside me. A baby-Emotional is growing inside me."

Dua could not speak. She stumbled back and then rushed for the door in so pell-mell a fashion that the Hard Ones could not get out of the way in time. She struck the appendage of the one in front, passing deep into it, and then pulled free with a harsh sound.

The Hard One's appendage fell limp and his expression seemed contorted with pain. Odeen tried to dodge around him to follow Dua, but the Hard One said, with apparent difficulty. "Let her go for now. There is enough harm done. We will take care."

ODEEN FOUND himself living through a nightmare. Dua was gone. The Hard Ones were gone. Only Tritt was still there; silent.

How could it have happened, Odeen thought in tortured fashion. How could Tritt have found his way alone to the Hard-caverns? How could he have taken a storage battery charged at the Positron Pump and designed to yield radiation in much more concentrated form than Sunlight and dared—

Odeen would not have had the courage to chance it. How could Tritt; stumbling, ignorant Tritt? Or was he unusual, too? Odeen, the clever Rational; Dua, the curious Emotional; and Tritt, the daring Parental?

He said, "How could you do it, Tritt?"

Tritt retorted hotly. "What did I do? I fed her. I fed her better than she had ever been fed before. Now we have a baby-Emotional initiated at last. Haven't we waited long enough? We would have waited forever, if we had waited for Dua."

"But don't you understand, Tritt? You might have hurt her. It wasn't ordinary Sunlight. It was an experimental radiational source that could have been too concentrated to be safe."

"I don't understand what you're saying, Odeen. How could it do harm? I tasted the kind of food the Hard Ones made before. It tasted bad. You've tasted it, too. It tasted just awful and it never hurt us. It tasted so bad, Dua wouldn't touch it. Then I came on the food-ball. It tasted *good*. I ate some and it was delicious. How can anything delicious hurt. You see, Dua ate it. She liked it. And it started the baby-Emotional. How can I have done wrong?"

Odeen despaired of explaining. He said, "Dua is going to be very angry."

"She'll get over it."

"I wonder. Tritt, she's not like ordinary Emotionals. That's what makes her so hard to live with, but so wondeful when we *can* live with her. She may never want to melt with us again."

Tritt's outline was sturdily plane-surfaced. Then he said, "Well, what of it?"

"What *of* it? *You* ask. Do you want to give up melting?"

"No, but if she won't she won't. I have my third baby and I don't care any more. I know all about the Soft Ones in the old days. They used to have two triad-births sometimes. But I don't care. One is plenty."

"But, Tritt, babies aren't all there is to melting."

"What else? I heard you say once you learned faster after you melted. Then learn slower. I don't care. I have my third baby."

Odeen turned away, trembling, and flowed jerkily out of the chamber. What was the use of scolding Tritt? Tritt wouldn't understand. He wasn't sure he understood himself.

Once the third baby was born, and grown a little, surely there would come a time to pass on. It would be he, Odeen, who would have to give the signal, who would have to say when, and it would have to be done without fear. Anything else would be disgrace, or worse, and yet he could not face it without melting, even now that all three children would have been formed.

Melting, somehow, would eliminate the fear. . . . Maybe it was because melting was like passing on. There was a period of time when you were not conscious, yet it did not hurt. It was like not existing and yet it was desirable.

With enough melting, he could gain the courage to pass on without fear and without—

Oh, Sun and all the stars, its wasn't "passing on." Why use that phrase so solemnly. He knew the other word that was never used except by children who wanted to shock their elders somehow. It was *dying*. He had to get ready to die without fear, and to have Dua and Tritt die with him.

And he didn't know how. . . . Not without melting . . .

— 4c —

TRITT REMAINED alone in the room, frightened, frightened, but sturdily resolved to remain unmoved. He had his third baby. He could feel it within.

That was what counted.

That was all that counted.

Yet why, then, deep inside, did he have a stubborn faint feeling that it *wasn't* all that counted?

— 5a —

DUA WAS ashamed almost beyond endurance. It took a long time for her to battle down the shame; battle it down enough to give herself room to think. She had hastened—hastened—moving blindly out and away from the horror of the home-cavern; scarcely caring that she did not know where she was going or even where she was.

It was night, when no decent Soft One would be on the surface, not even the most frivolous Emotional. And it would be a considerable time before the Sun rose. Dua was glad. The Sun was food and at the moment, she *hated* food and what had been done to her.

It was cold, too, but Dua was only distantly aware of it. Why should she care about cold, she thought, when she had been fattened in order that she might do her duty—fattened, mind and body. After that, cold and starvation were almost her friends.

She saw through Tritt. Poor thing; he was so easy to see through; his actions were pure instinct and he was to be praised that he had followed them so bravely. He had come back so daringly from the Hard-caverns with the food-ball (and she—she herself had sensed him and would have known what was happening if Tritt hadn't been so paralyzed at what he was doing that he had dared not think of it, and if *she* had not been so paralyzed at what *she* was doing and at the new depth of sensation it brought her that she would not take care to sense what most she needed to).

Tritt brought it back undetected and had arranged the pitiful booby trap, decorating her feeder to entice her. And she had come back, flushed with awareness of her rock-probing thinness, filled with the shame of it and with pity for Tritt. With all that shame and pity, she ate, and helped initiate birth.

Since then she had eaten but sparingly as was her custom and never at the feeder, but then there had been no impulse to. Tritt had not driven her. He had looked contented (of course) so there was nothing to reactivate the shame. And Tritt left the food-ball in place. He didn't dare risk taking it back; he had what he wanted; it was best and easiest to leave it there and think of it no more.

—Till he was caught.

But clever Odeen must have seen through Tritt's plan, must have spied the new connections to the electrodes, must have understood Tritt's purpose. Undoubtedly, he said nothing to Tritt; that would have embarrassed and frightened the poor right-ling and Odeen always watched over Tritt with loving care.

Of course, Odeen didn't have to say anything. He needed only to fill in the gaps in Tritt's clumsy plan and make it work.

Dua was under no illusions now. She would have detected the taste of the food-ball; noticed its extraordinary tang; caught the way in which it began to fill her while giving her no sensations of fullness—had it not been that Odeen had occupied her with talk.

It had been a conspiracy between the two of them, whether Tritt was consciously part of it or not. How could she have believed that Odeen was suddenly a careful, painstaking teacher? How could she have failed to see the ulterior motive? Their concern for her was their concern for the completion of the new triad, and that in itself was an indication of how little they thought of her.

Well—

She paused long enough to feel her own weariness and she worked herself into a crevice in the rock that would shield her from the thin, cold wind. Two of the seven stars were in her field of vision and she watched them absently, occupying her outer senses in trivia so that she might concentrate the more in internal thought.

She was disillusioned.

"Betrayed," she mutterd to herself. "Betrayed!"

Could they see no further than themselves?

That Tritt would be willing to see all destroyed if he were not secure in his babies was to be taken for granted. But he was a creature of instinct. What of Odeen?

Odeen reasoned, and did that mean that for the purpose of exercising his reason, he would sacrifice all else? Was everything produced by reason its own excuse for being—at any cost? Because Estwald had devised the Positron Pump, did it have to be used in order that the whole world, Hard and Soft alike, be placed at its mercy, and at the mercy of the people of the other Universe? What if the other people stopped and if the world was left without a Positron Pump and with a dangerously cooled Sun?

No, they wouldn't stop, those other people; for they had been persuaded to start and they would be persuaded to keep going until they were destroyed—and then they would be needed no longer by the Rationals, Hard or Soft—just as she, Dua, would have to pass on (be *destroyed*) now that she was needed no longer.

She and the other people, both being betrayed.

Almost without being aware of it, she was cushioning deeper and deeper into the rock. She buried herself, out of sight of the stars, out of touch with the wind, unaware of the world. She was pure thought.

It was Estwald whom she hated. He was the personification of all that was selfish and hard. He had devised the Positron Pump and would destroy a whole world of perhaps tens of thousands without conscience. He was so withdrawn that he never made his appearance and so powerful that even the other Hard Ones seemed afraid of him.

Well, then, she would fight him. She would stop him.

The people of the other Universe had helped set up the Positron Pump through communications of some sort. Odeen had mentioned those. Where would such communications be kept? What would they be like? How could they be used for further communication?

It was remarkable how clearly she could think. Remarkable. There was fierce enjoyment in this, that she would use reason to overcome the cruel reasoners.

They wouldn't be able to stop her, for she could go where no Hard One could go, where no Rational or Parental could—and where no other Emotional would.

She might be caught eventually, but at the moment she didn't care. She was going to fight to have her way—at any price—at any price—though to do it meant she would have to go through rock, live in rock, skirt the Hard-caverns, steal food from their stored energy batteries when she had to, flock with the other Emotionals and feed on Sunlight when she could.

But in the end she would teach them all a lesson and after that they could do as they wished. She would even be ready to pass on then—but only then—

— 5b —

ODEEN WAS present when the new baby-Emotional was born, perfect in every way, but he had not been able to feel enthusiasm over it. Even Tritt, who cared for it perfectly, as a Parental must, seemed subdued in his ecstasies.

A long time had passed and it was as though Dua had vanished. She had not passed on. A Soft One could not pass on except when the whole triad did; but she was not with them, either. It was as though she had passed on, without passing on.

Odeen had seen her once, only once, not very long after her wild fight on the news that she had initiated the new baby.

He had passed a cluster of Emotionals, sunning themselves, when he was moving over the surface on some foolish notion that he might find her. They had tittered at the rare sight of a Rational moving in the vicinity of an Emotional cluster and had thinned in mass-provocation, with no thought among the foolish lot of them but to advertise the fact that they were Emotionals.

Odeen felt only contempt for them and there was no answering stir along his own smooth curves at all. He thought of Dua instead and of how different she was from all of them. Dua never thinned for any reason other than her own inner needs. She had never tried to attract anyone and was the more attractive for that. If she could have brought herself to join the flock of empty-heads she would be easily recognized (he felt sure) by the fact that she alone would *not* thin, but would probably thicken, precisely because the others thinned.

And as he thought that, Odeen scanned the sunning Emotionals and noted that one indeed had not.

He stopped and then hastened toward her, oblivious to the Emotionals in his way, oblivious to their wild screeching as they flicked smokily out of his path and chattered desperately in their attempts to avoid coalescing one with the other—at least not in the open, and with a Rational watching.

It *was* Dua. She did not try to leave. She kept her ground and said nothing.

"Dua," he said humbly, "aren't you coming home?"

"I have no home, Odeen," she said. Not angrily, not in hate—and all the more dreadfully for that reason.

"How can you blame Tritt for what he did, Dua? You know the poor fellow can't reason."

"But you can, Odeen. And you occupied my mind while he arranged to feed my body, didn't you? Your reason told you that I was much more likely to be trapped by you than by him."

"Dua, *no!*"

"No, what? Didn't you make a big show of teaching me, of educating me."

"I did, but it wasn't a show, it was real. And it was not because of what Tritt had done. I didn't *know* what Tritt had done."

"I can't believe that." She flowed away without haste. He followed after. They were alone now, the Sun shining redly down upon them.

She turned to him. "Let me ask you one question, Odeen? Why did you want to teach me?"

Odeen said, "Because I *wanted* to. Because I *enjoy* teaching and because I would rather teach than do anything else—but learn."

"And melt, of course. . . . Never mind," she added to ward him off. "Don't explain that you are talking of reason and not of instinct. If you really mean what you say about enjoying teaching; if I can really ever believe what you say; then perhaps you can understand something I'm going to tell you.

"I've been learning a great deal since I left you, Odeen. Never mind how. I have. There's no Emotional left in me at all, except physiologically. Inside, where it counts, I'm all Rational, except that I hope I have more feeling for others than Rationals have. And one thing I've learned is what we really are, Odeen; you and I and Tritt and all the other triads on this planet; what we really are and always were."

"What is that?" asked Odeen. He was prepared to listen for as long as might be necessary, and as quietly, if only she would come back with him when she had said her say. He would perform any penance, do anything that might be required. Only she must come back—and something dim and dark inside him knew that she had to come back voluntarily.

"What we are? Why, nothing, really Odeen," she said lightly, almost laughing. "Isn't that strange? The Hard Ones are the only living species on the face of the world. Haven't they taught you that? There is only one species because you and I, the Soft Ones, are not really alive. We're machines, Odeen. We must be because only the Hard ones are alive. Haven't they taught you that, Odeen?"

"But, Dua, that's nonsense," said Odeen, nonplused.

Dua's voice grew harsher. "Machines, Odeen! Made by the Hard Ones!

Destroyed by the Hard Ones! *They* are alive, the Hard Ones. Only they. They don't talk about it much. They don't have to. They all know it. But I've learned to think, Odeen, and I've worked it out from the small clues I've had. They live tremendously long lives, but die eventually. They no longer give birth; the Sun yields too little energy for that. And since they die very infrequently, but don't give birth at all, their numbers are very slowly declining. And there are no young ones to provide new blood and new thoughts, so the old, long-lived Hard Ones get terribly bored. So what do you suppose they do, Odeen?''

''What?'' There was a kind of fascination about this. A repulsive fascination.

''They manufacture mechanical children, whom they can teach. You said it yourself, Odeen. You would rather teach than do anything else but learn—and melt, of course. The Rationals are made in the mental image of the Hard Ones, and the Hard Ones don't melt, and learning is terribly complex for them since they already know so much. What is left for them but the fun of teaching. Rationals were created for no purpose but to be taught. Emotionals and Parentals were created because they were necessary for the self-perpetuating machinery that made new Rationals. And new Rationals were needed constantly because the old ones were used up, were taught all they could be taught. And when old Rationals had absorbed what they could, they were destroyed and were taught, in advance, to call the destruction process ''passing on'' to spare their feelings. And of course, Emotionals and Parentals passed on with them. As long as they had helped form a new triad there was no further use for them.''

''But that's all wrong, Dua,'' Odeen managed to say. He had no arguments to pose against her nightmare scheme, but he knew with a certainty past argument that she was wrong. (Or did a little pang of doubt deep inside suggest that the certainty might have been implanted in him, to begin with?—No, surely no, for then would not Dua be certain with an implanted certainty, too, that this was wrong?—Or was she an imperfect Emotional without the proper implantations and without— Oh, what was he *thinking*. He was as crazy as she was.)

Dua said, ''You look upset, Odeen. Are you sure I'm all wrong? Of course, now they have the Positron Pump and they now have all the energy they need, or will have. Soon they will be giving birth again. Maybe they are doing so already. And they won't need any Soft-One machines at all, and we will all be destroyed; I beg pardon, we will all pass on.''

''No, Dua,'' said Odeen, strenuously, as much to himself as to her. ''I don't know how you got those notions, but the Hard Ones aren't like that. We are not destroyed.''

''Don't lie to yourself, Odeen. They *are* like that. They are prepared to destroy a whole world of other-beings for their benefit; a whole Universe if they have to. Would they stop at destroying a few Soft Ones for their comfort?— But they made one mistake. Somehow the machinery went wrong and a Rational mind got into an Emotional body. I'm a Left-Em, do you know that? They called me that when I was a child, and they were right. I can reason like a Rational and I can feel like an Emotional. And I will fight the Hard Ones with that combination.''

Odeen felt wild. Dua must surely be mad, yet he dared not say so. He had to cajole her somehow and bring her back. He said with strenuous sincerity, ''Dua, we're not destroyed when we pass on.''

''No? What does happen then?''

"I—I don't know. I think we enter another world, a better and happier world, and become like—like—well, much better than we are."

Dua laughed. "Where did you hear that? Did the Hard Ones tell you that?"

"No, Dua, I'm *sure* that this must be so out of my own thoughts. I've been thinking a great deal about it since you left."

Dua said, "Then think less and you'll be less foolish. Poor Odeen! Good-bye." She flowed away once more, thinly. There was an air of weariness about her.

Odeen called out, "But wait, Dua. Surely you want to see your new baby-mid."

She did not answer.

He cried out. "When will you come home?"

She did not answer.

And he followed no more, but looked after her in deepest misery as she dwindled.

He did not tell Tritt he had seen Dua. What was the use? Nor did he see her again. He began haunting the favored sunning-sites of the Emotionals in the region; doing so even though occasional Parentals emerged to watch him in stupid suspicion (Tritt was a mental giant compared to most Parentals).

The lack of her hurt more with each passing day. And with each pasing day, he realized that there was a gathering fright inside himself over her absence. He didn't know why.

He came back to home-cavern one day to find Losten waiting for him. Losten was standing there, grave and polite while Tritt was showing him the new baby and striving to keep the handful of mist from touching the Hard One.

Losten said, "It is indeed a beauty, Tritt. Derala is its name?"

"Derola," corrected Tritt. "I don't know when Odeen will be back. He wanders about a lot—"

"Here I am, Losten," said Odeen, hastily. "Tritt, take the baby away; there's a good fellow."

Tritt did so, and Losten turned to Odeen with quite obvious relief, saying, "You must be very happy to have completed the triad."

Odeen tried to answer with some polite inconsequence, but could maintain only a miserable silence. He had recently been developing a kind of comradeship, a vague sense of equality with the Hard Ones, that enabled them to talk together on a level. Somehow Dua's madness had spoiled it. Odeen knew she was wrong and yet he approached Losten once more as stiffy as in the long-gone days when he thought of himself as a far inferior creature to them, as a—machine?

Losten said, "Have you see Dua?" This was a real question, and not politeness. Odeen could tell easily.

"Only once, H—" (He almost said "Hard-sir" as though he were a child again, or a Parental.) "Only once, Losten. She won't come home."

"She *must* come home," said Losten, softly.

"I don't know how to arrange that."

Losten regarded him somberly. "Do you know what she is doing?"

Odeen dared not look at the other. Had he discovered Dua's wild theories? What would be done about that?

He made a negative sign without speaking.

Losten said, "She is a most unusual Emotional, Odeen. You know that, don't you?"

"Yes," sighed Odeen.

"So are you in your way, and Tritt in his. I doubt that any Parental in the world would have had either the courage or the initiative to steal an energy-battery or the perverse ingenuity to put it to use as he did. The three of you make up the most unusual triad of which we have any record."

"Thank you."

"But there are uncomfortable aspects to the triad, too; things we didn't count on. We wanted you to teach Dua as the mildest and best possible way in which to cajole her into performing her function voluntarily. We did not count on Tritt's quixotic action at just that moment. Nor, to tell you the truth, did we count on her wild reaction to the fact that the world in the other Universe must be destroyed."

"I ought to have been careful how I answered her questions," said Odeen miserably.

"It wouldn't have helped. She was finding out for herself. We didn't count on that either. Odeen, I am sorry, but I must tell you this—Dua has become a deadly danger; she is trying to stop the Poistron Pump."

"But how can she? She can't reach it, and even if she could, she lacks the knowledge to do anything about it."

"Oh, but she *can* reach it." Losten hesitated, then said, "She remains infused in the rock of the world where she is safe from us."

It took awhile for Odeen to grasp the clear meaning of the words. He said, "No grown Emotional would—Dua would never—"

"She would. She does. Don't waste time arguing the point. . . . She can penetrate anywhere in the caverns. Nothing is hidden from her. She has studied those communications we have received from the other Universe. We don't know that of certain knowledge, but there is no other way of explaining what is happening."

"Oh, oh, oh." Odeen rocked back and forth, his surface opaque with shame and grief. "Does Estwald know of all this?"

Losten said, grimly, "Not yet; though he must know someday."

"But what will she do with those communications?"

"She is using them to work out a method for sending some of her own in the other direction."

"But she cannot know how to translate or transmit."

"She is learning both. She knows more about those communications than Estwald himself. She is a frightening phenomenon, an Emotional who can reason and who is out of control."

Odeen shivered. Out of control? How machine-like a reference!

He said, "It can't be that bad."

"It can. She has communicated already and I fear she is advising the other creatures to stop their half of the Poistron Pump. If they do that before their Sun explodes, we will be helpless at this end."

"But then—"

"She must be stopped, Odeen."

"B—But, how? Are you going to blast—" His voice failed. Dimly, he knew that the Hard One had devices for digging caverns out of the world's rock; devices scarcely used since the world's population had begun declining ages ago. Would they locate Dua in the rock and blast it and her?

"No," said Losten, forcefully. "We cannot harm Dua."

"Estwald might—"

"Estwald cannot harm her, either."

"Then what's to be done?"

"It's you, Odeen. Only you. We're helpless, so we must depend on you."

"On *me?* But what can I do?"

"Think about it," said Losten, urgently. *Think* about it."

"Think about *what?"*

"I can't say more than that," said Losten, in apparent agony. "Think! There is so little time."

He turned and left, moving rapidly for a Hard One, moving as though he did not trust himself to stay and perhaps say too much.

And Odeen could only look after him, dismayed, confused—lost.

— 5c —

THERE WAS a great deal for Tritt to do. Babies required much care, but even two young-lefts and two young-rights together did not make up the sum of a single baby-mid—particularly not a mid as perfect as Derola. She had to be exercised and soothed, protected from percolating into whatever she touched, cajoled into condensing and resting.

It was a long time before he saw Odeen again and, actually, he didn't care. Derola took up all his time. But then he came across Odeen in the corner of his own alcove, iridescent with thought.

Tritt remembered, suddenly. He said, "Was Losten angry about Dua?"

Odeen came to himself with a start. "Losten?—Yes, he was angry. Dua is doing great harm."

"She should come home, shouldn't she?"

Odeen was staring at Tritt. "Tritt," he said, "we're going to have to persuade Dua to come home. We must find her first. You can do it. With a new baby, your Parental sensitivity is very high. You can use it to find Dua."

"No," said Tritt, shocked. "It's used for Derola. It would be wrong to use it for Dua. Besides, if she wants to stay away so long when a baby-mid is longing for her—and she was once a baby-mid herself—maybe we might just learn to do without her."

"But, Tritt, don't you ever want to melt again?"

"Well, the triad is now complete."

"That's not all there is to melting."

Tritt said, "But where do we have to go to find her? Little Derola needs me. She's a tiny baby. I don't want to leave her."

"The Hard Ones will arrange to have Derola taken care of. You and I will go the Hard-caverns and find Dua."

Tritt thought about that. He didn't care about Dua. He didn't even care about Odeen, somehow. There was only Derola. He said, "Someday. Someday, when Derola is older. Not till then."

"Tritt,' said Odeen, urgently, "we must find Dua. Otherwise—otherwise the babies will be taken away from us."

"By whom?" said Tritt.

"By the Hard Ones."

Tritt was silent. There was nothing he could say. He had never heard of such a thing. He could not conceive of such a thing.

Odeen said, "Tritt, we must pass on. I know why, now. I've been thinking about it ever since Losten— But never mind that. Dua and you must pass on, too. Now that I know why, you will feel you must and I hope—I think—Dua will feel she must, too. And we must pass on *soon,* for Dua is destroying the world."

Tritt was backing away. "Don't look at me like that, Odeen. . . . You're making me. . . . You're making me."

"I'm not making you, Tritt," said Odeen, sadly. "It's just that I know now and so you must. . . . But we must find Dua."

"No, no." Tritt was in agony, trying to resist. There was something terribly new about Odeen, and existence was approaching an end inexorably. There would be no Tritt and no baby-mid. Where every other Parental had his baby-mid for a long time, Tritt would have lost his almost at once.

It wasn't fair. Oh, it wasn't fair.

Tritt panted. "It's Dua's fault. Let *her* pass on first."

Odeen said, with deadening calm, "There's no other way but for all of us—"

And Tritt knew that was so—that was so—that was so—

— 6a —

DUA FELT thin and cold, wispy. Her attempts to rest in the open and absorb Sunlight had ended after Odeen had found her that time. Her feeding at the Hard Ones' batteries was erratic. She dared not remain too long outside the safety of rock, so she ate in quick gulps, and she never got enough.

She was conscious of hunger, continuously, all the more so since it seemed to tire her to remain in the rock. It was as though she were being punished for all that long time in which she haunted the Sunset and ate so skimpily.

If it were not for the work she was doing, she could not bear the weariness and hunger. Sometimes she hoped that the Hard Ones would destroy her—but only after she was finished.

The Hard Ones were helpless as long as she was in the rock. Sometimes she sensed them outside the rock in the open. They were afraid. Sometimes she thought the fear was *for* her, but that couldn't be. How could they be afraid for her; afraid that she would pass on out of sheer lack of food, out of sheer exhaustion. It must be that they were afraid *of* her; afraid of a machine that did not work as they had designed it to work; appalled at so great a prodigy; struck helpless with the terror of it.

Carefully, she avoided them. She always knew where they were, so they could not catch her nor stop her.

They could not watch all places always. She thought she could even blank what little perception they had.

She swirled out of the rock and studied the recorded duplicates of the communications they had received from the other Universe. They did not know that was what she was after. If they hid them, she would find them in whatever new place. If they destroyed them, it didn't matter. Dua could remember them.

She did not understand them, at first, but with her stay in the rocks, her senses grew steadily sharper, and she seemed to understand without understanding. Without knowing what the symbols meant, they inspired feelings within her.

She picked out markings and placed them where they would be sent to the other Universe. The markings were F-E-E-R. What that could possibly mean she had no idea, but its shape inspired her with a feeling of fear and she did her best to impress that feeling of fear upon the markings. Perhaps the other-creatures, studying the markings, would also feel fear.

When the answers came, Dua could sense excitement in them. She did not always get the answers that were sent. Sometimes the Hard Ones found them first. Surely, they must know what she was doing. Still, they couldn't read the messages, couldn't even sense the emotions that went along with them.

So she didn't care. She would not be stopped, till she was done—whatever the Hard Ones found out.

She waited for a message that would carry the feeling she wanted. It came: P-U-M-P B-A-D.

It carried the fear and hatred she wanted. She sent it back in extended form— more fear—more hatred— Now the other people would understand. Now they would stop the Pump. The Hard Ones would have to find some other way, some other source of energy; they must not obtain it through the death of all those thousands of other Universe creatures.

She was resting too much, declining into a kind of stupor, within the rock. Desperately she craved food and waited so that she could crawl out. Even more desperately than she wanted the food in the storage battery, she wanted the storage battery to be dead. She wanted to suck the last bit of food out of it and know that no more would come and that her task was done.

She emerged at last and remained recklessly long, sucking in the contents of one of the batteries. She wanted to withdraw its last, empty it, see that no more was entering—but it was an endless source—endless—endless.

She stirred and drew away from the battery in disgust. The Positron Pumps were still going then. Had her messages not persuaded the other Universe creatures to stop the Pumps? Had they not received them? Had they not sensed their meaning?

She had to try again. She had to make it plain beyond plain. She would include every combination of signals that to her seemed to carry the feeling of danger; every combination that would get across the plea to stop.

Desperately she began to fuse the symbols into metal; drawing without reserve on the energy she had just sucked out of the battery; drawing on it till it was all gone and she was more weary than ever: PUMP NOT STOP NOT STOP WE NOT STOP PUMP WE NOT HEAR DANGER NOT HEAR NOT HEAR YOU STOP PLEASE STOP YOU STOP SO WE STOP PLEASE YOU STOP DANGER DANGER DANGER DANGER STOP STOP YOU STOP PUMP.

It was all she could. There was nothing left in her but a racking pain. She placed the message where it could be transferred and she did not wait for the Hard Ones to send the message unwittingly. Through an agonizing haze, she manipulated the controls as she had seen them do, finding the energy for it somehow.

The message disappeared and so did the cavern in a purple shimmer of vertigo. She was—passing on—out of sheer—exhaustion.

Odeen—Tri—

— 6b —

ODEEN CAME. He had been flowing faster than ever he had flowed before. He had been following Tritt's sharp new-baby sense perception, but now he was close enough for his own blunter sense to detect her nearness. He could on his own account feel the flickering and fading consciousness of Dua, and he raced forward while Tritt did his best to clump along, gasping and calling, "Faster—faster—"

Odeen found her in a state of collapse, scarcely alive, smaller than he had ever seen an adult Emotional.

"Tritt," he said, "bring the battery here. No—no—don't try to carry her. She's too thin to carry. Hurry. If she sinks into the floor—"

The Hard Ones began to gather. They were late, of course, with their inability to sense other life-forms at a distance. If it had depended only on them, it would have been too late to save her. She would not have passed on; she would truly have been destroyed—and—and more than she knew would have been destroyed with her.

Now, as she was slowly gathering life out of the energy supply, the Hard Ones stood silently near them.

Odeen rose; a new Odeen who knew what was happening exactly. Imperiously, he ordered them away with an angry gesture—and they left. Silently. Without objection.

Dua stirred.

Tritt said, "Is she all right, Odeen?"

"Quiet, Tritt," said Odeen. "Dua?"

"Odeen?" She stirred, spoke in a whisper. "I thought I had passed on."

"Not yet, Dua. Not yet. But first you must eat and rest."

"Is Tritt here, too?"

"Here I am, Dua," said Tritt.

"Don't try to bring me back," said Dua. "It's over. I've done what I wanted to do. The Positron Pump will—will stop soon, I'm sure. The Hard Ones will continue to need Soft Ones and they will take care of you two, or at least the children."

Odeen didn't say anything. He kept Tritt from saying anything, either. He let the radiation pour slowly into Dua, very slowly. He stopped at times to let her rest a bit, then he started again.

She began to mutter, "Enough. Enough." Her substance was writhing more strongly.

Still he fed her.

Finally, he spoke. He said, "Dua, you were wrong. We are not machines. I know exactly what we are. I would have come to you sooner, if I had found out earlier, but I didn't know till Losten begged me to think. And I did; very hard; and even so it is almost premature."

Dua moaned and Odeen stopped for a while.

He said, "Listen, Dua. There *is* a single species of life. The Hard Ones *are* the only living things in the world. You gathered that, and so far you were right. But that doesn't mean the Soft Ones aren't alive; it merely means we are part of the same single species. *The Soft Ones are the immature forms of the Hard Ones.* We are first children as Soft Ones, then adults as Soft Ones, then Hard Ones. Do you understand?"

Tritt said, in soft confusion, "What? What?"

Odeen said, "Not now, Tritt. Now now. You'll understand, too, but this is for Dua." He kept watching Dua, who was gaining opalescence.

He said, "Listen Dua, whenever we melt, whenever the triad melts, we become a Hard One. The Hard One is three-in-one, which is why he is hard. During the time of unconsciousness in melting we are a Hard One. But it is only temporary, and we can never remember the period afterward. We can never stay a Hard One long; we must come back. But all through our life we keep developing, with certain key stages marking it off. Each baby born marks a key stage. With the birth of third, the Emotional, there comes the possibility of the final stage, where the Rational's mind by itself, without the other two, can remember those flashes of Hard One existence. Then, and only then, he can guide a perfect melt that will form the Hard One forever, so that the triad can live a new and unified life of learning and intellect. I told you that passing on was like being born again. I was groping then for something I did not quite understand, but now I know."

Dua was looking at him, trying to smile. She said, "How can you pretend to believe that, Odeen? If that were so, wouldn't the Hard Ones have told you long ago; told all of us?"

"They couldn't, Dua. There was a time, long ages ago, when melting was just a putting together of the atoms of bodies. But evolution slowly developed minds. Listen to me, Dua; melting is a putting together of the minds, too, and that's much harder, much more delicate. To put it together properly and permanently, just so, the Rational must reach a certain pitch in development. That pitch is reached when he finds out, *for himself,* what it's all about: when his mind is finally keen enough to remember what has happened in all those temporary unions during melting. If the Rational were told, that development would be aborted and the time of the perfect melt could not be determined. The Hard One would form imperfectly. When Losten pleaded with me to think, he was taking a great chance. Even that may have been—I hope not—

"For it's especially true in our case, Dua. For many generations, the Hard Ones have been combining triads with great care to form particularly advanced Hard Ones and our triad was the best they'd ever obtained. Especially you, Dua. Especially you. Losten was once the triad whose baby-mid you were. Part of him was your Parental. He knew you. He brought you to Tritt and me."

Dua sat up. Her voice was almost normal. "Odeen! Are you making all this up just to soothe me?"

Tritt broke in. "No, Dua. I feel it, too. I feel it, too. I don't know what exactly, but I feel it."

"He does, Dua," said Odeen. "You will, too. Aren't you beginning to recall being a Hard One during our melt? Don't you want to melt now? One last time? One last time?"

He lifted her. There was a feverishness about her, and though she struggled a bit, she was thinning.

"If what you say is true, Odeen," she gasped. "If we are to be a Hard One; then it seems to me you are saying we'll be an *important* one. Is that so?"

"The most important. The best who was ever formed. I mean that. . . . Tritt, over there. It's not goodbye, Tritt. We'll be together, as we always wanted to be. Dua, too. You, too, Dua."

Dua said, "Then we can make Estwald understand the Pump can't continue. We'll force—"

The melting was beginning. One by one, the Hard Ones were entering again at the crucial moment. Odeen saw them imperfectly, for he was beginning to melt into Dua.

It was not like the other times; no sharp ecstasy; just a smooth, cool, utterly peaceful movement. He could feel himself become partly Dua, and all the world seemed pouring into his/her sharpening senses. The Positron Pumps were still going—he/she could tell—why were they still going?

He was Tritt, too, and a keen sharp sense of bitter loss filled his/her/his mind. Oh, my babies—

And he cried out, one last cry under the consciousness of Odeen, except that somehow it was the cry of Dua. "No, we can't stop Estwald. *We* are Estwald. *We*—"

The cry that was Dua's and yet not Dua's stopped and there was no longer any Dua; nor would there ever be Dua again. Nor Odeen. Nor Tritt.

- 7abc -

ESTWALD STEPPED forth and said sadly to the waiting Hard Ones, by way of vibrating air waves, "I am permanently with you now, and there is much to do—"

III
...CONTEND IN VAIN?

— 1 —

SELENE LINDSTROM smiled brightly and walked with the light springy touch that was startling when first seen by the tourists, but was soon recognized as having a grace of its own.

"It's time for lunch," she said, cheerfully. "All home-grown, ladies and gentlemen. You may not be used to the taste, but it's all nourishing. . . . Right here, sir. You won't mind sitting with the ladies, I know. . . . One moment. There will be seats for all. . . . Sorry, there will be a choice on the beverage, but not on the main course. That will be veal. . . . No, no. Artificial flavor and texture, but it's really quite good."

Then she sat down herself, with a slight sigh and an even slighter wavering of her pleasant expression.

One of the group sat down across from her.

"Do you mind?" he asked.

She looked at him, quickly, penetrating. She had the faculty of making quick judgments, of course, and he did not seem troublesome. She said, "Not at all. But aren't you with someone in this group?"

He shook his head. "No. I'm alone. Even if that were not the case, earthies are no great thrill to me."

She looked at him again. He was fiftyish and there was a weary look about him which only his bright, inquisitive eyes seemed to belie. He had the unmistakable look of the Earthman, laden down with gravity. She said, " 'Earthie' is a Moon-expression, and not a very nice one."

"I'm from Earth," he said, "so I can use it without offense, I hope. Unless you object."

Selene shrugged as though to say: Please yourself.

She had the faintly oriental look about the eyes so many of the Moon-girls had, but her hair was the color of honey and her nose was prominent. She was undeniably attractive without being in any way classically beautiful.

The Earthman was staring at the nameplate she wore on the blouse covering the upper slope of her high, not-too-large left breast. She decided it was really

98

the nameplate he was looking at, not the breast, though the blouse was semi-transparent when it caught the light at a particular angle and there was no garment beneath it.

He said, "Are there many Selenes here?"

"Oh, yes. Hundreds, I think. Also Cynthias, Dianas, and Artemises. Selene is a little tiresome. Half the Selenes I know are called 'Silly' and the other half 'Lena.' "

"Which are you?"

"Neither. I am Selene, all three syllables. SELL-uh-nee," she said, coming down heavily on the first syllable, "to those who use my first name at all."

There was a small smile on the Earthman's face that sat there as though he weren't quite used to it. He said, "And what if anyone asks you if you sell any, Selene?"

"They never ask me that again!" she said, firmly.

"But do they ask you?"

"There are fools always."

A waitress had reached their table and had placed the dishes before them with quick, smooth motions.

The Earthman was visibly impressed. He said to the waitress, "You make them seem to float down."

The waitress smiled and moved on.

Selene said, "Don't you try to do the same. She's used to the gravity and can handle it."

"And if I try, I'll drop everything? Is that it?"

"You'll make a gorgeous mess," she said.

"Well, I won't try."

"There's a good chance someone will before long, and the plate will flow down to the floor and they'll grab for it and miss, and ten to one knock themselves out of their chair. I'd warn them, but it never helps and they're just all the more embarrassed. Everyone else will laugh—the tourists, that is, because the rest of us have seen it too often to find it funny and because it's just a cleanup job."

The Earthman was lifting his fork carefully. "I see what you mean. Even the simplest motions seem queer."

"Actually, you get used to it quickly enough. At least to little things like eating. Walking is harder. I never saw an Earthman run efficiently out here. Not really efficiently."

For a while they ate in silence. Then he said, "What does the L. stand for?" He was looking at her nameplate again. It said, "Selene Lindstrom L."

"It just means Luna," she said, rather indifferently, "to distinguish me from the immigrants. I was born here."

"Really?"

"That's nothing to be surprised about. We've had a working society here for over half a century. Don't you think babies are born here? We have people here who were born here and are grandparents."

"How old are you?"

"Thirty-two," she said.

He looked startled, then mumbled, "Of course."

Selene raised her eyebrows. "You mean you understand? Most Earthmen have to have it explained."

The Earthman said, "I know enough to know that most of the visible signs of aging are the result of the inexorable victory of gravity over tissue—the sagging of cheek and the drooping of breast. With the Moon's gravity one-sixth that of Earth, it isn't really hard to understand that people will stay young-looking."

Selene said, "Only young-*looking*. It doesn't mean we have immortality here. The life-span is about that of Earth, but most of us are more comfortable in old age."

"That's not to be dismissed. . . . Of course, there are penalties, I suppose." He had just taken his first sip of his coffee. "You have to drink this—" He paused for a word and must have discarded it, for he used none.

"We could import food and beverages from Earth," she said, amused, "but only enough to feed a fraction of us a fraction of the time. There'd be no point to that when we can use the space for more vital items. Besides, we're used to this crud. . . . Or were you going to use a still stronger word?"

"Not for the coffee," he said. "I was going to save that for the food. But crud will do. . . . Tell me, Miss Lindstorm. I didn't see any mention on the tour itinerary of the proton synchrotron."

"The proton synchrotron?" She was finishing her coffee and her eyes were beginning to slide round the room, as though estimating the moment for getting them all to their feet again. "That's Terrestrial property and it's not open to tourists."

"You mean that's it's off-limits to Lunarites."

"Oh, no. Nothing of the sort. Most of its staff are Lunarites. It's just that it's the Terrestrial government that sets the rules. No tourists."

"I'd love to see it," he said.

She said, "I'm sure you would. . . . You've brought me luck; not one item of food, not one blessed man or woman has hit the floor."

She got to her feet and said, "Ladies and gentlemen, we'll be leaving in about ten minutes. Please leave the plates where they are. There are rest rooms for those who wish to use them and then we will visit the food-processing plants where meals such as you have just eaten are made possible."

— 2 —

SELENE'S QUARTERS were small, of course, and compact; but they were intricate. The windows were panoramic; star scenes that changed slowly and very randomly, never having any relationship to any real constellation. Each of the three windows could be made to undergo telescopic magnification, when Selene so desired.

Barron Neville hated that part of it. He would tend to turn it off rather savagely and say, "How can you stand it? You're the only one I know who has the bad taste to do such a thing. It's not as though these nebulae and star clusters exist, even."

And Selene would shrug, coolly, and say, "What's existence? How do you know the ones out there exist? Besides it gives me a sensation of freedom and motion. May I have that in my own quarters if I choose?"

Then Neville would mumble something and make a halfhearted attempt to restore the controls to where he had found them and Selene would say, "Let it go!"

The furniture was in smooth curves, and the walls were abstractly decorated in low-key, unobtrusive colors. Nowhere was there any representation of anything that might be considered a living thing.

"Living things are Earth," Selene would say, "not the Moon."

Now, when she entered, she found, as so often, Neville there; Barron, Neville, resting on the flimsy couch with one sandal on. The other lay beside him where it had dropped, and there was a line of red marks on his abdomen, just over his umbilicus, where he had been meditatively scratching.

She said, "Get us some coffee, won't you, Barron?" and slipped out of her own clothes in a long, graceful wiggle accompanied by a sigh of relief, letting them drop to the ground and then kicking them into the corner with one toe.

"What a relief to get out of them," she said. "It's the worst part of the job, having to dress like an Earthie."

Neville was in the kitchen corner. He paid no attention; he had heard it before. He said, "What's wrong with your water supply? It's way down."

"Is it?" she asked. "Well, I've been overusing, I suppose. Just be patient."

"Any trouble, today?"

Selene shrugged. "No. Very run of the mill. Just the usual bit about watching them teetering along and pretending they don't hate the food, and knowing they're wondering if they'll be asked to take off their clothes, I shouldn't be surprised. . . . Disgusting possibility."

"Are you taking up prudery?" He brought the two small cups of coffee to the table.

"In this case prudery is required. They're wrinkled, sagging, paunchy, and full of germs. I don't care what the quarantine regulations are like; they're full of germs. . . . What's new on your side?"

Barron shook his head. He was heavily-built for a Lunarite, and there was an almost-sullen narrowing of his eyes that had become a built-in feature. Except for that his features were even, and remarkably handsome, Selene thought.

He said, "Nothing startling. We're still waiting out the change in Commissioner. We'll have to see what this Gottstein is like."

"Can he make difficulties?"

"None more than are being made. After all, what can they do? They can't infiltrate. You can't disguise an Earthie as a Lunarite." But he looked uneasy just the same.

Selene sipped at her coffee and looked at him shrewdly. "Some Lunarites might be Earthies inside."

"Yes, and I'd like to know which. Sometimes I don't think I can trust— Oh, well. I'm wasting incredible amounts of time with my synchrotron project and getting nowhere. I'm having no luck with priorities."

"They probably don't trust you, and I don't blame them. If only you didn't slink around so conspiratorially."

"I do no such thing. It would give me great pleasure to walk out of the synchrotron room and never return, but then they *would* become suspicious. . . . If you've been raising hell with your water supply, Selene, I suppose we can't have a second cup."

"No, we can't. But it if comes to that, you've been helping me waste water. You've had two showers here in the last week."

"I'll give you a water credit. I didn't know you were counting."

"I'm not counting—my water level is."

She finished her own cup of coffee and stared at its emptiness thoughtfully. She said, "They always make faces over it. The tourists do. And I can never figure out why, either. It tastes fine to me. Did you ever taste Earth-coffee, Barron?"

"No," he said, briefly.

"I did. Once. Some tourist had smuggled in packets of what he called instant coffee. He offered me some in exchange for you-know-what. Seemed to think it was an even trade."

"And you had some?"

"I was curious. It was bitter and metallic. I hated it. Then I told him that miscegenation was against Lunarite custom and he turned rather bitter and metallic himself."

"You never told me this. He didn't try anything, did he?"

"It's not particularly your business, is it? And, no, he didn't try anything. If he had tried, at the wrong gravity for him, I'd have bounced him from here to corridor 1."

Then she went on. "Oh, yes. I picked up another Earthie today. Insisted on sitting with me."

"And what did he offer you in exchange for the screwing you so delicately call you-know-what?"

"Just sat there."

"And stared at your breasts?"

"They're there to be stared at, but actually he didn't. He stared at my nameplate. . . . Besides, what's it to you what he fantasied? Fantasies are free and I don't have to fulfill them. What do you think *I*'m fantasizing? Bed with an Earthman? With all the action you would expect of someone trying to handle a gravitational field he isn't used to? I wouldn't say it hasn't been done, but not by me, and not that I've ever heard any good of it. Is that settled? Can I get back to the Earthie? Who's nearly fifty? And who obviously wasn't terrifically handsome even when he was twenty? . . . Interesting appearance, though; I'll grant him that."

"All right. I can do without a thumbnail sketch. What about him?"

"He asked about the proton synchrotron!"

Neville rose to his feet, swaying a little as was almost inevitable after quick movement at low gravity. "*What* did he ask about the synchrotron?"

"Nothing. Why are you so excited? You asked me to tell you anything that was out of the way with any tourist at any time and this seemed out of the way. No one ever asked me about the synchrotron before."

"All *right*." He paused a little, then in a normal voice, said, "Why was he interested in the synchrotron?"

Selene said, "I haven't the faintest idea. He just asked if he could see it. It could be that he's a tourist with an interest in science. For all I know, it was just a ploy to get me interested in him."

"And I suppose you are. What's his name?"

"I don't know. I didn't ask him."

"Why not?"

"Because I'm *not* interested in him. Which way do you want it to be? Besides, his asking shows he's a tourist. If he were a physicist, he wouldn't have to ask. He'd be there."

"My dear Selene," said Neville. "Let me spell it out. Under the present circumstances, anyone who asks to see the proton synchrotron is a peculiar fellow we want to know about. And why should he ask *you?*'' He walked hastily to the other end of the room and back as though wearing off a little energy. Then he said, ''You're the expert at that nonsense. Do *you* find him of interest?''

''Sexually?''

''You know what I mean. *Don't play games, Selene.*''

Selene said with clear reluctance. ''He's interesting, even disturbing. But I don't know why. He said nothing. He did nothing.''

''Interesting and disturbing, is he? Then you will see him again.''

''And do what?''

''How do I know? That's your bit. Find out his name. Find out anything else you can. You've got some brains, so use them on a little practical nosiness for a change.''

''Oh, well,'' she said, ''orders from on high. All right.''

— 3 —

THERE WAS no way of telling the Commissioner's quarters, by size alone, from those of any Lunarite. There was no space on the Moon, not even for Terrestrial officials; no luxurious waste, even as a symbol of the home planet. Nor, for that matter, was there any way of changing the overwhelming fact about the Moon—that it was underground at low gravity—even for the greatest Earthman who ever lived.

''Man is still the creature of his environment,'' sighed Luiz Montez. ''I've been two years on the Moon and there have been times when I have been tempted to stay on but— I'm getting on in years. I've just passed my fortieth and if I intend ever to go back to Earth, it had better be now. Any older and I won't be able to readjust to full-gravity.''

Konrad Gottstein was only thirty-four and looked, if anything, younger. He had a wide, round, large-featured face, the kind of face one didn't see among the Lunarites, the kind of face that was something they would draw as part of an Earthie caricature. He was not heavily-built—it did not pay to send heavily-built Earthmen to the Moon—and his head seemed too large for his body.

He said (and he spoke Planetary Standard with a perceptibly different accent from that of Montez), ''You sound apologetic.''

''I am. I am,'' said Montez. Where Gottstein's face was intrinsically good-natured in appearance, the long thin lines of Montez' face were almost comically tragic. ''I am apologetic in both senses. I am embarrassed to be leaving the Moon, since it is an attractive world filled with excitement. And I am embarrassed about the embarrassment; ashamed that I should be reluctant to take up Earth's burden—gravity and all.''

''Yes, I imagine taking back the other five-sixths will be hard,'' said Gottstein. ''I've been on the Moon only a few days and already I feel that one-sixth g is perfectly fine.''

''You won't feel that when the constipation starts and you start living on mineral oil,'' said Montez with a sigh, ''but that will pass. . . And don't think you can imitate the light gazelle just because you feel light. There's an art to it.''

"So I understand."

"So you *think* you understand, Gottstein. You haven't see the kangaroo walk, have you?"

"On television."

"That doesn't really give you the feel of it. You have to try it. It's the proper mode for crossing level lunar surface at high speed. The feet move together backward and launch you on what would be a simple broad jump on Earth. While you're in mid-air, they come forward; begin moving back just *before* they hit the ground again; keep you launched; and so on. The motion seems slow by Earth standards with only a low gravity whipping you on, but each leap is in excess of twenty feet and the amount of muscular effort required to keep you in the air—if there were air—is minimal. The sensation is like flying—"

"Have you tried it? Can you do it?"

"I've tried it, but no Earthman can really do it. I've kept it up for as many as five leaps in a row, enough to get the sensation; just enough to want to do more, but then there is the inevitable miscalculation, a loss of synchronization, and you tumble and slide for a quarter of a mile. The Lunarites are polite and never laugh at you. Of course, it's easy for them. They start as children and pick it up at once without trouble."

"It's their world," said Gottstein, chuckling. "Think how they'd be on Earth."

"They wouldn't be on Earth. They can't. I suppose that's an advantage on our side. We can be either on Moon or on Earth. They can live only on the Moon. We tend to forget that because we confuse the Lunarites with Immies."

"With what?"

"That's what they call the Earth-immigrants; those who live on the Moon more or less permanently but were born and raised on the Earth. The immigrants can, of course, return to the Earth, but the real Lunarites have neither the bones nor the muscles to withstand the Earth's gravity. There were some tragedies in that respect in the Moon's early history."

"Oh?"

"Oh, yes. People who returned with their Moon-born children. We tend to forget. We've had our own Crisis and a few dying children don't seem important in the light of the huge casualties of the late Twentieth and all that followed. Here on the Moon, though, every dead Lunarite who succumbed to the gravity of Earth is remembered. . . . It helps them feel a world apart, I think."

Gottstein said, "I thought I had been thoroughly briefed on Earth, but it seems I will still have a lot to learn."

"Impossible to learn everything about the Moon from a post on Earth, so I have left you a full report as my predecessor did for me. You'll find the Moon fascinating and, in some ways, excruciating. I doubt that you've eaten Lunar rations on Earth and if you're going by description only, you will not be prepared for the reality. . . But you'll have to learn to like it. It's bad policy to ship Earth-items here. We've got to eat and drink the local products."

"You've been doing it for two years. I guess I'll survive."

"I've not been doing it steadily. There are periodic furloughs to Earth. Those are obligatory, whether you want them or not. They've told you that, I'm sure."

"Yes," said Gottstein.

"Despite any exercises you do here, you will have to subject yourself to full gravity now and then just to remind your bones and muscles what it's like. And when you're on Earth, you'll *eat*. And occasionally, some food is smuggled in.''

Gottstein said, ''My luggage was carefully inspected, of course, but it turned out there was a can of corned beef in my coat pocket. I had overlooked it. So did they.''

Montez smiled slowly and said, hesitantly, ''I suspect you are now going to offer to share it.''

''No,'' said Gottstein, judiciously, wrinkling his large button nose. ''I was going to say with all the tragic nobility I could muster, 'Here, Montez, have it all! Thy need is greater than mine.' '' He stumbled a bit in trying to say this, since he rarely used second person singular in Planetary Standard.

Montez smiled more broadly, and then let it vanish. He shook his head. ''No. In a week, I'll have all the Earth-food I can eat. You won't. Your mouthfuls will be few in the next few years and you will spend too much time regretting your present generosity. You keep it all. . . . I insist. I would but be earning your hatred ex post facto.''

He seemed serious, his hand on the other's shoulder, his eyes looking straight into Gottstein's. ''Besides,'' he said, ''there is something I want to talk to you about that I've been putting off because I don't know how to approach it and this food would be an excuse for further sidetracking.''

Gottstein put away the Earth-can at once. There was no way in which his face could match the other's seriousness, but his voice was grave and steady. ''Is there something you could not put into your dispatches, Montez?''

''There was something I *tried* to put in, Gottstein, but between my not knowing how to phrase it and Earth's reluctance to grasp my meaning, we ended up not communicating. You may do better. I hope you do. One of the reasons I have not asked to have my tour of duty extended is that I can no longer take the responsibility of my failure to communicate.''

''You make it sound serious.''

''I wish I could make it sound serious. Frankly, it sounds silly. Thre are only some ten thousand people in the Lunar colony. Rather less than half are native Lunarites. They're hampered by an insufficiency of resources, an insufficiency of space, a harsh world, and yet—and yet—''

''And yet?'' said Gottstein, encouragingly.

''There is something going on here—I don't know exactly what—which may be dangerous.''

''How can it be dangerous? What can they do? Make war against the Earth?'' Gottstein's face trembled on the brink of a smile-crease.

''No, no. It's more subtle than that.'' Montez passed his hand over his face, rubbing his eyes petulantly. ''Let me be frank with you. Earth has lost its nerve.''

''What does that mean?''

''Well, what would you call it? Just about the time the Lunar colony was being established, Earth went through the Great Crisis. I don't have to tell you about that.''

''No, you don't,'' said Gottstein, with distaste.

''The population is two billion now from its six billion peak.''

''Earth is much better for that, isn't it?''

''Oh, undoubtedly, though I wish there had been a better way of achieving the drop. . . . But it's left behind a permanent distrust of technology; a vast inertia; a lack of desire to risk change because of the possible side-effects. Great and possibly dangerous efforts have been abandoned because the danger was feared more than greatness was desired.''

"I take it you refer to the program on genetic engineering."

"That's the most spectacular case of course, but not the only one," said Montez, bitterly.

"Frankly, I can't get excited over the abandonment of genetic engineering. It was a tissue of failures.''

"We lost our chance at intuitionism.''

"There has never been any evidence that intuitionism is desirable, and considerable indications of its undesirability. . . Besides what about the Lunar colony itself? This certainly is no indication of stagnation on Earth.''

"It is,'' said Montez, vigorously. "The Lunar colony is a hangover, a last remnant of the period before the Crisis; something that was carried through as a last sad forward thrust of mankind before the great retreat.''

"That's too dramatic, Montez.''

"I don't think so. The Earth has retreated. Mankind has retreated, everywhere but on the Moon. The Lunar colony is man's frontier not just physically, but psychologically, too. Here is a world that doesn't have a web of life to disrupt; that doesn't have a complex environment in delicate balance to upset. Everything on the Moon that is of any use to man is man-made. The Moon is a world constructed by man from the start and out of basics. There is no past.''

"Well?''

"On Earth, we are unmanned by our longing for a pastoral past that never really existed; and that, if it had existed, could never exist again. In some respects, much of the ecology was disrupted in the Crisis and we are making do with the remnants so that we are frightened, always frightened. . . . On the Moon, there is no past to long for or dream about. There is no direction but forward.''

Montez seemed to be catching fire with his own words. He said, "Gottstein, I have watched it for two years; you will watch it for a least that much longer. There is a fire here on the Moon; a restless burning. They expand in every direction. They expand physically. Every month, new corridors are bored, new living quarters established, a new population potential made room for. They expand as far as resources are concerned. They find new construction materials, new water sources, new lodes of specialized minerals. They expand their sun-power battery-banks, enlarge their electronics factories. . . . I suppose you know that these ten thousand people here on the Moon are now the major source for Earth's supply of mini-electronic devices and fine biochemicals.''

"I know they're an important source.''

"Earth lies to itself for comfort's sake. The Moon is the major source. At the present rate, it may become the sole source in the near future. . . . It's growing intellectually, too. Gottstein, I imagine there isn't a bright science-oriented youngster on Earth who doesn't vaguely—or perhaps not so vaguely—dream of going to the Moon one day. With Earth in retreat from technology, the Moon is where the action is.''

"You're referring to the proton synchrotron, I suppose?''

"That's one example. When was the last new synchrotron built on Earth? But it's just the biggest and most dramatic item; not the only or even the most important. If you want to know the most important scientific device on the Moon—''

"Something so secret I haven't been told?"

"No, something so obvious that no one seems to notice. It's the ten thousand brains here. The ten thousand best human brains there are. The only close-knit group of ten thousand human brains that are, in principle and by emotion, science-oriented."

Gottstein moved restlessly and tried to shift his chair's position. It was bolted to the floor and wouldn't move, but in the attempt to do so, Gottstein found himself skittering out of the chair. Montez reached out an arm to steady him.

Gottstein flushed. "Sorry."

"You'll get used to the gravity."

Gottstein said, "But aren't you making it out a lot worse than it is? Earth isn't a know-nothing planet altogether. We did develop the Electron Pump. That's a purely Terrestrial accomplishment. No Lunarite had anything to do with it."

Montez shook his head and muttered a few words in his native Spanish. They didn't sound like placid words. He said, "Have you ever met Frederick Hallam?"

Gottstein smiled. "Yes, as a matter of fact I have. The Father of the Electron Pump. I believe he has the phrase tattooed on his chest."

"The mere fact that you smile and make that remark proves my point, really. Ask yourself: Could a man like Hallam really have fathered the Electron Pump? For the unthinking multitude, the story will do, but the fact is—and you must know it if you stop to think about it—there is no father to the Electron Pump. The para-people, the people in the para-Universe, whoever they are and whatever that is, invented it. Hallam was their accidental instrument. All of Earth is their accidental instrument."

"We were clever enough to take advantage of their initiative."

"Yes, as cows are clever enough to eat the hay we provide for them. The Pump is no sign that man is forward-looking. Quite the reverse."

"If the Pump is a backward step, then I say good for backwardness. I wouldn't want to do without it."

"Who would? But the point is it fits Earth's present mood perfectly. Infinite energy at virtually zero cost, except for maintenance, and with zero pollution besides. But there are no Electron Pumps on the Moon."

Gottstein said, "I imagine there's no need for them. The Solar batteries supply what the Lunarites require. Infinite energy at virtually zero cost, except for maintenance, and with zero pollution besides. . . . Isn't that the litany?"

"Yes, indeed, but the Solar batteries are entirely man-made. That's the point I'm making. An Electron Pump was projected for the Moon; installation was attempted."

"And?"

"And it didn't work. The para-people didn't accept the tungsten. Nothing happened."

"I didn't know that. Why not?"

Montez lifted his shoulders and eyebrows expressively. "How is one to know? We might assume, for instance, that the para-people live on a world without a satellite; that they have no conception of separate worlds in close proximity, each populated; that, having found one, they did not seek another. Who knows?—The point is, that the para-people didn't bite and we ourselves, without them, could do nothing."

"We ourselves," repeated Gottstein, thoughtfully. "By that, you mean the Earthmen?"

"Yes."

"And the Lunarites?"

"They were not involved."

"Were they interested?"

"I don't know. That's where my uncertainty—and fear—chiefly rests. The Lunarites—the native Lunarites, particularly—do not feel like Earthmen. I don't know what their plans are or what they intend. I can't find out."

Gottstein looked thoughtful. "But what *can* they do? Do you have any reason to suppose they intend to do us harm; or that they can do Earth harm even if they intend it?"

"I can't answer that question. They are an attractive and intelligent people. It seems to me they lack real hatred or real rage or even real fear. But perhaps that is what only seems to me. What bothers me most is that I don't know."

"The scientific equipment on the Moon is run by Earth, I believe."

"That is correct. The proton synchrotron is. The radio telescope on the trans-terrestrial side is. The three-hundred-inch optical telescope is. . . . The large equipment, that is, all of which has been in existence for fifty years."

"And what's been done since?"

"Very little by Earthmen."

"What about the Lunarites?"

"I'm not sure. Their scientists work in the large installations, but I once tried to check time cards. There are gaps."

"Gaps?"

"They spend considerable time *away* from the large installations. It is as though they had laboratories of their own."

"Well, if they produce mini-electronic devices and fine bio-chemicals, isn't that to be expected?"

"Yes, but— Gottstein, I don't know. I fear my ignorance."

There was a moderately long pause. Gottstein said, "Montez, I take it you are telling me all this so that I will be careful; so that I will try to find out what the Lunarites are doing?"

"I suppose that's about it," said Montez, unhappily.

"But you don't even know that they're doing anything at all."

"I feel that they are."

Gottstein said, "It's odd, then. I should be trying to talk you out of all this fearful mysticism of yours—but it's odd—"

"What is?"

"The same vessel that brought me to the Moon brought someone else to the Moon. I mean, a large party came, but one face in particular triggered something. I didn't talk to him—had no occasion to—and I dismissed the matter. But now our talk is pushing a button, and he suddenly comes back to mind—"

"Yes?"

"I was on a committee once that dealt with Electron Pump matters. A question of safety." He smiled briefly. "Earth's lost nerve, you might say. We worry about safety everywhere—and a good thing, damn it, lost nerve or not. The details escape me but in connection with that hearing, I saw that face that now I saw on the vessel. I'm convinced of it."

"Does that have significance, do you think?"

"I'm not sure. I associate that face with something disturbing. If I keep on thinking, it may come back to me. In any case, I had better get a list of the passengers and see if any name means something to me. Too bad, Montez, but I think you're getting me started."

"Not bad at all," said Montez. "I'm glad of it. As for this man; it may be he is only a tourist of no consequence and will be gone in two weeks, but I am glad to have you thinking about the matter—"

Gottstein did not seem to be listening. "He is a physicist, or a scientist of some sort," he muttered. "I'm certain of it and I associate him with danger—"

—————————————————

— 4 —

"HELLO," SAID Selene, cheerfully.

The Earthman turned around. Recognition took almost no time at all. "Selene! Am I right? Selene!"

"Right! Correctly pronounced. Are you enjoying yourself?"

The Earthman said gravely, "Very much. It makes me realize how unique our century is. It was not so long ago I was on Earth, feeling tired of my world, tired of myself. Then I thought: Well, if I were living a hundred years ago, the only way I could leave the world would be to die, but now—I can go to the Moon." He smiled without real gaiety.

Selene said, "Are you happier now that you are on the Moon?"

"A little." He looked about. "Don't you have a crowd of tourists to take care of?"

"Not today," she said, cheerfully. "It's my day off. Who knows, I may take two or three. It's a dull job."

"What a shame, then, that you bump into a tourist on your day off."

"I didn't bump into you. I came looking for you. And a hard job that was, too. You shouldn't wander off by yourself."

The Earthman looked at her with interest. "Why should you look for me? Are you fond of Earthmen?"

"No," she said, with easy frankness. "I'm sick of them. I dislike them on principle and being constantly associated with them in my job makes it worse."

"Yet you come looking for me and there isn't a way on Earth—on the Moon, I mean—that I can convince myself I am young and handsome."

"Even if you were, it wouldn't help. Earthmen don't interest me, as everyone but Barron knows."

"Then why do you come looking for me?"

"Because there are other ways of being interested and because Barron is interested."

"And who is Barron? Your boyfriend?"

Selene laughed. "Barron Neville. He's a lot more than a boy and lot more than a friend. We have sex when we feel like it."

"Well, that's what I meant. Do you have children?"

"One boy. He's ten. He spends most of his time in the boys'-compound. To spare you the next question, he's not Barron's. I may have a child by Barron if we're still together when I'm assigned another child—*if* I'm assigned another child. . . . I am pretty sure I will be.''

"You're quite frank."

"About things I don't consider secret? Of course. . . Now what would you like to do?"

They had been walking along a corridor of milk-white rock, into the glazed surface of which were inset dusky bits of ''Moon-gems'' that lay about for the taking in most sections of the Lunar surface. She wore sandals which scarcely seemed to touch the ground; he wore thick-soled boots which leadenly helped weight him down to keep his steps from becoming torture.

The corridor was one-way. Occasionally, a small electric cart would overtake them and move nearly silently past.

The Earthman said, ''Now what would I like to do? That is a broad-beamed invitation. Would you like to set boundary conditions so that my answers will not innocently offend you?''

"Are you a physicist?"

The Earthman hesitated. ''Why do you ask?''

"Just to hear what you would say. I know you're a physicist."

"How?"

"No one says 'set boundary conditions' unless they are. Especially if the first thing they want to see on the Moon is the proton synchrotron.''

"Is that why you've come looking for me? Because I seem to be a physicist?"

"That's why Barron sent me looking for you. Because *he's* a physicist. I came because I thought you were rather unusual for an Earthman.''

"In what way?"

"Nothing terribly complimentary—if it's compliments you're fishing for. It's just that you seem not to like Earthmen.''

"How can you tell that?"

"I watched you look at the others in the party. Besides, I can always tell somehow. It's the Earthies who don't like Earthies who tend to stay on the Moon. Which brings me back to the question. . . . What would you like to do? And I'll set the boundary conditions. I mean, as far as sight-seeing is concerned.''

The Earthman looked at her sharply. ''That's peculiar, Selene. You have a day off. Your job is sufficiently uninteresting or distasteful so that you are glad to have the day off and would be willing to make it two or three. Yet your way of spending it is to volunteer to resume your job for me particularly. . . . Just because of a little interest.''

"Barron's interest. He's busy now and there's no harm in entertaining you until he's ready. . . . Besides, it's different. Can't you see it's different? On my job I'm riding herd on a couple of dozen Earthies— Don't you mind my using the term?''

"I use it myself."

"Because you're an Earthman. Some Earth-people consider it a term of derision and resent it when a Lunarite uses it.''

"You mean when a Lunie uses it?"

Selene flushed. She said, ''Yes. That's about it.''

"Well, then, let's neither of us cry out at words. Go ahead, you were telling me about your job.''

"On my job, there are these Earthies whom I have to keep from killing themselves and whom I have to take here and there and give little speeches to and make sure they eat and drink and walk by the book. They see their little pet sights and do their little pet things, and I have to be terribly polite and motherly.''

"Awful," said the Earthman.

"But you and I can do as we please, I hope, and you are willing to take your chances and I don't have to watch what I say."

"I told you that you're perfectly welcome to call me Earthie."

"All right, then. I'll have a busman's holiday. What would you like to do?"

"That's an easy one to answer. I want to see the proton synchrotron."

"Not that. Maybe Barron can arrange it after you see him."

"Well, if I can't see the synchrotron, I don't know what else there is to see. I know the radio telescope is on the other side and I don't suppose there's any novelty in it, anyway. . . . You tell me. What doesn't the average tourist get to see?"

"A number of things. There are the algae rooms—not the antiseptic processing plants, which you've seen—but the farms themselves. However, the smell is pretty strong there and I don't suppose an Earthie—Earthman—would find it particularly appetizing. Earth—men have trouble with the food as it is."

"Does that surprise you? Have you ever tasted Earth-food?"

"Not really. I probably wouldn't like it, though. It all depends on what you're used to."

"I suppose so," said the Earthman, sighing. "If you ate a real steak, you'd probably gag at the fat and fiber."

"We could go to the outskirts where the new corridors are being driven into bedrock, but you'll have to wear special protective garments. There are the factories—"

"You make the choice, Selene."

"I will, if you will tell me something honestly."

"I can't promise without hearing the question."

"I said that Earthies that didn't like Earthies tended to stay on the Moon. You didn't correct me. Do you intend to stay on the Moon?"

The Earthman stared at the toes of his clumsy boots. He said, "Selene, I had trouble getting a visa to the Moon. They said I might be too old for the trip and that if I stayed any length of time I might find it impossible to return to Earth. So I told them I planned to stay on the Moon permanently."

"You weren't lying?

"I wasn't sure at the time. But I think I'll stay here now."

"I should have thought that they would have been less willing than ever to let you go under those conditions."

"Why?"

"Generally, the Earth authorities don't like to send physicists to the Moon on a permanent basis."

The Earthman's lips twitched. "In that respect, I had no trouble."

"Well, then, if you're going to be one of us, I think you ought to visit the gymnasium. Earthies often want to but we don't encourage them as a general rule—though it's not forbidden outright. Immigrants are a different thing."

"Why?"

"Well, for one thing, we exercise in the nude or near-nude. Why not?" She sounded aggrieved, as though weary of repeating a defensive position. "The temperature is controlled; the environment is clean. It's just that where people from Earth are expected to be, nudity becomes unsettling. Some Earthies are shocked; some are titillated; and some are both. Well, we're not going to dress in the gymnasium for their sake, and we're not going to cope with them, either; so we keep them out.''

"But immigrants?''

"They have to get used to it. In the end, they'll be discarding clothes, too. And they'll need the gymnasium even more than the native Lunarites do.''

"I'll be honest with you, Selene. If I encounter female nudity, I'll find it titillating, too. I'm not quite so old that I won't.''

"Well, titillate, then,'' she said, indifferently, "but to yourself. Agreed?''

"Do we have to get undressed too?'' He looked at her with amused interest.

"As spectators? No. We could, but we don't have to. You would feel uncomfortable if you did this early in the game and you wouldn't be a particularly inspiring sight to the rest of us—''

"You *are* frank!''

"Do you think it would be? Be honest. And as for myself, I have no wish to put you under a special strain in your private titillation. So we might both just as well stay clothed.''

"Will there be any objection? I mean to my being there as an Earthie of uninspirational appearance?''

"Not if I'm with you.''

"Very well, then, Selene. Is it far away?''

"We are there. Just through here.''

"Ah, then, you were planning to come here all the time.''

"I thought it might be interesting.''

"Why?''

Selene smiled suddenly. "I just thought.''

The Earthman shook his head. "I'm beginning to think you never just think. Let me guess. If I'm to stay on the Moon, I will need to exercise now and then in order to keep muscles, bones, and all my organs, perhaps, in condition.''

"Quite true. So do all of us, immigrants from Earth in particular. The day will come when the gymnasium will be a daily grind for you.''

They stepped through a door and the Earthman stared in astonishment. "This is the first place I've seen that looks like Earth.''

"In what way?''

"Why it's big. I didn't imagine you would have such big rooms on the Moon. Desks, office machinery, women at the desks—''

"Bare-breasted women,'' said Selene, gravely.

"That part isn't Earthlike, I admit.''

"We've got a hold-chute, too, and an elevator for Earthies. There are many levels. . . . But wait.''

She approached a woman at one of the nearer desks, talking in a rapid, low voice while the Earthman stared at everything with amiable curiosity.

Selene returned. "No trouble. And it turns out we're going to have a melee. A rather good one; I know the teams.''

"This place is very impressive. Really.''

"If you still mean its size, it's not nearly big enough. We have three gymnasiums. This is the largest.''

"I'm somehow pleased that in the Spartan surroundings of the Moon, you can afford to waste so much room on frivolity.''

"Frivolity!" Selene sounded offended. "Why do you think this is frivolity?"

"Melees? Some sort of game?"

"You might call it a game. On Earth you can do such things for sports; ten men doing, ten thousand watching. It's not so on the Moon; what's frivolous for you is necessary for us. . . . This way; we'll take the elevator, which means a little waiting perhaps."

"Didn't mean to get you angry."

"I'm not really angry but you must be reasonable. You Earthmen have been adapted to Earth-gravity for all the three hundred million years since life crawled onto dry land. Even if you don't exercise, you get by. We've had no time at all to adapt to Moon-gravity."

"You look different enough."

"If you're born and reared under Moon-gravity, your bones and muscles are, naturally, slimmer and less massive than an Earthie's would be, but that's superficial. There isn't a bodily function we possess, however subtle—digestion, rates of hormonal secretions—that isn't maladjusted to gravity and that doesn't require a deliberate regimen of exercise. If we can arrange exercise in the form of fun and games that does not make it frivolity. . . . Here's the elevator."

The Earthman hung back in momentary alarm, but Selene said, with residual impatience, as though still seething over the necessity of defense. "I suppose you're going to tell me it looks like a wickerwork basket. Every Earthman who uses it says so. With Moon-gravity, it doesn't have to be any more substantial."

The elevator moved downward slowly. They were the only ones on board. The Earthman said, "I suspect this isn't much used."

Selene smiled again. "You're right. The hold-chute is much more popular, and much more fun."

"What is it?"

"Exactly what the name implies. . . . Here we are. We only had to drop two levels. . . . It's just a vertical tube you can drop through, with handholds. We don't encourage Earthies to use it."

"Too risky?"

"Not in itself. You can climb down as though it were a ladder. However, there are always youngsters swinging down at considerable speed and Earthies don't know how to keep out of the way. Collisions are always discomforting. But you'll get to use it in time. . . . In fact, what you'll see now is a kind of large hold-chute designed for recklessness."

She led him to a circular railing around which a number of individuals were leaning and talking. All were more or less in the nude. Sandals were common and usually hip-purse was slung over one shoulder. Some wore briefs. One was scooping a greenish-mash out of a container and was eating it.

The Earthman wrinkled his nose slightly as he passed that one. He said, "The dental problem must be severe on the Moon."

"It isn't good," Selene agreed. "If we ever get the chance, we'll select for an edentate jaw."

"Toothlessness?"

"Maybe not entirely. We might keep the incisors and canines for cosmetic reasons and for occasionally useful tasks. They're easily cleaned, too. But why should we want useless molars? It's just a hangover from an Earthie past."

"Are you making any progress in that direction?"

"No," she said stiffly. "Genetic engineering is illegal. Earth insists."

She was leaning over the railing. "They call this the Moon's playground," she said.

The Earthman looked down. It was a large cylindrical opening with pink smooth walls to which metal bars were attached in what seemed a random configuration. Here and there, a bar stretched across a portion of the cylinder, sometimes across its entire width. It was perhaps four or five hundred feet deep and about fifty feet across.

No one seemed to be paying particular attention either to the playground or to the Earthman. Some had looked at him indifferently as he passed, seeming to weigh his clothed state, his facial appearance, and then had turned away. Some made a casual hand gesture to Selene's direction before turning away, but all turned away. The no-interest signal, however subdued, could not have been more blatant.

The Earthman turned to the cylindrical opening. There were slim figures at the bottom, foreshortened because they were seen from above. Some wore wisps of clothing in red, some in blue. Two teams, he decided. Clearly the wisps served protective functions, since all wore gloves and sandals, protective bands about knees and elbows. Some wore brief bands about the hips, some about the chests.

"Oh," he muttered. "Men and women."

Selene said, "Right! The sexes compete equally but the idea is to prevent the uncontrolled swinging of parts that might hamper the guided fall. There's a sexual difference there which also involves vulnerability to pain. It's not modesty."

The Earthman said, "I think I've read of this."

"You may have," said Selene, indifferently. "Not much seems to get out. Not that *we* have any objection, but the Terrestrial government prefers to keep news of the Moon to a minimum."

"Why, Selene?"

"You're an Earthman. You tell me. . . . Our theory here on the Moon is that we embarrass the Earth. Or at least the Earth government."

On either side of the cylinder now, two individuals were rising rapidly and the patter of light drumbeats was heard in the background. At first, the climbers seemed to be going up a ladder, rung by rung, but their speed increased and by the time they were halfway up, they were striking each hold as they passed, making an ostentatious slapping noise.

"Couldn't do that on Earth as gracefully," said the Earthman, admiringly. "Or at all," he amended.

"It's not just low-gravity," said Selene. "Try it, if you think so. This takes endless hours of practice."

The climbers reached the railing and swung up to a headstand. They performed a simultaneous somersault and began to fall.

"They can move quickly when they want to," said the Earthman.

"Umm," said Selene, through the patter of applause. "I suspect that when Earthmen—I mean the real Earthmen, the ones who have never even visited the Moon—think of moving around the Moon, they think of the surface and of spacesuits. That's often slow, of course. The mass, with the spacesuit added, is huge, which means high inertia and a small gravity to overcome it."

"Quite right," said the Earthman. "I've seen the classic motion pictures of the early astronauts that all school children see and the movements are like those underwater. The picture gets imprinted, even when we know better."

"You'd be surprised how fast we can move on the surface these days, spacesuit and all," said Selene. "And here, underground, without spacesuits, we can move as quickly as on Earth. The slower whip of gravity is made up for by the proper use of muscles."

"But you can move slowly, too." The Earthman was watching the acrobats. They had gone up with speed and were going down with deliberate slowness. They were floating, slapping the handholds to delay the drop rather than, as before, to accelerate the rise. They reached the ground and two others replaced them. And then two more. And then two more. From each team alternately, pairs competed in virtuosity.

Each pair went up in unison; each pair rose and fell in a more complicated pattern. One pair kicked off simultaneously to cross the tube in a low parabola, convex upward, each reaching the handhold the other had abandoned, and somehow skimming past each other in mid-air without touching. That evoked louder applause.

The Earthman said, "I suspect I lack the experience to appreciate the finer points of skill. Are these all native Lunarites?"

"They have to be," said Selene. "The gymnasium is open to all Lunar citizens and some immigrants are fairly good, considering. For this kind of virtuosity, however, you must depend on babies that are conceived and born here. They have the proper physical adaptation, at least more than native Earthmen have, and they get the proper childhood training. Most of these performers are under eighteen."

"I imagine it's dangerous, even at Moon-gravity levels."

"Broken bones aren't very uncommon. I don't think there's been an actual death, but there's been at least one case of broken spine and paralysis. That was a terrible accident; I was actually watching— Oh, wait now; we're going to have the ad libs now."

"The what?"

"Till now, we've had set pieces. The climbs were according to a fixed pattern."

The percussion beat seemed softer as one climber rose and suddenly launched into mid-air. He caught a transverse bar one-handed, circling it once vertically, and let go.

The Earthman watched closely. He said, "Amazing. He gets around those bars exactly like a gibbon."

"A what?" asked Selene.

"A gibbon. A kind of ape; in fact, the only ape still existing in the wild. They—" He looked at Selene's expression and said, "I don't mean it as an insult, Selene; they are graceful creatures."

Selene said, frowning, "I've seen pictures of apes."

"You probably haven't seen gibbons in motion. . . . I dare say that Earthies might call Lunarites 'gibbons' and mean it insultingly, about the level of what you mean by 'Earthie.' But I don't mean it so."

He leaned both elbows on the railing and watched the movements. It was like dancing in the air. He said, "How do you treat Earth-immigrants here on the Moon, Selene? I mean immigrants who mean to stay here life-long. Since they lack true Lunarite abilities—"

"That makes no difference. Immies are citizens. There's no discrimination; no legal discrimination."

"What does that mean? No *legal* discrimination?"

"Well, you said it yourself. There are some things they can't do. There *are* differences. Their medical problems are different and they've usually had a worse medical history. If they come in middle age, they look—old."

The Earthman looked away, embarrasssed. "Can they intermarry? I mean, immigrants and Lunarites."

"Certainly. That is, they can interbreed."

"Yes, that's what I meant."

"Of course. No reason why an immigrant can't have some worthwhile genes. Heavens, my father was an immie, though I'm second-generation Lunarite on my mother's side."

"I suppose your father must have come when he was quite—Oh, *good Lord*—" He froze at the railing, then drew a shuddering sigh. "I thought he was going to miss that bar."

"Not a chance," said Selene. "That's Marco Fore. He likes to do that, reach out at the last moment. Actually, it's bad form to do that and a real champion doesn't. Still—My father was twenty-two when he arrived."

"I suppose that's the way. Still young enough to be adaptable; no emotional complications back on Earth. From the standpoint of the Earthie male, I imagine it must be rather nice to have a sexual attachment with a—"

"Sexual attachment!" Selene's amusement seemed to cover a very real sense of shock. "You don't suppose my father had sex with my mother. If my mother heard you say that she'd set *you* right in a hurry."

"But—"

"Artificial insemination was what it was for goodness sake. Sex with an *Earthman?*"

The Earthman looked solemn. "I thought you said there was no discrimination."

"That's not discrimination. That's a matter of physical fact. An Earthman can't handle the gravity field properly. However practiced he might be, under the stress of passion, he might revert. I wouldn't risk it. The clumsy fool might snap his arm or leg—or worse, mine. Gene mixtures are one thing; sex is quite another."

"I'm sorry. . . . Isn't artificial insemination against the law?"

She was watching the gymnastics with absorption. "That's Marco Fore again. When he isn't trying to be uselessly spectacular, he really is good; and his sister is almost as good. When they work together it's really a poem of motion. Look at them now. They'll come together and circle the same bar as though they have a single body stretched across. He's a little too flamboyant at times, but you can't fault his muscular control. . . . Yes, artificial insemination is against Earth's law, but it's allowed where medical reasons are involved, and, of course, that's often the case, or said to be."

All the acrobats had now climbed to the top and were in a great circle just below the railing; all the reds on one side, the blues on the other. All arms on the side of the interior were raised and the applause was loud. Quite a crowd had now gathered at the rail.

"You ought to have some seating arrangement," said the Earthman.

"Not at all. This isn't a show. This is exercise. We don't encourage any more spectators than can stand comfortably about the railing. We're supposed to be down there, not up here."

"You mean you can do that sort of thing, Selene?"

"After a fashion, of course. Any Lunarite can. I'm not as good as they are. I haven't joined any teams— There's going to be the melee now, the free-for-all. This is the really dangerous part. All ten are going to be in the air and each side is going to try to send members of the other side into a fall."

"A real fall."

"As real as possible."

"Are there injuries occasionally?"

"Occasionally. In theory, this sort of thing is frowned upon. That *is* considered frivolous, and we don't have so large a population that we can afford to incapacitate anyone without real cause. Still, the melee is popular and we can't raise the votes to outlaw it."

"Which side do you vote on, Selene?"

Selene blushed. "Oh, never mind. You watch this!"

The percussion rhythm had suddenly grown thunderous and each of the individuals in the huge well darted outward like an arrow. There was wild confusion in mid-air but when they parted again, each ended firmly on a bar-grip. There was the tension of waiting. One launched; another followed; and the air was filled with flashing bodies again. Over and over it happened.

Selene said, "The scoring is intricate. There is a point for every launch; a point for every touch; two points for every miss inflicted; ten points for a grounding; various penalties for various kinds of fouling."

"Who keeps the score?"

"There are umpires watching who make the preliminary decisions and there are television tapes in case of appeals. Very often even the tapes can't decide."

There was a sudden excited cry when a girl in blue moved past a boy in red and slapped his flank resoundingly. The boy who received the blow had writhed away, but not successfully, and grabbing at a wall bar with improper balance struck that wall ungracefully with his knee.

"Where were his eyes?" demanded Selene indignantly. "He didn't see her coming."

The action grew hotter and the Earthman tired of trying to make sense of the knotted flights. Occasionally, a leaper touched a bar and did not retain his hold. Those were the times when every spectator leaned over the railing as though ready to launch himself into space in sympathy. At one time, Marco Fore was struck in the wrist and someone cried "Foul!"

Fore missed his handhold and fell. To the Earthman's eyes, the fall, under Moon-gravity, was slow, and Fore's lithe body twisted and turned, reaching for bar after bar, without quite making it. The others waited, as though all maneuvering was suspended during a fall.

Fore was moving quite rapidly now, though twice he had slowed himself without quite being able to maintain a handhold.

He was nearly to the ground when a sudden spidery lunge caught a transverse bar with the right leg and he hung suspended and swinging, head downward, about ten feet above the ground. Arms outspread, he paused while the applause rang out and then he had twisted upright and jumped into a rapid climb.

The Earthman said, "Was he fouled?"

"If Jean Wong actually grabbed Marco's wrist instead of pushing it, it was a foul. The umpire has ruled a fair block, however, and I don't think Marco will appeal. He fell a lot farther than he had to. He likes these last-minute saves and someday he'll miscalculate and hurt himself. . . . Oh, oh.''

The Earthman looked up in sudden inquiry, but Selene's eyes weren't upon him. She said, "That's someone from the Commissioner's office and he must be looking for you.''

"Why—''

"I don't see why he should come here to find anyone else. You're the unusual one.''

"But there's no reason—'' began the Earthman.

Yet the messenger, who had the build of an Earthman himself or an Earth-immigrant, and who seemed uneasy to be the center of the stares of a couple of dozen slight, nude figures who seemed to tinge their scorn with indifference, came directly toward him.

"Sir,'' he began. "Commissioner Gottstein requests that you accompany me—''

— 5 —

BARRON NEVILLE'S quarters were somehow harsher than Selene's. His books were on bold display, his computer-outlet was unmasked in one corner, and his large desk was in disarray. His windows were blank.

Selene entered, folded her arms, and said, "If you live like a slob, Barron, how do you expect to have your thoughts neat?''

"I'll manage,'' said Barron, grumpily. "How is it you haven't brought the Earthman with you?''

"The Commissioner got to him first. The new Commissioner.''

"Gottstein?''

"That's right. Why weren't you ready sooner?''

"Because it took time to find out. I won't work blind.''

Selene said, "Well, then, we'll just have to wait.''

Neville bit at a thumbnail and then inspected the result severely. "I don't know whether I ought to like the situation or not. . . . What did you think of him?''

"I *liked* him,'' said Selene, definitely. "He was rather pleasant, considering he was an Earthie. He let me guide him. He was interested. He made no judgments. He didn't patronize. . . . And I didn't go out of my way to avoid insulting him, either.''

"Did he ask any further about the synchrotron?''

"No, but then he didn't have to.''

"Why not?''

"I told him *you* wanted to see him, and I said you were a physicist. So I imagine he'll ask you whatever he wants to ask you when he sees you.''

"Didn't he think it strange that he should be talking to a female tourist guide who just happens to know a physicist?''

"Why strange? I said you were my sex-partner. There's no accounting for sex attraction and a physicist may well condescend to a lowly tourist guide.''

"Shut up, Selene."

"Oh—Look, Barron, it seems to me that if he were spinning some sort of fancy web, if he approached me *because* he planned to get to you through me, he would have shown some trace of anxiety. The more complicated and silly any plot, the more rickety it is and the more anxious the plotter. I deliberately acted casual. I talked about everything but the synchrotron. I took him to a gymnastics show."

"And?"

"And he was interested. Relaxed and interested. Whatever he has on his mind, it isn't involuted."

"You're sure of that? Yet the Commissioner got to him before I did. You consider that good?"

"Why should I consider it bad? An open invitation to a meeting of some sort delivered in front of a couple of dozen Lunarites isn't particularly involuted, either."

Neville leaned back with his hands clasped at the nape of his neck. "Selene, please don't insist on making judgments, when I don't ask you to. It's irritating. The man is not a physicist in the first place. Did he tell you he was?"

Selene paused to think. "I called him a physicist. He didn't deny it but I don't recall that he actually said he was. And yet—and yet, I'm *sure* he is."

"It's a lie of omission, Selene. He may be a physicist in his own mind, but the fact is that he isn't trained as a physicist and he doesn't work as one. He has had scientific training; I'll grant him that; but he has no scientific job of any kind. He couldn't get one. There isn't a lab on Earth that would give him working room. He happens to be on Fred Hallam's crud-list and he's been top man there for a long time."

"Are you sure?"

"Believe me, I checked. Didn't you just criticize me for taking so long. . . . And it sounds so good that it's too good."

"Why too good? I don't see what you're getting at."

"Doesn't it seem to you we ought to trust him? After all, he's got a grievance against Earth."

"You can certainly argue that way, if your facts are right."

"Oh, my facts are right, at least in the sense that they're what turns up, if you dig for them. But maybe we're *supposed* to argue that way."

"Barron, that's disgusting. How can you weave these conspiracy theories into everything? Ben didn't sound—"

"Ben?" said Neville, sardonically.

"Ben!" repeated Selene, firmly. "Ben didn't sound like a man with a grievance or like a man trying to make me think he sounded like a man with a grievance."

"No, but he managed to make you think he was someone to be liked. You did say you *liked* him, didn't you? With emphasis? Maybe that's exactly what he was trying to do."

"I'm not that easy to fool and you know it."

"Well, I'll just have to wait till *I* see him."

"The hell with you, Barron. I've associated with thousands of Earthies of all kinds. It's my job. And you have no reason whatsoever to speak sarcastically about my judgment. You know you have every reason to trust it."

"All right. We'll see. Don't get angry. It's just that we'll have to wait now. . . . And as long as we do,'' he rose lithely to his feet, ''guess what I'm thinking?''

''I don't have to.'' Selene rose as smoothly, and with an almost invisible motion of her feet slid sideways, well away from him. ''But think it by yourself. I'm not in the mood.''

''Are you annoyed because I've impugned your judgment?''

''I'm annoyed because— Oh, hell why don't you keep your room in better condition?'' And she left.

— 6 —

''*I WOULD LIKE,*'' said Gottstein, ''to offer you some Earthside luxury, Doctor, but, as a matter of principle, I have been allowed to bring none. The good people of the Moon resent the artificial barriers imposed by special treatment for men from Earth. It seems better to soothe their sensibilities by assuming the Lunarite pose as far as possible though I'm afraid my gait will give me away. Their confounded gravity is impossible.''

The Earthman said ''I find this so also. I congratulate you on your new post—''

''Not yet quite mine, sir.''

''Still, my congratulations. Yet I can't help wondering why you have asked to see me.''

''We were shipmates. We arrived not so long ago on the same vessel.''

The Earthman waited politely.

Gottstein said, ''And my acquaintance with you is a longer one than that. We met—briefly—some years ago.''

The Earthman said quietly, ''I'm afraid I don't recall—''

''I'm not surprised at that. There is no reason for you to remember. I was, for a time, on the staff of Senator Burt, who headed—still heads, in fact—the Commitee on Technology and the Environment. It was at a time when he was rather anxious to get the goods on Hallam—Frederick Hallam.''

The Earthman seemed, quite suddenly, to sit a little straighter. ''Did you know Hallam?''

''You're the second person to ask me that since my coming to the Moon. Yes, I did. Not intimately. I've known others who've met him. Oddly enough, their opinion usually coincided with mine. For a person who is apparently idolized by the planet, Hallam inspired little personal liking on the part of those who knew him.''

''Little? None at all, I think,'' said the Earthman.

Gottstein ignored the interruption. ''It was my job, at the time—or at least, my assignment from the senator—to investigate the Electron Pump and see if its establishment and growth were accompanied by undue waste and personal profit-taking. It was a legitimate concern for what was essentially a watch-dog committee, but the senator was, between us, hoping to find something of damage to Hallam. He was anxious to decrease the strangle-hold that man was gaining on the scientific establishment. There, he failed.''

"That much would be obvious. Hallam is stronger than ever right now."

"There was no graft to speak of; certainly none that could be traced to Hallam. The man is rigidly honest."

"In that sense, I am sure. Power has its own market value not necessarily measured in credit-bills."

"But what interested me at the time, though it was something I could not then follow up, was that I did come across someone whose complaint was not against Hallam's power, but against the Electron Pump itself. I was present at the interview, but I did not conduct it. You were the complainant, were you not?"

The Earthman said, cautiously, "I remember the incident to which you refer, but I still don't remember you."

"I wondered then how anyone could possibly object to the Electron Pump on scientific grounds. You impressed me sufficiently so that when I saw you on the ship, something stirred; and then, eventually, it came back. I have not referred to the passenger list but let me check my memory. Aren't you Dr. Benjamin Andrew Denison?"

The Earthman sighed. "Benjamin *Allan* Denison. Yes. But why does this come up now? The truth is, Commissioner, I don't want to drag up matters of the past. I'm here on the Moon and rather anxious to start again; from the start, if necessary. Damn it, I considered changing my name."

"That wouldn't have helped. It was your face I recognized. I have no objection to your new life, Dr. Denison. I would not in any way interfere. But I would like to pry a little for reasons that do not directly involve you. I don't remember, quite, your objection to the Electron Pump. Could you tell me?"

Denison's head bent. The silence lengthened itself and the Commissioner-Appointee did not interrupt. He even stifled a small clearing of the throat.

Denison said, "Truly, it was nothing. It was a guess I made; a fear about the alteration in the intensity of the strong nuclear field. Nothing!"

"Nothing?" Gottstein did clear his throat now. "Please don't mind if I strive to understand this. I told you that you interested me at the time. I was unable to follow it up then and I doubt that I could dig the information out of the records now. The whole thing is classified—the senator did very poorly at the time and he isn't interested in publicity over it. Still, some details come back. You were once a colleague of Hallam's; you were not a physicist."

"That's right. I was a radiochemist. So was he."

"Stop me if I remember incorrectly, but your early record was a very good one, right?"

"There were objective criteria in my favor. I had no illusions about myself. I was a brilliant worker."

"Amazing how it comes back. Hallam, on the other hand, was not."

"Not particularly."

"And yet afterward things did not go well with you. In fact, when we interviewed you—I think you volunteered to see us—you were working for a toy manufacturer—"

"Cosmetics," said Denison, in a strangled voice. "Male cosmetics. That didn't help gain me a respectful hearing."

"No, it wouldn't. I'm sorry. You were a salesman."

"Sales manager. I was still brilliant. I rose to vice-president before breaking off and coming to the Moon."

"Did Hallam have something to do with that? I mean with you leaving science?'

"Commissioner," said Denison. "Please! It really doesn't matter any longer. I was there when Hallam first discovered the tungsten conversion and when the chain of events began that led to the Electron Pump. Exactly what would have happened if I had not been there, I can't say. Hallam and I might both have been dead of radiation poisoning a month later or of a nuclear explosion six weeks later. I don't know. But I *was* there and, partly because of me, Hallam is what he is now; and because of my part in it, I am what I am now. The hell with the details. Does that satisfy you? Because it will have to."

"I think it satisfies me. You had a personal grudge against Hallam, then?"

"I certainly had no affection for him, in those days. I have no affection for him now, for that matter."

"Would you say, then, that your objection to the Electron Pump was inspired by your anxiety to destroy Hallam."

Denison said, "I object to this cross-examination."

"Please? Nothing of what I ask is intended to be used against you. This is for my own benefit because I am concerned about the Pump and about a number of things."

"Well, then, I suppose you might work out some emotional involvement. Because I disliked Hallam I was ready to believe that his popularity and greatness had a false foundation. I thought about the Electron Pump, hoping to find a flaw."

"And you therefore found one?"

"No," said Denison forcefully, bringing his fist down on the arm of the chair and moving perceptibly upward from his seat in reaction. "Not 'therefore.' I found a flaw but it was an honest one. Or so it seemed to me. I certainly didn't invent a flaw merely to puncture Hallam."

"No question of *inventing,* Doctor," said Gottstein soothingly. "I don't dream of making such an implication. Yet we all know that in trying to determine something on the boundary line of the known, it is necessary to make assumptions. The assumptions can be made over a gray area of uncertainty and one can shade them in one direction or another with perfect honesty, but in accord with—uh—the emotions of the moment. You made your assumptions, perhaps, on the anti-Hallam edge of the possible."

"This is a profitless discussion, sir. At the time, I thought I had a valid point. However, I am not a physicist. I am—was—a radiochemist."

"Hallam was a radiochemist, too, but he is now the most famous physicist in the world."

"He's still a radiochemist. A quarter-century out of date."

"Not so, you. You worked hard to become a physicist."

Denison smoldered. "You really investigated me."

"I told you; you impressed me. Amazing how it comes back. But now I'll pass on to something a little different. Do you know a physicist named Peter Lamont?"

Reluctantly—"I've met him."

"Would you say he was brilliant, too?"

"I don't know him well enough to say and I hate to overuse the word."

"Would you say he knew what he was talking about?"

"Barring information to the contrary, I would say, yes."

Carefully, the Commissioner leaned back in his seat. It had a spindle look about it and by Earth standards it would not have supported his weight. He said, "Would you care to say how you came to know Lamont? Was it by reputation only? Did you meet?"

Denison said, "We had some direct conversations. He was planning to write a history of the Electron Pump; how it started; a full account of all the legendary crap that's grown up around it. I was flattered that Lamont came to me; that he seemed to have found out something about me. Damn it, Commissioner, I was flattered that he knew I was alive. But I couldn't really say much. What would have been the use? I would have gained nothing but some sneers and I am tired of it; tired of brooding; tired of self-pity."

"Do you know anything about what Lamont has been doing the last few years?"

"What is it you're thinking of, Commissioner?" asked Denison, cautiously.

"About a year ago, maybe a little more, Lamont spoke to Burt. I am not on the senator's staff any longer, but we see each other occasionally. He talked to me about it. He was concerned. He thought Lamont might have made a valid point against the Electron Pump and yet could see no practical way of taking up the matter. I, too, was concerned—"

"Concern everywhere," said Denison, sardonically.

"But now, I wonder. If Lamont talked to you and—"

"Stop! Stop right there, Commissioner. I think I see you sidling toward a point and I don't want you to move any further. If you expect me to tell you that Lamont stole my idea, that once again I am being treated badly, you are wrong. Let me tell you as forcefully as I can; I had no valid theory. It was purely a guess. It worried me; I presented it; it was not believed; I was discouraged. Since I had no way of demonstrating its value, I gave up. I did not mention it in my discussion with Lamont; we never went past the early days of the Pump. What he came up with later, however much it may have resembled my guess, was arrived at independently. It seems to be much more solid and to be based on rigid mathematical analysis. I lay claim to no priority; to *none*."

"You seem to know about Lamont's theory."

"It made the rounds in recent months. The fellow can't publish and no one takes him seriously, but it was passed along the grapevine. It even reached *me*."

"I see, Doctor. But *I* take it seriously. To me the warning was second time round, you understand. The report of the first warning—from you—had never reached the senator. It had nothing to do with financial irregularities, which were what was then on his mind. The actual head of the investigating panel—not myself—considered it—you will forgive me—crackpot. I did not. When the matter came up again, I grew disturbed. It was my intention to meet with Lamont, but a number of physicists whom I consulted—"

"Including Hallam?"

"No, I did not see Hallam. A number of those I consulted advised me that Lamont's work was utterly without foundation. Even so, I was considering seeing him when I was asked to take up this position, and here I am, and here *you* are. So you see why I had to see you. In your opinion is there merit in the theories advanced by yourself and by Dr. Lamont?"

"You mean is continued use of the Electron Pump going to blow up the Sun, or maybe the entire arm of the Galaxy?"

"Yes, that's exactly what I mean."

"How can I tell you? All I have is my own guess, which is just a guess. As for Lamont's theory, I have not studied it in detail; it has not been published. If I saw it, the mathematics might be beyond me. . . . Besides, what's the difference? Lamont won't convince anyone. Hallam has ruined him as earlier he ruined me, and the public generally would find it against their short-term interest to believe him even if he went over Hallam's head, so to speak. They don't want to give up the Pump, and it's a lot easier to refuse to accept Lamont's theory than to try to do something about it."

"But you're still concerned about it, aren't you?"

"In the sense that I think we might indeed destroy ourselves and that I wouldn't like to see that happen, of course."

"So you've come to the Moon, now, to do something that Hallam, your old enemy, would prevent your doing on Earth."

Denison said, slowly, "You, too, like to make guesses."

"Do I?" said Gottstein, indifferently. "Perhaps I am brilliant, too. Is my guess correct?"

"It may be. I haven't given up hope of returning to science. If anything I do were to lift the specter of doom from mankind, either by showing that it does not exist or that it does exist and must be removed, I would be pleased."

"I see. Dr. Denison, to discuss another point at the moment, my predecessor, the retiring Commissioner, Mr. Montez, tells me that the growing edge of science is here on the Moon. He seems to think a disproportionate quantity of the brains and initiative of mankind is here."

"He may be right," said Denison. "I don't know."

"He may be right," agreed Gottstein, thoughtfully. "If so, doesn't it strike you that this may be inconvenient for your purpose. Whatever you do, men may say and think it was accomplished through the Lunar scientific structure. You personally might gain little in the way of recognition, however valuable the results you present. . . Which, of course, would be unjust."

"I am tired of the rat-race of credit, Commissioner Gottstein. I want some interest in life, more interest than I can find as vice-president in charge of Ultra-sonic Depilatories. I'll find it in a return to science. If I accomplish something in my own eyes, I will be satisfied."

"Let us say that that would be insufficient for me. What credit you earn, you should receive; and it should be quite possible for me, as Commissioner, to present the facts to the Terrestrial community in such a way as to preserve for you what is yours. Surely you are human enough to want what is your own."

"You are kind. And in return?"

"You are cynical. But justly so. In return I want your help. The retiring Commissioner, Mr. Montez, is not certain as to the lines of scientific research being undertaken on the Moon. Communications between the peoples of Earth and Moon are not perfect, and coordination of the efforts on both worlds is clearly for the benefit of all. It is understandable that there's distrust, I suppose, but if you can do anything to break down that distrust, it will be as valuable to us as your scientific findings might be."

"Surely, Commissioner, you can't feel that I'm the ideal man to bear witness to the Lunarites as to how fair-meaning and well-disposed the Earth's scientific establishment is."

"You mustn't confuse one vengeful scientist with the men of the Earth as a whole, Dr. Denison. Let's put it this way. I would appreciate being kept aware of your scientific findings so that I could help you retain your fair share of credit; and in order to understand your findings properly—I am not a professional scientist myself, remember—it would be helpful if you were to explain them in the light of the present state of science on the Moon. Is it agreed?''

Denison said, "You ask a hard thing. Preliminary results, prematurely disclosed, whether through carelessness or over-enthusiasm, can do tremendous harm to a reputation. I would hate to talk about anything to anyone until I was sure of my ground. My earlier experience with the committee on which you served would certainly encourage me to be cautious.''

"I quite understand," said Gottstein, heartily. "I would leave it to you to decide when I might usefully be informed. . . . But I have kept you late and you probably want to sleep.''

Which was a dismissal. Denison left, and Gottstein looked after him thoughtfully.

— 7 —

DENISON OPENED the door by hand. There was a contact that would have opened it automatically, but in the blur of waking, he could not find it.

The dark-haired man, with a face that was somehow scowling in repose, said, "I'm sorry. . . . Am I early?''

Denison repeated the last word to give him time to absorb matters. "Early? . . . No. I . . . I'm late, I think.''

"I called. We made an appointment—''

And now Denison had it. "Yes. You're Dr. Neville.''

"That's right. May I come in?''

He stepped in as he asked. Denison's room was small, and held a rumpled bed that took up most of the available space. The ventilator was sighing softly.

Neville said with meaningless courtesy, "Slept well, I hope?''

Denison looked down at his pajamas and passed his hand over his rumpled hair. "No," he said abruptly. "I had an abominable night. May I be excused long enough to make myself more presentable?''

"Of course. Would you like to have me prepare breakfast meanwhile? You may be unacquainted with the equipment.''

"It would be a favor," said Denison.

He emerged some twenty minutes later, washed and shaved, wearing trousers and an undershirt. He said, "I trust I didn't break the shower. It went off and I couldn't turn it on again.''

"The water's rationed. You only get so much. This is the Moon, Doctor. I've taken the liberty of preparing scrambled eggs and hot soup for the two of us.''

"Scrambled—''

"We call it that. Earthmen wouldn't, I suppose.''

Denison said, "Oh!'' He sat down with something less than enthusiasm and tasted the pasty yellow mixture that clearly was what the other meant by scrambled eggs. He tried not to make a face at the first taste and then manfully swallowed it and dug in for a second forkful.

"You'll get used to it with time," said Neville, "and it's highly nourishing. I might warn you that the high-protein content and the low gravity will cut your need for food."

"Just as well," said Denison, clearing his throat.

Neville said, "Selene tells me that you intend to stay on the Moon."

Denison said, "That was my intention." He rubbed his eyes. "I've had a terrible night, though. It tests my resolution."

"How many times did you fall out of bed?"

"Twice. . . . I take it that the situation is a common one."

"For men of Earth, an invariable one. Awake, you can make yourself walk with due regard for the Moon's gravity. Asleep, you toss as you would on Earth. But at least falling is not painful at low gravity."

"The second time, I slept on the floor awhile before waking. Didn't remember falling. What the hell do you do about it?"

"You mustn't neglect your periodic checks on heartbeat, blood pressure, and so on, just to make sure the gravity change isn't introducing too much of a strain."

"I've been amply warned of that," said Denison with distaste. "In fact, I have fixed appointments for the next month. And pills."

"Well," said Neville, as if dismissing a triviality, "within a week you'll probably have no trouble at all. . . . And you'll need proper clothing. Those trousers will never do and that flimsy upper garment serves no purpose."

"I presume there's some place I can buy clothes."

"Of course. If you can get her when she's off duty, Selene will be glad to help, I'm sure. She assures me you're a decent sort, Doctor."

"I'm delighted she thinks so." Denison, having swallowed a spoonful of the soup, looked at it as though he were wondering what to do with the rest. Grimly, he continued the task of downing it.

"She judged you to be a physicist, but of course she's wrong."

"I was trained as a radiochemist."

"You haven't worked at that either for a long time, Doctor. We may be out of it up here, but we're not that far out of it. You're one of Hallam's victims."

"Are there so many you speak of them as a group?"

"Why not? The whole Moon is one of Hallam's victims."

"The Moon?"

"In a manner of speaking."

"I don't understand."

"We have no Electron Pump Stations on the Moon. None have been established because there has been no cooperation from the para-Universe. No samples of tungsten have been accepted."

"Surely, Dr. Neville, you don't intend to imply that this is Hallam's doing."

"In a negative way, yes. Why must it be only the para-Universe which can initiate a Pump Station. Why not ourselves?"

"As far as I know, we lack the knowledge to take the initiative."

"And we will continue to lack the knowledge if research into the matter is forbidden."

"Is it forbidden?" Denison asked, with a faint note of surprise.

"In effect. If none of the work necessary to expand knowledge in that direction finds adequate priorities at the proton synchrotron or at any of the other large equipment—all controlled by Earth and all under the influence of Hallam— then the research is effectively forbidden.''

Denison rubbed his eyes. ''I suspect I will have to sleep again before long. . . . I beg your pardon. I did not mean to imply you were boring me. But tell me, is the Electron Pump so important to the Moon? Surely the Solar batteries are effective and sufficient.''

''They tie us to the Sun, Doctor. They tie us to the *surface*.''

''Well— But why does Hallam take this adverse interest in the matter, do you suppose, Dr. Neville?''

''You know better than I, if you know him personally, as I do not. He prefers not to make it clear to the public generally that the entire Electron Pump establishment is the product of the para-men, with ourselves merely servants of the masters. And if, on the Moon, we advance to the point where we ourselves know what we are doing, then the birth of the true Electron Pump technology will date from our moment, not from his.''

Denison said, ''Why do you tell me all this?''

''To avoid wasting my time. Ordinarily, we welcome physicists from Earth. We feel cut off here on the Moon, victims of deliberate Terrestrial policy against us, and a physicist-visitor can be helpful, even if only to give us a feeling of lesser isolation. A physicist-immigrant is even more helpful and we like to explain the situation to him and encourage him to work with us. I am sorry that you are not, after all, a physicist.''

Denison said, impatiently, ''But I never said I was.''

''And yet you asked to see the synchrotron. Why?''

''Is that really what's bothering you? My dear sir, let me try to explain. My scientific career was ruined half a life-time ago. I have decided to see some sort of rehabilitation, some sort of renewed meaning, to my life as far away from Hallam as I could get—which means here on the Moon. I was trained as a radiochemist, but that has not permanently paralyzed me as far as any other field of endeavor is concern. Para-physics is the great field of today and I have done my best to self-educate myself there, feeling that this will offer me my best hope for rehabilitation.''

Neville nodded. ''I see,'' he said with clear dubiousness.

''By the way, since you mentioned the Electron Pump— Have you heard anything about the theories of Peter Lamont?''

Neville eyed the other narrowly. ''No. I don't think I know the man.''

''Yes, he is not yet famous. And probably never will be; chiefly for the same reason I'll never be. He crossed Hallam. . . . His name came up recently and I've been giving him some thought. It was one way of occupying the sleepless portion of last night.'' And he yawned.

Neville said, impatiently, ''Yes, Doctor? What of this man? What is his name?''

''Peter Lamont. He has some interesting thoughts on para-theory. He believes that with continued use of the Pump, the strong nuclear interaction will grow basically more intense in the space of the Solar system and that the Sun will slowly heat up and, at some crucial point, undergo a phase-change that will produce an explosion.''

''Nonsense! Do you know the amount of change produced, on a cosmic scale, of any use of the Pump on a human scale? Even granted that you are only self-educated in physics, you ought have no difficulty in seeing that the Pump can't possibly make any appreciable change in general Universal conditions during the lifetime of the Solar system.''

"Do you think so?''

"Of course. Don't you?'' said Neville.

"I'm not sure. Lamont's grinding a personal axe. I've met him briefly and he impressed me as an intense and very emotional fellow. Considering what Hallam has done to him, he is probably driven by overwhelming anger.''

Neville frowned. He said, "Are you sure he is on the outs with Hallam?''

"I'm an expert on the subject.''

"It doesn't occur to you that the initiation of that kind of doubt—that the Pump is dangerous—might be used as but another device to keep the Moon from developing Stations of its own?''

"At the cost of creating universal alarm and despondency? Of course not. That would be cracking walnuts with nuclear explosions. No, I'm sure Lamont is sincere. In fact, in my own bumbling way, I had similar notions once.''

"Because you, too, are drive by hate for Hallam.''

"I'm not Lamont. I imagine I don't react the same way he does. In fact, I had some dim hope I would be able to investigate the matter on the Moon, without Hallam's interference and without Lamont's emotionalism.''

"Here on the Moon?''

"Here on the Moon. I thought perhaps I might get the use of the synchrotron.''

"And that was your interest in it?''

Denison nodded.

Neville said, "You really think you will get the use of the synchrotron? Do you know how far back the requisitions have piled up?''

"I thought perhaps I might get the cooperation of some of the Lunar scientists.''

Neville laughed and shook his head. "We have almost as little chance as you. . . . However, I'll tell you what we can do. We have established laboratories of our own. We can give you space; we might even have some minor instrumentation for you. How useful our facilities would be to you, I can't say, but you might be able to do something.''

"Do you suppose I would have any means there of making observations useful to para-theory?''

"It would depend partly on your ingenuity, I suppose. Do you expect to prove the theories of this man, Lamont?''

"Or disprove them. Perhaps.''

"You'll disprove them, if anything at all. I have no fears about that.

Denison said, "It's quite clear, isn't it, and I'm not a physicist by training? Why do you so readily offer me working-space?''

"Because you're from Earth. I told you that we value that, and perhaps your self-education as a physicist will be of additional value. Selene vouches for you, something I attach more importance to than I should, perhaps. And we are fellow-sufferers at the hands of Hallam. If you wish to rehabilitate yourself, we will help you.''

"But pardon me if I am cynical. What do you expect to get out of it?''

"Your help. There is a certain amount of misunderstanding between the scientists of the Earth and the Moon. You are a man of Earth who has come voluntarily to the Moon and you could act as a bridge between us to the benefit of both. You have already had contact with the new Commissioner and it may be possible that, as you rehabilitate yourself, you will rehabilitate us as well.''

''You mean that if what I do weakens Hallam's influence, that will benefit Lunar science as well.''

''Whatever you do is sure to be useful. . . . But perhaps I ought to leave you to catch up with your sleep. Call on me during the next couple of days and I will see about placing you in a laboratory. And''—he looked about—''getting you somewhat more comfortable quarters as well.''

They shook hands and Neville left.

— 8 —

GOTTSTEIN SAID, ''I suppose that, however annoying this position of yours may have been, you are getting ready to leave it today with a small pang.''

Montez shrugged eloquently. ''A very large pang, when I think of the return to full gravity. The difficulty of breathing—the aching feet—the perspiration. I'll be a bath of perspiration constantly.''

''It will be my turn someday.''

''Take my advice. Never stay here longer than two months at a time. I don't care what the doctors tell you or what kind of isometric exercises they put you through—get back to Earth every sixty days and stay at least a week. You've got to keep the feel of it.''

''I'll bear that in mind. . . . Oh, I've been in touch with my friend.''

''Which friend is that?''

''The man who was on the vessel with me when I came in. I thought I remembered him and I did. A man named Denison; a radiochemist. What I remembered of him was accurate enough.''

''Ah?''

''I remembered a certain interesting irrationality of his, and tried to probe it. He resisted in quite a shrewd fashion. He sounded rational; so rational, in fact, that I grew suspicious. There's a kind of attractive rationality developed by certain types of crackpots; a kind of defense mechanism.''

''Oh, Lord,'' said Montez, clearly harassed. ''I'm not sure I follow you. If you don't mind, I'm going to sit down for a moment. Between trying to determine whether everything is properly packed and thinking about Earth's gravity, I'm out of breath. . . . What kind of irrationality?''

''He tried to tell us once that there was danger in the use of the Electron Pumps. He thought it would blow up the Universe.''

''Indeed? And will it?''

''I hope not. At the time it was dismissed rather brusquely. When scientists work on a subject at the limit of understanding, they grow edgy, you know. I knew a psychiatrist once who called it the 'Who knows?' phenomenon. If nothing you do will give you the knowledge you need, you end by saying, 'Who knows what will happen?' and imagination tells you.''

''Yes, but if physicists go around saying such things, even a few of them—''

"But they don't. Not officially. There's such a thing as scientific responsibility and the journals are careful not to print nonsense. . . . Or what they consider nonsense. Actually, you know, the subject's come up again. A physicist named Lamont spoke to Senator Burt, to that self-appointed environmental messiah, Chen, and to a few others. He also insists on the possibility of cosmic explosion. No one believes him but the story spreads in a thin sort of way and gets better with the retelling."

"And this man here on the Moon believes it."

Gottstein smiled broadly. "I suspect he does. Hell, in the middle of the night, when I have trouble sleeping—I keep falling out of bed, by the way—I believe it myself. He probably hopes to test the theory experimentally, here."

"Well?"

"Well, let him. I hinted we would help him."

Montez shook his head. "That's risky. I don't like the official encouragement of crackpot notions."

"You know, it's just barely possible they may not be entirely crackpot, but that's not the point. The point is that if we can get him established here on the Moon, we may find out, through him, what's going on here. He's anxious for rehabilitation and I hinted that rehabilitation would come through us if he cooperated. . . . I'll see to it that you are discreetly kept posted. As between friends, you know."

"Thank you," said Montez. "And good-bye."

— 9 —

NEVILLE CHAFED. "No. I don't like him."

"Why not? Because he's an Earthie?" Selene brushed a bit of fluff from her right breast, then caught it and looked at it critically. "That's not from my blouse. I tell you the air-recirculation is abominable."

"This Denison is worthless. He is not a para-physicist. He's a self-educated man in the field, he says, and proves it by coming here with ready-made damn-fool notions."

"Like what?"

"He thinks that the Electron Pump is going to explode the Universe."

"Did he say that?"

"I know he thinks that. . . . Oh, I know the arguments. I've heard them often enough. But it's not so, that's all."

"Maybe," said Selene, raising her eyebrows, "you just don't want it to be so."

"Don't *you* start," said Neville.

There was a short pause. Selene said, "Well, what will you do with him?"

"I'll give him a place to work. He may be worthless as a scientist, but he'll have his uses just the same. He'll be conspicuous enough; the Commissioner has been talking to him already."

"I know."

"Well, he has a romantic history as someone with a wrecked career trying to rehabilitate himself."

"Really?"

"Really. I'm sure you'll love it. If you ask him about it, he'll tell you. And that's good. If we have a romantic Earthman working on the Moon on a crackpot project, he'll make a perfect object to preoccupy the Commissioner. He'll be misdirection; window-dressing. And it may even be that through him, who knows, we might just possibly get a better idea of what goes on there on Earth. . . . You'd better continue to be friendly with him, Selene."

— 10 —

SELENE LAUGHED, and the sound was metallic in Denison's earpiece. Her figure was lost in the spacesuit she wore.

She said, "Now come, Ben, there's no reason to be afraid. You're an old hand by now—you've been here a month."

"Twenty-eight days," mumbled Denison. He felt smothered in his own suit.

"A month," insisted Selene. "It was well past half-Earth when you came; it is well-past half-Earth now." She pointed to the brilliant curve of the Earth in the southern sky.

"Well, but wait. I'm not as brave out here as I am underground. What if I fall?"

"What if you do? The gravity is weak by your standards, the slope is gentle, your suit is strong. If you fall, just let yourself slide and roll. It's almost as much fun that way, anyhow."

Denison looked about doubtfully. The Moon lay beautiful in the cold light of the Earth. It was black and white; a mild and delicate white as compared with the Sunlit views he had seen when he had taken a trip a week before to inspect the Solar batteries that stretched from horizon to horizon along the floor of Mare Imbrium. And the black was somehow softer, too, through lack of the blazing contrast of true day. The stars were supernally bright and the Earth—the Earth—was infinitely inviting with its swirls of white on blue, and its peeping glimpse of tan.

"Well," he said, "do you mind if I hang on to you?"

"Of course not. And we won't go all the way up. It will be the beginner's slope for you. Just try to keep in time with me. I'll move slowly."

Her steps were long, slow, and swinging, and he tried to keep in synchronization. The up-sloping ground beneath them was dusty and with each step he kicked up a fine power that settled quickly in the airlessness. He matched her stride for stride, but with an effort.

"Good," said Selene, her arm locked in his, steadying him. "You're very good for an Earthie—no, I ought to stay Immie—"

"Thank you."

"That's not much better, I suppose. Immie from Immigrant is as insulting as Earthie for Earthman. Shall I just say you're simply very good for a man your age."

"*No!* That's much worse." Denison was gasping a little and he could feel his forehead moistening.

Selene said, "Each time you reach the point where you're about to put your foot down, give a little push with your other foot. That will lengthen your stride and make it all the easier. No, no—watch me."

Denison paused thankfully and watched Selene, somehow slim and graceful despite the grotesquerie of the suit once she moved, take off into low, loping leaps. She returned and knelt at his feet.

"Now you take a slow step, Ben, and I'll hit your foot when I want it to shove."

They tried several times, and Denison said, "That's worse than running on Earth. I better rest."

"All right. It's just that your muscles aren't used to the proper coordination. It's yourself you're fighting, you know, not gravity. . . . Well, sit down and catch your breath. I won't take you up much farther."

Denison said, "Will I do any damage to the pack if I lie down on my back?"

"No, of course not, but it's not a good idea. Not on the bare ground. It's only a 120 degrees absolute; 150 degrees below zero, if you prefer, and the smaller the area of contact the better. I'd sit down."

"All right." Gingerly, Denison sat down with a grunt. Deliberately, he faced northward, away fom the Earth. "Look at those stars!"

Selene sat facing him, at right angles. He could see her face now and then, dimly through the faceplate, when the Earthlight caught it at the proper angle.

She said, "Don't you see the stars on Earth?"

"Not like this. Even when there are no clouds, the air on Earth absorbs some of the light. Temperature differences in the atmosphere make them twinkle, and city lights, even distant city lights, wash them out."

"Sounds disgusting."

"Do you like it out here, Selene? On the surface?"

"I'm not crazy about it really, but I don't mind it too much, now and then. It's part of my job to bring tourists out here, of course."

"And now you have to do it for me."

"Can't I convince you it's not the same thing at all, Ben? We've got a set route for the tourists. It's very tame, very uninteresting. You don't think we'd take them out here to the slide, do you? This is for Lunarites—and Immies. Mostly Immies, actually."

"It can't be very popular. There's no one here but ourselves."

"Oh, well. There are particular days for this sort of thing. You should see this place on race days. You wouldn't like it then, though."

"I'm not sure I like it *now*. Is gliding a sport for Immies, particularly?"

"Rather. Lunarites don't like the surface generally."

"How about Dr. Neville?"

"You mean, how he feels about the surface?"

"Yes."

"Frankly, I don't think he's ever been up here. He's a real city boy. Why do you ask?"

"Well, when I asked permission to go along on the routine servicing of the Solar batteries, he was perfectly willing to have me go, but he wouldn't go himself. I rather asked him to, I think, so I could have someone answer my questions, if there were any, and his refusal was rather strong."

"I hope there was someone else to answer your questions."

"Oh, yes. He was an Immie, too, come to think of it. Maybe that explains Dr. Neville's attitude toward the Electron Pump."

"What do you mean?"

"Well—" Denison leaned back and kicked his legs up alternately, watching them rise and fall slowly with a certain lazy pleasure. "Hey, that's not bad. Look, Selene— What I mean is that Neville is so intent on developing a Pump Station on the Moon when the Solar batteries are so adaquate for the job. We couldn't use Solar batteries on the Earth, where the Sun is never as unfailing, as prolonged, as bright, as radiant in all wave lengths. There's no a single planetary body in the Solar system, no body of any size, that is more suitable for the use of the batteries than the Moon is. Even Mercury is too hot. But the use does tie you to the surface, and if you don't like the surface—"

Selene rose to her feet suddenly, and said, "All right, Ben, you've rested enough. Up! Up!"

He struggled to his feet and said, "A Pump Station, however, would mean that no Lunarite would ever have to come out on the surface, if he didn't want to."

"Uphill we go, Ben. We'll go to that ridge up ahead. See it, where the Earthlight cuts off in a horizontal line?"

They made their way up the final stretch silently. Denison was aware of the smoother area to their side; a wide swathe of slope from which most of the dust had been brushed.

"That's too smooth for a beginner to work up," Selene said, answering his thoughts. "Don't get too ambitious or you'll want me to teach you the kangaroo-hop next."

She made a kangaroo-hop as she spoke, turned about face almost before landing, and said, "Right here. Sit down and I'll adjust—"

Denison did, facing downhill. He looked down the slope uncertainly. "Can I really glide on it?"

"Of course. The gravity is weaker on the Moon than on the Earth, so you press against the ground much less strongly, and that means there is much less friction. Everything is more slippery on the Moon than on the Earth. That's why the floors in our corridors and apartments seemed unfinished to you. Would you like to hear me give my little lecture on the subject? The one I give the tourists?"

"No, Selene."

"Besides, we're going to use gliders, of course." She had a small cartridge in her hand. Clamps and a pair of thin tubes were attached to it.

"What is that?" asked Ben.

"Just a small liquid-gas reservoir. It will emit a jet of vapor just under your boots. The thin gas layer between boots and ground will reduce friction to virtually zero. You'll move as though you were in clear space."

Denison said uneasily, "I disapprove. Surely, it's wasteful to use gas in this fashion on the Moon."

"Oh, now. What gas do you think we use in these gliders? Carbon dioxide? Oxygen? This is waste gas to begin with. It's argon. It come out of the Moon's soil in ton-lots, formed by the billions of years of breakdown of potassium-40. . . . That's part of my lecture, too, Ben. . . . The argon has only a few specialized uses on the Moon. We could use it for gliding for a million years without exhausting the supply. . . . All right. Your gliders are on. Now wait till I put mine on.''

"How do they work?''

"It's quite automatic. You just start sliding and that will trip the contact and start the vapor. You've only got a few minutes supply; but that's all you need.''

She stood up and helped him to his feet. "Face down-hill. . . . Come on, Ben, this is a gentle slope. Look at it. It looks perfectly level.''

"No, it doesn't,'' said Denison, sulkily. "It looks like a cliff to me.''

"Nonsense. Now listen to me and remember what I told you. Keep your feet about six inches apart and one just a few inches ahead of the other. It doesn't matter which one is ahead. Keep your knees bent. Don't lean into the wind because there isn't any. Don't try to look up or back, but you can look from side to side if you have to. Most of all, when you finally hit level, don't try to stop too soon; you'll be going faster than you think. Just let the glider expire and then friction will bring you to a slow halt.''

"I'll never remember all that.''

"Yes, you will. And I'll be right at your side to help. And if you do fall and I don't catch you, don't try to do anything. Just relax and let yourself tumble or slide. There are no boulders anywhere that you can collide with.''

Denison swallowed and looked ahead. The southward slide was gleaming in Earthlight. Minute unevennesses caught more than their share of light, leaving tiny uphill patches in darkness so that there was a vague mottling of the surface. The bulging half-circle of Earth rode the black sky almost directly ahead.

"Ready?'' said Selene. Her gauntleted hand was between his shoulders.

"Ready,'' said Denison faintly.

"Then off you go,'' she said. She pushed and Denison felt himself begin to move. He moved quite slowly at first. He turned toward her, wobbling, and she said, "Don't worry. I'm right at your side.''

He could feel the ground beneath his feet—and then he couldn't. The glider had been activated.

For a moment he felt as though he were standing still. There was no push of air against his body, no feel of anything sliding past his feet. But when he turned toward Selene again, he noticed that the lights and shadows to one side were moving backward at a slowly increasing speed.

"Keep your eyes on the Earth,'' Selene's voice said in his ear, "till you build up speed. The faster you go, the more stable you'll be. Keep your knees bent. . . . You're doing very well, Ben.''

"For an Immie,'' gasped Denison.

"How does it feel?''

"Like flying,'' he said. The pattern of light and dark on either side was moving backward in a blur. He looked briefly to one side, then the other, trying to convert the sensation of a backward flight of the surroundings into one of a forward flight of his own. Then, as soon as he succeeded, he found he had to look forward hastily at the Earth to regain his sense of balance. "I suppose that's not a good comparison to use to you. You have no experience of flying on the Moon.''

"Now I know, though. Flying must be like gliding—I know what *that* is.''

She was keeping up with him easily.

Denison was going fast enough now so that he got the sensation of motion even when he looked ahead. The Moonscape ahead was opening before him and flowing past on either side. He said, "How fast do you get to go in a glide?"

"A good Moon-race," said Selene, "has been clocked at speeds in excess of a hundred miles an hour—on steeper slopes than this one, of course. You'll probably reach a top of thirty-five."

"It feels a lot faster than that somehow."

"Well, it isn't. We're leveling off now, Ben, and you haven't fallen. Now just hang on; the glider will die off and you'll feel friction. Don't do anything to help it. Just keep going."

Selene had barely completed her remarks when Denison felt the beginning of pressure under his boots. There was at once an overwhelming sensation of speed and he clenched his fists hard to keep from throwing his arms up in an almost reflex gesture against the collision that wasn't going to happen. He knew that if he threw up his arms, he would go over backward.

He narrowed his eyes, held his breath till he thought his lungs would explode, and then Selene said, "Perfect, Ben, perfect. I've never known an Immie to go through his first slide without a fall, so if you do fall, there'll be nothing wrong. No disgrace."

"I don't intend to fall," whispered Denison. He caught a large, ragged breath, and opened his eyes wide. The Earth was as serene as ever, as uncaring. He was moving more slowly now—more slowly—more slowly—

"Am I standing still now, Selene?" he asked. "I'm not sure."

"You're standing still. Now don't move. You've got to rest before we make the trip back to town. . . . Damn it, I left it somewhere around here when we came up."

Denison watched her with disbelief. She had climbed up with him, had glided down with him. Yet he was half-dead with weariness and tension, and she was in the air with long kangaroo-leaps. She seemed a hundred yards away when she said, "Here it is!" and her voice was as loud in his ears as when she was next to him.

She was back in a moment, with a folded, paunchy sheet of plastic under her arm.

"Remember," she said, cheerily, "when you asked what it was on our way up and I said we'd be using it before we came down?" She unfolded it and spread it on the dusty surface of the Moon.

"A Lunar Lounge is its full name," she said, "but we just call it a lounge. We take the adjective for granted here on this world." She inserted a cartridge and tripped a lever.

It began to fill. Somehow Denison had expected a hissing noise, but of course there was no air to carry sound.

"Before you question our conservation policies again," said Selene, "this is argon also."

It blossomed into a mattress on six, stubby legs. "It will hold you," she said. "It makes very little actual contact with the ground and the vacuum all around will conserve its heat."

"Don't tell me it's hot," said Denison, amazed.

"The argon is heated as it pours in, but only relatively. It ends up at 270 degrees absolute, almost warm enough to melt ice, and quite warm enough to keep your insulated suit from losing heat faster than you can manufacture it. Go ahead. Lie down."

Denison did so, with a sensation of enormous luxury.

"Great!" he said with a long sigh.

"Mamma Selene thinks of everything," she said.

She came from behind him now, gliding around him, her feet placed heel to heel as though she were on skates, and then let them fly out from under her, as she came down gracefully on hip and elbow on the ground just beside him.

Denison whistled. "How did you do that?"

"Lots of practice! And don't you try it. You'll break your elbow. I warn you though. If I get too cold, I'm going to have to crowd you on the lounge."

"Safe enough," he said, "with both of us in suits."

"Ah, there speaks my brave lecher. . . . How do you feel?"

"All right, I guess. What an experience!"

"What an experience? You set a record for non-falls. Do you mind if I tell the folks back in town about this?"

"No. Always like to be appreciated. . . . You're not going to expect me to do this again, are you?"

"Right now? Of course not. I wouldn't myself. We'll just rest awhile, make sure your heart action is back to normal, and then we'll go back. If you'll reach your legs in my direction, I'll take your gliders off. Next time, I'll show you how to handle the gliders yourself."

"I'm not sure that there will be a next time."

"Of course there'll be. Didn't you enjoy it?"

"A little. In between terror."

"You'll have less terror next time, and still less the time after, and eventually you'll just experience the enjoyment and I'll make a racer out of you."

"No, you won't. I'm too old."

"Not on the Moon. You just *look* old."

Denison could feel the ultimate quiet of the Moon soaking into him as he lay there. He was facing the Earth this time. Its steady presence in the sky had, more than anything else, given him the sensation of stability during his recent glide and he felt grateful to it.

He said, "Do you often come out here, Selene? I mean, by yourself, or just one or two others? You know, when it isn't fiesta time?"

"Practically never. Unless there are people around, this is too much for me. That I'm doing it now, actually, surprises me."

"Uh-huh," said Denison, noncommittally.

"You're not surprised?"

"Should I be? My feeling is that each person does what he does either because he wants to or he must and in either case that's his business, not mine."

"Thanks, Ben. I mean it; it's good to hear. One of the nice things about you, Ben, is that for an Immie, you're willing to let us be ourselves. We're underground people, we Lunarites, cave people, corridor people. And what's wrong with that?"

"Nothing."

"Not to hear the Earthies talk. And I'm a tourist guide and have to listen to them. There isn't anything they say that I haven't heard a million times, but what I hear most of all"—and she dropped into the clipped accents of the typical Earthie speaking Planetary Standard "—'But, dear, however can all you people live in *caves* all the time? Doesn't it give you a terrible *closed-in* feeling? Don't you ever want to see blue sky and trees and ocean and feel wind and smell flowers—'

"Oh, I could go on and on, Ben. Then they say, 'But I suppose you don't know what blue sky and sea and trees are like so you don't miss them.' . . . As if we don't receive Earth-televison and as if we don't have full access to Earth-literature, both optical and auditory—and olfactory sometimes, too."

Denison was amused. He said, "What's the official answer to remarks like that?"

"Nothing much. We just say, 'We're quite used to it, madam.' Or 'sir' if it's a man. Usually it's a woman. The men are too interested in studying our blouses and wondering when we take them off, I suppose. You know what I'd like to tell the idiots?"

"Please tell me. As long as you have to keep the blouse on, it being inside the suit, at least get that off your chest."

"Funny, funny word play! . . . I'd like to tell them, 'Look, madam, why the hell should we be interested in your damned world? We don't want to be hanging on the outside of my planet and waiting to fall off or get blown off. We don't want raw air puffing at us and dirty water falling on us. We don't want your damned germs and your smelly grass and your dull blue sky and your dull white clouds. We can see Earth in our own sky when we want to, and we don't often want to. The Moon is our home and it's what we make it; exactly what we make it. We own it and we build our own ecology, and we don't need you here being sorry for us going our own way. Go back to your own world and let your gravity pull your breasts down to your knees.' That's what I'd say."

Denison said, "All right. Whenever you get too close to saying that to some Earthie, you come say it to me and you'll feel better."

"You know what? Every once in a while, some Immie suggests that we build an Earth-park on the Moon; some little spot with Earth-plants brought in as seeds or seedlings; maybe some animals. A touch of home—that's the usual expression."

"I take it you're against that."

"Of course, I'm against it. A touch of whose home? The *Moon* is our home. An Immie who wants a touch of home had better get back to *his* home. Immies can be worse than Earthies sometimes."

"I'll keep that in mind," said Denison.

"Not you—so far," said Selene.

There was silence for a moment and Denison wonderd if Selene were going to suggest a return to the caverns. On the one hand, it wouldn't be long before he would feel a fairly strenuous craving to visit a rest-room. On the other, he had never felt so relaxed. He wondered how long the oxygen in his pack would hold out.

Then Selene said, "Ben, do you mind if I ask you a question?"

"Not at all. If it's my private life that interests you, I am without secrets. I'm five-foot-nine, weigh twenty-eight pounds on the Moon, had one wife long ago, now divorced, one child, a daughter, grown-up and married, attended University of—"

"No, Ben. I'm serious. Can I ask about your work?"

"Of course you can, Selene. I don't know how much I can explain to you, though."

"Well— You know that Barron and I—"

"Yes, I know," said Denison, brusquely.

"We talk together. He tells me things sometimes. He said you think the Electron Pump might make the Universe explode."

"Our section of the Universe. It might convert a part of our Galactic arm into a quasar."

"Really? Do you really think so?"

Denison said, "When I came to the Moon, I wasn't sure. Now I am. I am personally convinced that this will happen."

"When do you think it will happen?"

"That I can't say exactly. Maybe a few years from now. Maybe a few decades."

There was a short silence between them. Then Selene said, in a subdued voice. "Barron doesn't think so."

"I know he doesn't. I'm not trying to convert him. You don't beat refusal to believe in a frontal attack. That's Lamont's mistake."

"Who's Lamont?"

"I'm sorry, Selene. I'm talking to myself."

"No, Ben. Please tell me. I'm interested. Please."

Denison turned to one side, facing her. "All right," he said. "I have no objection to telling you. Lamont, a physicist back on Earth, tried in his way to alert the world to the dangers of the Pump. He failed. Earthmen want the Pump; they want the free energy; they want it enough to refuse to believe they can't have it."

"But why should they want it, if it means death?"

"All they have to do is refuse to believe it means death. The easiest way to solve a problem is to deny it exists. Your friend, Dr. Neville, does the same thing. He dislikes the surface, so he forces himself to believe that Solar batteries are no good—even though to any impartial observer they would seem the perfect energy source for the Moon. He wants the Pump so he can stay underground, so he refuses to believe that there can be any danger from it."

Selene said, "I don't think Barron would refuse to believe something for which valid evidence existed. Do you really have the evidence?"

"I think I do. It's most amazing really, Selene. The whole thing depends on certain subtle factors of quark-quark interactions. Do you know what that means?"

"You don't have to explain. I've talked so much to Barron about all sorts of things that I might be able to follow."

"Well, I thought I would need the Lunar proton synchrotron for the purpose. It's twenty-five miles across, has superconducting magnets, and can dispose of energies of 20,000 Bev and more. It turns out, though, that you people have something you call a Pionizer, which fits into a moderate sized room and does all the work of the synchrotron. The Moon is to be congratulated on a most amazing advance."

"Thank you," said Selene, complacently. "I mean on behalf of the Moon."

"Well, then, my Pionizer results can show the rate of increase of intensity of strong nuclear interaction; and the increase is what Lamont says it is and not what the orthodox theory would have it be."

"And have you shown it to Barron?"

"No, I haven't. And if I do, I expect Neville to reject it. He'll say the results are marginal. He'll say I've made an error. He'll say that I haven't taken all factors into account. He'll say I've used inadequate controls. . . . What he'll really be saying is that he wants the Electron Pump and won't give it up.''

''You mean there's no way out.''

''Of course there is, but not the direct way. Not Lamont's way.''

''What's that?''

''Lamont's solution is to force abandonment of the Pump, but you can't just move backward. You can't push the chicken back into the egg, wine back into the grape, the boy back into the womb. If you want the baby to let go of your watch, you don't just try to explain that he ought to do it—you offer him something he would rather have.''

''And what's that?''

''Ah, that's where I'm not so sure. I do have an idea, a simple idea—perhaps too simple to work—based on the quite obvious fact that the number two is ridiculous and can't exist.''

There was a silence that lasted for a minute or so and then Selene, her voice as absorbed as his, said, ''Let me guess your meaning.''

''I don't know that I have any,'' said Denison.

''Let me guess, anyway. It could make sense to suppose that our own Universe is the only one that can exist or does exist, because it is the only one we live in and directly experience. Once, however, evidence arises that there is a second Universe as well, the one we call the para-Universe, then it becomes absolutely ridiculous to suppose that there are two and only two Universes. If a second Universe can exist, then an infinite number can. Between one and the infinite in cases such as these, there are no sensible numbers. Not only two, but any finite number, is ridiculous and can't exist.''

Denison said, ''That's exactly my reas—'' And silence fell again.

Denison heaved himself into a sitting position and looked down on the suit-encased girl. He said, ''I think we had better go back to town.''

She said, ''I was just guessing.''

He said, ''No, you weren't. Whatever it was, it wasn't *just* guessing.''

— 11 —

BARRON NEVILLE stared at her, quite speechless for a while. She looked calmly back at him. Her window panorama had been changed again. One of them now showed the Earth, a little more than half full.

Finally, he said, ''Why?''

She said, ''It was an accident, really, I saw the point and I was too enthusiastic not to speak. I should have told you days ago but I was afraid your reaction would be exactly what it is.''

''So he knows. You *fool!*''

She frowned. ''What does he know? Only what he would have guessed sooner or later—that I'm not really a tourist guide—that I'm your Intuitionist. An Intuitionist who knows no mathematics, for heaven's sake. So what if he knows that? What does it matter if I have intuition? How many times have you told me that my intuition has no value till it is backed by mathematical rigor and experimental observation? How many times have you told me that the most compelling intuition could be wrong? Well, then, what value will he place on mere Intuitionism?''

Neville grew white, but Selene couldn't tell whether that was out of anger or apprehension. He said, ''You're different. Hasn't your intuition always proved right? When you were sure of it?''

''Ah, but he doesn't know that, does he?''

''He'll guess it. He'll see Gottstein.''

''What will he tell Gottstein? He still has no idea of what we're really after.''

''Doesn't he?''

''No.'' She had stood up, walked away. Now she turned to him and shouted, ''*No!* It's cheap of you to imply that I would betray you and the rest. If you don't accept my integrity then accept my common sense. There's no point in telling them. What's the use of it to them, or to us, if we're all going to be destroyed?''

''Oh, please, Selene!'' Neville waved his hand in disgust. ''Not that.''

''No. You listen. He talked to me and described his work. You hide me like a secret weapon. You tell me that I'm more valuable than any instrument or any ordinary scientist. You play your games of conspiracy, insisting that everyone must continue to think me a tourist guide and nothing more so that my great talents will always be available to the Lunarites. To *you*. And what do you accomplish?''

''We have you, haven't we? How long do you suppose you would have remained free, if they—''

''You keep saying things like that. But who's been imprisoned? Who's been stopped? Where is the evidence of the great conspiracy you see all around you? The Earthmen keep you and your team from their large instruments much more because you goad them into it than out of any malice on their part. And that's done us good, rather than harm, since it's forced us to invent other instruments that are more subtle.''

''Based on *your* theoretical insight, Selene.''

Selene smiled. ''I know. Ben was very complimentary about them.''

''You and your Ben. What the *hell* do you want with that miserable Earthie?''

''He's an Immigrant. And what I want is information. Do you give me any? You're so damned afraid I'll be caught, you don't dare let me be seen talking to any physicist; only you, and you're my— For that reason only, probably.''

''No, Selene.'' He tried to manage a soothing tone, but there was far too much impatience to it.

''No, I don't care about that really. You've told me I have this one task and I've tried to concentrate on it and sometimes I think I have it, mathematics or not. I can visualize it; the kind of things that must be done—and then it slips away. But what's the use of it, when the Pump will destroy us all anyway. . . . Haven't I told you I distrusted the exchange of field intensities?''

Neville said, ''I'll ask you again. Are you ready to tell me that the Pump *will* destroy us? Never mind 'might,' never mind 'could'; never mind anything but 'will.' ''

Selene shook her head angrily. ''I can't. It's so marginal. I can't say it will. But isn't a simple 'might' sufficient in such a case?''

''Oh, Lord.''

''Don't turn up your eyes. Don't *sneer!* You've never tested the matter. I told you how it might be tested.''

"You were never this worried about it till you started listening to this Earthie of yours."

"He's an Immigrant. Aren't you going to test it?"

"No! I told you your suggestions were impractical. You're not an experimentalist, and what looks good in your mind doesn't necessarily work in the real world of instruments, of randomness, and of uncertainty."

"The so-called real world of your *laboratory.*" Her face was flushed and angry and she held her clenched fists at chin-level. "You waste so much time trying to get a vacuum good enough— There's a vacuum up there, up *there* on the surface where I'm pointing, with temperatures that, at times, are halfway down toward absolute zero. Why don't you try experiments on the surface?"

"It would have been useless."

"How do you *know?* You just won't try. Ben Denison tried. He took the trouble to devise a system he could use on the surface and he set it up when he went to inspect the Solar batteries. He wanted you to come and you wouldn't. Do you remember? It was a very simple thing, something even I could describe to you now that it's been described to me. He ran it at day-temperatures and again at night-temperatures and that was enough to guide him to a new line of research with the Pionizer."

"How simple you make it sound."

"How simple it *is.* Once he found out I was an Intuitionist, he talked to me as you never did. He explained his reasons for thinking that the strengthening of the strong nuclear interaction is indeed accumulating catastrophically in the neighborhood of Earth. It will only be a few years before the Sun explodes and sends the strengthening, in ripples—"

"No, no, no, *no,*" shouted Neville, "I've seen his results and I'm not impressed."

"You've *seen* them?"

"Yes, of course. Do you suppose I let him work in our laboratories without making sure I know what he's doing? I've seen his results and they're worth *nothing*. He deals with tiny deviations that are well within the experimental error. If he wants to believe that those deviations have significance and if you want to believe them, go ahead. But no amount of belief will make them have that significance if, in fact, they don't.

"What do *you* want to believe, Barron?"

"I want the truth."

"But haven't you decided in advance what the truth must be by your own gospel? You want the Pump Station of the Moon, don't you, so that you need have nothing to do with the surface; and anything that might prevent that is not the truth—by definition."

"I won't argue with you. I want the Pump Station, and even more—I want the other. One's no good without the other. Are you sure you haven't—"

"I *haven't.*"

"Will you?"

Selene whirled on him again, her feet tapping raidly on the ground in such a way as to keep her bobbing in the air to the tune of an angry clatter.

"I won't tell him anything," she said, "but I must have more information. You have no information for me, but he may have; or he may get it with the experiments you won't do. I've got to talk to him and find out what he is going to find out. If you get between him and me, you'll never have what you want.

And you needn't fear his getting it before I do. He's too used to Earth thinking; he won't make that last step. I will.''

''All right. And don't forget the difference between Earth and Moon, either. This is your world; you have no other. This man, Denison, this Ben, this *Immigrant,* having come from Earth to the Moon, can, if he chooses, return from Moon to Earth. You can never go to the Earth; never. You are a Lunarite forever.''

''A Moon-maiden,'' said Selene, derisively.

''No maiden,'' said Neville. ''Though you may have to wait a long while before I confirm the matter once again.''

She seemed unmoved at that.

He said, ''And about this big danger of explosion. If the risk involved in changing the basic constants of a Universe is so great, why haven't the para-men, who are so far advanced beyond us in technology, stopped Pumping?''

And he left.

She faced the closed door with bunched jaw muscles. Then she said, ''Because conditions are different for them and for us, you incredible jerk.'' But she was speaking to herself; he was gone.

She kicked the lever that let down her bed, threw herself into it and seethed. How much closer was she now to the real object for which Barron and those others had now been aiming for years?

No closer.

Energy! Everyone searched for energy! The magic word! The cornucopia! The one key to universal plenty! . . . And yet energy wasn't all.

If one found energy, one could find the other, too. If one found the key to energy, the key to the other would be obvious. She *knew* the key to the other would be obvious if she could but grasp some subtle point that would appear obvious the moment it was grasped. (Good heavens, she had been so infected by Barron's chronic suspicion that even in her thoughts she was calling it ''the other.'')

No Earthman would get that subtle point because no Earthman had reason to look for it.

Ben Denison would find it for her, then, without finding it for himself.

Except that— If the Universe was to be destroyed, what did anything matter?

— 12 —

DENISON TRIED to beat down his self-consciousness. Time and again, he made a groping motion as though to hitch upward the pants he wasn't wearing. He wore only sandals and the barest of briefs, which were uncomfortably tight. And, of course, he carried the blanket.

Selene, who was similarly accoutered, laughed. ''Now, Ben, there's nothing wrong with your bare body, barring a certain flabbiness. It's perfectly in fashion here. In fact, take off your briefs if they're binding you.''

''No!'' muttered Denison. He shifted the blanket so that it draped over his abdomen and she snatched it from him.

She said, "Now give me that thing. What kind of a Lunarite will you make if you bring your Earth puritanism here? You *know* that prudery is only the other side of prurience. The words are even on the same page in the dictionary."

"I have to get used to it, Selene."

"You might start by looking at me once in awhile, without having your glance slide off me as though I were coated with oil. You look at other women quite efficiently, I notice."

"If I look at you—"

"Then you'll seem too interested and you'll be embarrassed. But if you look hard, you'll get used to it, and you'll stop noticing. Look, I'll stand still and you stare. I'll take off my briefs."

Denison groaned, "Selene, there are people all around and you're making intolerable fun of me. Please keep walking and let me get used to the situation."

"All right, but I hope you notice the people who pass us don't look at us."

"They don't look at *you*. They look at me all right. They've probably never seen so old-looking and ill-shaped a person."

"They probably haven't," agreed Selene, cheerfully, "but they'll just have to get used to it."

Denison walked on in misery, conscious of every gray hair on his chest and of every quiver of his paunch. It was only when the passageway thinned out and the people passing them were fewer in number that he began to feel a certain relief.

He looked about him curiously now, not as aware of Selene's conical breasts as he had been, nor of her smooth thighs. The corridor seemed endless.

"How far have we come?" he asked.

"Are you tired?" Selene was contrite. "We could have taken a scooter. I forget you're from Earth."

"I should hope you do. Isn't that the idea for an immigrant? I'm not the least bit tired. Hardly the least bit tired at any rate. What I am is a little cold."

"Purely your imagination, Ben," said Selene, firmly. "You just think you ought to feel cold because so much of you is bare. Put it out of your head."

"Easy to say," he sighed. "I'm walking well, I hope."

"Very well. I'll have you kangarooing yet."

"And participating in glider races down the surface slopes. Remember, I'm moderately advanced in years. But really, how far have we come?"

"Two miles, I should judge."

"Good Lord! How many miles of corridors are there altogether?"

"I'm afraid I don't know. The residential corridors make up comparatively little of the total. There are the mining corridors, the geological ones, the industrial, the mycological. . . . I'm sure there must be several hundred miles altogether."

"Do you have maps?"

"Of course there are maps. We can't work blind."

"I mean you, personally."

"Well, no, not with me, but I don't need maps for this area; it's quite familiar to me. I used to wander about here as a child. These are old corridors. Most of the new corridors—and we average two or three miles of new corridors a year, I think—are in the north. I couldn't work my way through them, without a map, for untold sums. Maybe not even with a map."

"Where are we heading?"

"I promised you an unusual sight—no, not me, so don't say it—and you'll have it. It's the Moon's most unusual mine and it's completely off the ordinary tourist trails.''

"Don't tell me you've got diamonds on the Moon?''

"Better than that.''

The corridor walls were unfinished here—gray rock, dimly but adequately lit by patches of electroluminescence. The temperature was comfortable and at a steady mildness, with ventilation so gently effective there was no sensation of wind. It was hard to tell here that a couple of hundred feet above was a surface subjected to alternate frying and freezing as the Sun came and went on its grand biweekly swing from horizon to horizon and then underneath and back.

"Is all this airtight?" asked Denison, suddenly uncomfortably aware that he was not far below the bottom of an ocean of vacuum that extended upward through all infinity.

"Oh, yes. Those walls are impervious. They're all booby-trapped, too. If the air pressure drops as much as ten percent in any section of the corridors there is such a hooting and howling from sirens as you have never heard and such a flashing of arrows and blazing of signs directing you to safety as you have never seen.''

"How often does this happen?''

"Not often. I don't think anyone has been killed through air-lack for at least five years." Then, with sudden defensiveness, "You have natural catastrophes on Earth. A big quake or a tidal wave can kill thousands.''

"No argument, Selene." He threw up his hands. "I surrender.''

"All right," she said. "I didn't mean to get excited. . . . Do you hear that?'' She stopped, in an attitude of listening.

Denison listened, too, and shook his head. Suddenly, he looked around. "It's so quiet. Where is everybody? Are you sure we're not lost?''

"This isn't a natural cavern with unknown passageways. You have those on Earth, haven't you? I've seen photographs.''

"Yes, most of them are limestone caves, formed by water. That certainly can't be the case of the Moon, can it?''

"So we can't be lost," said Selene, smiling. "If we're alone, put it down to superstition.''

"To what?" Denison looked startled and his face creased in an expression of disbelief.

"Don't do that," she said. "You get all lined. That's right. Smooth out. You look much better than you did when you first arrived, you know. That's low gravity and exercise.''

"And trying to keep up with nude young ladies who have an uncommon amount of off-time and an uncommon lack of better things to do than to go on busmen's holidays.''

"Now you're treating me like a tourist guide again, and I'm not nude.''

"At that, even nudity is less frightening than Intuitionism. . . . But what's this about superstition?''

"Not really superstition, I suppose, but most of the people of the city tend to stay away from this part of the corridor-complex.''

"But why?''

"Because of what I'm going to show you." They were walking again. "Hear it now?''

She stopped and Denison listened anxiously. He said, "You mean that small tapping sound? Tap—tap— Is that what you mean?"

She ran ahead in slow, loping strides with the slow-motion movement of the Lunarite in unhurried flight. He followed her, attempting to ape the gait.

"Here—here—"

Denison's eyes followed Selene's eagerly pointing finger. "Good Lord," he said. "Where's it coming from?"

There was a drip of what was clearly water. A slow dripping, with each drip striking a small ceramic trough that led into the rock wall.

"From the rocks. We do have water on the Moon, you know. Most of it we can bake out of gypsum; enough for our purposes, since we conserve it pretty well."

"I know. I know. I've never yet been able to manage one complete shower. How you people manage to stay clean I don't know."

"I *told* you. First, wet yourself. Then turn off the water and smear just a little detergent on you. You rub it—Oh, Ben, I'm not going through it yet again. And there's nothing on the Moon to get you all that dirty anyway. . . . But that's not what we're talking about. In one or two places there are actually water deposits, usually as ice near the surface in a mountain shadow. If we locate it, it drips out. This one has been dripping since the corridor was first driven through, and that was eight years ago."

"But why the superstition?"

"Well, obviously, water is the great material resource on which the Moon depends. We drink it, wash with it, grow our food with it, make our oxygen with it, keep everything going with it. Free water can't help but get a lot of respect. Once this drip was discovered, plans to extend the tunnels in this direction were abandoned till it stopped. The corridor walls were even left unfinished."

"That sounds like superstition right there."

"Well—a kind of awe, maybe. It wasn't expected to last for more than a few months; such drips never do. Well, after this one had passed its first anniversary, it began to seem eternal. In fact, that's what it's called: 'The Eternal.' You'll even find it marked that way on the maps. Naturally people have come to attach importance to it; a feeling that if it stops it will mean some sort of bad fortune."

Denison laughed.

Selene said, warmly, "No one *really* believes it, but everyone part-believes it. You see, it's not really eternal and it must stop some time. As a matter of fact, the rate of drip is only about a third of what it was when it was first discovered, so that it is slowly drying. I imagine people feel that if it happened to stop when they were actually here, they would share in the bad fortune. At least, that's the rational way of explaining their reluctance to come here."

"I take it that you don't believe this."

"Whether I believe it or not isn't the point. You see I'm quite certain that it won't stop sharply enough for anyone to be able to take the blame. It will just drip slower and slower and slower and no one will ever be able to pinpoint the exact time when it stopped. So why worry?"

"I agree with you."

"I do, however," she said, making the transition smoothly, "have other worries, and I'd like to discuss them with you while we're alone." She spread out the blanket and sat on it, cross-legged.

"Which is why you really brought me here?" He dropped to hip and elbow, facing her.

She said, "See, you can look at me easily now. You're getting used to me. . . . And, really, there were surely times on Earth when near nudity wasn't something to be exclaimed over."

"Times and places," agreed Denison, "but not since the passing of the Crisis. In my lifetime—"

"Well, on the Moon, do as the Lunarites do is a good enough guide for behavior."

"Are you going to tell me why you really brought me here? Or shall I suspect you of planning seduction?"

"I could carry through seduction quite comfortably at home, thank you. This is different. The surface would have been best, but getting ready to go out on the surface would have attracted a great deal of attention. Coming here didn't, and this place is the only spot in town where we can be reasonably safe from interruption." She hesitated.

"Well?" said Denison.

"Barron is angry. Very angry, in fact."

"I'm not surprised. I warned you he would if you told him that I knew you were an Intuitionist. Why did you feel it so necessary to tell him?"

"Because it is difficult to keep things for long from my—companion. Probably, though, he doesn't consider me that any longer."

"I'm sorry."

"Oh, it was turning sour anyway. It's lasted long enough. What bothers me more—much more—is that he violently refuses to accept your interpretation of the Pionizer experiments you ran after the surface observations."

"I told you the way it would be."

"He said he had seen your results."

"He glanced at them and grunted."

"It's rather disillusioning. Does everyone just believe what he wants to?"

"As long as possible. Sometimes longer."

"What about you?"

"You mean, am I human? Certainly. I don't believe I'm really old. I believe I'm quite attractive. I believe you seek out my company because you think I'm charming—even when you insist on turning the conversation to physics."

"No! I mean it!"

"Well, I suspect Neville told you that the data I had gathered were not significant beyond the margin of error, which makes them doubtful, and that's true enough. . . . And yet I prefer to believe they have the meaning I expected them to have to begin with."

"Just because you want to believe that?"

"Not *just* because. Look at it this way. Suppose there is no harm in the Pump, but that I insist on thinking there *is* harm. In that case, I will turn out to be a fool and my scientific reputation will be badly damaged. But I *am* a fool in the eyes of the people who count, and I have no scientific reputation."

"Why is that, Ben? You've hinted around the tale several times. Can't you tell me the whole story?"

"You'd be surprised how little there is to tell. At the age of twenty-five I was still such a child that I had to amuse myself by insulting a fool for no reason other than that he was a fool. Since his folly was not his fault, I was the greater fool to do it. My insult drove him to heights he couldn't possibly have scaled otherwise—"

"You're talking of Hallam?"

"Yes, of course. And as he rose, I fell. And eventually, it dropped me to—the Moon."

"Is that so bad?"

"No, I rather think it's good. So let's say he did me a favor, long-way round. . . . And let's get back to what I'm talking about. I've just explained that if I believe the Pump to be harmful and am wrong, I lose nothing. On the other hand, if I believe the Pump to be harmless and am wrong, I will be helping to destroy the world. To be sure, I've lived most of my life already and I suppose I can argue myself into believing that I have no great cause to love humanity. However, only a few people have hurt me, and if I hurt everyone in return that is unconscionable usury.

"Then, too, if you'd rather have a less noble reason, Selene, consider my daughter. Just before I left for the Moon, she had applied for permission to have a child. She'll probably get it and before long I'll be—if you don't mind my saying so—a grandfather. Somehow I'd like to see my grandchild have a normal life expectancy. So I prefer to believe the Pump is dangerous and to act on that belief."

Selene said, intensely, "But here's my point. Is the Pump dangerous or is it not? I mean, the truth, and not what anyone wants to believe."

"I should ask *you* that. You're the Intuitionist. What does your intuition say?"

"But that's what bothers me, Ben. I can't make it really certain either way. I tend to feel the Pump is harmful, but maybe that's because I want to believe that."

"All right. Maybe you do. Why?"

Selene smiled ruefully and shrugged her shoulders. "It would be fun for Barron to be wrong. When he thinks he's certain, he's so *vituperatively* certain."

"I know. You want to see his face when he's forced to back down. I'm well aware of how intense such a desire can be. For instance, if the Pump *were* dangerous and I could prove it, I might conceivably be hailed as the savior of humanity, and yet I swear that I'd be more interested in the look on Hallam's face. I'm not proud of that feeling so I suspect that what I'll do is insist on an equal share of the credit with Lamont, who deserves it after all, and confine my pleasure to watching Lamont's face when *he* watches Hallam's face. The pettishness will then be one place removed. . . . But I'm beginning to speak nonsense. . . . Selene?"

"Yes, Ben?"

"When did you find out you were an Intuitionist?"

"I don't quite know."

"You took physics in college, I imagine."

"Oh, yes. Some math, too, but I was never good at that. Come to think of it, I wasn't particularly good in physics, either. I used to guess the answers when I was desperate; you know, guess what I was supposed to do to get the right answers. Very often, it worked and then I would be asked to explain why I had done what I did and I couldn't do that very well. They suspected me of cheating but could never prove it."

"They didn't suspect Intuitionism?"

"I don't think so. But then, I didn't either. Until—well, one of my first sex-mates was a physicist. In fact, he was the father of my child, assuming he really supplied the sperm-sample. He had a physics problem and he told me about it when we were lying in bed afterward, just to have something to talk about, I suppose. And I said, 'You know what it sounds like to me?' and told him. He tried it just for the fun of it, he said, and it worked. In fact, that was the first step to the Pionizer, which you said was much better than the proton synchrotron.''

"You mean that was *your* idea?" Denison put his finger under the dripping water and paused as he was about to put it in his mouth. "Is this water safe?"

"It's perfectly sterile," said Selene, "and it goes into the general reservoir for treatment. It's saturated with sulfates, carbonates, and a few other items, however. You won't like the taste."

Denison rubbed his finger on his briefs. *You* invented the Pionizer?''

"Not invented. I had the original concept. It took lots of development, mostly by Barron.''

Denison shook his head. "You know, Selene, you're an amazing phenomenon. You should be under observation by the molecular biologists.''

"Should I? That's not my idea of a thrill.''

"About half a century ago, there came the climax to the big trend toward genetic engineering—''

"I know. It flopped and was thrown out of court. It's illegal now—that whole type of study—insofar as research can be made illegal. I know people who've done work on it just the same.''

"I dare say. On Intuitionism?''

"No. I don't think so.''

"Ah. But that's my point. At the height of the push for genetic engineering, there was this attempt to stimulate Intuitionism. Almost all the great scientists had intuitive ability, of course, and there was the feeling that this was the single great key to creativity. One could argue that superior capacity for intuition was the product of a particular gene combination and there were all sorts of speculations as to which gene combination that was.''

"I suspect that there are many possible types that would satisfy.''

"And I suspect that if you are consulting your intuition here, you are correct. But there were also those who insisted that one gene, or one small related group of genes, was of particular importance to the combination so that you might speak of an Intuition Gene. . . . Then the whole thing collapsed.''

"As I said.''

"But before it collapsed," Denison went on, "there had been attempts to alter genes to increase the intensity of Intuitionism and there were those who insisted that some success had been achieved. The altered genes entered the gene pool, I'm positive, and if you happened to inherit— Were any of your grandparents involved in the program?''

"Not as far as I know," said Selene, "but I can't rule it out. One of them might have been, for all I can say. . . . If you don't mind. I'm not going to investigate the matter. I don't want to know.''

"Perhaps not. The whole field grew fearfully unpopular with the general public and anyone who can be considered the product of genetic engineering would not exactly be greeted gladly. . . . Intuitionism, they said, for instance, was inseparable from certain undesirable characteristics.''

"Well, thank you.''

"They said. To possess intuition is to inspire a certain envy and enmity in others. Even as gentle and saint-like an Intuitionist as Michael Faraday aroused the envy and hatred of Humphry Davy. Who's to say that it doesn't take a certain flaw in character to be capable of arousing envy. And in your case—"

Selene said, "Surely, I don't rouse your envy and hatred?"

"I don't think so. What about Neville, though?"

Selene was silent.

Denison said, "By the time you got to Neville, you were well-known as an Intuitionist, I suppose."

"Not *well* known, I would say. Some physicists suspected it, I'm sure. However, they don't like to give up credit here any more than on Earth, and I suppose they convinced themselves, more or less, that whatever I had said to them was just a meaningless guess. But Barron knew, of course."

"I see." Denison paused.

Selene's lips twitched. "Somehow I get the feeling that you want to say: 'Oh, *that's* why he bothers with you.' "

"No, of course not, Selene. You're quite attractive enough to be desired for your own sake."

"I think so, too, but every little bit helps and Barron was bound to be interested in my Intuitionism. Why shouldn't he be? Only he insisted I keep my job as tourist guide. He said I was an important natural resource of the Moon and he didn't want Earth monopolizing me the way they monopolized the synchrotron."

"An odd thought. But perhaps it was that the fewer who knew of your Intuitionism, the fewer would suspect your contribution to what would otherwise be put to his sole credit."

"Now you sound like Barron himself!"

"Do I? And is it possible he gets rather annoyed with you when your Intuitionism is working particularly well."

Selene shrugged. "Barron is a suspicious man. We all have our faults."

"Is it wise to be alone with me, then?"

Selene said, sharply, "Now don't get hurt because I defend him. He doesn't really suspect the possibility of sexual misbehavior between us. You're from Earth. In fact, I might as well tell you he encourages our companionship. He thinks I can learn from you."

"And have you?" asked Denison, coldly.

"I have. . . . Yet though that may be *his* chief reason for encouraging our friendship, it isn't mine."

"What's yours?"

"As you well know," said Selene, "and as you want to hear me say, I enjoy your company. Otherwise, I could get what I want in considerably less time."

"All right, Selene. Friends?"

"Friends! Absolutely."

"What have you learned from me, then? May I know?"

"That would take awhile to explain. You know that the reason we can't set up a Pump Station anywhere we want to is that we can't locate the para-Universe, even though they can locate us. That might be because they are much more intelligent or much more technologically advanced than we are—"

"Not necessarily the same thing," muttered Denison.

"I know. That's why I put in the 'or.' But it might also be that we are neither particularly stupid nor particularly backward. It might be something as simple as the fact that they offer the harder target. If the strong nuclear interaction is stronger in the para-Universe, they'd be bound to have much smaller Suns and, very likely, much smaller planets. Their individual world would be harder to locate than ours would be.

"Or then again," she went on, "suppose it's the electromagnetic field they detect. The electromagnetic field of a planet is much larger than the planet itself and is much easier to locate. And that would mean that while they can detect the Earth, they can't detect the Moon, which has no electromagnetic field to speak of. That's why, perhaps, we've failed to set up a Pump Station on the Moon. And, if their small planets lack a significant electromagnetic field, we can't locate them."

Denison said, "It's an attractive thought."

"Next, consider the inter-Universal exchange in properties that serves to weaken their strong nuclear interaction, cooling their Suns, while strengthening ours, heating and exploding our Suns. What might that imply? Suppose they can collect energy one-way without our help but only at ruinously low efficiencies. Under ordinary circumstances that would therefore be utterly impractical. They would need us to help direct concentrated energy in their direction by supplying tungsten-186 to them and accepting plutonium-186 in return. But suppose our Galactic arm implodes into a quasar. That would produce an energy concentration in the neighborhood of the Solar system enormously greater than now exists and one that might persist for over a million years.

"Once that quasar forms, even a ruinously low efficiency becomes sufficient. It wouldn't matter to them, therefore, whether we are destroyed or not. In fact, we might argue that it would be safer for them if we did explode. Until we do, we might end the Pump for any of a variety of reasons and they would be helpless to start it again. After the explosion, they are home free; no one could interfere. . . . And that's why people who say, 'If the Pump is dangerous, why don't those terribly clever para-men stop it?' don't know what they're talking about."

"Did Neville give you that argument?"

"Yes, he did."

"But the para-Sun would keep cooling down, wouldn't it?"

"What does that matter?" said Selene, impatiently. "With the Pump, they wouldn't be dependent on their Sun for anything."

Denison took a deep breath. "You can't possibly know this, Selene, but there was a rumor on Earth that Lamont received a message from the para-men to the effect that the Pump was dangerous, but that they couldn't stop it. No one took it seriously, of course, but suppose it's true. Suppose Lamont did receive such a message. Might it be that some of the para-men were humanitarian enough to wish not to destroy a world with cooperating intelligences upon it, and were prevented by the opposition of an oh-so-practical majority?"

Selene nodded. "I suppose that's possible. . . . All this I knew, or rather, intuited, before you came on the scene. But then you said that nothing between one and the infinite made any sense. Remember?"

"Of course."

"All right. The differences between our Universe and the para-Universe lie so obviously in the strong nuclear interaction that so far it's all that's been studied. But there is more than one interaction; there are four. In addition to the strong nuclear, there is the electromagnetic, the weak nuclear, and the gravitational, with intensity ratios of $130:1:10^{-10}:10^{-42}$. But if four, why not an infinite number, with all the others too weak to be detectable or to influence our Universe in any way."

Denison said, "If an interaction is too weak to be detectable or to exert influence in any way, then by any operational definition, it doesn't exist."

"In *this* Universe," said Selene, with a snap. "Who knows what does or does not exist in the para-Universe? With an infinite number of possible interactions, each of which can vary infinitely in intensity compared to any one of them taken as standard, the number of different possible Universes that can exist is infinite."

"Possibly the infinity of the continuum; aleph-one, rather than aleph-null." Selene frowned. "What does that mean?"

"It's not important. Go on."

Selene said, "Instead, then, of trying to work with the one para-Universe that has impinged itself on us and which may not suit our needs at all, why don't we instead try to work out which Universe, out of all the infinite possibilities, best suits us, and is most easily located. Let us *design* a Universe, for after all, whatever we design must exist, and search for it."

Denison smiled. "Selene, I've thought of exactly the same thing. And while there's no law that states I can't be completely wrong, it's very unlikely that anyone as brilliant as myself can be completely wrong when anyone as brilliant as yourself comes to exactly the same conclusion independently. . . . Do you know what?"

"What?" asked Selene.

"I'm beginning to like your damned Moon food. Or getting used to it, anyway. Let's go back home and eat, and then we can start working out our plans. . . . And you know what else?"

"What?"

"As long as we'll be working together, how about one kiss—as experimentalist to intuitionist."

Selene considered. She said, "We've both of us kissed and been kissed a good many times, I suppose. How about doing it as man to woman?"

"I think I can manage that. But what do I do so as not to be clumsy about it? What are the Moon-rules for kissing?"

"Follow instinct," said Selene, casually.

Carefully, Denison placed his arms behind his back and leaned toward Selene. Then, after a while, he placed his arms behind her back.

— 13 —

"*AND THEN* I actually kissed him back," said Selene, thoughtfully.

"Oh, did you?" said Barron Neville, harshly. "Well, that's valor beyond the call of duty."

"I don't know. It wasn't that bad. In fact," (and she smiled) "he was rather touching about it. He was afraid he would be clumsy and began by putting his arms behind his back so that he wouldn't crush me, I suppose."

"Spare me the details."

"Why, what the hell do you care?" she fired up, suddenly. "You're Mister Platonic, aren't you?"

"Do you want it differently? Now?"

"You needn't perform to order."

"But *you* had better. When do you expect to give us what we need?"

"As soon as I can," she said, tonelessly.

"Without his knowing?"

"He's interested only in energy."

"And in saving the world," mocked Neville. "And in being a hero. And in showing everybody. And in kissing you."

"He admits to all that. What do you admit to?"

"Impatience," said Neville, angrily. "Lots of impatience."

— 14 —

"*I AM GLAD,*" said Denison, deliberately, "that the daytime is over." He held out his right arm and stared at it, encased in its protective layers. "The Lunar Sun is one thing I can't get used to and don't want to get used to. Even this suit seems a natural thing to me in comparison."

"What's wrong with the Sun?" asked Selene.

"Don't tell me you like it, Selene!"

"No, of course not. I hate it. But then I never see it. You're an— You're used to the Sun."

"Not the way it is here on the Moon. It shines out of a black sky here. It dazzles the stars away, instead of muffling them. It is hot, hard, and dangerous. It is an enemy, and while it's in the sky, I can't help but feel that none of our attempts at reducing field intensity will succeed."

"That's superstition, Ben," said Selene, with a distant edge of exasperation. "The Sun has nothing to do with it. We were in the crater shadow anyway and it was just like night. Stars and all."

"Not quite," said Denison. "Anytime we looked northward, Selene, we could see that stretch of Sunlight glittering. I hated to look northward, yet the direction dragged at my eyes. Every time I looked at it I could feel the hard ultraviolet springing at my viewplate."

"That's imagination. In the first place there's no ultraviolet to speak of in reflected light; in the second, your suit protects you against radiation."

"Not against heat. Not very much."

"But it's night now."

"Yes," said Denison with satisfaction, "and this I like." He looked about with a continuing wonder. Earth was in the sky, of course, in its accustomed place; a fat crescent, now, bellying to the southwestward. The constellation Orion was above it, a hunter rising up out of the brilliant curved chair of Earth. The horizon glittered in the dim crescent-Earth light.

"It's beautiful," he said. Then: "Selene, is the Pionizer showing anything?"

Selene, who was looking at the skies with no comment, stepped toward the maze of equipment that, over the past three alternations of day and night, had been assembled there in the shadow of the crater.

"Not yet," she said, "but that's good news really. The field intensity is holding at just over fifty."

"Not low enough," said Denison.

Selene said, "It can be lowered further. I'm sure that all the parameters are suitable."

"The magnetic field, too?"

"I'm not sure about the magnetic field."

"If we strengthen that, the whole thing becomes unstable."

"It shouldn't. I know it shouldn't."

"Selene, I trust your intuition against everything but the facts. It *does* get unstable. We've tried it."

"I know, Ben. But not quite with this geometry. It's been holding to fifty-two a phenomenally long time. Surely, if we begin to hold it there for hours instead of minutes, we ought to be able to strengthen the magnetic field tenfold for a period of minutes instead of seconds. . . . Let's try."

"Not yet," said Denison

Selene hesitated, then stepped back, turning away. She said, "You still don't miss Earth, do you, Ben?"

"No. It's rather odd, but I don't. I would have thought it inevitable that I miss blue sky, green earth, flowing water—all the cliché adjective-noun combinations peculiar to Earth. I miss none of them. I don't even dream about them."

Selene said, "This sort of thing does happen sometime. At least, there are Immies who say they experience no homesickness. They're in the minority, of course, and no one has ever been able to decide what this minority has in common. Guesses run all the way from serious emotional deficiency, no capacity to feel anything; to serious emotional excess, a fear to admit homesickness lest it lead to breakdown."

"In my case, I think it's plain enough. Life on Earth was not very enjoyable for two decades and more, while here I work at last in a field I have made my own. And I have your help. . . . More than that, Selene, I have your company."

"You are kind," said Selene, gravely, "to place company and help in the relationship you do. You don't seem to need much help. Do you pretend to seek it for the sake of my company?"

Denison laughed softly. "I'm not sure which answer would flatter you more."

"Try the truth."

"The truth is not so easy to determine when I value each so much." He turned back to the Pionizer. "The field intensity still holds, Selene."

Selene's faceplate flinted in the Earthlight. She said, "Barron says that non-homesickness is natural and the sign of a healthy mind. He says that though the human body was adapted to Earth's surface and requires adjustment to the Moon, the human brain was not and does not. The human brain is so different, qualitatively, from all other brains that it can be considered a new phenomenon. It has had no time to be really fixed to Earth's surface and can, without adjustment, fit other environments. He says that enclosure in the caverns of the Moon may actually suit it best of all, for that is but a larger version of its enclosure in the cavern of the skull."

"Do you believe that?" asked Denison, amused.

"When Barron talks, he can make things sound very plausible."

"I think it can be made equally plausible to claim that the comfort to be found in the caverns of the Moon is the result of the fulfillment of the return-to-the-womb fantasy. In fact," he added, thoughtfully, "considering the controlled temperature and pressure, the nature and digestibility of the food, I could make a good case for considering the Lunar colony—I beg your pardon, Selene—the Lunar city a deliberate reconstruction of the fetal environment."

Selene said, "I don't think Barron would agree with you for a minute."

"I'm sure he wouldn't," said Denison. He looked at the Earth-crescent, watching the distant cloud banks on edge. He fell into silence, absorbed in the view, and even though Selene moved back to the Pionizer, he remained in place.

He watched Earth in its nest of stars and looked toward the serrated horizon where, every once in a while, it seemed to him he saw a puff of smoke where a small meteorite might be landing.

He had pointed out a similar phenomenon, with some concern, to Selene during the previous Lunar night. She had been unconcerned.

She said, "The Earth does shift slightly in the sky because of the Moon's libration and every once in a while a shaft of Earth-light tops a small rise and falls on a bit of soil beyond. It comes into view like a tiny puff of rising dust. It's common. We pay no attention."

Denison had said, "But it could be a meteorite sometimes. Don't meteorites ever strike?"

"Of course they do. You're probably hit by several every time you're out. Your suit protects you."

"I don't mean micro-dust particles. I mean sizable meteorites that would really kick up the dust. Meteorites that could kill you."

"Well, they fall, too, but they are few and the Moon is large. No one has been hit yet."

And as Denison watched the sky and thought of that, he saw what, in the midst of his momentary preoccupation, he took to be a meteorite. Light streaking through the sky could, however, be a meteorite only on Earth with its atmosphere and not on the airless Moon.

The light in the sky was man-made and Denison had not yet sorted out his impressions when it became, quite clearly, a small rocket-vessel sinking rapidly to a landing beside him.

A single suited figure emerged, while a pilot remained within, barely seen as a dark splotch against the highlights.

Denison waited. The etiquette of the spacesuit required the newcomer joining any group to announce himself first.

"Commissioner Gottstein here," the new voice said, "as you can probably tell from my wobble."

"Ben Denison here," said Denison.

"Yes. I thought as much."

"Have you come here looking for me?"

"Certainly."

"In a space-skipper? You might—"

"I might," said Gottstein, "have used Outlet P-4, which is less than a thousand yards from here. Yes, indeed. But I wasn't looking only for you."

"Well, I won't ask for the meaning of what you say."

"There's no reason for me to be coy. Surely you have not expected me to be uninterested in the fact that you have been carrying on experiments on the Lunar surface.''

"It's been no secret and anyone might be interested.''

"Yet no one seems to know the details of the experiments. Except, of course, that in some way you are working on matters concerning the Electron Pump.''

"It's a reasonable assumption.''

"Is it? It seemed to me that experiments of such a nature, to have any value at all, would require a rather enormous setup. This is not of my own knowledge, you understand. I consulted those who would know. And, it is quite obvious, you are not working on such a setup. It occurred to me, therefore, that you might not be the proper focus of my interest. While my attention was drawn to you, others might be undertaking more important tasks.''

"Why should I be used as distraction?''

"I don't know. If I knew, I would be less concerned.''

"So I have been under observation.''

Gottstein chuckled. "That, yes. Since you have arrived. But while you have been working here on the surface, we have observed this entire region for miles in every direction. Oddly enough, it would seem that you, Dr. Denison, and your companion, are the only ones on the Lunar surface for any but the most routine of purposes.''

"Why is that odd?''

"Because it means that you really think you're doing something with your gimcrack contraption, whatever it is. I can't believe that you are incompetent, so I think it would be worth listening to you if you tell me what you are doing.''

"I am experimenting in para-physics, Commissioner, precisely as rumor has it. To which I can add that so far my experiments have been only partly successful.''

"Your companion is, I imagine, Selene Lindstrom L., a tourist guide.''

"Yes.''

"An unusual choice as an assistant.''

"She is intelligent, eager, interested, and extremely attractive.''

"And willing to work with an Earthman?''

"And quite willing to work with an Immigrant who will be a Lunar citizen as soon as he qualifies for the status.''

Selene was approaching now. Her voice rang in their ears. "Good day, Commissioner. I would have liked not to overhear and intrude on a private conversation, but, in a spacesuit, overhearing is inevitable anywhere within the horizon.''

Gottstein turned. "Hello, Miss Lindstrom. I did not expect to talk in secrecy. Are you interested in para-physics?''

"Oh, yes.''

"You are not disheartened by the failures of the experiment.''

"They are not entirely failures,'' she said. "They are less a failure than Dr. Denison thinks at present.''

"What?'' Denison turned sharply on his heel, nearly overbalancing himself and sending out a spurt of dust.

All three were facing the Pionizer now, and above it, just about five feet above it, light shone like a fat star.

Selene said, "I raised the intensity of the magnetic field, and the nuclear field remained stable, in being—then eased further and further and—"

"Leaked!" Denison said, "Damn it. I didn't see it happen."

Selene said, "I'm sorry, Ben. First you were lost in your own thoughts, then the Commissioner arrived, and I couldn't resist the chance of trying on my own."

Gottstein said, "But just what is it that I see there?"

Denison said, "Energy being spontaneously given off by matter leaking from another Universe into ours."

And even as he said that the light blinked out and many yards away, a farther, dimmer star came into simultaneous being.

Denison lunged toward the Pionizer, but Selene, all Lunar grace, propelled herself across the surface more efficiently and was there first. She killed the field structure and the distant star went out.

She said, "The leak-point isn't stable, you see."

"Not on a small scale," said Denison, "but considering that a shift of a light-year is as theoretically possible as a shift of a hundred yards, one of a hundred yards only is miraculous stability."

"Not miraculous enough," said Selene, flatly.

Gottstein interrupted. "Let me guess what you're talking about. You mean that the matter can leak through here, or there, or anywhere in our Universe—at random."

"Not quite at random, Commissioner," said Denison. "The probability of leakage drops with distance from the Pionizer, and rather sharply I should say. The sharpness depends on a variety of factors and I think we've tightened the situation remarkably. Even so, a flip of a few hundred yards is quite probable and, as a matter of fact, you saw it happen."

"And it might have shifted to somewhere within the city or within our own helmets, perhaps."

Denison said, impatiently, "No no. The leak, at least by the techniques we use, is heavily dependent on the density of matter already present in this Universe. The chances are virtually nil that the leak-position would shift from a place of essential vacuum to one where an atmosphere even a hundredth as dense as that within the city or within our helmets would exist. It would be impractical to expect to arrange the leak anywhere but into a vacuum in the first place, which is why we had to make the attempt up here on the surface."

"Then this is not like the Electron Pump?"

"Not at all," said Denison. "In the Electron Pump there is a two-way transfer of matter, here a one-way leak. Nor are the Universes involved the same."

Gottstein said, "I wonder if you would have dinner with me this evening, Dr. Denison?"

Denison hesitated. "Myself only?"

Gottstein attempted a bow in the direction of Selene but could accomplish only a grotesque parody of it in his spacesuit. "I would be charmed to have Miss Lindstrom's company on another occasion, but on this one I must speak with you alone, Dr. Denison."

"Oh, go ahead," said Selene, crisply, as Denison still hesitated. "I have a heavy schedule tomorrow anyway and you'll need time to worry about the leak-point instability."

Denison said, uncertainly, "Well, then—Selene, will you let me know when your next free day is?"

"I always do, don't I? And we'll be in touch before then anyway. . . . Why don't you two go on? I'll take care of the equipment."

— 15 —

BARRON NEVILLE shifted from foot to foot in the fashion made necessary by the restricted quarters and by the Moon's gravity. In a larger room under a world's stronger pull, he would have walked hastily up and back. Here, he tilted from side to side, in a repetitive back-and-forth glide.

"Then you're positive it works. Right Selene? You're positive?"

"I'm positive," said Selene. "I've told you five times by actual count."

Neville didn't seem to be listening. He said in a low, rapid voice, "It doesn't matter that Gottstein was there, then? He didn't try to stop the experiment?"

"No. Of course not."

"There was no indication that he would try to exert authority—"

"No, Barron, what kind of authority could he exert? Will Earth send a police force? Besides—oh, you know they can't stop us."

Neville stopped moving, stood motionless for a while. "They don't know? They still don't know?"

"Of course they don't. Ben was looking at the stars and then Gottstein came. So I tried for the field-leak, got it, and I had already gotten the other. Ben's setup—"

"Don't call it his setup. It was your idea, wasn't it?"

Selene shook her head. "I made vague suggestions. The details were Ben's."

"But you can reproduce it now. For Luna's sake, we don't have to go to the Earthie for it, do we?"

"I think I can reproduce enough of it now so that our people can fill it in."

"All right, then. Let's get started."

"Not yet. Oh, damn it, Barron, not yet."

"Why not yet?"

"We need the energy, too."

"But we have that."

"Not *quite*. The leak-point is unstable; pretty badly unstable."

"But that can be fixed up. You said so."

"I said I *thought* it could."

"That's good enough for me."

"Just the same, it would be better to have Ben work out the details and stabilize it."

There was a silence between them. Neville's thin face slowly twisted into something approaching hostility. "You don't think I can do it? Is that it?"

Selene said, "Will you come out on the surface with me and work on it?"

There was another silence. Neville said, unsteadily, "I don't appreciate your sarcasm. And I don't want to have to wait long."

"I can't command the laws of nature. But I think it won't be long. . . . Now if you don't mind, I need my sleep. I've got my tourists tomorrow."

For a moment, Neville seemed on the point of gesturing to his own bed-alcove as though offering hospitality, but the gesture, if that was what it was, did not really come to birth and Selene made no sign of understanding or even anticipating. She nodded warily, and left.

— 16 —

"*I HAD HOPED*, to be frank," said Gottstein, smiling over what passed for dessert—a sticky, sweet concoction—"that we would have seen each other more often."

Denison said, "It is kind of you to take such an interest in my work. If the leak-instability can be corrected, I think my achievement—and that of Miss Lindstrom—will have been a most significant one."

"You speak carefully, like a scientist. . . . I won't insult you by offering the Lunar equivalent of a liqueur; that is the one approximation to Earth's cuisine I have simply made up my mind not to tolerate. Can you tell me, in lay language, what makes the achievement significant?"

"I can try," said Denison, cautiously. "Suppose we start with the para-Universe. It has a more intense strong nuclear interaction than our Universe has so that relatively small masses of protons in the para-Universe can undergo the fusion reaction capable of supporting a star. Masses equivalent to our stars would explode violently in the para-Universe which has many more, but much smaller, stars than ours does.

"Suppose, now, that we had a much less intense strong nuclear interaction than that which prevails in our Universe. In that case, huge masses of protons would have so little tendency to fuse that a very large mass of hydrogen would be needed to support a star. Such an anti-para-Universe—one that was the opposite of the para-Universe, in other words—would consist of considerably fewer but of far larger stars than our Universe does. In fact, if the strong nuclear interaction were made sufficiently weak, a Universe would exist which consisted of a single star containing all the mass in that Universe. It would be a very dense star, but relatively non-reactive and giving off no more radiation than our single Sun does, perhaps."

Gottstein said, "Am I wrong, or isn't that the situation that prevailed in our own Universe before the time of the big bang—one vast body containing all the universal mass."

"Yes," said Denison, "as a matter of fact, the anti-para-Universe I am picturing consists of what some call a cosmic egg; or 'cosmeg' for short. A cosmeg-Universe is what we need if we are to probe for one-way leakage. The para-Universe we are now using with its tiny stars is virtually empty space. You can probe and probe and touch nothing."

"The para-men reached us, however."

"Yes, possibly by following magnetic fields. There is some reason to think that there are no planetary magnetic fields of significance in the para-Universe, which deprives us of the advantage they have. On the other hand, if we probe the cosmeg-Universe, we cannot fail. The cosmeg is, itself, the entire Universe, and wherever we probe we strike matter.''

"But how do you probe for it?"

Denison hesitated. "That is the part I find difficult to explain. Pions are the mediating particles of the strong nuclear interaction. The intensity of the interaction depends on the mass of the pions and that mass can, under certain specialized conditions, be altered. The Lunar physicists have developed an instrument they call the Pionizer, which can be made to do just such a thing. Once the pion's mass is decreased, or increased for that matter, it is, effectively, part of another Universe; it becomes a gateway, a crossing point. If it is decreased sufficiently, it can be made part of a cosmeg-Universe and that's what we want.''

Gottstein said, "And you can suck in matter from the—the—cosmeg-Universe?"

"That part is easy. Once the gateway forms, the influx is spontaneous. The matter enters with its own laws and is stable when it arrives. Gradually the laws of our own Universe soak in, the strong interaction grows stronger, and the matter fuses and begins to give off enormous energy.''

"But if it is super-dense, why doesn't it just expand in a puff of smoke?"

"That, too, would yield energy, but that depends on the electromagnetic field and in this particular case the strong interaction takes precedence, because we control the electromagnetic field. It would take quite a time to explain that.''

"Well, then, the globe of light that I saw on the surface was cosmeg material fusing?"

"Yes, Commissioner.''

"And that energy can be harnessed for useful purposes?''

"Certainly. And in any quantity. What you saw was the arrival in our Universe of micromicrogram masses of cosmeg. There's nothing, in theory, to prevent our bringing it over in ton-lots.''

"Well, then, this can be used to replace the Electron Pump.''

Denison shook his head. "No. The use of cosmeg energy also alters the properties of the Universes in question. The strong interaction gradually grows more intense in the cosmeg-Universe and less intense in ours as the laws of nature cross over. That means that the cosmeg slowly undergoes fusion at a greater rate and gradually warms up. Eventually—''

"Eventually," said Gottstein, crossing his arms across his chest and narrowing his eyes, thoughtfully, "it explodes in a big bang.''

"That's my feeling.''

"Do you suppose that's what happened to our own Universe ten billion years ago?''

"Perhaps. Cosmogonists have wondered why the original cosmic egg exploded at some one point in time and not at another. One solution was to imagine an oscillating Universe in which the cosmic egg was formed and then *at once* exploded. The oscillating Universe has been eliminated as a possibility and the conclusion is that the cosmic egg had to exist for some long period of time and then went through a crisis of instability which arose for some unknown reason.''

"But which may have been the result of the tapping of its energy across the Universes.''

"Possibly, but not necessarily by some intelligence. Perhaps there are occasional spontaneous leaks."

"And when the big bang takes place," said Gottstein, "can we still extract energy from the cosmeg-Universe?"

"I'm not sure, but surely that is not an immediate worry. The leakage of our strong-interaction field into the cosmeg-Universe must very likely continue for millions of years before pushing it past the critical point. And there must be other cosmeg-Universes; an infinite number, perhaps.

"What about the change in our own Universe?"

"The strong interaction weakens. Slowly, very slowly, our Sun cools off."

"Can we use cosmeg energy to make up for that?"

"That would not be necessary, Commissioner," said Denison, earnestly. "While the strong interaction here in our Universe weakens as a result of the cosmeg pump, it strengthens through the action of the ordinary Electron Pump. If we adjust the energy productions of the two then, though the laws of nature change in the cosmeg-Universe and in the para-Universe, they do not change in ours. We are a highway but not the terminus in either direction.

"Nor need we be disturbed on behalf of the terminuses. The para-men on their side may have adjusted themselves to the cooling off of their Sun which may be pretty cool to begin with. As for the cosmeg-Universe, there is no reason to suspect life can exist there. Indeed, it is by inducing the conditions required for the big bang that we may be setting up a new kind of Universe that will eventually grow hospitable to life."

For a while, Gottstein said nothing. His plump face, in repose, seemed emotionless. He nodded to himself as though following the line of his thoughts.

Finally, he said, "You know, Denison, I think this is what will set the world on its ear. Any difficulty in persuading the scientific leadership that the Electron Pump is destroying the world should now disappear."

Denison said, "The emotional reluctance to accept that no longer exists. It will be possible to present the problem and the solution at the same time."

"When would you be willing to prepare a paper to this effect if I guarantee speedy publication?"

"Can you guarantee that?"

"In a government-published pamphlet, if no other way."

"I would prefer to try to neutralize the leak-instability before reporting."

"Of course."

"And I think it would be wise," said Denison, "to arrange to have Dr. Peter Lamont as co-author. He can make the mathematics rigorous; something I cannot do. Besides, it was through his work that I took the course I have followed. One more point, Commissioner—"

"Yes."

"I would suggest that the Lunar physicists be involved. One of their number, Dr. Barron Neville, might well be a third author."

"But why? Aren't you introducing unnecessary complications now?"

"It was their Pionizer that made everything possible."

"There can be appropriate mention of that. . . . But did Dr. Barron actually work on the project with you?"

"Not directly."

"Then why involve him?"

Denison looked down and brushed his hand thoughtfully over the weave of his pants leg. He said, "It would be the diplomatic thing to do. We would need to set up the cosmeg pump on the Moon."

"Why not on Earth?"

"In the first place, we need a vacuum. This is a one-way transfer and not a two-way as in the case of the Electron Pump, and the conditions necessary to make it practical are different in the two cases. The surface of the Moon has its vacuum ready-made in vast quantities; while to prepare one on Earth would involve an enormous effort."

"Yet it could be done, couldn't it?"

"Secondly," said Denison, "if we have two vast energy sources from opposite directions with our own Universe between, there would be something like a short circuit if the two outlets were too close together. Separation by a quarter-million miles of vacuum, with the Electron Pump operating only on Earth and the cosmeg pump operating only on the Moon, would be ideal—in fact, necessary. And if we are to operate on the Moon, it would be wise, even decent, to take the sensibilities of the Lunar physicists into account. We ought to give them a share."

Gottstein smiled. "Is this the advice of Miss Lindstrom?"

"I'm sure it would be, but the suggestion is reasonable enough to have occurred to me independently."

Gottstein rose, stretched, and then jumped in place two or three times in the eerily slow fashion imposed by Lunar gravity. He flexed his knees each time. He sat down again and said, "Ever try that, Dr. Denison?"

Denison shook his head.

"It's supposed to help the circulation in the lower extremities. I do it whenever I feel my legs may be going to sleep. I'll be heading back for a short visit to Earth before long and I'm trying to keep from getting too used to Lunar gravity. . . . Shall we talk of Miss Lindstrom, Dr. Denison?"

Denison said in a quite changed tone, "What about her?"

"She is a tourist guide."

"Yes. You said so earlier."

"As I also said, she is an odd assistant for a physicist."

"Actually, I'm an amateur physicist only, and I suppose she is an amateur assistant."

Gottstein was no longer smiling. "Don't play games, Doctor. I have taken the trouble to find out what I can about her. Her record is quite revealing, or would have been if it had occurred to anyone to look at it before this. I believe she is an Intuitionist."

Denison said, "Many of us are. I have no doubt you are an Intuitionist yourself, after a fashion. I certainly know that I am, after a fashion."

"There is a difference, Doctor. You are an accomplished scientist and I, I hope, am an accomplished administrator. . . . Yet while Miss Lindstrom is enough of an Intuitionist to be useful to you in advanced theoretical physics, she is, in actual fact, a tourist guide."

Denison hesitated. "She has little formal training, Commissioner. Her Intuitionism is at an unusually high level but it is under little conscious control."

"Is she the result of the one-time genetic engineering program?"

"I don't know. I wouldn't be surprised if that were so, however."

"Do you trust her?"

"In what way? She has helped me."

"Do you know that she is the wife of Dr. Barron Neville?"

"There is an emotional connection; not a legal one, I believe."

"None of the connections are what we would call legal here on the Moon. The same Neville you want to invite as third author of the paper you are to write?"

"Yes."

"Is that merely a coincidence?"

"No. Neville was interested in my arrival and I believe he asked Selene to help me in my work."

"Did she tell you this?"

"She said he was interested in me. That was natural enough, I suppose."

"Does it occur to you, Dr. Denison, that she may be working in her own interests and in those of Dr. Neville?"

"In what way would their interests differ from ours? She has helped me without reservation."

Gottstein shifted position and moved his shoulders as though he were going through muscle-pulling exercises. He said, "Dr. Neville must know that a woman so close to himself is an Intuitionist. Wouldn't he use her? Why would she remain a tourist guide, if not to mask her abilities—for a purpose."

"I understand Dr. Neville frequently reasons in this fashion. I find it difficult to suspect unnecessary conspiracies."

"How do you know they are unnecessary. . . . When my space-skipper was hovering over the Moon's surface just before the ball of radiation formed over your equipment, I was looking down at you. You were not at the Pionizer."

Denison thought back. "No, I wasn't. I was looking at the stars; rather a tendency of mine on the surface."

"What was Miss Lindstrom doing?"

"I didn't see. She said she strengthened the magnetic field and the leak finally broke through."

"Is it customary for her to manipulate the equipment without you?"

"No. But I can understand the impulse."

"And would there have been some sort of an ejection?"

"I don't understand you."

"I'm not sure I understand myself. There was a dim sparkle in the Earthlight, as though something was flying through the air. I don't know what."

"I don't either," said Denison.

"You can't think of anything that might naturally have to do with the experiment that—"

"No."

"Then what was Miss Lindstrom doing?"

"I still don't know."

For a moment, the silence was heavy between them. Then the Commissioner said, "As I see it then, you will try to correct the leak-instability and will be thinking about the preparation of a paper. I will get matters into motion at the other end and on my shortly forthcoming visit to Earth will make arrangements to have the paper published and will alert the government."

It was a clear dismissal. Denison rose and the Commissioner said easily, "And think about Dr. Neville and Miss Lindstrom."

IT WAS a heavier star of radiation, a fatter one, a brighter one. Denison could feel its warmth on his faceplate, and backed away. There was a distinct x-ray component in the radiation and though this shielding should take care of that there was no point in placing it under a strain.

"I guess we can't question it," he muttered. "The leak-point is stable."

"I'm sure of it," said Selene, flatly.

"Then let's turn if off and go back to the city."

They moved slowly and Denison felt oddly dispirited. There was no uncertainty any more; no excitement. From this point on, there was no chance of failure. The government was interested; more and more, it would be out of his own hands.

He said, "I suppose I can begin the paper now."

"I suppose so," said Selene, carefully.

"Have you talked to Barron again?"

"Yes, I have."

"Any difference in his attitude?"

"None at all. He will not participate. Ben—"

"Yes?"

"I really don't think it's any use talking to him. He will not cooperate in any project with the Earth government."

"But you've explained the situation?"

"Completely."

"And he still won't."

"He's asked to see Gottstein, and the Commissioner agreed to an interview after he returns from his Earth visit. We'll have to wait till then. Maybe Gottstein can have some effect on him, but I doubt it."

Denison shrugged, a useless maneuver inside his spacesuit. "I don't understand him."

"I do," said Selene, softly.

Denison did not respond directly. He shoved the Pionizer and its attendant apparatus into its rocky shelter and said, "Ready?"

"Ready."

They slipped into the surface entrance at Outlet P-4 in silence and Denison climbed down the entry ladder. Selene dropped past him, braking in quick holds at individual rungs. Denison had learned to do that, but he was dispirited and climbed down in a kind of rebellious refusal to accept acclimation.

They removed their suits in the staging areas, placed them in their lockers. Denison said, "Would you join me for lunch, Selene?"

Selene said uneasily, "You seem upset. Is something wrong?"

"Reaction, I think. Lunch?"

"Yes, of course."

They ate in Selene's quarters. She insisted, saying, "I want to talk to you and I can't do it properly in the cafeteria."

And when Denison was chewing slowly at something that had a faint resemblance to peanut-flavored veal, she said, "Ben, you haven't said a word, and you've been like this for a week."

"No, I haven't," said Denison, frowning.

"Yes, you have." She looked into his eyes with concern. "I'm not sure how good my intuition is outside physics, but I suppose there's something you don't want to tell me.''

Denison shrugged. "They're making a fuss about all this back on Earth. Gottstein has been pulling at strings as tough as cables in advance of his trip back. Dr. Lamont is being lionized, and they want me to come back once the paper is written.''

"Back to Earth?''

"Yes. It seems I'm a hero, too.''

"You should be.''

"Complete rehabilitation,'' said Denison, thoughtfully, "is what they offer. It's clear I can get a position in any suitable university or government agency on Earth.''

"Isn't that what you wanted?''

"It's what I imagine Lamont wants, and would enjoy, and will certainly get. But I don't want it.''

Selene said, "What *do* you want then?''

"I want to stay on the Moon.''

"Why?''

"Because it's the cutting edge of humanity and I want to be part of that cutting edge. I want to work at the establishment of cosmeg pumps and that will be only here on the Moon. I want to work on para-theory with the kind of instruments you can dream up and handle, Selene. . . . I want to be with you, Selene. But will you stay with me?''

"I am as interested in para-theory as you are.''

Denison said, "But won't Neville pull you off the job now?''

"Barron pull me off?'' She said, tightly, "Are you trying to insult me, Ben?''

"Not at all.''

"Well, then, do I misunderstand you? Are you suggesting that I'm working with you because Barron ordered me to?''

"Didn't he?''

"Yes, he did. But that's not why I'm here. I *choose* to be here. He may think he can order me about but he can only do so when his orders coincide with my will, as in your case they did. I resent his thinking he can order me otherwise, and I resent your thinking it, too.''

"You two are sex-partners.''

"We have been, yes, but what has that to do with it? By that argument, I can order him about as easily as he me.''

"Then you *can* work with me, Selene?''

"Certainly,'' she said, coldly. "If I choose to.''

"But do you choose to?''

"As of now, yes.''

And Denison smiled. "The chance that you might not choose to, or even might not be able to, is, I think, what has really been worrying me this past week. I dreaded the end of the project if it meant the end of you. I'm sorry, Selene, I don't mean to plague you with a sentimental attachment of an old Earthie—''

"Well, there's nothing old Earthie about your mind, Ben. There are other attachments than sexual. I like being with you.''

There was a pause and Denison's smile faded, then returned, perhaps a thought more mechanically. "I'm glad for my mind.''

Denison looked away, shook his head slightly, then turned back. She watched him carefully, almost anxiously.

Denison said, "Selene, there's more than energy involved in the cross-Universe leaks. I suspect you've been thinking about that."

The silence stretched out now, painfully, and finally Selene said, "Oh, that—"

For a while the two stared at each other—Denison embarrassed, Selene almost furtive.

— 18 —

GOTTSTEIN SAID, "I haven't got my Moon-legs quite yet, but this isn't anything compared to what it cost me to get my Earth-legs. Denison, you had better not dream of returning. You'll never make it."

"I have no intention of returning, Commissioner," said Denison.

"In a way, it's too bad. You could be emperor by acclamation. As for Hallam—"

Denison said, wistfully, "I would have liked to see his face, but that's a small ambition."

"Lamont, of course, is receiving the lion's share. He's on the spot."

"I don't mind that. He deserves a good deal. . . . Do you think Neville will really join us?"

"No question. He's on his way at this moment. . . . Listen," Gottstein's voice dropped one conspiratorial note in pitch. "Before he comes, would you like a bar of chocolate?"

"What?"

"A bar of chocolate. With almonds. *One.* I have some."

Denison's face, from initial confusion, suddenly lit with comprehension. *"Real* chocolate?"

"Yes."

"Certain—" His face hardened. "No, Commissioner."

"No?"

"No! If I taste real chocolate then, for the few minutes it's in my mouth, I'm going to miss Earth; I'm going to miss everything about it. I can't afford that. I don't want it. . . . Don't even show it to me. Don't let me smell it or see it."

The Commissioner looked discomfited. "You're right." He made an obvious attempt to change the subject. "The excitement on Earth is overwhelming. Of course, we made a considerable effort to save Hallam's face. He'll continue to hold some position of importance, but he'll have little real say."

"He's getting more consideration than he gave others," said Denison, resignedly.

"It's not for his sake. You can't smash a personal image that has been built to a level of such importance; it would reflect on science itself. The good name of science is more important than Hallam either way."

"I disapprove of that in principle," said Denison, warmly. "Science must take what blows it deserves."

"A time and place for— There's Dr. Neville."

Gottstein composed his face. Denison shifted his chair to face the entrance.

Barron Neville entered solemnly. Somehow there was less than ever of the Lunar delicacy about his figure. He greeted the two curtly, sat down, and crossed his legs. He was clearly waiting for Gottstein to speak first.

The Commissioner said, "I am glad to see you, Dr. Neville. Dr. Denison tells me that you refuse to append your name to what I am sure will be a classic paper on the cosmeg pump."

"No need to do so," said Neville. "What happens on Earth is of no interest to me."

"You are aware of the cosmeg pump experiments? Of its implications?"

"All of them. I know the situation as well as you two do."

"Then I will proceed without preliminaries. I have returned from Earth, Dr. Neville, and it is quite settled as to what will be the course of future procedure. Large cosmeg pump stations will be set up on three different places on the Lunar surface in such a way that one will always be in the night-shadow. Half the time, two will be. Those in the night-shadow will be constantly generating energy, most of which will simply radiate into space. The purpose will be not so much to use the energy for practical purposes, as to counteract the changes in field intensities introduced by the Electron Pump."

Denison interrupted. "For some years, we will have to overbalance the Electron Pump to restore our section of the Universe to the point at which it was before the pump began operation."

Neville nodded. "Will Luna City have the use of any of it?"

"If necessary. We feel the Solar batteries will probably supply what you need, but there is no objection to supplementation."

"That is kind of you," said Neville, not bothering to mask the sarcasm. "And who will build and run the cosmeg pump stations?"

"Lunar workers, we hope," said Gottstein.

"Lunar workers, you know," said Neville. "Earth workers would be too clumsy to work effectively on the Moon."

"We recognize that," said Gottstein. "We trust the men of the Moon will cooperate."

"And who will decide how much energy to generate, how much to apply for any local purpose, how much to radiate away? Who decides policy?"

Gottstein said, "The government would have to. It's a matter of planetary decision."

Neville said, "You see, then, it will be Moonmen who do the work; Earthmen who run the show."

Gottstein said, calmly, "No. All of us work who work best; all of us administer who can best weigh the total problem."

"I hear the words," said Neville, "but it boils down anyway to us working and you deciding. . . . No, Commissioner. The answer is no."

"You mean you won't build the cosmeg pump stations?"

"We'll build them, Commissioner, but they'll be ours. We'll decide how much energy to put out and what use to make of it."

"That would scarcely be efficient. You would have to deal constantly with the Earth government since the cosmeg pump energy will have to balance the Electron Pump energy."

"I dare say it will, more or less, but we have other things in mind. You might as well know now. Energy is not the only conserved phenomenon that becomes limitless once universes are crossed."

Denison interrupted. "There are a number of conservation laws. We realize that."

"I'm glad you do," said Neville, turning a hostile glare in his direction. "They include those of linear momentum and angular momentum. As long as any object responds to the gravitational field in which it is immersed, and to that only, it is in free fall and can retain its mass. In order to move in any other way than free fall, it must accelerate in a non-gravitational way and for that to happen, part of itself must undergo an opposite change."

"As in a rocketship," said Denison, "which must eject mass in one direction in order that the rest might accelerate in the opposite direction."

"I'm sure you understand, Dr. Denison," said Neville, "but I explain for the Commissioner's sake. The loss of mass can be minimized if its velocity is increased enormously, since momentum is equal to mass multiplied by velocity. Nevertheless, however great the velocity, some mass must be thrown away. If the mass which must be accelerated is enormous in the first place, then the mass which must be discarded is also enormous. If the Moon, for instance—"

"The *Moon!*" said Gottstein, explosively.

"Yes, the Moon," said Neville, calmly. "If the Moon were to be driven out of its orbit and sent out of the Solar system, the conservation of momentum would make it a colossal undertaking, and probably a thoroughly impractical one. If, however, momentum could be transferred to the cosmeg in another Universe, the Moon could accelerate at any convenient rate without loss of mass at all. It would be like poling a barge upstream, to give you a picture I obtained from some Earth-book I once read."

"But why? I mean why should you want to move the Moon?"

"I should think that would be obvious. Why do we need the suffocating presence of the Earth? We have the energy we need; we have a comfortable world through which we have room to expand for the next few centuries, at least. Why not go our own way? In any case, we will. I have come to tell you that you cannot stop us and to urge you to make no attempt to interfere. We shall transfer momentum and we shall pull out. We of the Moon know precisely how to go about building cosmeg pump stations. We will use what energy we need for ourselves and produce excess in order to neutralize the changes your own power stations are producing."

Denison said, sardonically, "It sounds kind of you to produce excess for our sake, but it isn't for our sake, of course. If our Electron Pump explode the Sun, that will happen long before you can move out of even the inner Solar system and you will vaporize wherever you are."

"Perhaps," said Neville, "but in any case we *will* produce an excess, so that won't happen."

"But you can't do that," said Gottstein, excitedly. "You can't move out. If you get out too far, the cosmeg pump will no longer neutralize the Electron Pump, eh, Denison?"

Denison shrugged. "Once they are as far off as Saturn, more or less, there may be trouble, if I may trust a mental calculation I have just made. It will, however, be many years before they recede to such a distance and by that time, we will surely have constructed space stations in what was once the orbit of the Moon and place cosmeg pumps on them. Actually, we don't need the Moon. It can leave—except that it won't."

Neville smiled briefly. "What makes you think we won't? We can't be stopped. There is no way Earthmen can impose their will on us."

"You won't leave, because there's no sense to doing so. Why drag the entire Moon away? To build up respectable accelerations will take years where the Moon-mass is concerned. You'll creep. Build starships instead; miles-long ships that are cosmeg-powered and have independent ecologies. With a cosmeg momentum-drive, you can then do wonders. If it takes twenty years to build the ships, they will nevertheless accelerate at a rate that will enable them to overtake the Moon's place within a year even if the Moon starts accelerating today. The ships will be able to change course in a tiny fraction of the time the Moon will."

"And the unbalanced cosmeg pumps? What will that do to the Universe."

"The energy required by a ship, or even by a number, will be far less than that required by a planet and will be distributed throughout large sections of the Universe. It will be millions of years before any significant change takes place. That is well worth the maneuverability you gain. The Moon will move so slowly it might as well be left in space."

Neville said, scornfully, "We're in no hurry to get anywhere—except away from Earth."

Denison said, "There are advantages in having Earth as a neighbor. You have the influx of the Immigrants. You have cultural intercourse. You have a planetary world of two billion people just over the horizon. Do you want to give all that up?"

"Gladly."

"Is that true of the people of the Moon generally? Or just of you? There's something intense about you, Neville. You won't go out on the surface. Other Lunarites do. They don't like it particularly, but they do. The interior of the Moon isn't their womb, as it is in your case. It isn't their prison, as it is yours. There is a neurotic factor in you that is absent in most Lunarities, or at least considerably weaker. If you take the Moon away from Earth, you make it into a prison for all. It will become a one-world prison from which no man—and not you only—can emerge, not even to the extent of seeing another inhabited world in the sky. Perhaps that is what you want."

"I want independence; a free world; a world untouched by the outside."

"You can build ships, any number. You can move outward at near-light velocities without difficulty, once you transfer momentum to the cosmeg. You can explore the entire Universe in a single lifetime. Wouldn't you like to get on such a ship?"

"No," said Neville, with clear distaste.

"Wouldn't you? Or is it couldn't? Is it that you must take the Moon with you wherever you go. Why must all the others accept your need?"

"Because that's the way it's going to be," said Neville.

Denison's voice remained level but his cheeks reddened. "Who gave you the right to say that? There are many citizens of Luna City who may not feel as you do."

"That is none of your concern."

"That is *precisely* my concern. I am in Immigrant who will qualify for citizenship soon. I do not wish to have my choice made for me by someone who cannot emerge on the surface and who wants his personal prison made into a prison for all. I have left Earth forever, but only to come to the Moon, only to remain a quarter-million miles from the home-planet. I have not contracted to be taken forever away for an unlimited distance."

"Then return to Earth," said Neville, indifferently. "There is still time."

"And what of the other citizens of Luna? The other Immigrants?"

"The decision is made."

"It is not made. . . . Selene!"

Selene entered, her face solemn, her eyes a little defiant. Neville's legs uncrossed. Both shoes came down flat upon the ground.

Neville said, "How long have you been waiting in the next room, Selene?"

"Since before you arrived, Barron," she said.

Neville looked from Selene to Denison and back again. "You two—" he began, finger pointing from one to the other and back.

"I don't know what you mean by 'you two,' " said Selene, "but Ben found out about the momentum quite a while ago."

"It wasn't Selene's fault," said Denison. "The Commissioner spotted something flying at a time when no one could possibly have known he would be observing. It seemed to me that Selene might be testing something I was not thinking of and transfer of momentum eventually occurred to me. After that—"

"Well, then, you knew," said Neville. "It doesn't matter."

"It does, Barron," said Selene. "I talked about it with Ben. I found that I didn't always have to accept what you said. Perhaps I can't ever go to Earth. Perhaps I don't even want to. But I found I liked it in the sky where I could see it if I wanted to. I didn't want an empty sky. Then I talked to others of the Group. Not everybody wants to leave. Most people would rather build the ships and let those go who wish to go while allowing those to remain behind who wish to remain."

Neville's breath was coming hard. "You *talked* about it. Who gave you the right to—"

"I *took* the right, Barron. Besides, it doesn't matter any more. You'll be outvoted."

"Because of—" Neville rose to his feet and took a menacing step toward Denison.

The Commissioner said, "Please don't get emotional, Dr. Neville. You may be of Luna, but I don't think you can man-handle both of us."

"All three," said Selene, "and I'm of Luna, too. I did it, Barron; not they."

Then Denison said, "Look, Neville—for all Earth cares, the Moon can go. Earth can build its space stations. It's the citizens of Luna City who care. Selene cares and I care and the rest. You are not being debarred from space, from escape, from freedom. In twenty years at the outside, all who want to go will go, including you if you can bring yourself to leave the womb. And those who want to stay will stay."

Slowly, Neville seated himself again. There was the look of defeat on his face.

– 19 –

IN SELENE'S apartment every window now had a view of the Earth. She said, "The vote did go against him, you know, Ben. Quite heavily."

"I doubt that he'll give up, though. If there's friction with Earth during the building of the stations, public opinion on the Moon may swing back."

"There needn't be friction."

"No, there needn't. In any case, there are no happy endings in history, only crisis points that pass. We've passed this one safely, I think, and we'll be sorry about the others as they come and as they can be foreseen. Once the starships are built, the tension will surely subside considerably."

"We'll live to see that, I'm sure."

"You will, Selene."

"You, too. Ben. Don't overdramatize your age. You're only forty-eight."

"Would you go on one of the starships, Selene?"

"No. I'd be too old and I still wouldn't want to lose Earth in the sky. My son might go. . . . Ben."

"Yes, Selene."

"I have applied for a second son. The application has been accepted. Would you contribute?"

Denison's eyes lifted and looked straight into hers. She did not look away. He said, "Artificial insemination?"

She said, "Of course. . . . The gene combination should be interesting."

Denison's eyes dropped. "I would be flattered, Selene."

Selene said, defensively, "That's just good sense, Ben. It's important to have good gene combinations. There's nothing wrong with some *natural* genetic engineering."

"None at all."

"It doesn't mean that I don't want it for other reasons, too. . . . Because I like you."

Denison nodded and remained silent.

Selene said, almost angrily, "Well, there's more to love than sex."

Denison said, "I agree to that. At least, I love you even with sex subtracted."

And Selene said, "And for that matter, there's more to sex than acrobatics."

Denison said, "I agree to that, too."

And Selene said, "And besides— Oh, damn it, you could try to learn."

Denison said softly, "If you would try to teach."

Hesitantly, he moved toward her. She did not move away.

He stopped hesitating.

C-CHUTE

EVEN FROM the cabin into which he and the other passengers had been herded, Colonel Anthony Windham could still catch the essence of the battle's progress. For a while, there was silence, no jolting, which meant the spaceships were fighting at astronomical distance in a duel of energy blasts and powerful force-field defenses.

He knew that could have only one end. Their Earth ship was only an armed merchantman and his glimpse of the Kloro enemy just before he had been cleared off deck by the crew was sufficient to show it to be a light cruiser.

And in less than half an hour, there came those hard little shocks he was waiting for. The passengers swayed back and forth as the ship pitched and veered, as though it were an ocean liner in a storm. But space was calm and silent as ever. It was their pilot sending desperate bursts of steam through the steam-tubes, so that by reaction the ship would be sent rolling and tumbling. It could only mean that the inevitable had occurred. The Earth ship's screens had been drained and it no longer dared withstand a direct hit.

Colonel Windham tried to steady himself with his aluminum cane. He was thinking that he was an old man; that he had spent his life in the militia and had never seen a battle; that now, with a battle going on around him, he was old and fat and lame and had no men under his command.

They would be boarding soon, those Kloro monsters. It was their way of fighting. They would be handicapped by spacesuits and their casualties would be high, but they wanted the Earth ship. Windham considered the passengers. For a moment, he thought, *if they were armed and I could lead them—*

He abandoned the thought. Porter was in an obvious state of funk and the young boy, Leblanc, was hardly better. The Polyorketes brothers—dash it, he couldn't tell them apart—huddled in a corner speaking only to one another. Mullen was a different matter. He sat perfectly erect, with no signs of fear or any other emotion in his face. But the man was just about five feet tall and had undoubtedly never held a gun of any sort in his hands in all his life. He could do nothing.

And there was Stuart, with his frozen half-smile and the high-pitched sarcasm which saturated all he said. Windham looked sidelong at Stuart now as Stuart sat there, pushing his dead-white hands through his sandy hair. With those artificial hands he was useless, anyway.

Windham felt the shuddering vibration of ship-to-ship contact, and in five minutes, there was the noise of the fight through the corridors. One of the Polyorketes brothers screamed and dashed for the door. The other called, "Aristides! Wait!" and hurried after.

It happened so quickly. Aristides was out the door and into the corridor, running in brainless panic. A carbonizer glowed briefly and there was never even a scream. Windham, from the doorway, turned in horror at the blackened stump of what was left. Strange—a lifetime in uniform and he had never before seen a man killed in violence.

It took the combined force of the rest to carry the other brother back struggling into the room.

The noise of battle subsided.

Stuart said, "That's it. They'll put a prize crew of two aboard and take us to one of their home planets. We're prisoners of war, naturally."

"Only two of the Kloros will stay aboard?" asked Windham, astonished.

Stuart said, "It is their custom. Why do you ask, Colonel? Thinking of leading a gallant raid to retake the ship?"

Windham flushed. "Simply a point of information, dash it." But the dignity and tone of authority he tried to assume failed him, he knew. He was simply an old man with a limp.

And Stuart was probably right. He had lived among the Kloros and knew their ways.

John Stuart had claimed from the beginning that the Kloros were gentlemen. Twenty-four hours of imprisonment had passed, and now he repeated the statement as he flexed the fingers of his hands and watched the crinkles come and go in the soft artiplasm.

He enjoyed the unpleasant reaction it aroused in the others. People were made to be punctured; windy bladders, all of them. And they had hands of the same stuff as their bodies.

There was Anthony Windham, in particular. Colonel Windham, he called himself, and Stuart was willing to believe it. A retired colonel who had probably drilled a home guard militia on a village green, forty years ago, with such lack of distinction that he was not called back to service in any capacity, even during the emergency of Earth's first interstellar war.

"Dashed unpleasant thing to be saying about the enemy, Stuart. Don't know that I like your attitude." Windham seemed to push the words through his clipped mustache. His head had been shaven, too, in imitation of the current military style, but now a gray stubble was beginning to show about a centered bald patch. His flabby cheeks dragged downward. That and the fine red lines on his thick nose gave him a somewhat undone appearance, as though he had been wakened too suddenly and too early in the morning.

Stuart said, "Nonsense. Just reverse the present situation. Suppose an Earth warship had taken a Kloro liner. What do you think would have happened to any Kloro civilians aboard?"

"I'm sure the Earth fleet would observe all the interstellar rules of war," Windham said stiffly.

"Except that there aren't any. If we landed a prize crew on one of their ships, do you think we'd take the trouble to maintain a chlorine atmosphere for the benefit of the survivors; allow them to keep their non-contraband possessions;

give them the use of the most comfortable stateroom, etcetera, etcetera, etcetera?''

Ben Porter said, ''Oh, shut up, for God's sake. If I hear your etcetera, etcetera once again, I'll go nuts.''

Stuart said, ''Sorry!'' He wasn't.

Porter was scarcely responsible. His thin face and beaky nose glistened with perspiration, and he kept biting the inside of his cheek until he suddenly winced. He put his tongue against the sore spot, which made him look even more clownish.

Stuart was growing weary of baiting them. Windham was too flabby a target and Porter could do nothing but writhe. The rest were silent. Demetrios Polyorketes was off in a world of silent internal grief for the moment. He had not slept the night before, most probably. At least, whenever Stuart woke to change his position—he himself had been rather restless—there had been Polyorketes' thick mumble from the next cot. It said many things, but the moan to which it returned over and over again was, ''Oh, my brother!''

He sat dumbly on his cot now, his red eyes rolling at the other prisoners out of his broad swarthy, unshaven face. As Stuart watched, his face sank into calloused palms so that only his mop of crisp and curly black hair could be seen. He rocked gently, but now that they were all awake, he made no sound.

Claude Leblanc was trying very unsuccessfully, to read a letter. He was the youngest of the six, scarcely out of college, returning to Earth to get married. Stuart had found him that morning weeping quietly, his pink and white face flushed and blotched as though it were a heartbroken child's. He was very fair, with almost a girl's beauty about his large blue eyes and full lips. Stuart wondered what kind of girl it was who had promised to be his wife. He had seen her picture. Who on the ship had not? She had the characterless prettiness that makes all pictures of fiancees indistinguishable. It seemed to Stuart that if he were a girl, however, he would want someone a little more pronouncedly masculine.

That left only Randolph Mullen. Stuart frankly did not have the least idea what to make of him. He was the only one of the six that had been on the Arcturian worlds for any length of time. Stuart, himself, for instance, had been there only long enough to give a series of lectures on astronautical engineering at the provincial engineering institute. Colonel Windham had been on a Cook's tour; Porter was trying to buy concentrated alien vegetables for his canneries on Earth; and the Polyorketes brothers had attempted to establish themselves in Arcturus as truck farmers and, after two growing seasons, gave it up, had somehow unloaded at a profit, and were returning to Earth.

Randolph Mullen, however, had been in the Arcturian system for seventeen years. How did voyagers discover so much about one another so quickly? As far as Stuart knew, the little man had scarcely spoken aboard ship. He was unfailingly polite, always stepped to one side to allow another to pass, but his entire vocabulary appeared to consist only of ''Thank you,'' and ''Pardon me.'' Yet the word had gone around that this was his first trip to Earth in seventeen years.

He was a little man, very precise, almost irritatingly so. Upon awaking that morning, he had made his cot neatly, shaved, bathed and dressed. The habit of years seemed not in the least disturbed by the fact that he was a prisoner of the Kloros now. He was unobtrusive about it, it had to be admitted, and gave no impression of disapproving of the sloppiness of the others. He simply sat there, almost apologetic, trussed in his overconservative clothing, and hands loosely clasped in his lap. The thin line of hair on his upper lip, far from adding character to his face, absurdly increased its primness.

He looked like someone's idea of a caricature of a bookkeeper. And the queer thing about it all, Stuart thought, was that that was exactly what he was. He had noticed it on the registry—Randolph Fluellen Mullen; occupation, bookkeeper; employers, Prime Paper Box Co.; 27 Tobias Avenue, New Warsaw, Arcturus II.

"Mr. Stuart?"

Stuart looked up. It was Leblanc, his lower lip trembling slightly. Stuart tried to remember how one went about being gentle. He said, "What is it, Leblanc?"

"Tell me, when will they let us go?"

"How should I know?"

"Everyone says you lived on a Kloro planet, and just now you said they were gentlemen."

"Well, yes. But even gentlemen fight wars in order to win. Probably, we'll be interned for the duration."

"But that could be *years!* Margaret is waiting. She'll think I'm *dead!*"

"I suppose they'll allow messages to be sent through once we're on their planet."

Porter's hoarse voice sounded in agitation. "Look here, if you know so much about these devils, what will they do to us while we're interned? What will they feed us? Where will they get oxygen for us? They'll kill us, I tell you." And as an afterthought, "I've got a wife waiting for me, too," he added.

But Stuart had heard him speaking of his wife in the days before the attack. He wasn't impressed. Porter's nail-bitten fingers were pulling and plucking at Stuart's sleeve. Stuart drew away in sharp revulsion. He couldn't stand those ugly hands. It angered him to desperation that such monstrosities should be real while his own white and perfectly shaped hands were only mocking imitations grown out of an alien latex.

He said, "They won't kill us. If they were going to, they would have done it before now. Look, we capture Kloros too, you know, and it's just a matter of common sense to treat your prisoners decently if you want the other side to be decent to your men. They'll do their best. The food may not be very good, but they're better chemists than we are. It's what they're best at. They'll know exactly what food factors we'll need and how many calories. We'll live. They'll see to that."

Windham rumbled, "You sound more and more like a blasted greenie sympathizer, Stuart. It turns my stomach to hear an Earthman speak well of the green fellas the way you've been doing. Burn it, man, where's your loyalty?"

"My loyalty's where it belongs. With honesty and decency, regardless of the shape of the being it appears in." Stuart held up his hands. "See these? Kloros made them. I lived on one of their planets for six months. My hands were mangled in the conditioning machinery of my own quarters. I thought the oxygen supply they gave me was a little poor—it wasn't, by the way—and I tried making the adjustments on my own. It was my fault. You should never trust yourself with the machines of another culture. By the time someone among the Kloros could put on an atmosphere suit and get to me, it was too late to save my hands.

"They grew these artiplasm things for me and operated. You know what that meant? It meant designing equipment and nutrient solutions that would work in oxygen atmosphere. It meant that their surgeons had to perform a delicate operation while dressed in atmosphere suits. And now I've got hands again." He laughed harshly, and clenched them into weak fists. "Hands—"

Windham said, "And you'd sell your loyalty to Earth for that?"

"Sell my loyalty? You're mad. For years, I hated the Kloros for this. I was a master pilot on the Trans-Galactic Spacelines before it happened. Now? Desk job. Or an occasional lecture. It took me a long time to pin the fault on myself and to realize that the only role played by the Kloros was a decent one. They have their code of ethics, and it's as good as ours. If it weren't for the stupidity of some of their people—and, by God, of some of ours—we wouldn't be at war. And after it's over—"

Polyorketes was on his feet. His thick fingers curved inward before him and his dark eyes glittered. "I don't like what you say, mister."

"Why don't you?"

"Because you talk too nice about these damned green bastards. The Kloros were good to you, eh? Well, they weren't good to my brother. They killed him. I think maybe I kill you, you damned greenie spy."

And he charged.

Stuart barely had time to raise his arms to meet the infuriated farmer. He gasped out, "What the hell—" as he caught one wrist and heaved a shoulder to block the other which groped toward his throat.

His antiplasm hand gave way. Polyorketes wrenched free with scarcely an effort.

Windham was bellowing incoherently, and Leblanc was calling out in his reedy voice, "Stop it! Stop it!" But it was little Mullen who threw his arms about the farmer's neck from behind and pulled with all his might. He was not very effective; Polyorketes seemed scarcely aware of the little man's weight upon his back. Mullen's feet left the floor so that he tossed helplessly to right and left. But he held his grip and it hampered Polyorketes sufficiently to allow Stuart to break free long enough to grasp Windham's aluminum cane.

He said, "Stay away, Polyorketes."

He was gasping for breath and fearful of another rush. The hollow aluminum cylinder was scarcely heavy enough to accomplish much, but it was better than having only his weak hands to defend himself with.

Mullen had loosed his hold and was now circling cautiously, his breathing roughened and his jacket in disarray.

Polyorketes, for a moment, did not move. He stood there, his shaggy head bent low. Then he said, "It is no use, I must kill Kloros. Just watch your tongue, Stuart. If it keeps on rattling too much, you're liable to get hurt. Really hurt, I mean."

Stuart passed a forearm over his forehead and thrust the cane back at Windham, who seized it with his left hand, while mopping his bald pate vigorously with a handkerchief in his right.

Windham said, "Gentlemen, we must avoid this. It lowers our prestige. We must remember the common enemy. We are Earthmen and we must act what we are—the ruling race of the Galaxy. We dare not demean ourselves before the lesser breeds."

"Yes, Colonel," said Stuart, wearily. "Give us the rest of the speech tomorrow."

He turned to Mullen, "I want to say thanks."

He was uncomfortable about it, but he had to. The little accountant had surprised him completely.

But Mullen said, in a dry voice that scarcely raised above a whisper, "Don't thank me, Mr. Stuart. It was the logical thing to do. If we are to be interned, we would need you as an interpreter, perhaps, one who would understand the Kloros."

Stuart stiffened. It was, he thought, too much of the bookkeeper type of reasoning, too logical, too dry of juice. Present risk and ultimate advantage. The assets and debits balanced neatly. He would have liked Mullen to leap to his defense out of—well, out of what? Out of pure, unselfish decency?

Stuart laughed silently at himself. He was beginning to expect idealism of human beings, rather than good, straightforward, self-centered motivation.

Polyorketes was numb. His sorrow and rage were like acid inside him, but they had no words to get out. If he were Stuart, big-mouth, white-hands Stuart, he could talk and talk and maybe feel better. Instead, he had to sit there with half of him dead; with no brother, no Aristides—

It happened so quickly. If he could only go back and have one second more warning, so that he might snatch Aristides, hold him, save him.

But mostly he hated the Kloros. Two months ago, he had hardly ever heard of them, and now he hated them so hard, he would be glad to die if he could kill a few.

He said, without looking up, "What happened to start this war, eh?"

He was afraid Stuart's voice would answer. He hated Stuart's voice. But it was Windham, the bald one.

Windham said, "The immediate cause, sir, was a dispute over mining concessions in the Wyandotte system. The Kloros had poached on Earth's property."

"Room for both, Colonel!"

Polyorketes looked up at that, snarling. Stuart could not be kept quiet for long. He was speaking again; the cripple-hand, wiseguy, Kloros-lover.

Stuart was saying, "Is that anything to fight over, Colonel? We can't use one another's worlds. Their chlorine planets are useless to us and our oxygen ones are useless to them. Chlorine is deadly to us and oxygen is deadly to them. There's no way we could maintain permanent hostility. Our races just don't coincide. Is there reason to fight then because both races want to dig iron out of the same airless planetoids where there are millions like them in the Galaxy?"

Windham said, "There is the question of planetary honor—"

"Planetary fertilizer. How can it excuse a ridiculous war like this one? It can only be fought on outposts. It has to come down to a series of holding actions and eventually be settled by negotiations that might just as easily have been worked out in the first place. Neither we nor the Kloros will gain a thing."

Grudgingly, Polyorketes found that he agreed with Stuart. What did he and Aristides care where Earth or the Kloros got their iron?"

Was that something for Aristides to die over?

The little warning buzzer sounded.

Polyorketes' head shot up and he rose slowly, his lips drawing back. Only one thing could be at the door. He waited, arms tense, fists balled. Stuart was edging toward him. Polyorketes saw that and laughed to himself. Let the Kloro come in, and Stuart, along with all the rest, could not stop him.

Wait, Aristides, wait just a moment, and a fraction of revenge will be paid back.

The door opened and a figure entered, completely swathed in a shapeless, billowing travesty of a spacesuit.

An odd, unnatural, but not entirely unpleasant voice began, "It is with some misgivings, Earthmen, that my companion and myself—"

It ended abruptly as Polyorketes, with a roar, charged once again. There was no science in the lunge. It was sheer bull-momentum. Dark head low, burly arms spread out with the hair-tufted fingers in choking position, he clumped on. Stuart was whirled to one side before he had a chance to intervene, and was spun tumbling across a cot.

The Kloro might have, without undue exertion, straightarmed Polyorketes to a halt, or stepped aside, allowing the whirlwind to pass. He did neither. With a rapid movement, a hand-weapon was up and a gentle pinkish line of radiance connected it with the plunging Earthman. Polyorketes stumbled and crashed down, his body maintaining its last curved position, one foot raised, as though a lightning paralysis had taken place. It toppled to one side and he lay there, eyes all alive and wild with rage.

The Kloro said, "He is not permanently hurt." He seemed not to resent the offered violence. Then he began again, "It is with some misgiving, Earthmen, that my companion and myself were made aware of a certain commotion in this room. Are you in any need which we can satisfy?"

Stuart was angrily nursing his knee which he had scraped in colliding with the cot. He said, "No, thank you, Kloro."

"Now, look here," puffed Windham, "this is a dashed outrage. We demand that our release be arranged."

The Kloro's tiny, insectlike head turned in the fat old man's direction. He was not a pleasant sight to anyone unused to him. He was about the height of an Earthman, but the top of him consisted of a thin stalk of a neck with a head that was the merest swelling. It consisted of a blunt triangular proboscis in front and two bulging eyes on either side. That was all. There was no brain pan and no brain. What corresponded to the brain in a Kloro was located in what would be an Earthly abdomen, leaving the head as a mere sensory organ. The Kloro's spacesuit followed the outlines of the head more or less faithfully, the two eyes being exposed by two clear semicircles of glass, which looked faintly green because of the chlorine atmosphere inside.

One of the eyes was now cocked squarely at Windham, who quivered uncomfortably under the glance, but insisted, "You have no right to hold us prisoner. We are noncombatants."

The Kloro's voice, sounding thoroughly artificial, came from a small attachment of chromium mesh on what served as its chest. The voice box was manipulated by compressed air under the control of one or two of the many delicate, forked tendrils that radiated from two circles about its upper body and were, mercifully enough, hidden by the suit.

The voice said, "Are you serious, Earthman? Surely you have heard of war and rules of war and prisoners of war."

It looked about, shifting eyes with quick jerks of its head, staring at a particular object first with one, then with another. It was Stuart's understanding that each eye transferred a separate message to the abdominal brain, which had to coordinate the two to obtain full information.

Windham had nothing to say. No one had. The Kloro, its four main limbs, roughly arms and legs in pairs, had a vaguely human appearance under the masking of the suit, if you looked no higher than its chest, but there was no way of telling what it felt.

They watched it turn and leave.

Porter coughed and said in a strangled voice, "God, smell that chlorine. If they don't do something, we'll all die of rotted lungs."

Stuart said, "Shut up. There isn't enough chlorine in the air to make a mosquito sneeze, and what there is will be swept out in two minutes. Besides, a little chlorine is good for you. It may kill your cold virus."

Windham coughed and said, "Stuart, I feel that you might have said something to your Kloro friend about releasing us. You are scarcely as bold in their presence, dash it, as you are once they are gone."

"You heard what the creature said, Colonel. We're prisoners of war, and prisoner exchanges are negotiated by diplomats. We'll just have to wait."

Leblanc, who had turned pasty white at the entrance of the Kloro, rose and hurried into the privy. There was the sound of retching.

An uncomfortable silence fell while Stuart tried to think of something to say to cover the unpleasant sound. Mullen filled in. He had rummaged through a little box he had taken from under his pillow.

He said, "Perhaps Mr. Leblanc had better take a sedative before retiring. I have a few. I'd be glad to give him one." He explained his generosity immediately, "Otherwise he may keep the rest of us awake, you see."

"Very logical," said Stuart, dryly. "You'd better save one for Sir Launcelot here; save half a dozen." He walked to where Polyorketes still sprawled and knelt at his side. "Comfortable, baby?"

Windham said, "Deuced poor taste speaking like that, Stuart."

"Well, if you're so concerned about him, why don't you and Porter hoist him onto his cot?"

He helped them to do so. Polyorketes' arms were trembling erratically now. From what Stuart knew of the Kloro's nerve weapons, the man should be in an agony of pins and needles about now.

Stuart said, "And don't be too gentle with him, either. The damned fool might have gotten us all killed. And for what?"

He pushed Polyorketes' stiff carcass to one side and sat at the edge of the cot. He said, "Can you hear me, Polyorketes?"

Polyorketes' eyes gleamed. An arm lifted abortively and fell back.

"Okay then, listen. Don't try anything like that again. The next time it may be the finish for all of us. If you had been a Kloro and he had been an Earthman, we'd be dead now. So just get one thing through your skull. We're sorry about your brother and it's a rotten shame, but it was his own fault."

Polyorketes tried to heave and Stuart pushed him back.

"No, you keep on listening," he said. "Maybe this is the only time I'll get to talk to you when you *have* to listen. Your brother had no right leaving passenger's quarters. There was no place for him to go. He just got in the way of our own men. We don't even know for certain that it was a Kloro gun that killed him. It might have been one of our own."

"Oh, I say, Stuart," objected Windham.

Stuart whirled at him. "Do you have proof it wasn't? Did you see the shot? Could you tell from what was left of the body whether it was Kloro energy or Earth energy?"

Polyorketes found his voice, driving his unwilling tongue into a fuzzy verbal snarl. "Damned stinking greenie bastard."

"Me?" said Stuart. "I know what's going on in your mind, Polyorketes. You think that when the paralysis wears off, you'll ease your feelings by slamming me around. Well, if you do, it will probably be curtains for all of us."

He rose, put his back against the wall. For the moment, he was fighting all of them. "None of you know the Kloros the way I do. The physical differences you see are not important. The differences in their temperament are. They don't understand our views on sex, for instance. To them, it's just a biological reflex like breathing. They attach no importance to it. But they *do* attach importance to social groupings. Remember, their evolutionary ancestors had lots in common with our insects. They always assume that any group of Earthmen they find together makes up a social unit.

"That means just about everything to them. I don't understand exactly *what* it means. No Earthman can. But the result is that they never break up a group, just as we don't separate a mother and her children if we can help it. One of the reasons they may be treating us with kid gloves right now is that they imagine we're all broken up over the fact that they killed one of us, and they feel guilt about it.

"But this is what you'll have to remember. We're going to be interned together and *kept* together for the duration. I don't like the thought. I wouldn't have picked any of you for cointernees and I'm pretty sure none of you would have picked me. But there it is. The Kloros could never understand that our being together on the ship is only accidental.

"That means we've got to get along somehow. That's not just goodie-goodie talk about birds in their little nest agreeing. What do you think would have happened if the Kloros had come in earlier and found Polyorketes and myself trying to kill each other? You don't know? Well, what do you suppose *you* would think of a mother you caught trying to kill her children?

"That's it, then. They would have killed every one of us as a bunch of Kloro-type perverts and monsters. Got that? How about you, Polyorketes? Have *you* got it? So let's call names if we have to, but let's keep our hands to ourselves. And now, if none of you mind, I'll massage my hands back into shape—these synthetic hands that I got from the Kloros and that one of my own kind tried to mangle again."

For Claude Leblanc, the worst was over. He had been sick enough, sick with many things; but sick most of all over having ever left Earth. It had been a great thing to go to college off Earth. It had been an adventure and had taken him away from his mother. Somehow, he had been sneakingly glad to make that escape after the first month of frightened adjustment.

And then on the summer holidays, he had been no longer Claude, the shy-spoken scholar, but Leblanc, space traveler. He had swaggered the fact for all it was worth. It made him feel such a man to talk of stars and Jumps and the customs and environments of other worlds; it had given him courage with Margaret. She had loved him for the dangers he had undergone—

Except that this had been the first one, really, and he had not done so well. He knew it and was ashamed and wished he were like Stuart.

He used the excuse of mealtime to approach. He said, "Mr. Stuart."

Stuart looked up and said shortly, "How do you feel?"

Leblanc felt himself blush. He blushed easily and the effort not to blush only made it worse. He said, "Much better, thank you. We are eating. I thought I'd bring you your ration."

Stuart took the offered can. It was standard space ration; thoroughly synthetic, concentrated, nourishing and, somehow, unsatisfying. It heated automatically when the can was opened, but could be eaten cold, if necessary. Though a combined fork-spoon utensil was enclosed, the ration was of a consistency that made the use of fingers practical and not particularly messy.

Stuart said, "Did you hear my little speech?"

"Yes, sir. I want you to know you can count on me."

"Well, good. Now go and eat."

"May I eat here?"

"Suit yourself."

For a moment, they ate in silence, and then Leblanc burst out, "You are so sure of yourself, Mr. Stuart! It must be very wonderful to be like that!"

"Sure of myself? Thanks, but there's your self-assured one."

Leblanc followed the direction of the nod in surprise. "Mr. Mullen? That little man? Oh, no!"

"You don't think he's self-assured?"

Leblanc shook his head. He looked at Stuart intently to see if he could detect humor in his expression. "That one is just cold. He has no emotion in him. He's like a little machine. I find him repulsive. You're different, Mr. Stuart. You have it all inside, but you control it. I would like to be like that."

And as though attracted by the magnetism of the mention, even though unheard, of his name, Mullen joined them. His can of ration was barely touched. It was still steaming gently as he squatted opposite them.

His voice had its usual quality of furtively rustling underbrush. "How long, Mr. Stuart, do you think the trip will take?"

"Can't say, Mullen. They'll undoubtedly be avoiding the usual trade routes and they'll be making more Jumps through hyper-space than usual to throw off possible pursuit. I wouldn't be surprised if it took as long as a week. Why do you ask? I presume you have a very practical and logical reason?"

"Why, yes. Certainly." He seemed quite shellbacked to sarcasm. He said, "It occurred to me that it might be wise to ration the rations, so to speak."

"We've got enough food and water for a month. I checked on that first thing."

"I see. In that case, I will finish the can." He did, using the all-purpose utensil daintily and patting a handkerchief against his unstained lips from time to time.

Polyorketes struggled to his feet some two hours later. He swayed a bit, looking like the Spirit of Hangover. He did not try to come closer to Stuart, but spoke from where he stood.

He said, "You stinking greenie spy, you watch yourself."

"You heard what I said before, Polyorketes."

"I heard. But I also heard what you said about Aristides. I won't bother with you, because you're a bag of nothing but noisy air. But wait, someday you'll blow your air in one face too many and it will be let out of you."

"I'll wait," said Stuart.

Windham hobbled over, leaning heavily on his cane. "Now, now," he called with a wheezing joviality that overlaid his sweating anxiety so thinly as to emphasize it. "We're all Earthmen, dash it. Got to remember that; keep it as a glowing light of inspiration. Never let down before the blasted Kloros. We've got to forget private feuds and remember only that we are Earthmen united against alien blighters."

Stuart's comment was unprintable.

Porter was right behind Windham. He had been in a close conference with the shaven-headed colonel for an hour, and now he said with indignation, "It doesn't help to be a wiseguy, Stuart. You listen to the colonel. We've been doing some hard thinking about the situation."

He had washed some of the grease off his face, wet his hair and slicked it back. It did not remove the little tic on his right cheek just at the point where his lips ended, or make his hangnail hands more attractive in appearance.

"All right, Colonel," said Stuart. "What's on your mind?"

Windham said, "I prefer to have all the men together."

"Okay, call them."

Leblanc hurried over; Mullen approached with greater deliberation.

Stuart said, "You want that fellow?" He jerked his head at Polyorketes.

"Why, yes. Mr. Polyorketes, may we have you, old fella?"

"Ah, leave me alone."

"Go ahead," said Stuart, "leave him alone. I don't want him."

"No, no," said Windham. "This is a matter for all Earthmen. Mr. Polyorketes, we must have you."

Polyorketes rolled off one side of his cot. "I'm close enough, I can hear you."

Windham said to Stuart, "Would they—the Kloros, I mean—have this room wired?"

"No," said Stuart. "Why should they?"

"Are you sure?"

"Of course I'm sure. They didn't know what happened when Polyorketes jumped me. They just heard the thumping when it started rattling the ship."

"Maybe they were trying to give us the impression the room wasn't wired."

"Listen, Colonel, I've never known a Kloro to tell a deliberate lie—"

Polyorketes interrupted calmly, "That lump of noise just *loves* the Kloros."

Windham said hastily, "Let's not begin that. Look, Stuart, Porter and I have been discussing matters and we have decided that you know the Kloros well enough to think of some way of getting us back to Earth."

"It happens that you're wrong. I can't think of any way."

"Maybe there is some way we can take the ship back from the blasted green fellas," suggested Windham. "Some weakness they may have. Dash it, you know what I mean."

"Tell me, Colonel, what are you after? Your own skin or Earth's welfare?"

"I resent that question. I'll have you know that while I'm as careful of my own life as anyone has a right to be, I'm thinking of Earth primarily. And I think that's true of all of us."

"Damn right," said Porter, instantly. Leblanc looked anxious, Polyorketes resentful; and Mullen had no expression at all.

"Good," said Stuart. "Of course, I don't think we can take the ship. They're armed and we aren't. But there's this. You know why the Kloros took this ship intact. It's because they need ships. They may be better chemists than Earthmen are, but Earthmen are better astronautical engineers. We have bigger, better and more ships. In fact, if our crew had had a proper respect for military axioms in the first place, they would have blown the ship up as soon as it looked as though the Kloros were going to board."

Leblanc looked horrified. "And kill the passengers?"

"Why not? You heard what the good colonel said. Every one of us puts his own lousy little life after Earth's interests. What good are we to Earth alive right now? None at all. What harm will this ship do in Kloro hands? A hell of a lot, probably."

"Just why," asked Mullen, "did our men refuse to blow up the ship? They must have had a reason."

"They did. It's the firmest tradition of Earth's military men that there must never be an unfavorable ratio of casualties. If we had blown ourselves up, twenty fighting men and seven civilians of Earth would be dead as compared with an enemy casualty total of zero. So what happens? We let them board, kill twenty-eight—I'm sure we killed at least that many—and let them have the ship."

"Talk, talk, talk," jeered Polyorketes.

"There's a moral to this," said Stuart. "We can't take the ship away from the Kloros. We *might* be able to rush them, though, and keep them busy long enough to allow one of us enough time to short the engines."

"What?" yelled Porter, and Windham shushed him in fright.

"Short the engines," Stuart repeated. "That would destroy the ship, of course, which is what we want to do, isn't it?"

Leblanc's lips were white. "I don't think that would work."

"We can't be sure till we try. But what have we to lose by trying?"

"Our lives, damn it!" cried Porter. "You insane maniac, you're crazy."

"If I'm a maniac," said Stuart, "and insane to boot, then naturally I'm crazy. But just remember that if we lose our lives, which is overwhelmingly probable, we lose nothing of value to Earth; whereas if we destroy the ship, as we just barely might, we do Earth a lot of good. What patriot would hesitate? Who here would put himself ahead of his world?" He looked about in the silence. "Surely not you, Colonel Windham."

Windham coughed tremendously. "My dear man, that is not the question. There must be a way to save the ship for Earth *without* losing our lives, eh?"

"All right. You name it."

"Let's all think about it. Now there are only two of the Kloros aboard ship. If one of us could sneak up on them and—"

"How? The rest of the ship's all filled with chlorine. We'd have to wear a spacesuit. Gravity in their part of the ship is hopped up to Kloro level, so whoever is patsy in the deal would be clumping around, metal on metal, slow and heavy. Oh, he could sneak up on them, sure—like a skunk trying to sneak downwind."

"Then we'll drop it all," Porter's voice shook. "Listen, Windham, there's not going to be any destroying the ship. My life means plenty to me and if any of you try anything like that, I'll call the Kloros. I mean it."

"Well," said Stuart, "there's hero number one."

Leblanc said, "I want to go back to Earth, but I—"

Mullen interrupted, "I don't think our chances of destroying the ship are good enough unless—"

"Heroes number two and three. What about you, Polyorketes? You would have the chance of killing two Kloros."

"I want to kill them with my bare hands," growled the farmer, his heavy fists writhing. "On their planet, I will kill dozens."

"That's a nice safe promise for now. What about you, Colonel? Don't you want to march to death and glory with me?"

"Your attitude is very cynical and unbecoming, Stuart. It's obvious that if the rest are unwilling, then your plan will fall through."

"Unless I do it myself, huh?"

"You won't, do you hear?" said Porter, instantly.

"Damn right I won't," agreed Stuart. "I don't claim to be a hero. I'm just an average patriot, perfectly willing to head for any planet they take me to and sit out the war."

Mullen said, thoughtfully, "Of course, there *is* a way we could surprise the Kloros."

The statement would have dropped flat except for Polyorketes. He pointed a black-nailed, stubby forefinger and laughed harshly. "Mr. Bookkeeper!" he said. "Mr. Bookkeeper is a big shot talker like this damned greenie spy, Stuart. All right, Mr. Bookkeeper, go ahead. You make big speeches also. Let the words roll like an empty barrel."

He turned to Stuart and repeated venomously, "Empty barrel! Cripple-hand empty barrel. No good for anything but talk."

Mullen's soft voice could make no headway until Polyorketes was through, but then he said, speaking directly to Stuart, "We might be able to reach them from outside. This room has a C-chute I'm sure."

"What's a C-chute?" asked Leblanc.

"Well—" began Mullen, and then stopped, at a loss.

Stuart said, mockingly, "It's a euphemism, my boy. Its full name is 'casualty chute.' It doesn't get talked about, but the main rooms on any ship would have them. They're just little airlocks down which you slide a corpse. Burial at space. Always lots of sentiment and bowed heads, with the captain making a rolling speech of the type Polyorketes here wouldn't like."

Leblanc's face twisted. "Use *that* to leave the ship?"

"Why not? Superstitious? Go on, Mullen."

The little man had waited patiently. He said, "Once outside, one could re-enter the ship by the steam-tubes. It can be done—with luck. And then you would be an unexpected visitor in the control room."

Stuart stared at him curiously. "How do you figure this out? What do *you* know about steam-tubes?"

Mullen coughed. "You mean because I'm in the paper-box business? Well—" He grew pink, waited a moment, then made a new start in a colorless, unemotional voice. "My company, which manufactures fancy paper boxes and novelty containers, made a line of spaceship candy boxes for the juvenile trade some years ago. It was designed so that if a string were pulled, small pressure containers were punctured and jets of compressed air shot out through the mock steam-tubes, sailing the box across the room and scattering candy as it went. The sales theory was that the youngsters would find it exciting to play with the ship and fun to scramble for the candy.

"Actually, it was a complete failure. The ship would break dishes and sometimes hit another child in the eye. Worse still, the children would not only scramble for the candy but would fight over it. It was almost our worst failure. We lost thousands.

"Still, while the boxes were being designed, the entire office was extremely interested. It was like a game, very bad for efficiency and office morale. For a while, we all became steam-tube experts. I read quite a few books on ship construction. On my own time, however, not the company's."

Stuart was intrigued. He said, "You know it's a video sort of idea, but it might work if we had a hero to spare. Have we?"

"What about you?" demanded Porter, indignantly. "You go around sneering at us with your cheap wisecracks. I don't notice you volunteering for anything."

"That's because I'm no hero, Porter. I admit it. My object is to stay alive, and shimmying down steam-tubes is no way to go about staying alive. But the rest of you are noble patriots. The colonel says so. What about you, Colonel? You're the senior hero here."

Windham said, "If I were younger, blast it, and if you had your hands, I would take pleasure, sir, in trouncing you soundly."

"I've no doubt of it, but that's no answer."

"You know very well that at my time of life and with my leg—" he brought the flat of his hand down upon his stiff knee—"I am in no position to do anything of the sort, however much I should wish to."

"Ah, yes," said Stuart, "and I, myself, am crippled in the hands, as Polyorketes tells me. That saves us. And what unfortunate deformities do the rest of us have?"

"Listen," cried Porter, "I want to know what this is all about. How can anyone go down the steam-tubes? What if the Kloros use them while one of us is inside?"

"Why, Porter, that's part of the sporting chance. It's where the excitement comes in."

"But he'd be boiled in the shell like a lobster."

"A pretty image, but inaccurate. The steam wouldn't be on for more than a very short time, maybe a second or two, and the suit insulation would hold that long. Besides, the jet comes scooting out at several hundred miles a minute, so that you would be blown clear of the ship before the steam could even warm you. In fact, you'd be blown quite a few miles out into space, and after that you would be quite safe from the Kloros. Of course, you couldn't get back to the ship."

Porter was sweating freely. "You don't scare me for one minute, Stuart."

"I don't? Then you're offering to go? Are you sure you've thought out what being stranded in space means? You're all alone, you know; really all alone. The steam-jet will probably leave you turning or tumbling pretty rapidly. You won't feel that. You'll seem to be motionless. But all the stars will be going around and around so that they're just streaks in the sky. They won't ever stop. They won't even slow up. Then your heater will go off, your oxygen will give out, and you will die very slowly. You'll have lots of time to think. Or, if you are in a hurry, you could open your suit. That wouldn't be pleasant, either. I've seen faces of men who had a torn suit happen to them accidentally, and it's pretty awful. But it would be quicker. Then——''

Porter turned and walked unsteadily away.

Stuart said, lightly, "Another failure. One act of heroism still ready to be knocked down to the highest bidder with nothing offered yet."

Polyorketes spoke up and his harsh voice roughed the words. "You keep on talking, Mr. Big Mouth. You just keep banging that empty barrel. Pretty soon, we'll kick your teeth in. There's one boy I think would be willing to do it now, eh, Mr. Porter?"

Porter's look at Stuart confirmed the truth of Polyorketes' remarks, but he said nothing.

Stuart said, "Then what about you, Polyorketes? You're the bare-hand man with guts. Want me to help you into a suit?"

"I'll ask you when I want help."

"What about you, Leblanc?"

The young man shrank away.

"Not even to get back to Margaret?"

But Leblanc could only shake his head.

"Mullen?"

"Well—I'll try."

"You'll what?"

"I said, yes, I'll try. After all, it's my idea."

Stuart looked stunned. "You're serious? How come?"

Mullen's prim mouth pursed. "Because no one else will."

"But that's no reason. Especially for you."

Mullen shrugged.

There was a thump of a cane behind Stuart. Windham brushed past.

He said, "Do you really intend to go, Mullen?"

"Yes, Colonel."

"In that case, dash it, let me shake your hand. I like you. You're an—an Earthman, by heaven. Do this, and win or die, I'll bear witness for you."

Mullen withdrew his hand awkwardly from the deep and vibrating grasp of the other.

And Stuart just stood there. He was in a very unusual position. He was, in fact, in the particular position of *all* positions in which he most rarely found himself.

He had nothing to say.

The quality of tension had changed. The gloom and frustration had lifted a bit, and the excitement of conspiracy had replaced it. Even Polyorketes was fingering the spacesuits and commenting briefly and hoarsely on which he considered preferable.

Mullen was having a certain amount of trouble. The suit hung rather limply upon him even though the adjustable joints had been tightened nearly to minimum. He stood there now with only the helmet to be screwed on. He wiggled his neck.

Stuart was holding the helmet with an effort. It was heavy, and his artiplasmic hands did not grip it well. He said, "Better scratch your nose if it itches. It's your last chance for a while." He didn't add, "Maybe forever," but he thought it.

Mullen said, tonelessly, "I think perhaps I had better have a spare oxygen cylinder."

"Good enough."

"With a reducing value."

Stuart nodded. "I see what you're thinking of. If you do get blown clear of the ship, you could try to blow yourself back by using the cylinder as an action-reaction motor."

They clamped on the headpiece and buckled the spare cylinder to Mullen's waist. Polyorketes and Leblanc lifted him up to the yawning opening of the C-chute. It was ominously dark inside, the metal lining of the interior having been painted a mournful black. Stuart thought he could detect a musty odor about it, but that, he knew, was only imagination.

He stopped the proceedings when Mullen was half within the tube. He tapped upon the little man's faceplate.

"Can you hear me?"

Within, there was a nod.

"Air coming through all right? No last-minute troubles?"

Mullen lifted his armored arm in a gesture of reassurance.

"Then remember, don't use the suit-radio out there. The Kloros might pick up the signals."

Reluctantly, he stepped away. Polyorketes' brawny hands lowered Mullen until they could hear the thumping sound made by the steel-shod feet against the outer valve. The inner valve then swung shut with a dreadful finality, its beveled silicone gasket making a slight soughing noise as it crushed hard. They clamped it into place.

Stuart stood at the toggle-switch that controlled the outer valve. He threw it and the gauge that marked the air pressure within the tube fell to zero. A little pinpoint of red light warned that the outer valve was open. Then the light disappeared, the valve closed, and the gauge climbed slowly to fifteen pounds again.

They opened the inner valve again and found the tube empty.

Polyorketes spoke first. He said, "The little son-of-a-gun. He went!" He looked wonderingly at the others. "A little fellow with guts like that."

Stuart said, "Look, we'd better get ready in here. There's just a chance that the Kloros may have detected the valves opening and closing. If so, they'll be here to investigate and we'll have to cover up."

"How?" asked Windham.

"They won't see Mullen anywhere around. We'll say he's in the head. The Kloros know that it's one of the peculiar characteristics of Earthmen that they resent intrusion on their privacy in lavatories, and they'll make no effort to check. If we can hold them off—"

"What if they wait, or if they check the spacesuits?" asked Porter.

Stuart shrugged, "Let's hope they don't. And listen, Polyorketes, don't make any fuss when they come in."

Polyorketes grunted, "With that little guy out there? What do you think I am?" He stared at Stuart without animosity, then scratched his curly hair vigorously. "You know, I laughed at him. I thought he was an old woman. It makes me ashamed."

Stuart cleared his throat. He said, "Look, I've been saying some things that maybe weren't too funny after all, now that I come to think of it. I'd like to say I'm sorry if I have."

He turned away morosely and walked toward his cot. He heard the steps behind him, felt the touch on his sleeve. He turned; it was Leblanc.

The youngster said softly, "I keep thinking that Mr. Mullen is an old man."

"Well, he's not a kid. He's about forty-five or fifty, I think."

Leblanc said, "Do you think, Mr. Stuart, that *I* should have gone, instead? I'm the youngest here. I don't like the thought of having let an old man go in my place. It makes me feel like the devil."

"I know. If he dies, it will be too bad."

"But he volunteered. We didn't make him, did we?"

"Don't try to dodge responsibility, Leblanc. It won't make you feel better. There isn't one of us without a stronger motive to run the risk than he had." And Stuart sat there silently, thinking.

Mullen felt the obstruction beneath his feet yield and the walls about him slip away quickly, too quickly. He knew it was the puff of air escaping, carrying him with it, and he dug arms and legs frantically against the wall to brake himself. Corpses were supposed to be flung well clear of the ship, but he was no corpse—for the moment.

His feet swung free and threshed. He heard the *clunk* of one magnetic boot against the hull just as the rest of his body puffed out like a tight cork under air pressure. He teetered dangerously at the lip of the hole in the ship—he had changed orientation suddenly and was looking down on it—then took a step backward as its lid came down of itself and fitted smoothly against the hull.

A feeling of unreality overwhelmed him. Surely, it wasn't he standing on the outer surface of a ship. Not Randolph F. Mullen. So few human beings could ever say they had, even those who traveled in space constantly.

He was only gradually aware that he was in pain. Popping out of that hole with one foot clamped to the hull had nearly bent him in two. He tried moving, cautiously, and found his motions to be erratic and almost impossible to control. He *thought* nothing was broken, though the muscles of his left side were badly wrenched.

And then he came to himself and noticed that the wristlights of his suit were on. It was by their light that he had stared into the blackness of the C-chute. He stirred with the nervous thought that from within, the Kloros might see the twin spots of moving light just outside the hull. He flicked the switch upon the suit's midsection.

Mullen had never imagined that, standing on a ship, he would fail to see its hull. But it was dark, as dark below as above. There were the stars, hard and bright little nondimensional dots. Nothing more. Nothing more anywhere. Under his feet, not even the stars—*not even to his feet.*

He bent back to look at the stars. His head swam. They were moving slowly. Or, rather, they were standing still and the ship was rotating, but he could not tell his eyes that. *They* moved. His eyes followed—down and behind the ship. New stars up and above from the other side. A black horizon. The ship existed only as a region where there were no stars.

No stars? Why, there was one almost at his feet. He nearly reached for it; then he realized that it was only a glittering reflection in the mirroring metal.

They were moving thousands of miles an hour. The stars were. The ship was. He was. But it meant nothing. To his senses, there was only silence and darkness and that slow wheeling of the stars. His eyes followed the wheeling—

And his head in its helmet hit the ship's hull with a soft bell-like ring.

He felt about in panic with his thick, insensitive, spunsilicate gloves. His feet were still firmly magnetized to the hull, that was true, but the rest of his body was bent backward at the knees in a right angle. There was no gravity outside the ship. If he bent back, there was nothing to pull the upper part of his body down and tell his joints they were bending. His body stayed as he put it.

He pressed wildly against the hull and his torso shot upward and refused to stop when upright. He fell forward.

He tried more slowly, balancing with both hands against the hull, until he squatted evenly. Then upward. Very slowly. Straight up. Arms out to balance.

He was straight now, aware of his nausea and light-headedness.

He looked about. My God, where were the steam-tubes? He couldn't see them. They were black on black, nothing on nothing.

Quickly, he turned on the wrist-lights. In space, there were no beams, only elliptical, sharply defined spots of blue steel, winking light back at him. Where they struck a rivet, a shadow was cast, knife-sharp and as black as space, the lighted region illuminated abruptly and without diffusion.

He moved his arms, his body swaying gently in the opposite direction; action and reaction. The vision of a steam-tube with its smooth cylindrical sides sprang at him.

He tried to move toward it. His foot held firmly to the hull. He pulled and it slogged upward, straining against quicksand that eased quickly. Three inches up and it had almost sucked free; six inches up and he thought it would fly away.

He advanced it and let it down, felt it enter the quicksand. When the sole was within two inches of the hull, it snapped down; out of control, hitting the hull ringingly. His spacesuit carried the vibrations, amplifying them in his ears.

He stopped in absolute terror. The dehydrators that dried the atmosphere within his suit could not handle the sudden gush of perspiration that drenched his forehead and armpits.

He waited, then tried lifting his foot again—a bare inch, holding it there by main force and moving it horizontally. Horizontal motion involved no effort at all; it was motion perpendicular to the lines of magnetic force. But he had to keep the foot from snapping down as he did so, and then lower it slowly.

He puffed with the effort. Each step was agony. The tendons of his knees were cracking, and there were knives in his side.

Mullen stopped to let the perspiration dry. It wouldn't do to steam up the inside of his faceplate. He flashed his wristlights, and the steam-cylinder was right ahead.

The ship had four of them, at ninety degree intervals, thrusting out at an angle from the midgirdle. They were the "fine adjustment" of the ship's course. The coarse adjustment was the powerful thrusters back and front which fixed final velocity by their accelerative and the decelerative force, and the hyperatomics that took care of the space-swallowing Jumps.

But occasionally the direction of flight had to be adjusted slightly and then the steam-cylinders took over. Singly, they could drive the ship up, down, right, left. By twos, in appropriate ratios of thrust, the ship could be turned in any desired direction.

The device had been unimproved in centuries, being too simple to improve. The atomic pile heated the water content of a closed container into steam, driving it, in less than a second, up to temperatures where it would have broken down into a mixture of hydrogen and oxygen, and then into a mixture of electrons and ions. Perhaps the breakdown actually took place. No one ever bothered testing; it worked, so there was no need to.

At the critical point, a needle valve gave way and the steam thrust madly out in a short but incredible blast. And the ship, inevitably and majestically, moved in the opposite direction, veering about its own center of gravity. When the degrees of turn were sufficient, an equal and opposite blast would take place and the turning would be canceled. The ship would be moving at its original velocity, but in a new direction.

Mullen had dragged himself out to the lip of the steam-cylinder. He had a picture of himself—a small speck teetering at the extreme end of a structure thrusting out of an ovoid that was tearing through space at ten thousand miles an hour.

But there was no air-stream to whip him off the hull, and his magnetic soles held him more firmly than he liked.

With lights on, he bent down to peer into the tube and the ship dropped down precipitously as his orientation changed. He reached out to steady himself, but he was not falling. There was no up or down in space except for what his confused mind chose to consider up or down.

The cylinder was just large enough to hold a man, so that it might be entered for repair purposes. His light caught the rungs almost directly opposite his position at the lip. He puffed a sigh of relief with what breath he could muster. Some ships didn't have ladders.

He made his way to it, the ship appearing to slip and twist beneath him as he moved. He lifted an arm over the lip of the tube, feeling for the rung, loosened each foot, and drew himself within.

The knot in his stomach that had been there from the first was a convulsed agony now. If they should choose to manipulate the ship, if the steam should whistle out now—

He would never hear it; never know it. One instant he would be holding a rung, feeling slowly for the next with a groping arm. The next moment he would be alone in space, the ship a dark, dark nothingness lost forever among the stars. There would be, perhaps, a brief glory of swirling ice crystals drifting with him, shining in his wrist-lights and slowly approaching and rotating about him, attracted by his mass like infinitesimal planets to an absurdly tiny Sun.

He was trickling sweat again, and now he was also conscious of thirst. He put it out of his mind. There would be no drinking until he was out of his suit—if ever.

Up a rung; up another; and another. How many were there? His hand slipped and he stared in disbelief at the glitter that showed under his light.

Ice?

Why not? The steam, incredibly hot as it was, would strike metal that was at nearly absolute zero. In the few split-seconds of thrust, there would not be time for the metal to warm above the freezing point of water. A sheet of ice would condense that would sublime slowly into the vacuum. It was the speed of all that happened that prevented the fusion of the tubes and of the original water-container itself.

His groping hand reached the end. Again the wrist-lights. He stared with crawling horror at the steam nozzle, half an inch in diameter. It looked dead, harmless. But it always would, right up to the micro-second before—

Around it was the outer steam lock. It pivoted on a central hub that was springed on the portion toward space, screwed on the part toward the ship. The springs allowed it to give under the first wild thrust of steam pressure before the ship's mighty inertia could be overcome. The steam was bled into the inner chamber, breaking the force of the thrust, leaving the total energy unchanged, but spreading it over time so that the hull itself was in that much less danger of being staved in.

Mullen braced himself firmly against a rung and pressed against the outer lock so that it gave a little. It was stiff, but it didn't have to give much, just enough to catch on the screw. He felt it catch.

He strained against it and turned it, feeling his body twist in the opposite direction. It held tight, the screw taking up the strain as he carefully adjusted the small control switch that allowed the springs to fall free. How well he remembered the books he had read!

He was in the interlock space now, which was large enough to hold a man comfortably, again for convenience in repairs. He could no longer be blown away from the ship. If the steam blast were turned on now, it would merely drive him against the inner lock—hard enough to crush him to a pulp. A quick death he would never feel, at least.

Slowly, he unhooked his spare oxygen cylinder. There was only an inner lock between himself and the control room now. This lock opened outward into space so that the steam blast could only close it tighter, rather than blow it open. And it fitted tightly and smoothly. There was absolutely no way to open it from without.

He lifted himself above the lock, forcing his bent back against the inner surface of the interlock area. It made breathing difficult. The spare oxygen cylinder dangled at a queer angle. He held its metal-mesh hose and straightened it, forcing it against the inner lock so that vibration thudded. Again—again—

It would *have* to attract the attention of the Kloros. They would *have* to investigate.

He would have no way of telling when they were about to do so. Ordinarily, they would first let air into the interlock to force the outer lock shut. But now the outer lock was on the central screw, well away from its rim. Air would suck about it ineffectually, dragging out into space.

Mullen kept on thumping. Would the Kloros look at the airgauge, note that it scarcely lifted from zero, or would they take its proper working for granted?

Porter said, "He's been gone an hour and a half."

"I know," said Stuart.

They were all restless, jumpy, but the tension among themselves had disappeared. It was as though all the threads of emotion extended to the hull of the ship.

Porter was bothered. His philosophy of life had always been simple—take care of yourself because no one will take care of you for you. It upset him to see it shaken.

He said, "Do you suppose they've caught him?"

"If they had, we'd hear about it," replied Stuart, briefly.

Porter felt, with a miserable twinge, that there was little interest on the part of the others in speaking to him. He could understand it; he had not exactly earned their respect. For the moment, a torrent of self-excuse poured through his mind. The others had been frightened, too. A man had a right to be afraid. No one likes to die. At least, he hadn't broken like Aristides Polyorketes. He hadn't wept like Leblanc. He—

But there was Mullen, out there on the hull.

"Listen," he cried, "why did he do it?" They turned to look at him, not understanding, but Porter didn't care. It bothered him to the point where it had to come out. "I want to know why Mullen is risking his life."

"The man," said Windham, "is a patriot—"

"No, none of that!" Porter was almost hysterical. "That little fellow had no emotion at all. He just has reasons and I want to know what those reasons are, because—"

He didn't finish the sentence. Could he say that if those reasons applied to a little middle-aged bookkeeper, they might apply even more forcibly to himself?

Polyorketes said, "He's one brave damn little fellow."

Porter got to his feet. "Listen," he said, "he may be stuck out there. Whatever he's doing, he may not be able to finish it alone. I—I volunteer to go out after him."

He was shaking as he said it and he waited in fear for the sarcastic lash of Stuart's tongue. Stuart was staring at him, probably with surprise, but Porter dared not meet his eyes to make certain.

Stuart said, mildly, "Let's give him another half-hour."

Porter looked up, startled. There was no sneer on Stuart's face. It was even friendly. They *all* looked friendly.

He said, "And then—"

"And then all those who volunteer will draw straws or something equally democratic. Who volunteers, besides Porter?"

They all raised their hands; Stuart did, too.

But Porter was happy. He had volunteered first. He was anxious for the half-hour to pass.

It caught Mullen by surprise. The outer lock flew open and the long, thin, snakelike, almost headless neck of a Kloro sucked out, unable to fight the blast of escaping air.

Mullen's cylinder flew away, almost tore free. After one wild moment of frozen panic, he fought for it, dragging it above the airstream, waiting as long as he dared to let the first fury die down as the air of the control room thinned out, then bringing it down with force.

It caught the sinewy neck squarely, crushing it. Mullen, curled above the lock, almost entirely protected from the stream, raised the cylinder again and plunging it down again striking the head, mashing the staring eyes to liquid ruin. In the near-vacuum, green blood was pumping out of what was left of the neck.

Mullen dared not vomit, but he wanted to.

With eyes averted, he backed away, caught the outer lock with one hand and imparted a whirl. For several seconds, it maintained that whirl. At the end of the screw, the springs engaged automatically and pulled it shut. What was left of the atmosphere tightened it and the laboring pumps could now begin to fill the control room once again.

Mullen crawled over the mangled Kloro and into the room. It was empty.

He had barely time to notice that when he found himself on his knees. He rose with difficulty. The transition from nongravity to gravity had taken him entirely by surprise. It was Klorian gravity, too, which meant that with this suit, he carried a fifty percent overload for his small frame. At least, though, his heavy metal clogs no longer clung so exasperatingly to the metal underneath. Within the ship, floors and wall were of cork-covered aluminum alloy.

He circled slowly. The neckless Kloro had collapsed and lay with only an occasional twitch to show it had once been a living organism. He stepped over it, distastefully, and drew the steam-tube lock shut.

The room had a depressing bilious cast and the lights shone yellow-green. It was the Kloro atmosphere, of course.

Mullen felt a twinge of surprise and reluctant admiration. The Kloros obviously had some way of treating materials so that they were impervious to the oxidizing effect of chlorine. Even the map of Earth on the wall, printed on glossy plastic-backed paper, seemed fresh and untouched. He approached, drawn by the familiar outlines of the continents—

There was a flash of motion caught in the corner of his eyes. As quickly as he could in his heavy suit, he turned, then screamed. The Kloro he had thought dead was rising to its feet.

Its neck hung limp, an oozing mass of tissue mash, but its arms reached out blindly, and the tentacles about its chest vibrated rapidly like innumerable snakes' tongues.

It was blind, of course. The destruction of its neck-stalk had deprived it of all sensory equipment, and partial asphyxiation had disorganized it. But the brain remained whole and safe in the abdomen. It still lived.

Mullen backed away. He circled, trying clumsily and unsuccessfully to tiptoe, though he knew that what was left of the Kloro was also deaf. It blundered on its way, struck a wall, felt to the base and began sidling along it.

Mullen cast about desperately for a weapon, found nothing. There was the Kloro's holster, but he dared not reach for it. Why hadn't he snatched it at the very first? Fool!

The door to the control room opened. It made almost no noise. Mullen turned, quivering.

The other Kloro entered, unharmed, entire. It stood in the doorway for a moment, chest-tendrils stiff and unmoving; its neck-stalk stretched forward; its horrible eyes flickering first at him and then at its nearly dead comrade.

And then its hand moved quickly to its side.

Mullen, without awareness, moved as quickly in pure reflex. He stretched out the hose of the spare oxygen-cylinder, which, since entering the control room, he had replaced in its suit-clamp, and cracked the valve. He didn't bother reducing the pressure. He let it gash out unchecked so that he nearly staggered under the backward push.

He could *see* the oxygen stream. It was a pale puff, billowing out amid the chlorine-green. It caught the Kloro with one hand on the weapon's holster.

The Kloro threw its hands up. The little beak on its head-nodule opened alarmingly but noiselessly. It staggered and fell, writhed for a moment, then lay still. Mullen approached and played the oxygen-stream upon its body as though he were extinguishing a fire. And then he raised his heavy foot and brought it down upon the center of the neck-stalk and crushed it on the floor.

He turned to the first. It was sprawled, rigid.

The whole room was pale with oxygen, enough to kill whole legions of Kloros, and his cylinder was empty.

Mullen stepped over the dead Kloro, out of the control room and along the main corridor toward the prisoners' room.

Reaction had set in. He was whimpering in blind, incoherent fright.

Stuart was tired. False hands and all, he was at the controls of a ship once again. Two light cruisers of Earth were on the way. For better than twenty-four hours he had handled the controls virtually alone. He had discarded the chlorinating equipment, rerigged the old atmospherics, located the ship's position in space, tried to plot a course, and sent out carefully guarded signals—which had worked.

So when the door of the control room opened, he was a little annoyed. He was too tired to play conversational handball. Then he turned, and it was Mullen stepping inside.

Stuart said, "For God's sake, get back into bed, Mullen!"

Mullen said, "I'm tired of sleeping, even though I never thought I would be a while ago."

"How do you feel?"

"I'm stiff all over. Especially my side." He grimaced and stared involuntarily around.

"Don't look for the Kloros," Stuart said. "We dumped the poor devils." He shook his head. "I was sorry for them. To themselves, *they're* the human beings, you know, and *we're* the aliens. Not that I'd rather they'd killed you, you understand."

"I understand."

Stuart turned a sidelong glance upon the little man who sat looking at the map of Earth and went on, "I owe you a particular and personal apology, Mullen. I didn't think much of you."

"It was your privilege," said Mullen in his dry voice. There was no feeling in it.

"No, it wasn't. It is no one's privilege to despise another. It is only a hard-won right after long experience."

"Have you been thinking about this?"

"Yes, all day. Maybe I can't explain. It's these hands." He held them up before him, spread out. "It was hard knowing that other people had hands of their own. I had to hate them for it. I always had to do my best to investigate and belittle their motives, point up their deficiencies, expose their stupidities. I had to do anything that would prove to myself that they weren't worth envying."

Mullen moved restlessly. "This explanation is not necessary."

"It is. It is!" Stuart felt his thoughts intently, strained to put them into words. "For years I've abandoned hope of finding any decency in human beings. Then you climbed into the C-chute."

"You had better understand," said Mullen, "that I was motivated by practical and selfish considerations. I will not have you present me to myself as a hero."

"I wasn't intending to. I know that you would do nothing without a reason. It was what your action did to the rest of us. It turned a collection of phonies and fools into decent people. And not by magic either. They were decent all along. It was just that they needed something to live up to and you supplied it. And— I'm one of them. I'll have to live up to you, too. For the rest of my life, probably."

Mullen turned away uncomfortably. His hand straightened his sleeves, which were not in the least twisted. His finger rested on the map.

He said, "I was born in Richmond, Virginia, you know. Here it is. I'll be going there first. Where were you born?"

"Toronto," said Stuart.

"That's right here. Not very far apart on the map, is it?"

Stuart said, "Would you tell me something?"

"If I can."

"Just why *did* you go out there?"

Mullen's precise mouth pursed. He said, dryly, "Wouldn't my rather prosaic reason ruin the inspirational effect?"

"Call it intellectual curiosity. Each of the rest of us had such obvious motives. Porter was scared to death of being interned; Leblanc wanted to get back to his sweetheart; Polyorketes wanted to kill Kloros; and Windham was a patriot according to his lights. As for me, I thought of myself as a noble idealist, I'm afraid. Yet in none of us was the motivation strong enough to get us into a spacesuit and out the C-chute. Then what made *you* do it, *you,* of all people?"

"Why the phrase, 'of all people'?"

"Don't be offended, but you seem devoid of all emotion."

"Do I?" Mullen's voice did not change. It remained precise and soft, yet somehow a tightness had entered it. "That's only training, Mr. Stuart, and self-discipline; not nature. A small man can have no respectable emotions. Is there anything more ridiculous than a man like myself in a state of rage? I'm five feet and one-half inch tall, and one hundred and two pounds in weight, if you care for exact figures. I insist on the half inch and the two pounds.

"Can I be dignified? Proud? Draw myself to my full height without inducing laughter? Where can I meet a woman who will not dismiss me instantly with a giggle? Naturally, I've had to learn to dispense with external display of emotion.

"*You* talk about deformities. No one would notice your hands or know they were different, if you weren't so eager to tell people all about it the instant you meet them. Do you think that the eight inches of height I do not have can be hidden? That it is not the first and, in most cases, the only thing about me that a person will notice?"

Stuart was ashamed. He had invaded a privacy he ought not have. He said, "I'm sorry."

"Why?"

"I should not have forced you to speak of this. I should have seen for myself that you—that you—"

"That I what? Tried to prove myself? Tried to show that while I might be small in body, I held within it a giant heart?"

"I would not have put it mockingly."

"Why not? It's a foolish idea, and nothing like it is the reason I did what I did.

What would I have accomplished if that's what was in my mind? Will they take me to Earth now and put me up before the television cameras—pitching them low, of course, to catch my face, or standing me on a chair—and pin medals on me?''

"They are quite likely to do exactly that."

"And what good would it do me? They would say, 'Gee, and he's such a little guy.' And afterward, what? Shall I tell each man I meet, 'You know, I'm the fellow they decorated for incredible valor last month?' How many medals, Mr. Stuart, do you suppose it would take to put eight inches and sixty pounds on me?''

Stuart said, "Put that way, I see your point."

Mullen was speaking a trifle more quickly now; a controlled heat had entered his words, warming them to just a tepid room temperature. "There *were* days when I thought I would show them, the mysterious 'them' that includes all the world. I was going to leave Earth and carve out worlds for myself. I would be a new and even smaller Napoleon. So I left Earth and went to Arcturus. And what could I do on Arcturus that I could not have done on Earth? Nothing. I balance books. So I am past the vanity, Mr. Stuart, of trying to stand on tiptoe."

"Then why *did* you do it?"

"I left Earth when I was twenty-eight and came to the Arcturian System. I've been there ever since. This trip was to be my first vacation, my first visit back to Earth in all that time. I was going to stay on Earth for six months. The Kloros instead captured us and would have kept us interned indefinitely. But I couldn't—I *couldn't* let them stop me from traveling to Earth. No matter what the risk, I had to prevent their interference. It wasn't love of woman, or fear or hate, or idealism of any sort. It was stronger than any of those."

He stopped, and stretched out a hand as though to caress the map on the wall.

"Mr. Stuart," Mullen asked quietly, "haven't you ever been homesick?"

THE DEAD PAST

ARNOLD POTTERLEY, PH.D., was a Professor of Ancient History. That, in itself, was not dangerous. What changed the world beyond all dreams was the fact that he *looked* like a Professor of Ancient History.

Thaddeus Araman, Department Head of the Division of Chronoscopy, might have taken proper action if Dr. Potterley had been owner of a large, square chin, flashing eyes, aquiline nose and broad shoulders.

As it was, Thaddeus Araman found himself staring over his desk at a mild-mannered individual, whose faded blue eyes looked at him wistfully from either side of a low-bridged button nose; whose small, neatly dressed figure seemed stamped "milk-and-water" from thinning brown hair to the neatly brushed shoes that completed a conservative middle-class costume.

Araman said pleasantly, "And now what can I do for you, Dr. Potterley?"

Dr. Potterley said in a soft voice that went well with the rest of him, "Mr. Araman, I came to you because you're top man in chronoscopy."

Araman smiled. "Not exactly. Above me is the World Commissioner of Research and above him is the Secretary-General of the United Nations. And above both of them, of course, are the sovereign peoples of Earth."

Dr. Potterley shook his head. "They're not interested in chronoscopy. I've come to you, sir, because for two years I have been trying to obtain permission to do some time viewing—chronoscopy, that is—in connection with my researches on ancient Carthage. I can't obtain such permission. My research grants are all proper. There is no irregularity in any of my intellectual endeavors and yet—"

"I'm sure there is no question of irregularity," said Araman soothingly. He flipped the thin reproduction sheets in the folder to which Potterley's name had been attached. They had been produced by Multivac, whose vast analogical mind kept all the department records. When this was over, the sheets could be destroyed, then reproduced on demand in a matter of minutes.

And while Araman turned the pages, Dr. Potterley's voice continued in a soft monotone.

The historian was saying, "I must explain that my problem is quite an important one. Carthage was ancient commercialism brought to its zenith. Pre-Roman Carthage was the nearest ancient analogue to pre-atomic America, at least insofar as its attachment to trade, commerce and business in general was

197

concerned. They were the most daring seamen and explorers before the Vikings; much better at it than the overrated Greeks.

"To know Carthage would be very rewarding, yet the only knowledge we have of it is derived from the writings of its bitter enemies, the Greeks and Romans. Carthage itself never wrote in its own defense or, if it did, the books did not survive. As a result, the Carthaginians have been one of the favorite sets of villains of history and perhaps unjustly so. Time viewing may set the record straight."

He said much more.

Araman said, still turning the reproduction sheets before him, "You must realize, Dr. Potterley, that chronoscopy, or time viewing, if you prefer, is a difficult process."

Dr. Potterley, who had been interrupted, frowned and said, "I am asking for only certain selected views at times and places I would indicate."

Araman sighed. "Even a few views, even one . . . It is an unbelievably delicate art. There is the question of focus, getting the proper scene in view and holding it. There is the synchronization of sound, which calls for completely independent circuits."

"Surely my problem is important enough to justify considerable effort."

"Yes, sir. Undoubtedly," said Araman at once. To deny the importance of someone's research problem would be unforgivably bad manners. "But you must understand how long-drawn-out even the simplest view is. And there is a long waiting line for the chronoscope and an even longer waiting line for the use of Multivac which guides us in our use of the controls."

Potterley stirred unhappily. "But can nothing be done? For two years—"

"A matter of priority, sir. I'm sorry. . . . Cigarette?"

The historian started back at the suggestion, eyes suddenly widening as he stared at the pack thrust out toward him. Araman looked surprised, withdrew the pack, made a motion as though to take a cigarette for himself and thought better of it.

Potterley drew a sigh of unfeigned relief as the pack was put out of sight. He said, "Is there any way of reviewing matters, putting me as far forward as possible. I don't know how to explain—"

Araman smiled. Some had offered money under similar circumstances which, of course, had gotten them nowhere, either. He said, "The decisions on priority are computer-processed. I could in no way alter those decisions arbitrarily."

Potterley rose stiffly to his feet. He stood five and a half feet tall. "Then, good day, sir."

"Good day, Dr. Potterley. And my sincerest regrets."

He offered his hand and Potterley touched it briefly.

The historian left, and a touch of the buzzer brought Araman's secretary into the room. He handed her the folder.

"These," he said, "may be disposed of."

Alone again, he smiled bitterly. Another item in his quarter-century's service to the human race. Service through negation.

At least this fellow had been easy to dispose of. Sometimes academic pressure had to be applied and even withdrawal of grants.

Five minutes later, he had forgotten Dr. Potterley. Nor, thinking back on it later, could he remember feeling any premonition of danger.

During the first year of his frustration, Arnold Potterley had experienced only that—frustration. During the second year, though, his frustration gave birth to an idea that first frightened and then fascinated him. Two things stopped him from trying to translate the idea into action, and neither barrier was the undoubted fact that his notion was a grossly unethical one.

The first was merely the continuing hope that the government would finally give its permission and make it unnecessary for him to do anything more. That hope had perished finally in the interview with Araman just completed.

The second barrier had been not a hope at all but a dreary realization of his own incapacity. He was not a physicist and he knew no physicists from whom he might obtain help. The Department of Physics at the university consisted of men well stocked with grants and well immersed in specialty. At best, they would not listen to him. At worst, they would report him for intellectual anarchy and even his basic Carthaginian grant might easily be withdrawn.

That he could not risk. And yet chronoscopy was the only way to carry on his work. Without it, he would be no worse off if his grant were lost.

The first hint that the second barrier might be overcome had come a week earlier than his interview with Araman, and it had gone unrecognized at the time. It had been at one of the faculty teas. Potterley attended these sessions unfailingly because he conceived attendance to be a duty, and he took his duties seriously. Once there, however, he conceived it to be no responsibility of his to make light conversation or new friends. He sipped abstemiously at a drink or two, exchanged a polite word with the dean or such department heads as happened to be present, bestowed a narrow smile on others and finally left early.

Ordinarily, he would have paid no attention, at that most recent tea, to a young man standing quietly, even diffidently, in one corner. He would never have dreamed of speaking to him. Yet a tangle of circumstance persuaded him this once to behave in a way contrary to his nature.

That morning at breakfast, Mrs. Potterley had announced somberly that once again she had dreamed of Laurel; but this time a Laurel grown up, yet retaining the three-year-old face that stamped her as their child. Potterley had let her talk. There had been a time when he fought her too frequent preoccupation with the past and death. Laurel would not come back to them, either through dreams or through talk. Yet if it appeased Caroline Potterley—let her dream and talk.

But when Potterley went to school that morning, he found himself for once affected by Caroline's inanities. Laurel grown up! She had died nearly twenty years ago; their only child, then and ever. In all that time, when he thought of her, it was as a three-year-old.

Now he thought: But if she were alive now, she wouldn't be three, she'd be nearly twenty-three.

Helplessly, he found himself trying to think of Laurel as growing progressively older; as finally becoming twenty-three. He did not quite succeed.

Yet he tried. Laurel using make-up. Laurel going out with boys. Laurel—getting married!

So it was that when he saw the young man hovering at the outskirts of the coldly circulating group of faculty men, it occurred to him quixotically that, for all he knew, a youngster just such as this might have married Laurel. That youngster himself, perhaps. . . .

Laurel might have met him, here at the university, or some evening when he might be invited to dinner at the Potterleys'. They might grow interested in one another. Laurel would surely have been pretty and this youngster looked well. He was dark in coloring, with a lean intent face and an easy carriage.

The tenuous daydream snapped, yet Potterley found himself staring foolishly at the young man, not as a strange face but as a possible son-in-law in the might-have-been. He found himself threading his way toward the man. It was almost a form of autohypnotism.

He put out his hand. "I am Arnold Potterley of the History Department. You're new here, I think?"

The youngster looked faintly astonished and fumbled with his drink, shifting it to his left hand in order to shake with his right. "Jonas Foster is my name, sir. I'm a new instructor in physics. I'm just starting this semester."

Potterley nodded. "I wish you a happy stay here and great success."

That was the end of it, then. Potterley had come uneasily to his senses, found himself embarrassed and moved off. He stared back over his shoulder once, but the illusion of relationship had gone. Reality was quite real once more and he was angry with himself for having fallen prey to his wife's foolish talk about Laurel.

But a week later, even while Araman was talking, the thought of that young man had come back to him. An instructor in physics. A new instructor. Had he been deaf at the time? Was there a short circuit between ear and brain? Or was it an automatic self-censorship because of the impending interview with the Head of Chronoscopy?

But the interview failed, and it was the thought of the young man with whom he had exchanged two sentences that prevented Potterley from elaborating his pleas for consideration. He was almost anxious to get away.

And in the autogiro express back to the university, he could almost wish he were superstitious. He could then console himself with the thought that the casual meaningless meeting had really been directed by a knowing and purposeful Fate.

Jonas Foster was not new to academic life. The long and rickety struggle for the doctorate would make anyone a veteran. Additional work as a postdoctorate teaching fellow acted as a booster shot.

But now he was Instructor Jonas Foster. Professorial dignity lay ahead. And he now found himself in a new sort of relationship toward other professors.

For one thing, they would be voting on future promotions. For another, he was in no position to tell so early in the game which particular member of the faculty might or might not have the ear of the dean or even of the university president. He did not fancy himself as a campus politician and was sure he would make a poor one, yet there was no point in kicking his own rear into blisters just to prove that to himself.

So Foster listened to this mild-mannered historian who, in some vague way, seemed nevertheless to radiate tension, and did not shut him up abruptly and toss him out. Certainly that was his first impulse.

He remembered Potterley well enough. Potterley had approached him at that tea (which had been a grizzly affair). The fellow had spoken two sentences to him stiffly, somehow glassy-eyed, had then come to himself with a visible start and hurried off.

It had amused Foster at the time, but now . . .

Potterley might have been deliberately trying to make his acquaintance, or, rather, to impress his own personality on Foster as that of a queer sort of duck, eccentric but harmless. He might now be probing Foster's views, searching for unsettling opinions. Surely, they ought to have done so before granting him his appointment. Still . . .

Potterley might be serious, might honestly not realize what he was doing. Or he might realize quite well what he was doing; he might be nothing more or less than a dangerous rascal.

Foster mumbled, "Well, now—" to gain time, and fished out a package of cigarettes, intending to offer one to Potterley and to light it and one for himself very slowly.

But Potterley said at once, "Please, Dr. Foster. No cigarettes."

Foster looked startled. "I'm sorry, sir."

"No. The regrets are mine. I cannot stand the odor. An idiosyncrasy. I'm sorry."

He was positively pale. Foster put away the cigarettes.

Foster, feeling the absence of the cigarette, took the easy way out. "I'm flattered that you ask my advice and all that, Dr. Potterley, but I'm not a neutrinics man. I can't very well do anything professional in that direction. Even stating an opinion would be out of line, and frankly, I'd prefer that you didn't go into any particulars."

The historian's prim face set hard. "What do you mean, you're not a neutrinics man? You're not anything yet. You haven't received any grant, have you?"

"This is only my first semester."

"I know that. I imagine you haven't even applied for any grant yet."

Foster half-smiled. In three months at the university, he had not succeeded in putting his initial requests for research grants into good enough shape to pass on to a professional science writer, let alone to the Research Commission.

(His Department Head, fortunately, took it quite well. "Take your time now, Foster," he said, "and get your thoughts well organized. Make sure you know your path and where it will lead, for, once you receive a grant, your specialization will be formally recognized and, for better or for worse, it will be yours for the rest of your career." The advice was trite enough, but triteness has often the merit of truth, and Foster recognized that.)

Foster said, "By education and inclination, Dr. Potterley, I'm a hyperoptics man with a gravitics minor. It's how I described myself in applying for this position. It may not be my official specialization yet, but it's going to be. It can't be anything else. As for neutrinics, I never even studied the subject."

"Why not?" demanded Potterley at once.

Foster stared. It was the kind of rude curiosity about another man's professional status that was always irritating. He said, with the edge of his own politeness just a trifle blunted, "A course in neutrinics wasn't given at my university."

"Good Lord, where did you go?"

"M.I.T.," said Foster quietly.

"And they don't teach neutrinics?"

"No, they don't." Foster felt himself flush and was moved to a defense. "It's a highly specialized subject with no great value. Chronoscopy, perhaps, has some value, but it is the only practical application and that's a dead end."

The historian stared at him earnestly. "Tell me this. Do you know where I can find a neutrinics man?"

"No, I don't," said Foster bluntly.

"Well, then, do you know a school which teaches neutrinics?"

"No, I don't."

Potterley smiled tightly and without humor.

Foster resented that smile, found he detected insult in it and grew sufficiently annoyed to say, "I would like to point out, sir, that you're stepping out of line."

"What?"

"I'm saying that, as a historian, your interest in any sort of physics, your *professional* interest, is———" He paused, unable to bring himself quite to say the word.

"Unethical?"

"That's the word, Dr. Potterley."

"My researches have driven me to it," said Potterley in an intense whisper.

"The Research Commission is the place to go. If they permit———"

"I have gone to them and have received no satisfaction."

"Then obviously you must abandon this." Foster knew he was sounding stiffly virtuous, but he wasn't going to let this man lure him into an expression of intellectual anarchy. It was too early in his career to take stupid risks.

Apparently, though, the remark had its effect on Potterley. Without any warning, the man exploded into a rapid-fire verbal storm of irresponsibility.

Scholars, he said, could be free only if they could freely follow their own free-swinging curiosity. Research, he said, forced into a predesigned pattern by the powers that held the purse strings became slavish and had to stagnate. No man, he said, had the right to dictate the intellectual interests of another.

Foster listened to all of it with disbelief. None of it was strange to him. He had heard college boys talk so in order to shock their professors and he had once or twice amused himself in that fashion, too. Anyone who studied the history of science knew that many men had once thought so.

Yet it seemed strange to Foster, almost against nature, that a modern man of science could advance such nonsense. No one would advocate running a factory by allowing each individual worker to do whatever pleased him at the moment, or of running a ship according to the casual and conflicting notions of each individual crewman. It would be taken for granted that some sort of centralized supervisory agency must exist in each case. Why should direction and order benefit a factory and a ship but not scientific research?

People might say that the human mind was somehow qualitatively different from a ship or factory but the history of intellectual endeavor proved the opposite.

When science was young and the intricacies of all or most of the known was within the grasp of an individual mind, there was no need for direction, perhaps. Blind wandering over the uncharted tracts of ignorance could lead to wonderful finds by accident.

But as knowledge grew, more and more data had to be absorbed before worthwhile journeys into ignorance could be organized. Men had to specialize. The researcher needed the resources of a library he himself could not gather, then of instruments he himself could not afford. More and more, the individual researcher gave way to the research team and the research institution.

The funds necessary for research grew greater as tools grew more numerous.

What college was so small today as not to require at least one nuclear micro-reactor and at least one three-stage computer?

Centuries before, private individuals could no longer subsidize research. By 1940, only the government, large industries and large universities or research institutions could properly subsidize basic research.

By 1960, even the largest universities depended entirely upon government grants, while research institutions could not exist without tax concessions and public subscriptions. By 2000, the industrial combines had become a branch of the world government and, thereafter, the financing of research and therefore its direction naturally became centralized under a department of the government.

It all worked itself out naturally and well. Every branch of science was fitted neatly to the needs of the public, and the various branches of science were co-ordinated decently. The material advance of the last half-century was argument enough for the fact that science was not falling into stagnation.

Foster tried to say a very little of this and was waved aside impatiently by Potterley who said, "You are parroting official propaganda. You're sitting in the middle of an example that's squarely against the official view. Can you believe that?"

"Frankly, no."

"Well, why do you say time viewing is a dead end? Why is neutrinics unimportant? You say it is. You say it categorically. Yet you've never studied it. You claim complete ignorance of the subject. It's not even given in your school——"

"Isn't the mere fact that it isn't given proof enough?"

"Oh, I see. It's not given because it's unimportant. And it's unimportant because it's not given. Are you satisified with that reasoning?"

Foster felt a growing confusion. "It's in the books."

"That's all. The books say neutrinics is unimportant. Your professors tell you so because they read it in the books. The books say so because professors write them. Who says it from personal experience and knowledge? Who does research in it? Do you know of anyone?"

Foster said, "I don't see that we're getting anywhere, Dr. Potterley. I have work to do——"

"One minute. I just want you to try this on. See how it sounds to you. I say the government is actively suppressing basic research in neutrinics and chronoscopy. They're suppressing application of chronoscopy."

"Oh, no."

"Why not? They could do it. There's your centrally directed research. If they refuse grants for research in any portion of science, that portion dies. They've killed neutrinics. They can do it and have done it."

"But why?"

"I don't know why. I want you to find out. I'd do it myself if I knew enough. I came to you because you're a young fellow with a brand-new education. Have your intellectual arteries hardened already? Is there no curiosity in you? Don't you want to *know?* Don't you want *answers?*"

The historian was peering intently into Foster's face. Their noses were only inches apart, and Foster was so lost that he did not think to draw back.

He should, by rights, have ordered Potterley out. If necessary, he should have thrown Potterley out.

It was not respect for age and position that stopped him. It was certainly not that Potterley's arguments had convinced him. Rather, it was a small point of college pride.

Why didn't M.I.T. give a course in neutrinics? For that matter, now that he came to think about it, he doubted that there was a single book on neutrinics in the library. He could never recall having seen one.

He stopped to think about that.

And that was ruin.

Caroline Potterley had once been an attractive woman. There were occasions, such as dinners or university functions, when, by considerable effort, remnants of the attractiveness could be salvaged.

On ordinary occasions, she sagged. It was the word she applied to herself in moments of self-abhorrence. She had grown plumper with the years, but the flaccidity about her was not a matter of fat entirely. It was as though her muscles had given up and grown limp so that she shuffled when she walked, while her eyes grew baggy and her cheeks jowly. Even her graying hair seemed tired rather than merely stringy. Its straightness seemed to be the result of a supine surrender to gravity, nothing else.

Caroline Potterley looked at herself in the mirror and admitted this was one of her bad days. She knew the reason, too.

It had been the dream of Laurel. The strange one, with Laurel grown up. She had been wretched ever since.

Still, she was sorry she had mentioned it to Arnold. He didn't say anything; he never did any more; but it was bad for him. He was particularly withdrawn for days afterward. It might have been that he was getting ready for that important conference with the big government official (he kept saying he expected no success), but it might also have been her dream.

It was better in the old days when he would cry sharply at her, "Let the dead past *go,* Caroline! Talk won't bring her back, and dreams won't either."

It had been bad for both of them. Horribly bad. She had been away from home and had lived in guilt ever since. If she had stayed at home, if she had not gone on an unnecessary shopping expedition, there would have been two of them available. One would have succeeded in saving Laurel.

Poor Arnold had not managed. Heaven knew he tried. He had nearly died himself. He had come out of the burning house, staggering in agony, blistered, choking, half-blinded, with the dead Laurel in his arms.

The nightmare of that lived on, never lifting entirely.

Arnold slowly grew a shell about himself afterward. He cultivated a low-voiced mildness through which nothing broke, no lightning struck. He grew puritanical and even abandoned his minor vices, his cigarettes, his penchant for an occasional profane exclamation. He obtained his grant for the preparation of a new history of Carthage and subordinated everything to that.

She tried to help him. She hunted up his references, typed his notes and microfilmed them. Then that ended suddenly.

She ran from the desk suddenly one evening, reaching the bathroom in bare time and retching abominably. Her husband followed her in confusion and concern.

"Caroline, what's wrong?"

It took a drop of brandy to bring her around. She said, "Is it true? What they did?"

"Who did?"

"The Carthaginians."

He stared at her and she got it out by indirection. She couldn't say it right out.

The Carthaginians, it seemed, worshiped Moloch, in the form of a hollow, brazen idol with a furnace in its belly. At times of national crisis, the priests and the people gathered, and infants, after the proper ceremonies and invocations, were dextrously hurled, alive, into the flames.

They were given sweetmeats just before the crucial moment, in order that the efficacy of the sacrifice not be ruined by displeasing cries of panic. The drums rolled just after the moment, to drown out the few seconds of infant shrieking. The parents were present, presumably gratified, for the sacrifice was pleasing to the gods. . . .

Arnold Potterley frowned darkly. Vicious lies, he told her, on the part of Carthage's enemies. He should have warned her. After all, such propagandistic lies were not uncommon. According to the Greeks, the ancient Hebrews worshiped an ass's head in their Holy of Holies. According to the Romans, the primitive Christians were haters of all men who sacrificed pagan children in the catacombs.

"Then they didn't do it?" asked Caroline.

"I'm sure they didn't. The primitive Phoenicians may have. Human sacrifice is commonplace in primitive cultures. But Carthage in her great days was not a primitive culture. Human sacrifice often gives way to symbolic actions such as circumcision. The Greeks and Romans might have mistaken some Carthaginian symbolism for the original full rite, either out of ignorance or out of malice."

"Are you sure?"

"I can't be sure yet, Caroline, but when I've got enough evidence, I'll apply for permission to use chronoscopy, which will settle the matter once and for all."

"Chronoscopy?"

"Time viewing. We can focus on ancient Carthage at some time of crisis, the landing of Scipio Africanus in 202 B.C., for instance, and see with our own eyes exactly what happens. And you'll see, I'll be right."

He patted her and smiled encouragingly, but she dreamed of Laurel every night for two weeks thereafter and she never helped him with his Carthage project again. Nor did he ever ask her to.

But now she was bracing herself for his coming. He had called her after arriving back in town, told her he had seen the government man and that it had gone as expected. That meant failure, and yet the little telltale sign of depression had been absent from his voice and his features had appeared quite composed in the teleview. He had another errand to take care of, he said, before coming home.

It meant he would be late, but that didn't matter. Neither one of them was particular about eating hours or cared when packages were taken out of the freezer or even which packages or when the selfwarming mechanism was activated.

When he did arrive, he surprised her. There was nothing untoward about him in any obvious way. He kissed her dutifully and smiled, took off his hat and asked if all had been well while he was gone. It was all almost perfectly normal. Almost.

She had learned to detect small things, though, and his pace in all this was a trifle hurried. Enough to show her accustomed eye that he was under tension.

She said, "Has something happened?"

He said, "We're going to have a dinner guest night after next, Caroline. You don't mind?"

"Well, no. Is it anyone I know?"

"No. A young instructor. A newcomer. I've spoken to him." He suddenly whirled toward her and seized her arms at the elbow, held them a moment, then dropped them in confusion as though disconcerted at having shown emotion.

He said, "I almost didn't get through to him. Imagine that. Terrible, *terrible*, the way we have all bent to the yoke; the affection we have for the harness about us."

Mrs. Potterley wasn't sure she understood, but for a year she had been watching him grow quietly more rebellious; little by little more daring in his criticism of the government. She said, "You haven't spoken foolishly to him, have you?"

"What do you mean, foolishly? He'll be doing some neutrinics for me."

"Neutrinics" was trisyllabic nonsense to Mrs. Potterley, but she knew it had nothing to do with history. She said faintly, "Arnold, I don't like you to do that. You'll lose your position. It's—"

"It's intellectual anarchy, my dear," he said. "That's the phrase you want. Very well. I am an anarchist. If the government will not allow me to push my researches, I will push them on my own. And when I show the way, others will follow. . . . And if they don't, it makes no difference. It's Carthage that counts and human knowledge, not you and I."

"But you don't know this young man. What if he is an agent for the Commission of Research."

"Not likely and I'll take that chance." He made a fist of his right hand and rubbed it gently against the palm of his left. "He's on my side now. I'm sure of it. He can't help but be. I can recognize intellectual curiosity when I see it in a man's eyes and face and attitude, and it's a fatal disease for a tame scientist. Even today it takes time to beat it out of a man and the young ones are vulnerable. . . . Oh, why stop at anything? Why not build our own chronoscope and tell the government to go to——"

He stopped abruptly, shook his head and turned away.

"I hope everything will be all right," said Mrs. Potterley, feeling helplessly certain that everything would not be, and frightened, in advance, for her husband's professorial status and the security of their old age.

It was she alone, of them all, who had a violent presentiment of trouble. Quite the wrong trouble, of course.

Jonas Foster was nearly half an hour late in arriving at the Potterleys' off-campus house. Up to that very evening, he had not quite decided he would go. Then, at the last moment, he found he could not bring himself to commit the social enormity of breaking a dinner appointment an hour before the appointed time. That, and the nagging of curiosity.

The dinner itself passed interminably. Foster ate without appetite. Mrs. Potterley sat in distant absent-mindedness, emerging out of it only once to ask if he were married and to make a deprecating sound at the news that he was not.

Dr. Potterley himself asked neutrally after his professional history and nodded his head primly.

It was as staid, stodgy—boring, actually—as anything could be.

Foster thought: He seems so harmless.

Foster had spent the last two days reading up on Dr. Potterley. Very casually, of course, almost sneakily. He wasn't particularly anxious to be seen in the Social Science Library. To be sure, history was one of those borderline affairs and historical works were frequently read for amusement or edification by the general public.

Still, a physicist wasn't quite the "general public." Let Foster take to reading histories and he would be considered queer, sure as relativity, and after a while the Head of the Department would wonder if his new instructor were really "the man for the job."

So he had been cautious. He sat in the more secluded alcoves and kept his head bent when he slipped in and out at odd hours.

Dr. Potterley, it turned out, had written three books and some dozen articles on the ancient Mediterranean worlds, and the later articles (all in "Historical Reviews") had all dealt with pre-Roman Carthage from a sympathetic viewpoint.

That, at least, checked with Potterley's story and had soothed Foster's suspicions somewhat. . . . And yet Foster felt that it would have been much wiser, much safer, to have scotched the matter at the beginning.

A scientist shouldn't be too curious, he thought in bitter dissatisfaction with himself. It's a dangerous trait.

After dinner, he was ushered into Potterley's study and he was brought up sharply at the threshold. The walls were simply lined with books.

Not merely films. There were films, of course, but these were far outnumbered by the books—print on paper. He wouldn't have thought so many books would exist in usable condition.

That bothered Foster. Why should anyone want to keep so many books at home? Surely all were available in the university library, or, at the very worst, at the Library of Congress, if one wished to take the minor trouble of checking out a microfilm.

There was an element of secrecy involved in a home library. It breathed of intellectual anarchy. That last thought, oddly, calmed Foster. He would rather Potterley be an authentic anarchist than a play-acting *agent provocateur*.

And now the hours began to pass quickly and astonishingly.

"You see," Potterley said, in a clear, unflurried voice, "it was a matter of finding, if possible, anyone who had ever used chronoscopy in his work. Naturally, I couldn't ask baldly, since that would be unauthorized research."

"Yes," said Foster dryly. He was a little surprised such a small consideration would stop the man.

"I used indirect methods——"

He had. Foster was amazed at the volume of correspondence dealing with small disputed points of ancient Mediterranean culture which somehow managed to elicit the casual remark over and over again: "Of course, having never made use of chronoscopy——" or, "Pending approval of my request for chronoscopic data, which appear unlikely, at the moment——"

"Now these aren't blind questionings," said Potterley. "There's a monthly booklet put out by the Institute for Chronoscopy in which items concerning the past as determined by time viewing are printed. Just one or two items.

"What impressed me first was the triviality of most of the items, their insipidity. Why should such researches get priority over my work? So I wrote to people who would be most likely to do research in the directions described in the booklet. Uniformly, as I have shown you, they did *not* make use of the chronoscope. Now let's go over it point by point."

At last Foster, his head swimming with Potterley's meticulously gathered details, asked, "But why?"

"I don't know why," said Potterley, "but I have a theory. The original invention of the chronoscope was by Sterbinski—you see, I know that much—and it was well publicized. But then the government took over the instrument and decided to suppress further research in the matter or any use of the machine. But then, people might be curious as to why it wasn't being used. Curiosity is such a vice, Dr. Foster."

Yes, agreed the physicist to himself.

"Imagine the effectiveness, then," Potterley went on, "of pretending that the chronoscope *was* being used. It would then be not a mystery, but a commonplace. It would no longer be a fitting object for legitimate curiosity or an attractive one for illicit curiosity."

"*You* were curious," pointed out Foster.

Potterley looked a trifle restless. "It was different in my case," he said angrily. "I have something that *must* be done, and I wouldn't submit to the ridiculous way in which they kept putting me off."

A bit paranoid, too, thought Foster gloomily.

Yet he had ended up with something, paranoid or not. Foster could no longer deny that something peculiar was going on in the matter of neutrinics.

But what was Potterley after? That still bothered Foster. If Potterley didn't intend this as a test of Foster's ethics, what *did* he want?

Foster put it to himself logically. If an intellectual anarchist with a touch of paranoia wanted to use a chronoscope and was convinced that the powers-that-be were deliberately standing in his way, what would he do?

Supposing it were I, he thought. What would I do?

He said slowly, "Maybe the chronoscope doesn't exist at all?"

Potterley started. There was almost a crack in his general calmness. For an instant, Foster found himself catching a glimpse of something not at all calm.

But the historian kept his balance and said, "Oh, no, there *must* be a chronoscope."

"Why? Have you seen it? Have I? Maybe that's the explanation of everything. Maybe they're not deliberately holding out on a chronoscope they've got. Maybe they haven't got it in the first place."

"But Sterbinski lived. He built a chronoscope. That much is a fact."

"The book says so," said Foster coldly.

"Now listen." Potterley actually reached over and snatched at Foster's jacket sleeve. "I need the chronoscope. I must have it. Don't tell me it doesn't exist. What we're going to do is find out enough about neutrinics to be able to ——"

Potterley drew himself up short.

Foster drew his sleeve away. He needed no ending to that sentence. He supplied it himself. He said, "Build one of our own?"

Potterley looked sour as though he would rather not have said it point-blank. Nevertheless, he said, "Why not?"

"Because that's out of the question," said Foster. "If what I've read is correct, then it took Sterbinski twenty years to build his machine and several millions in composite grants. Do you think you and I can duplicate that illegally? Suppose we had the time, which we haven't, and suppose I could learn enough out of books, which I doubt, where would we get the money and equipment? The chronoscope is supposed to fill a five-story building, for Heaven's sake."

"Then you won't help me?"

"Well, I'll tell you what. I have one way in which I may be able to find out something——"

"What is that?" asked Potterley at once.

"Never mind. That's not important. But I may be able to find out enough to tell you whether the government is deliberately suppressing research by chronoscope. I may confirm the evidence you already have or I may be able to prove that your evidence is misleading. I don't know what good it will do you in either case, but it's as far as I can go. It's my limit."

Potterley watched the young man go finally. He was angry with himself. Why had he allowed himself to grow so careless as to permit the fellow to guess that he was thinking in terms of a chronoscope of his own. That was premature.

But then why did the young fool have to suppose that a chronoscope might not exist at all?

It *had* to exist. It *had* to. What was the use of saying it didn't?

And why couldn't a second one be built? Science had advanced in the fifty years since Sterbinski. All that was needed was knowledge.

Let the youngster gather knowledge. Let him think a small gathering would be his limit. Having taken the path to anarchy, there would be no limit. If the boy were not driven onward by something in himself, the first steps would be error enough to force the rest. Potterley was quite certain he would not hesitate to use blackmail.

Potterley waved a last good-by and looked up. It was beginning to rain.

Certainly! Blackmail if necessary, but he would not be stopped.

Foster steered his car across the bleak outskirts of town and scarcely noticed the rain.

He *was* a fool, he told himself, but he couldn't leave things as they were. He had to know. He damned his streak of undisciplined curiosity, but he had to know.

But he would go no further than Uncle Ralph. He swore mightily to himself that it would stop there. In that way, there would be no evidence against him, no real evidence. Uncle Ralph would be discreet.

In a way, he was secretly ashamed of Uncle Ralph. He hadn't mentioned him to Potterley partly out of caution and partly because he did not wish to witness the lifted eyebrow, the inevitable half-smile. Professional science writers, however useful, were a little outside the pale, fit only for patronizing contempt. The fact that, as a class, they made more money than did research scientists only made matters worse, of course.

Still, there were times when a science writer in the family could be convenient. Not being really educated, they did not have to specialize.

Consequently, a good science writer knew practically everything. . . . And Uncle Ralph was one of the best.

Ralph Nimmo had no college degree and was rather proud of it. "A degree," he once said to Jonas Foster, when both were considerably younger, "is a first step down a ruinous highway. You don't want to waste it so you go on to graduate work and doctoral research. You end up a thoroughgoing ignoramus on everything in the world except for one subdivisional sliver of nothing.

"On the other hand, if you guard your mind carefully and keep it blank of any clutter of information till maturity is reached, filling it only with intelligence and training it only in clear thinking, you then have a powerful instrument at your disposal and you can become a science writer."

Nimmo received his first assignment at the age of twenty-five, after he had completed his apprenticeship and been out in the field for less than three months. It came in the shape of a clotted manuscript whose language would impart no glimmering of understanding to any reader, however qualified, without careful study and some inspired guesswork. Nimmo took it apart and put it together again (after five long and exasperating interviews with the authors, who were biophysicists), making the language taut and meaningful and smoothing the style to a pleasant gloss.

"Why not?" he would say tolerantly to his nephew, who countered his strictures on degrees by berating him with his readiness to hang on the fringes of science. "The fringe is important. Your scientists can't write. Why should they be expected to? They aren't expected to be grand masters at chess or virtuosos at the violin, so why expect them to know how to put words together? Why not leave that for specialists, too?"

"Good Lord, Jonas, read your literature of a hundred years ago. Discount the fact that the science is out of date and that some of the expressions are out of date. Just try to read it and make sense out of it. It's just jaw-cracking, amateurish. Pages are published uselessly; whole articles which are either noncomprehensible or both."

"But you don't get recognition, Uncle Ralph," protested young Foster, who was getting ready to start his college career and was rather starry-eyed about it. "You could be a terrific researcher."

"I get recognition," said Nimmo. "Don't think for a minute I don't. Sure, a biochemist or a state-meterologist won't give me the time of day, but they pay me well enough. Just find out what happens when some first-class chemist finds the Commission has cut his year's allowance for science writing. He'll fight harder for enough funds to afford me, or someone like me, than to get a recording ionograph."

He grinned broadly and Foster grinned back. Actually, he was proud of his paunchy, round-faced, stub-fingered uncle, whose vanity made him brush his fringe of hair futilely over the desert on his pate and made him dress like an unmade haystack because such negligence was his trademark. Ashamed, but proud, too.

And now Foster entered his uncle's cluttered apartment in no mood at all for grinning. He was nine years older now and so was Uncle Ralph. For nine years, papers in every branch of science had come to him for polishing and a little of each had crept into his capacious mind.

Nimmo was eating seedless grapes, popping them into his mouth one at a time. He tossed a bunch to Foster who caught them by a hair, then bent to retrieve individual grapes that had torn loose and fallen to the floor.

"Let them be. Don't bother," said Nimmo carelessly. "Someone comes in here to clean once a week. What's up? Having trouble with your grant application write-up?"

"I haven't really got into that yet."

"You haven't? Get a move on, boy. Are you waiting for me to offer to do the final arrangement?"

"I couldn't afford you, Uncle."

"Aw, come on. It's all in the family. Grant me all popular publication rights and no cash need change hands."

Foster nodded. "If you're serious, it's a deal."

"It's a deal."

It was a gamble, of course, but Foster knew enough of Nimmo's science writing to realize it could pay off. Some dramatic discovery of public interest on primitive man or on a new surgical technique, or on any branch of spationautics could mean a very cash-attracting article in any of the mass media of communication.

It was Nimmo, for instance, who had written up, for scientific consumption, the series of papers by Bryce and co-workers that elucidated the fine structure of two cancer viruses, for which job he asked the picayune payment of fifteen hundred dollars, provided popular publication rights were included. He then wrote up, exclusively, the same work in semidramatic form for use in trimensional video for a twenty-thousand-dollar advance plus rental royalties that were still coming in after five years.

Foster said bluntly, "What do you know about neutrinics, Uncle?"

"Neutrinics?" Nimmo's small eyes looked surprised. "Are you working in that? I thought it was pseudo-gravitic optics."

"It is p.g.o. I just happen to be asking about neutrinics."

"That's a devil of a thing to be doing. You're stepping out of line. You know that, don't you?"

"I don't expect you to call the Commission because I'm a little curious about things."

"Maybe I should before you get into trouble. Curiosity is an occupational danger with scientists. I've watched it work. One of them will be moving quietly along on a problem, then curiosity leads him up a strange creek. Next thing you know they've done so little on their proper problem, they can't justify for a project renewal. I've seen more——"

"All I want to know," said Foster patiently, "is what's been passing through your hands lately on neutrinics."

Nimmo leaned back, chewing at a grape thoughtfully. "Nothing. Nothing ever. I don't recall ever getting a paper on neutrinics."

"What!" Foster was openly astonished. "Then who does get the work?"

"Now that you ask," said Nimmo, "I don't know. Don't recall anyone talking about it at the annual conventions. I don't think much work is being done there."

"Why not?"

"Hey, there, don't bark. I'm not doing anything. My guess would be——"

Foster was exasperated. "Don't you know?"

"Hmp. I'll tell you what I know about neutrinics. It concerns the applications of neutrino movements and the forces involved——"

"Sure. Sure. Just as electronics deals with the applications of electron movements and the forces involved, and pseudo-gravitics deals with the applications of artificial gravitational fields. I didn't come to you for that. Is that all you know?"

"And," said Nimmo with equanimity, "neutrinics is the basis of time viewing and that *is* all I know."

Foster slouched back in his chair and massaged one lean cheek with great intensity. He felt angrily dissatisfied. Without formulating it explicitly in his own mind, he had felt sure, somehow, that Nimmo would come up with some late reports, bring up interesting facets of modern neutrinics, send him back to Potterley able to say that the elderly historian was mistaken, that his data was misleading, his deductions mistaken.

Then he could have returned to his proper work.

But now . . .

He told himself angrily: So they're not doing much work in the field. Does that make it deliberate suppression? What if neutrinics is a sterile discipline? Maybe it is. I don't know. Potterley doesn't. Why waste the intellectual resources of humanity on nothing? Or the work might be secret for some legitimate reason. It might be . . .

The trouble was, he had to know. He couldn't leave things as they were now. *He couldn't!*

He said, "Is there a text on neutrinics, Uncle Ralph? I mean a clear and simple one. An elementary one."

Nimmo thought, his plump cheeks puffing out with a series of sighs. "You ask the damnedest questions. The only one I ever heard of was Sterbinski and somebody. I've never seen it, but I viewed something about it once. . . . Sterbinski and LaMarr, that's it."

"Is that the Sterbinski who invented the chronoscope?"

"I think so. Proves the book ought to be good."

"Is there a recent edition? Sterbinski died thirty years ago."

Nimmo shrugged and said nothing.

"Can you find out?"

They sat in silence for a moment, while Nimmo shifted his bulk to the creaking tune of the chair he sat on. Then the science writer said, "Are you going to tell me what this is all about?"

"I can't. Will you help me anyway, Uncle Ralph? Will you get me a copy of the text?"

"Well, you've taught me all I know on pseudo-gravitics. I should be grateful. Tell you what—I'll help you on one condition."

"Which is?"

The older man was suddenly very grave. "That you be careful, Jonas. You're obviously way out of line whatever you're doing. Don't blow up your career just because you're curious about something you haven't been assigned to and which is none of your business. Understand?"

Foster nodded, but he hardly heard. He was thinking furiously.

*   *   *

A full week later, Ralph Nimmo eased his rotund figure into Jonas Foster's on-campus two-room combination and said, in a hoarse whisper, "I've got something."

"What?" Foster was immediately eager.

"A copy of Sterbinski and LaMarr." He produced it, or rather a corner of it, from his ample topcoat.

Foster almost automatically eyed door and windows to make sure they were closed and shaded respectively, then held out his hand.

The film case was flaking with age, and when he cracked it the film was faded and growing brittle. He said sharply, "Is this all?"

"Gratitude, my boy, gratitude!" Nimmo sat down with a grunt, and reached into a pocket for an apple.

"Oh, I'm grateful, but it's so old."

"And lucky to get it at that. I tried to get a film run from the Congressional Library. No go. The book was restricted."

"Then how did you get this?"

"Stole it." He was biting crunchingly around the core. "New York Public."

"What?"

"Simple enough. I had access to the stacks, naturally. So I stepped over a chained railing when no one was around, dug this up, and walked out with it. They're very trusting out there. Meanwhile, they won't miss it in years. . . . Only you'd better not let anyone see it on you, nephew."

Foster stared at the film as though it were literally hot.

Nimmo discarded the core and reached for a second apple. "Funny thing, now. There's nothing more recent in the whole field of neutrinics. Not a monograph, not a paper, not a progress note. Nothing since the chronoscope."

"Uh-huh," said Foster absently.

Foster worked evenings in the Potterley home. He could not trust his own on-campus rooms for the purpose. The evening work grew more real to him than his own grant applications. Sometimes he worried about it but then that stopped, too.

His work consisted, at first, simply in viewing and reviewing the text film. Later it consisted in thinking (sometimes while a section of the book ran itself off through the pocket projector, disregarded).

Sometimes Potterley would come down to watch, to sit with prim, eager eyes, as though he expected thought processes to solidify and become visible in all their convolutions. He interfered in only two ways. He did not allow Foster to smoke and sometimes he talked.

It wasn't conversation talk, never that. Rather it was a low-voiced monologue with which, it seemed, he scarcely expected to command attention. It was much more as though he were relieving a pressure within himself.

Carthage! Always Carthage!

Carthage, the New York of the ancient Mediterranean. Carthage, commercial empire and queen of the seas. Carthage, all that Syracuse and Alexandria pretended to be. Carthage, maligned by her enemies and inarticulate in her own defense.

She had been defeated once by Rome and then driven out of Sicily and

Sardinia, but came back to more than recoup her losses by new dominions in Spain, and raised up Hannibal to give the Romans sixteen years of terror.

In the end, she lost again a second time, reconciled herself to fate and built again with broken tools a limping life in shrunken territory, succeeding so well that jealous Rome deliberately forced a third war. And then Carthage, with nothing but bare hands and tenacity, built weapons and forced Rome into a two-year war that ended only with complete destruction of the city, the inhabitants throwing themselves into their flaming houses rather than surrender.

"Could people fight so for a city and a way of life as bad as the ancient writers painted it? Hannibal was a better general than any Roman and his soldiers were absolutely faithful to him. Even his bitterest enemies praised him. There was a Carthaginian. It is fashionable to say that he was an atypical Carthaginian, better than the others, a diamond placed in garbage. But then why was he so faithful to Carthage, even to his death after years of exile? They talk of Moloch——"

Foster didn't always listen but sometimes he couldn't help himself and he shuddered and turned sick at the bloody tale of child sacrifice.

But Potterley went on earnestly, "Just the same, it isn't true. It's a twenty-five-hundred-year-old canard started by the Greeks and Romans. They had their own slaves, their crucifixions and torture, their gladiatorial contests. They weren't holy. The Moloch story is what later ages would have called war propaganda, the big lie. I can prove it was a lie. I can prove it and, by Heaven, I will—I will——"

He would mumble that promise over and over again in his earnestness.

Mrs. Potterley visited him also, but less frequently, usually on Tuesdays and Thursdays when Dr. Potterley himself had an evening course to take care of and was not present.

She would sit quietly, scarcely talking, face slack and doughy, eyes blank, her whole attitude distant and withdrawn.

The first time, Foster tried, uneasily, to suggest that she leave.

She said tonelessly, "Do I disturb you?"

"No, of course not," lied Foster restlessly. "It's just that—that——" He couldn't complete the sentence.

She nodded, as though accepting an invitation to stay. Then she opened a cloth bag she had brought with her and took out a quire of vitron sheets which she proceeded to weave together by rapid, delicate movements of a pair of slender, tetra-faceted depolarizers, whose battery-fed wires made her look as though she were holding a large spider.

One evening, she said softly, "My daughter, Laurel, is your age."

Foster started, as much at the sudden unexpected sound of speech as at the words. He said, "I didn't know you had a daughter, Mrs. Potterley."

"She died. Years ago."

The vitron grew under the deft manipulations into the uneven shape of some garment Foster could not yet identify. There was nothing left for him to do but mutter inanely, "I'm sorry."

Mrs. Potterley sighed. "I dream about her often." She raised her blue, distant eyes to him.

Foster winced and looked away.

Another evening she asked, pulling at one of the vitron sheets to loosen its gentle clinging to her dress, "What is time viewing anyway?"

That remark broke into a particularly involved chain of thought, and Foster said snappishly, "Dr. Potterley can explain."

"He's tried to. Oh, my, yes. But I think he's a little impatient with me. He calls it chronoscopy most of the time. Do you actually see things in the past, like the trimensionals? Or does it just make little dot patterns like the computer you use?"

Foster stared at his hand computer with distaste. It worked well enough, but every operation had to be manually controlled and the answers were obtained in code. Now if he could use the school computer . . . Well, why dream, he felt conspicuous enough, as it was, carrying a hand computer under his arm every evening as he left his office.

He said, "I've never seen the chronoscope myself, but I'm under the impression that you actually see pictures and hear sound."

"You can hear people talk, too?"

"I think so." Then, half in desperation, "Look here, Mrs. Potterley, this must be awfully dull for you. I realize you don't like to leave a guest all to himself, but really, Mrs. Potterley, you mustn't feel compelled——"

"I don't feel compelled," she said. "I'm sitting here, waiting."

"Waiting? For what?"

She said composedly, "I listened to you that first evening. The time you first spoke to Arnold. I listened at the door."

He said, "You did?"

"I know I shouldn't have, but I was awfully worried about Arnold. I had a notion he was going to do something he oughtn't and I wanted to hear what. And then when I heard——" She paused, bending close over the vitron and peering at it.

"Heard what, Mrs. Potterley?"

"That you wouldn't build a chronoscope."

"Well, of course not."

"I thought maybe you might change your mind."

Foster glared at her. "Do you mean you're coming down here hoping I'll build a chronoscope, waiting for me to build one?"

"I hope you do, Dr. Foster. Oh, I hope you do."

It was as though, all at once, a fuzzy veil had fallen off her face, leaving all her features clear and sharp, putting color into her cheeks, life into her eyes, the vibrations of something approaching excitement into her voice.

"Wouldn't it be wonderful," she whispered, "to have one? People of the past could live again. Pharoahs and kings and—just people. I hope you build one, Dr. Foster. I really—hope——"

She choked, it seemed, on the intensity of her own words and let the vitron sheets slip off her lap. She rose and ran up the basement stairs, while Foster's eyes followed her awkwardly fleeing body with astonishment and distress.

It cut deeper into Foster's nights and left him sleepless and painfully stiff with thought. It was almost a mental indigestion.

His grant requests went limping in, finally, to Ralph Nimmo. He scarcely had any hope for them. He thought numbly: They won't be approved.

If they weren't, of course, it would create a scandal in the department and probably mean his appointment at the university would not be renewed, come the end of the academic year.

He scarcely worried. It was the neutrino, the neutrino, only the neutrino. Its trail curved and veered sharply and led him breathlessly along uncharted pathways that even Sterbinski and LaMarr did not follow.

He called Nimmo. "Uncle Ralph, I need a few things. I'm calling from off the campus."

Nimmo's face in the video plate was jovial, but his voice was sharp. He said, "What you need is a course in communication. I'm having a hell of a time pulling your application into one intelligible piece. If that's what you're calling about——"

Foster shook his head impatiently. "That's *not* what I'm calling about. I need these." He scribbled quickly on a piece of paper and held it up before the receiver.

Nimmo yiped. "Hey, how many tricks do you think I can wangle?"

"You can get them, Uncle. You know you can."

Nimmo reread the list of items with silent motions of his plump lips and looked grave.

"What happens when you put those things together?" he asked. Foster shook his head. "You'll have the exclusive popular publication rights to whatever turns up, the way it's always been. But please don't ask any questions now."

"I can't do miracles, you know."

"Do this one. You've got to. You're a science writer, not a research man. You don't have to account for anything. You've got friends and connections. They can look the other way, can't they, to get a break from you next publication time?"

"Your faith, nephew, is touching. I'll try."

Nimmo succeeded. The material and equipment were brought over late one evening in a private touring car. Nimmo and Foster lugged it in with the grunting of men unused to manual labor.

Potterley stood at the entrance of the basement after Nimmo had left. He asked softly, "What's this for?"

Foster brushed the hair off his forehead and gently massaged a sprained wrist. He said, "I want to conduct a few simple experiments."

"Really?" The historian's eyes glittered with excitement.

Foster felt exploited. He felt as though he were being led along a dangerous highway by the pull of pinching fingers on his nose; as though he could see the ruin clearly that lay in wait at the end of the path, yet walked eagerly and determinedly. Worst of all, he felt the compelling grip on his nose to be his own.

It was Potterley who began it, Potterley who stood there now, gloating; but the compulsion was his own.

Foster said sourly, "I'll be wanting privacy now, Potterley. I can't have you and your wife running down here and annoying me."

He thought: If that offends him, let him kick me out. Let him put an end to this.

In his heart, though, he did not think being evicted would stop anything.

But it did not come to that. Potterley was showing no signs of offense. His mild gaze was unchanged. He said, "Of course, Dr. Foster, of course. All the privacy you wish."

Foster watched him go. He was left still marching along the highway, perversely glad of it and hating himself for being glad.

He took to sleeping over on a cot in Potterley's basement and spending his weekends there entirely.

During that period, preliminary word came through that his grants (as doctored by Nimmo) had been approved. The Department Head brought the word and congratulated him.

Foster stared back distantly and mumbled, "Good. I'm glad," with so little conviction that the other frowned and turned away without another word.

Foster gave the matter no further thought. It was a minor point, worth no notice. He was planning something that really counted, a climactic test for that evening.

One evening, a second and third and then, haggard and half beside himself with excitement, he called in Potterley.

Potterley came down the stairs and looked about at the homemade gadgetry. He said, in his soft voice, "The electric bills are quite high. I don't mind the expense, but the City may ask questions. Can anything be done?"

It was a warm evening, but Potterley wore a tight collar and a semijacket. Foster, who was in his undershirt, lifted bleary eyes and said shakily, "It won't be for much longer, Dr. Potterley. I've called you down to tell you something. A chronoscope can be built. A small one, of course, but it can be built."

Potterley seized the railing. His body sagged. He managed a whisper. "Can it be built here?"

"Here in the basement," said Foster wearily.

"Good Lord. You said——"

"I know what I said," cried Foster impatiently. "I said it couldn't be done. I didn't know anything then. Even Sterbinski didn't know anything."

Potterley shook his head. "Are you sure? You're not mistaken, Dr. Foster? I couldn't endure it if——"

Foster said, "I'm not mistaken. Damn it, sir, if just theory had been enough, we could have had a time viewer over a hundred years ago, when the neutrino was first postulated. The trouble was, the original investigators considered it only a mysterious particle without mass or charge that could not be detected. It was just something to even up the bookkeeping and save the law of conservation of mass energy."

He wasn't sure Potterley knew what he was talking about. He didn't care. He needed a breather. He had to get some of this out of his clotting thoughts. . . . And he needed background for what he would have to tell Potterley next.

He went on. "It was Sterbinski who first discovered that the neutrino broke through the space-time cross-sectional barrier, that it traveled through time as well as through space. It was Sterbinski who first devised a method for stopping neutrinos. He invented a neutrino recorder and learned how to interpret the pattern of the neutrino stream. Naturally, the stream had been affected and deflected by all the matter it had passed through in its passage through time, and the deflections could be analyzed and converted into the images of the matter that had done the deflecting. Time viewing was possible. Even air vibrations could be detected in this way and converted into sound."

Potterley was definitely not listening. He said, "Yes. Yes. But when can you build a chronoscope?"

Foster said urgently, "Let me finish. Everything depends on the method used to detect and analyze the neutrino stream. Sterbinski's method was difficult and roundabout. It required mountains of energy. But I've studied pseudo-gravitics, Dr. Potterley, the science of artificial gravitational fields. I've specialized in the behavior of light in such fields. It's a new science. Sterbinski knew nothing of it. If he had, he would have seen—anyone would have—a much better and more efficient method of detecting neutrinos using a pseudo-gravitic field. If I had known more neutrinics to begin with, I would have seen it at once."

Potterley brightened a bit. "I knew it," he said. "Even if they stop research in neutrinics there is no way the government can be sure that discoveries in other segments of science won't reflect knowledge on neutrinics. So much for the value of centralized direction of science. I thought this long ago, Dr. Foster, before you ever came to work here."

"I congratulate you on that," said Foster, "but there's one thing——"

"Oh, never mind all this. Answer me. Please. When can you build a chronoscope?"

"I'm trying to tell you something, Dr. Potterley. A chronoscope won't do you any good." (This is it, Foster thought.)

Slowly, Potterley descended the stairs. He stood facing Foster. "What do you mean? Why won't it help me?"

"You won't see Carthage. It's what I've got to tell you. It's what I've been leading up to. You can never see Carthage."

Potterley shook his head slightly. "Oh, no, you're wrong. If you have the chronoscope, just focus it properly——"

"No, Dr. Potterley. It's not a question of focus. There are random factors affecting the neutrino stream, as they affect all subatomic particles. What we call the uncertainty principle. When the stream is recorded and interpreted, the random factor comes out as fuzziness, or 'noise' as the communications boys speak of it. The further back in time you penetrate, the more pronounced the fuzziness, the greater the noise. After a while, the noise drowns out the picture. Do you understand?"

"More power," said Potterley in a dead kind of voice.

"That won't help. When the noise blurs out detail, magnifying detail magnifies the noise, too. You can't see anything in a sun-burned film by enlarging it, can you? Get this through your head, now. The physical nature of the universe sets limits. The random thermal motions of air molecules set limits to how weak a sound can be detected by any instrument. The length of a light wave or of an electron wave sets limits to the size of objects that can be seen by any instrument. It works that way in chronoscopy, too. You can only time view so far."

"How far? How far?"

Foster took a deep breath. "A century and a quarter. That's the most."

"But the monthly bulletin the Commission puts out deals with ancient history almost entirely." The historian laughed shakily. "You must be wrong. The government has data as far back as 3000 B.C."

"When did you switch to believing them?" demanded Foster, scornfully. "You began this business by proving they were lying; that no historian had made use of the chronoscope. Don't you see why now? No historian, except one interested in contemporary history, could. No chronoscope can possibly see back in time further than 1920 under any conditions.''

"You're wrong. You don't know everything," said Potterley.

"The truth won't bend itself to your convenience either. Face it. The government's part in this is to perpetuate a hoax.''

"Why?''

"I don't know why.''

Potterley's snubby nose was twitching. His eyes were bulging. He pleaded. "It's only theory, Dr. Foster. Build a chronoscope. Build one and try.''

Foster caught Potterley's shoulders in a sudden, fierce grip. "Do you think I haven't? Do you think I would tell you this before I had checked it every way I knew? I *have* built one. It's all around you. Look!''

He ran to the switches at the power leads. He flicked them on, one by one. He turned a resistor, adjusted other knobs, put out the cellar lights. "Wait. Let it warm up.''

There was a small glow near the center of one wall. Potterley was gibbering incoherently, but Foster only cried again, "Look!''

The light sharpened and brightened, broke up into a light-and-dark pattern. Men and women! Fuzzy. Features blurred. Arms and legs mere streaks. An old-fashioned ground car, unclear but recognizable as one of the kind that had once used gasoline-powered internal-combustion engines, sped by.

Foster said, "Mid-twentieth century, somewhere. I can't hook up an audio yet so this is soundless. Eventually, we can add sound. Anyway, mid-twentieth is almost as far back as you can go. Believe me, that's the best focusing that can be done.''

Potterley said, "Build a larger machine, a stronger one. Improve your circuits.''

"You can't lick the Uncertainty Principle, man, any more than you can live on the sun. There are physical limits to what can be done.''

"You're lying. I won't believe you. I——''

A new voice sounded, raised shrilly to make itself heard.

"Arnold! Dr. Foster!''

The young physicist turned at once. Dr. Potterley froze for a long moment, then said, without turning, "What is it, Caroline? Leave us.''

"No!'' Mrs. Potterley descended the stairs. "I heard. I couldn't help hearing. Do you have a time viewer here, Dr. Foster? Here in the basement?''

"Yes, I do, Mrs. Potterley. A kind of time viewer. Not a good one. I can't get sound yet and the picture is darned blurry, but it works.''

Mrs. Potterley clasped her hands and held them tightly against her breast. "How wonderful. How wonderful.''

"It's not at all wonderful,'' snapped Potterley. "The young fool can't reach further back than——''

"Now, look,'' began Foster in exasperation.

"Please!'' cried Mrs. Potterley. "Listen to me. Arnold, don't you see that as long as we can use it for twenty years back, we can see Laurel once again? What do we care about Carthage and ancient times? It's Laurel we can see. She'll be alive for us again. Leave the machine here, Dr. Foster. Show us how to work it.''

Foster stared at her then at her husband. Dr. Potterley's face had gone white.

Though his voice stayed low and even, its calmness was somehow gone. He said, "You're a fool!"

Caroline said weakly, "Arnold!"

"You're a fool, I say. What will you see? The past. The dead past. Will Laurel do one thing she did not do? Will you see one thing you haven't seen? Will you live three years over and over again, watching a baby who'll never grow up no matter how you watch?"

His voice came near to cracking, but held. He stopped closer to her, seized her shoulder and shook her roughly. "Do you know what will happen to you if you do that? They'll come to take you away because you'll go mad. Yes, mad. Do you want mental treatment? Do you want to be shut up, to undergo the psychic probe?"

Mrs. Potterley tore away. There was no trace of softness or vagueness about her. She had twisted into a virago. "I want to see my child, Arnold. She's in that machine and I want her."

"She's *not* in the machine. An image is. Can't you understand? An image! Something that's not real!"

"I want my child. Do you hear me?" She flew at him, screaming, fists beating. *"I want my child."*

The historian retreated at the fury of the assault, crying out. Foster moved to step between, when Mrs. Potterley dropped, sobbing wildly, to the floor.

Potterley turned, eyes desperately seeking. With a sudden heave, he snatched at a Lando-rod, tearing it from its support, and whirling away before Foster, numbed by all that was taking place, could move to stop him.

"Stand back!" gasped Potterley, "or I'll kill you. I swear it."

He swung with force, and Foster jumped back.

Potterley turned with fury on every part of the structure in the cellar, and Foster, after the first crash of glass, watched dazedly.

Potterley spent his rage and then he was standing quietly amid shards and splinters, with a broken Lando-rod in his hand. He said to Foster in a whisper, "Now get out of here! Never come back! If any of this cost you anything, send me a bill and I'll pay for it. I'll pay double."

Foster shrugged, picked up his shirt and moved up the basement stairs. He could hear Mrs. Potterley sobbing loudly, and, as he turned at the head of the stairs for a last look, he saw Dr. Potterley bending over her, his face convulsed with sorrow.

Two days later, with the school day drawing to a close, and Foster looking wearily about to see if there were any data on his newly approved projects that he wished to take home, Dr. Potterley appeared once more. He was standing at the open door of Foster's office.

The historian was neatly dressed as ever. He lifted his hand in a gesture that was too vague to be a greeting, too abortive to be a plea. Foster stared stonily.

Potterley said, "I waited till five, till you were . . . May I come in?"

Foster nodded.

Potterley said, "I suppose I ought to apologize for my behavior. I was dreadfully disappointed; not quite master of myself. Still, it was inexcusable."

"I accept your apology," said Foster. "Is that all?"

"My wife called you, I think."

"Yes, she has."

"She has been quite hysterical. She told me she had but I couldn't be quite sure——"

"Could you tell me—would you be so kind as to tell me what she wanted?"

"She wanted a chronoscope. She said she had some money of her own. She was willing to pay."

"Did you—make any commitments?"

"I said I wasn't in the manufacturing business."

"Good," breathed Potterley, his chest expanding with a sigh of relief. "Please don't take any calls from her. She's not—quite——"

"Look, Dr. Potterley," said Foster, "I'm not getting into any domestic quarrels, but you'd better be prepared for something. Chronoscopes can be built by anybody. Given a few simple parts that can be bought through some etherics sales center, it can be built in the home workshop. The video part, anyway."

"But no one else will think of it beside you, will they? No one has."

"I don't intend to keep it secret."

"But you can't publish. It's illegal research."

"That doesn't matter any more, Dr. Potterley. If I lose my grants, I lose them. If the university is displeased, I'll resign. It just doesn't matter."

"But you can't do that!"

"Till now," said Foster, "you didn't mind my risking loss of grants and position. Why do you turn so tender about it now? Now let me explain something to you. When you first came to me, I believed in organized and directed research; the situation as it existed, in other words. I considered you an intellectual anarchist, Dr. Potterley, and dangerous. But, for one reason or another, I've been an anarchist myself for months now and I have achieved great things.

"Those things have been achieved not because I am a brilliant scientist. Not at all. It was just that scientific research had been directed from above and holes were left that could be filled in by anyone who looked in the right direction. And anyone might have if the government hadn't actively tried to prevent it.

"Now understand me. I still believe directed research can be useful. I'm not in favor of a retreat to total anarchy. But there must be a middle ground. Directed research can retain flexibility. A scientist must be allowed to follow his curiosity, at least in his spare time."

Potterley sat down. He said ingratiatingly, "Let's discuss this, Foster. I appreciate your idealism. You're young. You want the moon. But you can't destroy yourself through fancy notions of what research must consist of. I got you into this. I am responsible and I blame myself bitterly. I was acting emotionally. My interest in Carthage blinded me and I was a damned fool."

Foster broke in. "You mean you've changed completely in two days? Carthage is nothing? Government suppression of research is nothing?"

"Even a damned fool like myself can learn, Foster. My wife taught me something. I understand the reason for government suppression of neutrinics now. I didn't two days ago. And, understanding, I approve. You saw the way my wife reacted to the news of a chronoscope in the basement. I had envisioned a chronoscope used for research purposes. All *she* could see was the personal pleasure of returning neurotically to a personal past, a dead past. The pure researcher, Foster, is in the minority. People like my wife would outweigh us.

"For the government to encourage chronoscopy would have meant that everyone's past would be visible. The government officers would be subjected to blackmail and improper pressure, since who on Earth has a past that is absolutely clean? Organized government might become impossible.''

Foster licked his lips. ''Maybe. Maybe the government has some justification in its own eyes. Still, there's an important principle involved here. Who knows what other scientific advances are being stymied because scientists are being stifled into walking a narrow path? If the chronoscope becomes the terror of a few politicians, it's a price that must be paid. The public must realize that science must be free and there is no more dramatic way of doing it than to publish my discovery, one way or another, legally or illegally.''

Potterley's brow was damp with perspiration, but his voice remained even. ''Oh, not just a few politicians, Dr. Foster. Don't think that. It would be my terror, too. My wife would spend her time living with our dead daughter. She would retreat further from reality. She would go mad living the same scenes over and over. And not just my terror. There would be others like her. Children searching for their dead parents or their own youth. We'll have a whole world living in the past. Midsummer madness.''

Foster said, ''Moral judgments can't stand in the way. There isn't one advance at any time in history that mankind hasn't had the ingenuity to pervert. Mankind must also have the ingenuity to prevent. As for the chronoscope, your delvers into the dead past will get tired soon enough. They'll catch their loved parents in some of the things their loved parents did and they'll lose their enthusiasm for it all. But all this is trivial. With me, it's a matter of important principle.''

Potterley said, ''Hang your principle. Can't you understand men and women as well as principle? Don't you understand that my wife will live through the fire that killed our baby? She won't be able to help herself. I know her. She'll follow through each step, trying to prevent it. She'll live it over and over again, hoping each time that it won't happen. How many times do you want to kill Laurel?'' A huskiness had crept into his voice.

A thought crossed Foster's mind. ''What are you really afraid she'll find out, Dr. Potterley? What happened the night of the fire?''

The historian's hands went up quickly to cover his face and they shook with his dry sobs. Foster turned away and stared uncomfortably out the window.

Potterley said after a while, ''It's a long time since I've had to think of it. Caroline was away. I was baby-sitting. I went into the baby's bedroom midevening to see if she had kicked off the bedclothes. I had my cigarette with me . . . I smoked in those days. I must have stubbed it out before putting it in the ashtray on the chest of drawers. I was always careful. The baby was all right. I returned to the living room and fell asleep before the video. I awoke, choking, surrounded by fire. I don't know how it started.''

''But you think it may have been the cigarette, is that it?'' said Foster. ''A cigarette which, for once, you forgot to stub out?''

''I don't know. I tried to save her, but she was dead in my arms when I got out.''

''You never told your wife about the cigarette, I suppose.''

Potterley shook his head. ''But I've lived with it.''

''Only now, with a chronoscope, she'll find out. Maybe it wasn't the cigarette. Maybe you did stub it out. Isn't that possible?''

The scant tears had dried on Potterley's face. The redness had subsided. He said, ''I can't take the chance. . . . But it's not just myself, Foster. The past has its terrors for most people. Don't loose those terrors on the human race.''

Foster paced the floor. Somehow, this explained the reason for Potterley's rabid, irrational desire to boost the Carthaginians, deify them, most of all disprove the story of their fiery sacrifices to Moloch. By freeing them of the guilt of infanticide by fire, he symbolically freed himself of the same guilt.

So the same fire that had driven him on to causing the construction of a chronoscope was now driving him on to the destruction.

Foster looked sadly at the older man. "I see your position, Dr. Potterley, but this goes above personal feelings. I've got to smash this throttling hold on the throat of science."

Potterley said, savagely, "You mean you want the fame and wealth that goes with such a discovery."

"I don't know about the wealth, but that, too, I suppose. I'm not more than human."

"You won't suppress your knowledge?"

"Not under any circumstances."

"Well, then——" and the historian got to his feet and stood for a moment, glaring.

Foster had an odd moment of terror. The man was older than he, smaller, feebler, and he didn't look armed. Still . . .

Foster said, "If you're thinking of killing me or anything insane like that, I've got the information in a safety-deposit vault where the proper people will find it in case of my disappearance or death."

Potterley said, "Don't be a fool," and stalked out.

Foster closed the door, locked it and sat down to think. He felt silly. He had no information in any safety-deposit vault, of course. Such a melodramatic action would not have occurred to him ordinarily. But now it had.

Feeling even sillier, he spent an hour writing out the equations of the application of pseudo-gravitic optics to neutrinic recording, and some diagrams of the engineering details of construction. He sealed it in an envelope and scrawled Ralph Nimmo's name over the outside.

He spent a rather restless night and the next morning, on the way to school, dropped the envelope off at the bank, with appropriate instructions to an official, who made him sign a paper permitting the box to be opened after his death.

He called Nimmo to tell him of the existence of the envelope, refusing querulously to say anything about its contents.

He had never felt so ridiculously self-conscious as at that moment.

That night and the next, Foster spent in only fitful sleep, finding himself face to face with the highly practical problem of the publication of data unethically obtained.

The *Proceedings of the Society for Pseudo-Gravitics,* which was the journal with which he was best acquainted, would certainly not touch any paper that did not include the magic footnote: "The work described in this paper was made possible by Grant No. so-and-so from the Commission of Research of the United Nations."

Nor, doubly so, would the *Journal of Physics.*

There were always the minor journals who might overlook the nature of the article for the sake of the sensation, but that would require a little financial negotiation on which he hesitated to embark. It might, on the whole, be better to pay the cost of publishing a small pamphlet for general distribution among scholars. In that case, he would even be able to dispense with the services of a science writer, sacrificing polish for speed. He would have to find a reliable printer. Uncle Ralph might know one.

He walked down the corridor to his office and wondered anxiously if perhaps he ought to waste no further time, give himself no further chance to lapse into indecision and take the risk of calling Ralph from his office phone. He was so absorbed in his own heavy thoughts that he did not notice that his room was occupied until he turned from the clothes closet and approached his desk.

Dr. Potterley was there and a man whom Foster did not recognize.

Foster stared at them. "What's this?"

Potterley said, "I'm sorry, but I had to stop you."

Foster continued staring. "What are you talking about?"

The stranger said, "Let me introduce myself." He had large teeth, a little uneven, and they showed prominently when he smiled. "I am Thaddeus Araman, Department Head of the Division of Chronoscopy. I am here to see you concerning information brought to me by Professor Arnold Potterley and confirmed by our own sources——"

Potterley said breathlessly, "I took all the blame, Dr. Foster. I explained that it was I who persuaded you against your will into unethical practices. I have offered to accept full responsibility and punishment. I don't wish you harmed in any way. It's just that chronoscopy must not be permitted!"

Araman nodded. "He has taken the blame as he says, Dr. Foster, but this thing is out of his hands now."

Foster said, "So? What are you going to do? Blackball me from all consideration for research grants?"

"That is in my power," said Araman.

"Order the university to discharge me?"

"That, too, is in my power."

"All right, go ahead. Consider it done. I'll leave my office now, with you. I can send for my books later. If you insist, I'll leave my books. Is that all?"

"Not quite," said Araman. "You must engage to do no further research in chronoscopy, to publish none of your findings in chronoscopy and, of course, to build no chronoscope. You will remain under surveillance indefinitely to make sure you keep that promise."

"Supposing I refuse to promise? What can you do? Doing research out of my field may be unethical, but it isn't a criminal offense."

"In the case of chronoscopy, my young friend," said Araman patiently, "it is a criminal offense. If necessary, you will be put in jail and kept there."

"Why?" shouted Foster. "What's magic about chronoscopy?"

Araman said, "That's the way it is. We cannot allow further developments in the field. My own job is, primarily, to make sure of that, and I intend to do my job. Unfortunately, I had no knowledge, nor did anyone in the department, that the optics of pseudo-gravity fields had such immediate application to chronoscopy. Score one for general ignorance, but henceforward research will be steered properly in that respect, too."

Foster said, "That won't help. Something else may apply that neither you nor I dream of. All science hangs together. It's one piece. If you want to stop one part, you've got to stop it all."

"No doubt that is true," said Araman, "in theory. On the practical side, however, we have managed quite well to hold chronoscopy down to the original Sterbinski level for fifty years. Having caught you in time, Dr. Foster, we hope to continue doing so indefinitely. And we wouldn't have come this close to disaster, either, if I had accepted Dr. Potterley at something more than face value."

He turned toward the historian and lifted his eyebrows in a kind of humorous self-deprecation. "I'm afraid, sir, that I dismissed you as a history professor and no more on the occasion of our first interview. Had I done my job properly and checked on you, this would not have happened."

Foster said abruptly, "Is anyone allowed to use the government chrono-scope?"

"No one outside our division under any pretext. I say that since it is obvious to me that you have already guessed as much. I warn you, though, that any repetition of that fact will be a criminal, not an ethical, offense."

"And your chronoscope doesn't go back more than a hundred twenty-five years or so, does it?"

"It doesn't."

"Then your bulletin with its stories of time viewing ancient times is a hoax?"

Araman said coolly, "With the knowledge you now have, it is obvious you know that for a certainty. However, I confirm your remark. The monthly bulletin is a hoax."

"In that case," said Foster, "I will not promise to suppress my knowledge of chronoscopy. If you wish to arrest me, go ahead. My defense at the trial will be enough to destroy the vicious card house of directed research and bring it tumbling down. Directing research is one thing; suppressing it and depriving mankind of its benefits is quite another."

Araman said, "Oh, let's get something straight, Dr. Foster. If you do not co-operate, you will go to jail directly. You will *not* see a lawyer, you will *not* be charged, you will *not* have a trial. You will simply stay in jail."

"Oh, no," said Foster, "you're bluffing. This is not the twentieth century, you know."

There was a stir outside, the clatter of feet, a high-pitched shout that Foster was sure he recognized. The door crashed open, the lock splintering, and three intertwined figures stumbled in.

As they did so, one of the men raised a blaster and brought its butt down hard on the skull of another.

There was a whoosh of expiring air, and the one whose head was struck went limp.

"Uncle Ralph!" cried Foster.

Araman frowned. "Put him down in that chair," he ordered, "and get some water."

Ralph Nimmo, rubbing his head with a gingerly sort of disgust, said, "There was no need to get rough, Araman."

Araman said, "The guard should have been rough sooner and kept you out of here, Nimmo. You'd have been better off."

"You know each other?" asked Foster.

"I've had dealings with the man," said Nimmo, still rubbing. "If he's here in your office, nephew, you're in trouble."

"And you, too," said Araman angrily. "I know Dr. Foster consulted you on neutrinics literature."

Nimmo corrugated his forehead, then straightened it with a wince as though the action had brought pain. "So?" he said. "What else do you know about me?"

"We will know everything about you soon enough. Meanwhile, that one item is enough to implicate you. What are you doing here?"

"My dear Dr. Araman," said Nimmo, some of his jauntiness restored, "day before yesterday, my jackass of a nephew called me. He had placed some mysterious information——"

"Don't tell him! Don't say anything!" cried Foster.

Araman glanced at him coldly. "We know all about it, Dr. Foster. The safety-deposit box has been opened and its contents removed."

"But how can you know——" Foster's voice died away in a kind of furious frustration.

"Anyway," said Nimmo, "I decided the net must be closing around him and, after I took care of a few items, I came down to tell him to get off this thing he's doing. It's not worth his career."

"Does that mean you know what he's doing?" asked Araman.

"He never told me," said Nimmo, "but I'm a science writer with a hell of a lot of experience. I know which side of an atom is electronified. The boy, Foster, specializes in pseudo-gravitic optics and coached me on the stuff himself. He got me to get him a textbook on neutrinics and I kind of ship-viewed it myself before handing it over. I can put the two together. He asked me to get him certain pieces of physical equipment, and that was evidence, too. Stop me if I'm wrong, but my nephew has built a semiportable, low-power chronoscope. Yes, or—yes?"

"Yes." Araman reached thoughtfully for a cigarette and paid no attention to Dr. Potterley (watching silently, as though all were a dream) who shied away, gasping, from the white cylinder. "Another mistake for me. I ought to resign. I should have put tabs on you, too, Nimmo, instead of concentrating too hard on Potterley and Foster. I didn't have much time of course and you've ended up safely here, but that doesn't excuse me. You're under arrest, Nimmo."

"What for?" demanded the science writer.

"Unauthorized research."

"I wasn't doing any. I can't, not being a registered scientist. And even if I did, it's not a criminal offense."

Foster said savagely, "No use, Uncle Ralph. This bureaucrat is making his own laws."

"Like what?" demanded Nimmo.

"Like life imprisonment without trial."

"Nuts," said Nimmo. "This isn't the twentieth cen——"

"I tried that," said Foster. "It doesn't bother him."

"Well, nuts," shouted Nimmo. "Look here, Araman. My nephew and I have relatives who haven't lost touch with us, you know. The professor has some also, I imagine. You can't just make us disappear. There'll be questions and a scandal. This *isn't* the twentieth century. So if you're trying to scare us, it isn't working."

The cigarette snapped between Araman's fingers and he tossed it away violently. He said, "Damn it, I don't know *what* to do. It's never been like this before. . . . Look! You three fools know nothing of what you're trying to do. You understand nothing. Will you listen to me?"

"Oh, we'll listen," said Nimmo grimly.

(Foster sat silently, eyes angry, lips compressed. Potterley's hands writhed like two intertwined snakes.)

Araman said, "The past to you is the dead past. If any of you have discussed the matter, it's dollars to nickels you've used that phrase. The dead past. If you knew how many times I've heard those three words, you'd choke on them, too.

"When people think of the past, they think of it as dead, far away and gone, long ago. We encourage them to think so. When we report time viewing, we always talk of views centuries in the past, even though you gentlemen know seeing more than a century or so is impossible. People accept it. The past means Greece, Rome, Carthage, Egypt, the Stone Age. The deader the better.

"Now you three know a century or a little more is the limit, so what does the past mean to you? Your youth. Your first girl. Your dead mother. Twenty years ago. Thirty years ago. Fifty years ago. The deader the better. . . . But when does the past really begin?"

He paused in anger. The others stared at him and Nimmo stirred uneasily.

"Well," said Araman, "when did it begin? A year ago? Five minutes ago? One second ago? Isn't it obvious that the past begins an instant ago? The dead past is just another name for the living present. What if you focus the chronoscope in the past of one-hundredth of a second ago? Aren't you watching the present? Does it begin to sink in?"

Nimmo said, "Damnation."

"Damnation," mimicked Araman. "After Potterley came to me with his story night before last, how do you suppose I checked up on both of you? I did it with the chronoscope, spotting key moments to the very instant of the present."

"And that's how you knew about the safety-deposit box?" said Foster.

"And every other important fact. Now what do you suppose would happen if we let news of a home chronoscope get out? People might start out by watching their youth, their parents and so on, but it wouldn't be long before they'd catch on to the possibilities. The housewife will forget her poor, dead mother and take to watching her neighbor at home and her husband at the office. The businessman will watch his competitor; the employer his employee.

"There will be no such thing as privacy. The party line, the prying eye behind the curtain will be nothing compared to it. The video stars will be closely watched at all times by everyone. Every man his own peeping Tom and there'll be no getting away from the watcher. Even darkness will be no escape because chronoscopy can be adjusted to the infrared and human figures can be seen by their own body heat. The figures will be fuzzy, of course, and the surroundings will be dark, but that will make the titillation of it all the greater, perhaps. . . . Hmp, the men in charge of the machine now experiment sometimes in spite of the regulations against it."

Nimmo seemed sick. "You can always forbid private manufacture——"

Araman turned on him fiercely. "You can, but do you expect it to do good? Can you legislate successfully against drinking, smoking, adultery or gossiping over the back fence? And this mixture of nosiness and prurience will have a worse grip on humanity than any of those. Good Lord, in a thousand years of trying we haven't been able to wipe out the heroin traffic and you talk about legislating against a device for watching anyone you please at any time you please that can be built in a home workshop."

Foster said suddenly, "I won't publish."

Potterley burst out, half in sobs, "None of us will talk. I regret——"

Nimmo broke in. "You said you didn't tab me on the chronoscope, Araman."

"No time," said Araman wearily. "Things don't move any faster on the chronoscope than in real life. You can't speed it up like the film in a book viewer. We spent a full twenty-four hours trying to catch the important moments during the last six months of Potterley and Foster. There was no time for anything else and it was enough."

"It wasn't," said Nimmo.

"What are you talking about?" There was a sudden infinite alarm on Araman's face.

"I told you my nephew, Jonas, had called me to say he had put important information in a safety-deposit box. He acted as though he were in trouble. He's my nephew. I had to try to get him off the spot. It took a while, then I came here to tell him what I had done. I told you when I got here, just after your man conked me that I had taken care of a few items."

"What? For Heaven's sake——"

"Just this: I sent the details of the portable chronoscope off to half a dozen of my regular publicity outlets."

Not a word. Not a sound. Not a breath. They were all past any demonstration.

"Don't stare like that," cried Nimmo. "Don't you see my point? I had popular publication rights. Jonas will admit that. I knew he couldn't publish scientifically in any legal way. I was sure he was planning to publish illegally and was preparing the safety-deposit box for that reason. I thought if I put through the details prematurely, all the responsibility would be mine. His career would be saved. And if I were deprived of my science-writing license as a result, my exclusive possession of the chronometric data would set me up for life. Jonas would be angry, I expected that, but I could explain the motive and we would split the take fifty-fifty. . . . Don't stare at me like that. How did I know——"

"Nobody knew anything," said Araman bitterly, "but you all just took it for granted that the government was stupidly bureaucratic, vicious, tyrannical, given to suppressing research for the hell of it. It never occurred to any of you that we were trying to protect mankind as best we could."

"Don't sit there talking," wailed Potterley. "Get the names of the people who were told——"

"Too late," said Nimmo, shrugging. "They've had better than a day. There's been time for the word to spread. My outfits will have called any number of physicists to check my data before going on with it and they'll call one another to pass on the news. Once scientists put neutrinics and pseudo-gravitics together, home chronoscopy becomes obvious. Before the week is out, five hundred people will know how to build a small chronoscope and how will you catch them all?" His plum cheeks sagged. "I suppose there's no way of putting the mushroom cloud back into that nice, shiny uranium sphere."

Araman stood up. "We'll try, Potterley, but I agree with Nimmo. It's too late. What kind of a world we'll have from now on, I don't know, I can't tell, but the world we know has been destroyed completely. Until now, every custom, every habit, every tiniest way of life has always taken a certain amount of privacy for granted, but that's all gone now."

He saluted each of the three with elaborate formality.

"You have created a new world among the three of you. I congratulate you. Happy goldfish bowl to you, to me, to everyone, and may each of you fry in hell forever. Arrest rescinded."

HOSTESS

ROSE SMOLLETT was happy about it; almost triumphant. She peeled off her gloves, put her hat away, and turned her brightening eyes upon her husband.

She said, "Drake, we're going to have him here."

Drake looked at her with annoyance. "You've missed supper. I thought you were going to be back by seven."

"Oh, that doesn't matter. I ate something on the way home. But, Drake, we're going to have him here!"

"*Who* here? What are you talking about?"

"The doctor from Hawkin's Planet! Didn't you realize that was what today's conference was about? We spent all day talking about it. It's the most exciting thing that could possibly have happened!"

Drake Smollett removed the pipe from the vicinity of his face. He stared first at it and then at his wife. "Let me get this straight. When you say the doctor from Hawkin's Planet, do you mean the Hawkinsite you've got at the Institute?"

"Well, of course. Who else could I possibly mean?"

"And may I ask what the devil you mean by saying we'll have him here?"

"Drake, don't you understand?"

"What is there to understand? Your Institute may be interested in the thing, but I'm not. What have we do with it personally? It's Institute business, isn't it?"

"But, darling," Rose said, patiently, "the Hawkinsite would like to stay at a private house somewhere, where he won't be bothered with official ceremony, and where he'll be able to proceed more according to his own likes and dislikes. I find it quite understandable."

"Why at *our* house?"

"Because our place is convenient for the purpose, I suppose. They asked if I would allow it, and frankly," she added with some stiffness, "I consider it a privilege."

"Look!" Drake put his fingers through his brown hair and succeeded in rumpling it. "We've got a convenient little place here—granted! It's not the most elegant place in the world, but it does well enough for us. However, I don't see where we've got room for extraterrestrial visitors."

* * *

229

Rose began to look worried. She removed her glasses and put them away in their case. "He can stay in the spare room. He'll take care of it himself. I've spoken to him and he's very pleasant. Honestly, all we have to do is show a certain amount of adaptability."

Drake said, "Sure, just a little adapatability! The Hawkinsites breathe cyanide. We'll just adapt ourselves to that, I suppose!"

"He carries the cyanide in a little cylinder. You won't even notice it."

"And what else about them won't I notice?"

"*Nothing* else. They're perfectly harmless. Goodness, they're even vegetarians."

"And what does that mean? Do we feed him a bale of hay for dinner?"

Rose's lower lip trembled. "Drake, you're being deliberately hateful. There are many vegetarians on Earth; they don't eat hay."

"And what about us? Do we eat meat ourselves or will that make us look like cannibals to him? I won't live on salads to suit him; I warn you."

"You're being quite ridiculous."

Rose felt helpless. She had married late in life, comparatively. Her career had been chosen; she herself had seemed well settled in it. She was a fellow in biology at the Jenkins Institute for Natural Sciences, with over twenty publications to her credit. In a word, the line was hewed, the path cleared; she had been set for a career and spinsterhood. And now, at thirty-five, she was still a little amazed to find herself a bride of less than a year.

Occasionally, it embarrassed her, too, since she sometimes found that she had not the slightest idea of how to handle her husband. What *did* one do when the man of the family became mulish? That was not included in any of her courses. As a woman of independent mind and career, she couldn't bring herself to cajolery.

So she looked at him steadily and said simply, "It means very much to me."

"Why?"

"Because, Drake, if he stays here for any length of time, I can study him really closely. Very little work has been done on the biology and psychology of the individual Hawkinsites or of any of the extraterrestrial intelligences. We have some on their sociology and history, of course, but that's all. Surely, you must see the opportunity. He stays here; we watch him, speak to him, observe his habits—"

"Not interested."

"Oh, Drake, I don't understand you."

"You're going to say I'm not usually like this, I suppose."

"Well, you're not."

Drake was silent for a while. He seemed withdrawn and his high cheekbones and large chin were twisted and frozen into a brooding position.

He said, finally, "Look, I've heard a bit about the Hawkinsites in the way of my own business. You say there have been investigations of their sociology, but not of their biology. Sure. It's because Hawkinsites don't like to be studied as specimens any more than we would. I've spoken to men who were in charge of security groups watching various Hawkinsite missions on Earth. The missions stay in the rooms assigned to them and don't leave for anything but the most important official business. They have nothing to do with Earthmen. It's quite obvious that they are as revolted by us as I personally am by them.

"In fact, I just don't understand why this Hawkinsite at the Institute should be any different. It seems to me to be against all the rules to have him come here by himself, anyway—and to have him want to stay in an Earthman's home just puts the maraschino cherry on top."

Rose said, wearily, "This is different. I'm surprised you can't understand it, Drake. He's a doctor. He's coming here in the way of medical research, and I'll grant you that he probably doesn't enjoy staying with human beings and will find us perfectly horrible. But he must stay just the same! Do you suppose human doctors enjoy going into the tropics, or that they are particularly fond of letting themselves be bitten by infected mosquitoes?"

Drake said sharply, "What's this about mosquitoes? What have they to do with it?"

"Why, nothing," Rose answered, surprised. "It just came to my mind, that's all. I was thinking of Reed and his yellow fever experiments."

Drake shrugged. "Well, have it your own way."

For a moment, Rose hesitated. "You're not angry about this, are you?" To her own ears she sounded unpleasantly girlish.

"No."

And that, Rose knew, meant that he was.

Rose surveyed herself doubtfully in the full-length mirror. She had never been beautiful and was quite reconciled to the fact; so much so that it no longer mattered. Certainly, it would not matter to a being from Hawkin's Planet. What *did* bother her was this matter of being a hostess under the very queer circumstances of having to be tactful to an extraterrestrial creature and, at the same time, to her husband as well. She wondered which would prove the more difficult.

Drake was coming home late that day; he was not due for half an hour. Rose found herself inclined to believe that he had arranged that purposely in a sullen desire to leave her alone with her problem. She found herself in a state of mild resentment.

He had called her just before noon at the Institute and had asked abruptly, "When are you taking him home?"

She answered curtly, "In about three hours."

"All right. What's his name? His Hawkinsite name?"

"Why do you want to know?" She could not keep the chill from her words.

"Let's call it a small investigation of my own. After all, the thing will be in my house."

"Oh, for heaven's sake, Drake, don't bring your job home with you!"

Drake's voice sounded tinny and nasty in her ears. "Why not, Rose? Isn't that exactly what you're doing?"

It was, of course, so she gave him the information he wanted.

This was the first time in their married life that they had had even the semblance of a quarrel, and, as she sat there before the full-length mirror, she began to wonder if perhaps she ought not make an attempt to see his side of it. In essence, she had married a policeman. Of course he was more than simply a policeman; he was a member of the World Security Board.

It had been a surprise to her friends. The fact of the marriage itself had been the biggest surprise, but if she had decided on marriage, the attitude was, why not with another biologist? Or, if she had wanted to go afield, an anthropologist, perhaps; even a chemist; but why, of all people, a policeman? Nobody had exactly said those things, naturally, but it had been in the very atmosphere at the time of her marriage.

She had resented it then, and ever since. A man could marry whom he chose, but if a doctor of philosophy, female variety, chose to marry a man who never went past the bachelor's degree, there was shock. Why should there be? What business was it of theirs? He was handsome, in a way, intelligent, in another way, and she was perfectly satisfied with her choice.

Yet how much of this same snobbishness did she bring home with her? Didn't she always have the attitude that her own work, her biological investigations, were important, while his job was merely something to be kept within the four walls of his little office in the old U.N. buildings on the East River?

She jumped up from her seat in agitation and, with a deep breath, decided to leave such thoughts behind her. She desperately did not want to quarrel with him. And she just wasn't going to interfere with him. She was committed to accepting the Hawkinsite as guest, but otherwise she would let Drake have his own way. He was making enough of a concession as it was.

Harg Tholan was standing quietly in the middle of the living room when she came down the stairs. He was not sitting, since he was not anatomically constructed to sit. He stood on two sets of limbs placed close together, while a third pair entirely different in construction were suspended from a region that would have been the upper chest in a human being. The skin of his body was hard, glistening and ridged, while his face bore a distant resemblance to something alienly bovine. Yet he was not completely repulsive, and he wore clothes of a sort over the lower portion of his body in order to avoid offending the sensibilities of his human hosts.

He said, "Mrs. Smollett, I appreciate your hospitality beyond my ability to express it in your language," and he drooped so that his forelimbs touched the ground for a moment.

Rose knew this to be a gesture signifying gratitude among the beings of Hawkin's Planet. She was grateful that he spoke English as well as he did. The construction of his mouth, combined with an absence of incisors, gave a whistling sound to the sibilants. Aside from that, he might have been born on Earth for all the accent his speech showed.

She said, "My husband will be home soon, and then we will eat."

"Your husband?" For a moment, he said nothing more, and then added, "Yes, of course."

She let it go. If there was one source of infinite confusion among the five intelligent races of the known Galaxy, it lay in the differences among them with regard to their sex life and the social institutions that grew around it. The concept of husband and wife, for instance, existed only on Earth. The other races could achieve a sort of intellectual understanding of what it meant, but never an emotional one.

She said, "I have consulted the Institute in preparing your menu. I trust you will find nothing in it that will upset you."

The Hawkinsite blinked its eyes rapidly. Rose recalled this to be a gesture of amusement.

He said, "Proteins are proteins, my dear Mrs. Smollett. For those trace factors which I need but are not supplied in your food, I have brought concentrates that will be most adequate."

And proteins *were* proteins. Rose knew this to be true. Her concern for the creature's diet had been largely one of formal politeness. In the discovery of life on the planets of the outer stars, one of the most interesting generalizations that had developed was the fact that, although life could be formed on the basis of substances other than proteins—even on elements other than carbon—it remained true that the only known intelligences were proteinaceous in nature. This meant that each of the five forms of intelligent life could maintain themselves over prolonged periods on the food of any of the other four.

She heard Drake's key in the door and went stiff with apprehension.

She had to admit he did well. He strode in, and, without hesitation, thrust his hand out at the Hawkinsite, saying firmly, "Good evening, Dr. Tholan."

The Hawkinsite put out his large and rather clumsy forelimb and the two, so to speak, shook hands. Rose had already gone through that procedure and knew the queer feeling of a Hawkinsite hand in her own. It had felt rough and hot and dry. She imagined that, to the Hawkinsite, her own and Drake's felt cold and slimy.

At the time of the formal greeting, she had taken the opportunity to observe the alien hand. It was an excellent case of converging evolution. Its morphological development was entirely different from that of the human hand, yet it had brought itself into a fairly approximate similarity. There were four fingers but no thumb. Each finger had five independent ball-and-socket joints. In this way, the flexibility lost with the absence of the thumb was made up for by the almost tentacular properties of the fingers. What was even more interesting to her biologist's eyes was the fact that each Hawkinsite finger ended in a vestigial hoof, very small and, to the layman, unidentifiable as such, but clearly adapted at one time to running, just as man's had been to climbing.

Drake said, in friendly enough fashion, "Are you quite comfortable, sir?"

The Hawkinsite answered, "Quite. Your wife has been most thoughtful in all her arrangements."

"Would you care for a drink?"

The Hawkinsite did not answer but looked at Rose with a slight facial contortion that indicated some emotion which, unfortunately, Rose could not interpret. She said, nervously, "On Earth there is the custom of drinking liquids which have been fortified with ethyl alcohol. We find it stimulating."

"Oh, yes. I am afraid, then, that I must decline. Ethyl alcohol would interfere most unpleasantly with my metabolism."

"Why, so it does to Earthmen, too, but I understand, Dr. Tholan," Drake replied. "Would you object to *my* drinking?"

"Of course not."

Drake passed close to Rose on his way to the sideboard and she caught only one word. He said, "God!" in a tightly controlled whisper, yet he managed to put seventeen exclamation points after it.

*   *   *

The Hawkinsite *stood* at the table. His fingers were models of dexterity as they wove their way around the cutlery. Rose tried not to look at him as he ate. His wide lipless mouth split his face alarmingly as he ingested food, and, in chewing, his large jaws moved disconcertingly from side to side. It was another evidence of his ungulate ancestry. Rose found herself wondering if, in the quiet of his own room, he would later chew his cud, and was then panic-stricken lest Drake get the same idea and leave the table in disgust. But Drake was taking everything quite calmly.

He said, "I imagine, Dr. Tholan, that the cylinder at your side holds cyanide?"

Rose started. She had actually not noticed it. It was a curved metal object, something like a water canteen, that fitted flatly against the creature's skin, half-hidden behind its clothing. But, then, Drake had a policeman's eyes.

The Hawkinsite was not in the least disconcerted. "Quite so," he said, and his hoofed fingers held out a thin, flexible hose that ran up his body, its tint blending into that of his yellowish skin, and entered the corner of his wide mouth. Rose felt slightly embarrassed, as though at the display of intimate articles of clothing.

Drake said, "And does it contain pure cyanide?"

The Hawkinsite humorously blinked his eyes. "I hope you are not considering possible danger to Earthites. I know the gas is highly poisonous to you and I do not need a great deal. The gas contained in the cylinder is five percent hydrogen cyanide, the remainder oxygen. None of it emerges except when I actually suck at the tube, and that need not be done frequently."

"I see. And you really must have the gas to live?"

Rose was slightly appalled. One simply did not ask such questions without careful preparation. It was impossible to foresee where the sensitive points of an alien psychology might be. And Drake *must* be doing this deliberately, since he could not help realizing that he could get answers to such questions as easily from herself. Or was it that he preferred not to ask her?

The Hawkinsite remained apparently unperturbed. "Are you not a biologist, Mr. Smollett?"

"No, Dr. Tholan."

"But you are in close association with Mrs. *Dr.* Smollett."

Drake smiled a bit. "Yes, I am married to a Mrs. doctor, but just the same I am not a biologist; merely a minor government official. My wife's friends," he added, "call me a policeman."

Rose bit the inside of her cheek. In this case it was the Hawkinsite who had impinged upon the sensitive point of an alien psychology. On Hawkin's Planet, there was a tight caste system and intercaste associations were limited. But Drake wouldn't realize that.

The Hawkinsite turned to her. "May I have your permission, Mrs. Smollett, to explain a little of our biochemistry to your husband? It will be dull for you, since I am sure you must understand it quite well already."

She said, "By all means do, Dr. Tholan."

He said, "You see, Mr. Smollett, the respiratory system in your body and in the bodies of all air-breathing creatures on Earth is controlled by certain metal-containing enzymes, I am taught. The metal is usually iron, though sometimes it is copper. In either case, small traces of cyanide would combine with these metals and immobilize the respiratory system of the terrestrial living cell. They would be prevented from using oxygen and killed in a few minutes.

"The life on my own planet is not quite so constituted. The key respiratory compounds contain neither iron nor copper; no metal at all, in fact. It is for this reason that my blood is colorless. Our compounds contain certain organic groupings which are essential to life, and these groupings can only be maintained intact in the presence of a small concentration of cyanide. Undoubtedly, this type of protein has developed through millions of years of evolution on a world which has a few tenths of a percent of hydrogen cyanide occurring naturally in the atmosphere. Its presence is maintained by a biological cycle. Various of our native micro-organisms liberate the free gas."

"You make it extremely clear, Dr. Tholan, and very interesting," Drake said. "What happens if you don't breathe it? Do you just go, like that?" He snapped his fingers.

"Not quite. It isn't equivalent to the presence of cyanide for you. In my case, the absence of cyanide would be equivalent to slow strangulation. It happens sometimes, in ill-ventilated rooms on my world, that the cyanide is gradually consumed and falls below the minimum necessary concentration. The results are very painful and difficult to treat."

Rose had to give Drake credit; he really sounded interested. And the alien, thank heaven, did not mind the catechism.

The rest of the dinner passed without incident. It was almost pleasant.

Throughout the evening, Drake remained that way; interested. Even more than that—absorbed. He drowned her out, and she was glad of it. *He* was the one who was really colorful and it was only her job, her specialized training, that stole the color from him. She looked at him gloomily and thought, *Why did he marry me?*

Drake sat, one leg crossed over the other, hands clasped and tapping his chin gently, watching the Hawkinsite intently. The Hawkinsite faced him, standing in his quadruped fashion.

Drake said, "I find it difficult to keep thinking of you as a doctor."

The Hawkinsite laughingly blinked his eyes. "I understand what you mean," he said. "I find it difficult to think of you as a policeman. On my world, policemen are very specialized and distinctive people."

"Are they?" said Drake, somewhat drily, and then changed the subject. "I gather that you are not here on a pleasure trip."

"No, I am here very much on business. I intend to study this queer planet you call Earth, as it has never been studied before by any of my people."

"Queer?" asked Drake. "In what way?"

The Hawkinsite looked at Rose. "Does he know of the Inhibition Death?"

Rose felt embarrassed. "His work is important," she said. "I am afraid that my husband has little time to listen to the details of my work." She knew that this was not really adequate and she felt herself to be the recipient, yet again, of one of the Hawkinsite's unreadable emotions.

The extraterrestrial creature turned back to Drake. "It is always amazing to me to find how little you Earthmen understand your own unusual characteristics. Look, there are five intelligent races in the Galaxy. These have all developed independently, yet have managed to converge in remarkable fashion. It is as though, in the long run, intelligence requires a certain physical makeup to flourish. I leave that question for philosophers. But I need not belabor the point, since it must be a familiar one to you.

"Now when the differences among the intelligences are closely investigated, it is found over and over again that it is you Earthmen, more than any of the others, who are unique. For instance, it is only on Earth that life depends upon metal enzymes for respiration. Your people are the only ones which find hydrogen cyanide poisonous. Yours is the only form of intelligent life which is carnivorous. Yours is the only form of life which has not developed from a grazing animal. And, most interesting of all, yours is the only form of intelligent life known which stops growing upon reaching maturity."

Drake grinned at him. Rose felt her heart suddenly race. It was the nicest thing about him, that grin, and he was using it perfectly naturally. It wasn't forced or false. He was *adjusting* to the presence of this alien creature. He was being pleasant—and he must be doing it for her. She loved that thought and repeated it to herself. He was doing it for her; he was being nice to the Hawkinsite for her sake.

Drake was saying with his grin, "You don't look very large, Dr. Tholan, I should say that you are an inch taller than I am, which would make you six feet two inches tall. Is it that you are young, or is it that the others on your world are generally small?"

"Neither," said the Hawkinsite. "We grow at a diminishing rate with the years, so that at my age it would take fifteen years to grow an additional inch, but—and this is the important point—we never *entirely* stop. And, of course, as a consequence, we never entirely die."

Drake gasped and even Rose felt herself sitting stiffly upright. This was something new. This was something which, to her knowledge, the few expeditions to Hawkin's Planet had never brought back. She was torn with excitement but held an exclamation back and let Drake speak for her.

He said, "They don't entirely die? You're not trying to say, sir, that the people on Hawkin's Planet are immortal?"

"No people are truly immortal. If there were no other way to die, there would always be accident, and if that fails, there is boredom. Few of us live more than several centuries of your time. Still, it is unpleasant to think that death may come involuntarily. It is something which, to us, is extremely horrible. It bothers me even as I think of it now, this thought that *against my will and despite all care,* death may come."

"We," said Drake, grimly, "are quite used to it."

"You Earthmen live with the thought; we do not. And this is why we are disturbed to find that the incidence of Inhibition Death has been increasing in recent years."

"You have not yet explained," said Drake, "just what the Inhibition Death is, but let me guess. Is the Inhibition Death a pathological cessation of growth?"

"Exactly."

"And how long after growth's cessation does death follow?"

"Within the year. It is a waiting disease, a tragic one, and absolutely incurable."

"What causes it?"

*   *   *

The Hawkinsite paused a long time before answering, and even then there was something strained and uneasy about the way he spoke. "Mr. Smollett, we know nothing about the cause of the disease."

Drake nodded thoughtfully. Rose was following the conversation as though she were a spectator at a tennis match.

Drake said, "And why do you come to Earth to study this disease?"

"Because again Earthmen are unique. They are the only intelligent beings who are immune. The Inhibition Death affects *all* the other races. Do your biologists know that, Mrs. Smollett?"

He had addressed her suddenly, so that she jumped slightly. She said, "No, they don't."

"I am not surprised. That piece of information is the result of very recent research. The Inhibition Death is easily diagnosed incorrectly and the incidence is much lower on the other planets. In fact, it is a strange thing, something to philosophize over, that the incidence of the Death is highest on my world, which is closest to Earth, and lower on each more distant planet—so that it is lowest on the world of the star Tempora, which is farthest from Earth, while Earth itself is immune. Somewhere in the biochemistry of the Earthite, there is the secret of that immunity. How interesting it would be to find it."

Drake said, "But look here, you can't say Earth is immune. From where I sit, it looks as if the incidence is a hundred percent. All Earthmen stop growing and all Earthmen die. We've *all* got the Inhibition Death."

"Not at all. Earthmen live up to seventy years after the cessation of growth. That is not the Death as *we* know it. *Your* equivalent disease is rather one of unrestrained growth. Cancer, you call it. But come, I bore you."

Rose protested instantly. Drake did likewise with even more vehemence, but the Hawkinsite determinedly changed the subject. It was then that Rose had her first pang of suspicion, for Drake circled Harg Tholan warily with his words, worrying him, jabbing at him, attempting always to get the information back to the point where the Hawkinsite had left off. Not baldly, not unskillfully, but Rose knew him, and could tell what he was after. And what could he be after but that which was demanded by his profession? And, as though in response to her thoughts, the Hawkinsite took up the phrase which had begun careening in her mind like a broken record on a perpetual turntable.

He asked, "Did you not say you were a policeman?"

Drake said, curtly, "Yes."

"Then there is something I would like to request you to do for me. I have been wanting to all this evening, since I discovered your profession, and yet I hesitate. I do not wish to be troublesome to my host and hostess."

"We'll do what we can."

"I have a profound curiosity as to how Earthmen live; a curiosity which is not perhaps shared by the generality of my countrymen. So I wonder, could you show me through one of the police departments on your planet?"

"I do not belong to a police department in exactly the way you imagine," said Drake, cautiously. "However, I am known to the New York police department. I can manage it without trouble. Tomorrow?"

"That would be most convenient for me. Would I be able to visit the Missing Persons Bureau?"

"The what?"

The Hawkinsite drew his four standing legs closer together, as if he were becoming more intense. "It is a hobby of mine, a little queer corner of interest I have always had. I understand you have a group of police officers whose sole duty it is to search for men who are missing."

"And women and children," added Drake. "But why should that interest you so particularly?"

"Because there again you are unique. There is no such thing as a missing person on our planet. I can't explain the mechanism to you, of course, but among the people of the other worlds, there is always an awareness of one another's presence, especially if there is a strong, affectionate tie. We are always aware of each other's exact location, no matter where on the planet we might be."

Rose grew excited again. The scientific expeditions to Hawkin's Planet had always had the greatest difficulty in penetrating the internal emotional mechanisms of the natives, and here was one who talked freely, who would explain! She forgot to worry about Drake and intruded into the conversation. "Can you feel such awareness even now? On Earth?"

The Hawkinsite said, "You mean across space? No, I'm afraid not. But you see the importance of the matter. All the uniquenesses of Earth should be linked. If the lack of this sense can be explained, perhaps the immunity to Inhibition Death can be, also. Besides, it strikes me as very curious that any form of intelligent community life can be built up among people who lack this community awareness. How can an Earthman tell, for instance, when he has formed a congenial sub-group, a family? How can you two, for instance, know that there is a true tie between you?"

Rose found herself nodding. How strongly she missed such a sense!

But Drake only smiled. "We have our ways. It is as difficult to explain what we call 'love' to you as it is for you to explain your sense to us."

"I suppose so. Yet tell me truthfully, Mr. Smollett—if Mrs. Smollett were to leave this room and enter another without your having seen her do so, would you really not be aware of her location?"

"I really would not."

The Hawkinsite said, "Amazing." He hesitated, then added, "Please do not be offended at the fact that I find it revolting as well."

After the light in the bedroom had been put out, Rose went to the door three times, opening it a crack and peering out. She could feel Drake watching her. There was a hard kind of amusement in his voice as he asked, finally, "What's the matter?"

She said, "I want to talk to you."

"Are you afraid our friend can hear?"

Rose was whispering. She got into bed and put her head on his pillow so that she could whisper better. She said, "Why were you talking about the Inhibition Death to Dr. Tholan?"

"I am taking an interest in your work, Rose. You've always wanted me to take an interest."

"I'd rather you weren't sarcastic." She was almost violent, as nearly violent as she could be in a whisper. "I know that there's something of your own interest in this—of *police* interest, probably. What is it?"

He said, "I'll talk to you tomorrow."

"No, right now."

He put his hand under her head, lifting it. For a wild moment she thought he was going to kiss her—just kiss her on impulse the way husbands sometimes did, or as she imagined they sometimes did. Drake never did, and he didn't now.

He merely held her close and whispered, "Why are you so interested?"

His hand was almost brutally hard upon the nape of her neck, so that she stiffened and tried to draw back. Her voice was more than a whisper now. "Stop it, Drake."

He said, "I want no questions from you and no interference. You do your job, and I'll do mine."

"The nature of my job is open and known."

"The nature of my job," he retorted, "isn't, by definition. But I'll tell you this. Our six-legged friend is here in this house for some definite reason. You weren't picked as biologist in charge for any random reason. Do you know that two days ago, he'd been inquiring about me at the Commission?"

"You're joking."

"Don't believe that for a minute. There are depths to this that you know nothing about. But that's my job and I won't discuss it with you any further. Do you understand?"

"No, but I won't question you if you don't want me to."

"Then go to sleep."

She lay stiffly on her back and the minutes passed, and then the quarter-hours. She was trying to fit the pieces together. Even with what Drake had told her, the curves and colors refused to blend. She wondered what Drake would say if he knew she had a recording of that night's conversation!

One picture remained clear in her mind at that moment. It hovered over her mockingly. The Hawkinsite, at the end of the long evening, had turned to her and said gravely, "Good night, Mrs. Smollett. You are a most charming hostess."

She had desperately wanted to giggle at the time. How could he call her a charming hostess? To him, she could only be a horror, a monstrosity with two few limbs and a too-narrow face.

And then, as the Hawkinsite delivered himself of this completely meaningless piece of politeness, Drake had turned white! For one instant, his eyes had burned with something that looked like terror.

She had never before known Drake to show fear of anything, and the picture of that instant of pure panic remained with her until all her thoughts finally sagged into the oblivion of sleep.

It was noon before Rose was at her desk the next day. She had deliberately waited until Drake and the Hawkinsite had left, since only then was she able to remove the small recorder that had been behind Drake's armchair the previous evening. She had had no original intention of keeping its presence secret from him. It was just that he had come home so late, and she couldn't say anything about it with the Hawkinsite present. Later on, of course, things had changed—

The placing of the recorder had been only a routine maneuver. The Hawkinsite's statements and intonations needed to be preserved for future intensive studies by various specialists at the Institute. It had been hidden in order to avoid the distortions of self-consciousness that the visibility of such a device would bring, and now it couldn't be shown to the members of the Institute at all. It would have to serve a different function altogether. A rather nasty function.

She was going to spy on Drake.

She touched the little box with her fingers and wondered, irrelevantly, how Drake was going to manage, that day. Social intercourse between inhabited worlds was, even now, not so commonplace that the sight of a Hawkinsite on the city streets would not succeed in drawing crowds. But Drake would manage, she knew. Drake always managed.

She listened once again to the sounds of last evening, repeating the interesting moments. She was dissatisfied with what Drake had told her. Why should the Hawkinsite have been interested in the two of them particularly? Yet Drake wouldn't lie. She would have liked to check at the Security Commission, but she knew she could not do that. Besides, the thought made her feel disloyal; Drake would definitely not lie.

But, then again, why should Harg Tholan not have investigated them? He might have inquired similarly about the families of all the biologists at the Institute. It would be no more than natural to attempt to choose the home he would find most pleasant by his own standards, whatever they were.

And if he had—even if he had investigated only the Smolletts—why should that create the great change in Drake from intense hostility to intense interest? Drake undoubtedly had knowledge he was keeping to himself. Only heaven knew how much.

Her thoughts churned slowly through the possibilities of interstellar intrigue. So far, to be sure, there were no signs of hostility or ill-feeling among any of the five intelligent races known to inhabit the Galaxy. As yet they were spaced at intervals too wide for enmity. Even the barest contact among them was all but impossible. Economic and political interests just had no points at which to conflict.

But that was only her idea and she was not a member of the Security Commission. If there *were* conflict, if there *were* danger, if there *were* any reason to suspect that the mission of a Hawkinsite might be other than peaceful—Drake would know.

Yet was Drake sufficiently high in the councils of the Security Commission to know, offhand, the dangers involved in the visit of a Hawkinsite physician? She had never thought of his position as more than that of a very minor functionary in the Commission; he had never presented himself as more. And yet—

Might he be more?

She shrugged at the thought. It was reminiscent of twentieth-century spy novels and of costume dramas of the days when there existed such things as atom bomb secrets.

The thought of costume dramas decided her. Unlike Drake, she wasn't a real policeman, and she didn't know how a real policeman would go about it. But she knew how such things were done in the old dramas.

She drew a piece of paper toward her and, with a quick motion, slashed a vertical pencil mark down its center. She headed one column "Harg Tholan," the other "Drake." Under "Harg Tholan" she wrote "bonafide" and thoughtfully put three question marks after it. After all, was he a doctor at all, or was he what could only be described as an interstellar agent? What proof had even the Institute of his profession except his own statements? Was that why Drake had quizzed him so relentlessly concerning the Inhibition Death? Had he boned up in advance and tried to catch the Hawkinsite in an error?

For a moment, she was irresolute; then, springing to her feet, she folded the paper, put it in the pocket of her short jacket, and swept out of her office. She said nothing to any of those she passed as she left the Institute. She left no word at the reception desk as to where she was going, or when she would be back.

Once outside, she hurried into the third level tube and waited for an empty compartment to pass. The two minutes that elapsed seem unbearably long. It was all she could do to say, "New York Academy of Medicine," into the mouthpiece just above the seat.

The door of the little cubicle closed, and the sound of the air flowing past the compartment hissed upward in pitch.

The New York Academy of Medicine had been enlarged both vertically and horizontally in the past two decades. The library, alone, occupied one entire wing of the third floor. Undoubtedly, if all the books, pamphlets and periodicals it contained were in their original printed form, rather than in microfilm, the entire building, huge though it was, would not have been sufficiently vast to hold them. As it was, Rose knew there was already talk of limiting printed works to the last five years, rather than to the last ten, as was now the case.

Rose, as a member of the Academy, had free entry to the library. She hurried toward the alcoves devoted to extraterrestrial medicine and was relieved to find them unoccupied.

It might have been wiser to have enlisted the aid of a librarian, but she chose not to. The thinner and smaller the trail she left, the less likely it was that Drake might pick it up.

And so, without guidance, she was satisfied to travel along the shelves, following the titles anxiously with her fingers. The books were almost all in English, though some were in German or Russian. None, ironically enough, were in extraterrestrial symbolisms. There was a room somewhere for such originals, but they were available only to official translators.

Her traveling eye and finger stopped. She had found what she was looking for.

She dragged half a dozen volumes from the shelf and spread them out upon the small dark table. She fumbled for the light switch and opened the first of the volumes. It was entitled *Studies on Inhibition*. She leafed through it and then turned to the author index. The name of Harg Tholan was there.

One by one, she looked up the references indicated, then returned to the shelves for translations of such original papers as she could find.

She spent more than two hours in the Academy. When she was finished, she knew this much—there was a Hawkinsite doctor named Harg Tholan, who was an expert on the Inhibition Death. He was connected with the Hawkinsite research organization with which the Institute had been in correspondence. Of course, the Harg Tholan she knew might simply be impersonating an actual doctor to make the role more realistic, but why should that be necessary?

*　　*　　*

She took the paper out of her pocket and, where she had written "bonafide" with three question marks, she now wrote a YES in capitals. She went back to the Institute and at 4 P.M. was once again at her desk. She called the switchboard to say that she would not answer any phone calls and then she locked her door.

Underneath the column headed "Harg Tholan" she now wrote two questions: "Why did Harg Tholan come to Earth alone?" She left considerable space. Then, "What is his interest in the Missing Persons Bureau?"

Certainly, the Inhibition Death was all the Hawkinsite said it was. From her reading at the Academy, it was obvious that it occupied the major share of medical effort on Hawkin's Planet. It was more feared there than cancer was on Earth. If they had thought the answer to it lay on Earth, the Hawkinsites would have sent a full-scale expedition. Was it distrust and suspicion on their part that made them send only one investigator?

What was it Harg Tholan had said the night before? The incidence of the Death was highest upon his own world, which was closest to Earth, lowest upon the world farthest from Earth. Add to that the fact implied by the Hawkinsite, and verified by her own readings at the Academy, that the incidence had expanded enormously since interstellar contact had been made with Earth . . .

Slowly and reluctantly she came to one conclusion. The inhabitants of Hawkin's Planet might have decided that somehow Earth had discovered the cause of the Inhibition Death, and was deliberately fostering it among the alien peoples of the Galaxy, with the intention, perhaps, of becoming supreme among the stars.

She rejected this conclusion with what was almost panic. It could not be; it was impossible. In the first place, Earth *wouldn't* do such a horrible thing. Secondly, it *couldn't*.

As far as scientific advance was concerned, the beings of Hawkin's Planet were certainly the equals of Earthmen. The Death had occurred there for thousands of years and their medical record was one of total failure. Surely, Earth, in its long-distance investigations into alien biochemistry, could not have succeeded so quickly. In fact, as far as she knew, there were no investigations to speak of into Hawkinsite pathology on the part of Earth biologists and physicians.

Yet all the evidence indicated that Harg Tholan had come in suspicion and had been received in suspicion. Carefully, she wrote down under the question, "Why did Harg Tholan come to Earth alone?" the answer, "Hawkin's Planet *believes* Earth is causing the Inhibition Death."

But, then, what was this business about the Bureau of Missing Persons? As a scientist, she was rigorous about the theories she developed. *All* the facts had to fit in, not merely some of them.

Missing Persons Bureau! If it was a false trail, deliberately intended to deceive Drake, it had been done clumsily, since it came only after an hour of discussion of the Inhibition Death.

Was it intended as an opportunity to study Drake? If so, why? Was this perhaps the *major* point? The Hawkinsite had investigated Drake before coming to them. Had he come because Drake was a policeman with entry to Bureaus of Missing Persons?

But why? Why?

*   *   *

She gave it up and turned to the column headed "Drake."

And there a question wrote itself, not in pen and ink upon the paper, but in the much more visible letters of thought on mind. *Why did he marry me?* thought Rose, and she covered her eyes with her hands so that the unfriendly light was excluded.

They had met quite by accident somewhat more than a year before, when he had moved into the apartment house in which she then lived. Polite greetings had somehow become friendly conversation and this, in turn, had led to occasional dinners in a neighborhood restaurant. It had been very friendly and normal and an excitingly new experience, and she had fallen in love.

When he asked her to marry him, she was pleased—and overwhelmed. At the time, she had many explanations for it. He appreciated her intelligence and friendliness. She was a nice girl. She would make a good wife, a splendid companion.

She had tried all those explanations and had half-believed every one of them. But half-belief was not enough.

It was not that she had any definite fault to find in Drake as a husband. He was always thoughtful, kind and a gentleman. Their married life was not one of passion, and yet it suited the paler emotional surges of the late thirties. She wasn't nineteen. What did she expect?

That was it; she wasn't nineteen. She wasn't beautiful, or charming, or glamorous. What did she expect? Could she have expected Drake—handsome and rugged, whose interest in intellectual pursuits was quite minor, who neither asked about her work in all the months of their marriage, nor offered to discuss his own with her? Why, then, did he marry her?

But there was no answer to that question, and it had nothing to do with what Rose was trying to do now. It was extraneous, she told herself fiercely; it was a childish distraction from the task she had set herself. She was acting like a girl of nineteen, after all, with no chronological excuse for it.

She found that the point of her pencil had somehow broken, and took a new one. In the column headed "Drake" she wrote, "Why is he suspicious of Harg Tholan?" and under it she put an arrow pointing to the other column.

What she had already written there was sufficient explanation. If Earth were spreading the Inhibition Death, or if Earth knew it was suspected of such a deed, then, obviously, it would be preparing for eventual retaliation on the part of the aliens. In fact, the setting would actually be one of preliminary maneuvering for the first interstellar war of history. It was an adequate but horrible explanation.

Now there was left the second question, the one she could not answer. She wrote it slowly, "Why Drake's reaction to Tholan's words, 'You are a most charming hostess'?"

She tried to bring back the exact setting. The Hawkinsite had said it innocuously, matter-of-factly, politely, and Drake had frozen at the sound of it. Over and over, she had listened to that particular passage in the recording. An Earthman might have said it in just such an inconsequential tone on leaving a routine cocktail party. The recording did not carry the sight of Drake's face; she had only her memory for that. Drake's eyes had become alive with fear and hate, and Drake was one who feared practically nothing. What was there to fear in the phrase, "You are a most charming hostess," that could upset him so? Jealousy? Absurd. The feeling that Tholan had been sarcastic? Maybe, though unlikely. She was sure Tholan was sincere.

She gave it up and put a large question mark under that second question. There were two of them now, one under "Harg Tholan" and one under "Drake." Could there be a connection between Tholan's interest in missing persons and Drake's reaction to a polite party phrase? She could think of none.

She put her head down upon her arms. It was getting dark in the office and she was very tired. For a while, she must have hovered in that queer land between waking and sleeping, when thoughts and phrases lose the control of the conscious and disport themselves erratically and surrealistically through one's head. But, no matter where they danced and leaped, they always returned to that one phrase, "You are a most charming hostess." Sometimes she heard it in Harg Tholan's cultured, lifeless voice, and sometimes in Drake's vibrant one. When Drake said it, it was full of love, full of a love she never heard from him. She liked to hear him say it.

She startled herself to wakefulness. It was quite dark in the office now, and she put on the desk light. She blinked, then frowned a little. Another thought must have come to her in that fitful half-sleep. There had been another phrase which had upset Drake. What was it? Her forehead furrowed with mental effort. It had not been last evening. It was not anything in the recorded conversation, so it must have been before that. Nothing came and she grew restless.

Looking at her watch, she gasped. It was almost eight. They would be at home waiting for her.

But she did not want to go home. She did not want to face them. Slowly, she took up the paper upon which she had scrawled her thoughts of the afternoon, tore it into little pieces and let them flutter into the little atomic-flash ashtray upon her desk. They were gone in a little flare and nothing was left of them.

If only nothing were left of the thoughts they represented as well.

It was no use. She would have to go home.

They were not there waiting for her, after all. She came upon them getting out of a gyrocab just as she emerged from the tubes on to street level. The gyrocabbie, wide-eyed, gazed after his fares for a moment, then hovered upward and away. By unspoken mutual consent, the three waited until they had entered the apartment before speaking.

Rose said disinterestedly, "I hope you have had a pleasant day, Dr. Tholan."

"Quite. And a fascinating and profitable one as well, I think."

"Have you had a chance to eat?" Though Rose had not herself eaten, she was anything but hungry.

"Yes, indeed."

Drake interrupted, "We had lunch and supper sent up to us. Sandwiches." He sounded tired.

Rose said, "Hello, Drake." It was the first time she had addressed him.

Drake scarcely looked at her. "Hello."

The Hawkinsite said, "Your tomatoes are remarkable vegetables. We have nothing to compare with them in taste on our own planet. I believe I ate two dozen, as well as an entire bottle of tomato derivative."

"Ketchup," explained Drake, briefly.

Rose said, "And your visit at the Missing Persons Bureau, Dr. Tholan? You say you found it profitable?"

"I should say so. Yes."

Rose kept her back to him. She plumped up sofa cushions as she said, "In what way?"

"I find it most interesting that the large majority of missing persons are males. Wives frequently report missing husbands, while the reverse is practically never the case."

Rose said, "Oh, that's not mysterious, Dr. Tholan. You simply don't realize the economic setup we have on Earth. On this planet, you see, it is the male who is usually the member of the family that maintains it as an economic unit. He is the one whose labor is repaid in units of currency. The wife's function is generally that of taking care of home and children."

"Surely this is not universal!"

Drake put in, "More or less. If you are thinking of my wife, she is an example of the minority of women who are capable of making their own way in the world."

Rose looked at him swiftly. Was he being sarcastic?

The Hawkinsite said, "Your implication, Mrs. Smollett, is that women, being economically dependent upon their male companions, find it less feasible to disappear?"

"That's a gentle way of putting it," said Rose, "but that's about it."

"And would you call the Missing Persons Bureau of New York a fair sampling of such cases in the planet at large?"

"Why, I should think so."

The Hawkinsite said, abruptly, "And is there, then, an economic explanation for the fact that since interstellar travel has been developed, the percentage of young males among the missing is more pronounced than ever?"

It was Drake who answered, with a verbal snap. "Good Lord, that's even less of a mystery than the other. Nowadays, the runaway has all space to disappear into. Anyone who wants to get away from trouble need only hop the nearest space freighter. They're always looking for crewmen, no questions asked, and it would be almost impossible to locate the runaway after that, if he really wanted to stay out of circulation."

"And almost always young men in their first year of marriage."

Rose laughed suddenly. She said, "Why, that's just the time a man's troubles seem the greatest. If he survives the first year, there is usually no need to disappear at all."

Drake was obviously not amused. Rose thought again that he looked tired and unhappy. *Why* did he insist on bearing the load alone? And then she thought that perhaps he had to.

The Hawkinsite said, suddenly, "Would it offend you if I disconnected for a period of time?"

Rose said, "Not at all. I hope you haven't had too exhausting a day. Since you come from a planet whose gravity is greater than that of Earth's, I'm afraid we too easily presume that you would show greater endurance than we do."

"Oh, I'm not tired in a physical sense." He looked for a moment at her legs and blinked very rapidly, indicating amusement. "You know, I keep expecting Earthmen to fall either forward or backward in view of their meager equipment of standing limbs. You must pardon me if my comment is overfamiliar, but your mention of the lesser gravity of Earth brought it to my mind. On my planet, two legs would simply not be enough. But this is all beside the point at the moment. It is just that I have been absorbing so many new and unusual concepts that I feel the desire for a little disconnection."

Rose shrugged inwardly. Well, that was as close as one race could get to another, anyway. As nearly as the expeditions to Hawkin's Planet could make out, Hawkinsites had the faculty for disconnecting their conscious mind from all its bodily functions and allowing it to sink into an undisturbed meditative process for periods of time lasting up to terrestrial days. Hawkinsites found the process pleasant, even necessary sometimes, though no Earthman could truly say what function it served.

Conversely, it had never been entirely possible for Earthmen to explain the concept of "sleep" to a Hawkinsite, or to any extraterrestrial. What an Earthman would call sleep or a dream, a Hawkinsite would view as an alarming sign of mental disintegration. Rose thought uneasily, *Here is another way Earthmen are unique.*

The Hawkinsite was backing away, drooping so that his forelimbs swept the floor in polite farewell. Drake nodded curtly at him as he disappeared behind the bend in the corridor. They heard his door open, close, then silence.

After minutes in which the silence was thick between them, Drake's chair creaked as he shifted restlessly. With a mild horror, Rose noticed blood upon his lips. She thought to herself, *He's in some kind of trouble. I've got to talk to him. I can't let it go on like this.*

She said, "Drake!"

Drake seemed to look at her from a far, far distance. Slowly, his eyes focused closer at hand and he said, "What is it? Are you through for the day, too?"

"No, I'm ready to begin. It's the tomorrow you spoke of. Aren't you going to speak to me?"

"Pardon me?"

"Last night, you said you would speak to me tomorrow. I am ready now."

Drake frowned. His eyes withdrew beneath a lowered brow and Rose felt some of her resolution begin to leave her. He said, "I thought it was agreed that you would not question me about my business in this matter."

"I think it's too late for that. I know too much about your business by now."

"What do you mean?" he shouted, jumping to his feet. Recollecting himself, he approached, laid his hands upon her shoulders and repeated in a lower voice, "What do you mean?"

Rose kept her eyes upon her hands, which rested limply in her lap. She bore the painfully gripping fingers patiently, and said slowly, "Dr. Tholan thinks that Earth is spreading the Inhibition Death purposely. That's it, isn't it?"

She waited. Slowly, the grip relaxed and he was standing there, hands at his side, face baffled and unhappy. He said, "Where did you get that notion?"

"It's true, isn't it?"

He said breathlessly, unnaturally, "I want to know exactly why you say that. Don't play foolish games with me, Rose. This is for keeps."

"If I tell you, will you answer one question?"

"What question?"

"Is Earth spreading the disease deliberately, Drake?"

Drake flung his hands upward. "Oh, for Heaven's sake!"

He knelt before her. He took both her hands in his and she could feel their trembling. He was forcing his voice into soothing, loving syllables.

He was saying, "Rose dear, look, you've got something red-hot by the tail and you think you can use it to tease me in a little husband-wife repartee. Now, I'm not asking much. Just tell me exactly what causes you to say what—what you have just said." He was terribly earnest about it.

"I was at the New York Academy of Medicine this afternoon. I did some reading there."

"But why? What made you do it?"

"You seemed so interested in the Inhibition Death, for one thing. And Dr. Tholan made those statements about the incidence increasing since interstellar travel, and being the highest on the planet nearest Earth." She paused.

"And your reading?" he prompted. "What about your reading, Rose?"

She said, "It backs him up. All I could do was to skim hastily into the direction of their research in recent decades. It seems obvious to me, though, that at least some of the Hawkinsites are considering the possibility the Inhibition Death originates on Earth."

"Do they say so outright?"

"No. Or, if they have, I haven't seen it." She gazed at him in surprise. In a matter like this, certainly the government would have investigated Hawkinsite research on the matter. She said, gently. "Don't you know about Hawkinsite research in the matter, Drake? The government—"

"Never mind about that." Drake had moved away from her and now he turned again. His eyes were bright. He said, as though making a wonderful discovery, "Why, you're an expert in this!"

Was she? Did he find that out only now that he needed her? Her nostrils flared and she said flatly, "I am a biologist."

He said, "Yes, I know that, but I mean your particular specialty is growth. Didn't you once tell me you had done work on growth?"

"You might call it that. I've had twenty papers published on the relationship of nucleic acid 'fine structure' and embryonic development on my Cancer Society grant."

"Good. I should have thought of that." He was choked with a new excitement. "Tell me, Rose—Look, I'm sorry if I lost my temper with you a moment ago. You'd be as competent as anyone to understand the direction of their researches if you read about it, wouldn't you?"

"Fairly competent, yes."

"Then tell me how they think the disease is spread. The details, I mean."

"Oh, now look, that's asking a little too much. I spent a few hours in the Academy, that's all. I'd need much more time than that to be able to answer your question."

"An intelligent guess, at least. You can't imagine how important it is."

She said, doubtfully, "Of course, 'Studies on Inhibition,' is a major treatise in the field. It would summarize all of the available research date."

"Yes? And how recent is it?"

"It's one of those periodic things. The last volume is about a year old."

"Does it have any account of *his* work in it?" His finger jabbed in the direction of Harg Tholan's bedroom.

"More than anyone else's. He's an outstanding worker in the field. I looked over his papers especially."

"And what are his theories about the origin of the disease? Try to remember, Rose."

She shook her head at him. "I could swear he blames Earth, but he admits they know nothing about how the disease is spread. I could swear to that, too."

He stood stiffly before her. His strong hands were clenched into fists at his side and his words were scarcely more than a mutter. "It could be a matter of complete overestimation. Who knows—"

He whirled away. "I'll find out about this right now, Rose. Thank you for your help."

She ran after him. "What are you going to do?"

"Ask him a few questions." He was rummaging through the drawers of his desk and now his right hand withdrew. It held a needle-gun.

She cried, "No, Drake!"

He shook her off roughly, and turned down the corridor toward the Hawkinsite's bedroom.

Drake threw the door open and entered. Rose was at his heels, still trying to grasp his arm, but now she stopped and looked at Harg Tholan.

The Hawkinsite was standing there motionless, eyes unfocused, his four standing limbs sprawled out in four directions as far as they would go. Rose felt ashamed of intruding, as though she were violating an intimate rite. But Drake, apparently unconcerned, walked to within four feet of the creature and stood there. They were face to face, Drake holding the needle-gun easily at a level of about the center of the Hawkinsite's torso.

Drake said, "Now keep quiet. He'll gradually become aware of me."

"How do you know?"

The answer was flat. "I *know*. Not get out of here."

But she did not move and Drake was too absorbed to pay her further attention.

Portions of the skin on the Hawkinsite's face were beginning to quiver slightly. It was rather repulsive and Rose found herself preferring not to watch.

Drake said suddenly, "That's about all, Dr. Tholan. Don't throw in connection with any of the limbs. Your sense organs and voice box will be quite enough."

The Hawkinsite's voice was dim. "Why do you invade my disconnection chamber?" Then, more strongly, "and why are you armed?"

His head wobbled slightly atop a still frozen torso. He had, apparently, followed Drake's suggestion against limb connection. Rose wondered how Drake knew such partial reconnection to be possible. She herself had not known of it.

The Hawkinsite spoke again. "What do you want?"

And this time Drake answered. He said, "The answer to certain questions."

"With a gun in your hand? I would not humor your discourtesy so far."

"You would not merely be humoring me. You might be saving your own life."

"That would be a matter of considerable indifference to me, under the circumstances. I am sorry, Mr. Smollett, that the duties toward a guest are so badly understood on Earth."

"You are not guest of mine, Dr. Tholan," said Drake. "You entered my house on false pretenses. You had some reason for it, some way you had planned of using me to further your own purposes. I have no compunction in reversing the process."

"You had better shoot. It will save time."

"You are convinced that you will answer no questions? That, in itself, is suspicious. It seems that you consider certain answers to be more important than your life."

"I consider the principles of courtesy to be very important. You, as an Earthman, may not understand."

"Perhaps not. But I, as an Earthman, understand one thing." Drake had jumped forward, faster than Rose could cry out, faster than the Hawkinsite could connect his limbs. When he sprang backward, the flexible hose of Harg Tholan's cyanide cylinder was in his hand. At the corner of the Hawkinsite's wide mouth, where the hose had once been affixed, a droplet of colorless liquid oozed sluggishly from a break in the rough skin, and slowly solidified into a brown jellylike globule, as it oxidized.

Drake yanked at the hose and the cylinder jerked free. He plunged home the knob that controlled the needle valve at the head of the cylinder and the small hissing ceased.

"I doubt," said Drake, "that enough will have escaped to endanger us. I hope, however, that you realize what will happen to you *now,* if you do not answer the questions I am going to ask you—and answer them in such a way that I am convinced you are being truthful."

"Give me back my cylinder," said the Hawkinsite, slowly. "If not, it will be necessary for me to attack you and then it will be necessary for you to kill me."

Drake stepped back. "Not at all. Attack me and I shoot your legs from under you. You will lose them; all four, if necessary, but you will still live, in a horrible way. You will live to die of cyanide lack. It would be a most uncomfortable death. I am only an Earthman and I can't appreciate its true horrors, but you can, can't you?"

The Hawkinsite's mouth was open and something within quivered yellow-green. Rose wanted to throw up. She wanted to scream. *Give him back the cylinder, Drake!* But nothing would come. She couldn't even turn her head.

Drake said, "You have about an hour, I think, before the effects are irreversible. Talk quickly, Dr. Tholan, and you will have your cylinder back."

"And after that—" said the Hawkinsite.

"After that, what does it matter to you? Even if I kill you then, it will be a clean death; not cyanide lack."

Something seemed to pass out of the Hawkinsite. His voice grew guttural and his words blurred as though he no longer had the energy to keep his English perfect. He said, "What are your questions?" and as he spoke, his eyes followed the cylinder in Drake's hand.

Drake swung it deliberately, tantalizingly, and the creature's eyes followed—followed—

Drake said, "What are your theories concerning the Inhibition Death? Why did you really come to Earth? What is your interest in the Missing Persons Bureau?"

Rose found herself waiting in breathless anxiety. These were the questions she would like to have asked, too. Not in this manner, perhaps, but in Drake's job, kindness and humanity had to take second place to necessity.

She repeated that to herself several times in an effort to counteract the fact that she found herself loathing Drake for what he was doing to Dr. Tholan.

The Hawkinsite said, "The proper answer would take more than the hour I have left me. You have bitterly shamed me by forcing me to talk under duress. On my own planet, you could not have done so under any circumstances. It is only here, on this revolting planet, that I can be deprived of cyanide."

"You are wasting your hour, Dr. Tholan."

"I would have told you this eventually, Mr. Smollett. I needed your help. It is why I came here."

"You are still not answering my questions."

"I will answer them now. For years, in addition to my regular scientific work, I have been privately investigating the cells of my patients suffering from Inhibition Death. I have been forced to use the utmost secrecy and to work without assistance, since the methods I used to investigate the bodies of my patients were frowned upon by my people. Your society would have similar feelings against human vivisection, for instance. For this reason, I could not present the results I obtained to my fellow physicians until I had verified my theories here on Earth."

"What were your theories?" demanded Drake. The feverishness had returned to his eyes.

"It became more and more obvious to me as I proceeded with my studies that the entire direction of research into the Inhibition Death was wrong. The answer was neither bacterial nor viral."

Rose interrupted, "Surely, Dr. Tholan, it isn't psychosomatic."

A thin, gray, translucent film had passed over the Hawkinsite's eyes. He no longer looked at them. He said, "No, Mrs. Smollett, it is not psychosomatic. It is a true infection, but more subtle than could be expected of either bacteria or viruses. I worked with Inhibition Death patients of other races than my own, and the conclusion was eventually forced upon me. There is a whole variety of infection never yet suspected by the medical science of any of the planets."

Rose said, faintly, "This is wild, impossible. You must be mistaken, Dr. Tholan."

"I am not mistaken. Until I came to Earth, I thought I might be. But my stay at the Institute, my researches at the Missing Persons Bureau have convinced me that this is not so. What is so impossible about the concept of a supremely subtle, yet unsuspected class of infections? The very subtlety would militate against their discovery. In your history and in ours, there were thousands of years in which the causes of bacterial infections were unknown. And when tools were developed capable of studying bacteria, viruses remained unknown for generations.

"Is it impossible to proceed a step further? Bacteria, by and large, are extracellular creatures. They compete with the cells of the body for foodstuffs, sometimes too successfully, and they release their waste products, or toxins, into the bloodstream. The virus goes a step further. It lives within the cell, utilizing cellular machinery for its own purposes. You know all this, Mrs. Smollett, so I need not elaborate. Perhaps your husband knows it as well."

"Go on," said Drake.

"Proceed one more stage, then. Imagine a parasite that lives not only inside the cell, but inside the *chromosomes* of the cell. In other words, a parasite that takes its place along with the genes, so that it is something we might call a pseudo-gene. It would have a hand in the manufacture of enzymes, which is the primary function of genes, and in that way a very firm finger in the biochemistry of the terrestrial organism."

Rose said, "Why particularly the terrestrial?"

"Have you not surmised that the pseudo-gene I speak of is a native of Earth? Terrestrial beings from the beginning have lived with it, have adapted to it, are unconscious of it. These pseudo-genes feed on the *organization* of the body. Bacteria feed on the foodstuffs, viruses on the cells, pseudo-genes on the economy of the cellular macrostructure as a whole through their control of the body's biochemistry. It is why the higher species of terrestrial animals, including man, do not grow after maturity, and, eventually, die what is called natural death. It is the inevitable end result of this universal parasitic infestation."

"A disease of the soul—" Rose said, wistfully.

The Hawkinsite said, "What is the soul?"

"For heaven's sake," said Drake, abruptly, "do not get mystical, Rose!"

She flushed. "I'm sorry. Go on, Dr. Tholan."

"As a pseudo-gene, it is perfectly obvious how the universal disease is transmitted. It is placed along with the true genes in every ovum or spermatazoon formed by the infected organism. Every organism is already infected at the moment of conception. But there is another form of transmission—there *must* be to account for all the facts. Chemically, genes and viruses are similar, since both are nuclear proteins. A pseudo-gene can, therefore, exist independently of the chromosomes.

"Perhaps it infects a virus, or perhaps it forms a virus-like body itself at some stage of its development. As such, it can be transmitted in the ordinary fashion of other viral infections—by contact, by air, through waste materials and so on. Naturally, Earthmen have nothing to fear from such contact; they are already infected. On Earth, such a process is purely vestigial, dating back to the days when infections could yet be made. It is different on the extraterrestrial worlds, however."

"I see," said Rose.

"I don't," objected Drake, bluntly.

*　　*　　*

The Hawkinsite sighed. "We of the other worlds have not lived with these parasites for millions of years, as man and his ancestors had. We have not adapted ourselves to it. Our weak strains have not been killed off gradually through hundreds of generations until only the resistants were left. So, where Earthmen could survive the infection for decades with little harm, we others, once infected by the viral stage of the disease, die a quick death within a year."

Rose said, "And is that why the incidence has increased since interstellar travel between Earth and the other planets began?"

"Yes. There were infections previously. It has long been suspected that bacterial spores and virus molecules can drift off into space and through it. Absolute zero will not kill them, but rather keep them alive indefinitely. Statistically, a certain percentage of them will reach other planets. Before space travel there were cases which could be accounted for, perhaps, by such a mechanism. Since then, it has increased ten thousand times and more."

For a moment there was silence, and then the Hawkinsite said with a sudden access of energy, "Give me back my cylinder. You have your answer."

Drake said, coolly, "What about the Missing Persons Bureau?" He was swinging the cylinder again; but now the Hawkinsite did not follow its movements. The gray translucent film on his eyes had deepened and Rose wondered whether that was simply an expression of weariness or an example of the changes induced by cyanide lack.

The Hawkinsite said, "As we are not well adapted to the pseudo-genes that infest man, neither are they well adapted to us. It can live on us, but it cannot reproduce with ourselves alone as the source of its life. Infections of Inhibition Death before the advent of space travel set off tiny epidemics that would last through ten or twenty transfers, growing gradually milder, until it died out altogether. Now, the disease transfers indefinitely, getting milder where thorough quarantines are imposed and then, suddenly, and erratically, growing completely virulent again."

Rose looked at him with a growing horror. "What are you implying, Dr. Tholan?"

He said, "The Earthman remains the prime host for the parasite. An Earthman may infect one of us if he remains among us. But the pseudo-gene, once located within our cells, cannot maintain its vigor indefinitely. Sooner or later, within twenty infections, perhaps, it must somehow return to an Earthman, if it expects to continue reproduction. Before interstellar travel this was possible only by returning through space, which was so unlikely as to be considered zero. Now—"

Rose said faintly, "The missing persons."

"Yes. They are the intermediate hosts. Almost all the young men who disappeared in the last decade were space-travelers. They had been on other inhabited planets at least once in their lives. Once the period of incubation within the human being has transpired, they return to an outer planet. He disappears, as far as Earth is concerned."

"But this is impossible," insisted Rose. "What you say implies that the pseudo-gene can control the actions of its host! This cannot be!"

"Why not? They control the biochemistry, at least in part, by their very role as pseudo-genes. There is no intelligence, or even instinct, behind their control. It is purely chemical. If adrenalin is injected into your bloodstream, there is no imposition of a superior intelligence that makes your heart double its rate, your breathing quicken, your clotting time decrease, your blood vessels dilate—purely chemical.

"—But I am quite ill now and cannot speak much longer. I have only this to say. In this pseudo-gene, your people and mine have a common enemy. Earthmen, too, need not die involuntarily. I thought that perhaps if I found myself unable to return to my own world with my information, due to my own infection, perhaps, I might bring it to the authorities on Earth, and ask their help in stamping out this menace. Imagine my pleasure when I found that the husband of one of the biologists at the Institute was a member of one of Earth's most important investigating bodies. Naturally, I did what I could to be a guest at his home in order that I might deal with him privately; convince him of the terrible truth; utilize his position to help in the attack on the parasites.

"This is, of course, now impossible. I cannot blame you too far. As Earthmen, you cannot be expected to understand thoroughly the psychology of my people. Nevertheless, you must understand this. I can have no further dealing with either of you. I could not even bear to remain any longer on Earth."

Drake said, "Then you, alone, of all your people have any knowledge of this theory of yours."

"I alone."

Drake held out the cylinder. "Your cyanide, Dr. Tholan."

The Hawkinsite groped for it eagerly. His supple fingers manipulated the hose and the needle valve with the utmost delicacy. In the space of ten seconds, he had it in place and was inhaling the gas in huge breaths. His eyes were growing clear and transparent.

Drake waited until the Hawkinsite's breathing had subsided to normal, and then, without expression, he raised his needle-gun and fired.

Rose screamed. The Hawkinsite remained standing. His four lower limbs were incapable of buckling, but his head lolled and, from his suddenly flaccid mouth, the cyanide hose fell, disregarded.

Once again, Drake closed the needle valve and now he tossed the cylinder aside and stood there somberly, looking at the dead creature.

There was no external mark to show that Tholan had been killed. The needle-gun's pellet, thinner than the needle which gave the gun its name, entered the body noiselessly and easily, and exploded with devastating effect only within the abdominal cavity.

Rose ran from the room, still screaming.

Drake pursued her, seized her arm. She heard the hard, brisk sounds of his palms upon her face without feeling them and subsided into little bubbling sobs.

Drake said, "I told you to have nothing to do with this. Now, what do you think you're going to do?"

She said, "Let me go. I want to leave. I want to go away."

"Because of something it was my job to do? You heard what the creature was saying. Do you suppose I could allow him to return to his world and spread those lies? They would believe him. And what do you think would happen then? Can you guess what an interstellar war might be like? They would imagine they would have to kill us all to stop the disease.''

With an effort that seemed to turn her inside out, Rose steadied. She looked firmly into Drake's eyes and said, ''What Dr. Tholan said were no lies and no mistakes, Drake.''

''Oh, come now, you're hysterical. You need sleep.''

''No, Drake. I know what he said is so because the Security Commission knows all about that same theory, and knows it to be true.''

''Why do you say such a preposterous thing?''

''Because you let that slip yourself twice.''

Drake said, ''Sit down.''

She did so, and he stood there, looking curiously at her.

He said, ''So I have given myself away twice, have I? You've had a busy day of detection, my dear. You have facets you keep well hidden.'' He sat down and crossed his legs.

Rose thought, *Yes, I've had a busy day.* She could see the electric clock on the kitchen wall from where she sat and it was more than two hours past midnight. Harg Tholan had entered their house thirty-five hours before; and now he lay murdered in the spare bedroom.

Drake said, ''Well, aren't you going to tell me where I pulled my two boners?''

''You turned white when Harg Tholan referred to me as a charming hostess. Hostess has a double meaning, you know, Drake. A host is one who harbors a parasite.''

''Number one,'' said Drake. ''What's number two?''

''That's something you did before Harg Tholan entered the house. I've been trying to remember it for hours. Do *you* remember, Drake? You spoke about how unpleasant it was for Hawkinsites to associate with Earthmen, and I said Harg Tholan was a doctor and had to. I asked you if you thought that human doctors particularly enjoyed going to the tropics, or letting infected mosquitoes bite them. Do you remember how upset you became?''

Drake laughed shortly. ''I had no idea I was so transparent. Mosquitoes are hosts for the malaria and yellow fever parasites.'' He sighed. ''I've done my best to keep you out of this, Rose. I tried to keep the Hawkinsite away. I tried threatening you. Now, there's nothing left but to tell you the truth. I must, because only the truth—or death—will keep you quiet. And I don't want to kill you.''

Rose shrank back in her chair, eyes wide.

Drake said, ''The Commission knows the truth, yes. It does us no good. We can only do all in our power to prevent the other worlds from finding out.''

''But that is impossible! The truth can't be held down forever. Harg Tholan found out. You've killed him, but another extraterrestrial will repeat the same discovery—over and over again. You can't kill them all.''

''We know that, too,'' agreed Drake. ''But we have no choice.''

''Why?'' cried Rose. ''Harg Tholan gave you the solution. He made no suggestions or threats regarding enmity and war between worlds. He said something, instead, for which I admired him. He suggested that we combine

with the other intelligences and help to wipe out the parasite. And we can—we
can! If we, in common with all the others, put every scrap of effort into it—''

''You mean we can trust him? Does he speak for his government? Or for the
other races?''

''Can we dare to refuse the risk?''

Drake said, ''No, Rose, you don't understand.'' He reached toward her and
took one of her cold, unresisting hands between both of his. He went on, ''I may
seem silly trying to teach you anything about your specialty, but I want you to
hear me out. Harg Tholan was right. Man and his prehistoric ancestors have been
living with this pseudo-gene for uncounted ages; certainly for a much longer
period than we have been truly *Homo sapiens*. In that interval, we have not only
become adapted to it, we have become dependent upon it. It is no longer a case
of parasitism. It is a case of mutual cooperation.''

She tore her hand away, ''What are you talking about?''

''We have a disease of our own, remember. It is a reverse disease; one of
unrestrained growth. We've mentioned it already as a contrast to the Inhibition
Death. Well, what is the cause of cancer? How long have biologists, physiologists, biochemists and all the others been working on it? How much success have
they had with it? Why? Can't you answer that for yourself now?''

Rose frowned at him. She said, slowly, ''No, I can't. What are you talking
about?''

''It's all very well to say that if we could remove the parasite, we would once
again have the privilege of eternal growth and life if we wanted it; or at least until
we got tired of being too big or of living too long, and did away with ourselves
neatly. But how many millions of years has it been since the human body has had
occasion to grow in such an unrestrained fashion? Can it do so any longer? Is the
chemistry of the body adjusted to that? Has it got the proper whatchamacallits?''

''Enzymes,'' prompted Rose in a whisper.

''Yes, enzymes. It's impossible for us. If, for any reason, the pseudo-gene, as
Harg Tholan calls it, does leave the human body, or if its relationship to the
human mind is in any way impaired, growth does take place, but not in any
orderly fashion. We call the growth cancer.

''And there you have it, Rose. There's no way of getting rid of the parasite.
We're together for all eternity. So that to get rid of their Inhibition Death,
extraterrestrials must first wipe out all vertebrate life on Earth. There is no other
solution for them, and so we must keep knowledge of it from them. Do you
understand?''

She rose from her chair. Her mouth was dry and it was difficult to talk. ''I
understand, Drake.''

She noticed that his forehead was damp and that there was a line of
perspiration down each cheek.

She said tightly, ''And now you'll have to get it out of the apartment.''

''I know. I've made arrangements. It's late at night and I'll be able to get the
body out of the building. From there on—'' he turned to her—''I don't know
when I'll be back.''

Rose said again, ''I understand, Drake.''

Harg Tholan was heavy. Drake had to drag him through the apartment. Rose turned away, retching. She hid her eyes until she heard the front door close. She whispered again to herself, "I understand, Drake."

It was 3 A.M. Nearly an hour had passed since she had heard the front door click gently into place behind Drake and his burden. She didn't know where he was going, what he intended doing—

She sat there numbly. There was no desire to sleep; no desire to move. She kept her mind traveling in tight circles, away from the thing she knew and which she wanted not to know.

Pseudo-genes!

Was it only a coincidence or was it some queer racial memory, some tenuous long-sustained wisp of tradition or insight, stretching back through incredible millennia, that kept current the odd myths of human beginnings? The stories of the golden ages, the Garden of Eden in which Man had eternal life, until he lost it.

She had called the pseudo-genes a disease of the soul. Was that the memory again? The memory of the world in which sin entered, in which the soul grew diseased, and into which, as a consequence, death entered?

Yet despite her efforts, the circle of her thoughts expanded, and returned to Drake. She shoved and it returned; she counted to herself, she recited the names of the objects in her field of vision, she cried, *No, no, no,* and it returned. It kept returning.

Drake had lied to her. It had been a plausible story. It would have held good under most circumstances; but Drake was not a biologist.

Cancer could not be, as Drake had said, a disease that was an expression of a lost ability for any normal growth.

Cancer attacked children while they were still growing; it could even attack embryonic tissue. It attacked fish, which, like extraterrestrials, never stopped growing while they lived, and died only by disease or accident. It attacked plants, for many of which the same could be said.

Cancer had nothing to do with the presence or absence of normal growth. It was the general disease of life, to which *no* tissues of *any* multicellular organism were completely immune.

He should not have bothered lying. He should not have allowed some obscure sentimental weakness to persuade him to avoid the necessity of killing her in that manner. She would tell them at the Institute. The parasite *could* be beaten! Its absence would *not* cause cancer. But who would believe her?

She put her hands over her eyes and rocked gently to and fro. The young men who disappeared were usually in the first year of their marriage. Whatever the process of rejuvenation among the strains of the pseudo-genes, it must involve close association with another strain—as in the case of conjugation among the protozoa. That was how the pseudo-genes had to spread infection; through the formation of the gametes and their subsequent fertilization, a mixing of strains.

Drake had been on Hawkin's Planet. He knew too much about Hawkinsites not to have been there at least once.

She could feel her thoughts slowly disconnect. They would be coming to her. They would be saying, *Where is Harg Tholan?* And she would answer, *With my husband.* Only they would say, *Where is your husband?* because he would be gone, too.

She knew that, anyway. He needed her no longer. He would never return. They would never find him, because he would be out in space. She would report them both, Drake Smollett and Harg Tholan, to the Missing Persons Bureau.

She wanted to weep, but couldn't. She was dry-eyed and it was very painful. And then she began to giggle. She couldn't stop; it just went on.

After all, it was very funny. She had looked for the answers to so many questions and had found them all. She had even found the answer to the question she thought had no bearing on the subject.

She had finally learned why Drake had married her.

Not a conjugal relationship—

Conjugation.

"IN A GOOD CAUSE—"

IN THE Great Court, which stands as a patch of untouched peace among the fifty busy square miles devoted to the towering buildings that are the pulse beat of the United Worlds of the Galaxy, stands a statue.

It stands where it can look at the stars at night. There are other statues ringing the court, but this one stands in the center and alone.

It is not a very good statue. The face is too noble and lacks the lines of living. The brow is a shade too high, the nose a shade too symmetrical, the clothing a shade too carefully disposed. The whole bearing is by far too saintly to be true. One can suppose that the man in real life might have frowned at times, or hiccuped, but the statue seems to insist that such imperfections were impossible.

All this, of course, is understandable overcompensation. The man had no statues raised to him while alive, and succeeding generations, with the advantage of hindsight, felt guilty.

The name on the pedestal reads "Richard Sayama Altmayer." Underneath it is a short phrase and, vertically arranged, three dates. The phrase is: *"In a good cause, there are no failures."* The three dates are June 17, 2755; September 5, 2788; December 21, 2800—the years being counted in the usual manner of the period, that is, from the date of the first atomic explosion in 1945 of the ancient era.

None of those dates represents either his birth or death. They mark neither a date of marriage or of the accomplishment of some great deed or, indeed, of anything that the inhabitants of the United Worlds can remember with pleasure and pride. Rather, they are the final expression of the feeling of guilt.

Quite simply and plainly, they are the three dates upon which Richard Sayama Altmayer was sent to prison for his opinions.

1—*JUNE 17, 2755*

At the age of twenty-two, certainly, Dick Altmayer was fully capable of feeling fury. His hair was as yet dark brown and he had not grown the mustache which, in later years, would be so characteristic of him. His nose was, of course, thin and high-bridged, but the contours of his face were youthful. It would only be later that the growing gauntness of his cheeks would convert that nose into the prominent landmark that it now is in the minds of trillions of school children.

Geoffrey Stock was standing in the doorway, viewing the results of his friend's fury. His round face and cold, steady eyes were there, but he had yet to put on the first of the military uniforms in which he was to spend the rest of his life.

He said, "Great Galaxy!"

Altmayer looked up. "Hello, Jeff."

"What's been happening, Dick? I thought your principles, pal, forbid destruction of any kind. Here's a bookviewer that looks somewhat destroyed." He picked up the pieces.

Altmayer said, "I was holding the viewer when my wave-receiver came through with an official message. You know which one, too."

"I know. It happened to me, too. Where is it?"

"On the floor. I tore it off the spool as soon as it belched out at me. Wait, let's dump it down the atom chute."

"Hey, hold on. You can't—"

"Why not?"

"Because you won't accomplish anything. You'll have to report."

"And just why"

"Don't be an ass, Dick."

"This is a matter of principle, by Space."

"Oh, nuts! You can't fight the whole planet."

"I don't intend to fight the whole planet; just the few who get us into wars."

Stock shrugged. "That means the whole planet. That guff of yours of leaders tricking poor innocent people into fighting is just so much space-dust. Do you think that if a vote were taken the people wouldn't be overwhelmingly in favor of fighting this fight?"

"That means nothing, Jeff. The government has control of—"

"The organs of propaganda. Yes, I know. I've listened to you often enough. But why not report, anyway?"

Altmayer turned away.

Stock said, "In the first place, you might not pass the physical examination."

"I'd pass. I've been in Space."

"That doesn't mean anything. If the doctors let you hop a liner, that only means you don't have a heart murmur or an aneurysm. For military duty aboard ship in Space you need more than just that. How do you know you qualify?"

"That's a side issue, Jeff, and an insulting one. It's not that I'm afraid to fight."

"Do you think you can stop the war this way?"

"I wish I could," Altmayer's voice almost shook as he spoke. "It's this idea I have that all mankind should be a single unit. There shouldn't be wars or space-fleets armed only for destruction. The Galaxy stands ready to be opened to the united efforts of the human race. Instead, we have been factioned for nearly two thousand years, and we throw away all the Galaxy."

Stock laughed, "We're doing all right. There are more than eighty independent planetary systems."

"And are we the only intelligences in the Galaxy?"

"Oh, the Diaboli, your particular devils," and Stock put his fists to his temples and extended the two forefingers, waggling them.

"And yours, too, and everybody's. They have a single government extending over more planets than all those occupied by our precious eighty independents."

"Sure, and their nearest planet is only fifteen hundred light years away from Earth and they can't live on oxygen planets anyway."

Stock got out of his friendly mood. He said, curtly, "Look, I dropped by here to say that I was reporting for examination next week. Are you coming with me?"

"No."

"You're really determined."

"I'm really determined."

"You know you'll accomplish nothing. There'll be no great flame ignited on Earth. It will be no case of millions of young men being excited by your example into a no-war strike. You will simply be put in jail."

"Well, then, jail it is."

And jail it was. On June 17, 2755, of the atomic era, after a short trial in which Richard Sayama Altmayer refused to present any defense, he was sentenced to jail for the term of three years or for the duration of the war, whichever should be longer. He served a little over four years and two months, at which time the war ended in a definite though not shattering Santannian defeat. Earth gained complete control of certain disputed asteroids, various commercial advantages, and a limitation of the Santannian navy.

The combined human losses of the war were something over two thousand ships with, of course, most of their crews, and in addition, several millions of lives due to the bombardment of planetary surfaces from space. The fleets of the two contending powers had been sufficiently strong to restrict this bombardment to the outposts of their respective systems, so that the planets of Earth and Santanni, themselves, were little affected.

The war conclusively established Earth as the strongest single human military power.

Geoffrey Stock fought throughout the war, seeing action more than once and remaining whole in life and limb despite that. At the end of the war he had the rank of major. He took part in the first diplomatic mission sent out by Earth to the worlds of the Diaboli, and that was the first step in his expanding role in Earth's military and political life.

2—SEPTEMBER 5, 2788

They were the first Diaboli ever to have appeared on the surface of Earth itself. The projection posters and the newscasts of the Federalist party made that abundantly clear to any who were unaware of that. Over and over, they repeated the chronology of events.

It was toward the beginning of the century that human explorers first came across the Diaboli. They were intelligent and had discovered interstellar travel independently somewhat earlier than had the humans. Already the galactic volume of their dominions was greater than that which was human-occupied.

Regular diplomatic relationships between the Diaboli and the major human powers had begun twenty years earlier, immediately after the war between Santanni and Earth. At that time, outposts of Diaboli power were already within twenty light years of the outermost human centers. Their missions went everywhere, drawing trade treaties, obtaining concessions on unoccupied asteroids.

And now they were on Earth itself. They were treated as equals and perhaps as more than equals by the rulers of the greatest center of human population in the Galaxy. The most damning statistic of all was the most loudly proclaimed by the Federalists. It was this: Although the number of living Diaboli was somewhat less than the total number of living humans, humanity had opened up not more than five new worlds to colonization in fifty years, while the Diaboli had begun the occupation of nearly five hundred.

"A hundred to one against us," cried the Federalists, "because they are one political organization and we are a hundred." But relatively few on Earth, and fewer in the Galaxy as a whole, paid attention to the Federalists and their demands for Galactic Union.

The crowds that lined the streets along which nearly daily the five Diaboli of the mission traveled from their specially conditioned suite in the best hotel of the city to the Secretariat of Defense were, by and large, not hostile. Most were merely curious, and more than a little revolted.

The Diaboli were not pleasant creatures to look at. They were larger and considerably more massive than Earthmen. They had four stubby legs set close together below and two flexibly-fingered arms above. Their skin was wrinkled and naked and they wore no clothing. Their broad, scaly faces wore no expressions capable of being read by Earthmen, and from flattened regions just above each large-pupilled eye there sprang short horns. It was these last that gave the creatures their names. At first they had been called devils, and later the politer Latin equivalent.

Each wore a pair of cylinders on its back from which flexible tubes extended to the nostrils; there they clamped on tightly. These were packed with soda-lime which absorbed the, to them, poisonous carbon dioxide from the air they breathed. Their own metabolism revolved about the reduction of sulfur and sometimes those foremost among the humans in the crowd caught a foul whiff of the hydrogen sulfide exhaled by the Diaboli.

The leader of the Federalists was in the crowd. He stood far back where he attracted no attention from the police who had roped off the avenues and who now maintained a watchful order on the little hoppers that could be maneuvered quickly through the thickest crowd. The Federalist leader was gaunt-faced, with a thin and prominently bridged nose and straight, graying hair.

He turned away, "I cannot bear to look at them."

His companion was more philosophic. He said, "No uglier in spirit, at least, then some of our handsome officials. These creatures are at least true to their own."

"You are sadly right. Are we entirely ready?"

"Entirely. There won't be one of them alive to return to his world."

"Good! I will remain here to give the signal."

The Diaboli were talking as well. This fact could not be evident to any human, no matter how close. To be sure, they could communicate by making ordinary sounds to one another but that was not their method of choice. The skin between their horns could, by the actions of muscles which differed in their construction from any known to humans, vibrate rapidly. The tiny waves which were transmitted in this manner to the air were too rapid to be heard by the human ear and too delicate to be detected by any but the most sensitive of human instrumentation. At that time, in fact, humans remained unaware of this form of communication.

A vibration said, "Did you know that this is the planet of origin of the Two-legs?"

"No." There was a chorus of such no's, and then one particular vibration said, "Do you get that from the Two-leg communications you have been studying, queer one?"

"Because I study the communications? More of our people should do so instead of insisting so firmly on the complete worthlessness of Two-leg culture. For one thing, we are in a much better position to deal with the Two-legs if we know something about them. Their history is interesting in a horrible way. I am glad I brought myself to view their spools."

"And yet," came another vibration, "from our previous contacts with Two-legs, one would be certain that they did not know their planet of origin. Certainly there is no veneration of this planet, Earth, or any memorial rites connected with it. Are you sure the information is correct?"

"Entirely so. The lack of ritual, and the fact that this planet is by no means a shrine, is perfectly understandable in the light of Two-leg history. The Two-legs on the other worlds would scarcely concede the honor. It would somehow lower the independent dignity of their own worlds."

"I don't quite understand."

"Neither do I, exactly, but after several days of reading I think I catch a glimmer. It would seem that, originally, when interstellar travel was first discovered by the Two-legs, they lived under a single political unit."

"Naturally."

"Not for these Two-legs. This was an unusual stage in their history and did not last. After the colonies on the various worlds grew and came to reasonable maturity, their first interest was to break away from the mother world. The first in the series of interstellar wars among these Two-legs began then."

"Horrible. Like cannibals."

"Yes, isn't it? My digestion has been upset for days. My cud is sour. In any case, the various colonies gained independence, so that now we have the situation of which we are well aware. All of the Two-leg kingdoms, republics, aristocracies, etc., are simply tiny clots of worlds, each consisting of a dominant world and a few subsidiaries which, in turn, are forever seeking their independence or being shifted from one dominant to another. This Earth is the strongest among them and yet less than a dozen worlds owe it allegiance."

"Incredible that these creatures should be so blind to their own interests. Do they not have a tradition of the single government that existed when they consisted of but one world?"

"As I said that was unusual for them. The single government had existed only a few decades. Prior to that, their very planet itself was split into a number of subplanetary political units."

"Never heard anything like it." For a while, the supersonics of the various creatures interfered with one another.

"It's a fact. It is simply the nature of the beast."

And with that, they were at the Secretariat of Defense.

The five Diaboli stood side by side along the table. They stood because their anatomy did not admit of anything that could correspond to "sitting." On the other side of the table, five Earthmen stood as well. It would have been more convenient for the humans to sit but, understandably, there was no desire to make the handicap of smaller size any more pronounced than it already was. The table was a rather wide one; the widest, in fact, that could be conveniently obtained. This was out of respect for the human nose, for from the Diaboli, slightly so as they breathed, much more so when they spoke, there came the gentle and continuous drift of hydrogen sulfide. This was a difficulty rather unprecedented in diplomatic negotiations.

Ordinarily the meetings did not last for more than half an hour, and at the end of this interval the Diaboli ended their conversations without ceremony and turned to leave. This time, however, the leave-taking was interrupted. A man entered, and the five human negotiators made way for him. He was tall, taller than any of the other Earthmen, and he wore a uniform with the ease of long usage. His face was round and his eyes cold and steady. His black hair was rather thin but as yet untouched by gray. There was an irregular blotch of scar tissue running from the point of his jaw downward past the line of his high, leather-brown collar. It might have been the result of a hand energy-ray, wielded by some forgotten human enemy in one of the five wars in which the man had been an active participant.

"Sirs," said the Earthman who had been chief negotiator hitherto, "may I introduce the Secretary of Defense?"

The Diaboli were somewhat shocked and, although their expressions were in repose and inscrutable, the sound plates on their foreheads vibrated actively. Their strict sense of hierarchy was disturbed. The Secretary was only a Two-leg, but by Two-leg standards, he outranked them. They could not properly conduct official business with him.

The Secretary was aware of their feelings but had no choice in the matter. For at least ten minutes, their leaving must be delayed and no ordinary interruption could serve to hold back the Diaboli.

"Sirs," he said, "I must ask your indulgence to remain longer this time."

The central Diabolus replied in the nearest approach to English any Diabolus could manage. Actually, a Diabolus might be said to have two mouths. One was hinged at the outermost extremity of the jawbone and was used in eating. In this capacity, the motion of the mouth was rarely seen by human beings, since the Diaboli much preferred to eat in the company of their own kind, exclusively. A narrower mouth opening, however, perhaps two inches in width, could be used in speaking. It pursed itself open, revealing the gummy gap where a Diabolus' missing incisors ought to have been. It remained open during speech, the necessary consonantal blockings being performed by the palate and back of the tongue. The result was hoarse and fuzzy, but understandable.

The Diabolus said, "You will pardon us, already we suffer." And by his forehead, he twittered unheard, "They mean to suffocate us in their vile atmosphere. We must ask for larger poison-absorbing cylinders."

The Secretary of Defense said, "I am in sympathy with your feelings, and yet this may be my only opportunity to speak with you. Perhaps you would do us the honor to eat with us."

The Earthman next the Secretary could not forbear a quick and passing frown. He scribbled rapidly on a piece of paper and passed it to the Secretary, who glanced momentarily at it.

It read, "No. They eat sulfuretted hay. Stinks unbearably." The Secretary crumpled the note and let it drop.

The Diabolus said, "The honor is ours. Were we physically able to endure your strange atmosphere for so long a time, we would accept most gratefully."

And via forehead, he said with agitation, "They cannot expect us to eat with them and watch them consume the corpses of dead animals. My cud would never be sweet again."

"We respect your reasons," said the Secretary. "Let us then transact our business now. In the negotiations that have so far proceeded, we have been unable to obtain from your government, in the persons of you, their representatives, any clear indication as to what the boundaries of your sphere of influence are in your own minds. We have presented several proposals in this matter."

"As far as the territories of Earth are concerned, Mr. Secretary, a definition has been given."

"But surely you must see that this is unsatisfactory. The boundaries of Earth and your lands are nowhere in contact. So far, you have done nothing but state this fact. While true, the mere statement is not satisfying."

"We do not completely understand. Would you have us discuss the boundaries between ourselves and such independent human kingdoms as that of Vega?"

"Why, yes."

"That cannot be done, sir. Surely, you realize that any relations between ourselves and the sovereign realm of Vega cannot be possibly any concern of Earth. They can be discussed only with Vega."

"Then you will negotiate a hundred times with the hundred human world systems?"

"It is necessary. I would point out, however, that the necessity is imposed not by us but by the nature of your human organization."

"Then that limits our field of discussion drastically." The Secretary seemed abstracted. He was listening, not exactly to the Diaboli opposite, but, rather, it would seem, to something at a distance.

And now there was a faint commotion, barely heard from outside the Secretariat. The babble of distant voices, the brisk crackle of energy-guns muted by distance to nearly nothingness, and the hurried click-clacking of police hoppers.

The Diaboli showed no indication of hearing, nor was this simply another affectation of politeness. If their capacity for receiving supersonic sound waves was far more delicate and acute than almost anything human ingenuity had ever invented, their reception for ordinary sound waves was rather dull.

The Diabolus was saying, "We beg leave to state our surprise. We were of the opinion that all this was known to you."

A man in police uniform appeared in the doorway. The Secretary turned to him and, with the briefest of nods, the policeman departed.

The Secretary said suddenly and briskly, "Quite. I merely wished to ascertain once again that this was the case. I trust you will be ready to resume negotiations tomorrow?"

"Certainly, sir."

One by one, slowly, with a dignity befitting the heirs of the universe, the Diaboli left.

An Earthman said, "I'm glad they refused to eat with us."

"I knew they couldn't accept," said the Secretary, thoughtfully. "They're vegetarian. They sicken thoroughly at the very thought of eating meat. I've seen them eat, you know. Not many humans have. They resemble our cattle in the business of eating. They bolt their food and then stand solemnly about in circles, chewing their cuds in a great community of thought. Perhaps they intercommunicate by a method we are unaware of. The huge lower jaw rotates horizontally in a slow, grinding process—''

The policeman had once more appeared in the doorway.

The Secretary broke off, and called, ''You have them all?''

''Yes, sir.''

''Do you have Altmayer?''

''Yes, sir.''

''Good.''

The crowd had gathered again when the five Diaboli emerged from the Secretariat. The schedule was strict. At 3:00 P.M. each day they left their suite and spent five minutes walking to the Secretariat. At 3:35, they emerged therefrom once again and returned to their suite, the way being kept clear by the police. They marched stolidly, almost mechanically, along the broad avenue.

Halfway in their trek there came the sounds of shouting men. To most of the crowd, the words were not clear but there was the crackle of an energy-gun and the pale blue fluorescence split the air overhead. Police wheeled, their own energy-guns drawn, hoppers springing seven feet into the air, landing delicately in the midst of groups of people, touching none of them, jumping again almost instantly. People scattered and their voices were joined to the general uproar.

Through it all, the Diaboli, either through defective hearing or excessive dignity, continued marching as mechanically as ever.

At the other end of the gathering, almost diametrically opposing the region of excitement, Richard Sayama Altmayer stroked his nose in a moment of satisfaction. The strict chronology of the Diaboli had made a split-second plan possible. The first diversionary disturbance was only to attract the attention of the police. It was now—

And he fired a harmless sound pellet into the air.

Instantly, from four directions, concussion pellets split the air. From the roofs of buildings lining the way, snipers fired.

Each of the Diaboli, torn by the shells, shuddered and exploded as the pellets detonated within them. One by one, they toppled.

And from nowhere, the police were at Altmayer's side. He stared at them with some surprise.

Gently, for in twenty years he had lost his fury and learned to be gentle, he said, ''You come quickly, but even so you come too late.'' He gestured in the direction of the shattered Diaboli.

The crowd was in simple panic now. Additional squadrons of police, arriving in record time, could do nothing more than herd them off into harmless directions.

The policeman, who now held Altmayer in a firm grip, taking the sound gun from him and inspecting him quickly for further weapons, was a captain by rank. He said, stiffly, ''I think you've made a mistake, Mr. Altmayer. You'll notice you've drawn no blood.'' And he, too, waved toward where the Diaboli lay motionless.

Altmayer turned, startled. The creatures lay there on their sides, some in pieces, tattered skin shredding away, frames distorted and bent, but the police captain was correct. There was no blood, no flesh. Altmayer's lips, pale and stiff, moved soundlessly.

The police captain interpreted the motion accurately enough. He said, "You are correct, sir, they are robots."

And from the great doors of the Secretariat of Defense, the true Diaboli emerged. Clubbing policemen cleared the way, but another way, so that they need not pass the sprawled travesties of plastic and aluminum which for three minutes had played the role of living creatures.

The police captain said, "I'll ask you to come without trouble, Mr. Altmayer. The Secretary of Defense would like to see you."

"I am coming, sir." A stunned frustration was only now beginning to overwhelm him.

Geoffrey Stock and Richard Altmayer faced one another for the first time in almost a quarter of a century, there in the Defense Secretary's private office. It was a rather strait-laced office: a desk, an armchair, and two additional chairs. All were a dull brown in color, the chairs being topped by brown foamite which yielded to the body enough for comfort, not enough for luxury. There was a micro-viewer on the desk and a little cabinet big enough to hold several dozen opto-spools. On the wall opposite the desk was a trimensional view of the old *Dauntless,* the Secretary's first command.

Stock said, "It is a little ridiculous meeting like this after so many years. I find I am sorry."

"Sorry about what, Jeff?" Altmayer tried to force a smile, "I am sorry about nothing but that you tricked me with those robots."

"You were not difficult to trick," said Stock, "and it was an excellent opportunity to break your party. I'm sure it will be quite discredited after this. The pacifist tries to force war; the apostle of gentleness tries assassination."

"War against the true enemy," said Altmayer sadly. "But you are right. It is a sign of desperation that this was forced on me."—Then, "How did you know my plans?"

"You still overestimate humanity, Dick. In any conspiracy the weakest points are the people that compose it. You had twenty-five co-conspirators. Didn't it occur to you that at least one of them might be an informer, or even an employee of mine?"

A dull red burned slowly on Altmayer's high cheekbones. "Which one?" he said.

"Sorry. We may have to use him again."

Altmayer sat back in his chair wearily. "What have you gained?"

"What have *you* gained? You are as impractical now as on that last day I saw you; the day you decided to go to jail rather than report for induction. You haven't changed."

Altmayer shook his head, "The truth doesn't change."

Stock said impatiently, "If it is truth, why does it always fail? Your stay in jail accomplished nothing. The war went on. Not one life was saved. Since then, you've started a political party; and every cause it has backed has failed. Your conspiracy has failed. You're nearly fifty, Dick, and what have you accomplished? Nothing.''

Altmayer said, ''And you went to war, rose to command a ship, then to a place in the Cabinet. They say you will be the next Coordinator. You've accomplished a great deal. Yet success and failure do not exist in themselves. Success in what? Success in working the ruin of humanity. Failure in what? In saving it? I wouldn't change places with you. Jeff, remember this. In a good cause, there are no failures; there are only delayed successes.''

''Even if you are executed for this day's work?''

''Even if I am executed. There will be someone else to carry on, and his success will be my success.''

''How do you envisage this success? Can you really see a union of worlds, a Galactic Federation? Do you want Santanni running our affairs? Do you want a Vegan telling you what to do? Do you want Earth to decide its own destiny or to be at the mercy of any random combination of powers?''

''We would be at their mercy no more than they would be at ours.''

''Except that we are the richest. We would be plundered for the sake of the depressed worlds of the Sirius Sector.''

''And pay the plunder out of what we would save in the wars that would no longer occur.''

''Do you have answers for all questions, Dick?''

''In twenty years we have been asked all questions, Jeff.''

''Then answer this one. How would you force this union of yours on unwilling humanity?''

''That is why I wanted to kill the Diaboli.'' For the first time, Altmayer showed agitation. ''It would mean war with them, but all humanity would unite against the common enemy. Our own political and ideological differences would fade in the face of that.''

''You really believe that? Even when the Diaboli have never harmed us? They cannot live on our worlds. They must remain on their own worlds of sulfide atmosphere and oceans which are sodium sulfate solutions.''

''Humanity knows better, Jeff. They are spreading from world to world like an atomic explosion. They block space-travel into regions where there are unoccupied oxygen worlds, the kind *we* could use. They are planning for the future; making room for uncounted future generations of Diaboli, while we are being restricted to one corner of the Galaxy, and fighting ourselves to death. In a thousand years we will be their slaves; in ten thousand we will be extinct. Oh, yes, they are the common enemy. Mankind knows that. You will find that out sooner than you think, perhaps.''

The Secretary said, ''Your party members speak a great deal of ancient Greece of the preatomic age. They tell us that the Greeks were a marvelous people, the most culturally advanced of their time, perhaps of all times. They set mankind on the road it has never yet left entirely. They had only one flaw. They could not unite. They were conquered and eventually died out. And we follow in their footsteps now, eh?''

''You have learned your lesson well, Jeff.''

''But have you, Dick?''

''What do you mean?''

''Did the Greeks have no common enemy against whom they could unite?''

Atlmayer was silent.

Stock said, "The Greeks fought Persia, their great common enemy. Was it not a fact that a good proportion of the Greek states fought on the Persian side?"

Altmayer said finally, "Yes. Because they thought Persian victory was inevitable and they wanted to be on the winning side."

"Human beings haven't changed, Dick. Why do you suppose the Diaboli are here? What is it we are discussing?"

"I am not a member of the government."

"No," said Stock, savagely, "but I am. The Vegan League has allied itself with the Diaboli."

"I don't believe you. It can't be."

"It can be and is. The Diaboli have agreed to supply them with five hundred ships at any time they happen to be at war with Earth. In return, Vega abandons all claims to the Nigellian star cluster. So if you had really assassinated the Diaboli, it would have been war, but with half of humanity probably fighting on the side of your so-called common enemy. We are trying to prevent that."

Altmayer said slowly, "I am ready for trial. Or am I to be executed without one?"

Stock said, "You are still foolish. If we shoot you, Dick, we make a martyr. If we keep you alive and shoot only your subordinates, you will be suspected of having turned state's evidence. As a presumed traitor, you will be quite harmless in the future."

And so, on September 5th, 2788, Richard Sayama Altmayer, after the briefest of secret trials, was sentenced to five years in prison. He served his full term. The year he emerged from prison, Geoffrey Stock was elected Coordinator of Earth.

3—DECEMBER 21, 2800

Simon Devoire was not at ease. He was a little man, with sandy hair and a freckled, ruddy face. He said, "I'm sorry I agreed to see you, Altmayer. It won't do you any good. It might do me harm."

Altmayer said, "I am an old man. I won't hurt you." And he was indeed a very old man somehow. The turn of the century found his years at two thirds of a century, but he was older than that, older inside and older outside. His clothes were too big for him, as if he were shrinking away inside them. Only his nose had not aged; it was still the thin, aristocratic, high-beaked Altmayer nose.

Devoire said, "It's not you I'm afraid of."

"Why not? Perhaps you think I betrayed the men of '88."

"No, of course not. No man of sense believes that you did. But the days of the Federalists are over, Altmayer."

Altmayer tried to smile. He felt a little hungry; he hadn't eaten that day—no time for food. Was the day of the Federalists over? It might seem so to others. The movement had died on a wave of ridicule. A conspiracy that fails, a "lost cause," is often romantic. It is remembered and draws adherents for generations, *if* the loss is at least a dignified one. But to shoot at living creatures and find the mark to be robots; to be outmaneuvered and outfoxed; to be made ridiculous—that is deadly. It is deadlier than treason, wrong, and sin. Not many had believed Altmayer had bargained for his life by betraying his associates, but the universal laughter killed Federalism as effectively as though they had.

But Altmayer had remained stolidly stubborn under it all. He said, "The day of the Federalists will never be over, while the human race lives."

"Words," said Devoire impatiently. "They meant more to me when I was younger. I am a little tired now."

"Simon, I need access to the subetheric system."

Devoire's face hardened. He said, "And you thought of me. I'm sorry, Altmayer, but I can't let you use my broadcasts for your own purposes."

"You were a Federalist once."

"Don't rely on that," said Devoire. "That's in the past. Now I am—nothing. I am a Devoirist, I suppose. I want to live."

"Even if it is under the feet of the Diaboli? Do you want to live when they are willing; die when they are ready?"

"Words!"

"Do you approve of the all-Galactic conference?"

Devoire reddened past his usual pink level. He gave the sudden impression of a man with too much blood for his body. He said smolderingly, "Well, why not? What does it matter how we go about establishing the Federation of Man? If you're still a Federalist, what have you to object to in a united humanity?"

"United under the Diaboli?"

"What's the difference? Humanity can't unite by itself. Let us be driven to it, as long as the fact is accomplished. I am sick of it all, Altmayer, sick of all our stupid history. I'm tired of trying to be an idealist with nothing to be idealistic over. Human beings are human beings and that's the nasty part of it. Maybe we've *got* to be whipped into line. If so, I'm perfectly willing to let the Diaboli do the whipping."

Altmayer said gently, "You're very foolish, Devoire. It won't be a real union, you know that. The Diaboli called this conference so that they might act as umpires on all current interhuman disputes to their own advantage, and remain the supreme court of judgment over us hereafter. You know they have no intention of establishing a real central human government. It will only be a sort of interlocking directorate; each human government will conduct its own affairs as before and pull in various directions as before. It is simply that we will grow accustomed to running to the Diaboli with our little problems."

"How do you know that will be the result?"

"Do you seriously think any other result is possible?"

Devoire chewed at his lower lip, "Maybe not!"

"Then see through a pane of glass, Simon. Any true independence we now have will be lost."

"A lot of good this independence has ever done us. Besides, what's the use? We can't stop this thing. Coordinator Stock is probably no keener on the conference than you are, but that doesn't help him. If Earth doesn't attend, the union will be formed without us, and then we will face war with the rest of humanity and the Diaboli. And that goes for any other government that wants to back out."

"What if *all* the governments back out? Wouldn't the conference break up completely?"

"Have you ever known all the human governments to do *anything* together? You never learn, Altmayer."

"There are new facts involved."

"Such as? I know I am foolish for asking, but go ahead."

Altmayer said, "For twenty years most of the Galaxy has been shut to human ships. You know that. None of us has the slightest notion of what goes on within the Diaboli sphere of influence. And yet some human colonies exist within that sphere."

"So?"

"So occasionally, human beings escape into the small portion of the Galaxy that remains human and free. The government of Earth receives reports; reports which they don't dare make public. But not *all* officials of the government can stand the cowardice involved in such actions forever. One of them has been to see me. I can't tell you which one, of course. So I have documents, Devoire; official, reliable, and true."

Devoire shrugged, "About what?" He turned the desk chronometer rather ostentatiously so that Altmayer could see its gleaming metal face on which the red, glowing figures stood out sharply. They read 22:31, and even as it was turned, the 1 faded and the new glow of a 2 appeared.

Altmayer said, "There is a planet called by its colonists Chu Hsi. It did not have a large population; two million, perhaps. Fifteen years ago the Diaboli occupied worlds on various sides of it; and in all those fifteen years, no human ship ever landed on the planet. Last year the Diaboli themselves landed. They brought with them huge freight ships filled with sodium sulfate and bacterial cultures that are native to their own worlds."

"What? You can't make me believe it."

"Try," said Altmayer, ironically. "It is not difficult. Sodium sulfate will dissolve in the oceans of any world. In a sulfate ocean, their bacteria will grow, multiply, and produce hydrogen sulfide in tremendous quantities which will fill the oceans and the atmosphere. They can then introduce their plants and animals and eventually themselves. Another planet will be suitable for Diaboli life—and unsuitable for any human. It would take time, surely, but the Diaboli have time. They are a united people and . . ."

"Now, look," Devoire waved his hand in disgust, "that just doesn't hold water. The Diaboli have more worlds than they know what to do with."

"For their present purposes, yes, but the Diaboli are creatures that look toward the future. Their birth rate is high and eventually they will fill the Galaxy. And how much better off they would be if they were the only intelligence in the universe."

"But it's impossible on purely physical grounds. Do you know how many millions of tons of sodium sulfate it would take to fill up the oceans to their requirements?"

"Obviously a planetary supply."

"Well, then, do you suppose they would strip one of their own worlds to create a new one? Where is the gain?"

"Simon, Simon, there are millions of planets in the Galaxy which through atmospheric conditions, temperature, or gravity are forever uninhabitable either to humans or to Diaboli. Many of these are quite adequately rich in sulfur."

Devoire considered, "What about the human beings on the planet?"

"On Chu Hsi? Euthanasia—except for the few who escaped in time. Painless I suppose. The Diaboli are not needlessly cruel, merely efficient."

Altmayer waited. Devoire's fist clenched and unclenched.

Altmayer said, "Publish this news. Spread it out on the interstellar subetheric web. Broadcast the documents to the reception centers on the various worlds.

You can do it, and when you do, the all-Galactic conference will fall apart.''
    Devoire's chair tilted forward. He stood up. ''Where's your proof?''
    ''Will you do it?''
    ''I want to see your proof.''
    Altmayer smiled, ''Come with me.''

    They were waiting for him when he came back to the furnished room he was
living in. He didn't notice them at first. He was completely unaware of the small
vehicle that followed him at a slow pace and a prudent distance. He walked with
his head bent, calculating the length of time it would take for Devoire to put the
information through the reaches of Space; how long it would take for the
receiving stations on Vega and Santanni and Centaurus to blast out the news;
how long it would take to spread it over the entire Galaxy. And in this way he
passed, unheeding, between the two plain-clothes men who flanked the entrance
of the rooming house.
    It was only when he opened the door to his own room that he stopped and
turned to leave but the plain-clothes men were behind him now. He made no
attempt at violent escape. He entered the room instead and sat down, feeling so
old. He thought feverishly, I need only hold them off an hour and ten minutes.
    The man who occupied the darkness reached up and flicked the switch that
allowed the wall lights to operate. In the soft wall glow, the man's round face
and balding gray-fringed head were startlingly clear.
    Altmayer said gently, ''I am honored with a visit by the Coordinator himself.''
    And Stock said, ''We are old friends, you and I, Dick. We meet every once
in a while.''
    Altmayer did not answer.
    Stock said, ''You have certain government papers in your possession, Dick.''
    Altmayer said, ''If you think so, Jeff, you'll have to find them.''
    Stock rose wearily to his feet. ''No heroics, Dick. Let me tell you what those
papers contained. They were circumstantial reports of the sulfation of the planet,
Chu Hsi. Isn't that true?''
    Altmayer looked at the clock.
    Stock said, ''If you are planning to delay us, to angle us as though we were
fish, you will be disappointed. We know where you've been, we know Devoire
has the papers, we know exactly what he's planning to do with them.''
    Altmayer stiffened. The thin parchment of his cheeks trembled. He said,
''How long have you known?''
    ''As long as you have, Dick. You are a very predictable man. It is the very
reason we decided to use you. Do you suppose the Recorder would really come
to see you as he did, without our knowledge?''
    ''I don't understand.''
    Stock said, ''The Government of Earth, Dick, is not anxious that the
all-Galactic conference be continued. However, we are not Federalists; we know
humanity for what it is. What do you suppose would happen if the rest of the
Galaxy discovered that the Diaboli were in the process of changing a salt-oxygen
world into a sulfate-sulfide one?
    ''No, don't answer. You are Dick Altmayer and I'm sure you'd tell me that
with one fiery burst of indignation, they'd abandon the conference, join together
in a loving and brotherly union, throw themselves at the Diaboli, and overwhelm
them.''

Stock paused such a long time that for a moment it might have seemed he would say no more. Then he continued in a half a whisper, "Nonsense. The other worlds would say that the Government of Earth for purposes of its own had initiated a fraud, had forged documents in a deliberate attempt to disrupt the conference. The Diaboli would deny everything, and most of the human worlds would find it to their interests to believe the denial. They would concentrate on the iniquities of the Diaboli. So you see, we could sponsor no such exposé."

Altmayer felt drained, futile. "Then you will stop Devoire. It is always that you are so sure of failure beforehand; that you believe the worst of your fellow man—"

"Wait! I said nothing of stopping Devoire. I said only that the government could not sponsor such an exposé and we will not. But the exposé will take place just the same, except that afterward we will arrest Devoire and yourself and denounce the whole thing as vehemently as will the Diaboli. The whole affair would then be changed. The Government of Earth will have dissociated itself from the claims. It will then seem to the rest of the human government that for our own selfish purposes we are trying to hide the actions of the Diaboli, that we have, perhaps, a special understanding with them. They will fear that special understanding and unite against us. But *then* to be against us will mean that they are also against the Diaboli. They will insist on believing the expose to be the truth, the documents to be real—and the conference will break up."

"It will mean war again," said Altmayer hopelessly, "and not against the real enemy. It will mean fighting among the humans and a victory all the greater for the Diaboli when it is all over."

"No war," said Stock. "No government will attack Earth with the Diaboli on our side. The other governments will merely draw away from us and grind a permanent anti-Diaboli bias into their propaganda. Later, if there should be war between ourselves and the Diaboli, the other governments will at least remain neutral."

He looks very old, thought Altmayer. We are all old, dying men. Aloud, he said, "Why would you expect the Diaboli to back Earth? You may fool the rest of mankind by pretending to attempt suppression of the facts concerning the planet Chu Hsi, but you won't fool the Diaboli. They won't for a moment believe Earth to be sincere in its claim that it believes the documents to be forgeries."

"Ah, but they will." Geoffrey Stock stood up, "You see, the documents *are* forgeries. The Diaboli may be planning sulfation of planets in the future, but to our knowledge, they have not tried it yet."

On December 21, 2800, Richard Sayama Altmayer entered prison for the third and last time. There was no trial, no definite sentence, and scarcely a real imprisonment in the literal sense of the word. His movements were confined and only a few officials were allowed to communicate with him, but otherwise his comforts were looked to assiduously. He had no access to news, of course, so that he was not aware that in the second year of this third imprisonment of his, the war between Earth and the Diaboli opened with the surprise attack near Sirius by an Earth squadron upon certain ships of the Diaboli navy.

In 2802, Geoffrey Stock came to visit Altmayer in his confinement. Altmayer rose in surprise to greet him.

"You're looking well, Dick," Stock said.

He himself was not. His complexion had grayed. He still wore his naval captain's uniform, but his body stooped slightly within it. He was to die within the year, a fact of which he was not completely unaware. It did not bother him much. He thought repeatedly, I have lived the years I've had to live.

Altmayer, who looked the older of the two, had yet more than nine years to live. He said, "An unexpected pleasure, Jeff, but this time you can't have come to imprison me. I'm in prison already."

"I've come to set you free, if you would like."

"For what purpose, Jeff? Surely you have a purpose? A clever way of using me?"

Stock's smile was merely a momentary twitch. He said. "A way of using you, truly, but this time you will approve. . . .We are at war."

"With whom?" Altmayer was startled.

"With the Diaboli. We have been at war for six months."

Altmayer brought his hands together, thin fingers interlacing nervously, "I've heard nothing of this."

"I know." The Coordinator clasped his hands behind his back and was distantly surprised to find that they were trembling. He said, "It's been a long journey for the two of us, Dick. We've had the same goal, you and I—No, let me speak. I've often wanted to explain my point of view to you, but you would never have understood. You weren't the kind of man to understand, until I had the results for you. I was twenty-five when I first visited a Diaboli world, Dick. I knew then it was either they or we."

"I said so," whispered Altmayer, "from the first."

"Merely saying so was not enough. You wanted to force the human governments to unite against them and that notion was politically unrealistic and completely impossible. It wasn't even desirable. Humans are not Diaboli. Among the Diaboli, individual consciousness is low, almost nonexistent. Ours is almost overpowering. They have no such thing as politics; we have nothing else. They can never disagree, can have nothing but a single government. We can never agree; if we had a single island to live on, we would split it in three.

"But our very disagreements are our strength! Your Federalist party used to speak of ancient Greece a great deal once. Do you remember? But your people always missed the point. To be sure, Greece could never unite and was therefore ultimately conquered. But even in her state of disunion, she defeated the gigantic Persian Empire. Why?

"I would like to point out that the Greek city-states over centuries had fought with one another. They were forced to specialize in things military to an extent far beyond the Persians. Even the Persians themselves realized that, and in the last century of their imperial existence, Greek mercenaries formed the most valued parts of their armies.

"The same might be said of the small nation-states of preatomic Europe, which in centuries of fighting had advanced their military arts to the point where they could overcome and hold for two hundred years the comparatively gigantic empires of Asia.

"So it is with us. The Diaboli, with vast extents of galactic space, have never fought a war. Their military machine is massive, but untried. In fifty years, only such advances have been made by them as they have been able to copy from the various human navies. Humanity, on the other hand, has competed ferociously in warfare. Each government has raced to keep ahead of its neighbors in military science. They've had to! It was our own disunion that made the terrible race for survival necessary, so that in the end almost any one of us was a match for all the Diaboli, provided only that none of us would fight on their side in a general war.

"It was toward the prevention of such a development that all of Earth's diplomacy has been aimed. Until it was certain that in a war between Earth and the Diaboli, the rest of humanity would be at least neutral, there could be no war, and no union of human governments could be allowed, since the race for military perfection must continue. Once we were sure of neutrality, through the hoax that broke up the conference two years ago, we sought the war, and now we have it."

Altmayer, through all this, might have been frozen. It was a long time before he could say anything.

Finally, "What if the Diaboli are victorious after all?"

Stock said, "They aren't. Two weeks ago, the main fleets joined action and theirs was annihilated with practically no loss to ourselves, although we were greatly outnumbered. We might have been fighting unarmed ships. We had stronger weapons of greater range and more accurate sighting. We had three times their effective speed since we had antiacceleration devices which they lacked. Since the battle a dozen of the other human governments have decided to join the winning side and have declared war on the Diaboli. Yesterday the Diaboli requested that negotiations for an armistice be opened. The war is practically over; and henceforward the Diaboli will be confined to their original planets with only such future expansions as we permit."

Altmayer murmured incoherently.

Stock said, "And now union becomes necessary. After the defeat of Persia by the Greek city-states, they were ruined because of their continued wars among themselves, so that first Macedon and then Rome conquered them. After Europe colonized the Americas, cut up Africa, and conquered Asia, a series of continued European wars led to European ruin.

"Disunion until conquest; union thereafter! But now union is easy. Let one subdivision succeed by itself and the rest will clamor to become part of that success. The ancient writer, Toynbee, first pointed out this difference between what he called a 'dominant minority' and a 'creative minority.'

"We are a creative minority now. In an almost spontaneous gesture, various human governments have suggested the formation of a United Worlds organization. Over seventy governments are willing to attend the first sessions in order to draw up a Charter of Federation. The others will join later, I am sure. We would like you to be one of the delegates from Earth, Dick."

Altmayer found his eyes flooding, "I—I don't understand your purpose. Is this all true?"

"It is all exactly as I say. You were a voice in the wilderness, Dick, crying for union. Your words will carry much weight. What did you once say: 'In a good cause, there are no failures.' "

"No!" said Altmayer, with sudden energy. "It seems your cause was the good one."

Stock's face was hard and devoid of emotion, "You were always a misunderstander of human nature, Dick. When the United Worlds is a reality and when generations of men and women look back to these days of war through their centuries of unbroken peace, they will have forgotten the purpose of my methods. To them, they will represent war and death. *Your* calls for union, *your* idealism, will be remembered forever.''

He turned away and Altmayer barely caught his last words: ''And when they build their statues, they will build none for me.''

In the Great Court, which stands as a patch of untouched peace among the fifty busy square miles devoted to the towering buildings that are the pulse beat of the United Worlds of the Galaxy, stands a statue . . .

THE KEY

KARL JENNINGS knew he was going to die. He had a matter of hours to live and much to do.

There was no reprieve from the death sentence, not here on the Moon, not with no communications in operation.

Even on Earth there were a few fugitive patches where, without radio handy, a man might die without the hand of his fellow man to help him, without the heart of his fellow man to pity him, without even the eye of his fellow man to discover the corpse. Here on the Moon, there were few spots that were otherwise.

Earthmen knew he was on the Moon, of course. He had been part of a geological expedition—no, selenological expedition! Odd, how his Earth-centered mind insisted on the "geo-."

Wearily he drove himself to think, even as he worked. Dying though he was, he still felt that artificially imposed clarity of thought. Anxiously he looked about. There was nothing to see. He was in the dark of the eternal shadow of the northern interior of the wall of the crater, a blackness relieved only by the intermittent blink of his flash. He kept that intermittent, partly because he dared not consume its power source before he was through and partly because he dared not take more than the minimum chance that it be seen.

On his left hand, toward the south along the nearby horizon of the Moon, was a crescent of bright white Sunlight. Beyond the horizon, and invisible, was the opposite lip of the crater. The Sun never peered high enough over the lip of his own edge of the crater to illuminate the floor immediately beneath his feet. He was safe from radiation—from that at least.

He dug carefully but clumsily, swathed as he was in his spacesuit. His side ached abominably.

The dust and broken rock did not take up the "fairy castle" appearance characteristic of those portions of the Moon's surface exposed to the alternation of light and dark, heat and cold. Here, in eternal cold, the slow crumbling of the crater wall had simply piled fine rubble in a heterogeneous mass. It would not be easy to tell there had been digging going on.

He misjudged the unevenness of the dark surface for a moment and spilled a cupped handful of dusty fragments. The particles dropped with the slowness characteristic of the Moon and yet with the appearance of a blinding speed, for there was no air resistance to slow them further still and spread them out into a dusty haze.

Jennings' flash brightened for a moment, and he kicked a jagged rock out of the way.

He hadn't much time. He dug deeper into the dust.

A little deeper and he could push the Device into the depression and begin covering it. Strauss must not find it.

Strauss!

The other member of the team. Half-share in the discovery. Half-share in the renown.

If it were merely the whole share of the credit that Strauss had wanted, Jennings might have allowed it. The discovery was more important than any individual credit that might go with it. But what Strauss wanted was something far more, something Jennings would fight to prevent.

One of the few things Jennings was willing to die to prevent.

And he was dying.

They had found it together. Actually, Strauss had found the ship; or, better, the remains of the ship; or, better still, what just conceivably might have been the remains of something analogous to a ship.

"Metal," said Strauss, as he picked up something ragged and nearly amorphous. His eyes and face could just barely be seen through the thick lead glass of the visor, but his rather harsh voice sounded clearly enough through the suit radio.

Jennings came drifting over from his own position half a mile away. He said, "Odd! There is no free metal on the Moon."

"There shouldn't be. But you know well enough they haven't explored more than one per cent of the Moon's surface. Who knows what can be found on it?"

Jennings grunted assent and reached out his gauntlet to take the object.

It was true enough that almost anything might be found on the Moon for all anyone really knew. Theirs was the first privately financed selenographic expedition ever to land on the Moon. Till then, there had been only government-conducted shotgun affairs, with half a dozen ends in view. It was a sign of the advancing space age that the Geological Society could afford to send two men to the Moon for selenological studies only.

Strauss said, "It looks as though it once had a polished surface."

"You're right," said Jennings. "Maybe there's more about."

They found three more pieces, two of trifling size and one a jagged object that showed traces of a seam.

"Let's take them to the ship," said Strauss.

They took the small skim boat back to the mother ship. They shucked their suits once on board, something Jennings at least was always glad to do. He scratched vigorously at his ribs and rubbed his cheeks till his light skin reddened into welts.

Strauss eschewed such weakness and got to work. The laser beam pock-marked the metal and the vapor recorded itself on the spectrograph. Titanium-steel, essentially, with a hint of cobalt and molybdenum.

"That's artificial, all right," said Strauss. His broad-boned face was as dour and as hard as ever. He showed no elation, although Jennings could feel his own heart begin to race.

It may have been the excitement that trapped Jennings into beginning, "This is a development against which we must steel ourselves—" with a faint stress on "steel" to indicate the play on words.

Strauss, however, looked at Jennings with an icy distaste, and the attempted set of puns was choked off.

Jennings sighed. He could never swing it, somehow. Never could! He remembered at the University—Well, never mind. The discovery they had made was worth a far better pun than any he could construct for all Strauss's calmness.

Jennings wondered if Strauss could possibly miss the significance.

He knew very little about Strauss, as a matter of fact, except by selenological reputation. That is, he had read Strauss's papers and he presumed Strauss had read his. Although their ships might well have passed by night in their University days, they had never happened to meet until after both had volunteered for this expedition and had been accepted.

In the week's voyage, Jennings had grown uncomfortably aware of the other's stocky figure, his sandy hair and china-blue eyes, and the way the muscles over his prominent jawbones worked when he ate. Jennings, himself, much slighter in build, also blue-eyed, but with darker hair, tended to withdraw automatically from the heavy exudation of the other's power and drive.

Jennings said, "There's no record of any ship ever having landed on this part of the Moon. Certainly none has crashed."

"If it were part of a ship," said Strauss, "it should be smooth and polished. This is eroded and, without an atmosphere here, that means exposure to micrometeor bombardment over many years."

Then he *did* see the significance. Jennings said, with an almost savage jubilation, "It's a non-human artifact. Creatures not of Earth once visited the Moon. Who knows how long ago?"

"Who knows?" agreed Strauss dryly.

"In the report—"

"Wait," said Strauss imperiously. "Time enough to report when we have something to report. If it was a ship, there will be more to it than what we now have."

But there was no point in looking further just then. They had been at it for hours, and the next meal and sleep were overdue. Better to tackle the whole job fresh and spend hours at it. They seemed to agree on that without speaking.

The Earth was low on the eastern horizon, almost full in phase, bright and blue-streaked. Jennings looked at it while they ate and experienced, as he always did, a sharp homesickness.

"It looks peaceful enough," he said, "but there are six billion people busy on it."

Strauss looked up from some deep inner life of his own and said, "Six billion people ruining it!"

Jennings frowned. "You're not an Ultra, are you?"

Strauss said, "What the hell are you talking about?"

Jennings felt himself flush. A flush always showed against his fair skin, turning it pink at the slightest upset of the even tenor of his emotions. He found it intensely embarrassing.

He turned back to his food, without saying anything.

For a whole generation now, the Earth's population had held steady. No further increase could be afforded. Everyone admitted that. There were those, in fact, who said that "no higher" wasn't enough; the population had to drop. Jennings himself sympathized with that point of view. The globe of the Earth was being eaten alive by its heavy freight of humanity.

But *how* was the population to be made to drop? Randomly, by encouraging the people to lower the birth rate still further, as and how they wished? Lately there had been the slow rise of a distant rumble which wanted not only a population drop but a selected drop—the survival of the fittest, with the self-declared fit choosing the criteria of fitness.

Jennings thought: I've insulted him, I suppose.

Later, when he was almost asleep, it suddenly occurred to him that he knew virtually nothing of Strauss's character. What if it were his intention to go out now on a foraging expedition of his own so that he might get sole credit for—?

He raised himself on his elbow in alarm, but Strauss was breathing heavily, and even as Jennings listened, the breathing grew into the characteristic burr of a snore.

They spent the next three days in a single-minded search for additional pieces. They found some. They found more than that. They found an area glowing with the tiny phosphorescence of Lunar bacteria. Such bacteria were common enough, but nowhere previously had their occurrence been reported in concentration so great as to cause a visible glow.

Strauss said, "An organic being, or his remains, may have been here once. He died, but the microorganisms within him did not. In the end they consumed him."

"And spread perhaps," added Jennings. "That may be the source of Lunar bacteria generally. They may not be native at all but may be the result of contamination instead—eons ago."

"It works the other way, too," said Strauss. "Since the bacteria are completely different in very fundamental ways from any Earthly form of microorganism, the creatures they parasitized—assuming this was their source— must have been fundamentally different too. Another indication of extraterrestrial origin."

The trail ended in the wall of a small crater.

"It's a major digging job," said Jennings, his heart sinking. "We had better report this and get help."

"No," said Strauss somberly. "There may be nothing to get help for. The crater might have formed a million years after the ship had crash-landed."

"And vaporized most of it, you mean, and left only what we've found?"

Strauss nodded.

Jennings said, "Let's try anyway. We can dig a bit. If we draw a line through the finds we've made so far and just keep on . . ."

Strauss was reluctant and worked halfheartedly, so that it was Jennings who made the real find. Surely that counted! Even though Strauss had found the first piece of metal, Jennings had found the artifact itself.

It *was* an artifact—cradled three feet underground under the irregular shape of a boulder which had fallen in such a way that it left a hollow in its contact with the Moon's surface. In that hollow lay the artifact, protected from everything for a million years or more; protected from radiation, from micrometeors, from temperature change, so that it remained fresh and new forever.

Jennings labeled it at once the Device. It looked not remotely similar to any instrument either had ever seen, but then, as Jennings said, why should it?

"There are no rough edges that I can see," he said. "It may not be broken."

"There may be missing parts, though."

"Maybe," said Jennings, "but there seems to be nothing movable. It's all one piece and certainly oddly uneven." He noted his own play on words, then went on with a not-altogether-successful attempt at self-control. "*This* is what we need. A piece of worn metal or an area rich in bacteria is only material for deduction and dispute. But this is the real thing—a Device that is clearly of extraterrestrial manufacture."

It was on the table between them now, and both regarded it gravely.

Jennings said, "Let's put through a preliminary report, now."

"No!" said Strauss, in sharp and strenuous dissent. "Hell, no!"

"Why not?"

"Because if we do, it becomes a Society project. They'll swarm all over it and we won't be as much as a footnote when all is done. No!" Strauss looked almost sly. "Let's do all we can with it and get as much out of it as possible before the harpies descend."

Jennings thought about it. He couldn't deny that he too wanted to make certain that no credit was lost. But still—

He said, "I don't know that I like to take the chance, Strauss." For the first time he had an impulse to use the man's first name, but fought it off. "Look, Strauss," he said, "it's not right to wait. If this is of extraterrestrial origin, then it must be from some other planetary system. There isn't a place in the Solar System, outside the Earth, that can possibly support an advanced life form."

"Not proven, really," grunted Strauss, "but what if you're right?"

"Then it would mean that the creatures of the ship had interstellar travel and therefore had to be far in advance, technologically, of ourselves. Who knows what the Device can tell us about their advanced technology. It might be the key to—who knows what. It might be the clue to an unimaginable scientific revolution."

"That's romantic nonsense. If this is the product of a technology far advanced over ours, we'll learn nothing from it. Bring Einstein back to life and show him a microprotowarp and what would he make of it?"

"We can't be certain that we won't learn."

"So what, even so? What if there's a small delay? What if we assure credit for ourselves? What if we make sure that we ourselves go along with this, that we don't let go of it?"

"But Strauss"—Jennings felt himself moved almost to tears in his anxiety to get across his sense of the importance of the Device—"what if we crash with it? What if we don't make it back to Earth? We can't risk this thing." He tapped it then, almost as though he were in love with it. "We should report it now and have them send ships out here to get it. It's too precious to—"

At the peak of his emotional intensity, the Device seemed to grow warm under his hand. A portion of its surface, half-hidden under a flap of metal, glowed phosphorescently.

Jennings jerked his hand away in a spasmodic gesture and the Device darkened. But it was enough; the moment had been infinitely revealing.

He said, almost choking, "It was like a window opening into your skull. I could see into your mind."

"I read yours," said Strauss, "or experienced it, or entered into it, or whatever you choose." He touched the Device in his cold, withdrawn way, but nothing happened.

"You're an Ultra," said Jennings angrily. "When I touched this"—And he did so. "It's happening again. I see it. Are you a madman? Can you honestly believe it is humanly decent to condemn almost all the human race to extinction and destroy the versatility and variety of the species?"

His hand dropped away from the Device again, in repugnance at the glimpses revealed, and it grew dark again. Once more, Strauss touched it gingerly and again nothing happened.

Strauss said, "Let's not start a discussion, for God's sake. This thing is an aid to communication—a telepathic amplifier. Why not? The brain cells have each their electric potentials. Thought can be viewed as a wavering electromagnetic field of microintensities—"

Jennings turned away. He didn't want to speak to Strauss. He said, "We'll report it now. I don't give a damn about credit. Take it all. I just want it out of our hands."

For a moment Strauss remained in a brown study. Then he said, "It's more than a communicator. It responds to emotion and it amplifies emotion."

"What are you talking about?"

"Twice it started at your touch just now, although you'd been handling it all day with no effect. It still has no effect when I touch it."

"Well?"

"It reacted to you when you were in a state of high emotional tension. That's the requirement for activation, I suppose. And when you raved about the Ultras while you were holding it just now, I felt as you did, for just a moment."

"So you should."

"But, listen to me. Are you sure *you're* so right. There isn't a thinking man on Earth that doesn't know the planet would be better off with a population of one billion rather than six billion. If we used automation to the full—as now the hordes won't allow us to do—we could probably have a completely efficient and viable Earth with a population of no more than, say, five million. Listen to me, Jennings. Don't turn away, man."

The harshness in Strauss's voice almost vanished in his effort to be reasonably winning. "But we can't reduce the population democratically. You know that. It isn't the sex urge, because uterine inserts solved the birth control problem long ago; you know that. It's a matter of nationalism. Each ethnic group wants other groups to reduce themselves in population first, and I agree with them. I want my ethnic group, *our* ethnic group, to prevail. I want the Earth to be inherited by the elite, which means by men like ourselves. We're the true men, and the horde of half-apes who hold us down are destroying us all. They're doomed to death anyway; why not save ourselves?"

"No," said Jennings strenuously. "No one group has a monopoly on humanity. Your five million-images, trapped in a humanity robbed of its variety and versatility, would die of boredom—and serve them right."

"Emotional nonsense, Jennings. You don't believe that. You've just been trained to believe it by our damn-fool equalitarians. Look, this Device is just what we need. Even if we can't build any others or understand how this one works, this one Device might do. If we could control or influence the minds of key men, then little by little we can superimpose our views on the world. We already have an organization. You must know that if you've seen my mind. It's better motivated and better designed than any other organization on Earth. The brains of mankind flock to us daily. Why not you too? This instrument is a key, as you see, but not just a key to a bit more knowledge. It is a key to the final solution of men's problems. Join us! Join us!'' He had reached an earnestness that Jennings had never heard in him.

Strauss's hand fell on the Device, which flickered a second or two and went out.

Jennings smiled humorlessly. He saw the significance of that. Strauss had been deliberately trying to work himself into an emotional state intense enough to activate the Device and had failed.

"You can't work it," said Jennings. "You're too darned supermannishly self-controlled and can't break down, can you?" He took up the Device with hands that were trembling, and it phosphoresced at once.

"Then *you* work it. Get the credit for saving humanity."

"Not in a hundred million years," said Jennings, gasping and barely able to breathe in the intensity of his emotion. "I'm going to report this now."

"No," said Strauss. He picked up one of the table knives. "It's pointed enough, sharp enough."

"You needn't work so hard to make your point," said Jennings, even under the stress of the moment conscious of the pun. "I can see your plans. With the Device you can convince anyone that I never existed. You can bring about an Ultra victory."

Strauss nodded. "You read my mind perfectly."

"But you won't," gasped Jennings. "Not while I hold this." He was willing Strauss into immobility.

Strauss moved raggedly and subsided. He held the knife out stiffly and his arm trembled, but he did not advance.

Both were perspiring freely.

Strauss said between clenched teeth, "You can't keep it—up all—day."

The sensation was clear, but Jennings wasn't sure he had the words to describe it. It was, in physical terms, like holding a slippery animal of vast strength, one that wriggled incessantly. Jennings had to concentrate on the feeling of immobility.

He wasn't familiar with the Device. He didn't know how to use it skillfully. One might as well expect someone who had never seen a sword to pick one up and wield it with the grace of a musketeer.

"Exactly," said Strauss, following Jennings' train of thought. He took a fumbling step forward.

Jennings knew himself to be no match for Strauss's mad determination. They both knew that. But there was the skim boat. Jennings had to get away. With the Device.

But Jennings had no secrets. Strauss saw his thought and tried to step between the other and the skim boat.

Jennings redoubled his efforts. Not immobility, but unconsciousness. Sleep, Strauss, he thought desperately. Sleep!

Strauss slipped to his knees, heavy-lidded eyes closing.

Heart pounding, Jennings rushed forward. If he could strike him with something, snatch the knife—

But his thoughts had deviated from their all-important concentration on sleep, so that Strauss's hand was on his ankle, pulling downward with raw strength.

Strauss did not hesitate. As Jennings tumbled, the hand that held the knife rose and fell. Jennings felt the sharp pain and his mind reddened with fear and despair.

It was the very access of emotion that raised the flicker of the Device to a blaze. Strauss's hold relaxed as Jennings silently and incoherently screamed fear and rage from his own mind to the other.

Strauss rolled over, face distorted.

Jennings rose unsteadily to his feet and backed away. He dared do nothing but concentrate on keeping the other unconscious. Any attempt at violent action would block out too much of his own mind force, whatever it was; too much of his unskilled bumbling mind force that could not lend itself to really effective use.

He backed toward the skim boat. There would be a suit on board—bandages—

The skim boat was not really meant for long-distance runs. Nor was Jennings, any longer. His right side was slick with blood despite the bandages. The interior of his suit was caked with it.

There was no sign of the ship itself on his tail, but surely it would come sooner or later. Its power was many times his own; it had detectors that would pick up the cloud of charge concentration left behind by his ion-drive reactors.

Desperately Jennings had tried to reach Luna Station on his radio, but there was still no answer, and he stopped in despair. His signals would merely aid Strauss in pursuit.

He might reach Luna Station bodily, but he did not think he could make it. He would be picked off first. He would die and crash first. He wouldn't make it. He would have to hide the Device, put it away in a safe place, *then* make for Luna Station.

The Device . . .

He was not sure he was right. It might ruin the human race, but it was infinitely valuable. Should he destroy it altogether? It was the only remnant of non-human intelligent life. It held the secrets of an advanced technology; it was an instrument of an advanced science of the mind. Whatever the danger, consider the value—the potential value—

No, he must hide it so that it could be found again—but only by the enlightened Moderates of the government. Never by the Ultras . . .

The skim boat flickered down along the northern inner rim of the crater. He knew which one it was, and the Device could be buried here. If he could not reach Luna Station thereafter, either in person or by radio, he would have to at least get away from the hiding spot; well away, so that his own person would not give it away. And he would have to leave *some* key to its location.

He was thinking with an unearthly clarity, it seemed to him. Was it the influence of the Device he was holding? Did it stimulate his thinking and guide him to the perfect message? Or was it the hallucination of the dying, and would none of it make any sense to anyone? He didn't know, but he had no choice. He had to try.

For Karl Jennings knew he was going to die. He had a matter of hours to live and much to do.

*   *   *

H. Seton Davenport of the American Division of the Terrestrial Bureau of Investigation rubbed the star-shaped scar on his left cheek absently. "I'm aware, sir, that the Ultras are dangerous."

The Division Head, M. T. Ashley, looked at Davenport narrowly. His gaunt cheeks were set in disapproving lines. Since he had sworn off smoking once again, he forced his groping fingers to close upon a stick of chewing gum, which he shelled, crumpled, and shoved into his mouth morosely. He was getting old, and bitter, too, and his short iron-gray mustache rasped when he rubbed his knuckles against it.

He said, "You don't know how dangerous. I wonder if anyone does. They are small in numbers, but strong among the powerful who, after all, are perfectly ready to consider themselves the elite. No one knows for certain who they are or how many."

"Not even the Bureau?"

"The Bureau is held back. We ourselves aren't free of the taint, for that matter. Are you?"

Davenport frowned. "I'm not an Ultra."

"I didn't say you were," said Ashley. "I asked if you were free of the taint. Have you considered what's been happening to the Earth in the last two centuries? Has it never occurred to you that a moderate decline in population would be a good thing? Have you never felt that it would be wonderful to get rid of the unintelligent, the incapable, the insensitive, and leave the rest. *I* have, damn it."

"I'm guilty of thinking that sometimes, yes. But considering something as a wish-fulfillment idea is one thing, but planning it as a practical scheme of action to be Hitlerized through is something else."

"The distance from wish to action isn't as great as you think. Convince yourself that the end is important enough, that the danger is great enough, and the means will grow increasingly less objectionable. Anyway, now that the Istanbul matter is taken care of, let me bring you up to date on this matter. Istanbul was of no importance in comparison. Do you know Agent Ferrant?"

"The one who's disappeared? Not personally."

"Well, two months ago, a stranded ship was located on the Moon's surface. It had been conducting a privately financed selenographic survey. The Russo-American Geological Society, which had sponsored the flight, reported the ship's failure to report. A routine search located it without much trouble within a reasonable distance of the site from which it had made its last report.

"The ship was not damaged but its skim boat was gone and with it one member of the crew. Name—Karl Jennings. The other man, James Strauss, was alive but in delirium. There was no sign of physical damage to Strauss, but he was quite insane. He still is, and that's important."

"Why?" put in Davenport.

"Because the medical team that investigated him reported neurochemical and neuroelectrical abnormalities of unprecedented nature. They'd never seen a case like it. Nothing human could have brought it about."

A flicker of a smile crossed Davenport's solemn face. "You suspect extraterrestrial invaders?"

"Maybe," said the other, with no smile at all. "But let me continue. A routine search in the neighborhood of the stranded ship revealed no signs of the skim boat. Then Luna Station reported receipt of weak signals of uncertain origin. They had been tabbed as coming from the western rim of Mare Imbrium, but it was uncertain whether they were of human origin or not, and no vessel was believed to be in the vicinity. The signals had been ignored. With the skim boat in mind, however, the search party headed out for Imbrium and located it. Jennings was aboard, dead. Knife wound in one side. It's rather surprising he had lived as long as he did.

"Meanwhile the medicos were becoming increasingly disturbed at the nature of Strauss's babbling. They contacted the Bureau and our two men on the Moon—one of them happened to be Ferrant—arrived at the ship.

"Ferrant studied the tape recordings of the babblings. There was no point in asking questions, for there was, and is, no way of reaching Strauss. There is a high wall between the universe and himself—probably a permanent one. However, the talk in delirium, although heavily repetitious and disjointed, can be made to make sense. Ferrant put it together like a jigsaw puzzle.

"Apparently Strauss and Jennings had come across an object of some sort which they took to be of ancient and non-human manufacture, an artifact of some ship wrecked eons ago. Apparently it could somehow be made to twist the human mind."

Davenport interrupted. "And it twisted Strauss's mind? Is that it?"

"That's exactly it. Strauss was an Ultra—we can say 'was' for he's only technically alive—and Jennings did not wish to surrender the object. Quite right, too. Strauss babbled of using it to bring about the self-liquidation, as he called it, of the undesirable. He wanted a final, ideal population of five million. There was a fight in which only Jennings, apparently, could handle the mind-thing, but in which Strauss had a knife. When Jennings left, he was knifed, but Strauss's mind had been destroyed."

"And where was the mind-thing?"

"Agent Ferrant acted decisively. He searched the ship and the surroundings again. There was no sign of anything that was neither a natural Lunar formation nor an obvious product of human technology. There was nothing that could be the mind-thing. He then searched the skim boat and its surroundings. Again nothing."

"Could the first search team, the ones who suspected nothing—could they have carried something off?"

"They swore they did not, and there is no reason to suspect them of lying. Then Ferrant's partner—"

"Who was he?"

"Gorbansky," said the District Head.

"I know him. We've worked together."

"I know you have. What do you think of him?"

"Capable and honest."

"All right. Gorbansky found something. Not an alien artifact. Rather, something most routinely human indeed. It was an ordinary white three-by-five card with writing on it, spindled, and in the middle finger of the right gauntlet. Presumably Jennings had written it before his death and, also presumably, it represented the key to where he had hidden the object."

"What reason is there to think he had hidden it?"

"I said we had found it nowhere."

"I mean, what if he had destroyed it, as something too dangerous to leave intact?"

"That's highly doubtful. If we accept the conversation as reconstructed from Strauss's ravings—and Ferrant built up what seems a tight word-for-word record of it—Jennings thought the mind-thing to be of key importance to humanity. He called it 'the clue to an unimaginable scientific revolution.' He wouldn't destroy something like that. He would merely hide it from the Ultras and try to report its whereabouts to the government. Else why leave a clue to its whereabouts?"

Davenport shook his head, "You're arguing in a circle, chief. You say he left a clue because you think there is a hidden object, and you think there is a hidden object because he left a clue."

"I admit that. Everything is dubious. Is Strauss's delirium meaningful? Is Ferrant's reconstruction valid? Is Jennings' clue really a clue? Is there a mind-thing, or a Device, as Jennings called it, or isn't there? There's no use asking such questions. Right now, we must act on the assumption that there is such a Device and that it must be found."

"Because Ferrant disappeared?"

"Exactly."

"Kidnapped by the Ultras?"

"Not at all. The card disappeared with him."

"Oh—I see."

"Ferrant has been under suspicion for a long time as a secret Ultra. He's not the only one in the Bureau under suspicion either. The evidence didn't warrant open action; we can't simply lay about on pure suspicion, you know, or we'll gut the Bureau from top to bottom. He was under surveillance."

"By whom?"

"By Gorbansky, of course. Fortunately Gorbansky had filmed the card and sent the reproduction to the headquarters on Earth, but he admits he considered it as nothing more than a puzzling object and included it in the information sent to Earth only out of a desire to be routinely complete. Ferrant—the better mind of the two, I suppose—did see the significance and took action. He did so at great cost, for he has given himself away and has destroyed his future usefulness to the Ultras, but there is a chance that there will be no need for future usefulness. If the Ultras control the Device—"

"Perhaps Ferrant has the Device already."

"He was under surveillance, remember. Gorbanksy swears the Device did not turn up anywhere."

"Gorbansky did not manage to stop Ferrant from leaving with the card. Perhaps he did not manage to stop him from obtaining the Device unnoticed, either."

Ashley tapped his fingers on the desk between them in an uneasy and uneven rhythm. He said at last, "I don't want to think that. If we find Ferrant, we may find out how much damage he's done. Till then, we must search for the Device. If Jennings hid it, he must have tried to get away from the hiding place. Else why leave a clue? It wouldn't be found in the vicinity."

"He might not have lived long enough to get away."

Again Ashley tapped, "The skim boat showed signs of having engaged in a long, speedy flight and had all but crashed at the end. That is consistent with the view that Jennings was trying to place as much space as possible between himself and some hiding place."

"Can you tell from what direction he came?"

"Yes, but that's not likely to help. From the condition of the side vents, he had been deliberately tacking and veering."

Davenport sighed. "I suppose you have a copy of the card with you."

"I do. Here it is." He flipped a three-by-five replica toward Davenport. Davenport studied it for a few moments. It looked like this:

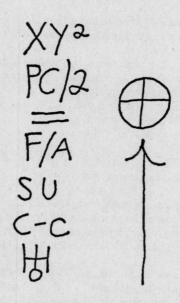

Davenport said, "I don't see any significance here."

"Neither did I, at first, nor did those I first consulted. But consider. Jennings must have thought that Strauss was in pursuit; he might not have known that Strauss had been put out of action, at least, not permanently. He was deadly afraid, then, that an Ultra would find him before a Moderate would. He dared not leave a clue too open. This"—and the Division Head tapped the reproduction— "must represent a clue that is opaque on the surface but clear enough to anyone sufficiently ingenious."

"Can we rely on that?" asked Davenport doubtfully. "After all, he was a dying, frightened man, who might have been subjected to this mind-altering object himself. He need not have been thinking clearly, or even humanly. For instance, why didn't he make an effort to reach Lunar Station? He ended half a circumference away almost. Was he too twisted to think clearly? Too paranoid to trust even the Station? Yet he must have tried to reach them at first since they picked up signals. What I'm saying is that this card, which looks as though it is covered with gibberish, *is* covered with gibberish."

Ashley shook his head solemnly from side to side, like a tolling bell. "He was in panic, yes. And I suppose he lacked the presence of mind to try to reach Lunar Station. Only the need to run and escape possessed him. Even so this can't be gibberish. It hangs together too well. Every notation on the card can be made to make sense, and the whole can be made to hang together."

"Where's the sense, then?" asked Davenport.

"You'll notice that there are seven items on the left side and two on the right. Consider the left-hand side first. The third one down looks like an equals sign. Does an equals sign mean anything to you, anything in particular?"

"An algebraic equation."

"That's general. Anything particular?"

"No."

"Suppose you consider it as a pair of parallel lines?"

"Euclid's fifth postulate?" suggested Davenport, groping.

"Good! There is a crater called Euclides on the Moon—the Greek name of the mathematician we call Euclid."

Davenport nodded. "I see your drift. As for F/A, that's force divided by acceleration, the definition of mass by Newton's second law of motion—"

"Yes, and there is a crater called Newton on the Moon also."

"Yes, but wait awhile, the lowermost item is the astronomic symbol for the planet Uranus, and there is certainly no crater—or any other lunar object, so far as I know—that is name Uranus."

"You're right there. But Uranus was discovered by William Herschel, and the H that makes up part of the astronomic symbol is the initial of his name. As it happens, there is a crater named Herschel on the Moon—three of them, in fact, since one is named for Caroline Herschel, his sister, and another for John Herschel, his son."

Davenport thought awhile, then said, "PC/2—Pressure times half the speed of light. I'm not familiar with that equation."

"Try craters. Try P for Ptolemaeus and C for Copernicus."

"And strike an average? Would that signify a spot exactly between Ptolemaeus and Copernicus?"

"I'm disappointed, Davenport," said Ashley sardonically. "I thought you knew your history of astronomy better than that. Ptolemy, or Ptolemaeus in Latin, presented a geocentric picture of the Solar System with the Earth at the center, while Copernicus presented a heliocentric one with the Sun at the center. One astronomer attempted a compromise, a picture halfway between that of Ptolemy and Copernicus—"

"Tycho Brahe!" said Davenport.

"Right. And the crater Tycho is the most conspicuous feature on the Moon's surface."

"All right. Let's take the rest. The C-C is a common way of writing a common type of chemical bond, and I think there is a crater named Bond."

"Yes, named for an American Astronomer, W. C. Bond."

"The item on top, XY^2. Hmm. XYY. An X and two Y's. Wait! Alfonso X. He was the royal astronomer in medieval Spain who was called Alfonso the Wise. X the Wise. XYY. The crater Alphonsus."

"Very good. What's SU?"

"That stumps me, chief."

"I'll tell you one theory. It stands for Soviet Union, the old name for the Russian Region. It was the Soviet Union that first mapped the other side of the Moon, and maybe it's a crater there. Tsiolkovsky, for instance. You see, then, the symbols on the left can each be interpreted as standing for a crater: Alphonsus, Tycho, Euclides, Newton, Tsiolkovsky, Bond, Herschel."

"What about the symbols on the right-hand side?"

"That's perfectly transparent. The quartered circle is the astronomic symbol for the Earth. An arrow pointing to it indicates that Earth must be directly overhead.''

"Ah," said Davenport, "the Sinus Medii—the Middle Bay—over which the Earth is perpetually at zenith. That's not a crater, so it's on the right-hand side, away from the other symbols.''

"All right," said Ashley. "The notations all make sense, or they can be made to make sense, so there's at least a good chance that this isn't gibberish and that it is trying to tell us something. But what? So far we've got seven craters and a non-crater mentioned, and what does that mean? Presumably, the Device can only be in one place.''

"Well," said Davenport heavily, "a crater can be a huge place to search. Even if we assume he hugged the shadow to avoid Solar radiation, there can be dozens of miles to examine in each case. Suppose the arrow pointing to the symbol for the Earth defines the crater where he hid the Device, the place from which the Earth can be seen nearest the zenith.''

"That's been thought of, old man. It cuts out one place and leaves us with seven pinpointed craters, the southernmost extremity of those north of the Lunar equator and the northernmost extremity of those south. But which of the seven?''

Davenport was frowning. So far, he hadn't thought of anything that hadn't already been thought of. "Search them all," he said brusquely.

Ashley crackled into brief laughter. "In the weeks since this has all come up, we've done exactly that.''

"And what have you found?''

"Nothing. We haven't found a thing. We're still looking, though.''

"Obviously one of the symbols isn't interpreted correctly.''

"Obviously!''

"You said yourself there were three craters named Herschel. The symbol SU, if it means the Soviet Union and therefore the other side of the Moon, can stand for any crater on the other side: Lomonosov, Jules Verne, Joliet-Curie, any of them. For that matter, the symbol of the Earth might stand for the crater Atlas, since he is pictured as supporting the Earth in some versions of the myth. The arrow might stand for the Straight Wall.''

"There's no argument there, Davenport. But even if we get the right interpretation for the right symbol, how do we recognize it from among all the wrong interpretations, or from among the right interpretations of the wrong symbols? Somehow there's got to be something that leaps up at us from this card and gives us so clear a piece of information that we can tell it at once as the real thing from among all the red herrings. We've all failed and we need a fresh mind, Davenport. What do you see here?''

"I'll tell you one thing we could do," said Davenport reluctantly. "We can consult someone I— Oh, my God!'' He half-rose.

Ashley was all controlled excitement at once. "What do you see?''

Davenport could feel his hand trembling. He hoped his lips weren't. He said, "Tell me, have you checked on Jennings' past life?''

"Of course.''

"Where did he go to college?''

"Eastern University.''

A pang of joy shot through Davenport, but he held on. That was not enough. "Did he take a course in extraterrology?''

"Of course, he did. That's routine for a geology major.''

"All right, then don't you know who teaches extraterrology at Eastern University?"

Ashley snapped his fingers. "That oddball. What's-his-name—Wendell Urth."

"Exactly, an oddball who is brilliant man in his way. An oddball who's acted as a consultant for the Bureau on several occasions and given perfect satisfaction every time. An oddball I was going to suggest we consult this time and then noticed that this card was *telling* us to do so. An arrow pointing to the symbol for the Earth. A rebus that couldn't mean more clearly 'Go to Urth,' written by a man who was once a student of Urth and would know him."

Ashley stared at the card, "By God, it's possible. But what could Urth tell us about the card that we can't see for ourselves?"

Davenport said, with polite patience, "I suggest we ask him, sir."

Ashley looked about curiously, half-wincing as he turned from one direction to another. He felt as though he had found himself in some arcane curiosity shop, darkened and dangerous, from which at any moment some demon might hurtle forth squealing.

The lighting was poor and the shadows many. The walls seemed distant, and dismally alive with book-films from floor to ceiling. There was a Galactic Lens in soft three-dimensionality in one corner and behind it were star charts that could dimly be made out. A map of the Moon in another corner might, however, possibly be a map of Mars.

Only the desk in the center of the room was brilliantly lit by a tight-beamed lamp. It was littered with papers and opened printed books. A small viewer was threaded with film, and a clock with an old-fashioned round-faced dial hummed with subdued merriment.

Ashley found himself unable to recall that it was late afternoon outside and that the sun was quite definitely in the sky. Here, within, was a place of eternal night. There was no sign of any window, and the clear presence of circulating air did not spare him a claustrophobic sensation.

He found himself moving closer to Davenport, who seemed insensible to the unpleasantness of the situation.

Davenport said in a low voice, "He'll be here in a moment, sir."

"Is it always like this?" asked Ashley.

"Always. He never leaves this place, as far as I know, except to trot across the campus and attend his classes."

"Gentlemen! Gentlemen!" came a reedy, tenor voice. "I am so glad to see you. It is good of you to come."

A round figure of a man bustled in from another room, shedding shadow and emerging into the light.

He beamed at them, adjusting round, thick-lensed glasses upward so that he might look through them. As his fingers moved away, the glasses slipped downward at once to a precarious perch upon the round nubbin of his snub nose. "I am Wendell Urth," he said.

The scraggly gray Van Dyke on his pudgy, round chin did not in the least add to the dignity which the smiling face and the stubby ellipsoidal torso so noticeably lacked.

"Gentlemen! It is good of you to come," Urth repeated, as he jerked himself backward into a chair from which his legs dangled with the toes of his shoes a full inch above the floor. "Mr. Davenport remembers, perhaps, that it is a matter of—uh—some importance to me to remain here. I do not like to travel, except to walk, of course, and a walk across campus is quite enough for me."

Ashley looked baffled as he remained standing, and Urth stared at him with a growing bafflement of his own. He pulled a handkerchief out and wiped his glasses, then replaced them, and said, "Oh, I see the difficulty. You want chairs. Yes. Well, just take some. If there are things on them, just push them off. Push them off. Sit down, please."

Davenport removed the books from one chair and placed them carefully on the floor. He pushed the chair toward Ashley. Then he took a human skull off a second chair and placed the skull even more carefully on Urth's desk. Its mandible, insecurely wired, unhinged as he transferred it, and it sat there with jaw askew.

"Never mind," said Urth, affably, "it will not hurt. Now tell me what is on your mind, gentlemen?"

Davenport waited a moment for Ashley to speak, then, rather gladly, took over. "Dr. Urth, do you remember a student of yours named Jennings? Karl Jennings?"

Urth's smile vanished momentarily with the effort of recall. His somewhat protuberant eyes blinked. "No," he said at last. "Not at the moment."

"A geology major. He took your extraterrology course some years ago. I have his photograph here, if that will help."

Urth studied the photograph handed him with nearsighted concentration, but still looked doubtful.

Davenport drove on. "He left a cryptic message which is the key to a matter of great importance. We have so far failed to interpret it satisfactorily, but this much we see—it indicates we are to come to you."

"Indeed? How interesting! For what purpose are you to come to me?"

"Presumably for your advice on interpreting the message."

"May I see it?"

Silently Ashley passed the slip of paper to Wendell Urth. The extraterrologist looked at it casually, turned it over, and stared for a moment at the blank back. He said, "Where does it say to ask me?"

Ashley looked startled, but Davenport forestalled him by saying, "The arrow pointing to the symbol of the Earth. It seems clear."

"It is clearly an arrow pointing to the symbol for the planet Earth. I suppose it might literally mean 'go to the Earth' if this were found on some other world."

"It was found on the Moon, Dr. Urth, and it could, I suppose, mean that. However, the reference to you seemed clear once we realized that Jennings had been a student of yours."

"He took a course in extraterrology here at the University?"

"That's right."

"In what year, Mr. Davenport?"

"In '18."

"Ah. The puzzle is solved."

"You mean the significance of the message?" said Davenport.

"No, no. The message has no meaning to me. I mean the puzzle of why it is that I did not remember him, for I remember him now. He was a very quiet fellow, anxious, shy, self-effacing—not at all the sort of person anyone would remember. Without this''—and he tapped the message—''I might never have remembered him.''

''Why does the card change things?'' asked Davenport.

''The reference to me is a play on words. Earth—Urth. Not very subtle, of course, but that is Jennings. His unattainable delight was the pun. My only clear memory of him is his occasional attempts to perpetrate puns. I enjoy puns, I adore puns, but Jennings—yes, I remember him well now—was atrocious at it. Either that, or distressingly obvious at it, as in this case. He lacked all talent for puns, yet craved them so much—''

Ashley suddenly broke in. ''This message consists entirely of a kind of wordplay, Dr. Urth. At least, we believe so, and that fits in with what you say.''

''Ah!'' Urth adjusted his glasses and peered through them once more at the card and the symbols it carried. He pursed his plump lips, then said cheerfully, ''I make nothing of it.''

''In that case—'' began Ashley, his hands balling into fists.

''But if you tell me what it's all about,'' Urth went on, ''then perhaps it might mean something.''

Davenport said quickly, ''May I, sir? I am confident that this man can be relied on—and it may help.''

''Go ahead,'' muttered Ashley. ''At this point, what can it hurt?''

Davenport condensed the tale, giving it in crisp, telegraphic sentences, while Urth listened carefully, moving his stubby fingers over the shining milk-white desktop as though he were sweeping up invisible cigar ashes. Toward the end of the recital, he hitched up his legs and sat with them crossed like an amiable Buddha.

When Davenport was done, Urth thought a moment, then said, ''Do you happen to have a transcript of the conversation reconstructed by Ferrant?''

''We do,'' said Davenport. ''Would you like to see it?''

''Please.''

Urth placed the strip of microfilm in a scanner and worked his way rapidly through it, his lips moving unintelligibly at some points. Then he tapped the reproduction of the cryptic message. ''And this, you say, is the key to the entire matter? The crucial clue?''

''We think it is, Dr. Urth.''

''But it is not the original. It is a reproduction.''

''That is correct.''

''The original has gone with this man, Ferrant, and you believe it to be in the hands of the Ultras.''

''Quite possibly.''

Urth shook his head and looked troubled. ''Everyone knows my sympathies are not with the Ultras. I would fight them by all means, so I don't want to seem to be hanging back, but—what is there to say that this mind-affecting object exists at all? You have only the ravings of a psychotic and your dubious deductions from the reproduction of a mysterious set of marks that may mean nothing at all.''

''Yes, Dr. Urth, but we can't take chances.''

''How certain are you that this copy is accurate? What if the original has something on it that this lacks, something that makes the message quite clear, something without which the message must remain impenetrable?''

''We are certain the copy is accurate.''

"What about the reverse side? There is nothing on the back of this reproduction. What about the reverse of the original?"

"The agent who made the reproduction tells us that the back of the original was blank."

"Men can make mistakes."

"We have no reason to think he did, and we must work on the assumption that he didn't. At least until such time as the original is regained."

"Then you assure me," said Urth, "that any interpretation to be made of this message must be made on the basis of exactly what one sees here."

"We think so. We are virtually certain," said Davenport with a sense of ebbing confidence.

Urth continued to look troubled. He said, "Why not leave the instrument where it is? If neither group finds it, so much the better. I disapprove of any tampering with minds and would not contribute to making it possible."

Davenport placed a restraining hand on Ashley's arm, sensing the other was about to speak. Davenport said, "Let me put it to you, Dr. Urth, that the mind-tampering aspect is not the whole of the Device. Suppose an Earth expedition to a distant primitive planet had dropped an old-fashioned radio there, and suppose the native population had discovered electric current but had not yet developed the vacuum tube.

"The population might discover that if the radio was hooked up to a current, certain glass objects within it would grow warm and would glow, but of course they would receive no intelligible sound, merely, at best, some buzzes and crackles. However, if they dropped the radio into a bathtub while it was plugged in, a person in that tub might be electrocuted. Should the people of this hypothetical planet therefore conclude that the device they were studying was designed solely for the purpose of killing people?"

"I see your analogy," said Urth. "You think that the mind-tampering property is merely an incidental function of the Device?"

"I'm sure of it," said Davenport earnestly. "If we can puzzle out its real purpose, earthly technology may leap ahead centuries."

"Then you agree with Jennings when he said"—here Urth consulted the microfilm—" 'It might be the key to—who knows what? It might be the clue to an unimaginable scientific revolution.' "

"Exactly!"

"And yet the mind-tampering aspect is there and is infinitely dangerous. Whatever the radio's purpose, it *does* electrocute."

"Which is why we can't let the Ultras get it."

"Or the government either, perhaps?"

"But I must point out that there is a reasonable limit to caution. Consider that men have always held danger in their hands. The first flint knife in the old Stone Age; the first wooden club before that could kill. They could be used to bend weaker men to the will of stronger ones under threat of force and that, too, is a form of mind-tampering. What counts, Dr. Urth, is not the Device itself, however dangerous it may be in the abstract, but the intentions of the men who make use of the Device. The Ultras have the declared intention of killing off more than 99.9 per cent of humanity. The government, whatever the faults of the men composing it, would have no such intention."

"What *would* the government intend?"

"A scientific study of the Device. Even the mind-tampering aspect itself could yield infinite good. Put to enlightened use, it could educate us concerning the physical basis of mental function. We might learn to correct mental disorders or cure the Ultras. Mankind might learn to develop greater intelligence generally.''

"How can I believe that such idealism will be put into practice?''

"*I* believe so. Consider that you face a possible turn to evil by the government if you help us, but you risk the certain and declared evil purpose of the Ultras if you don't.''

Urth nodded thoughtfully. "Perhaps you're right. And yet I have a favor to ask of you. I have a niece who is, I believe, quite fond of me. She is constantly upset over the fact that I steadfastly refuse to indulge in the lunacy of travel. She states that she will not rest content until someday I accompany her to Europe or North Carolina or some other outlandish place—''

Ashley leaned forward earnestly, brushing Davenport's restraining gesture to one side. "Dr. Urth, if you help us find the Device and if it can be made to work, then I assure you that we will be glad to help you free yourself of your phobia against travel and make it possible for you to go with your niece anywhere you wish.''

Urth's bulging eyes widened and he seemed to shrink within himself. For a moment he looked wildly about as though he were already trapped, *"No!"* he gasped. "Not at all! Never!''

His voice dropped to an earnest, hoarse whisper. "Let me explain the nature of my fee. If I help you, if you retrieve the Device and learn its use, if the fact of my help becomes public, then my niece will be on the government like a fury. She is a terribly headstrong and shrill-voiced woman who will raise public subscriptions and organize demonstrations. She will stop at nothing. And yet you must not give in to her. You must *not!* You must resist all pressures. I wish to be left alone exactly as I am now. That is my absolute and minimum fee.''

Ashley flushed. "Yes, of course, since that is your wish.''

"I have your word?''

"You have my word.''

"Please remember. I rely on you too, Mr. Davenport.''

"It will be as you wish,'' soothed Davenport. "And now, I presume, you can interpret the items?''

"The items?'' asked Urth, seeming to focus his attention with difficulty on the card. "You mean these markings, XY^2 and so on?''

"Yes. What do they mean?''

"I don't know. Your interpretations are as good as any, I suppose.''

Ashley exploded. "Do you mean that all this talk about helping us is nonsense? What was this maundering about a fee, then?''

Wendell Urth looked confused and taken aback. "I would like to help you.''

"But you don't know what these items mean.''

"I—I don't. But I know what this message means.''

"You do?'' cried Davenport.

"Of course. Its meaning is transparent. I suspected it halfway through your story. And I was sure of it once I read the reconstruction of the conversations between Strauss and Jennings. You would understand it yourself, gentlemen, if you would only stop to think.''

"See here,'' said Ashley in exasperation, "you said you don't know what the items mean.''

"I don't. I said I know what the *message* means.''

"What is the message if it is not the items? Is it the paper, for Heaven's sake?"

"Yes, in a way."

"You mean invisible ink or something like that?"

"No! Why is it so hard for you to understand, when you yourself stand on the brink?"

Davenport leaned toward Ashley and said in a low voice, "Sir, will you let me handle it, please?"

Ashley snorted, then said in a stifled manner, "Go ahead."

"Dr. Urth," said Davenport, "will you give us your analysis?"

"Ah! Well, all right." The little extraterrologist settled back in his chair and mopped his damp forehead on his sleeve. "Let's consider the message. If you accept the quartered circle and the arrow as directing you to me, that leaves seven items. If these indeed refer to seven craters, six of them, at least, must be designed merely to distract, since the Device surely cannot be in more than one place. It contained no movable or detachable parts—it was all one piece.

"Then, too, none of the items are straightforward. SU might, by your interpretation, mean any place on the other side of the Moon, which is an area the size of South America. Again PC/2 can mean 'Tycho,' as Mr. Ashley says, or it can mean 'halfway between Ptolemaeus and Copernicus,' as Mr. Davenport thought, or for that matter 'halfway between Plato and Cassini.' To be sure, XY^2 could mean 'Alfonsus'—very ingenious interpretation, that—but it could refer to some co-ordinate system in which the Y co-ordinate was the square of the X co-ordinate. Similarly $C = C$ would mean 'Bond' or it could mean 'halfway between Cassini and Copernicus.' F/A could mean 'Newton' or it could mean 'between Fabricius and Archimedes.'

"In short, the items have so many meanings that they are meaningless. Even if one of them had meaning, it could not be selected from among the others, so that it is only sensible to suppose that all the items are merely red herrings.

"It is necessary, then, to determine what about the message is completely unambiguous, what is perfectly clear. The answer to that can only be that it *is* a message, that it *is* a clue to a hiding place. That is the one thing we are certain about, isn't it?"

Davenport nodded, then said cautiously, "At least, we think we are certain of it."

"Well, you have referred to this message as the key to the whole matter. You have acted as though it were the crucial clue. Jennings himself referred to the Device as a key or a clue. If we combine this serious view of the matter with Jennings' penchant for puns, a penchant which may have been heightened by the mind-tampering Device he was carrying— So let me tell you a story.

"In the last half of the sixteenth century, there lived a German Jesuit in Rome. He was a mathematician and astronomer of note and helped Pope Gregory XIII reform the calendar in 1582, performing all the enormous calculations required. This astronomer admired Copernicus but he did not accept the heliocentric view of the Solar System. He clung to the older belief that the Earth was the center of the Universe.

"In 1650, nearly forty years after the death of this mathematician, the Moon was mapped by another Jesuit, the Italian astronomer, Giovanni Battista Riccioli. He named the craters after astronomers of the past and since he too rejected Copernicus, he selected the largest and most spectacular craters for those who placed the Earth at the center of the Universe—for Ptolemy, Hipparchus, Alfonso X, Tycho Brahe. The biggest crater Riccioli could find he reserved for his German Jesuit predecessor.

"This crater is actually only the second largest of the craters visible from Earth. The only larger crater is Bailly, which is right on the Moon's limb and is therefore very difficult to see from the Earth. Riccioli ignored it, and it was named for an astronomer who lived a century after his time and who was guillotined during the French Revolution."

Ashley was listening to all this restlessly. "But what has this to do with the message?"

"Why, everything," said Urth, with some surprise. "Did you not call this message the key to the whole business? Isn't it the crucial clue?"

"Yes, of course."

"Is there any doubt that we are dealing with something that is a clue or key to something else?"

"No, there isn't," said Ashley.

"Well, then— The name of the German Jesuit I have been speaking of is Christoph Klau—pronounced 'klow.' Don't you see the pun? Klau—clue?"

Ashley's entire body seemed to grow flabby with disappointment. "Far-fetched," he muttered.

Davenport said anxiously, "Dr. Urth, there is no feature on the Moon named Klau as far as I know."

"Of course not," said Urth excitedly. "That is the whole point. At this period of history, the last half of the sixteenth century, European scholars were Latinizing their names. Klau did so. In place of the German 'u', he made use of the equivalent letter, the Latin 'v'. He then added an 'ius' ending typical of Latin names and Christoph Klau became Christopher Clavius, and I suppose you are all aware of the giant crater we call Clavius."

"But—" began Davenport.

"Don't 'but' me," said Urth. "Just let me point out that the Latin word 'clavis' means 'key.' Now do you see the double and bilingual pun? Klau—clue, Clavius—clavis—key. In his whole life, Jennings could never have made a double, bilingual pun, without the Device. Now he could, and I wonder if death might not have been almost triumphant under the circumstances. And he directed you to me because he knew I would remember his penchant for puns and because he knew I loved them too."

The two men of the Bureau were looking at him wide-eyed.

Urth said solemnly, "I would suggest you search the shaded rim of Clavius, at that point where the Earth is nearest the zenith."

Ashley rose. "Where is your videophone?"

"In the next room."

Ashley dashed. Davenport lingered behind. "Are you sure, Dr. Urth?"

"Quite sure. But even if I am wrong, I suspect it doesn't matter."

"What doesn't matter?"

"Whether you find it or not. For if the Ultras find the Device, they will probably be unable to use it."

"Why do you say that?"

"You asked me if Jennings had ever been a student of mine, but you never asked me about Strauss, who was also a geologist. He was a student of mine a year or so after Jennings. I remember him well."

"Oh?"

"An unpleasant man. Very cold. It is the hallmark of the Ultras, I think. They are all very cold, very rigid, very sure of themselves. They can't empathize, or they wouldn't speak of killing off billions of human beings. What emotions they posses are icy ones, self-absorbed ones, feelings incapable of spanning the distance between two human beings."

"I think I see."

"I'm sure you do. The conversation reconstructed from Strauss's ravings showed us he coud not manipulate the Device. He lacked the emotional intensity, or the type of necessary emotion. I imagine all Ultras would. Jennings, who was not an Ultra, could manipulate it. Anyone who could use the Device would, I suspect, be incapable of deliberate cold-blooded cruelty. He might strike out of panic fear as Jennings struck at Strauss, but never out of calculation, as Strauss tried to strike at Jennings. In short, to put it tritely, I think the Device can be actuated by love, but never by hate, and the Ultras are nothing if not haters."

Davenport nodded. "I hope you're right. But then—why were you so suspicious of the government's motives if you felt the wrong men could not manipulate the Device?"

Urth shrugged. "I wanted to make sure you could bluff and rationalize on your feet and make yourself convincingly persuasive at a moment's notice. After all, you may have to face my niece."

LEST WE REMEMBER

— 1 —

THE PROBLEM with John Heath, as far as John Heath was concerned, was that he struck a dead average. He was sure of it. What was worse, he felt that Susan suspected it.

It meant he would never make a true mark in the world, never climb to the top of Quantum Pharmaceuticals, where he was a steady cog among the junior executives—never make the Quantum Leap.

Nor would he do it anywhere else, if he changed jobs.

He sighed inwardly. In just two more weeks he was going to be married and for her sake he yearned to be upwardly mobile. After all, he loved her madly and wanted to shine in her eyes.

But then, that was dead average for a young man about to be married.

Susan Collins looked at John lovingly. And why not? He was reasonably good-looking and intelligent and a steady, affectionate fellow besides. If he didn't blind her with his brilliance, he at least didn't upset her with an erraticism he didn't possess.

She patted the pillow she had placed behind his head when he sat down in the armchair and handed him his drink, making sure he had a firm grip before she let go.

She said, "I'm practicing to treat you well, Johnny. I've got to be an efficient wife."

John sipped at his drink. "I'm the one who'll have to be on my toes, Sue. Your salary is higher than mine."

"It's all going to go into one pocket once we're married. It will be the firm of Johnny and Sue keeping one set of books."

"You'll have to keep it," said John, despondently. "I'm bound to make mistakes if I try."

"Only because you're sure you will. When are your friends coming?"

"Nine, I think. Maybe nine-thirty. And they're not exactly friends. They're Quantum people from the research labs."

"You're sure they won't expect to be fed?"

"They said after dinner. I'm positive about that. It's business."

She looked at him quizzically. "You didn't say that before."

"Say what before?"

"That it was business. Are you sure?"

John felt confused. Any effort to remember *precisely* always left him confused. "They said so—I think."

Susan's look was that of good-natured exasperation, rather like the one she would have given a friendly puppy who is completely unaware its paws are muddy. "If you really thought," she said, "as often as you say 'I think' you wouldn't be so perennially uncertain. Don't you see it *can't* be business. If it were business, wouldn't they see you *at* business?"

"It's confidential," said John. "They didn't want to see me at work. Not even at my apartment."

"Why here, then?"

"Oh, I suggested that. I thought you ought to be around, anyway. They're going to have to deal with the firm of Johnny and Sue, right?"

"It depends," said Susan, "on what the confidential is all about. Did they give you any hints?"

"No, but it couldn't hurt to listen. It could be something that would give me a boost in standing at the firm."

"Why you?" asked Susan.

John looked hurt, "Why *not* me?"

"It just strikes me that someone at your job level doesn't require all that confidentiality and that—"

She broke off when the intercom buzzed. She dashed off to answer and came back to say, "They're on the way up."

— 2 —

TWO OF them were at the door. One was Boris Kupfer, whom John had already spoken to—large and restless, with a clear view of bluish stubble on his chin.

The other was David Anderson, smaller and more composed. His quick eyes moved this way and that, however, missing nothing.

"Susan," said John, uncertainly, still holding the door open. "These are the two colleagues of mine that I told you about. Boris—" He hit a blank in his memory banks and stopped.

"Boris Kupfer," said the larger man morosely, jingling some change in his pocket, "and David Anderson here. It's very kind of you, Miss—"

"Susan Collins."

"It's very kind of you to make your place of residence available to Mr. Heath and to us for a private conference. We apologize for trespassing on your time and your privacy in this manner—and if you could leave us to ourselves for a while, we will be further grateful."

Susan stared at him solemnly. "Do you want me to go to the movies, or just into the next room?"

"If you could visit a friend—"

"No," said Susan, firmly.

"You can dispose of your time as you please, of course. A movie, if you wish."

"When I said 'No,' " said Susan, "I meant I wasn't leaving. I want to know what this is about."

Kupfer seemed nonplussed. He stared at Anderson for a moment, then said, "It's confidential, as Mr. Heath explained to you, I hope."

John, looking uneasy, said, "I explained that. Susan understands—"

"Susan," said Susan, "doesn't understand and wasn't given to understand that she was to absent herself from the proceedings. This is my apartment and Johnny and I are being married in two weeks—exactly two weeks from today. We are the firm of Johnny and Sue and you'll have to deal with the firm."

Anderson's voice sounded for the first time, surprisingly deep and as smooth as though it had been waxed. "Boris, the young woman is right. As Mr. Heath's soon-to-be wife, she will have a great interest in what we have come here to suggest and it would be wrong to exclude her. She has so firm an interest in our proposal that if she were to wish to leave, I would urge her most strongly to remain."

"Well, then, my friends," said Susan, "what will you have to drink? Once I bring you those drinks, we can begin."

Both were seated rather stiffly and had sipped cautiously at their drinks, and then Kupfer said, "Heath, I don't suppose you know much about the chemical details of the company's work—the cerebro-chemicals, for instance."

"Not a bit," said John, uneasily.

"No reason you should," said Anderson, silkily.

"It's like this," said Kupfer, casting an uneasy glance at Susan—

"No reason to go into technical details," said Anderson, almost at the lower level of audibility.

Kupfer colored slightly. "Without technical details, Quantum Pharmaceuticals deals with cerebro-chemicals which are, as the name implies, chemicals that affect the cerebrum; that is, the higher functioning of the brain."

"It must be very complicated work," said Susan, with composure.

"It is," said Kupfer. "The mammalian brain has hundreds of characteristic molecular varieties found nowhere else, which serve to modulate cerebral activity, including aspects of what we might term the intellectual life. The work is under the closest corporate security, which is why Anderson wants no technical details. I *can* say this, though—we can go no further with animal experiments. We're up against a brick wall if we can't try the human response."

"Then why don't you?" said Susan. "What stops you?"

"Public reaction if something goes wrong!"

"Use volunteers, then."

"That won't help. Quantum Pharmaceuticals couldn't take the adverse publicity if something went wrong."

Susan looked at them mockingly. "Are you two working on your own, then?"

Anderson raised his hand to stop Kupfer. "Young woman," he said, "let me explain briefly in order to put an end to wasteful verbal fencing. If we succeed, we will be enormously rewarded. If we fail, Quantum Pharmaceuticals will disown us and we will pay what penalty there is to be paid, such as the ending of our careers. If you ask us, why we are willing to take this risk, the answer is, we do not think a risk exists. We are reasonably sure we will succeed; entirely sure we will do no harm. The corporation feels it cannot take the chance; but we feel we can. Now, Kupfer, proceed!''

Kupfer said, ''We have a memory chemical. It works with every animal we have tried. Their learning ability improves amazingly. It should work on human beings, too.''

John said, ''That sounds exciting.''

''It *is* exciting,'' said Kupfer. ''Memory is not improved by devising a way for the brain to store information more efficiently. All our studies show that the brain stores almost unlimited numbers of items perfectly and permanently. The difficulty lies in recall. How many times have you had a name at the tip of your tongue and couldn't get it? How many times have you failed to come up with something you *knew* you knew, and then did come up with it two hours later when you were thinking about something else. Am I putting it correctly, David?''

''You are,'' said Anderson. ''Recall is inhibited, we think, because the mammalian brain outraced its needs by developing a too-perfect recording system. A mammal stores more bits of information than it needs or is capable of using and if all of it was on tap at all times, it would never be able to choose among them quickly enough for appropriate reaction. Recall is inhibited, therefore, to insure that items emerge from memory storage in manipulable numbers, and with those items most desired not blurred by the accompaniment of numerous other items of no interest.

''There is a definite chemical in the brain that functions as a recall inhibitor, and we have a chemical that neutralizes the inhibitor. We call it a disinhibitor, and as far as we have been able to ascertain the matter, it has no deleterious side effects.''

Susan laughed. ''I see what's coming, Johnny. You can leave now, gentlemen. You just said that recall is inhibited to allow mammals to react more efficiently, and now you say that the disinhibitor has no deleterious side effects. Surely the disinhibitor will make the mammals react less efficiently; perhaps find themselves unable to react at all. And now you are going to propose that you try it on Johnny and see if you reduce him to catatonic immobility or not.''

Anderson rose, his thin lips quivering. He took a few rapid strides to the far end of the room and back. When he sat down, he was composed and smiling. ''In the first place, Miss Collins, it's a matter of dosage. We told you that the experimental animals all displayed enhanced learning ability. Naturally, we didn't eliminate the inhibitor entirely; we merely suppressed it in part. Secondly, we have reason to think the human brain *can* handle complete disinhibition. It is much larger than the brain of any animal we have tested and we all know its incomparable capacity for abstract thought.

''It is a brain designed for perfect recall, but the blind forces of evolution have not managed to remove the inhibiting chemical which, after all, was designed for and inherited from the lower animals.''

''Are you sure?'' asked John.

''You *can't* be sure,'' said Susan, flatly.

Kupfer said, ''We are sure, but we need the proof to convince others. That's why we have to try a human being.''

''John, in fact,'' said Susan.

''Yes.''

"Which brings us," said Susan, "to the key question. Why John?"

"Well," said Kupfer, slowly, "we need someone for whom chances of success are most nearly certain, and in whom it would be most demonstrable. We don't want someone so low in mental capacity that we must use dangerously large doses of the disinhibitor; nor do we want someone so bright that the effect will not be sufficiently noticeable. We need someone who's average. Fortunately, we have the full physical and psychological profiles of all the employees at Quantum and in this and, in fact, all other ways, Mr. Heath is ideal."

"Dead average?" said Susan.

John looked stricken at the use of the phrase he had thought his own innermost, and disgraceful, secret. "Come on, now," he said.

Ignoring John's outcry, Kupfer answered Susan, "Yes."

"And he won't be, if he submits to treatment?"

Anderson's lips stretched into another one of his cheerless smiles. "That's right. He won't be. This is something to think about if you're going to be married soon—the firm of Johnny and Sue, I think you called it. As it is, I don't think the firm will advance at Quantum, Miss Collins, for although Heath is a good and reliable employee he is, as you say, dead average. If he takes the disinhibitor, however, he will become a remarkable person and move upward with astonishing speed. Consider what that will mean to the firm."

"What does the firm have to lose?" asked Susan, grimly.

Anderson said, "I don't see how you can lose anything. It will be a sensible dose which can be administered at the laboratories tomorrow—Sunday. We will have the floor to ourselves; we will keep him under surveillance for a few hours. It is certain nothing could go wrong. If I could tell you of our painstaking experimentation and of our thoroughgoing exploration of all possible side effects—"

"On animals," said Susan, not giving an inch.

But John said, tightly, "I'll make the decision, Sue. I've had it up to here with that dead-average bit. It's worth some risk to me if it means getting off that dead-average dead end."

"Johnny," said Susan, "don't jump."

"I'm thinking of the firm, Sue. I want to contribute my share."

Anderson said, "Good, but sleep on it. We will leave two copies of an agreement we will ask you to look over and sign. Please don't show it to anybody whether you sign or not. We will be here tomorrow morning again to take you to the laboratory."

They smiled, rose, and left.

John read over the agreement with a troubled frown, then looked up. "You don't think I should be doing this, do you, Sue?"

"It worries me, sure."

"Look, if I have a chance to get away from that dead average—"

Susan said, "What's wrong with that? I've met so many nuts and cranks in my short life that I welcome a nice, average guy like you, Johnny. Listen, I'm dead average too."

"*You* dead average. With your looks? Your figure?"

Susan looked down upon herself with a touch of complacency. "Well, then, I'm just your dead-average gorgeous girl," she said.

— 3 —

THE INJECTION took place at 8 A.M. Sunday, no more than twelve hours after the proposition had been advanced. A thoroughly computerized body sensor was attached to John in a dozen places, while Susan watched with keen-eyed apprehension.

Kupfer said, "Please, Heath, relax. All is going well, but tension speeds the heart rate, raises the blood pressure, and skews our results."

"How can I relax?" muttered John.

Susan put in sharply, "Skews the results to the point where you don't know what's going on?"

"No, no," said Anderson. "Boris said all is going well and it is. It is just that our animals were always sedated before the injection, and we did not feel sedation would have been appropriate in this case. So if we can't have sedation, we must expect tension. Just breathe slowly and do your best to minimize it."

It was late afternoon before he was finally disconnected.

"How do you feel?" asked Anderson.

"Nervous," said John. "Otherwise, all right."

"No headache?"

"No. But I want to visit the bathroom. I can't exactly relax with a bedpan."

"Of course."

John emerged, frowning. "I don't notice any particular memory improvement."

"That will take some time and will be gradual. The disinhibitor must leak across the blood-brain barrier, you know," said Anderson.

— 4 —

IT WAS nearly midnight when Susan broke what had turned out to be an oppressively silent evening in which neither had much responded to the television.

She said, "You'll have to stay here overnight. I don't want you alone when we don't really know what's going to happen."

"I don't feel a thing," said John, gloomily. "I'm still me."

"I'll settle for that, Johnny," said Susan. "Do you feel any pains or discomforts or oddness at all?"

"I don't think so."

"I wish we hadn't done it."

"For the firm," said John, smiling weakly. "We've got to take some chances for the firm."

— 5 —

JOHN SLEPT poorly, and woke drearily, but on time. And he arrived at work on time, too, to start the new week.

By 11 A.M., however, his morose air had attracted the unfavorable attention of his immediate superior, Michael Ross. Ross was burly and black-browed and fit the stereotype of the stevedore without being one. John got along with him though he did not like him.

Ross said, in his bass-baritone, "What's happened to your cheery disposition, Heath—your jokes—your lilting laughter?" Ross cultivated a certain preciosity of speech as though he were anxious to negate the stevedore image.

"Don't exactly feel tip-top," said John, not looking up.

"Hangover?"

"No, sir," said John, coldly.

"Well, cheer up, then. You'll win no friends, scattering stinkweeds over the fields as you gambol along."

John would have liked to groan. Ross's subliterary affectations were wearisome at the best of times and this wasn't the best of times.

And to make matters worse, John smelled the foul odor of a rancid cigar and knew that James Arnold Prescott—the head of the sales division—could not be far behind.

Nor was he. He looked about, and said, "Mike, when and what did we sell Rahway last spring or thereabouts? There's some damned question about it and I think the details have been miscomputerized."

The question was not addressed to him, but John said quietly, "Forty-two vials of PCAP. That was on April 14, J.P., invoice number P-20543, with a five per cent discount granted on payment within thirty days. Payment, in full, received on May 8."

Apparently everyone in the room had heard that. At least, everyone looked up.

Prescott said, "How the hell do you happen to know all that?"

John stared at Prescott for a moment, a vast surprise on his face. "I just happened to remember, J.P."

"You did, eh? Repeat it."

John did, faltering a bit, and Prescott wrote it down on one of the papers on John's desk, wheezing slightly as the bend at his waist compressed his portly abdomen up against his diaphragm and made breathing difficult. John tried to duck the smoke from the cigar without seeming to do so.

Prescott said, "Ross, check this out on your computer and see if there's anything to it at all." He turned to John with an aggrieved look. "I don't like practical jokers. What would you have done if I had accepted these figures of yours and walked off with them?"

"I wouldn't have done anything. They're correct," said John, conscious of himself as the full center of attention.

Ross handed Prescott the readout. Prescott looked at it and said, "This is from the computer?"

"Yes, J.P."

Prescott stared at it, then said, with a jerk of his head toward John, "And what's he? Another computer? His figures were correct."

John tried a weak smile, but Prescott growled and left, the stench of his cigar a lingering reminder of his presence.

Ross said, "What the hell was that little bit of legerdemain, Heath? You found out what he wanted to know and looked it up in advance to get some kudos?"

"No, sir," said John, who was gathering confidence. "I just happened to remember. I have a good memory for these things."

"And took the trouble to keep it from your loyal companions all these years? There's no one here who had any idea you hid a good memory behind that unremarkable forehead of yours."

"No point in showing it, Mr. Ross, is there? Now when I have, it doesn't seem to have gained me any goodwill, does it?"

And it hadn't. Ross glowered at him and turned away.

— 6 —

JOHN'S EXCITEMENT over the dinner table at Gino's that night made it difficult for him to talk coherently, but Susan listened patiently and tried to act as a stabilizing force.

"You might just have happened to remember, you know," she said. "By itself it doesn't prove anything, Johnny."

"Are you crazy?" He lowered his voice at Susan's gesture and quick glance about. He repeated in a semiwhisper, "Are you crazy? You don't suppose it's the only thing I remember, do you? I think I can remember anything I ever heard. It's just a question of recall. For instance, quote some line out of Shakespeare."

"To be or not to be."

John looked scornful. "Don't be funny. Oh, well, it doesn't matter. The point is that if you recite any line, I can carry on from there for as long as you like. I read some of the plays for English Lit classes at college and some for myself and I can bring any of it back. I've tried. It flows! I suppose I can bring back any part of any book or article or newspaper I've ever read, or any TV show I've ever watched—word for word or scene for scene."

Susan said, "What will you do with all that?"

John said, "I don't have that consciously in my head at all times. Surely you don't—wait, let's order—"

Five minutes later, he said, "Surely you don't— My God, I haven't forgotten where we left off. Isn't it amazing? Surely you don't think I'm swimming in a mental sea of Shakespearean sentences at all times. The recall takes an effort; not much of one, but an effort."

"How does it work?"

"I don't know. How do you lift your arm? What orders do you give your muscles? You just will the arm to lift upward and it does so. It's no trouble to do so, but your arm doesn't lift *until* you want it to. Well, I remember anything I've ever read or seen when I want to but not when I don't want to. I don't know how I do it, but I do it."

The first course arrived and John tackled it happily.

Susan picked at her stuffed mushrooms. "It sounds exciting."

"Exciting? I've got the biggest, most wonderful toy in the world. My own brain. Listen, I can spell any word correctly and I'm pretty sure I won't ever make any grammatical mistake."

"Because you remember all the dictionaries and grammars you ever read?"
John looked at her sharply. "Don't be sarcastic, Sue."

"I wasn't being—"

He waved her silent. "I never used dictionaries as light reading. But I do remember words and sentences in my reading and they were correctly spelled and correctly parsed."

"Don't be sure. You've seen any word misspelled in every possible way and every possible example of twisted grammar, too."

"Those were exceptions. By far the largest number of times I've encountered literary English, I've encountered it used correctly. It outweighs accidents, errors, and ignorance. What's more, I'm sure I'm improving even as I sit here, growing more intelligent steadily."

"And you're not worried. What if—"

"What if I become *too* intelligent? Tell me how on Earth you think becoming too intelligent can be harmful."

"I was going to say," said Susan, coldly, "that what you're experiencing is not intelligence. It's only total recall."

"How do you mean 'only'? If I recall perfectly, if I use the English language correctly, if I know endless quantities of material, isn't that going to make me seem more intelligent? How else need one define intelligence? You aren't growing just a little jealous, are you, Sue?"

"No," more coldly still. "I can always get an injection of my own if I feel desperate about it."

John put down his fork. "You can't mean that."

"I don't, but what if I did?"

"Because you can't take advantage of your special knowledge to deprive me of my position."

"What position?"

The main course arrived and for a few moments, John was busy. Then he said, in a whisper, "My position as the first of the future. *Homo superior!* There'll never be too many of us. You heard what Kupfer said. Some are too dumb to make it. Some are too smart to change much. I'm the one!"

"*Dead* average." One corner of Susan's mouth lifted.

"Once I was. There'll be others like me eventually. Not many, but there'll be others. It's just that I want to make my mark before the others come along. It's for the firm, you know. Us!"

He remained lost in thought thereafter, testing his brain delicately.

Susan ate in an unhappy silence.

— 7 —

JOHN SPENT several days organizing his memories. It was like the preparation of an orderly reference book. One by one, he recalled all his experiences in the six years he had spent at Quantum Pharmaceuticals and all he had heard and all the papers and memos he had read.

There was no difficulty in discarding the irrelevant and unimportant and storing them in a "hold till further notice" compartment where they did not interfere with his analysis. Other items were put in order so that they established a natural progression.

Against that skeletal organization, he resurrected the scuttlebutt he had heard; the gossip, malicious or otherwise; casual phrases and interjections at conferences which he had not been conscious of hearing at the time. Those items which did not fit anywhere against the background he had built up in his head were worthless, empty of factual content. Those which did fit clicked firmly into place and could be seen as true by that mere fact.

The further the structure grew, and the more coherent, the more significant new items became and the easier it was to fit them in.

Ross stopped by John's desk on Thursday. He said, "I want to see you in my office at the nonce, Heath, if your legs will deign to carry you in that direction."

John rose uneasily. "Is it necessary? I'm busy."

"Yes, you look busy." Ross looked over the clear desk which, at the moment, held nothing but a studio photo of a smiling Susan. "You've been this busy all week. But you've asked me whether seeing me in my office is necessary. For me, no; but for you, vital. There's the door to my office. There's the door to the hell out of here. Choose one or the other and do it fast."

John nodded and, without undue hurry, followed Ross into his office.

Ross seated himself behind his desk but did not invite John to sit. He maintained a hard stare for a moment, then said, "What the hell's got into you this week, Heath. Don't you know what your job is?"

"To the extent that I have done it, it would seem that I do," said John. "The report on microcosmic is on your desk and complete and seven days ahead of deadline. I doubt that you can have complaints about it."

"You doubt, do you? Do I have permission to have complaints if I choose to after communing with my soul? Or am I condemned to applying to you for permission?"

"I apparently have not made myself plain, Mr. Ross. I doubt that you have *rational* complaints about it. To have those of the other variety is entirely up to you."

Ross rose now. "Listen, punk, if I decide to fire you, you won't get the news by word of mouth. It won't be anything I say that will give you the glad tidings. You will go through the door in a violent tumble and mine will be the propulsive force behind that tumble. Just keep that in your small brain and your tongue in your big mouth. Whether you've done your work or not is not at question right now. Whether you've done everyone else's is. Who and what gives you the right to manage everyone in this place?"

John said nothing.

Ross roared, "Well?"

John said, "Your order was 'keep your tongue in your big mouth.' "

Ross turned a dangerous red. "You will answer questions, however."

John said, "I am not aware that I have been managing anyone."

"There's not a person in the place you haven't corrected at least once. You have gone over Willoughby's head in connection with the correspondence on the TMP's; you have been in general files using Bronstein's computer access; and God knows what else I haven't yet been told about and all in the last two days. You are disrupting the work of this department and it must cease this moment. There must be dead calm, and instantaneously, or it will be tornado weather for you, my man."

John said, "If I have interfered in the narrow sense, it has been for the good of the company. In the case of Willoughby, his treatment of the TMP matter was putting Quantum Pharmaceuticals in violation of government regulations, something I have pointed out to you in one of several memos I have sent you which you apparently have not had occasion to read. As for Bronstein, he was simply ignoring general directions and costing the company fifty thousand in unnecessary tests, something I was easily able to establish by locating the necessary correspondence—merely to corroborate my clear memory of the situation."

Ross was swelling visibly through the talk. "Heath," he said, "you are usurping my role. You will, therefore, gather your personal effects and be off the premises before lunch, never to return. If you do, I will take extreme pleasure in helping you out again with my foot. Your official notice of dismissal will be in your hands, or down your throat, before your effects will be collected, work as quickly as you may."

John said, "Don't try to bully me, Ross. You've cost the company a quarter of a million dollars through incompetence and you know it."

There was a short pause as Ross deflated. He said, cautiously, "What are you talking about?"

"Quantum Pharmaceuticals went down to the wire on the Nutley bid and missed out because a certain piece of information that was in your hands stayed in your hands and never got to the Board of Directors. You either forgot or you didn't bother and in either case you are not the man for your job. You are either incompetent or have sold out."

"You're insane."

"No one need believe me. The information is in the computer, if one knows where to look and I know where to look. What's more, the knowledge is on file and will be on the desks of the interested parties two minutes after I leave these premises."

"If this were so," said Ross, speaking with difficulty, "you could not possibly know. This is a stupid attempt at blackmail by threat of slander."

"You know it's not slander. If you doubt that I have the information, let me tell you that there is one memorandum that is not in the records but can be reconstructed without too much difficulty from what is there. You would have to explain its absence and it will be presumed you have destroyed it. You know I'm not bluffing."

"It's still blackmail."

"Why? I'm making no demands and no threats. I'm merely explaining my actions of the past two days. Of course, if I'm forced to resign, I'll have to explain why I resigned, won't I?"

Ross said nothing.

John said, coolly, "Is my resignation being requested?"

"Get out of here!"

"With my job? Or without it?"

Ross said, "You have your job." His face was a study in hatred.

— 8 —

SUSAN HAD arranged a dinner at her apartment and had gone to considerable trouble for it. Never, in her own opinion, had she looked more enticing and never did she think it more important to move John, at least for a bit, away from his total concentration on his own mind.

She said, with an attempt at heartiness, "After all, we are celebrating the last nine days of single blessedness."

"We are celebrating more than that," said John with a grim smile. "It's only four days since I got the disinhibitor and already I've been able to put Ross in his place. He'll never bother me again."

"We each seem to have our own notion of sentiment," said Susan. "Tell me the details of *your* tender remembrance."

John told the tale crisply, repeating the conversation verbatim and without hesitation.

Susan listened stonily, without in any way rising to the gathering triumph in John's voice. "How *did* you know all that about Ross?"

John said, "There are no secrets, Sue. Things just *seem* secret because people don't remember. If you can recall every remark, every comment, every stray word made to you or in your hearing and consider them all in combination, you find that everyone gives himself away in everything. You can pick out meanings that will, in these days of computerization, send you straight to the necessary records. It can be done. I can do it. I have done it in the case of Ross. I can do it in the case of anybody with whom I associate."

"You can also get them furious."

"I got Ross furious. You can bet on that."

"Was that wise?"

"What can he do to me? I've got him cold."

"He has enough clout in the upper echelons—"

"Not for long. I have a conference set for 2 P.M. tomorrow with old man Prescott and his stinking cigar and I'll cut Ross off at the pass."

"Don't you think you're moving too quickly?"

"Moving too quickly? I haven't even begun. Prescott's just a stepping-stone. Quantum Pharmaceutical's just a stepping-stone."

"It's still too quick. Johnny, you need someone to direct you. You need—"

"I need *nothing*. With what I have," he tapped his temple, "there's no one and nothing that can stop me."

Susan said, "Well, look, let's not discuss that. We have different plans to make."

"Plans?"

"Our own. We're getting married in just under nine days. Surely," with heavy irony, "you haven't returned to the sad old days when you forgot things."

"I remember the wedding," said John, testily, "but at the moment I've got to reorganize Quantum. In fact, I've been thinking seriously of postponing the wedding till I have things well in hand."

"Oh? And when might that be?"

"That's hard to tell. Not long at the rate I'm taking hold. A month or two, I suppose. Unless," and he descended into sarcasm, "you think that's moving too quickly."

Susan was breathing hard. "Were you planning to consult with me on the matter?"

John raised his eyebrows. "Would it have been necessary? Where's the argument? Surely you see what's happening. We can't interrupt it and lose momentum. Listen, did you know I'm a mathematical wiz. I can multiply and divide as fast as a computer because at some time in my life I have come across almost every simple bit of arithmetic and I can *recall* the answers. I read a table of square roots and I can—"

Susan cried, "My God, Johnny, you *are* a kid with a new toy. You've lost your perspective. Instant recall is good for nothing but playing tricks with. It doesn't give you one bit more intelligence; not an ounce; not a speck more of judgment; not a whiff more of common sense. You're about as safe to have around as a little boy with a loaded grenade. You need looking after by someone with brains."

John scowled. "Do I? It seems to me that I'm getting what I want."

"Are you? Isn't it true that I'm what you want also?"

"What?"

"Go ahead, Johnny. You want me. Reach out and take me. Exercise that remarkable recall you have. Remember who I am, what I am, the things we can do, the warmth, the affection, the sentiment."

John, with his forehead still creased in uncertainty, extended his arms toward Susan.

She stepped out of them. "But you haven't got me, or anything about me. You can't remember me into your arms; you have to love me into them. The trouble is, you don't have the good sense to do it and you lack the intelligence to establish reasonable priorities. Here, take this and get out of my apartment or I'll hit you with something a lot heavier."

He stopped to pick up the engagement ring. "Susan—"

"I said, get out! The firm of Johnny and Sue is hereby dissolved."

Her face blazed anger and John turned meekly and left.

— 9 —

WHEN HE arrived at Quantum the next morning, Anderson was waiting for him with a look of anxious impatience on his face.

"Mr. Heath," he said, smiling, and rising.

"What do you want?" demanded John.

"We are private here, I take it?"

"The place isn't bugged as far as I know."

"You are to report to us day after tomorrow for examination. On Sunday. You recall that?"

"Of course, I recall that. I'm incapable of not recalling. I *am* capable of changing my mind, however. Why do I need an examination?"

"Why not, sir? It is quite plain from what Kupfer and I have picked up that the treatment seems to have worked splendidly. Actually, we don't want to wait till Sunday. If you can come with me today—now, in fact—it would mean a great deal to us, to Quantum, and, of course, to humanity.''

John said, curtly, ''You might have held on to me when you had me. You sent me about my business, allowing me to live and work unsupervised so that you could test me under field conditions, and get a better idea of how things would work out. It meant more risk for me, but you didn't worry about that, did you?''

''Mr. Heath, that was not in our minds. We—''

''Don't tell me that. I remember every last word you and Kupfer said to me last Sunday, and it's quite clear to me that that *was* in your minds. So if I take the risk, I accept the benefits. I have no intention of presenting myself as a biochemical freak who has achieved my ability at the end of a hypodermic needle. Nor do I want others of the sort wandering around. For now, I have a monopoly and I intend to use it. When I'm ready—not before—I will be willing to cooperate with you and benefit humanity. But just remember, I'm the one who will know when I'm ready, not you. So don't call me; I'll call you.''

Anderson managed a soft smile. ''As to that, Mr. Heath, how can you stop us from making our announcement? Those who have dealt with you this week will have no trouble in recognizing the change in you and in testifying to it.''

''Really? See here, Anderson, listen closely and do so without that foolish grin on your face. It irritates me. I told you I remember every word you and Kupfer spoke. I remember every nuance of expression, every sidelong glance. It all spoke volumes. I learned enough to check through sick-leave records with a good idea of what I was looking for. It would seem that I was not the first Quantum employee on whom you had tried the disinhibitor.''

Anderson was, indeed, not smiling. ''That is nonsense.''

''You know it is not, and you had better know I can prove it. I know the names of the men involved—one was a woman, actually—and the hospitals in which they were treated and the false history with which they were supplied. Since you did not warn me of this, when you used me as your fourth experimental animal on two legs, I owe you nothing but a prison sentence.''

Anderson said, ''I won't discuss this matter. Let me say this, though. The treatment will wear off, Heath. You won't keep your total recall. You will have to come back for further treatment and you can be sure it will be on our terms.''

John said, ''Nuts! You don't suppose I haven't investigated your reports—at least, those you haven't kept secret. And I already have a notion of what aspects you *have* kept secret. The treatment lasts longer in some cases than others. It invariably lasts longer where it is more effective. In my case, the treatment has been extraordinarily effective and it will endure a considerable time. By the time I come to you again, if I ever have to, I will be in a position where any failure on your part to cooperate will be swiftly devastating to you. Don't even think of it.''

''You ungrateful—''

''Don't bother me,'' said John, wearily. ''I have no time to listen to you froth. Go away, I have work to do.''

Anderson's face was a study in fear and frustration as he left.

IT WAS 2:30 P.M. when John walked into Prescott's office, for once not minding the cigar smoke. It would not be long, he knew, before Prescott would have to choose between his cigars and his position.

With Prescott were Arnold Gluck and Lewis Randall, so that John had the grim pleasure of knowing he was facing the three top men in the division.

Prescott rested his cigar on top of an ashtray and said, "Ross has asked me to give you half an hour, and that's all I will give you. You're the one with the trick memory, aren't you?"

"My name is John Heath, sir, and I intend to present you with a rationalization of procedure for the company; one that will make full use of the age of computers and electronic communication and will lay the groundwork for further modification as the technology improves."

The three men looked at each other.

Gluck, whose creased face was tanned a leathery-brown said, "Are you an expert in office management?"

"I don't have to be, sir. I have been here for six years and I recall every bit of the procedure in every transaction in which I have been involved. That means the pattern of such transactions is plain to me and its imperfections obvious. One can see toward what it is tending and where it is doing so wastefully and inefficiently. If you'll listen, I will explain. You will find it easy to understand."

Randall, whose red hair and freckles made him seem younger than he was, said sardonically, "Real easy, I hope, because we have trouble with hard concepts."

"You won't have trouble," said John.

"And you won't get a second more than twenty-one minutes," said Prescott, looking at his watch.

"It won't take that," said John. "I have it diagrammed and I can talk quickly."

It took fifteen minutes and the three management personnel were remarkably silent in that interval.

Finally Gluck said, with a hostile glance out of his small eyes, "It sounds as though you are saying we can get along with half the management we are employing these days."

"Less than half," said John, coolly, "and be the more efficient for it. We can't fire ordinary personnel at will because of the unions, though we can profitably lose them by attrition. Management is not protected, however, and can be let go. They'll have pensions if they're old enough and can get new jobs if they're young enough. Our thought must be for Quantum."

Prescott, who had maintained an ominous silence, now puffed furiously at his noxious cigar and said, "Changes like this have to be considered carefully and implemented, if at all, with the greatest of caution. What seems logical on paper can lose out in the human equation."

John said, "Prescott, if this reorganization is not accepted within a week, and if I am not placed in charge of its implementation, I will resign. I will have no trouble in finding employment with a smaller firm where this plan can be far more easily put into practice. Beginning with a small group of management people, I can expand in both quantity and efficiency of performance without additional hiring and within a year I'll drive Quantum into bankruptcy. It would be fun to do this if I am driven to it, so consider carefully. My half hour is up. Good-bye.'' And he left.

— 11 —

PRESCOTT LOOKED after him with a glance of frigid calculation. He said to the other two, "I think he means what he says and that he knows every facet of our operations better than we do. We can't let him go."

"You mean we've got to accept his plan," said Randall, shocked.

"I didn't say that. You two go, and remember this whole thing is confidential."

Gluck said, "I have the feeling that if we don't do something, all three of us will find ourselves on our butts in the street within a month."

"Very likely," said Prescott, "so we'll do something."

"What?"

"If you don't know, you won't get hurt. Leave it to me. Forget it for now and have a nice weekend."

When they were gone, he thought a while, chewing furiously on his cigar. He then turned to his telephone and dialed an extension. "Prescott here. I want you in my office first thing Monday morning. First thing. Hear me?"

— 12 —

ANDERSON LOOKED a trifle disheveled. He had had a bad weekend. Prescott, who had had a worse, said to him, malevolently, "You and Kupfer tried again, didn't you?"

Anderson said, softly, "It's better not to discuss that, Mr. Prescott. You remember it was agreed that in certain aspects of research, a distance was to be established. We were to take the risks or the glory, and Quantum was to share in the latter but not in the former."

"And your salary was doubled with a guarantee of all legal payments to be Quantum's responsibility; don't forget that. This man, John Heath, was treated by you and Kupfer, wasn't he? Come on. There's no mistaking it. There's no point in hiding it."

"Well, yes."

"And you were so brilliant that you turned him loose on us—this—this— tarantula."

"We didn't anticipate this would happen. When he didn't go into instant shock, we thought it was our first chance to test the process in the field. We thought he would break down after two or three days, or it would pass."

Prescott said, "If I hadn't been protected so damned well, I wouldn't have put the whole thing out of my mind and I would have guessed what had happened when that bastard first pulled the computer bit and produced the details of correspondence he had no business remembering. All right, we know where we are now. He's holding the company to ransom with a new plan of operations he can't be allowed to put through. Also, he can't be allowed to walk away from us.''

Anderson said, ''Considering Heath's capacity for recall and synthesis, is it possible that his plan of operations may be a good one?''

''I don't care if it is. That bastard is after my job and who knows what else and we've got to get rid of him.''

''How do you mean, rid of him? He could be of vital importance to the cerebro-chemical project.''

''Forget that. It's a disaster. You're creating a super-Hitler.''

Anderson said, in soft-voiced anguish, ''The effect will wear off.''

''Yes? When?''

''At this moment, I can't be sure.''

''Then I can't take chances. We've got to make our arrangements and do it tomorrow at the latest. We can't wait any longer.

— 13 —

JOHN WAS in high good humor. The manner in which Ross avoided him when he could and spoke to him deferentially when he had to affected the entire work force. There was a strange and radical change in the pecking order, with himself at the top.

Nor could John deny to himself that he liked it. He reveled in it. The tide was moving strongly and unbelievably swiftly. It was only nine days since the injection of the disinhibitor and every step had been forward.

Well, no, there had been Susan's silly rage at him, but he would deal with her later. When he showed her the heights to which he would climb in nine additional days—in ninety—

He looked up. Ross was at his desk, waiting for his attention but reluctant to do anything as crass as to attract that attention by as much as clearing his throat. John swiveled his chair, put his feet out before him in an attitude of relaxation, and said, ''Well, Ross?''

Ross said, carefully, ''I would like to see you in my office, Heath. Something important has come up and, frankly, you're the only one who can set it straight.''

John got slowly to his feet. ''Yes? What is it?''

Ross looked about mutely at the busy room, with at least five men in reasonable earshot. Then he looked toward his office door and held out an inviting arm.

John hesitated, but for years Ross had held unquestioned authority over him, and at this moment he reacted to habit.

Ross held his door open for John politely, stepped through himself and closed the door behind him, locking it unobtrusively and remaining in front of it. Anderson stepped out from the other side of the bookcase.

John said sharply, "What's all this about?"

"Nothing at all, Heath," said Ross, his smile turning into a vulpine grin. "We're just going to help you out of your abnormal state—take you back to normality. Don't move, Heath."

Anderson had a hypodermic in his hand. "Please, Heath, do not struggle. We wish you no harm."

"If I yell—" said John.

"If you make any sound," said Ross, "I will put a hammerlock on you and hold it till your eyes bug out. I would like to do that, so please try to yell."

John said, "I have the goods on both of you, safe on deposit. Anything that happens to me—"

"Mr. Heath," said Anderson, "nothing will happen to you. Something is going to *un*happen to you. We will put you back to where you were. That would happen anyway, but we will hurry it up just a little."

"So I'm going to hold you, Heath," said Ross, "and you won't move because if you do, you will disturb our friend with the needle and he might slip and give you more than the carefully calculated dose, and you might end up unable to remember anything at all."

Heath was backing away, breathless. "That's what you're planning. You think you'll be safe that way. If I forgot all about you, all about the information, all about its storage. But—"

"We're not going to hurt you, Heath," said Anderson.

John's forehead glistened with sweat. A near-paralysis gripped him.

"An amnesiac!" he said, huskily, and with a terror that only someone could feel at the possibility who himself had perfect recall.

"Then you won't remember this either, will you?" said Ross. "Go ahead, Anderson."

"Well," muttered Anderson, in resignation. "I'm destroying a perfect test-subject." He lifted John's flaccid arm and readied the hypodermic.

There was a knock at the door. A clear voice called, "John!"

Anderson froze almost automatically, looking up questioningly.

Ross had turned to look at the door. Now he turned back. "Shoot that stuff into him, Doc," he said in an urgent whisper.

The voice came again, "Johnny, I know you're in there. I've called the police. They're on the way."

Ross whispered again, "Go ahead. She's lying. And by the time they come, it's over. Who can prove anything?"

But Anderson was shaking his head vigorously. "It's his fiancée. She knows he was treated. She was there."

"You jackass."

There was the sound of a kick against the door and then the voice sounded in a muffled, "Let go of me. They've got— Let go!"

Anderson said, "Having her push the thing was the only way we could get him to agree. Besides, I don't think we have to do anything. Look at him."

John had collapsed in a corner, eyes glazed, and clearly in a state of unconscious trance.

Anderson said, "He's been terrified and that can produce a shock that will interfere with recall under normal conditions. I think the disinhibitor has been wiped out. Let her in and let *me* talk to her."

— 14 —

SUSAN LOOKED pale as she sat with her arm protectively about the shoulders of her ex-fiancé. "What happened?"

"You remember the injection of—"

"Yes, yes. What happened?"

"He was supposed to come to our office day before yesterday, Sunday, for a thorough examination. He didn't come. We worried and the reports from his superiors had me very perturbed. He was becoming arrogant, megalomaniacal, irascible— Perhaps you noticed. You're not wearing your engagement ring."

"We—quarreled," said Susan.

"Then you understand. He was— Well, if he were an inanimate device, we might say his motor was overheating as it sped faster and faster. This morning it seemed absolutely essential to treat him. We persuaded him to come here, locked the door and—"

"Injected him with something while I howled and kicked outside."

"Not at all," said Anderson. "We would have used a sedative, but we were too late. He had what I can only describe as a breakdown. You may search his body for fresh punctures, which, as his fiancée, I presume you may do without embarrassment, and you will find none."

Susan said, "I'll see about that. What happens, now?"

"I am sure he will recover. He will be his old self again."

"Dead average?"

"He will not have perfect recall, but until ten days ago, he never had. Naturally, the firm will give him indefinite leave on full salary. If any medical treatment is required, all medical expenses will be paid. And when he feels like it, he can return to active duty."

"Yes? Well, I will want all that in writing before the day is out, or I see my lawyer tomorrow."

"But Miss Collins," said Anderson, "you know that Mr. Heath volunteered. You were willing too."

"I think," said Susan, "that *you* know the situation was misrepresented to us and that you won't welcome an investigation. Just see to it that what you've just promised is in writing."

"You will have to, in return, sign an agreement to hold us guiltless of any misadventure your fiancé may have suffered."

"Possibly. I prefer to see what kind of misadventure it is first. Can you walk, Johnny?"

John nodded and said, a little huskily, "Yes, Sue."

"Then let's go."

— 15 —

JOHN HAD put himself outside a cup of good coffee and an omelet before Susan permitted discussion. Then he said, "What I don't understand is how you happened to be there?"

"Shall we say woman's intuition?"

"Let'say Susan's brains."

"All right. Let's! After I threw the ring at you, I felt self-pitying and aggrieved and after that wore off, I felt a severe sense of loss because, odd though it might seem to the average sensible person, I'm very fond of you."

"I'm sorry, Sue," said John, humbly.

"As well you should be. God, you were insupportable. But then I got to thinking that if you could get poor, loving me that furious, what must you be doing to your co-workers. The more I thought about it, the more I thought they might have a strong impulse to kill you. Now, don't get me wrong. I'm willing to admit you deserved killing, but only at *my* hands. I wouldn't dream of allowing anyone else to do it. I didn't hear from you—"

"I know, Sue. I had plans and I had no time—"

"You had to do it all in two weeks. I know, you idiot. By this morning I couldn't stand it anymore. I came to see how you were and found you behind a locked door."

John shuddered. "I never thought I'd welcome your kicking and screaming, but I did then. You stopped them."

"Will it upset you to talk about it?"

"I don't think so. I'm all right."

"Then what were they doing?"

"They were going to re-inhibit me. I thought they might be giving me an overdose and make me an amnesiac."

"Why?"

"Because they knew I had them all. I could ruin them and the company."

"You really could?"

"Absolutely."

"But they didn't actually inject you, did they? Or was that another of Anderson's lies?"

"They really didn't."

"Are you all right?"

"I'm not an amnesiac."

"Well, I hate to sound like a Victorian damsel, but I hope you have learned your lesson."

"If you mean, do I realize you were right, I do."

"Then just let me lecture you for one minute, so you don't forget again. You went about everything too rapidly, too openly, and with too much disregard for the possible violent counteraction of others. You had total recall and you mistook it for intelligence. If you had someone who was really intelligent to guide you—"

"I needed you, Sue."

"Well, you've got me now, Johnny."

"What do we do next, Sue?"

"First, we get that paper from Quantum and, since you're all right, we'll sign the release for them. Second, we get married on Saturday, just as we originally planned. Third, we'll see— But, Johnny?"

"Yes?"

"You're all right?"

"Couldn't be better, Sue. Now that we're together, everything's fine."

— 16 —

IT WASN'T a formal wedding. Less formal than they had originally planned and fewer guests. No one was there from Quantum, for instance—Susan had pointed out, quite firmly, that that would be a bad idea.

A neighbor of Susan's had brought a video-camera to record the proceedings, something that seemed to John to be the height of schlock, but Susan had wanted it.

And then the neighbor had said to him with a tragic shrug, "Can't get the damn thing to turn on. You'd think they'd give me one in working order. I'll have to make a phone call." He hastened down the steps to the pay phone in the chapel lobby.

John advanced to look at the camera curiously. An instruction booklet lay on a small table to one side. He picked it up and leafed through the pages with moderate speed, then put it back. He looked about him, but everyone was busy. No one seemed to be paying attention to him.

He slid the rear panel to one side, unobtrusively, and peered inside. He then turned away and gazed at the opposite wall thoughtfully. He was still gazing even as his right hand snaked in toward the mechanism and made a quick adjustment. After a brief interval he put the rear panel back and flicked a toggle switch.

The neighbor came bustling back, looking exasperated. "How am I going to follow directions I can't make head or—" He frowned, then said, "Funny. It's on. It must have been working all the time."

— 17 —

"YOU MAY kiss the bride," said the minister, benignly, and John took Susan in his arms and followed orders with enthusiasm.

Susan whispered through unmoving lips, "You fixed that camera. Why?"

He whispered back, "I wanted everything right for the wedding."

She whispered, "You wanted to show off."

They broke apart, looking at each other through love-misted eyes, then fell into another embrace, while the small audience stirred and tittered.

Susan whispered, "You do it again, and I'll skin you. As long as no one knows you still have it, no one will stop you. We'll have it all within a year, if you follow directions."

"Yes, dear," whispered John, humbly.

THE
MARTIAN WAY

— 1 —

FROM THE doorway of the short corridor between the only two rooms in the travel-head of the spaceship, Mario Esteban Rioz watched sourly as Ted Long adjusted the video dials painstakingly. Long tried a touch clockwise, then a touch counter. The picture was lousy.

Rioz knew it would stay lousy. They were too far from Earth and at a bad position facing the Sun. But then Long would not be expcted to know that. Rioz remained standing in the doorway for an additional moment, head bent to clear the upper lintel, body turned half sidewise to fit the narrow opening. Then he jerked into the galley like a cork popping out of a bottle.

"What are you after?" he asked.

"I thought I'd get Hilder," said Long.

Rioz propped his rump on the corner of a table shelf. He lifted a conical can of milk from the companion shelf just above his head. Its point popped under pressure. He swirled it gently as he waited for it to warm.

"What for?" he said. He upended the cone and sucked noisily.

"Thought I'd listen."

"I think it's a waste of power."

Long looked up, frowning. "It's customary to allow free use of personal video sets."

"Within reason," retorted Rioz.

Their eyes met challengingly. Rioz had the rangy body, the gaunt, cheek-sunken face that was almost the hallmark of the Martian Scavenger, those Spacers who patiently haunted the space routes between Earth and Mars. Pale blue eyes were set keenly in the brown, lined face which, in turn, stood darkly out against the white surrounding syntho-fur that lined the up-turned collar of his leathic space jacket.

Long was altogether paler and softer. He bore some of the marks of the Grounder, although no second-generation Martian could be a Grounder in the sense that Earthmen were. His own collar was thrown back and his dark brown hair freely exposed.

"What do you call within reason?" demanded Long.

Rioz's thin lips grew thinner. He said, "Considering that we're not even going to make expenses this trip, the way it looks, any power drain at all is outside reason."

Long said, "If we're losing money, hadn't you better get back to your post? It's your watch."

Rioz grunted and ran a thumb and forefinger over the stubble on his chin. He got up and trudged to the door, his soft, heavy boots muting the sound of his steps. He paused to look at the thermostat, then turned with a flare of fury.

"I *thought* it was hot. Where do you think you are?"

Long said, "Forty degrees isn't excesive."

"For you it isn't, maybe. But this is space, not a heated office at the iron mines." Rioz swung the thermostat control down to minimum with a quick thumb movement. "Sun's warm enough."

"The galley isn't on Sunside."

"It'll percolate through, damn it."

Rioz stepped through the door and Long stared after him for a long moment, then turned back to the video. He did not turn up the thermostat.

The picture was still flickering badly, but it would have to do. Long folded a chair down out of the wall. He leaned forward waiting through the formal announcement, the momentary pause before the slow dissolution of the curtain, the spotlight picking out the well-known bearded figure which grew as it was brought forward until it filled the screen.

The voice, impressive even through the flutings and croakings induced by the electron storms of twenty millions of miles, began:

"Friends! My fellow citizens of Earth . . ."

— 2 —

RIOZ'S EYE caught the flash of the radio signal as he stepped into the pilot room. For one moment, the palms of his hands grew clammy when it seemed to him that it was a radar pip; but that was only his guilt speaking. He should not have left the pilot room while on duty theoretically, though all Scavengers did it. Still, it was the standard nightmare, this business of a strike turning up during just those five minutes when one knocked off for a quick coffee because it seemed certain that space was clear. And the nightmare had been known to happen, too.

Rioz threw in the multi-scanner. It was a waste of power, but while he was thinking about it, he might as well make sure.

Space was clear except for the far-distant echoes from the neighboring ships on the scavenging line.

He hooked up the radio circuit, and the blond, long-nosed head of Richard Swenson, copilot of the next ship on the Marsward side, filled it.

"Hey Mario," said Swenson.

"Hi. What's new?"

There was a second and a fraction of pause between that and Swenson's next comment, since the speed of electromagnetic radiation is not infinite.

"What a day I've *had*."

"Something happened?" Rioz asked.

"I had a strike."

"Well, good."

"Sure, if I'd roped it in," said Swenson morosely.

"What happened?"

"Damn it, I headed in the wrong direction."

Rioz knew better than to laugh. He said, "How did you do that?"

"It wasn't my fault. The trouble was the shell was moving way out of the ecliptic. Can you imagine the stupidity of a pilot that can't work the release maneuver decently? How was I to know? I got the distance of the shell and let it go at that. I just assumed its orbit was in the usual trajectory family. Wouldn't you? I started along what I thought was a good line of intersection and it was five minutes before I noticed the distance was still going up. The pips were taking their sweet time returning. So then I took the angular projections of the thing, and it was too late to catch up with it."

"Any of the other boys getting it?"

"No. It's 'way out of the ecliptic and'll keep on going forever. That's not what bothers me so much. It was only an inner shell. But I hate to tell you how many tons of propulsion I wasted getting up speed and then getting back to station. You should have heard Canute."

Canute was Richard Swenson's brother and partner.

"Mad, huh?" said Rioz.

"Mad? Like to have killed me! But then we've been out five months now and it's getting kind of sticky. You know."

"I know."

"How are you doing, Mario?"

Rioz made a spitting gesture. "About that much this trip. Two shells in the last two weeks and I had to chase each one for six hours."

"Big ones?"

"Are you kidding? I could have scaled them down to Phobos by hand. This is the worst trip I've ever had."

"How much longer are you staying?"

"For my part, we can quit tomorrow. We've only been out two months and it's got so I'm chewing Long out all the time."

There was a pause over and above the electromagnetic lag.

Swenson said, "What's he like, anyway? Long, I mean."

Rioz looked over his shoulder. He could hear the soft, crackly mutter of the video in the galley. "I can't make him out. He says to me about a week after the start of the trip, 'Mario, why are you a Scavenger?' I just look at him and say 'To make a living. Why do you suppose?' I mean, what the hell kind of a question is that? Why is anyone a Scavenger?

"Anyway, he says, 'That's not it, Mario.' *He's* telling *me*, you see. He says, 'You're a Scavenger because this is a part of the Martian way.'"

Swenson said, "And what did he mean by that?"

Rioz shrugged. "I never asked him. Right now he's sitting in there listening to the ultra-microwave from Earth. He's listening to some Grounder called Hilder.''

''Hilder? A Grounder politician, an Assemblyman or something, isn't he?''

''That's right. At least, I think that's right. Long is always doing things like that. He brought about fifteen pounds of books with him, all about Earth. Just plain dead weight, you know.''

''Well, he's your partner. And talking about partners, I think I'll get back on the job. If I miss another strike, there'll be murder around here.''

He was gone and Rioz leaned back. He watched the even green line that was the pulse scanner. He tried the multi-scanner a moment. Space was still clear.

He felt a little better. A bad spell is always worse if the Scavengers all about you are pulling in shell after shell; if the shells go spiraling down to the Phobos scrap forges with everyone's brand welded on except your own. Then, too, he had managed to work off some of his resentment toward Long.

It was a mistake teaming up with Long. It was always a mistake to team up with a tenderfoot. They thought what you wanted was conversation, especially Long, with his eternal theories about Mars and its great new role in human progress. That was the way he said it—Human Progress: the Martian Way; the New Creative Minority. And all the time what Rioz wanted wasn't talk, but a strike, a few shells to call their own.

At that, he hadn't any choice, really. Long was pretty well known down on Mars and made good pay as a mining engineer. He was a friend of Commissioner Sankov and he'd been out on one or two short scavenging missions before. You can't turn a fellow down flat before a tryout, even though it did look funny. Why should a mining engineer with a comfortable job and good money want to muck around in space?

Rioz never asked Long that question. Scavenger partners are forced too close together to make curiosity desirable, or sometimes even safe. But Long talked so much that he answered the question.

''I had to come out here, Mario,'' he said. ''The future of Mars isn't in the mines; it's in space.''

Rioz wondered how it would be to try a trip alone. Everyone said it was impossible. Even discounting lost opportunities when one man had to go off watch to sleep or attend to other things, it was well known that one man alone in space would become intolerably depressed in a relatively short while.

Taking a partner along made a six-month trip possible. A regular crew would be better, but no Scavenger could make money on a ship large enough to carry one. The capital it would take in propulsion alone!

Even two didn't find it exactly fun in space. Usually you had to change partners each trip and you could stay out longer with some than with others. Look at Richard and Canute Swenson. They teamed up every five or six trips because they were brothers. And yet whenever they did, it was a case of constantly mounting tension and antagonism after the first week.

Oh well. Space was clear. Rioz would feel a little better if he went back in the galley and smoothed down some of the bickering with Long. He might as well show he was an old spacehead who took the irritations of space as they came.

He stood up, walked the three steps necessary to reach the short, narrow corridor that tied together the two rooms of the spaceship.

ONCE AGAIN Rioz stood in the doorway for a moment, watching. Long was intent on the flickering screen.

Rioz said gruffly, "I'm shoving up the thermostat. It's all right—we can spare the power."

Long nodded. "If you like."

Rioz took a hesitant step forward. Space was clear, so to hell with sitting and looking at a blank, green, pipless line. He said, "What's the Grounder been talking about?"

"History of space travel mostly. Old stuff, but he's doing it well. He's giving the whole works—color cartoons, trick photography, stills from old films, everything."

As if to illustrate Long's remarks, the bearded figure faded out of view, and a cross-sectional view of a spaceship flitted onto the screen. Hilder's voice continued, pointing out features of interest that appeared in schematic color. The communications system of the ship outlined itself in red as he talked about it, the storerooms, the proton micropile drive, the cybernetic circuits . . .

Then Hilder was back on the screen. "But this is only the travel-head of the ship. What moves it? What gets it off the Earth?"

Everyone knew what moved a spaceship, but Hilder's voice was like a drug. He made spaceship propulsion sound like the secret of the ages, like an ultimate revelation. Even Rioz felt a slight tingling of suspense, though he had spent the greater part of his life aboard ship.

Hilder went on. "Scientists call it different names. They call it the Law of Action and Reaction. Sometimes they call it Newton's Third Law. Sometimes they call it Conservation of Momentum. But we don't have to call it any name. We can just use our common sense. When we swim, we push water backward and move forward ourselves. When we walk, we push back against the ground and move forward. When we fly a gyro-flivver, we push air backward and move forward.

"Nothing can move forward unless something else moves backward. It's the old principal of 'You can't get something for nothing.'

"Now imagine a spaceship that weighs a hundred thousand tons lifting off Earth. To do that, something else must be moved downward. Since a spaceship is extremely heavy, a great deal of material must be moved downward. So much material, in fact, that there is no place to keep it all aboard ship. A special compartment must be built behind the ship to hold it."

Again Hilder faded out and the ship returned. It shrank and a truncated cone appeared behind it. In bright yellow, words appeared within it: MATERIAL TO BE THROWN AWAY.

"But now," said Hilder, "the total weight of the ship is much greater. You need still more propulsion and still more."

The ship shrank enormously to add on another larger shell and still another immense one. The ship proper, the travelhead, was a little dot on the screen, a glowing red dot.

Rioz said, "Hell, this is kindergarten stuff."

"Not to the people he's speaking to, Mario," replied Long. "Earth isn't Mars. There must be billions of Earth people who've never even seen a spaceship; don't know the first thing about it."

Hilder was saying, "When the material inside the biggest shell is used up, the shell is detached. It's thrown away, too."

The outermost shell came loose, wobbled about the screen.

"Then the second one goes," said Hilder, "and then, if the trip is a long one, the last is ejected."

The ship was just a red dot now, with three shells shifting and moving, lost in space.

Hilder said, "These shells represent a hundred thousand tons of tungsten, magnesium, aluminum, and steel. They are gone forever from Earth. Mars is ringed by Scavengers, waiting along the routes of space travel, waiting for the cast-off shells, netting and branding them, saving them for Mars. Not one cent of payment reaches Earth for them. They are salvage. They belong to the ship that finds them."

Rioz said, "We risk our investment and our lives. If we don't pick them up, no one gets them. What loss is that to Earth?"

"Look," said Long, "he's been talking about nothing but the drain that Mars, Venus and the Moon put on Earth. This is just another item of loss."

"They'll get their return. We're mining more iron every year."

"And most of it goes right back into Mars. If you can believe his figures, Earth has invested two hundred billion dollars in Mars and received back about five billion dollars' worth of iron. It's put five hundred billion dollars into the Moon and gotten back a little over twenty-five billion dollars of magnesium, titanium, and assorted light metals. It's put fifty billion dollars into Venus and gotten back nothing. And that's what the taxpayers of Earth are really interested in—tax money out; nothing in."

The screen was filled, as he spoke, with diagrams of the Scavengers on the route to Mars; little, grinning caricatures of ships, reaching out wiry, tenuous arms that groped for the tumbling, empty shells, seizing and snaking them in, branding them MARS PROPERTY in glowing letters, then scaling them down to Phobos.

Then it was Hilder again. "They tell us eventually they will return it all to us. Eventually! Once they are a going concern! We don't know when that will be. A century from now? A thousand years? A million? 'Eventually.' Let's take them at their word. Someday they will give us back all our metals. Someday they will grow their own food, use their own power, live their own lives.

"But one thing they can never return. Not in a hundred million years. *Water!*

"Mars has only a trickle of water because it is too small. Venus has no water at all because it is too hot. The Moon has none because it is too hot and too small. So Earth must supply not only drinking water and washing water for the Spacers, water to run their industries, water for the hydroponic factories they claim to be setting up—but even water to throw away by the millions of tons.

"What is the propulsive force that spaceships use? What is it they throw out behind so that they can accelerate forward? Once it was the gases generated from explosives. That was very expensive. Then the proton micropile was invented— a cheap power source that could heat up any liquid until it was a gas under the tremendous pressure. What is the cheapest and most plentiful liquid available? Why, water, of course.

"Each spaceship leaves Earth carrying nearly a million tons—not pounds, *tons*—of water, for the sole purpose of driving it into space so that it may speed up or slow down.

"Our ancestors burned the oil of Earth madly and wilfully. They destroyed its coal recklessly. We despise and condemn them for that, but at least they had this excuse—they thought that when the need arose, substitutes would be found. And they were right. We have our plankton farms and our proton micropiles.

"But there is no substitute for water. None! There never can be. And when our descendants view the desert we will have made of Earth, what excuse will they find for us? When the droughts come and grow——"

Long leaned forward and turned off the set He said, "That bothers me. The damn fool is deliberately——What's the matter?"

Rioz had risen uneasily to his feet. "I ought to be watching the pips."

"The hell with the pips." Long got up likewise, followed Rioz through the narrow corridor, and stood just inside the pilot room. "If Hilder carries this through, if he's got the guts to make a real issue out of it—*Wow!*"

He had seen it too. The pip was a Class A, racing after the outgoing signal like a greyhound after a mechanical rabbit.

Rioz was babbling, "Space was clear, I tell you, *clear*. For Mars' sake, Ted, don't just freeze on me. See if you can spot it visually."

Rioz was working speedily and with an efficiency that was the result of nearly twenty years of scavenging. He had the distance in two minutes. Then, remembering Swenson's experience, he measured the angle of declination and the radial velocity as well.

He yelled at Long, "One point seven six radians. You can't miss it, man."

Long held his breath as he adjusted the vernier. "It's only half a radian off the Sun. It'll only be crescent-lit."

He increased magnification as rapidly as he dared, watching for the one "star" that changed position and grew to have a form, revealing itself to be no star.

"I'm starting, anyway" said Rioz. "We can't wait."

"I've got it. I've got it." Magnification was still too small to give it a definite shape, but the dot Long watched was brightening and dimming rhythmically as the shell rotated and caught sunlight on cross sections of different sizes.

"Hold on."

The first of many fine spurts of steam squirted out of the proper vents, leaving long trails of micro-crystals of ice gleaming mistily in the pale beams of the distant Sun. They thinned out for a hundred miles or more. One spurt, then another, then another, as the Scavenger ship moved out of its stable trajectory and took up a course tangential to that of the shell.

"It's moving like a comet at perihelion!" yelled Rioz. "Those damned Grounder pilots knock the shells off that way on purpose. I'd like to—"

He swore his anger in a frustrated frenzy as he kicked steam backward and backward recklessly, till the hydraulic cushioning of his chair had soughed back a full foot and Long had found himself all but unable to maintain his grip on the guard rail.

"Have a heart," he begged.

But Rioz had his eye on the pips. "If you can't take it, man, stay on Mars!" The steam spurts continued to boom distantly. The radio came to life. Long managed to lean forward through what seemed like molasses and closed contact. It was Swenson, eyes glaring.

Swenson yelled, "Where the hell are you guys going? You'll be in my sector in ten seconds."

Rioz said, "I'm chasing a shell."

"In *my* sector?"

"It started in mine and you're not in position to get it. Shut off that radio, Ted."

The ship thundered through space, a thunder that could be heard only within the hull. And then Rioz cut the engines in stages large enough to make Long flail forward. The sudden silence was more ear-shattering than the noise that had preceded it.

Rioz said, "All right. Let me have the 'scope."

They both watched. The shell was a definite truncated cone now, tumbling with slow solemnity as it passed along among the stars.

"It's a Class A shell, all right," said Rioz with satisfaction. A giant among shells, he thought. It would put them into the black.

Long said, "We've got another pip on the scanner. I think it's Swenson taking after us."

Rioz scarcely gave it a glance. "He won't catch us."

The shell grew larger still, filling the visiplate.

Rioz's hands were on the harpoon lever. He waited, adjusted the angle microscopically twice, played out the length allotment. Then he yanked, tripping the release.

For a moment, nothing happened. Then a metal mesh cable snaked out onto the visiplate, moving toward the shell like a striking cobra. It made contact, but it did not hold. If it had, it would have snapped instantly like a cobweb strand. The shell was turning with a rotational momentum amounting to thousands of tons. What the cable did do was to set up a powerful magnetic field that acted as a brake on the shell.

Another cable and another lashed out. Rioz sent them out in an almost heedless expenditure of energy.

"I'll get this one! By Mars, I'll get this one."

With some two dozen cables stretching between ship and shell, he desisted. The shell's rotational energy, converted by breaking into heat, had raised its temperature to a point where its radiation could be picked up by the ship's meters.

Long said, "Do you want me to put our brand on?"

"Suits me. But you don't have to if you don't want to. It's my watch."

"I don't mind."

Long clambered into his suit and went out the lock. It was the surest sign of his newness to the game that he could count the number of times he had been out in space in a suit. This was the fifth time.

He went out along the nearest cable, hand over hand, feeling the vibration of the mesh against the metal of his mitten.

He burned their serial number in the smooth metal of the shell. There was nothing to oxidize the steel in the emptiness of space. It simply melted and vaporized, condensing some feet away from the energy beam, turning the surface it touched into a gray, powdery dullness.

Long swung back toward the ship.

Inside again, he took off his helmet, white and thick with frost that collected as soon as he had entered.

The first thing he heard was Swenson's voice coming over the radio in this almost unrecognizable rage: ". . . straight to the Commissioner. Damn it, there are rules to this game!"

Rioz sat back, unbothered. "Look, it hit my sector. I was late spotting it and I chased it into yours. You couldn't have gotten it with Mars for a backstop. That's all there is to it—You back, Long?"

He cut contact.

The signal button raged at him, but he paid no attention.

"He's going to the Commissioner?" Long asked.

"Not a chance. He just goes on like that because it breaks the monotony. He doesn't mean anything by it. He knows it's our shell. And how do you like that hunk of stuff, Ted?"

"Pretty good."

"Pretty good? It's terrific! Hold on. I'm setting it swinging."

The side jets spat steam and the ship started a slow rotation about the shell. The shell followed it. In thirty minutes, they were a gigantic bolo spinning in emptiness. Long checked the *Ephemeris* for the position of Deimos.

At a precisely calculated moment, the cables released their magnetic field and the shell went streaking off tangentially in a trajectory that would, in a day or so, bring it within pronging distance of the shell stores on the Martian satellite.

Rioz watched it go. He felt good. He turned to Long. "This is one fine day for us."

"What about Hilder's speech?" asked Long.

"What? Who? Oh, that. Listen, if I had to worry about everything some damned Grounder said, I'd never get any sleep. Forget it."

"I don't think we should forget it."

"You're nuts. Don't bother me about it, will you? Get some sleep instead."

— 4 —

TED LONG found the breadth and height of the city's main thoroughfare exhilarating. It had been two months since the Commissioner had declared a moratorium on scavenging and had pulled all ships out of space, but this feeling of a stretched-out vista had not stopped thrilling Long. Even the thought that the moratorium was called pending a decision on the part of Earth to enforce its new insistence on water economy, by deciding upon a ration limit for scavenging, did not cast him entirely down.

The roof of the avenue was painted a luminous light blue, perhaps as an old-fashioned imitation of Earth's sky. Ted wasn't sure. The walls were lit with the store windows that pierced it.

Off in the distance, over the hum of traffic and the sloughing noise of people's feet passing him, he could hear the intermittent blasting as new channels were being bored into Mars' crust. All his life he remembered such blastings. The ground he walked on had been part of solid, unbroken rock when he was born. The city was growing and would keep on growing— if Earth would only let it.

He turned off at a cross street, narrower, not quite as brilliantly lit, shop windows giving way to apartment houses, each with its row of lights along the front façade. Shoppers and traffic gave way to slower-paced individuals and to squawling youngsters who had as yet evaded the maternal summons to the evening meal.

At the last minute, Long remembered the social amenities and stopped off at a corner water store.

He passed over his canteen. "Fill'er up."

The plump storekeeper unscrewed the cap, cocked an eye into the opening. He shook it a little and let it gurgle. "Not much left," he said cheerfully.

"No," agreed Long.

The storekeeper trickled water in, holding the neck of the canteen close to the hose tip to avoid spillage. The volume gauge whirred. He screwed the cap back on.

Long passed over the coins and took his canteen. It clanked against his hip now with a pleasing heaviness. It would never do to visit a family without a full canteen. Among the boys, it didn't matter. Not as much, anyway.

He entered the hallway of No. 27, climbed a short flight of stairs, and paused with his thumb on the signal.

The sound of voices could be heard quite plainly.

One was a woman's voice, somewhat shrill. "It's all right for you to have your Scavenger friends here, isn't it? I'm supposed to be thankful you manage to get home two months a year. Oh, it's quite enough that you spend a day or two with me. After that, it's the Scavengers again."

"I've been home for a long time now," said a male voice, "and this is business. For Mars' sake, let up, Dora. They'll be here soon."

Long decided to wait a moment before signaling. It might give them a chance to hit a more neutral topic.

"What do I care if they come?" retorted Dora. "Let them hear me. And I'd just as soon the Commissioner kept the moratorium on permanently. You hear me?"

"And what would we live on?" came the male voice hotly. "You tell me that."

"I'll tell you. You can make a decent, honorable living right here on Mars, just like everybody else. I'm the only one in this apartment house that's a Scavenger widow. That's what I am—a widow. I'm worse than a widow, because if I were a widow, I'd at least have a chance to marry someone else——What did you say?"

"Nothing. Nothing at all."

"Oh, I know what you said. Now listen here, Dick Swenson——"

"I only said," cried Swenson, "that now I know why Scavengers usually don't marry."

"You shouldn't have either. I'm tired of having every person in the neighborhood pity me and smirk and ask when you're coming home. Other people can be mining engineers and administrators and even tunnel borers. At least tunnel borers' wives have a decent home life and their children don't grow up like vagabonds. Peter might as well not have a father——"

A thin boy-soprano voice made its way through the door. It was somewhat more distant, as though it were in another room. "Hey, Mom, what's a vagabond?"

Dora's voice rose a notch. "Peter! You keep your mind on your homework."

Swenson said in a low voice, "It's not right to talk this way in front of the kid. What kind of notions will he get about me?"

"Stay home then and teach him better notions."

Peter's voice called out again. "Hey, Mom, I'm going to be a Scavenger when I grow up."

Footsteps sounded rapidly. There was a momentary hiatus in the sounds, then a piercing, "Mom! Hey, Mom! Leggo my ear! What did I do?" and a snuffling silence.

Long seized the chance. He worked the signal vigorously.

Swenson opened the door, brushing down his hair with both hands.

"Hello, Ted," he said in a subdued voice. Then loudly, "Ted's here, Dora. Where's Mario, Ted?"

Long said, "He'll be here in a while."

Dora came bustling out of the next room, a small, dark woman with a pinched nose, and hair, just beginning to show touches of gray, combed off the forehead.

"Hello, Ted. Have you eaten?"

"Quite well, thanks. I haven't interrupted you, have I?"

"Not at all. We finished ages ago. Would you like some coffee?"

"I think so." Ted unslung his canteen and offered it.

"Oh, goodness, that's all right. We've plenty of water."

"I insist."

"Well, then——"

Back into the kitchen she went. Through the swinging door, Long caught a glimpse of dishes sitting in Secoterg, the "waterless cleaner that soaks up and absorbs grease and dirt in a twinkling. One ounce of water will rinse eight square feet of dish surface clean as clean. Buy Secoterg. Secoterg just cleans it right, makes your dishes shiny bright, does away with water waste——"

The tune started whining through his mind and Long crushed it with speech. He said, "How's Pete?"

"Fine, fine. The kid's in the fourth grade now. You know I don't get to see him much. Well, sir, when I came back last time, he looked at me and said . . ."

It went on for a while and wasn't too bad as bright sayings of bright children as told by dull parents go.

The door signal burped and Mario Rioz came in, frowning and red.

Swenson stepped to him quickly. "Listen, don't say anything about shell-snaring. Dora still remembers the time you fingered a Class A shell out of my territory and she's in one of her moods now."

"Who the hell wants to talk about shells?" Rioz slung off a fur-lined jacket, threw it over the back of the chair, and sat down.

Dora came through the swinging door, viewed the newcomer with a synthetic smile, and said, "Hello, Mario. Coffee for you, too?"

"Yeah," he said, reaching automatically for his canteen.

"Just use some more of my water, Dora," said Long quickly. "He'll owe it to me."

"Yeah," said Rioz.

"What's wrong, Mario?" asked Long.

Rioz said heavily, "Go on. Say you told me so. A year ago when Hilder made that speech, you told me so. Say it."

Long shrugged.

Rioz said, "They've set up the quota. Fifteen minutes ago the news came out."

"Well?"

"Fifty thousand tons of water per trip."

"What?" yelled Swenson, burning. "You can't get off Mars with fifty thousand!"

"That's the figure. It's a deliberate piece of gutting. No more scavenging."

Dora came out with the coffee and set it down all around.

"What's all this about no more scavenging?" She sat down very firmly and Swenson looked helpless.

"It seems," said Long, "that they're rationing us at fifty thousand tons and that means we can't make any more trips."

"Well, what of it?" Dora sipped her coffee and smiled gaily. "If you want my opinion, it's a good thing. It's time all you Scavengers found yourselves a nice, steady job here on Mars. I mean it. It's no life to be running all over space——"

"Please, Dora" said Swenson.

Rioz came close to a snort.

Dora raised her eyebrows. "I'm just giving my opinions."

Long said, "Please feel free to do so. But I would like to say something. Fifty thousand is just a detail. We know that Earth—or at least Hilder's party—wants to make political capital out of a campaign for water economy, so we're in a bad hole. We've got to get water somehow or they'll shut us down altogether, right?"

"Well, sure," said Swenson.

"But the question is how, right?"

"If it's only getting water," said Rioz in a sudden gush of words, "there's only one thing to do and you know it. If the Grounders won't give us water, we'll take it. The water doesn't belong to them just because their fathers and grandfathers were too damned sick-yellow ever to leave their fat planet. Water belongs to people wherever they are. We're people and the water's ours, too. We have a right to it."

"How do you propose taking it?" asked Long.

"Easy! They've got oceans of water on Earth. They can't post a guard over every square mile. We can sink down on the night side of the planet any time we want, fill our shells, then get away. How can they stop us?"

"In half a dozen ways, Mario. How do you spot shells in space up to distances of a hundred thousand miles? One thin metal shell in all that space. How? By radar. Do you think there's no radar on Earth? Do you think that if Earth ever gets the notion we're engaged in waterlegging, it won't be simple for them to set up a radar network to spot ships coming in from space?"

Dora broke in indignantly. "I'll tell you one thing, Mario Rioz. My husband isn't going to be part of any raid to get water to keep up his scavenging with."

"It isn't just scavenging," said Mario. "Next they'll be cutting down on everything else. We've got to stop them now."

"But we don't need their water, anyway," said Dora. "We're not the Moon or Venus. We pipe enough water down from the polar caps for all we need. We have a water tap right in this apartment. There's one in every apartment on this block."

Long said, "Home use is the smallest part of it. The mines use water. And what do we do about the hydroponic tanks?"

"That's right," said Swenson. "What about the hydroponic tanks, Dora? They've got to have water and it's about time we arranged to grow our own fresh food instead of having to live on the condensed crud they ship us from Earth.''

"Listen to him,'' said Dora scornfully. "What do you know about fresh food? You've never eaten any.''

"I've eaten more than you think. Do you remember those carrots I picked up once?''

"Well, what was so wonderful about them? If you ask me, good baked protomeal is much better. And healthier, too. It just seems to be the fashion now to be talking fresh vegetables because they're increasing taxes for these hydroponics. Besides, all this will blow over.''

Long said, "I don't think so. Not by itself, anyway. Hilder will probably be the next Coordinator, and then things may really get bad. If they cut down on food shipments, too——''

"Well, then,'' shouted Rioz, "what do we do? I still say take it! Take the water!''

"And I say we can't do that, Mario. Don't you see that what you're suggesting is the Earth way, the Grounder way? You're trying to hold on to the umbilical cord that ties Mars to Earth. Can't you get away from that? Can't you see the Martian way?''

"No, I can't. Suppose you tell me.''

"I will, if you'll listen. When we think about the Solar System, what do we think about? Mercury, Venus, Earth, Moon, Mars, Phobos, and Deimos. There you are—seven bodies, that's all. But that doesn't represent 1 per cent of the Solar System. We Martians are right at the edge of the other 99 per cent. Out there, farther from the Sun, there's unbelievable amounts of water!''

The others stared.

Swenson said uncertainly, "You mean the layers of ice on Jupiter and Saturn?''

"Not that specifically, but it *is* water, you'll admit. A thousand-mile-thick layer of water is a lot of water.''

"But it's all covered up with layers of ammonia or—or something, isn't it?'' asked Swenson. "Besides, we can't land on the major planets.''

"I know that,'' said Long, "but I haven't said that was the answer. The major planets aren't the only objects out there. What about the asteroids and the satellites? Vesta is a two-hundred-mile-diameter asteroid that's hardly more than a chunk of ice. One of the moons of Saturn is mostly ice. How about that?''

Rioz said, "Haven't you ever been in space, Ted?''

"You know I have. Why do you ask?''

"Sure, I know you have, but you still talk like a Grounder. Have you thought of the distances involved? The average asteroid is a hundred twenty million miles from Mars at the closest. That's twice the Venus-Mars hop and you know that hardly any liners do even that in one jump. They usually stop off at Earth or the Moon. After all, how long do you expect anyone to stay in space, man?''

"I don't know. What's your limit?''

"You know the limit. You don't have to ask me. It's six months. That's handbook data. After six months, if you're still in space, you're psychotherapy meat. Right, Dick?''

Swenson nodded.

"And that's just the asteroids,'' Rioz went on. "From Mars to Jupiter is three hundred thirty million miles, and to Saturn it's seven hundred million. How can anyone handle that kind of distance? Suppose you hit standard velocity or, to make it even, say you get up to a good two hundred kilomiles an hour. It would take you—let's see, allowing time for acceleration and deceleration—about six or seven months to get to Jupiter and nearly a year to get to Saturn. Of course, you could hike the speed to a million miles an hour, theoretically, but where would you get the water to do that?''

"Gee," said a small voice attached to a smutty nose and round eyes. "Saturn!''

Dora whirled in her chair. "Peter, march right back into your room!''

"Aw, Ma.''

"Don't 'Aw, Ma' me.'' She began to get out of the chair, and Peter scuttled away.

Swenson said, "Say, Dora, why don't you keep him company for a while? It's hard to keep his mind on homework if we're all out here talking.''

Dora sniffed obstinately and stayed put. "I'll sit right here until I find out what Ted Long is thinking of. I tell you right now I don't like the sound of it.''

Swenson said nervously, "Well, never mind Jupiter and Saturn. I'm sure Ted isn't figuring on that. But what about Vesta? We could make it in ten or twelve weeks there and the same back. And two hundred miles in diameter. That's four million cubic miles of ice!''

"So what?'' said Rioz. "What do we do on Vesta? Quarry the ice? Set up mining machinery? Say, do you know how long that would take?''

Long said, "I'm talking about Saturn, not Vesta.''

Rioz addressed an unseen audience. "I tell him seven hundred million miles and he keeps on talking.''

"All right," said Long, "suppose you tell me how you know we can only stay in space six months, Mario?''

"It's common knowledge, damn it.''

"Because it's in the *Handbook of Space Flight*. It's data compiled by Earth scientists from experience with Earth pilots and spacemen. You're still thinking Grounder style. You won't think the Martian way.''

"A Martian may be a Martian, but he's still a man.''

"But how can you be so blind? How many times have you fellows been out for over six months without a break?''

Rioz said, "That's different.''

"Because you're Martians? Because you're professional Scavengers?''

"No. Because we're not on a flight. We can put back for Mars any time we want to.''

"But you *don't* want to. That's my point. Earthmen have tremendous ships with libraries of films, with a crew of fifteen plus passengers. Still, they can only stay out six months maximum. Martian Scavengers have a two-room ship with only one partner. But we can stick it out more than six months.''

Dora said, "I suppose you want to stay in a ship for a year and go to Saturn.''

"Why not, Dora?'' said Long. "We can do it. Don't you see we can? Earthmen can't. They've got a real world. They've got open sky and fresh food, all the air and water they want. Getting into a ship is a terrible change for them. More than six months is too much for them for that very reason. Martians are different. We've been living on a ship our entire lives.''

"That's all Mars is—a ship. It's just a big ship forty-five hundred miles across with one tiny room in it occupied by fifty thousand people. It's closed in like a ship. We breathe packaged air and drink packaged water, which we repurify over and over. We eat the same food rations we eat aboard ship. When we get into a ship, it's the same thing we've known all our lives. W can stand it for a lot more than a year if we have to."

Dora said, "Dick, too?"

"We all can."

"Well, Dick can't. It's all very well for you, Ted Long, and this shell stealer here, this Mario, to talk about jaunting off for a year. You're not married. Dick is. He has a wife and he has a child and that's enough for him. He can just get a regular job right here on Mars. Why, my goodness, suppose you go to Saturn and find there's no water there. How'll you get back? Even if you had water left, you'd be out of food. It's the most ridiculous thing I ever heard of."

"No. Now listen," said Long tightly. "I've thought this thing out. I've talked to Commissioner Sankov and he'll help. But we've got to have ships and men. I can't get them. The men won't listen to me. I'm green. You two are known and respected. You're veterans. If you back me, even if you don't go yourselves, if you'll just help me sell this thing to the rest, get volunteers——"

"First," said Rioz grumpily, "you'll have to do a lot more explaining. Once we get to Saturn, where's the water?"

"That's the beauty of it," said Long. "That's why it's got to be Saturn. The water there is just floating around in space for the taking."

— 5 —

WHEN HAMISH Sankov had come to Mars, there was no such thing as a native Martian. Now there were two-hundred-odd babies whose grandfathers had been born on Mars—native in the third generation.

When he had come as a boy in his teens, Mars had been scarcely more than a huddle of grounded spaceships connected by sealed underground tunnels. Through the years, he had seen buildings grow and burrow widely, thrusting blunt snouts up into the thin, unbreathable atmosphere. He had seen huge storage depots spring up into which spaceships and their loads could be swallowed whole. He had seen the mines grow from nothing to a huge gouge in the Martian crust, while the population of Mars grew from fifty to fifty thousand.

It made him feel old, these long memories—they and the even dimmer memories induced by the presence of this Earthman before him. His visitor brought up those long-forgotten scraps of thought about a soft-warm world that was as kind and gentle to mankind as the mother's womb.

The Earthman seemed fresh from that womb. Not very tall, not very lean; in fact, distinctly plump. Dark hair with a neat little wave in it, a neat little mustache, and neatly scrubbed skin. His clothing was right in style and as fresh and neatly turned as plastek could be.

Sankov's own clothes were of Martian manufacture, serviceable and clean, but many years behind the times. His face was craggy and lined, his hair was pure white, and his Adam's apple wobbled when he talked.

The Earthman was Myron Digby, member of Earth's General Assembly. Sankov was Martian Commissioner.

Sankov said, "This all hits us hard, Assemblyman."

"It's hit most of us hard, too, Commissioner."

"Uh-huh. Can't honestly say then that I can make it out. Of course, you understand, I don't make out that I can understand Earth ways, for all that I was born there. Mars is a hard place to live, Assemblyman, and you have to understand that. It takes a lot of shipping space just to bring us food, water, and raw materials so we can live. There's not much room left for books and news films. Even video programs can't reach Mars, except for about a month when Earth is in conjunction, and even then nobody has much time to listen.

"My office gets a weekly summary film from Planetary Press. Generally, I don't have time to pay attention to it. Maybe you'd call us provincial, and you'd be right. When something like this happens, all we can do is kind of helplessly look at each other."

Digby said slowly, "You can't mean that your people on Mars haven't heard of Hilder's anti-Waster campaign."

"No, can't exactly say that. There's a young Scavenger, son of a good friend of mine who died in space"—Sankov scratched the side of his neck doubtfully—"who makes a hobby out of reading up on Earth history and things like that. He catches video broadcasts when he's out in space and he listened to this man Hilder. Near as I can make out, that was the first talk Hilder made about Wasters.

"The young fellow came to me with that. Naturally, I didn't take him very serious. I kept an eye on the Planetary Press films for a while after that, but there wasn't much mention of Hilder and what there was made him out to look pretty funny."

"Yes, Commissioner," said Digby, "it all seemed quite a joke when it started."

Sankov stretched out a pair of long legs to one side of his desk and crossed them at the ankles. "Seems to me it's still pretty much of a joke. What's his argument? We're using up water. Has he tried looking at some figures? I got them all here. Had them brought to me when this committee arrived.

"Seems that Earth has four hundred million cubic miles of water in its oceans and each cubic mile weighs four and a half billion tons. That's a lot of water. Now we use some of that heap in space flight. Most of the thrust is inside Earth's gravitational field, and that means the water thrown out finds its way back to the oceans. Hilder doesn't figure that in. When he says a million tons of water is used up per flight, he's a liar. It's less than a hundred thousand tons.

"Suppose, now, we have fifty thousand flights a year. We don't, of course; not even fifteen hundred. But let's say there are fifty thousand. I figure there's going to be considerable expansion as time goes on. With fifty thousand flights, one cubic mile of water would be lost to space each year. That means that in a million years, Earth would lose *one quarter of 1 per cent* of its total water supply!"

Digby spread his hands, palms upward, and let them drop. "Commissioner, Interplanetary Alloys had used figures like that in their campaign against Hilder, but you can't fight a tremendous, emotion-filled drive with cold mathematics. This man Hilder has invented a name, 'Wasters.' Slowly he has built this name up into a gigantic conspiracy; a gang of brutal, profitseeking wretches raping Earth for their own immediate benefit.

"He has accused the government of being riddled with them, the Assembly of being dominated by them, the press of being owned by them. None of this, unfortunately, seems ridiculous to the average man. He knows all too well what selfish men can do to Earth's resources. He knows what happened to Earth's oil during the Time of Troubles, for instance, and the way topsoil was ruined.

"When a farmer experiences a drought, he doesn't care that the amount of water lost in space flight isn't a droplet in a fog as far as Earth's over-all water supply is concerned. Hilder has given him something to blame and that's the strongest possible consolation for disaster. He isn't going to give that up for a diet of figures."

Sankov said, "That's where I get puzzled. Maybe it's because I don't know how things work on Earth, but it seems to me that there aren't just droughty farmers there. As near as I could make out from the news summaries, these Hilder people are a minority. Why is it Earth goes along with a few farmers and some crackpots that egg them on?"

"Because, Commissioner, there are such things as worried human beings. The steel industry sees that an era of space flight will stress increasingly the light, nonferrous alloys. The various miners' unions worry about extraterrestrial competition. Any Earthman who can't get aluminum to build a prefab is certain that it is because the aluminum is going to Mars. I know a professor of archaeology who's an anti-Waster because he can't get a government grant to cover his excavations. He's convinced that all government money is going into rocketry research and space medicine and he resents it."

Sankov said, "That doesn't sound like Earth people are much different from us here on Mars. But what about the General Assembly? Why do they have to go along with Hilder?"

Digby smiled sourly. "Politics isn't pleasant to explain. Hilder introduced this bill to set up a committee to investigate waste in space flight. Maybe three fourths or more of the General Assembly was against such an investigation as an intolerable and useless extension of bureaucracy—which it is. But then how could any legislator be against a mere investigation of waste? It would sound as though he had something to fear or to conceal. It would sound as though he were himself profiting from waste. Hilder is not in the least afraid of making such accusations, and whether true or not, they would be a powerful factor with the voters in the next election. The bill passed.

"And then there came the question of appointing the members of the committee. Those who were against Hilder shied away from membership, which would have meant decisions that would be continually embarrassing. Remaining on the side lines would make that one that much less a target for Hilder. The result is that I am the only member of the committee who is outspokenly anti-Hilder and it may cost me reelection."

Sankov said, "I'd be sorry to hear that, Assemblyman. It looks as though Mars didn't have as many friends as we thought we had. We wouldn't like to lose one. But if Hilder wins out, what's he after, anyway?"

"I should think," said Digby, "that that is obvious. He wants to be the next Global Co-ordinator."

"Think he'll make it?"

"If nothing happens to him, he will."

"And then what? Will he drop this Waster campaign then?"

"I can't say. I don't know if he's laid his plans past the Coordinacy. Still, if you want my guess, he couldn't abandon the campaign and maintain his popularity. It's gotten out of hand.''

Sankov scratched the side of his neck. ''All right. In that case, I'll ask you for some advice. What can we folks on Mars do? You know Earth. You know the situation. We don't. Tell us what to do.''

Digby rose and stepped to the window. He looked out upon the low domes of other buildings; red, rocky, completely desolate plain in between; a purple sky and a shrunken sun.

He said, without turning, ''Do you people really like it on Mars?''

Sankov smiled. ''Most of us don't exactly know any other world, Assemblyman. Seems to me Earth would be something queer and uncomfortable to them.''

''But wouldn't Martians get used to it? Earth isn't hard to take after this. Wouldn't your people learn to enjoy the privilege of breathing air under an open sky? You once lived on Earth. You remember what it was like.''

''I sort of remember. Still, it doesn't seem to be easy to explain. Earth is just there. It fits people and people fit it. People take Earth the way they find it. Mars is different. It's sort of raw and doesn't fit people. People got to make something out of it. They got to *build* a world, and not take what they find. Mars isn't much yet, but we're building, and when we're finished, we're going to have just what we like. It's sort of a great feeling to know you're building a world. Earth would be kind of unexciting after that.''

The Assemblyman said, ''Surely the ordinary Martian isn't such a philosopher that he's content to live this terribly hard life for the sake of a future that must be hundreds of generations away.''

''No-o, not just like that.'' Sankov put his right ankle on his left knee and cradled it as he spoke. ''Like I said, Martians are a lot like Earthmen, which means they're sort of human beings, and human beings don't go in for philosophy much. Just the same, there's something to living in a growing world, whether you think about it much or not.

''My father used to send me letters when I first came to Mars. He was an accountant and he just sort of stayed an accountant. Earth wasn't much different when he died from what it was when he was born. He didn't see anything happen. Every day was like every other day, and living was just a way of passing time until he died.

''On Mars, it's different. Every day there's something new—the city's bigger, the ventilation system gets another kick, the water lines from the poles get slicked up. Right now, we're planning to set up a news-film association of our own. We're going to call it Mars Press. If you haven't lived when things are growing all about you, you'll never understand how wonderful it feels.

''No, Assemblyman, Mars is hard and tough and Earth is a lot more comfortable, but seems to me if you take our boys to Earth, they'll be unhappy. They probably wouldn't be able to figure out why, most of them, but they'd feel lost; lost and useless. Seems to me lots of them would never make the adjustment.''

Digby turned away from the window and the smooth, pink skin of his forehead was creased into a frown. ''In that case, Commissioner, I am sorry for you. For all of you.''

''Why?''

''Because I don't think there's anything your people on Mars can do. Or the people on the Moon or Venus. It won't happen now; maybe it won't happen for a year or two, or even for five years. But pretty soon you'll all have to come back to Earth, unless——''

Sankov's white eyebrows bent low over his eyes. "Well?"

"Unless you can find another source of water besides the planet Earth."

Sankov shook his head. "Don't seem likely, does it?"

"Not very."

"And except for that, seems to you there's no chance?"

"None at all."

Digby said that and left, and Sankov stared for a long time at nothing before he punched a combination of the local communiline.

After a while, Ted Long looked out at him.

Sankov said, "You were right, son. There's nothing they can do. Even the ones that mean well see no way out. How did you know?"

"Commissioner," said Long, "when you've read all you can about the Time of Troubles, particularly about the twentieth century, nothing political can come as a real suprise."

"Well, maybe. Anyway, son, Assemblyman Digby is sorry for us, quite a piece sorry, you might say, but that's all. He says we'll have to leave Mars—or get water somewhere else. Only he thinks we can't get water somewhere else."

"You know we can, don't you, Commissioner?"

"I know we *might,* son. It's a terrible risk."

"If I find enough volunteers, the risk is our business."

"How is it going?

"Not bad. Some of the boys are on my side right now. I talked Mario Rioz into it, for instance, and you know he's one of the best."

"That's just it—the volunteers will be the best men we have. I hate to allow it."

"If we get back, it will be worth it."

"If! It's a big word, son."

"And a big thing we're trying to do."

"Well, I gave my word that if there was no help on Earth, I'll see that the Phobos water hole lets you have all the water you'll need. Good luck."

— 6 —

HALF A million miles above Saturn, Mario Rioz was cradled on nothing and sleep was delicious. He came out of it slowly and for a while, alone in his suit, he counted the stars and traced lines from one to another.

At first, as the weeks flew past, it was scavenging all over again, except for the gnawing feeling that every minute meant an additional number of thousands of miles away from all humanity. That made it worse.

They had aimed high to pass out of the ecliptic while moving through the Asteroid Belt. That had used up water and had probably been unnecessary. Although tens of thousands of worldlets look as thick as vermin in two-dimensional projection upon a photographic plate, they are nevertheless scattered so thinly through the quadrillions of cubic miles that make up their conglomerate orbit that only the most ridiculous of coincidences would have brought about a collision.

Still, they passed over the Belt and someone calculated the chances of collision with a fragment of matter large enough to do damage. The value was so low, so impossibly low, that it was perhaps inevitable that the notion of the "space-float" should occur to someone.

The days were long and many, space was empty, only one man was needed at the controls at any one time. The thought was a natural.

First, it was a particularly daring one who ventured out for fifteen minutes or so. Then another who tried half an hour. Eventually, before the asteroids were entirely behind, each ship regularly had its off-watch member suspended in space at the end of a cable.

It was easy enough. The cable, one of those intended for operations at the conclusion of their journey, was magnetically attached at both ends, one to the space suit to start with. Then you clambered out the lock onto the ship's hull and attached the other end there. You paused awhile, clinging to the metal skin by the electromagnets in your boots. Then you neutralized those and made the slightest muscular effort.

Slowly, ever so slowly, you lifted from the ship and even more slowly the ship's larger mass moved an equivalently shorter distance downward. You floated incredibly, weightlessly, in solid, speckled black. When the ship had moved far enough away from you, your gauntleted hand, which kept touch upon the cable, tightened its grip slightly. Too tightly, and you would begin moving back toward the ship and it toward you. Just tightly enough, and friction would halt you. Because your motion was equivalent to that of the ship, it seemed as motionless below you as though it had been painted against an impossible background while the cable between you hung in coils that had no reason to straighten out.

It was a half-ship to your eye. One half was lit by the light of the feeble sun, which was still too bright to look at directly without the heavy protection of the polarized space-suit visor. The other half was black on black, invisible.

Space closed in and it was like sleep. Your suit was warm, it renewed its air automatically, it had food and drink in special containers from which it could be sucked with a minimal motion of the head, it took care of wastes appropriately. Most of all, more than anything else, there was the delightful euphoria of weightlessness.

You never felt so well in your life. The days stopped being too long, they weren't long enough, and there weren't enough of them.

They had passed Jupiter's orbit at a spot some 30 degrees from its then position. For months, it was the brightest object in the sky, always excepting the glowing white pea that was the sun. At its brightest, some of the Scavengers insisted they could make out Jupiter as a tiny sphere, one side squashed out of true by the night shadow.

Then over a period of additional months it faded, while another dot of light grew until it was brighter than Jupiter. It was Saturn, first as a dot of brilliance, then as an oval, glowing splotch.

("Why oval?" someone asked, and after a while, someone else said, "The rings, of course," and it was obvious.)

Everyone space-floated at all possible times toward the end, watching Saturn incessantly.

("Hey, you jerk, come on back in, damn it. You're on duty." "Who's on duty? I've got fifteen minutes more by my watch." "You set your watch back. Besides, I gave you twenty minutes yesterday." "You wouldn't give two minutes to your grandmother." "Come on in, damn it, or I'm coming out anyway." "All right, I'm coming. Holy howlers, what a racket over a lousy minute." But no quarrel could possibly be serious, not in space. It felt too good.)

Saturn grew until at last it rivaled and then surpassed the Sun. The rings, set at a broad angle to their trajectory of approach, swept grandly about the planet, only a small portion being eclipsed. Then, as they approached, the span of the rings grew still wider, yet narrower as the angle of approach constantly decreased.

The larger moons showed up in the surrounding sky like serene fireflies.

Mario Rioz was glad he was awake so that he could watch again.

Saturn filled half the sky, streaked with orange, the night shadow cutting it fuzzily nearly one quarter of the way in from the right. Two round little dots in the brightness were shadows of two of the moons. To the left and behind him (he could look over his left shoulder to see, and as he did so, the rest of his body inched slightly to the right to conserve angular momentum) was the white diamond of the Sun.

Most of all he liked to watch the rings. At the left, they emerged from behind Saturn, a tight, bright triple band of orange light. At the right, their beginnings were hidden in the night shadow, but showed up closer and broader. They widened as they came, like the flare of a horn, growing hazier as they approached, until, while the eye followed them, they seemed to fill the sky and lose themselves.

From the position of the Scavenger fleet just inside the outer rim of the outermost ring, the rings broke up and assumed their true identity as a phenomenal cluster of solid fragments rather than the tight, solid band of light they seemed.

Below him, or rather in the direction his feet pointed, some twenty miles away, was one of the ring fragments. It looked like a large, irregular splotch, marring the symmetry of space, three quarters in brightness and the night shadow cutting it like a knife. Other fragments were farther off, sparkling like star dust, dimmer and thicker, until, as you followed them down, they became rings once more.

The fragments were motionless, but that was only because the ships had taken up an orbit about Saturn equivalent to that of the outer edge of the rings.

The day before, Rioz reflected, he had been on that nearest fragment, working along with more than a score of others to mold it into the desired shape. Tomorrow he would be at it again.

Today—today he was space-floating.

"Mario?" The voice that broke upon his earphones was questioning.

Momentarily Rioz was flooded with annoyance. Damn it, he wasn't in the mood for company.

"Speaking," he said.

"I thought I had your ship spotted. How are you?"

"Fine. That you, Ted?"

"That's right," said Long.

"Anything wrong on the fragment?"

"Nothing. I'm out here floating."

"You?"

"It gets me, too, occasionally. Beautiful, isn't it?"

"Nice," agreed Rioz.

"You know, I've read Earth books——"

"Grounder books, you mean." Rioz yawned and found it difficult under the circumstances to use the expression with the proper amount of resentment.

"—and sometimes I read descriptions of people lying on grass," continued Long. "You know that green stuff like thin, long pieces of paper they have all over the ground down there, and they look up at the blue sky with clouds in it. Did you ever see any films of that?"

"Sure. It didn't attract me. It looked cold."

"I suppose it isn't, though. After all, Earth is quite close to the Sun, and they say their atmosphere is thick enough to hold the heat. I must admit that personally I would hate to be caught under open sky with nothing on but clothes. Still, I imagine they like it."

"Grounders are nuts!"

"They talk about the trees, big brown stalks, and the winds, air movements, you know."

"You mean drafts. They can keep that, too."

"It doesn't matter. The point is they describe it beautifully, almost passionately. Many times I've wondered, 'What's it really like? Will I ever feel it or is this something only Earthmen can possibly feel?' I've felt so often that I was missing something vital. Now I know what it must be like. It's this. Complete peace in the middle of a beauty-drenched universe."

Rioz said, "They wouldn't like it. The Grounders, I mean. They're so used to their own lousy little world they wouldn't appreciate what it's like to float and look down on Saturn." He flipped his body slightly and began swaying back and forth about his center of mass, slowly, soothingly.

Long said, "Yes, I think so too. They're slaves to their planet. Even if they come to Mars, it will only be their children that are free. There'll be starships someday; great, huge things that can carry thousands of people and maintain their self-contained equilibrium for decades, maybe centuries. Mankind will spread through the whole Galaxy. But people will have to live their lives out on shipboard until new methods of interstellar travel are developed, so it will be Martians, not planet-bound Earthmen, who will colonize the Universe. That's inevitable. It's got to be. It's the Martian Way."

But Rioz made no answer. He had dropped off to sleep again, rocking and swaying gently, half a million miles above Saturn.

— 7 —

THE WORK shift of the ring fragment was the tail of the coin. The weightlessness, peace, and privacy of the space-float gave place to something that had neither peace nor privacy. Even the weightlessness, which continued, became more a purgatory than a paradise under the new conditions.

Try to manipulate an ordinarily non-portable heat projector. It could be lifted despite the fact that it was six feet high and wide and almost solid metal, since it weighed only a fraction of an ounce. But its inertia was exactly what it had always been, which meant that if it wasn't moved into position very slowly, it would just keep on going, taking you with it. Then you would have to hike the pseudo-grav field of your suit and come down with a jar.

Keralski had hiked the field a little too high and he came down a little too roughly, with the projector coming down with him at a dangerous angle. His crushed ankle had been the first casualty of the expedition.

Rioz was swearing fluently and nearly continuously. He continued to have the impulse to drag the back of his hand across his forehead in order to wipe away the accumulating sweat. The few times that he had succumbed to the impulse, metal had met silicone with a clash that rang loudly inside his suit, but served no useful purpose. The desiccators within the suit were sucking at maximum and, of course, recovering the water and restoring ion-exchanged liquid, containing a careful proportion of salt, into the appropriate receptacle.

Rioz yelled, "Damn it, Dick, wait till I give the word, will you?"

And Swenson's voice rang in his ears, "Well, how long am I supposed to sit here?"

"Till I say," replied Rioz.

He strengthened pseudo-grav and lifted the projector a bit. He released pseudo-grav, insuring that the projector would stay in place for minutes even if he withdrew support altogether. He kicked the cable out of the way (it stretched beyond the close "horizon" to a power source that was out of sight) and touched the release.

The material of which the fragment was composed bubbled and vanished under its touch. A section of the lip of the tremendous cavity he had already carved into its substance melted away and a roughness in its contour had disappeared.

"Try it now," called Rioz.

Swenson was in the ship that was hovering nearly over Rioz's head.

Swenson called, "All clear?"

"I told you to go ahead."

It was a feeble flicker of steam that issued from one of the ship's forward vents. The ship drifted down toward the ring fragment. Another flicker adjusted a tendency to drift sidewise. It came down straight.

A third flicker to the rear slowed it to a feather rate.

Rioz watched tensely. "Keep her coming. You'll make it. You'll make it."

The rear of the ship entered the hole, nearly filling it. The bellying walls came closer and closer to its rim. There was a grinding vibration as the ship's motion halted.

It was Swenson's turn to curse. "It doesn't fit," he said.

Rioz threw the projector groundward in a passion and went flailing up into space. The projector kicked up a white crystal-line dust all about it, and when Rioz came down under pseudo-grav, he did the same.

He said, "You went in on the bias, you dumb Grounder."

"I hit it level, you dirt-eating farmer."

Backward-pointing side jets of the ship were blasting more strongly than before, and Rioz hopped to get out of the way.

The ship scraped up from the pit, then shot into space half a mile before forward jets could bring it to a halt.

Swenson said tensely, "We'll spring half a dozen plates if we do this once again. Get it right, will you?"

"I'll get it right. Don't worry about it. Just you come in right."

Rioz jumped upward and allowed himself to climb three hundred yards to get an over-all look at the cavity. The gouge marks of the ship were plain enough. They were concentrated at one point halfway down the pit. He would get that.

It began to melt outward under the blaze of the projector.

Half an hour later the ship snuggled neatly into its cavity, and Swenson, wearing his space suit, emerged to join Rioz.

Swenson said, "If you want to step in and climb out of the suit, I'll take care of the icing."

"It's all right," said Rioz. "I'd just as soon sit here and watch Saturn."

He sat down at the lip of the pit. There was a six-foot gap between it and the ship. In some places about the circle, it was two feet; in a few places, even merely a matter of inches. You couldn't expect a better fit out of handwork. The final adjustment would be made by steaming ice gently and letting it freeze into the cavity between the lip and the ship.

Saturn moved visibly across the sky, its vast bulk inching below the horizon.

Rioz said, "How many ships are left to put in place?"

Swenson said, "Last I heard, it was eleven. We're in now, so that means only ten. Seven of the ones that are placed are iced in. Two or three are dismantled."

"We're coming along fine."

"There's plenty to do yet. Don't forget the main jets at the other end. And cables and the power lines. Sometimes I wonder if we'll make it. On the way out, it didn't bother me so much, but just now I was sitting at the controls and I was saying, 'We won't make it. We'll sit out here and starve and die with nothing but Saturn over us.' It makes me feel——"

He didn't explain how it made him feel. He just sat there.

Rioz said, "You think too damn much."

"It's different with you," said Swenson. "I keep thinking of Pete—and Dora."

"What for? She said you could go, didn't she? The Commissioner gave her that talk on patriotism and how you'd be a hero and set for life once you got back, and she said you could go. You didn't sneak out the way Adams did."

"Adams is different. That wife of his should have been shot when she was born. Some women can make hell for a guy, can't they? She didn't want him to go—but she'd probably rather he didn't come back if she can get his settlement pay."

"What's your kick, then? Dora wants you back, doesn't she?"

Swenson sighed. "I never treated her right."

"You turned over your pay, it seems to me. I wouldn't do that for any woman. Money for value received, not a cent more."

"Money isn't it. I get to thinking out here. A woman likes company. A kid needs his father. What am I doing 'way out here?"

"Getting set to go home."

"Ah-h, you don't understand."

— 8 —

TED LONG wandered over the ridged surface of the ring fragment with his spirits as icy as the ground he walked on. It had all seemed perfectly logical back on Mars, but that was Mars. He had worked it out carefully in his mind in perfectly reasonable steps. He could still remember exactly how it went.

It didn't take a ton of water to move a ton of ship. It was not mass equals mass, but mass times velocity equals mass times velocity. It didn't matter, in other words, whether you shot out a ton of water at a mile a second or a hundred pounds of water at twenty miles a second. You got the same final velocity out of the ship.

That meant the jet nozzles had to be made narrower and the steam hotter. But then the drawbacks appeared. The narrower the nozzle, the more energy was lost in friction and turbulence. The hotter the steam, the more refractory the nozzle had to be and the shorter its life. The limit in that direction was quickly reached.

Then, since a given weight of water could move considerably more than its own weight under the narrow-nozzle conditions, it paid to be big. The bigger the water-storage space, the larger the size of the actual travel-head, even in proportion. So they started to make liners heavier and bigger. But then the larger the shell, the heavier the bracings, the more difficult the weldings, the more exacting the engineering requirements. At the moment, the limit in that direction had been reached also.

And then he had put his finger on what had seemed to him to be the basic flaw—the original unswervable conception that the fuel had to be placed *inside* the ship; the metal had to be built to encircle a million tons of water.

Why? Water did not have to be water. It could be ice, and ice could be shaped. Holes could be melted into it. Travelheads and jets could be fitted into it. Cables could hold travelheads and jets stiffly together under the influence of magnetic field-force grips.

Long felt the trembling of the ground he walked on. He was at the head of the fragment. A dozen ships were blasting in and out of sheaths carved in its substance, and the fragment shuddered under the continuing impact.

The ice didn't have to be quarried. It existed in proper chunks in the rings of Saturn. That's all the rings were—pieces of nearly pure ice, circling Saturn. So spectroscopy stated and so it had turned out to be. He was standing on one such piece now, over two miles long, nearly one mile thick. It was almost a half a billion tons of water, all in one piece, and he was standing on it.

But now he was face to face with the realities of life. He had never told the men just how quickly he had expected to set up the fragment as a ship, but in his heart, he had imagined it would be two days. It was a week now and he didn't dare to estimate the remaining time. He no longer even had any confidence that the task was a possible one. Would they be able to control jets with enough delicacy through leads slung across two miles of ice to manipulate out of Saturn's dragging gravity?

Drinking water was low, though they could always distill more out of the ice. Still, the food stores were not in a good way either.

He paused, looked up into the sky, eyes straining. *Was* the object growing

345

larger? He ought to measure its distance. Actually, he lacked the spirit to add that trouble to the others. His mind slid back to greater immediacies.

Morale, at least, was high. The men seemed to enjoy being out Saturn-way. They were the first humans to penetrate this far, the first to pass the asteroids, the first to see Jupiter like a glowing pebble to the naked eye, the first to see Saturn—like that.

He didn't think fifty practical, case-hardened, shell-snatching Scavengers would take time to feel that sort of emotion But they did. And they were proud.

Two men and a half-buried ship slid up the moving horizon as he walked.

He called crisply, "Hello, there!"

Rioz answered, "That you, Ted?"

"You bet. Is that Dick with you?"

"Sure. Come on, sit down. We were just getting ready to ice in and we were looking for an excuse to delay."

"I'm not," said Swenson promptly. "When will we be leaving, Ted?"

"As soon as we get through. That's no answer, is it?"

Swenson said dispiritedly, "I suppose there isn't any other answer."

Long looked up, staring at the irregular bright splotch in the sky.

Rioz followed his glance. "What's the matter?"

For a moment, Long did not reply. The sky was black otherwise and the ring fragments were an orange dust against it. Saturn was more than three fourths below the horizon and the rings were going with it. Half a mile away a ship bounded past the icy rim of the planetoid into the sky, was orange-lit by Saturn-light, and sank down again.

The ground trembled gently.

Rioz said, "Something bothering you about the Shadow?"

They called it that. It was the nearest fragment of the rings, quite close considering that they were at the outer rim of the rings, where the pieces spread themselves relatively thin. It was perhaps twenty miles off, a jagged mountain, its shape clearly visible.

"How does it look to you?" asked Long.

Rioz shrugged. "Okay, I guess. I don't see anything wrong."

"Doesn't it seem to be getting larger?"

"Why should it?"

"Well, doesn't it?" Long insisted.

Rioz and Swenson stared at it thoughtfully.

"It does look bigger," said Swenson.

"You're just putting the notion into our minds," Rioz argued. "If it were getting bigger, it would be coming closer."

"What's impossible about that?"

"These things are on stable orbits."

"They were when we came here," said Long. "There, did you feel that?"

The ground had trembled again.

Long said, "We've been blasting this thing for a week now. First, twenty-five ships landed on it, which changed its momentum right there. Not much, of course. Then we've been melting parts of it away and our ships have been blasting in and out of it—all at one end, too. In a week, we may have changed its orbit just a bit. The two fragments, this one and the Shadow, might be converging."

"It's got plenty of room to miss us in." Rioz watched it thoughtfully.
"Besides, if we can't even tell for sure that it's getting bigger, how quickly can
it be moving? Relative to us, I mean."

"It doesn't have to be moving quickly. Its momentum is as large as ours,
so that, however gently it hits, we'll be nudged completely out of our orbit,
maybe in toward Saturn, where we don't want to go. As a matter of fact, ice
has a very low tensile strength, so that both planetoids might break up into
gravel."

Swenson rose to his feet. "Damn it, if I can tell how a shell is moving a
thousand miles away, I can tell what a mountain is doing twenty miles away."
He turned toward the ship.

Long didn't stop him.

Rioz said, "There's a nervous guy."

The neighboring planetoid rose to zenith, passed overhead, began sinking.
Twenty minutes later, the horizon opposite that portion behind which Saturn had
disappeared burst into orange flame as its bulk began lifting again.

Rioz called into his radio, "Hey, Dick, are you dead in there?"

"I'm checking," came the muffled response.

"Is it moving?" asked Long.

"Yes."

"Toward us?"

There was a pause. Swenson's voice was a sick one. "On the nose, Ted.
Intersection of orbits will take place in three days."

"You're crazy!" yelled Rioz.

"I checked four times," said Swenson.

Long thought blankly, What do we do now?

— 9 —

SOME OF the men were having trouble with the cables. They had to be laid
precisely; their geometry had to be very nearly perfect for the magnetic field to
attain maximum strength. In space, or even in air, it wouldn't have mattered.
The cables would have lined up automatically once the juice went on.

Here it was different. A gouge had to be plowed along the planetoid's surface
and into it the cable had to be laid. If it were not lined up within a few minutes
of arc of the calculated direction, a torque would be applied to the entire
planetoid, with consequent loss of energy, none of which could be spared. The
gouges then had to be redriven, the cables shifted and iced into the new
positions.

The men plodded wearily through the routine.

And then the word reached them:

"All hands to the jets!"

Scavengers could not be said to be the type that took kindly to discipline. It
was a grumbling, growling, muttering group that set about disassembling the jets
of the ships that yet remained intact, carrying them to the tail end of the

planetoid, grubbing them into position, and stringing the leads along the surface.

It was almost twenty-four hours before one of them looked into the sky and said, "Holy jeepers!" followed by something less printable.

His neighbor looked and said, "I'll be damned!"

Once they noticed, all did. It became the most astonishing fact in the Universe.

"Look at the Shadow!"

It was spreading across the sky like an infected wound. Men looked at it, found it had doubled its size, wondered why they hadn't noticed that sooner.

Work came to a virtual halt. They beseiged Ted Long.

He said, "We can't leave. We don't have the fuel to see us back to Mars and we don't have the equipment to capture another planetoid. So we've got to stay. Now the Shadow is creeping in on us because our blasting has thrown us out of orbit. We've got to change that by continuing the blasting. Since we can't blast the front end any more without endangering the ship we're building, let's try another way."

They went back to work on the jets with a furious energy that received impetus every half hour when the Shadow rose again over the horizon, bigger and more menacing than before.

Long had no assurance that it would work. Even if the jets would respond to the distant controls, even if the supply of water, which depended upon a storage chamber opening directly into the icy body of the planetoid, with built-in heat projectors steaming the propulsive fluid directly into the driving cells, were adequate, there was still no certainty that the body of the planetoid without a magnetic cable sheathing would hold together under the enormously disruptive stresses.

"Ready!" came the signal in Long's receiver.

Long called, "Ready!" and depressed the contact.

The vibration grew about him. The star field in the visiplate trembled.

In the rearview, there was a distant gleaming spume of swiftly moving ice crystals.

"It's blowing!" was the cry.

It kept on blowing. Long dared not stop. For six hours, it blew, hissing, bubbling, steaming into space; the body of the planetoid converted to vapor and hurled away.

The Shadow came closer until men did nothing but stare at the mountain in the sky, surpassing Saturn itself in spectacularity. Its every groove and valley was a plain scar upon its face. But when it passed through the planetoid's orbit, it crossed more than half a mile behind its then position.

The steam jet ceased.

Long bent in his seat and covered his eyes. He hadn't eaten in two days. He could eat now, though. Not another planetoid was close enough to interrupt them, even if it began an approach that very moment.

Back on the planetoid's surface, Swenson said, "All the time I watched that damned rock coming down, I kept saying to myself, 'This can't happen. We can't let it happen.' "

"Hell," said Rioz, "we were all nervous. Did you see Jim Davis? He was green. I was a little jumpy myself."

"That's not it. It wasn't just—dying, you know. I was thinking—I know it's funny, but I can't help it—I was thinking that Dora warned me I'd get myself killed, she'll never let me hear the last of it. Isn't that a crummy sort of attitude at a time like that?''

"Listen," said Rioz, "you wanted to get married, so you got married. Why come to me with your troubles?''

– 10 –

THE FLOTILLA, welded into a single unit, was returning over its mighty course from Saturn to Mars. Each day it flashed over a length of space it had taken nine days outward.

Ted Long had put the entire crew on emergency. With twenty-five ships embedded in the planetoid taken out of Saturn's rings and unable to move or maneuver independently, the co-ordination of their power sources into unified blasts was a ticklish problem. The jarring that took place on the first day of travel nearly shook them out from under their hair.

That, at least, smoothed itself out as the velocity raced upward under the steady thrust from behind. They passed the one-hundred-thousand-mile-an-hour mark late on the second day, and climbed steadily toward the million-mile mark and beyond.

Long's ship, which formed the needle point of the frozen fleet, was the only one which possessed a five-way view of space. It was an uncomfortable position under the circumstances. Long found himself watching tensely, imagining somehow that the stars would slowly begin to slip backward, to whizz past them, under the influence of the multi-ship's tremendous rate of travel.

They didn't, of course. They remained nailed to the black backdrop, their distance scorning with patient immobility any speed mere man could achieve.

The men complained bitterly after the first few days. It was not only that they were deprived of the space-float. They were burdened by much more than the ordinary pseudo-gravity field of the ships, by the effects of the fierce acceleration under which they were living. Long himself was weary to death of the relentless pressure against hydraulic cushions.

They took to shutting off the jet thrusts one hour out of every four and Long fretted.

It had been just over a year that he had last seen Mars shrinking in an observation window from this ship, which had then been an independent entity. What had happened since then? Was the colony still there?

In something like a growing panic, Long sent out radio pulses towards Mars daily, with the combined power of twenty-five ships behind it. There was no answer. He expected none. Mars and Saturn were on opposite sides of the Sun now, and until he mounted high enough above the ecliptic to get the Sun well beyond the line connecting himself and Mars, solar interference would prevent any signal from getting through.

High above the outer rim of the Asteroid Belt, they reached maximum velocity. With short spurts of power from first one side jet, then another, the huge vessel reversed itself. The composite jet in the rear began its mighty roaring once again, but now the result was deceleration.

They passed a hundred million miles over the Sun, curving down to intersect the orbit of Mars.

A week out of Mars, answering signals were heard for the first time, fragmentary, ether-torn, and incomprehensible, but they were coming from Mars. Earth and Venus were at angles sufficiently different to leave no doubt of that.

Long relaxed. There were still humans on Mars, at any rate.

Two days out of Mars, the signal was strong and clear and Sankov was at the other end.

Sankov said, "Hello, son. It's three in the morning here. Seems like people have no consideration for an old man. Dragged me right out of bed."

"I'm sorry, sir."

"Don't be. They were following orders. I'm afraid to ask, son. Anyone hurt? Maybe dead?"

"No deaths, sir. Not one."

"And—and the water? Any left?"

Long said, with an effort at nonchalance, "Enough."

"In that case, get home as fast as you can. Don't take any chances, of course."

"There's trouble, then."

"Fair to middling. When will you come down?"

"Two days. Can you hold out that long?"

"I'll hold out."

Forty hours later Mars had grown to a ruddy-orange ball that filled the ports and they were in final planet-landing spiral.

"Slowly," Long said to himself, "slowly." Under these conditions, even the thin atmosphere of Mars could do dreadful damage if they moved through it too quickly.

Since they came in from well above the ecliptic, their spiral passed from north to south. A polar cap shot whitely below them, then the much smaller one of the summer hemisphere, the large one again, the small one, at longer and longer intervals. The planet approached closer, the landscape began to show features.

"Prepare for landing!" called Long.

– 11 –

SANKOV DID his best to look placid, which was difficult considering how closely the boys had shaved their return. But it had worked out well enough.

Until a few days ago, he had no sure knowledge that they had survived. It seemed more likely—inevitable, almost—that they were nothing but frozen corpses somewhere in the trackless stretches from Mars to Saturn, new planetoids that had once been alive.

The Committee had been dickering with him for weeks before the news had come. They had insisted on his signature to the paper for the sake of appearances. It would look like an agreement, voluntarily and mutually arrived at. But Sankov knew well that, given complete obstinacy on his part, they would act unilaterally and be damned with appearances. It seemed fairly certain that Hilder's election was secure now and they would take the chance of arousing a reaction of sympathy for Mars.

So he dragged out the negotiations, dangling before them always the possibility of surrender.

And then he heard from Long and concluded the deal quickly.

The papers had lain before him and he had made a last statement for the benefit of the reporters who were present.

He said, "Total imports of water from Earth are twenty million tons a year. This is declining as we develop our own piping system. If I sign this paper agreeing to an embargo, our industry will be paralyzed, any possibilities of expansion will halt. It looks to me as if that can't be what's in Earth's mind, can it?"

Their eyes met his and held only a hard glitter. Assemblyman Digby had already been replaced and they were unanimous against him.

The Committee Chairman impatiently pointed out, "You have said all this before."

"I know, but right now I'm kind of getting ready to sign and I want it clear in my head. Is Earth set and determined to bring us to an end here?"

"Of course not. Earth is interested in conserving its irreplaceable water supply, nothing else."

"You have one and a half quintillion tons of water on Earth."

The Committee Chairman said, "We cannot spare water."

And Sankov had signed.

That had been the final note he wanted. Earth had one and a half quintillion tons of water and could spare none of it.

Now, a day and a half later, the Committee and the reporters waited in the spaceport dome. Through thick, curving windows, they could see the bare and empty grounds of Mars Spaceport.

The Committee Chairman asked with annoyance, "How much longer do we have to wait? And, if you don't mind, what are we waiting for?"

Sankov said, "Some of our boys have been out in space, out past the asteroids."

The Committee Chairman removed a pair of spectacles and cleaned them with a snowy-white handkerchief. "And they're returning?"

"They are."

The Chairman shrugged, lifted his eyebrows in the direction of the reporters.

In the smaller room adjoining, a know of women and children clustered about another window. Sankov stepped back a bit to cast a glance toward them. He would much rather have been with them, been part of their excitement and tension. He, like them, had waited over a year now. He, like them, had thought, over and over again, that the men must be dead.

"You see that?" said Sankov, pointing.

"Hey!" cried a reporter. "It's a ship!"

A confused shouting came from the adjoining room.

It wasn't a ship so much as a bright dot obscured by a drifting white cloud. The cloud grew larger and began to have form. It was a double streak against the sky, the lower ends billowing out and upward again. As it dropped still closer, the bright dot at the upper end took on a crudely cylindrical form.

It was rough and craggy, but where the sunlight hit, brilliant high lights bounced back.

The cylinder dropped toward the ground with the ponderous slowness characteristic of space vessels. It hung suspended on those blasting jets and settled down upon the recoil of tons of matter hurling downward like a tired man dropping into his easy chair.

And as it did so, a silence fell upon all within the dome. The women and children in one room, the politicians and reporters in the other remained frozen, heads craned incredulously upward.

The cylinder's landing flanges, extending far below the two rear jets, touched ground and sank into the pebbly morass. And then the ship was motionless and the jet action ceased.

But the silence continued in the dome. It continued for a long time.

Men came clambering down the sides of the immense vessel, inching down, down the two-mile trek to the ground, with spikes on their shoes and ice axes in their hands. They were gnats against the blinding surface.

One of the reporters croaked, "What is it?"

"That," said Sankov calmly, "happens to be a chunk of matter that spent its time scooting around Saturn as part of its rings. Our boys fitted it out with travel-head and jets and ferried it home. It just turns out the fragments in Saturn's rings are made up out of ice."

He spoke into a continuing deathlike silence. "That thing that looks like a spaceship is just a mountain of hard water. If it were standing like that on Earth, it would be melting into a puddle and maybe it would break under its own weight. Mars is colder and has less gravity, so there's no such danger.

"Of course, once we get this thing really organized, we can have water stations on the moons of Saturn and Jupiter and on the asteroids. We can scale in chunks of Saturn's rings and pick them up and send them on at the various stations. Our Scavengers are good at that sort of thing.

"We'll have all the water we need. That one chunk you see is just under a cubic mile—or about what Earth would send us in two hundred years. The boys used quite a bit of it coming back from Saturn. They made it in five weeks, they tell me, and used up about a hundred million tons. But, Lord, that didn't make any dent in all that mountain. Are you getting all this, boys?"

He turned to the reporters. There was no doubt they were getting it.

He said, "Then get this, too. Earth is worried about its water supply. It only has one and a half quintillion tons. It can't spare us a single ton out of it. Write down that we folks on Mars are worried about Earth and don't want anything to happen to Earth people. Write down that we'll sell water to Earth. Write down that we'll let them have million-ton lots for a reasonable fee. Write down that in ten years, we figure we can sell it in cubic-mile lots. Write down that Earth can quit worrying because Mars can sell it all the water it needs and wants."

The Committee Chairman was past hearing. He was feeling the future rushing in. Dimly he could see the reporters grinning as they wrote furiously.

Grinning.

He could hear the grin become laughter on Earth as Mars turned the tables so neatly on the anti-Wasters. He could hear the laughter thunder from every continent when word of the fiasco spread. And he could see the abyss, deep and black as space, into which would drop forever the political hopes of John Hilder and of every opponent of space flight left on Earth—his own included, of course.

In the adjoining room, Dora Swenson screamed with joy, and Peter, grown two inches, jumped up and down, calling, "Daddy! Daddy!"

Richard Swenson had just stepped off the extremity of the flange and, face showing clearly through the clear silicone of the headpiece, marched toward the dome.

"Did you ever see a guy look so happy?" asked Ted Long. "Maybe there's something in this marriage business."

"Ah, you've just been out in space too long," Rioz said.

NIGHTFALL

"If the stars should appear one night in a thousand years, how would men believe and adore, and preserve for many generations the remembrance of the city of God."

EMERSON

ATON 77, director of Saro University, thrust out a belligerent lower lip and glared at the young newspaperman in a hot fury.

Theremon 762 took that fury in his stride. In his earlier days, when his now widely syndicated column was only a mad idea in a cub reporter's mind, he had specialized in "impossible" interviews. It had cost him bruises, black eyes, and broken bones; but it had given him an ample supply of coolness and self-confidence.

So he lowered the outthrust hand that had been so pointedly ignored and calmly waited for the aged director to get over the worst. Astronomers were queer ducks, anyway, and if Aton's actions of the last two months meant anything, this same Aton was the queer-duckiest of the lot.

Aton 77 found his voice, and though it trembled with restrained emotion, the careful, somewhat pedantic phraseology, for which the famous astronomer was noted, did not abandon him.

"Sir," he said, "you display an infernal gall in coming to me with that impudent proposition of yours."

The husky telephotographer of the Observatory, Beenay 25, thrust a tongue's tip across dry lips and interposed nervously, "Now, sir, after all—"

The director turned to him and lifted a white eyebrow. "Do not interfere, Beenay. I will credit you with good intentions in bringing this man here; but I will tolerate no insubordination now."

Theremon decided it was time to take a part. "Director Aton, if you'll let me finish what I started saying, I think—"

"I don't believe, young man," retorted Aton, "that anything you could say now would count much as compared with your daily columns of these last two months. You have led a vast newspaper campaign against the efforts of myself and my colleagues to organize the world against the menace which it is now too late to avert. You have done your best with your highly personal attacks to make the staff of this Observatory objects of ridicule."

The director lifted a copy of the Saro City *Chronicle* from the table and shook it at Theremon furiously. "Even a person of your well-known impudence should have hesitated before coming to me with a request that he be allowed to cover today's events for his paper. Of all newsmen, you!"

Aton dashed the newspaper to the floor, strode to the window, and clasped his arms behind his back.

"You may leave," he snapped over his shoulder. He stared moodily out at the skyline where Gamma, the brightest of the planet's six suns, was setting. It had already faded and yellowed into the horizon mists, and Aton knew he would never see it again as a sane man.

He whirled. "No, wait, come here!" He gestured preemptorily, "I'll give you your story."

The newsman had made no motion to leave, and now he approached the old man slowly. Aton gestured outward. "Of the six suns, only Beta is left in the sky. Do you see it?"

The question was rather unnecessary. Beta was almost at zenith, its ruddy light flooding the landscape to an unusual orange as the brilliant rays of setting Gamma died. Beta was at aphelion. It was small; smaller than Theremon had ever seen it before, and for the moment it was undisputed ruler of Lagash's sky.

Lagash's own sun, Alpha, the one about which it revolved, was at the antipodes, as were the two distant companion pairs. The red dwarf Beta—Alpha's immediate companion—was alone, grimly alone.

Aton's upturned face flushed redly in the sunlight. "In just under four hours," he said, "civilization, as we know it, comes to an end. It will do so because, as you see, Beta is the only sun in the sky." He smiled grimly. "Print that! There'll be no one to read it."

"But if it turns out that four hours pass—and another four—and nothing happens?" asked Theremon softly.

"Don't let that worry you. Enough will happen."

"Granted! And *still*—if nothing happens?"

For a second time, Beenay 25 spoke. "Sir, I think you ought to listen to him."

Theremon said, "Put it to a vote, Director Aton."

There was a stir among the remaining five members of the Observatory staff, who till now had maintained an attitude of wary neutrality.

"That," stated Aton flatly, "is not necessary." He drew out his pocket watch. "Since your good friend, Beenay, insists so urgently, I will give you five minutes. Talk away."

"Good! Now, just what difference would it make if you allowed me to take down an eyewitness account of what's to come? If your prediction comes true, my presence won't hurt; for in that case my column would never be written. On the other hand, if nothing comes of it, you will just have to expect ridicule or worse. It would be wise to leave that ridicule to friendly hands."

Aton snorted. "Do you mean yours when you speak of friendly hands?"

"Certainly!" Theremon sat down and crossed his legs. "My columns may have been a little rough, but I gave you people the benefit of the doubt every time. After all, this is not the century to preach 'The end of the world is at hand' to Lagash. You have to understand that people don't believe the *Book of Revelations* anymore, and it annoys them to have scientists turn about-face and tell us the Cultists are right after all—"

"No such thing, young man," interrupted Aton. "While a great deal of our data has been supplied us by the Cult, our results contain none of the Cult's mysticism. Facts are facts, and the Cult's so-called mythology *has* certain facts behind it. We've exposed them and ripped away their mystery. I assure you that the Cult hates us now worse than you do.''

''I don't hate you. I'm just trying to tell you that the public is in an ugly humor. They're angry.''

Aton twisted his mouth in derision. ''Let them be angry.''

''Yes, but what about tomorrow?''

''There'll be no tomorrow!''

''But if there is. Say that there is—just to see what happens. That anger might take shape into something serious. After all, you know, business has taken a nosedive these last two months. Investors don't really believe the world is coming to an end, but just the same they're being cagy with their money until it's all over. Johnny Public doesn't believe you, either, but the new spring furniture might just as well wait a few months—just to make sure.

''You see the point. Just as soon as this is all over, the business interests will be after your hide. They'll say that if crackpots—begging your pardon—can upset the country's prosperity any time they want, simply by making some cockeyed prediction—it's up to the planet to prevent them. The sparks will fly, sir.''

The director regarded the columnist sternly. ''And just what were you proposing to do to help the situation?''

''Well''—Theremon grinned—''I was proposing to take charge of the publicity. I can handle things so that only the ridiculous side will show. It would be hard to stand, I admit, because I'd have to make you all out to be a bunch of gibbering idiots, but if I can get people laughing at you, they might forget to be angry. In return for that, all my publisher asks is an exclusive story.''

Beenay nodded and burst out, ''Sir, the rest of us think he's right. These last two months we've considered everything but the million-to-one chance that there is an error somewhere in our theory or in our calculations. We ought to take care of that, too.''

There was a murmur of agreement from the men grouped about the table, and Aton's expression became that of one who found his mouth full of something bitter and couldn't get rid of it.

''You may stay if you wish, then. You will kindly refrain, however, from hampering us in our duties in any way. You will also remember that I am in charge of all activities here, and in spite of your opinions as expressed in your columns, I will expect full cooperation and full respect—''

His hands were behind his back, and his wrinkled face thrust forward determinedly as he spoke. He might have continued indefinitely but for the intrusion of a new voice.

''Hello, hello, hello!'' It came in a high tenor, and the plump cheeks of the newcomer expanded in a pleased smile. ''What's this morgue-like atmosphere about here? No one's losing his nerve, I hope.''

Aton started in consternation and said peevishly, ''Now what the devil are you doing here, Sheerin? I thought you were going to stay behind in the Hideout.''

Sheerin laughed and dropped his tubby figure into a chair. ''Hideout be blowed! The place bored me. I wanted to be here, where things are getting hot. Don't you suppose I have my share of curiosity? I want to see these Stars the Cultists are forever speaking about.'' He rubbed his hands and added in a soberer tone, "It's freezing outside. The wind's enough to hang icicles on your nose. Beta doesn't seem to give any heat at all, at the distance it is."

The white-haired director ground his teeth in sudden exasperation. "Why do you go out of your way to do crazy things, Sheerin? What kind of good are you around here?"

"What kind of good am I around there?" Sheerin spread his palms in comical resignation. "A psychologist isn't worth his salt in the Hideout. They need men of action and strong, healthy women that can breed children. Me? I'm a hundred pounds too heavy for a man of action, and I wouldn't be a success at breeding children. So why bother them with an extra mouth to feed? I feel better over here."

Theremon spoke briskly. "Just what is the Hideout, sir?"

Sheerin seemed to see the columnist for the first time. He frowned and blew his ample cheeks out. "And just who in Lagash are you, redhead?"

Aton compressed his lips and then muttered sullenly, "That's Theremon 762, the newspaper fellow. I suppose you've heard of him."

The columnist offered his hand. "And, of course, you're Sheerin 501 of Saro University. I've heard of you." Then he repeated, "What is this Hideout, sir?"

"Well," said Sheerin, "we have managed to convince a few people of the validity of our prophecy of—er—doom, to be spectacular about it, and those few have taken proper measures. They consist mainly of the immediate members of the families of the Observatory staff, certain of the faculty of Saro University, but three quarters are women and children."

"I see! They're supposed to hide where the Darkness and the—er—Stars can't get at them, and then hold out when the rest of the world goes poof."

"If they can. It won't be easy. With all of mankind insane, with the great cities going up in flames—environment will not be conducive to survival. But they have food, water, shelter, and weapons—"

"They've got more," said Aton. "They've got all our records, except for what we will collect today. Those records will mean everything to the next cycle, and *that's* what must survive. The rest can go hang."

Theremon uttered a long, low whistle and sat brooding for several minutes. The men about the table had brought out a multi-chess board and started a six-member game. Moves were made rapidly and in silence. All eyes bent in furious concentration on the board. Theremon watched them intently and then rose and approached Aton, who sat apart in whispered conversation with Sheerin.

"Listen," he said, "let's go somewhere where we won't bother the rest of the fellows. I want to ask some questions."

The aged astronomer frowned sourly at him, but Sheerin chirped up, "Certainly. It will do me good to talk. It always does. Aton was telling me about your ideas concerning world reaction to a failure of the prediction—and I agree with you. I read your column pretty regularly, by the way, and as a general thing I like your views."

"Please, Sheerin," growled Aton.

"Eh? Oh, all right. We'll go into the next room. It has softer chairs, anyway."

There were softer chairs in the next room. There were also thick red curtains on the windows and a maroon carpet on the floor. With the bricky light of Beta pouring in, the general effect was one of dried blood.

Theremon shuddered. "Say, I'd give ten credits for a decent dose of white light for just a second. I wish Gamma or Delta were in the sky."

"What are your questions?" asked Aton. "Please remember that our time is limited. In a little over an hour and a quarter we're going upstairs, and after that there will be no time for talk."

"Well, here it is." Theremon leaned back and folded his hands on his chest. "You people seem so all-fired serious about this that I'm beginning to believe you. Would you mind explaining what it's all about?"

Aton exploded, "Do you mean to sit there and tell me that you've been bombarding us with ridicule without even finding out what we've been trying to say?"

The columnist grinned sheepishly. "It's not that bad, sir. I've got the general idea. You say there is going to be a world-wide Darkness in a few hours and that all mankind will go violently insane. What I want now is the science behind it."

"No, you don't. No, you don't," broke in Sheerin. "If you ask Aton for that—supposing him to be in the mood to answer at all—he'll trot out pages of figures and volumes of graphs. You won't make head or tail of it. Now if you were to ask me, I could give you the layman's standpoint."

"All right; I ask you."

"Then first I'd like a drink." He rubbed his hands and looked at Aton.

"Water?" grunted Aton.

"Don't be silly!"

"Don't you be silly. No alcohol today. It would be too easy to get my men drunk. I can't afford to tempt them."

The psychologist grumbled wordlessly. He turned to Theremon, impaled him with his sharp eyes, and began.

"You realize, of course, that the history of civilization on Lagash displays a cyclic character—but I mean, *cyclic!*"

"I know," replied Theremon cautiously, "that that is the current archaeological theory. Has it been accepted as a fact?"

"Just about. In this last century it's been generally agreed upon. This cyclic character is—or rather, was—one of the great mysteries. We've located series of civilizations, nine of them definitely, and indications of others as well, all of which have reached heights comparable to our own, and all of which, without exception, were destroyed by fire at the very height of their culture.

"And no one could tell why. All centers of culture were thoroughly gutted by fire, with nothing left behind to give a hint as to the cause."

Theremon was following closely. "Wasn't there a Stone Age, too?"

"Probably, but as yet practically nothing is known of it, except that men of that age were little more than rather intelligent apes. We can forget about that."

"I see. Go on!"

"There have been explanations of these recurrent catastrophes, all of a more or less fantastic nature. Some say that there are periodic rains of fire; some that Lagash passes through a sun every so often; some even wilder things. But there is one theory, quite different from all of these, that has been handed down over a period of centuries."

"I know. You mean this myth of the 'Stars' that the Cultists have in their *Book of Revelations*."

"Exactly," rejoined Sheerin with satisfaction. "The Cultists said that every two thousand and fifty years Lagash entered a huge cave, so that all the suns disappeared, and there came *total darkness all over the world!* And then, they say, things called Stars appeared, which robbed men of their souls and left them unreasoning brutes, so that they destroyed the civilization they themselves had built up. Of course they mix all this up with a lot of religio-mystic notions, but that's the central idea.''

There was a short pause in which Sheerin drew a long breath. ''And now we come to the Theory of Universal Gravitation.'' He pronounced the phrase so that the capital letters sounded—and at that point Aton turned from the window, snorted loudly, and stalked out of the room.

The two stared after him, and Theremon said, ''What's wrong?''

''Nothing in particular,'' replied Sheerin. ''Two of the men were due several hours ago and haven't shown up yet. He's terrifically short-handed, of course, because all but the really essential men have gone to the Hideout.''

''You don't think the two deserted, do you?''

''Who? Faro and Yimot? Of course not. Still, if they're not back within the hour, things would be a little sticky.'' He got to his feet suddenly, and his eyes twinkled. ''Anyway, as long as Aton is gone—''

Tiptoeing to the nearest window, he squatted, and from the low window box beneath withdrew a bottle of red liquid that gurgled suggestively when he shook it.

''I *thought* Aton didn't know this,'' he remarked as he trotted back to the table. ''Here! We've only got one glass so, as the guest, you can have it. I'll keep the bottle.'' And he filled the tiny cup with judicious care.

Theremon rose to protest, but Sheerin eyed him sternly. ''Respect your elders, young man.''

The newsman seated himself with a look of anguish on his face. ''Go ahead, then, you old villain.''

The psychologist's Adam's apple wobbled as the bottle upended, and then, with a satisfied grunt and a smack of the lips, he began again. ''But what do you know about gravitation?''

''Nothing, except that it is a very recent development, not too well established, and that the math is so hard that only twelve men in Lagash are supposed to understand it.''

''*Tcha!* Nonsense! Baloney! I can give you all the essential math in a sentence. The Law of Universal Gravitation states that there exists a cohesive force among all bodies of the universe, such that the amount of this force between any two given bodies is proportional to the product of their masses divided by the square of the distance between them.''

''Is that all?''

''That's enough! It took four hundred years to develop it.''

''Why that long? It sounded simple enough, the way you said it.''

''Because great laws are not divined by flashes of inspiration, whatever you may think. It usually takes the combined work of a world full of scientists over a period of centuries. After Genovi 41 discovered that Lagash rotated about the sun Alpha rather than vice versa—and that was four hundred years ago—astronomers have been working. The complex motions of the six suns were recorded and analyzed and unwoven. Theory after theory was advanced and checked and counterchecked and modified and abandoned and revived and converted to something else. It was a devil of a job.''

Theremon nodded thoughtfully and held out his glass for more liquor. Sheerin grudgingly allowed a few ruby drops to leave the bottle.

"It was twenty years ago," he continued after remoistening his own throat, "that it was finally demonstrated that the Law of Universal Gravitation accounted exactly for the orbital motions of the six suns. It was a great triumph."

Sheerin stood up and walked to the window, still clutching his bottle. "And now we're getting to the point. In the last decade, the motions of Lagash about Alpha were computed according to gravity, and *it did not account for the orbit observed;* not even when all perturbations due to the other suns were included. Either the law was invalid, or there was another, as yet unknown, factor involved."

Theremon joined Sheerin at the window and gazed out past the wooded slopes to where the spires of Saro City gleamed bloodily on the horizon. The newsman felt the tension of uncertainty grow within him as he cast a short glance at Beta. It glowered redly at zenith, dwarfed and evil.

"Go ahead, sir," he said softly.

Sheerin replied, "Astronomers stumbled about for years, each proposed theory more untenable than the one before—until Aton had the inspiration of calling in the Cult. The head of the Cult, Sor 5, had access to certain data that simplified the problem considerably. Aton set to work on a new track.

"What if there were another nonluminous planetary body such as Lagash? If there were, you know, it would shine only by reflected light, and if it were composed of bluish rock, as Lagash itself largely is, then, in the redness of the sky, the eternal blaze of the suns would make it invisible—drown it out completely."

Theremon whistled. "What a screwy idea!"

"You think *that's* screwy? Listen to this: Suppose this body rotated about Lagash at such a distance and in such an orbit and had such a mass that its attraction would exactly account for the deviations of Lagash's orbit from theory—do you know what would happen?"

The columnist shook his head.

"Well, sometimes this body would get in the way of a sun." And Sheerin emptied what remained in the bottle at a draft.

"And it does, I suppose," said Theremon flatly.

"Yes! But only one sun lies in its plane of revolution." He jerked a thumb at the shrunken sun above. "Beta! And it has been shown that the eclipse is alone in its hemisphere and at maximum distance, at which time the moon is invariably at minimum distance. The eclipse that results, with the moon seven times the apparent diameter of Beta, covers all of Lagash and lasts well over half a day, so that no spot on the planet escapes the effects. *That eclipse comes once every two thousand and forty-nine years.*"

Theremon's face was drawn into an expressionless mask. "And that's my story?"

The psychologist nodded. "That's all of it. First the eclipse—which will start in three quarters of an hour—then universal Darkness and, maybe, these mysterious Stars—then madness, and end of the cycle."

He brooded. "We had two months' leeway—we at the Observatory—and that wasn't enough time to persuade Lagash of the danger. Two centuries might not have been enough. But our records are at the Hideout, and today we photograph the eclipse. The next cycle will *start off* with the truth, and when the *next* eclipse comes, mankind will at last be ready for it. Come to think of it, that's part of your story too.''

A thin wind ruffled the curtains at the window as Theremon opened it and leaned out. It played coldly with his hair as he stared at the crimson sunlight on his hand. Then he turned in sudden rebellion.

"What is there in Darkness to drive *me* mad?"

Sheerin smiled to himself as he spun the empty liquor bottle with abstracted motions of his hand. "Have you ever experienced Darkness, young man?"

The newsman leaned against the wall and considered. "No. Can't say I have. But I know what it is. Just—uh—" He made vague motions with his fingers and then brightened. "Just no light. Like in caves."

"Have you ever been in a cave?"

"In a *cave!* Of course not!"

"I thought not. *I* tried last week—just to see—but I got out in a hurry. I went in until the mouth of the cave was just visible as a blur of light, with black everywhere else. I never thought a person my weight could run that fast."

Theremon's lip curled. "Well, if it comes to that, I guess I wouldn't have run if I had been there."

The psychologist studied the young man with an annoyed frown.

"My, don't you talk big! I dare you to draw the curtain."

Theremon looked his surprise and said, "What for? If we had four or five suns out there, we might want to cut the light down a bit for comfort, but now we haven't enough light as it is."

"That's the point. Just draw the curtain; then come here and sit down."

"All right." Theremon reached for the tasseled string and jerked. The red curtain slid across the wide window, the brass rings hissing their way along the crossbar, and a dusk-red shadow clamped down on the room.

Theremon's footsteps sounded hollowly in the silence as he made his way to the table, and then they stopped halfway. "I can't see you, sir," he whispered.

"Feel your way," ordered Sheerin in a strained voice.

"But I can't see you, sir." The newsman was breathing harshly. "I can't see anything."

"What did you expect?" came the grim reply. "Come here and sit down!"

The footsteps sounded again, waveringly, approaching slowly. There was the sound of someone fumbling with a chair. Theremon's voice came thinly. "Here I am. I feel . . . *ulp* . . . all right."

"You like it, do you?"

"N—no. It's pretty awful. The walls seem to be—" He paused. "They seem to be closing in on me. I keep wanting to push them away. But I'm not going *mad!* In fact, the feeling isn't as bad as it was."

"All right. Draw the curtain back again."

There were cautious footsteps through the dark, the rustle of Theremon's body against the curtain as he felt for the tassel, and then the triumphant *ro-o-osh* of the curtain slithering back. Red light flooded the room, and with a cry of joy Theremon looked up at the sun.

Sheerin wiped the moistness off his forehead with the back of a hand and said shakily, "And that was just a dark room."

"It can be stood," said Theremon lightly.

"Yes, a dark room can. But were you at the Jonglor Centennial Exposition two years ago?"

"No, it so happens I never got around to it. Six thousand miles was just a bit too much to travel, even for the exposition."

"Well, I was there. You remember hearing about the 'Tunnel of Mystery' that broke all records in the amusement area—for the first month or so, anyway?"

"Yes. Wasn't there some fuss about it?"

"Very little. It was hushed up. You see, that Tunnel of Mystery was just a mile-long tunnel—with no lights. You got into a little open car and jolted along through Darkness for fifteen minutes. It was very popular—while it lasted."

"Popular?"

"Certainly. There's a fascination in being frightened *when it's part of a game.* A baby is born with three instinctive fears: of loud noises, of falling, and of the absence of light. That's why it's considered so funny to jump at someone and shout 'Boo!' That's why it's such fun to ride a roller coaster. And that's why that Tunnel of Mystery started cleaning up. People came out of that Darkness shaking, breathless, half dead with fear, but they kept on paying to get in."

"Wait a while, I remember now. Some people came out dead, didn't they? There were rumors of that after it shut down."

The psychologist snorted. "Bah! Two or three died. That was nothing! They paid off the families of the dead ones and argued the Jonglor City Council into forgetting it. After all, they said, if people with weak hearts want to go through the tunnel, it was at their own risk—and besides, it wouldn't happen again. So they put a doctor in the front office and had every customer go through a physical examination before getting into the car. That actually *boosted* ticket sales."

"Well, then?"

"But you see, there was something else. People sometimes came out in perfect order, except that they refused to go into buildings—any buildings; including palaces, mansions, apartment houses, tenements, cottages, huts, shacks, lean-tos, and tents."

Theremon looked shocked. "You mean they refused to come in out of the open? Where'd they sleep?"

"In the open."

"They should have *forced* them inside."

"Oh, they did, they did. Whereupon these people went into violent hysterics and did their best to bat their brains out against the nearest wall. Once you got them inside, you couldn't keep them there without a strait jacket or a heavy dose of tranquilizer."

"They must have been crazy."

"Which is exactly what they were. One person out of every ten who went into that tunnel came out that way. They called in the psychologists, and we did the only thing possible. We closed down the exhibit." He spread his hands.

"What was the matter with these people?" asked Theremon finally.

"Essentially the same thing that was the matter with you when you thought the walls of the room were crushing in on you in the dark. There is a psychological term for mankind's instinctive fear of the absence of light. We call it 'claustrophobia,' because the lack of light is always tied up with enclosed places, so that fear of one is fear of the other. You see?"

"And those people of the tunnel?"

"Those people of the tunnel consisted of those unfortunates whose mentality did not quite possess the resiliency to overcome the claustrophobia that overtook them in the Darkness. Fifteen minutes without light is a long time; you only had two or three minutes, and I believe you were fairly upset.

"The people of the tunnel had what is called 'claustrophobic fixation.' Their latent fear of Darkness and enclosed places had crystalized and become active, and, as far as we can tell, permanent. That's what fifteen minutes in the dark will do."

There was a long silence, and Theremon's forehead wrinkled slowly into a frown. "I don't believe it's that bad."

"You mean you don't want to believe," snapped Sheerin. "You're afraid to believe. Look out the window!"

Theremon did so, and the psychologist continued without pausing. "Imagine Darkness—everywhere. No light, as far as you can see. The houses, the trees, the fields, the earth, the sky—black! And Stars thrown in, for all I know—whatever *they* are. Can you conceive it?"

"Yes, I can," declared Theremon truculently.

And Sheerin slammed his fist down upon the table in sudden passion. "You lie! You can't conceive that. Your brain wasn't built for the conception any more than it was built for the conception of infinity or of eternity. You can only talk about it. A fraction of the reality upsets you, and when the real thing comes, your brain is going to be presented with the phenomenon outside its limits of comprehension. You will go mad, completely and permanently! There is no question of it!"

He added sadly, "And another couple of millennia of painful struggle comes to nothing. Tomorrow there won't be a city standing unharmed in all Lagash."

Theremon recovered part of his mental equilibrium. "That doesn't follow. I still don't see that I can go loony just because there isn't a sun in the sky—but even if I did, and everyone else did, how does that harm the cities? Are we going to blow them down?"

But Sheerin was angry, too. "If you were in Darkness, what would you want more than anything else; what would it be that every instinct would call for? Light, damn you, *light!*"

"Well?"

"And how would you get light?"

"I don't know," said Theremon flatly.

"What's the *only* way to get light, short of a sun?"

"How should I know?"

They were standing face to face and nose to nose.

Sheerin said, "You burn something, mister. Ever see a forest fire? Ever go camping and cook a stew over a wood fire? Heat isn't the only thing burning wood gives off, you know. It gives off light, and people know that. And when it's dark they want light, and they're going to *get* it."

"So they burn wood?"

"So they burn whatever they can get. They've got to have light. They've got to burn something, and wood isn't handy—so they'll burn whatever is nearest. They'll have their light—and every center of habitation goes up in flames!"

Eyes held each other as though the whole matter were a personal affair of respective will powers, and then Theremon broke away wordlessly. His breathing was harsh and ragged, and he scarcely noted the sudden hubbub that came from the adjoining room behind the closed door.

Sheerin spoke, and it was with an effort that he made it sound matter-of-fact. "I think I heard Yimot's voice. He and Faro are probably back. Let's go in and see what kept them."

"Might as well!" muttered Theremon. He drew a long breath and seemed to shake himself. The tension was broken.

The room was in an uproar, with members of the staff clustering about two young men who were removing outer garments even as they parried the miscellany of questions being thrown at them.

Aton bustled through the crowd and faced the newcomers angrily. "Do you realize that it's less than half an hour before deadline? Where have you two been?"

Faro 24 seated himself and rubbed his hands. His cheeks were red with the outdoor chill. "Yimot and I have just finished carrying through a little crazy experiment of our own. We've been trying to see if we couldn't construct an arrangement by which we could simulate the appearance of Darkness and Stars so as to get an advance notion as to how it looked."

There was a confused murmur from the listeners, and a sudden look of interest entered Aton's eyes. "There wasn't anything said of this before. How did you go about it?"

"Well," said Faro, "the idea came to Yimot and myself long ago, and we've been working it out in our spare time. Yimot knew of a low one-story house down in the city with a domed roof—it had once been used as a museum, I think. Anyway, we bought it—"

"Where did you get the money?" interrupted Aton peremptorily.

"Our bank accounts," grunted Yimot 70. "It cost two thousand credits." Then, defensively, "Well, what of it? Tomorrow, two thousand credits will be two thousand pieces of paper. That's all."

"Sure," agreed Faro. "We bought the place and rigged it up with black velvet from top to bottom so as to get as perfect a Darkness as possible. Then we punched tiny holes in the ceiling and through the roof and covered them with little metal caps, all of which could be shoved aside simultaneously at the close of a switch. At least we didn't do that part ourselves; we got a carpenter and an electrician and some others—money didn't count. The point was that we could get the light to shine through those holes in the roof, so that we could get a starlike effect."

Not a breath was drawn during the pause that followed. Aton said stiffly, "You had no right to make a private—"

Faro seemed abashed. "I know, sir—but frankly, Yimot and I thought the experiment was a little dangerous. If the effect really worked, we half expected to go mad—from what Sheerin says about all this, we thought that would be rather likely. We wanted to take the risk ourselves. Of course if we found we could retain sanity, it occurred to us that we might develop immunity to the real thing, and then expose the rest of you the same way. But things didn't work out at all—"

"Why, what happened?"

It was Yimot who answered. "We shut ourselves in and allowed our eyes to get accustomed to the dark. It's an extremely creepy feeling because the total Darkness makes you feel as if the walls and ceiling are crushing in on you. But we got over that and pulled the switch. The caps fell away and the roof glittered all over with little dots of light—''

"Well?"

"Well—nothing. That was the whacky part of it. Nothing happened. It was just a roof with holes in it, and that's just what it looked like. We tried it over and over again—that's what kept us so late—but there just isn't any effect at all.''

There followed a shocked silence, and all eyes turned to Sheerin, who sat motionless, mouth open.

Theremon was the first to speak. "You know what this does to this whole theory you've built up, Sheerin, don't you?'' He was grinning with relief.

But Sheerin raised his hand. "Now wait a while. Just let me think this through.'' And then he snapped his fingers, and when he lifted his head there was neither surprise nor uncertainty in his eyes. "Of course—''

He never finished. From somewhere up above there sounded a sharp clang, and Beenay, starting to his feet, dashed up the stairs with a "What the devil!''

The rest followed after.

Things happened quickly. Once up in the dome, Beenay cast one horrified glance at the shattered photographic plates and at the man bending over them; and then hurled himself fiercely at the intruder, getting a death grip on his throat. There was a wild threshing, and as others of the staff joined in, the stranger was swallowed up and smothered under the weight of half a dozen angry men.

Aton came up last, breathing heavily. "Let him up!''

There was a reluctant unscrambling and the stranger, panting harshly, with his clothes torn and his forehead bruised, was hauled to his feet. He had a short yellow beard curled elaborately in the style affected by the Cultists.

Beenay shifted his hold to a collar grip and shook the man savagely. "All right, rat, what's the idea? These plates—''

"I wasn't after *them*,'' retorted the Cultist coldly. "That was an accident.''

Beenay followed his glowering stare and snarled, "I see. You were after the cameras themselves. The accident with the plates was a stroke of luck for you, then. If you had touched Snapping Bertha or any of the others, you would have died by slow torture. As it is—'' He drew his fist back.

Aton grabbed his sleeve. "Stop that! Let him go!''

The young technician wavered, and his arm dropped reluctantly. Aton pushed him aside and confronted the Cultist. "You're Latimer, aren't you?''

The Cultist bowed stiffly and indicated the symbol upon his hip. "I am Latimer 25, adjutant of the third class to his serenity, Sor 5.''

"And''—Aton's white eyebrows lifted—"you were with his serenity when he visited me last week, weren't you?''

Latimer bowed a second time.

"Now, then, what do you want?''

"Nothing that you would give me of your own free will.''

"Sor 5 sent you, I suppose—or is this your own idea?''

"I won't answer that question.''

"Will there be any further visitors?''

"I won't answer that, either.''

Aton glanced at his timepiece and scowled. "Now, man, what is it your master wants of me? I have fulfilled my end of the bargain.''

Latimer smiled faintly, but said nothing.

"I asked him," continued Aton angrily, "for data only the Cult could supply, and it was given me. For that, thank you. In return I promised to prove the essential truth of the creed of the Cult."

"There was no need to prove that," came the proud retort. "It stands proven by the *Book of Revelations*."

"For the handful that constitute the Cult, yes. Don't pretend to mistake my meaning. I offered to present scientific backing for your beliefs. And I did!"

The Cultist's eyes narrowed bitterly. "Yes, you did—with a fox's subtlety, for your pretended explanation backed our beliefs, and at the same time removed all necessity for them. You made of the Darkness and of the Stars a natural phenomenon and removed all its real significance. That was blasphemy."

"If so, the fault isn't mine. The facts exist. What can I do but state them?"

"Your 'facts' are a fraud and a delusion."

Aton stamped angrily. "How do you know?"

And the answer came with the certainty of absolute faith. "I know!"

The director purpled and Beenay whispered urgently. Aton waved him silent. "And what does Sor 5 want us to do? He still thinks, I suppose, that in trying to warn the world to take measures against the menace of madness, we are placing innumerable souls in jeopardy. We aren't succeeding, if that means anything to him."

"The attempt itself has done harm enough, and your vicious effort to gain information by means of your devilish instruments must be stopped. We obey the will of the Stars, and I only regret that my clumsiness prevented me from wrecking your infernal devices."

"It wouldn't have done you too much good," returned Aton. "All our data, except for the direct evidence we intend collecting right now, is already safely cached and well beyond possibility of harm." He smiled grimly. "But that does not affect your present status as an attempted burglar and criminal."

He turned to the men behind him. "Someone call the police at Saro City."

There was a cry of distaste from Sheerin. "Damn it, Aton, what's wrong with you? There's no time for that. Here"—he bustled his way forward—"let me handle this."

Aton stared down his nose at the psychologist. "This is not the time for your monkeyshines, Sheerin. Will you please let me handle this my own way? Right now you are a complete outsider here, and don't forget it."

Sheerin's mouth twisted eloquently. "Now why should we go to the impossible trouble of calling the police—with Beta's eclipse a matter of minutes from now—when this young man here is perfectly willing to pledge his word of honor to remain and cause no trouble whatsoever?"

The Cultist answered promptly, "I will do no such thing. You're free to do what you want, but it's only fair to warn you that just as soon as I get my chance I'm going to finish what I came out here to do. If it's my word of honor you're relying on, you'd better call the police."

Sheerin smiled in a friendly fashion. "You're a determined cuss, aren't you? Well, I'll explain something. Do you see that young man at the window? He's a strong, husky fellow, quite handy with his fists, and he's an outsider besides. Once the eclipse starts there will be nothing for him to do except keep an eye on you. Besides him, there will be myself—a little too stout for active fisticuffs, but still able to help."

"Well, what of it?" demanded Latimer frozenly.

"Listen and I'll tell you," was the reply. "Just as soon as the eclipse starts, we're going to take you, Theremon and I, and deposit you in a little closet with one door, to which is attached one giant lock and no windows. You will remain there for the duration."

"And afterward," breathed Latimer fiercely, "there'll be no one to let me out. I know as well as you do what the coming of the Stars means—I know it far better than you. With all your minds gone, you are not likely to free me. Suffocation or slow starvation, is it? About what I might have expected from a group of scientists. But I don't give my word. It's a matter of principle, and I won't discuss it further."

Aton seemed perturbed. His faded eyes were troubled. "Really, Sheerin, locking him—"

"Please!" Sheerin motioned him impatiently to silence. "I don't think for a moment things will go that far. Latimer has just tried a clever little bluff, but I'm not a psychologist just because I like the sound of the word." He grinned at the Cultist. "Come now, you don't really think I'm trying anything as crude as slow starvation. My dear Latimer, if I lock you in the closet, you are not going to see the Darkness, and you are not going to see the Stars. It does not take much knowledge of the fundamental creed of the Cult to realize that for you to be hidden from the Stars when they appear means the loss of your immortal soul. Now, I believe you to be an honorable man. I'll accept your word of honor to make no further effort to disrupt proceedings, if you'll offer it."

A vein throbbed in Latimer's temple, and he seemed to shrink within himself as he said thickly, "You have it!" And then he added with swift fury, "But it is my consolation that you will all be damned for your deeds of today." He turned on his heel and stalked to the high three-legged stool by the door.

Sheerin nodded to the columnist. "Take a seat next to him, Theremon—just as a formality. Hey, Theremon!"

But the newspaperman didn't move. He had gone pale to the lips. "Look at that!" The finger he pointed toward the sky shook, and his voice was dry and cracked.

There was one simultaneous gasp as every eye followed the pointing finger and, for one breathless moment, stared frozenly.

Beta was chipped on one side!

The tiny bit of encroaching blackness was perhaps the width of a fingernail, but to the staring watchers it magnified itself into the crack of doom.

Only for a moment they watched, and after that there was a shrieking confusion that was even shorter of duration and which gave way to an orderly scurry of activity—each man at his prescribed job. At the crucial moment there was no time for emotion. The men were merely scientists with work to do. Even Aton had melted away.

Sheerin said prosaically, "First contact must have been made fifteen minutes ago. A little early, but pretty good considering the uncertainties involved in the calculation." He looked about him and then tiptoed to Theremon, who still remained staring out the window, and dragged him away gently.

"Aton is furious," he whispered, "so stay away. He missed first contact on account of this fuss with Latimer, and if you get in his way he'll have you thrown out the window."

Theremon nodded shortly and sat down. Sheerin stared in surprise at him.

"The devil, man," he exclaimed, "you're shaking."

"Eh?" Theremon licked dry lips and then tried to smile. "I don't feel very well, and that's a fact."

The psychologist's eyes hardened. "You're not losing your nerve?"

"No!" cried Theremon in a flash of indignation. "Give me a chance, will you? I haven't really believed this rigmarole—not way down beneath, anyway—till just this minute. Give me a chance to get used to the idea. You've been preparing yourself for two months or more."

"You're right, at that," replied Sheerin thoughtfully. "Listen! Have you got a family—parents, wife, children?"

Theremon shook his head. "You mean the Hideout, I suppose. No, you don't have to worry about that. I have a sister, but she's two thousand miles away. I don't even know her exact address."

"Well, then, what about yourself? You've got time to get there, and they're one short anyway, since I left. After all, you're not needed here, and you'd make a darned fine addition—"

Theremon looked at the other wearily. "You think I'm scared stiff, don't you? Well, get this, mister, I'm a newspaperman and I've been assigned to cover a story. I intend covering it."

There was a faint smile on the psychologist's face. "I see. Professional honor, is that it?"

"You might call it that. But, man, I'd give my right arm for another bottle of that sockeroo juice even half the size of the one you hogged. If ever a fellow needed a drink, I do."

He broke off. Sheerin was nudging him violently. "Do you hear that? Listen!"

Theremon followed the motion of the other's chin and stared at the Cultist, who, oblivious to all about him, faced the window, a look of wild elation on his face, droning to himself the while in singsong fashion.

"What's he saying?" whispered the columnist.

"He's quoting *Book of Revelations,* fifth chapter," replied Sheerin. Then, urgently, "Keep quiet and listen, I tell you."

The Cultist's voice had risen in a sudden increase of fervor: " 'And it came to pass that in those days the Sun, Beta, held lone vigil in the sky for ever longer periods as the revolutions passed; until such time as for full half a revolution, it alone, shrunken and cold, shone down upon Lagash.

" 'And men did assemble in the public squares and in the highways, there to debate and to marvel at the sight, for a strange depression had seized them. Their minds were troubled and their speech confused, for the souls of men awaited the coming of the Stars.

" 'And in the city of Trigon, at high noon, Vendret 2 came forth and said unto the men of Trigon, "Lo, ye sinners! Though ye scorn the ways of righteousness, yet will the time of reckoning come. Even now the Cave approaches to swallow Lagash; yea, and all it contains."

" 'And even as he spoke the lip of the Cave of Darkness passed the edge of Beta so that to all Lagash it was hidden from sight. Loud were the cries of men as it vanished, and great the fear of soul that fell upon them.

" 'It came to pass that the Darkness of the Cave fell upon Lagash, and there was no light on all the surface of Lagash. Men were even as blinded, nor could one man see his neighbor, though he felt his breath upon his face.

" 'And in this blackness there appeared the Stars, in countless numbers, and to the strains of music of such beauty that the very leaves of the trees cried out in wonder.

" 'And in that moment the souls of men departed from them, and their abandoned bodies became even as beasts; yea, even as brutes of the wild; so that through the blackened streets of the cities of Lagash they prowled with wild cries.

" 'From the Stars there then reached down the Heavenly Flame, and where it touched, the cities of Lagash flamed to utter destruction, so that of man and of the works of man nought remained.

" 'Even then—' "

There was a subtle change in Latimer's tone. His eyes had not shifted, but somehow he had become aware of the absorbed attention of the other two. Easily, without pausing for breath, the timbre of his voice shifted and the syllables became more liquid.

Theremon, caught by surprise, stared. The words seemed on the border of familiarity. There was an elusive shift in the accent, a tiny change in the vowel stress; nothing more—yet Latimer had become thoroughly unintelligible.

Sheerin smiled slyly. "He shifted to some old-cycle tongue, probably their traditional second cycle. That was the language in which the *Book of Revelations* was originally written, you know."

"It doesn't matter; I've heard enough." Theremon shoved his chair back and brushed his hair back with hands that no longer shook. "I feel much better now."

"You do?" Sheerin seemed mildly surprised.

"I'll say I do. I had a bad case of jitters just a while back. Listening to you and your gravitation and seeing that eclipse start almost finished me. But this"— he jerked a contemptuous thumb at the yellow-bearded Cultist—"*this* is the sort of thing my nurse used to tell me. I've been laughing at that sort of thing all my life. I'm not going to let it scare me *now*."

He drew a deep breath and said with a hectic gaiety, "But if I expect to keep on the good side of myself, I'm going to turn my chair away from the window."

Sheerin said, "Yes, but you'd better talk lower. Aton just lifted his head out of that box he's got it stuck into and gave you a look that should have killed you."

Theremon made a mouth. "I forgot about the old fellow." With elaborate care he turned the chair from the window, cast one distasteful look over his shoulder, and said, "It has occurred to me that there must be considerable immunity against this Star madness."

The psychologist did not answer immediately. Beta was past its zenith now, and the square of bloody sunlight that outlined the window upon the floor had lifted into Sheerin's lap. He stared at its dusky color thoughtfully and then bent and squinted into the sun itself.

The chip in its side had grown to a black encroachment that covered a third of Beta. He shuddered, and when he straightened once more his florid cheeks did not contain quite as much color as they had had previously.

With a smile that was almost apologetic, he reversed his chair also. "There are probably two million people in Saro City that are all trying to join the Cult at once in one gigantic revival." Then, ironically, "The Cult is in for an hour of unexampled prosperity. I trust they'll make the most of it. Now, what was it you said?"

"Just this. How did the Cultists manage to keep the *Book of Revelations* going from cycle to cycle, and how on Lagash did it get written in the first place? There must have been some sort of immunity, for if everyone had gone mad, who would be left to write the book?"

Sheerin stared at his questioner ruefully. "Well, now, young man, there isn't any eyewitness answer to that, but we've got a few damned good notions as to what happened. You see, there are three kinds of people who might remain relatively unaffected. First, the very few who don't see the Stars at all: the seriously retarded or those who drink themselves into a stupor at the beginning of the eclipse and remain so to the end. We leave them out—because they aren't really witnesses.

"Then there are children below six, to whom the world as a whole is too new and strange for them to be too frightened at Stars and Darkness. They would be just another item in an already surprising world. You see that, don't you?"

The other nodded doubtfully. "I suppose so."

"Lastly, there are those whose minds are too coarsely grained to be entirely toppled. The very insensitive would be scarcely affected—oh, such people as some of our older, work-broken peasants. Well, the children would have fugitive memories, and that, combined with the confused, incoherent babblings of the half-mad morons, formed the basis for the *Book of Revelations.*

"Naturally, the book was based, in the first place, on the testimony of those least qualified to serve as historians; that is, children and morons; and was probably edited and re-edited through the cycles."

"Do you suppose," broke in Theremon, "that they carried the book through the cycles the way we're planning on handing on the secret of gravitation?"

Sheerin shrugged. "Perhaps, but their exact method is unimportant. They do it, somehow. The point I was getting at was that the book can't help but be a mass of distortion, even if it is based on fact. For instance, do you remember the experiment with the holes in the roof that Faro and Yimot tried—the one that didn't work?"

"Yes."

"You know why it didn't w—" He stopped and rose in alarm, for Aton was approaching, his face a twisted mask of consternation. *"What's happened?"*

Aton drew him aside and Sheerin could feel the fingers on his elbow twitching.

"Not so loud!" Aton's voice was low and tortured. "I've just gotten word from the Hideout on the private line."

Sheerin broke in anxiously. "They are in trouble?"

"Not *they.*" Aton stressed the pronoun significantly. "They sealed themselves off just a while ago, and they're going to stay buried till day after tomorrow. They're safe. But the *city*, Sheerin—it's a shambles. You have no idea—" He was having difficulty in speaking.

"Well?" snapped Sheerin impatiently. "What of it? It will get worse. What are you shaking about?" Then, suspiciously, "How do you feel?"

Aton's eyes sparked angrily at the insinuation, and then faded to anxiety once more. "You don't understand. The Cultists are active. They're rousing the people to storm the Observatory—promising them immediate entrance into grace, promising them salvation, promising them anything. What are we to do, Sheerin?"

Sheerin's head bent, and he stared in long abstraction at his toes. He tapped his chin with one knuckle, then looked up and said crisply, "Do? What is there to do? Nothing at all. Do the men know of this?"

"No, of course not!"

"Good! Keep it that way. How long till totality?"

"Not quite an hour."

"There's nothing to do but gamble. It will take time to organize any really formidable mob, and it will take more time to get them out here. We're a good five miles from the city—"

He glared out the window, down the slopes to where the farmed patches gave way to clumps of white houses in the suburbs; down to where the metropolis itself was a blur on the horizon—a mist in the waning blaze of Beta.

He repeated without turning. "It will take time. Keep on working and pray that totality comes first."

Beta was cut in half, the line of division pushing a slight concavity into the still-bright portion of the Sun. It was like a gigantic eyelid shutting slantwise over the light of a world.

The faint clatter of the room in which he stood faded into oblivion, and he sensed only the thick silence of the fields outside. The very insects seemed frightened mute. And things were dim.

He jumped at the voice in his ear. Theremon said, "Is something wrong?"

"Er? Er—no. Get back to the chair. We're in the way." They slipped back to their corner, but the psychologist did not speak for a time. He lifted a finger and loosened his collar. He twisted his neck back and forth but found no relief. He looked up suddenly.

"Are you having any difficulty in breathing?"

The newspaperman opened his eyes wide and drew two or three long breaths. "No. Why?"

"I looked out the window too long, I suppose. The dimness got me. Difficulty in breathing is one of the first symptoms of a claustrophobic attack."

Theremon drew another long breath. "Well, it hasn't got me yet. Say, here's another of the fellows."

Beenay had interposed his bulk between the light and the pair in the corner, and Sheerin squinted up at him anxiously. "Hello, Beenay."

The astronomer shifted his weight to the other foot and smiled feebly. "You won't mind if I sit down awhile and join in the talk? My cameras are set, and there's nothing to do till totality." He paused and eyed the Cultist, who fifteen minutes earlier had drawn a small, skin-bound book from his sleeve and had been poring intently over it ever since. "That rat hasn't been making trouble, has he?"

Sheerin shook his head. His shoulders were thrown back and he frowned his concentration as he forced himself to breathe regularly. He said, "Have you had any trouble breathing, Beenay?"

Beenay sniffed the air in his turn. "It doesn't seem stuffy to me."

"A touch of claustrophobia," explained Sheerin apologetically.

"Ohhh! It worked itself differently with me. I get the impression that my eyes are going back on me. Things seem to blur and—well, nothing is clear. And it's cold, too."

"Oh, it's cold all right. That's no illusion." Theremon grimaced. "My toes feel as if I've been shipping them cross-country in a refrigerating car."

"What we need," put in Sheerin, "is to keep our minds busy with extraneous affairs. I was telling you a while ago, Theremon, why Faro's experiments with the holes in the roof came to nothing.''

''You were just beginning,'' replied Theremon. He encircled a knee with both arms and nuzzled his chin against it.

''Well, as I started to say, they were misled by taking the *Book of Revelations* literally. There probably wasn't any sense in attaching any physical significance to the Stars. It might be, you know, that in the presence of total Darkness, the mind finds it absolutely necessary to create light. This illusion of light might be all the Stars there really are.''

''In other words,'' interposed Theremon, ''you mean the Stars are the results of the madness and not one of the causes. Then, what good will Beenay's photographs be?''

''To prove that it is an illusion, maybe; or to prove the opposite; for all I know. Then again—''

But Beenay had drawn his chair closer, and there was an expression of enthusiasm on his face. ''Say, I'm glad you two got onto this subject.'' His eyes narrowed and he lifted one finger. ''I've been thinking about these Stars and I've got a really cute notion. Of course it's strictly ocean foam, and I'm not trying to advance it seriously, but I think it's interesting. Do you want to hear it?''

He seemed half reluctant, but Sheerin leaned back and said, ''Go ahead! I'm listening.''

''Well, then, supposing there were other suns in the universe.'' He broke off a little bashfuly. ''I mean suns that are so far away that they're too dim to see. It sounds as if I've been reading some of that fantastic fiction, I suppose.''

''Not necessarily. Still, isn't that possibility eliminated by the fact that, according to the Law of Gravitation, they would make themselves evident by their attractive forces?''

''Not if they were far enough off,'' rejoined Beenay. ''Really far off—maybe as much as four light years, or even more. We'd never be able to detect perturbations then, because they'd be too small. Say that there were a lot of suns that far off; a dozen or two, maybe.''

Theremon whistled melodiously. ''What an idea for a good Sunday supplement article. Two dozen suns in a universe eight light years across. Wow! That would shrink our world into insignificance. The readers would eat it up.''

''Only an idea,'' said Beenay with a grin, ''but you see the point. During an eclipse, these dozen suns would become visible because there'd be no *real* sunlight to drown them out. Since they are so far off, they'd appear small, like so many little marbles. Of course the Cultists talk of millions of Stars, but that's probably exaggeration. There just isn't any place in the universe you could put a million suns—unless they touched each other.''

Sheerin had listened with gradually increasing interest. ''You've hit something there, Beenay. And exaggeration is just exactly what would happen. Our minds, as you probably know, can't grasp directly any number higher than five; above that there is only the concept of 'many.' A dozen would become a million just like that. A damn good idea!''

''And I've got another cute little notion,'' Beenay said. ''Have you ever thought what a simple problem gravitation would be if only you had a sufficiently simple system? Supposing you had a universe in which there was a planet with only one sun. The planet would travel in a perfect eclipse and the exact nature of the gravitatinal force would be so evident it could be accepted as an axiom. Astronomers on such a world would start off with gravity probably before they even invented the telescope. Naked-eye observation would be enough.''

"But would such a system be dynamically stable?'' questioned Sheerin doubtfully.

"Sure! They call it the 'one-and-one' case. It's been worked out mathematically, but it's the philosophical implications that interest me.''

"It's nice to think about,'' admitted Sheerin, "as a pretty abstraction—like a perfect gas, or absolute zero.''

"Of course,'' continued Beenay, "there's the catch that life would be impossible on such a planet. It wouldn't get enough heat and light, and if it rotated there would be total Darkness half of each day. You couldn't expect life—which is fundamentally dependent upon light—to develop under those conditions. Besides—''

Sheerin's chair went over backward as he sprang to his feet in a rude interruption. "Aton's brought out the lights.''

Beenay said, "Huh,'' turned to stare, and then grinned halfway around his head in open relief.

There were half a dozen foot-long, inch-thick rods cradled in Aton's arms. He glared over them at the assembled staff members.

"Get back to work, all of you. Sheerin, come here and help me!''

Sheerin trotted to the older man's side and, one by one, in utter silence, the two adjusted the rods in makeshift metal holders suspended from the walls.

With the air of one carrying through the most sacred item of a religious ritual, Sheerin scraped a large, clumsy match into spluttering life and passed it to Aton, who carried the flame to the upper end of one of the rods.

It hesitated there awhile, playing futilely about the tip, until a sudden, crackling flare cast Aton's lined face into yellow highlights. He withdrew the match and a spontaneous cheer rattled the window.

The rod was topped by six inches of wavering flame! Methodically, the other rods were lighted, until six independent fires turned the rear of the room yellow.

The light was dim, dimmer even than the tenuous sunlight. The flames reeled crazily, giving birth to drunken, swaying shadows. The torches smoked devilishly and smelled like a bad day in the kitchen. But they emitted yellow light.

There was something about yellow light, after four hours of somber, dimming Beta. Even Latimer had lifted his eyes from his book and stared in wonder.

Sheerin warmed his hands at the nearest, regardless of the soot that gathered upon them in a fine, gray powder, and muttered ecstatically to himself. "Beautiful! Beautiful! I never realized before what a wonderful color yellow is.''

But Theremon regarded the torches suspiciously. He wrinkled his nose at the rancid odor and said, "What are those things?''

"Wood,'' said Sheerin shortly.

"Oh, no, they're not. They aren't burning. The top inch is charred and the flame just keeps shooting up out of nothing.''

"That's the beauty of it. This is a really efficient artificial-light mechanism. We made a few hundred of them, but most went to the Hideout, of course. You see''—he turned and wiped his blackened hands upon his handkerchief—"you take the pithy core of coarse water reeds, dry them thoroughly, and soak them in animal grease. Then you set fire to it and the grease burns, little by little. These torches will burn for almost half an hour without stopping. Ingenious, isn't it? It was developed by one of our own young men at Saro University.''

After the momentary sensation, the dome had quieted. Latimer had carried his chair directly beneath a torch and continued reading, lips moving in the monotonous recital of invocations to the Stars. Beenay had drifted away to his cameras once more, and Theremon seized the opportunity to add to his notes on the article he was going to write for the Saro City *Chronicle* the next day—a procedure he had been following for the last two hours in a perfectly methodical, perfectly conscientious and, as he was well aware, perfectly meaningless fashion.

But, as the gleam of amusement in Sheerin's eyes indicated, careful note-taking occupied his mind with something other than the fact that the sky was gradually turning a horrible deep purple-red, as if it were one gigantic, freshly peeled beet; and so it fulfilled its purpose.

The air grew, somehow, denser. Dusk, like a palpable entity, entered the room, and the dancing circle of yellow light about the torches etched itself into ever-sharper distinction against the gathering grayness beyond. There was the odor of smoke and the presence of little chuckling sounds that the torches made as they burned; the soft pad of one of the men circling the table at which he worked, on hesitant tiptoes; the occasional indrawn breath of someone trying to retain composure in a world that was retreating into the shadow.

It was Theremon who first heard the extraneous noise. It was a vague, unorganized *impression* of sound that would have gone unnoticed but for the dead silence that prevailed within the dome.

The newspaperman sat upright and replaced his notebook. He held his breath and listened; then, with considerable reluctance, threaded his way between the solarscope and one of Beenay's cameras and stood before the window.

The silence ripped to fragments at his startled shout: "*Sheerin!*"

Work stopped! The psychologist was at his side in a moment. Aton joined him. Even Yimot 70, high in his little lean-back seat at the eyepiece of the gigantic solarscope, paused and looked downward.

Outside, Beta was a mere smoldering splinter, taking one last desperate look at Lagash. The eastern horizon, in the direction of the city, was lost in Darkness, and the road from Saro to the Observatory was a dull-red line bordered on both sides by wooded tracts, the trees of which had somehow lost individuality and merged into a continuous shadowy mass.

But it was the highway itself that held attention, for along it there surged another, and infinitely menacing shadowy mass.

Aton cried in a cracked voice, "The madmen from the city! They've come!"

"How long to totality?" demanded Sheerin.

"Fifteen minutes, but . . . but they'll be here in five."

"Never mind, keep the men working. We'll hold them off. This place is built like a fortress. Aton, keep an eye on our young Cultist just for luck. Theremon, come with me.''

Sheerin was out the door, and Theremon was at his heels. The stairs stretched below them in tight, circular sweeps about the central shaft, fading into a dank and dreary grayness.

The first momentum of their rush had carried them fifty feet down, so that the dim, flickering yellow from the open door of the dome had disappeared and both above and below the same dusky shadow crushed in upon them.

Sheerin paused, and his pudgy hand clutched at his chest. His eyes bulged and his voice was a dry cough. "I can't . . . breathe . . . Go down . . . yourself. Close all doors—"

Theremon took a few downward steps, then turned. "Wait! Can you hold out a minute?" He was panting himself. The air passed in and out of his lungs like so much molasses, and there was a little germ of screeching panic in his mind at the thought of making his way into the mysterious Darkness below by himself.

Theremon, after all, was afraid of the dark!

"Stay here," he said. "I'll be back in a second." He dashed upward two steps at a time, heart pounding—not altogether from the exertion—tumbled into the dome and snatched a torch from its holder. It was foul-smelling, and the smoke smarted his eyes almost blind, but he clutched that torch as if he wanted to kiss it for joy, and its flame streamed backward as he hurtled down the stairs again.

Sheerin opened his eyes and moaned as Theremon bent over him. Theremon shook him roughly. "All right, get a hold of yourself. We've got light."

He held the torch at tiptoe height and, propping the tottering psychologist by an elbow, made his way downward in the middle of the protecting circle of illumination.

The offices on the ground floor still possessed what light there was, and Theremon felt the horror about him relax.

"Here," he said brusquely, and passed the torch to Sheerin. "You can hear *them* outside."

And they could. Little scraps of hoarse, wordless shouts.

But Sheerin was right; the Observatory was built like a fortress. Erected in the last century, when the neo-Gavottian style of architecture was at its ugly height, it had been designed for stability and durability rather than for beauty.

The windows were protected by the grillwork of inch-thick iron bars sunk deep into the concrete sills. The walls were solid masonry that an earthquake couldn't have touched, and the main door was a huge oaken slab reinforced with iron. Theremon shot the bolts and they slid shut with a dull clang.

At the other end of the corridor, Sheerin cursed weakly. He pointed to the lock of the back door which had been neatly jimmied into uselessness.

"That must be how Latimer got in," he said.

"Well, don't stand there," cried Theremon impatiently. "Help drag up the furniture—and keep that torch out of my eyes. The smoke's killing me."

He slammed the heavy table up against the door as he spoke, and in two minutes had built a barricade which made up for what it lacked in beauty and symmetry by the sheer inertia of its massiveness.

Somewhere, dimly, far off, they could hear the battering of naked fists upon the door; and the screams and yells from outside had a sort of half reality.

That mob had set off from Saro City with only two things in mind: the attainment of Cultist salvation by the destruction of the Observatory, and a maddening fear that all but paralyzed them. There was no time to think of ground cars, or of weapons, or of leadership, or even of organization. They made for the Observatory on foot and assaulted it with bare hands.

And now that they were there, the last flash of Beta, the last ruby-red drop of flame, flickered feebly over a humanity that had left only stark, universal fear!

Theremon groaned, "Let's get back to the dome!"

In the dome, only Yimot, at the solarscope, had kept his place. The rest were clustered about the cameras, and Beenay was giving his instructions in a hoarse, strained voice.

"Get it straight, all of you. I'm snapping Beta just before totality and changing the plate. That will leave one of you to each camera. You all know about . . . about times of exposure—"

There was a breathless murmur of agreement.

Beenay passed a hand over his eyes. "Are the torches still burning? Never mind, I see them!" He was leaning hard against the back of a chair. "Now remember, don't try to look for good shots. Don't waste time trying to get t-two stars at a time in the scope field. One is enough. And . . . and if you feel yourself going, *get away from the camera.*"

At the door, Sheerin whispered to Theremon, "Take me to Aton. I don't see him."

The newsman did not answer immediately. The vague forms of the astronomers wavered and blurred, and the torches overhead had become only yellow splotches.

"It's dark," he whispered.

Sheerin held out his hand. "Aton." He stumbled forward. "Aton!"

Theremon stepped after and seized his arm. "Wait, I'll take you." Somehow he made his way across the room. He closed his eyes against the Darkness and his mind against the chaos within it.

No one heard them or paid attention to them. Sheerin stumbled against the wall. "Aton!"

The psychologist felt shaking hands touching him, then withdrawing, and a voice muttering, "Is that you, Sheerin?"

"Aton!" He strove to breathe normally. "Don't worry about the mob. The place will hold them off."

Latimer, the Cultist, rose to his feet, and his face twisted in desperation. His word was pledged, and to break it would mean placing his soul in mortal peril. Yet that word had been forced upon him and had not been given freely. The Stars would come soon! He could not stand by and allow—And yet his word was pledged.

Beenay's face was dimly flushed as it looked upward at Beta's last ray, and Latimer, seeing him bend over his camera, made his decision. His nails cut the flesh of his palms as he tensed himself.

He staggered crazily as he started his rush. There was nothing before him but shadows; the very floor beneath his feet lacked substance. And then someone was upon him and he went down with clutching fingers at his throat.

He doubled his knee and drove it hard into his assailant. "Let me up or I'll kill you."

Theremon cried out sharply and muttered through a blinding haze of pain. "You double-crossing rat!"

The newsman seemed conscious of everything at once. He heard Beenay croak, "I've got it. At your cameras, men!" and then there was the strange awareness that the last thread of sunlight had thinned out and snapped.

Simultaneously he heard one last choking gasp from Beenay, and a queer little cry from Sheerin, a hysterical giggle that cut off in a rasp—and a sudden silence, a strange, deadly silence from outside.

And Latimer had gone limp in his loosening grasp. Theremon peered into the Cultist's eyes and saw the blankness of them, staring upward, mirroring the feeble yellow of the torches. He saw the bubble of froth upon Latimer's lips and heard the low animal whimper in Latimer's throat.

With the slow fascination of fear, he lifted himself on one arm and turned his eyes toward the blood-curdling blackness of the window.

Through it shone the Stars!

Not Earth's feeble thirty-six hundred Stars visible to the eye; Lagash was in the center of a giant cluster. Thirty thousand mighty suns shone down in a soul-searing splendor that was more frighteningly cold in its awful indifference than the bitter wind that shivered across the cold, horribly bleak world.

Theremon staggered to his feet, his throat constricting him to breathlessness, all the muscles of his body writhing in an intensity of terror and sheer fear beyond bearing. He was going mad and knew it, and somewhere deep inside a bit of sanity was screaming, struggling to fight off the hopeless flood of black terror. It was very horrible to go mad and know that you were going mad—to know that in a little minute you would be here physically and yet all the real essence would be dead and drowned in the black madness. For this was the Dark—the Dark and the Cold and the Doom. The bright walls of the universe were shattered and their awful black fragments were falling down to crush and squeeze and obliterate him.

He jostled someone crawling on hands and knees, but stumbled somehow over him. Hands groping at his tortured throat, he limped toward the flame of the torches that filled all his mad vision.

"Light!" he screamed.

Aton, somewhere, was crying, whimpering horribly like a terribly frightened child. "Stars—all the Stars—we didn't know at all. We didn't know anything. We thought six stars in a universe is something the Stars didn't notice is Darkness forever and ever and ever and the walls are breaking in and we didn't know we couldn't know and anything—"

Someone clawed at the torch, and it fell and snuffed out. In the instant, the awful splendor of the indifferent Stars leaped nearer to them.

On the horizon outside the window, in the direction of Saro City, a crimson glow began growing, strengthening in brightness, that was not the glow of a sun.

The long night had come again.

PROFESSION

GEORGE PLATEN could not conceal the longing in his voice. It was too much to suppress. He said, "Tomorrow's the first of May. Olympics!"

He rolled over on his stomach and peered over the foot of his bed at his roommate. Didn't *he* feel it, too? Didn't *this* make some impression on him?

George's face was thin and had grown a trifle thinner in the nearly year and a half that he had been at the House. His figure was slight but the look in his blue eyes was as intense as it had ever been, and right now there was a trapped look in the way his fingers curled against the bedspread.

George's roommate looked up briefly from his book and took the opportunity to adjust the light-level of the stretch of wall near his chair. His name was Hali Omani and he was a Nigerian by birth. His dark brown skin and massive features seemed made for calmness, and mention of the Olympics did not move him.

He said, "I know, George."

George owed much to Hali's patience and kindness when it was needed, but even patience and kindness could be overdone. Was this a time to sit there like a statue built of some dark, warm wood?

George wondered if he himself would grow like that after ten years here and rejected the thought violently. No!

He said defiantly, "I think you've forgotten what May means."

The other said, "I remember very well what it means. It means nothing! You're the one who's forgotten that. May means nothing to you, George Platen, and," he added softly, "it means nothing to me, Hali Omani."

George said, "The ships are coming in for recruits. By June, thousands and thousands will leave with millions of men and women heading for any world you can name, and all that means nothing?"

"Less than nothing. What do you want me to do about it, anyway?" Omani ran his finger along a difficult passage in the book he was reading and his lips moved soundlessly.

George watched him. Damn it, he thought, yell, scream; you can do that much. Kick at me, do anything.

It was only that he wanted not to be so alone in his anger. He wanted not to be the only one so filled with resentment, not to be the only one dying a slow death.

It was better those first weeks when the Universe was a small shell of vague

379

light and sound pressing down upon him. It was better before Omani had wavered into view and dragged him back to a life that wasn't worth living.

Omani! He was old! He was at least thirty. George thought: Will I be like that at thirty? Will I be like that in twelve years?

And because he was afraid he might be, he yelled at Omani, "Will you stop reading that fool book?"

Omani turned a page and read on a few words, then lifted his head with its skullcap of crisply curled hair and said, "What?"

"What good does it do you to read the book?" He stepped forward, snorted "More electronics," and slapped it out of Omani's hands.

Omani got up slowly and picked up the book. He smoothed a crumpled page without visible rancor. "Call it the satisfaction of curiosity." he said. "I understand a little of it today, perhaps a little more tomorrow. That's a victory in a way."

"A victory. What kind of a victory? Is that what satisfies you in life? To get to know enough to be a quarter of a Registered Electronician by the time you're sixty-five?"

"Perhaps by the time I'm thirty-five."

"And then who'll want you? Who'll use you? Where will you go?"

"No one. No one. Nowhere. I'll stay here and read other books."

"And that satisfies you? Tell me! You've dragged me to class. You've got me to reading and memorizing, too. For what? There's nothing in it that satisfies me."

"What good will it do you to deny yourself satisfaction?"

"It means I'll quit the whole farce. I'll do as I planned to do in the beginning before you dovey-lovied me out of it. I'm going to force them to—to——"

Omani put down his book. He let the other run down and then said, "To what, George?"

"To correct a miscarriage of justice. A frame-up. I'll get that Antonelli and force him to admit he—he——"

Omani shook his head. "Everyone who comes here insists it's a mistake. I thought you'd passed that stage."

"Don't call it a stage," said George violently. "In my case, it's a fact. I've told you——"

"You've told me, but in your heart you know no one made any mistake as far as you were concerned."

"Because no one will admit it? You think any of them would admit a mistake unless they were forced to?——Well, I'll force them."

It was May that was doing this to George; it was Olympics month. He felt it bring the old wildness back and he couldn't stop it. He didn't want to stop it. He had been in danger of forgetting.

He said, "I was going to be a Computer Programmer and I *can* be one. I could be one today, regardless of what they say analysis shows." He pounded his mattress. "They're wrong. They *must* be."

"The analysts are never wrong."

"They *must* be. Do you doubt my intelligence?"

"Intelligence hasn't one thing to do with it. Haven't you been told that often enough? Can't you understand that?"

George rolled away, lay on his back, and stared somberly at the ceiling.

"What did you want to be, Hali?"

"I had no fixed plans. Hydroponicist would have suited me, I suppose."

"Did you think you could make it?"

"I wasn't sure."

George had never asked personal questions of Omani before. It struck him as queer, almost unnatural, that other people had had ambitions and ended here. Hydroponicist!

He said, "Did you think you'd make *this?*"

"No, but here I am just the same."

"And you're satisfied. Really, really satisfied. You're happy. You love it. You wouldn't be anywhere else."

Slowly, Omani got to his feet. Carefully, he began to unmake his bed. He said, "George, you're a hard case. You're knocking yourself out because you won't accept the facts about yourself. George, you're here in what you call the House, but I've never heard you give it its full title. Say it, George, say it. Then go to bed and sleep this off."

George gritted his teeth and showed them. He choked out, "No!"

"Then I will," said Omani, and he did. He shaped each syllable carefully. George was bitterly ashamed at the sound of it. He turned his head away.

For most of the first eighteen years of his life, George Platen had headed firmly in one direction, that of Registered Computer Programmer. There were those in his crowd who spoke wisely of Spationautics, Refrigeration Technology, Transportation Control, and even Administration. But George held firm.

He argued relative merits as vigorously as any of them, and why not? Education Day loomed ahead of them and was the great fact of their existence. It approached steadily, as fixed and certain as the calendar—the first day of November of the year following one's eighteenth birthday.

After that day, there were other topics of conversation. One could discuss with others some detail of the profession, or the virtues of one's wife and children, or the fate of one's space-polo team, or one's experiences in the Olympics. Before Education Day, however, there was only one topic that unfailingly and unwearyingly held everyone's interest, and that was Education Day.

"What are you going for? Think you'll make it? Heck, that's no good. Look at the records; quota's been cut. Logistics now——"

Or Hypermechanics now—— Or Communications now—— Or Gravitics now——

Especially Gravitics at the moment. Everyone had been talking about Gravitics in the few years just before George's Education Day because of the development of the Gravitic power engine.

Any world within ten light-years of a dwarf star, everyone said, would give its eyeteeth for any kind of Registered Gravitics Engineer.

The thought of that never bothered George. Sure it would; all the eyeteeth it could scare up. But George had also heard what had happened before in a newly developed technique. Rationalization and simplification followed in a flood. New models each year; new types of gravitic engines; new principles. Then all those eyeteeth gentlemen would find themselves out of date and superseded by later models with later educations. The first group would then have to settle down to unskilled labor or ship out to some backwoods world that wasn't quite caught up yet.

Now Computer Programmers were in steady demand year after year, century after century. The demand never reached wild peaks; there was never a howling bull market for Programmers; but the demand climbed steadily as new worlds opened up and as older worlds grew more complex.

He had argued with Stubby Trevelyan about that constantly. As best friends, their arguments had to be constant and vitriolic and, of course, neither ever persuaded or was persuaded.

But then Trevelyan had had a father who was a Registered Metallurgist and had actually served on one of the Outworlds, and a grandfather who had also been a Registered Metallurgist. He himself was intent on becoming a Registered Metallurgist almost as a matter of family right and was firmly convinced that any other profession was a shade less than respectable.

"There'll always be metal," he said, "and there's an accomplishment in molding alloys to specification and watching structures grow. Now what's a Programmer going to be doing. Sitting at a coder all day long, feeding some fool mile-long machine.

Even at sixteen, George had learned to be practical. He said simply, "There'll be a million Metallurgists put out along with you."

"Because it's good. A good profession. The best."

"But you get crowded out, Stubby. You can be way back in line. Any world can tape out its own Metallurgists, and the market for advanced Earth models isn't so big. And it's mostly the small worlds that want them. You know what per cent of the turnout of Registered Metallurgists· get tabbed for worlds with a Grade A rating. I looked it up. It's just 13.3 per cent. That means you'll have seven chances in eight of being stuck in some world that just about has running water. You may even be stuck on Earth; 2.3 per cent are."

Trevelyan said belligerently, "There's no disgrace in staying on Earth. Earth needs technicians, too. Good ones." His grandfather had been an Earth-bound Metallurgist, and Trevelyan lifted his finger to his upper lip and dabbed at an as yet nonexistent mustache.

George knew about Trevelyan's grandfather and, considering the Earth-bound position of his own ancestry, was in no mood to sneer. He said diplomatically, "No intellectual disgrace. Of course not. But it's nice to get into a Grade A world, isn't it?

"Now you take Programmers. Only the Grade A worlds have the kind of computers that really need first-class Programmers so they're the only ones in the market. And Programmer tapes are complicated and hardly any one fits. They need more Programmers than their own population can supply. It's just a matter of statistics. There's one first-class Programmer per million, say. A world needs twenty and has a population of ten million, they have to come to Earth for five to fifteen Programmers. Right?

"And you know how many Registered Computer Programmers went to Grade A planets last year? I'll tell you. Every last one. If you're a Programmer, you're a picked man. Yes, sir."

Trevelyan frowned. "If only one in a million makes it, what makes you think *you*'ll make it?"

George said guardedly, "I'll make it."

He never dared tell anyone; not Trevelyan; not his parents; of exactly what he was doing that made him so confident. But he wasn't worried. He was simply confident (that was the worst of the memories he had in the hopeless days afterward). He was as blandly confident as the average eight-year-old kid approaching Reading Day—that childhood preview of Education Day.

Of course, Reading Day had been different. Partly, there was the simple fact of childhood. A boy of eight takes many extraordinary things in stride. One day you can't read and the next day you can. That's just the way things are. Like the sun shining.

And then not so much depended upon it. There were no recruiters just ahead, waiting and jostling for the lists and scores on the coming Olympics. A boy or girl who goes through the Reading Day is just someone who has ten more years of undifferentiated living upon Earth's crawling surface; just someone who returns to his family with one new ability.

By the time Education Day came, ten years later, George wasn't even sure of most of the details of his own Reading Day.

Most clearly of all, he remembered it to be a dismal September day with a mild rain falling. (September for Reading Day; November for Education Day; May for Olympics. They made nursery rhymes out of it.) George had dressed by the wall lights, with his parents far more excited than he himself was. His father was a Registered Pipe Fitter and had found his occupation on Earth. This fact had always been a humiliation to him, although, of course, as anyone could see plainly, most of each generation must stay on Earth in the nature of things.

There had to be farmers and miners and even technicians on Earth. It was only the late-model, high-specialty professions that were in demand on the Outworlds, and only a few millions a year out of Earth's eight billion population could be exported. Every man and woman on Earth couldn't be among that group.

But every man and woman could hope that at least one of his children could be one, and Platen, Senior, was certainly no exception. It was obvious to him (and, to be sure, to others as well) that George was notably intelligent and quick-minded. He would be bound to do well and he would have to, as he was an only child. If George didn't end on an Outworld, they would have to wait for grandchildren before a next chance would come along, and that was too far in the future to be much consolation.

Reading Day would not prove much, of course, but it would be the only indication they would have before the big day itself. Every parent on Earth would be listening to the quality of reading when his child came home with it; listening for any particularly easy flow of words and building that into certain omens of the future. There were few families that didn't have at least one hopeful who, from Reading Day on, was the great hope because of the way he handled his trisyllabics.

Dimly, George was aware of the cause of his parents' tension, and if there was any anxiety in his young heart that drizzly morning, it was only the fear that his father's hopeful expression might fade out when he returned home with his reading.

The children met in the large assembly room of the town's Education hall. All over Earth, in millions of local halls, throughout that month, similar groups of children would be meeting. George felt depressed by the grayness of the room and by the other children, strained and stiff in unaccustomed finery.

Automatically, George did as all the rest of the children did. He found the small clique that represented the children on his floor of the apartment house and joined them.

Trevelyan, who lived immediately next door, still wore his hair childishly long and was years removed from the sideburns and thin, reddish mustache that he was to grow as soon as he was physiologically capable of it.

Trevelyan (to whom George was then known as Jaw-jee) said, "Bet you're scared."

"I am not," said George. Then, confidentially, "My folks got a hunk of printing up on the dresser in my room, and when I come home, I'm going to read it for them." (George's main suffering at the moment lay in the fact that he didn't quite know where to put his hands. He had been warned not to scratch his head or rub his ears or pick his nose or put his hands into his pockets. This eliminated almost every possibility.)

Trevelyan put *his* hands in his pockets and said, "My father isn't worried."

Trevelyan, Senior, had been a Metallurgist on Diporia for nearly seven years, which gave him a superior social status in his neighborhood even though he had retired and returned to Earth.

Earth discouraged these re-immigrants because of population problems, but a small trickle did return. For one thing the cost of living was lower on Earth, and what was a trifling annuity on Diporia, say, was a comfortable income on Earth. Besides, there were always men who found more satisfaction in displaying their success before the friends and scenes of their childhood than before all the rest of the Universe besides.

Trevelyan, Senior, further explained that if he stayed on Diporia, so would his children, and Diporia was a one-spaceship world. Back on Earth, his kids could end anywhere, even Novia.

Stubby Trevelyan had picked up that item early. Even before Reading Day, his conversation was based on the carelessly assumed fact that his ultimate home would be in Novia.

George, oppressed by thoughts of the other's future greatness and his own small-time contrast, was driven to belligerent defense at once.

"My father isn't worried either. He just wants to hear me read because he knows I'll be good. I suppose your father would just as soon not hear you because he knows you'll be all wrong."

"I will not be all wrong. Reading is *nothing*. On Novia, I'll *hire* people to read to me."

"Because *you* won't be able to read yourself, on account of you're *dumb!*"

"Then how come I'll be on Novia?"

And George, driven, made the great denial, "Who says you'll be on Novia? Bet you don't go anywhere."

Stubby Trevelyan reddened. "I won't be a Pipe Fitter like your old man."

"Take that back, you dumbhead."

"You take *that* back."

They stood nose to nose, not wanting to fight but relieved at having something familiar to do in this strange place. Furthermore, now that George had curled his hands into fists and lifted them before his face, the problem of what to do with his hands was, at least temporarily, solved. Other children gathered round excitedly.

But then it all ended when a woman's voice sounded loudly over the public address system. There was instant silence everywhere. George dropped his fists and forgot Trevelyan.

"Children," said the voice, "we are going to call out your names. As each child is called, he or she is to go to one of the men waiting along the side walls. Do you see them? They are wearing red uniforms so they will be easy to find. The girls will go to the right. The boys will go to the left. Now look about and see which man in red is nearest to you—"

George found his man at a glance and waited for his name to be called off. He had not been introduced before this to the sophistications of the alphabet, and the length of time it took to reach his own name grew disturbing.

The crowd of children thinned; little rivulets made their way to each of the red-clad guides.

When the name "George Platen" was finally called, his sense of relief was exceeded only by the feeling of pure gladness at the fact that Stubby Trevelyan still stood in his place, uncalled.

George shouted back over his shoulder as he left, "Yay, Stubby, maybe they don't want you."

That moment of gaiety quickly left. He was herded into a line and directed down corridors in the company of strange children. They all looked at one another, large-eyed and concerned, but beyond a snuffling, "Quitcher pushing" and "Hey, watch out" there was no conversation.

They were handed little slips of paper which they were told must remain with them. George stared at his curiously. Little black marks of different shapes. He knew it to be printing but how could anyone make words out of it? He couldn't imagine.

He was told to strip; he and four other boys who were all that now remained together. All the new clothes came shucking off and four eight-year-olds stood naked and small, shivering more out of embarrassment than cold. Medical technicians came past, probing them, testing them with odd instruments, pricking them for blood. Each took the little cards and made additional marks on them with little black rods that produced the marks, all neatly lined up, with great speed. George stared at the new marks, but they were no more comprehensible than the old. The children were ordered back into their clothes.

They sat on separate little chairs then and waited again. Names were called again and "George Platen" came third.

He moved into a large room, filled with frightening instruments with knobs and glassy panels in front. There was a desk in the very center, and behind it a man sat, his eyes on the papers piled before him.

He said, "George Platen?"

"Yes, sir," said George, in a shaky whisper. All this waiting and all this going here and there was making him nervous. He wished it were over.

The man behind the desk said, "I am Dr. Lloyed, George. How are you?"

The doctor didn't look up as he spoke. It was as though he had said those words over and over again and didn't have to look up any more.

"I'm all right."

"Are you afraid, George?"

"N—no, sir," said George, sounding afraid even in his own ears.

"That's good," said the doctor, "because there's nothing to be afraid of, you know. Let's see, George. It says here on your card that your father is named

Peter and that he's a Registered Pipe Fitter and your mother is named Amy and is a Registered Home Technician. Is that right?''

"Y—yes, sir.''

"And your birthday is February 13, and you had an ear infection about a year ago. Right?''

"Yes, sir.''

"Do you know how I know all these things?''

"It's on the card, I think, sir.''

"That's right.'' The doctor looked up at George for the first time and smiled. He showed even teeth and looked much younger than George's father. Some of George's nervousness vanished.

The doctor passed the card to George. "Do you know what all those things there mean, George?''

Although George knew he did not he was startled by the sudden request into looking at the card as though he might understand now through some sudden stroke of fate. But they were just marks as before and he passed the card back. "No, sir.''

"Why not?''

George felt a sudden pang of suspicion concerning the sanity of this doctor. Didn't he know why not?

George said, "I can't read, sir.''

"Would you like to read?''

"Yes, sir.''

"Why, George?''

George stared, appalled. No one had ever asked him that. He had no answer. He said falteringly, "I don't know, sir.''

"Printed information will direct you all through your life. There is so much you'll have to know even after Education Day. Cards like this one will tell you. Books will tell you. Television screens will tell you. Printing will tell you such useful things and such interesting things that not being able to read would be as bad as not being able to see. Do you understand?''

"Yes, sir.''

"Are you afraid, George?''

"No, sir.''

"Good. Now I'll tell you exactly what we'll do first. I'm going to put these wires on your forehead just over the corners of your eyes. They'll stick there but they won't hurt at all. Then, I'll turn on something that will make a buzz. It will sound funny and it may tickle you, but it won't hurt. Now if it does hurt, you tell me, and I'll turn it off right away, but it won't hurt. All right?''

George nodded and swallowed.

"Are you ready?''

George nodded. He closed his eyes while the doctor busied himself. His parents had explained this to him. They, too, had said it wouldn't hurt, but then there were always the older children. There were the ten- and twelve-year-olds who howled after the eight-year-olds waiting for Reading Day, "Watch out for the needle.'' There were the others who took you off in confidence and said, "They got to cut your head open. They use a sharp knife that big with a hook on it,'' and so on into horrifying details.

George had never believed them but he had had nightmares, and now he closed his eyes and felt pure terror.

He didn't feel the wires at his temple. The buzz was a distant thing, and there was the sound of his own blood in his ears, ringing hollowly as though it and he were in a large cave. Slowly he chanced opening his eyes.

The doctor had his back to him. From one of the instruments a strip of paper unwound and was covered with a thin, wavy purple line. The doctor tore off pieces and put them into a slot in another machine. He did it over and over again. Each time a little piece of film came out, which the doctor looked at. Finally, he turned toward George with a queer frown between his eyes.

The buzzing stopped.

George said breathlessly, "Is it over?"

The doctor said, "Yes," but he was still frowning.

"Can I read now?" asked George. He felt no different.

The doctor said, "What?" then smiled very suddenly and briefly. He said, "It works fine, George. You'll be reading in fifteen minutes. Now we're going to use another machine this time and it will take longer. I'm going to cover your whole head, and when I turn it on you won't be able to see or hear anything for a while, but it won't hurt. Just to make sure I'm going to give you a little switch to hold in your hand. If anything hurts, you press the little button and everything shuts off. All right?"

In later years, George was told that the little switch was strictly a dummy; that it was introduced solely for confidence. He never did know for sure, however, since he never pushed the button.

A large smoothly curved helmet with a rubbery inner lining was placed over his head and left there. Three or four little knobs seemed to grab at him and bite into his skull, but there was only a little pressure that faded. No pain.

The doctor's voice sounded dimly. "Everything all right, George?"

And then, with no real warning, a layer of thick felt closed down all about him. He was disembodied, there was no sensation, no universe, only himself and a distant murmur at the very ends of nothingness telling him something—telling him—telling him—

He strained to hear and understand but there was all that thick felt between.

Then the helmet was taken off his head, and the light was so bright that it hurt his eyes while the doctor's voice drummed at his ears.

The doctor said, "Here's your card, George. What does it say?"

George looked at his card again and gave out a strangled shout. The marks weren't just marks at all. They made up words. They were words just as clearly as though something were whispering them in his ears. He could *hear* them being whispered as he looked at them.

"What does it say, George?"

"It says—it says—"Platen, George. Born 13 February 6492 of Peter and Amy Platen in . . .' " He broke off.

"You can read, George," said the doctor. "It's all over."

"For good? I won't forget how?"

"Of course not." The doctor leaned over to shake hands gravely. "You will be taken home now."

It was days before George got over this new and great talent of his. He read for his father with such facility that Platen, Senior, wept and called relatives to tell the good news.

George walked about town, reading every scrap of printing he could find and wondering how it was that none of it had ever made sense to him before.

He tried to remember how it was not to be able to read and he couldn't. As far as his feeling about it was concerned, he had always been able to read. Always.

At eighteen, George was rather dark, of medium height, but thin enough to look taller. Trevelyan, who was scarcely an inch shorter, had a stockiness of build that made "Stubby" more than ever appropriate, but in this last year he had grown self-conscious. The nickname could no longer be used without reprisal. And since Trevelyan disapproved of his proper first name even more strongly, he was called Trevelyan or any decent variant of that. As though to prove his manhood further, he had most persistently grown a pair of sideburns and a bristly mustache.

He was sweating and nervous now, and George, who had himself grown out of "Jaw-jee" and into the curt monosyllabic gutterality of "George," was rather amused by that.

They were in the same large hall they had been in ten years before (and not since). It was as if a vague dream of the past had come to sudden reality. In the first few minutes George had been distinctly surprised at finding everything seem smaller and more cramped than his memory told him; then he made allowance for his own growth.

The crowd was smaller than it had been in childhood. It was exclusively male this time. The girls had another day assigned them.

Trevelyan leaned over to say, "Beats me the way they make you wait."

"Red tape," said George. "You can't avoid it."

Trevelyan said, "What makes *you* so damned tolerant about it?"

"I've got nothing to worry about."

"Oh, brother, you make me sick. I hope you end up Registered Manure Spreader just so I can see your face when you do." His somber eyes swept the crowd anxiously.

George looked about, too. It wasn't quite the system they used on the children. Matters went slower, and instructions had been given out at the start in print (an advantage over the pre-Readers). The names Platen and Trevelyan were well down the alphabet still, but this time the two knew it.

Young men came out of the education rooms, frowning and uncomfortable, picked up their clothes and belongings, then went off to analysis to learn the results.

Each, as he came out, would be surrounded by a clot of the thinning crowd. "How was it?" "How'd it feel?" "Whacha think ya made?" "Ya feel any different?"

Answers were vague and noncommittal.

George forced himself to remain out of those clots. You only raised your own blood pressure. Everyone said you stood the best chance if you remained calm. Even so, you could feel the palms of your hands grow cold. Funny that new tensions came with the years.

For instance, high-specialty professionals heading out for an Outworld were accompanied by a wife (or husband). It was important to keep the sex ratio in good balance on all worlds. And if you were going out to a Grade A world, what girl would refuse you? George had no specific girl in mind yet; he wanted none. Not now! Once he made Programmer; once he could add to his name, Registered

Computer Programmer, he could take his pick, like a sultan in a harem. The thought excited him and he tried to put it away. Must stay calm.

Trevelyan muttered, "What's it all about anyway? First they say it works best if you're relaxed and at ease. Then they put you through this and make it impossible for you to be relaxed and at ease."

"Maybe that's the idea. They're separating the boys from the men to begin with. Take it easy, Trev."

"Shut up."

George's turn came. His name was not called. It appeared in glowing letters on the notice board.

He waved at Trevelyan. "Take it easy. Don't let it get you."

He was happy as he entered the testing chamber. Actually happy.

The man behind the desk said, "George Platen?"

For a fleeting instant there was a razor-sharp picture in George's mind of another man, ten years earlier, who had asked the same question, and it was almost as though this were the same man and he, George, had turned eight again as he had stepped across the threshold.

But the man looked up and, of course, the face matched that of the sudden memory not at all. The nose was bulbous, the hair thin and stringy, and the chin wattled as though its owner had once been grossly overweight and had reduced.

The man behind the desk looked annoyed. "Well?"

George came to Earth. "I'm George Platen, sir."

"Say so, then. I'm Dr. Zachary Antonelli, and we're going to be intimately acquainted in a moment."

He stared at small strips of film, holding them up to the light owlishly.

George winced inwardly. Very hazily, he remembered that other doctor (he had forgotten the name) staring at such film. Could these be the same? The other doctor had frowned and this one was looking at him now as though he were angry.

His happiness was already just about gone.

Dr. Antonelli spread the pages of a thickish file out before him now and put the films carefully to one side. "It says here you want to be a Computer Programmer."

"Yes, doctor."

"Still do?"

"Yes, sir."

"It's a responsible and exacting position. Do you feel up to it?"

"Yes, sir."

"Most pre-Educates don't put down any specific profession. I believe they are afraid of queering it."

"I think that's right, sir."

"Aren't you afraid of that?"

"I might as well be honest, sir."

Dr. Antonelli nodded, but without any noticeable lightening of his expression. "Why do you want to be a Programmer?"

"It's a responsible and exacting position as you said, sir. It's an important job and an exciting one. I like it and I think I can do it."

Dr. Antonelli put the papers away, and looked at George sourly. He said,

"How do you know you like it? Because you think you'll be snapped up by some Grade A planet?"

George thought uneasily: He's trying to rattle you. Stay calm and stay frank.

He said, "I think a Programmer has a good chance, sir, but even if I were left on Earth, I know I'd like it." (That was true enough. I'm not lying, thought George.)

"All right, how do you know?"

He asked it as though he knew there was no decent answer and George almost smiled. He had one.

He said, "I've been reading about Programming, sir."

"You've been *what?*" Now the doctor looked genuinely astonished and George took pleasure in that.

"Reading about it, sir. I bought a book on the subject and I've been studying it."

"A book for Registered Programmers?"

"Yes, sir."

"But you couldn't understand it."

"Not at first. I got other books on mathematics and electronics. I made out all I could. I still don't know much, but I know enough to know I like it and to know I can make it." (Even his parents never found that secret cache of books or knew why he spent so much time in his own room or exactly what happened to the sleep he missed.)

The doctor pulled at the loose skin under his chin. "What was your idea in doing that, son?"

"I wanted to make sure I would be interested, sir."

"Surely you know that being interested means nothing. You could be devoured by a subject and if the physical make-up of your brain makes it more efficient for you to be something else, something else you will be. You know that, don't you?"

"I've been told that," said George cautiously.

"Well, believe it. It's true."

George said nothing.

Dr. Antonelli said, "Or do you believe that studying some subject will bend the brain cells in that direction, like that other theory that a pregnant woman need only listen to great music persistently to make a composer of her child. Do you believe that?"

George flushed. That had certainly been in his mind. By forcing his intellect constantly in the desired direction, he had felt sure that he would be getting a head start. Most of his confidence had rested on exactly that point.

"I never——" he began, and found no way of finishing.

"Well, it isn't true. Good Lord, youngster, your brain pattern is fixed at birth. It can be altered by a blow hard enough to damage the cells or by a burst blood vessel or by a tumor or by a major infection——each time, of course, for the worse. But it certainly can't be affected by your thinking special thoughts." He stared at George thoughtfully, then said, "Who told you to do this?"

George, now thoroughly disturbed, swallowed and said, "No one, doctor. My own idea."

"Who knew you were doing it after you started?"

"No one. Doctor, I meant to do no wrong."

"Who said anything about wrong? Useless is what I would say. Why did you keep it to yourself?"

"I—I thought they'd laugh at me." (He thought abruptly of a recent exchange with Trevelyan. George had very cautiously broached the thought, as of something merely circulating distantly in the very outermost reaches of his mind, concerning the possibility of learning something by ladling it into the mind by hand, so to speak, in bits and pieces. Trevelyan had hooted, "George, you'll be tanning your own shoes next and weaving your own shirts." He had been thankful then for his policy of secrecy.)

Dr. Antonelli shoved the bits of film he had first looked at from position to position in morose thought. Then he said, "Let's get you analyzed. This is getting me nowhere."

The wires went to George's temples. There was the buzzing. Again there came a sharp memory of ten years ago.

George's hands were clammy; his heart pounded. He should never have told the doctor about his secret reading.

It was his damned vanity, he told himself. He had wanted to show how enterprising he was, how full of initiative. Instead, he had showed himself superstitious and ignorant and aroused the hostility of the doctor. (He could tell the doctor hated him for a wise guy on the make.)

And now he had brought himself to such a state of nervousness, he was sure the analyzer would show nothing that made sense.

He wasn't aware of the moment when the wires were removed from his temples. The sight of the doctor, staring at him thoughtfully, blinked into his consciousness and that was that; the wires were gone. George dragged himself together with a tearing effort. He had quite given up his ambition to be a Programmer. In the space of ten minutes, it had all gone.

He said dismally, "I suppose no?"

"No what?"

"No Programmer?"

The doctor rubbed his nose and said, "You get your clothes and whatever belongs to you and go to room 15-C. Your files will be waiting for you there. So will my report."

George said in complete surprise. "Have I been Educated already? I thought this was just to——"

Dr. Antonelli stared down at his desk. "It will all be explained to you. You do as I say."

George felt something like panic. What was it they couldn't tell him? He wasn't fit for anything but Registered Laborer. They were going to prepare him for that; adjust him to it.

He was suddenly certain of it and he had to keep from screaming by main force.

He stumbled back to his place of waiting. Trevelyan was not there, a fact for which he would have been thankful if he had had enough self-possession to be meaningfully aware of his surroundings. Hardly anyone was left, in fact, and the few who were looked as though they might ask him questions were it not that they were too worn out by their tail-of-the-alphabet waiting to buck the fierce, hot look of anger and hate he cast at them.

What right had *they* to be technicians and he, himself, a Laborer? Laborer! He was *certain!*

He was led by a red-uniformed guide along the busy corridors lined with separate rooms each containing its groups, here two, there five: the Motor Mechanics, the Construction Engineers, the Agronomists—— There were hundreds of specialized Professions and most of them would be represented in this small town by one or two anyway.

He hated them all just then: the Statisticians, the Accountants, the lesser breeds and the higher. He hated them because they owned their smug knowledge now, knew their fate, while he himself, empty still, had to face some kind of further red tape.

He reached 15-C, was ushered in and left in an empty room. For one moment, his spirits bounded. Surely, if this were the Labor classification room, there would be dozens of youngsters present.

A door sucked into its recess on the other side of a waist-high partition and an elderly, white-haired man stepped out. He smiled and showed even teeth that were obviously false, but his face was still ruddy and unlined and his voice had vigor.

He said, "Good evening, George. Our own sector has only one of you this time, I see."

"Only one?" said George blankly.

"Thousands over the Earth, of course. Thousands. You're not alone."

George felt exasperated. He said, "I don't understand, sir. What's my classification? What's happening?"

"Easy, son. You're all right. It could happen to anyone." He held out his hand and George took it mechanically. It was warm and it pressed George's hand firmly. "Sit down, son. I'm Sam Ellenford."

George nodded impatiently. "I want to know what's going on, sir."

"Of course. To begin with, you can't be a Computer Programmer, George. You've guessed that, I think."

"Yes, I have," said George bitterly. "What will I be, then?"

"That's the hard part to explain, George." He paused, then said with careful distinctness, "Nothing."

"*What!*"

"Nothing!"

"But what does that mean? Why can't you assign me a profession?"

"We have no choice in the matter, George. It's the structure of your mind that decides that."

George went a sallow yellow. His eyes bulged. "There's something wrong with my mind?"

"There's *something* about it. As far as professional classification is concerned, I suppose you can call it wrong."

"But why?"

Ellenford shrugged. "I'm sure you know how Earth runs its Educational program, George. Practically any human being can absorb practically any body of knowledge, but each individual brain pattern is better suited to receiving some types of knowledge than others. We try to match mind to knowledge as well as we can within the limits of the quota requirements for each profession."

George nodded. "Yes, I know."

"Every once in a while, George, we come up against a young man whose mind is not suited to receiving a superimposed knowledge of any sort."

"You mean I can't be Educated?"

"That is what I mean."

"But that's crazy. I'm intelligent. I can understand——" He looked helplessly about as though trying to find some way of proving that he had a functioning brain.

"Don't misunderstand me, please," said Ellenford gravely. "You're intelligent. There's no question about that. You're even above average in intelligence. Unfortunately that has nothing to do with whether the mind ought to be allowed to accept superimposed knowledge or not. In fact, it is almost always the intelligent person who comes here."

"You mean I can't even be a Registered Laborer?" babbled George. Suddenly even that was better than the blank that faced him. "What's there to know to be a Laborer?"

"Don't underestimate the Laborer, young man. There are dozens of subclassifications and each variety has its own corpus of fairly detailed knowledge. Do you think there's no skill in knowing the proper manner of lifting a weight? Besides, for the Laborer, we must select not only minds suited to it, but bodies as well. You're not the type, George, to last long as a Laborer."

George was conscious of his slight build. He said, "But I've never heard of anyone without a profession."

"There aren't many," conceded Ellenford. "And we protect them."

"Protect them?" George felt confusion and fright grow higher inside him.

"You're a ward of the planet, George. From the time you walked through that door, we've been in charge of you." And he smiled.

It was a fond smile. To George it seemed the smile of ownership; the smile of a grown man for a helpless child.

He said, "You mean, I'm going to be in prison?"

"Of course not. You will simply be with others of your kind."

Your kind. The words made a kind of thunder in George's ear.

Ellenford said, "You need special treatment. We'll take care of you."

To George's own horror, he burst into tears. Ellenford walked to the other end of the room and faced away as though in thought.

George fought to reduce the agonized weeping to sobs and then to strangle those. He thought of his father and mother, of his friends, of Trevelyan, of his own shame——

He said rebelliously, "I learned to read."

"Everyone with a whole mind can do that. We've never found exceptions. It is at this stage that we discover—exceptions. And when you learned to read, George, we were concerned about your mind pattern. Certain peculiarities were reported even then by the doctor in charge."

"Can't you try Educating me? You haven't even tried. I'm willing to take the risk."

"The law forbids us to do that, George. But look, it will not be bad. We will explain matters to your family so they will not be hurt. At the place to which you'll be taken, you'll be allowed privileges. We'll get you books and you can learn what you will."

"Dab knowledge in by hand," said George bitterly. "Shred by shred. Then, when I die I'll know enough to be a Registered Junior Office Boy, Paper-Clip Division.''

"Yet I understand you've already been studying books."

George froze. He was struck devastatingly by sudden understanding. "That's it . . .''

"What is?"

"That fellow Antonelli. He's knifing me."

"No, George. You're quite wrong."

"Don't tell me that." George was in an ecstasy of fury. "That lousy bastard is selling me out because he thought I was a little too wise for him. I read books and tried to get a head start toward programming. Well, what do you want to square things? Money? You won't get it. I'm getting out of here and when I finish broadcasting this—''

He was screaming.

Ellenford shook his head and touched a contact.

Two men entered on catfeet and got on either side of George. They pinned his arms to his sides. One of them used an air-spray hypodermic in the hollow of his right elbow and the hypnotic entered his vein and had an almost immediate effect.

His screams cut off and his head fell forward. His knees buckled and only the men on either side kept him erect as he slept.

They took care of George as they said they would; they were good to him and unfailingly kind—about the way, George thought, he himself would be to a sick kitten he had taken pity on.

They told him that he should sit up and take some interest in life; and then told him that most people who came there had the same attitude of despair at the beginning and that he would snap out of it.

He didn't even hear them.

Dr. Ellenford himself visited him to tell him that his parents had been informed that he was away on special assignment.

George muttered, "Do they know——''

Ellenford assured him at once, "We gave no details."

At first George had refused to eat. They fed him intravenously. They hid sharp objects and kept him under guard. Hali Omani came to be his roommate and his stolidity had a calming effect.

One day, out of sheer desperate boredom, George asked for a book. Omani, who himself read books constantly, looked up, smiling broadly. George almost withdrew the request then, rather than give any of them satisfaction, then thought: What do I care?

He didn't specify the book and Omani brought one on chemistry. It was in big print, with small words and many illustrations. It was for teen-agers. He threw the book violently against the wall.

That's what he would be always. A teen-ager all his life. A pre-Educate forever and special books would have to be written for him. He lay smoldering in bed, staring at the ceiling, and after an hour had passed, he got up sulkily, picked up the book, and began reading.

*   *   *

It took him a week to finish it and then he asked for another.

"Do you want me to take the first one back?" asked Omani.

George frowned. There were things in the book he had not understood, yet he was not so lost to shame as to say so.

But Omani said, "Come to think of it, you'd better keep it. Books are meant to be read and reread."

It was that same day that he finally yielded to Omani's invitation that he tour the place. He dogged at the Nigerian's feet and took in his surroundings with quick hostile glances.

The place was no prison certainly. There were no walls, no locked doors; no guards. But it was a prison in that the inmates had no place to go outside.

It was somehow good to see others like himself by the dozen. It was so easy to believe himself to be the only one in the world so—maimed.

He mumbled, "How many people here anyway?"

"Two hundred and five, George, and this isn't the only place of the sort in the world. There are thousands."

Men looked up as he passed, wherever he went; in the gymnasium, along the tennis courts; through the library (he had never in his life imagined books could exist in such numbers; they were stacked, actually stacked, along long shelves). They stared at him curiously and he returned the looks savagely. At least *they* were no better than he; no call for *them* to look at him as though he were some sort of curiosity.

Most of them were in their twenties. George said suddenly, "What happens to the older ones?"

Omani said, "This place specializes in the younger ones." Then, as though he suddenly recognized an implication in George's question that he had missed earlier, he shook his head gravely and said, "They're not put out of the way, if that's what you mean. There are other Houses for older ones."

"Who cares?" mumbled George, who felt he was sounding too interested and in danger of slipping into surrender.

"You might. As you grow older, you will find yourself in a House with occupants of both sexes."

That surprised George somehow. "Women, too?"

"Of course. Do you suppose women are immune to this sort of thing?"

George thought of that with more interest and excitement than he had felt for anything since before that day when—— He forced his thought away from that.

Omani stopped at the doorway of a room that contained a small closed-circuit television set and a desk computer. Five or six men sat about the television. Omani said, "This is a classroom."

George said, "What's that?"

"The young men in there are being educated. Not," he added, quickly, "in the usual way."

"You mean they're cramming it in bit by bit."

"That's right. This is the way everyone did it in ancient times."

This was what they kept telling him since he had come to the House but what of it? Suppose there had been a day when mankind had not known the diatherm-oven. Did that mean he should be satisfied to eat meat raw in a world where others ate it cooked?

He said, "Why do they want to go through that bit-by-bit stuff?"

"To pass the time, George, and because they're curious."

"What good does it do them?"

"It makes them happier."

George carried that thought to bed with him.

The next day he said to Omani ungraciously, "Can you get me into a classroom where I can find out something about programming?"

Omani replied heartily, "Sure."

It was slow and he resented it. Why should someone have to explain something and explain it again? Why should he have to read and reread a passage, then stare at a mathematical relationship and not understand it at once? That wasn't how other people had to be.

Over and over again, he gave up. Once he refused to attend classes for a week.

But always he returned. The official in charge, who assigned reading, conducted the television demonstrations, and even explained difficult passages and concepts, never commented on the matter.

George was finally given a regular task in the gardens and took his turn in the various kitchen and cleaning details. This was represented to him as being an advance, but he wasn't fooled. The place might have been far more mechanized than it was, but they deliberately made work for the young men in order to give them the illusion of worth-while occupation, of usefulness. George wasn't fooled.

They were even paid small sums of money out of which they could buy certain specified luxuries or which they could put aside for a problematical use in a problematical old age. George kept his money in an open jar, which he kept on a closet shelf. He had no idea how much he had accumulated. Nor did he care.

He made no real friends though he reached the stage where a civil good day was in order. He even stopped brooding (or almost stopped) on the miscarriage of justice that had placed him there. He would go weeks without dreaming of Antonelli, of his gross nose and wattled neck, of the leer with which he would push George into a boiling quicksand and hold him under, till he woke screaming with Omani bending over him in concern.

Omani said to him on a snowy day in February, "It's amazing how you're adjusting."

But that was February, the thirteenth to be exact, his nineteenth birthday. March came, then April, and with the approach of May he realized he hadn't adjusted at all.

The previous May had passed unregarded while George was still in his bed, drooping and ambitionless. This May was different.

All over Earth, George knew, Olympics would be taking place and young men would be competing, matching their skills against one another in the fight for a place on a new world. There would be the holiday atmosphere, the excitement, the news reports, the self-contained recruiting agents from the worlds beyond space, the glory of victory or the consolations of defeat.

How much of fiction dealt with these motifs; how much of his own boyhood excitement lay in following the events of Olympics from year to year; how many of his own plans——

George Platen could not conceal the longing in his voice. It was too much to suppress. He said, "Tomorrow's the first of May. Olympics!"

And that led to his first quarrel with Omani and to Omani's bitter enunciation of the exact name of the institution in which George found himself.

Omani gazed fixedly at George and said distinctly, "A House for the Feeble-minded."

George Platen flushed. Feeble-minded!

He rejected it desperately. He said in a monotone, "I'm leaving." He said it on impulse. His conscious mind learned it first from the statement as he uttered it.

Omani, who had returned to his book, looked up. "What?"

George knew what he was saying now. He said it fiercely, "I'm leaving."

"That's ridiculous. Sit down, George, calm yourself."

"Oh, no. I'm here on a frame-up, I tell you. This doctor, Antonelli, took a dislike to me. It's the sense of power these petty bureaucrats have. Cross them and they wipe out your life with a stylus mark on some card file."

"Are you back to that?"

"And staying there till it's all straightened out. I'm going to get to Antonelli somehow, break him, force the truth out of him." George was breathing heavily and he felt feverish. Olympics month was here and he couldn't let it pass. If he did, it would be the final surrender and he would be lost for all time.

Omani threw his legs over the side of his bed and stood up. He was nearly six feet tall and the expression on his face gave him the look of a concerned Saint Bernard. He put his arm about George's shoulder, "If I hurt your feeling——"

George shrugged him off. "You just said what you thought was the truth, and I'm going to prove it isn't the truth, that's all. Why not? The door's open. There aren't any locks. No one ever said I couldn't leave. I'll just walk out."

"All right, but where will you go?"

"To the nearest air terminal, then to the nearest Olympics center. I've got money." He seized the open jar that held the wages he had put away. Some of the coins jangled to the floor.

"That will last you a week maybe. Then what?"

"By then I'll have things settled."

"By then you'll come crawling back here," said Omani earnestly, "with all the progress you've made to do over again. You're mad, George."

"Feeble-minded is the word you used before."

"Well, I'm sorry I did. Stay here, will you?"

"Are you going to try to stop me?"

Omani compressed his full lips. "No, I guess I won't. This is your business. If the only way you can learn is to buck the world and come back with blood on your face, go ahead. ——Well, go ahead."

George was in the doorway now, looking back over his shoulder. "I'm going,"—he came back to pick up his pocket grooming set slowly—"I hope you don't object to my taking a few personal belongings."

Omani shrugged. He was in bed again reading, indifferent.

George lingered at the door again, but Omani didn't look up. George gritted his teeth, turned and walked rapidly down the empty corridor and out into the night-shrouded grounds.

He had expected to be stopped before leaving the grounds. He wasn't. He had stopped at an all-night diner to ask directions to an air terminal and expected the proprietor to call the police. That didn't happen. He summoned a skimmer to take him to the airport and the driver asked no questions.

Yet he felt no lift at that. He arrived at the airport sick at heart. He had not realized how the outer world would be. He was surrounded by professionals. The diner's proprietor had had his name inscribed on the plastic shell over the cash register. So and so, Registered Cook. The man in the skimmer had his license up, Registered Chauffeur. George felt the bareness of his name and experienced a kind of nakedness because of it; worse, he felt skinned. But no one challenged him. No one studied him suspiciously and demanded proof of professional rating.

George thought bitterly: Who would imagine any human being without one?

He bought a ticket to San Francisco on the 3 A.M. plane. No other plane for a sizable Olympics center was leaving before morning and he wanted to wait as little as possible. As it was, he sat huddled in the waiting room, watching for the police. They did not come.

He was in San Francisco before noon and the noise of the city struck him like a blow. This was the largest city he had ever seen and he had been used to silence and calm for a year and a half now.

Worse, it was Olympics month. He almost forgot his own predicament in his sudden awareness that some of the noise, excitement, confusion was due to that.

The Olympics boards were up at the airport for the benefit of the incoming travelers, and crowds jostled around each one. Each major profession had its own board. Each listed directions to the Olympics Hall where the contest for that day for that profession would be given; the individuals competing and their city of birth; the Outworld (if any) sponsoring it.

It was a completely stylized thing. George had read descriptions often enough in the newsprints and films, watched matches on television, and even witnessed a small Olympics in the Registered Butcher classification at the county seat. Even that, which had no conceivable Galactic implication (there was no Outworlder in attendance, of course) aroused excitement enough.

Partly, the excitement was caused simply by the fact of competition, partly by the spur of local pride (oh, when there was a hometown boy to cheer for, though he might be a complete stranger), and, of course, partly by betting. There was no way of stopping the last.

George found it difficult to approach the board. He found himself looking at the scurrying, avid onlookers in a new way.

There must have been a time when they themselves were Olympic material. What had *they* done? Nothing!

If they had been winners, they would be far out in the Galaxy somewhere, not stuck here on Earth. Whatever they were, their professions must have made them Earth-bait from the beginning; or else they had made themselves Earth-bait by inefficiency at whatever high-specialized professions they had had.

Now these failures stood about and speculated on the chances of newer and younger men. Vultures!

How he wished they were speculating on him.

He moved down the line of boards blankly, clinging to the outskirts of the groups about them. He had eaten breakfast on the strato and he wasn't hungry. He was afraid, though. He was in a big city during the confusion of the beginning of Olympics competition. That was protection, sure. The city was full of strangers. No one would question George. No one would care about George.

No one would care. Not even the House, thought George bitterly. They cared for him like a sick kitten, but if a sick kitten up and wanders off, well, too bad, what can you do?

And now that he was in San Francisco, what did he do? His thoughts struck blankly against a wall. See someone? Whom? How? Where would he even stay? The money he had left seemed pitiful.

The first shamefaced thought of going back came to him. He could go to the police— He shook his head violently as though arguing with a material adversary.

A word caught his eye on one of the boards, gleaming there: *Metallurgist*. In smaller letters, *nonferrous*. At the bottom of a long list of names, in flowing script, *sponsored by Novia*.

It induced painful memories: himself arguing with Trevelyan, so certain that he himself would be a Programmer, so certain that a Programmer was superior to a Metallurgist, so certain that he was following the right course, so certain that he was clever——

So clever that he had to boast to that small-minded, vindictive Antonelli. He had been so sure of himself that moment when he had been called and had left the nervous Trevelyan standing there, so cocksure.

George cried out in a short, incoherent high-pitched gasp. Someone turned to look at him, then hurried on. People brushed past impatiently pushing him this way and that. He remained staring at the board, openmouthed.

It was as though the board had answered his thought. He was thinking "Trevelyan" so hard that it had seemed for a moment that of course the board would say "Trevelyan" back at him.

But that *was* Trevelyan, up there. And *Armand* Trevelyan (Stubby's hated first name; up in lights for everyone to see) and the right hometown. What's more, Trev had wanted Novia, aimed for Novia, insisted on Novia; and this competition was sponsored by Novia.

This had to be Trev; good old Trev. Almost without thinking, he noted the directions for getting to the place of competition and took his place in line for a skimmer.

Then he thought somberly: Trev made it! He wanted to be a Metallurgist, and he made it!

George felt colder, more alone than ever.

There was a line waiting to enter the hall. Apparently, Metallurgy Olympics was to be an exciting and closely fought one. At least, the illuminated sky sign above the hall said so, and the jostling crowd seemed to think so.

It would have been a rainy day, George thought, from the color of the sky, but San Francisco had drawn the shield across its breadth from bay to ocean. It was an expense to do so, of course, but all expenses were warranted where the comfort of Outworlders was concerned. They would be in town for the Olympics. They were heavy spenders. And for each recruit taken, there would be a fee both to Earth and to the local government from the planet sponsoring the Olympics. It paid to keep Outworlders in mind of a particular city as a pleasant place in which to spend Olympics time. San Francisco knew what it was doing.

George, lost in thought, was suddenly aware of a gentle pressure on his shoulder blade and a voice saying, "Are you in line here, young man?"

The line had moved up without George's having noticed the widening gap. He stepped forward hastily and muttered, "Sorry, sir."

There was the touch of two fingers on the elbow of his jacket and he looked about furtively.

The man behind him nodded cheerfully. He had iron-gray hair, and under his jacket he wore an old-fashioned sweater that buttoned down the front. He said, "I didn't mean to sound sarcastic."

"No offense."

"All right, then." He sounded cozily talkative. "I wasn't sure you might not simply be standing there, entangled with the line, so to speak, only by accident. I thought you might be a——"

"A what?" said George sharply.

"Why, a contestant, of course. You look young."

George turned away. He felt neither cozy nor talkative, and bitterly impatient with busybodies.

A thought struck him. Had an alarm been sent out for him? Was his description known, or his picture? Was Gray-hair behind him trying to get a good look at his face?

He hadn't seen any news reports. He craned his neck to see the moving strip of news headlines parading across one section of the city shield, somewhat lackluster against the gray of the cloudy afternoon sky. It was no use. He gave up at once. The headlines would never concern themselves with him. This was Olympics time and the only news worth headlining was the comparative scores of the winners and the trophies won by continents, nations, and cities.

It would go on like that for weeks, with scores calculated on a per capita basis and every city finding some way of calculating itself into a position of honor. His own town had once placed third in an Olympics covering Wiring Technician; third in the whole state. There was still a plaque saying so in Town Hall.

George hunched his head between his shoulders and shoved his hands in his pocket and decided that made him more noticeable. He relaxed and tried to look unconcerned, and felt no safer. He was in the lobby now, and no authoritative hand had yet been laid on his shoulder. He filed into the hall itself and moved as far forward as he could.

It was with an unpleasant shock that he noticed Gray-hair next to him. He looked away quickly and tried reasoning with himself. The man had been right behind him in line after all.

Gray-hair, beyond a brief and tentative smile, paid no attention to him and, besides, the Olympics was about to start. George rose in his seat to see if he could make out the position assigned to Trevelyan and at the moment that was all his concern.

The hall was moderate in size and shaped in the classical long oval, with the spectators in the two balconies running completely about the rim and the contestants in the linear trough down the center. The machines were set up, the progress boards above each bench were dark, except for the name and contest number of each man. The contestants themselves were on the scene, reading, talking together; one was checking his fingernails minutely. (It was, of course, considered bad form for any contestant to pay any attention to the problem before him until the instant of the starting signal.)

George studied the program sheet he found in the appropriate slot in the arm of his chair and found Trevelyan's name. His number was twelve and, to George's chagrin, that was at the wrong end of the hall. He could make out the figure of Contestant Twelve, standing with his hands in his pockets, back to his machine, and staring at the audience as though he were counting the house. George couldn't make out the face.

Still, that was Trev.

George sank back in his seat. He wondered if Trev would do well. He hoped, as a matter of conscious duty, that he would, and yet there was something within him that felt rebelliously resentful. George, professionless, here, watching. Trevelyan, Registered Metallurgist, Nonferrous, there, competing.

George wondered if Trevelyan had competed in his first year. Sometimes men did, if they felt particularly confident—or hurried. It involved a certain risk. However efficient the Educative process, a preliminary year on Earth ("oiling the stiff knowledge," as the expression went) insured a higher score.

If Trevelyan was repeating, maybe he wasn't doing so well. George felt ashamed that the thought pleased him just a bit.

He looked about. The stands were almost full. This would be a well-attended Olympics, which meant greater strain on the contestants—or greater drive, perhaps, depending on the individual.

Why Olympics, he thought suddenly? He had never known. Why was bread called bread?

Once he had asked his father: "Why do they call it Olympics, Dad?"

And his father had said: "Olympics means competition."

George had said: "Is when Stubby and I fight an Olympics, Dad?"

Platen, Senior, had said: "No. Olympics is a special kind of competition and don't ask silly questions. You'll know all you have to know when you get Educated."

George, back in the present, sighed and crowded down into his seat.

All you have to know!

Funny that the memory should be so clear now. "When you get Educated." No one ever said, "*If* you get Educated."

He always had asked silly questions, it seemed to him now. It was as though his mind had some instinctive foreknowledge of its inability to be Educated and had gone about asking questions in order to pick up scraps here and there as best it could.

And at the House they encouraged him to do so because they agreed with his mind's instinct. It was the only way.

He sat up suddenly. What the devil was he doing? Falling for that lie? Was it because Trev was there before him, an Educee, competing in the Olympics that he himself was surrendering?

He *wasn't* feeble-minded! *No!*

And the shout of denial in his mind was echoed by the sudden clamor in the audience as everyone got to his feet.

The box seat in the very center of one long side of the oval was filling with an entourage wearing the colors of Novia, and the word "Novia" went up above them on the main board.

Novia was a Grade A world with a large population and a thoroughly developed civilization, perhaps the best in the Galaxy. It was the kind of world that every Earthman wanted to live in someday; or, failing that, to see his children live in. (George remembered Trevelyan's insistence on Novia as a goal—and there he was competing for it.)

The lights went out in that section of the ceiling above the audience and so did the wall lights. The central trough, in which the contestants waited, became floodlit.

Again George tried to make out Trevelyan. Too far.

The clear, polished voice of the announcer sounded. "Distinguished Novian sponsors. Ladies. Gentlemen. The Olympics competition for Metallurgist, Nonferrous, is about to begin. The contestants are——"

Carefully and conscientiously, he read off the list in the program. Names. Home towns. Educative years. Each name received its cheers, the San Franciscans among them receiving the loudest. When Trevelyan's name was reached, George surprised himself by shouting and waving madly. The gray-haired man next to him surprised him even more by cheering likewise.

George could not help but stare in astonishment and his neighbor leaned over to say (speaking loudly in order to be heard over the hubbub), "No one here from my home town; I'll root for yours. Someone you know?"

George shrank back. "No."

"I noticed you looking in that direction. Would you like to borrow my glasses?"

"No. Thank you." (Why didn't the old fool mind his own business?)

The announcer went on with other formal details concerning the serial number of the competition, the method of timing and scoring and so on. Finally, he approached the meat of the matter and the audience grew silent as it listened.

"Each contestant will be supplied with a bar of nonferrous alloy of unspecified composition. He will be required to sample and assay the bar, reporting all results correctly to four decimals in per cent. All will utilize for this purpose a Beeman Microspectrograph, Model FX-2, each of which is, at the moment, not in working order."

There was an appreciative shout from the audience.

"Each contestant will be required to analyze the fault of his machine and correct it. Tools and spare parts are supplied. The spare part necessary may not be present, in which case it must be asked for, and time of delivery thereof will be deducted from final time. Are all contestants ready?"

The board above Contestant Five flashed a frantic red signal. Contestant Five ran off the floor and returned a moment later. The audience laughed good-naturedly.

"Are all contestants ready?"

The boards remained blank.

"Any questions?"

Still blank.

"You may begin."

There was, of course, no way anyone in the audience could tell how any contestant was progressing except for whatever notations went up on the notice board. But then, that didn't matter. Except for what professional Metallurgists there might be in the audience, none would understand anything about the contest professionally in any case. What was important was who won, who was second, who was third. For those who had bets on the standings (illegal, but unpreventable) that was all-important. Everything else might go hang.

George watched as eagerly as the rest, glancing from one contestant to the next, observing how this one had removed the cover from his microspectrograph with deft strokes of a small instrument; how that one was peering into the face of the thing; how still a third was setting his alloy bar into its holder; and how a fourth adjusted a vernier with such small touches that he seemed momentarily frozen.

Trevelyan was as absorbed as the rest. George had no way of telling how he was doing.

The notice board over Contestant Seventeen flashed: Focus plate out of adjustment.

The audience cheered wildly.

Contestant Seventeen might be right and he might, of course, be wrong. If the latter, he would have to correct his diagnosis later and lose time. Or he might never correct his diagnosis and be unable to complete his analysis or, worse still, end with a completely wrong analysis.

Never mind. For the moment, the audience cheered.

Other boards lit up. George watched for Board Twelve. That came on finally: "Sample holder off-center. New clamp depresser needed."

An attendant went running to him with a new part. If Trevelyan was wrong, it would mean useless delay. Nor would the time elapsed in waiting for the part be deducted. George found himself holding his breath.

Results were beginning to go up on Board Seventeen, in gleaming letters: aluminum, 41.2649; magnesium, 22.1914; copper. 10.1001.

Here and there, other boards began sprouting figures.

The audience was in bedlam.

George wondered how the contestants could work in such pandemonium, then wondered if that were not even a good thing. A first-class technician should work best under pressure.

Seventeen rose from his place as his board went red-rimmed to signify completion. Four was only two seconds behind him. Another, then another.

Trevelyan was still working, the minor constituents of his alloy bar still unreported. With nearly all contestants standing, Trevelyan finally rose, also. Then, tailing off, Five rose, and received an ironic cheer.

It wasn't over. Official announcements were naturally delayed. Time elapsed was something, but accuracy was just as important. And not all diagnoses were of equal difficulty. A dozen factors had to be weighed.

Finally, the announcer's voice sounded, "Winner in the time of four minutes and twelve seconds, diagnosis correct, analysis correct within an average of zero point seven parts per hundred thousand, Contestant Number—*Seventeen, Henry Anton Schmidt of——*"

What followed was drowned in the screaming. Number Eight was next and then Four, whose good time was spoiled by a five part in ten thousand error in the niobium figure. Twelve was never mentioned. He was an also-ran.

George made his way through the crowd to the Contestant's Door and found a large clot of humanity ahead of him. There would be weeping relatives (joy or sorrow, depending) to greet them, newsmen to interview the top-scorers, or the home-town boys, autograph hounds, publicity seekers and the just plain curious.

Girls, too, who might hope to catch the eye of a top-scorer, almost certainly headed for Novia (or perhaps a low-scorer who needed consolation and had the cash to afford it).

George hung back. He saw no one he knew. With San Francisco so far from home, it seemed pretty safe to assume that there would be no relatives to condole with Trev on the spot.

Contestants emerged, smiling weakly, nodding at shouts of approval. Policemen kept the crowds far enough away to allow a lane for walking. Each high-scorer drew a portion of the crowd off with him, like a magnet pushing through a mound of iron filings.

When Trevelyan walked out, scarcely anyone was left. (George felt somehow that he had delayed coming out until just that had come to pass.) There was a cigarette in his dour mouth and he turned, eyes downcast, to walk off.

It was the first hint of home George had had in what was almost a year and a half and seemed almost a decade and a half. He was almost amazed that Trevelyan hadn't aged, that he was the same Trev he had last seen.

George sprang forward. *"Trev!"*

Trevelyan spun about, astonished. He stared at George and then his hand shot out. "George Platen, *what* the devil——"

And almost as soon as the look of pleasure had crossed his face, it left. His hand dropped before George had quite the chance of seizing it.

"Were you in there?" A curt jerk of Trev's head indicated the hall.

"I was."

"To see me?"

"Yes."

"Didn't do so well, did I?" He dropped his cigarette and stepped on it, staring off to the street, where the emerging crowd was slowly eddying and finding its way into skimmers, while new lines were forming for the next scheduled Olympics.

Trevelyan said heavily, "So what? It's only the second time I missed. Novia can go shove after the deal I got today. There are planets that would jump at me fast enough—— But, listen, I haven't seen you since Education Day. Where did you go? Your folks said you were on special assignment but gave no details and you never wrote. You might have written."

"I should have," said George uneasily. "Anyway, I came to say I was sorry the way things went just now."

"Don't be," said Trevelyan. "I told you. Novia can go shove—— At that I should have known. They've been saying for weeks that the Beeman machine would be used. All the wise money was on Beeman machines. The damned Education tapes they ran through me were for Henslers and who uses Henslers? The worlds in the Goman Cluster if you want to call them worlds. Wasn't *that* a nice deal they gave me?"

"Can't you complain to——"

"Don't be a fool. They'll tell me my brain was built for Henslers. Go argue. *Everything* went wrong. I was the only one who had to send out for a piece of equipment. Notice that?"

"They deducted the time for that, though."

"Sure, but I lost time wondering if I could be right in my diagnosis when I noticed there wasn't any clamp depresser in the parts they had supplied. They

don't deduct for that. If it had been a Hensler, I would have *known* I was right.
How could I match up then? The top winner was a San Franciscan. So were three
of the next four. And the fifth guy was from Los Angeles. They get big-city
Educational tapes. The best available. Beeman spectrographs and all. How do I
compete wth them? I came all the way out here just to get a chance at a
Novian-sponsored Olympics in my classification and I might just as well have
stayed home. I knew it, I tell you, and that settles it. Novia isn't the only chunk
of rock in space. Of all the damned——"

He wasn't speaking to George. He wasn't speaking to anyone. He was just
uncorked and frothing. George realized that.

George said, "If you knew in advance that the Beemans were going to be
used, couldn't you have studied up on them?"

"They weren't in my tapes, I tell you."

"You could have read—books."

The last word had tailed off under Trevelyan's suddenly sharp look.

Trevelyan said, "Are you trying to make a big laugh out of this? You think
this is funny? How do you expect me to read some book and try to memorize
enough to match someone else who *knows*."

"I thought——"

"You try it. You try——" Then, suddenly, "What's your profession, by the
way?" He sounded thoroughly hostile.

"Well——".

"Come on, now. If you're going to be a wise guy with me, let's see what
you've done. You're still on Earth, I notice, so you're not a Computer
Programmer and your special assignment can't be much."

George said, "Listen, Trev, I'm late for an appointment." He backed away,
trying to smile.

"No, you don't." Trevelyan reached out fiercely, catching hold of George's
jacket. "You answer my question. Why are you afraid to tell me? What is it with
you? Don't come here rubbing a bad showing in my face, George, unless you can
take it, too. Do you hear me?"

He was shaking George in frenzy and they were struggling and swaying across
the floor, when the Voice of Doom struck George's ear in the form of a
policeman's outraged call.

"All right now. *All* right. Break it up."

George's heart turned to lead and lurched sickeningly. The policeman would
be taking names, asking to see identity cards, and George lacked one. He would
be questioned and his lack of profession would show at once; and before
Trevelyan, too, who ached with the pain of the drubbing he had taken and would
spread the news back home as a salve for his own hurt feelings.

George couldn't stand that. He broke away from Trevelyan and made to run,
but the policeman's heavy hand was on his shoulder. "Hold on, there. Let's see
your identity card."

Trevelyan was fumbling for his, saying harshly, "I'm Armand Trevelyan,
Metallurgist, Nonferrous. I was just competing in the Olympics. You better find
out about him, though, officer."

George faced the two, lips dry and throat thickened past speech.

Another voice sounded, quiet, well-mannered. "Officer. One moment."

The policeman stepped back. "Yes, sir?"

"This young man is my guest. What is the trouble?"

George looked about in wild surprise. It was the gray-haired man who had been sitting next to him. Gray-hair nodded benignly at George.

Guest? Was he mad?

The policeman was saying, "These two were creating a disturbance, sir."

"Any criminal charges? Any damages?"

"No, sir."

"Well, then, I'll be responsible." He presented a small card to the policeman's view and the latter stepped back at once.

Trevelyan began indignantly, "Hold on, now——" but the policeman turned on him.

"All right, now. Got any charges?"

"I just——"

"On your way. The rest of you—move on." A sizable crowd had gathered, which now, reluctantly, unknotted itself and raveled away.

George let himself be led to a skimmer but balked at entering.

He said, "Thank you, but I'm not your guest." (Could it be a ridiculous case of mistaken identity?)

But Gray-hair smiled and said, "You weren't but you are now. Let me introduce myself, I'm Ladislas Ingenescu, Registered Historian."

"But——"

"Come, you will come to no harm, I assure you. After all, I only wanted to spare you some trouble with a policeman."

"But why?"

"Do you want a reason? Well, then, say that we're honorary towns-mates, you and I. We both shouted for the same man, remember, and we townspeople must stick together, even if the tie is only honorary. Eh?"

And George, completely unsure of this man, Ingenescu, and of himself as well, found himself inside the skimmer. Before he could make up his mind that he ought to get off again, they were off the ground.

He thought confusedly: The man has some status. The policeman deferred to him.

He was almost forgetting that his real purpose here in San Francisco was not to find Trevelyan but to find some person with enough influence to force a reappraisal of his own capacity of Education.

It could be that Ingenescu was such a man. And right in George's lap.

Everything could be working out fine—fine. Yet it sounded hollow in his thought. He was uneasy.

During the short skimmer-hop, Ingenescu kept up an even flow of small-talk, pointing out the landmarks of the city, reminiscing about past Olympics he had seen. George, who paid just enough attention to make vague sounds during the pauses, watched the route of flight anxiously.

Would they head for one of the shield-openings and leave the city altogether?

No, they headed downward, and George sighed his relief softly. He felt safer in the city.

The skimmer landed at the roof-entry of a hotel and, as he alighted, Ingenescu said, "I hope you'll eat dinner with me in my room?"

George said, "Yes," and grinned unaffectedly. He was just beginning to realize the gap left within him by a missing lunch.

Ingenescu let George eat in silence. Night closed in and the wall lights went on automatically. (George thought: I've been on my own almost twenty-four hours.)

And then over the coffee, Ingenescu finally spoke again. He said, "You've been acting as though you think I intend you harm."

George reddened, put down his cup and tried to deny it, but the older man laughed and shook his head.

"It's so. I've been watching you closely since I first saw you and I think I know a great deal about you now."

George half rose in horror.

Ingenescu said, "But sit down. I only want to help you."

George sat down but his thoughts were in a whirl. If the old man knew who he was, why had he not left him to the policeman? On the other hand, why should he volunteer help?

Ingenescu said, "You want to know why I should want to help you? Oh, don't look alarmed. I can't read minds. It's just that my training enables me to judge the little reactions that give minds away, you see. Do you understand that?"

George shook his head.

Ingenescu said, "Consider my first sight of you. You were waiting in line to watch an Olympics, and your micro-reactions didn't match what you were doing. The expression of your face was wrong, the action of your hands was wrong. It meant that something, in general, was wrong, and the interesting thing was that, whatever it was, it was nothing common, nothing obvious. Perhaps, I thought, it was something of which your own conscious mind was unaware.

"I couldn't help but follow you, sit next to you. I followed you again when you left and eavesdropped on the conversation between your friend and yourself. After that, well, you were far too interesting an object of study—I'm sorry if that sounds cold-blooded—for me to allow you to be taken off by a policeman. —— Now tell me, what is it that troubles you?"

George was in an agony of indecision. If this was a trap, why should it be such an indirect, roundabout one? And he *had* to turn to someone. He had come to the city to find help and here was help being offered. Perhaps what was wrong was that it was being offered. It came too easy.

Ingenescu said, "Of course, what you tell me as a Social Scientist is a privileged communication. Do you know what that means?"

"No, sir."

"It means, it would be dishonorable for me to repeat what you say to anyone for any purpose. Moreover no one has the legal right to compel me to repeat it."

George said, with sudden suspicion, "I thought you were a Historian."

"So I am."

"Just now you said you were a Social Scientist."

Ingenescu broke into loud laughter and apologized for it when he could talk. "I'm sorry, young man, I shouldn't laugh, and I wasn't really laughing at you. I was laughing at Earth and it's emphasis on physical science, and the practical segments of it at that. I'll bet you can rattle off every subdivision of construction technology or mechanical engineering and yet you're a blank on social science."

"Well, then what *is* social science?"

"Social science studies groups of human beings and there are many high-specialized branches to it, just as there are to zoology, for instance. For instance, there are Culturists, who study the mechanics of cultures, their growth, development, and decay. Cultures," he aded, forestalling a question, "are all the aspects of a way of life. For instance it includes the way we make our living, the things we enjoy and believe, what we consider good and bad and so on. Do you understand?"

"I think I do."

"An Economist—not an Economic Statistician, now, but an Economist—specializes in the study of the way a culture supplies the bodily needs of its individual members. A Psychologist specializes in the individual member of a society and how he is affected by the society. A Futurist specializes in planning the future course of a society, and a Historian—— That's where I come in, now."

"Yes, sir."

"A Historian specializes in the past development of our own society and of societies with other cultures."

George found himself interested. "Was it different in the past?"

"I should say it was. Until a thousand years ago, there was no Education; not what we call Education, at least."

George said, "I know. People learned in bits and pieces out of books."

"Why, how do you know this?"

"I've heard it said," said George cautiously. Then, "Is there any use in worrying about what's happened long ago? I mean, it's all done with, isn't it?"

"It's never done with, my boy. The past explains the present. For instance, why is our Educational system what it is?"

George stirred restlessly. The man kept bringing the subject back to that. He said snappishly, "Because it's best."

"Ah, but why is it best? Now you listen to me for one moment and I'll explain. Then you can tell me if there is any use in history. Even before interstellar travel was developed——" He broke off at the look of complete astonishment on George's face. "Well, did you think we always had it?"

"I never gave it any thought, sir."

"I'm sure you didn't. But there was a time, four or five thousand years ago when mankind was confined to the surface of Earth. Even then, his culture had grown quite technological and his numbers had increased to the point where any failure in technology would have meant mass starvation and disease. To maintain the technological level and advance it in the face of an increasing population, more and more technicians and scientists had to be trained, and yet, as science advanced, it took longer and longer to train them.

"As first interplanetary and then interstellar travel was developed, the problem grew more acute. In fact, actual colonization of extra-Solar planets was impossible for about fifteen hundred years because of a lack of properly trained men.

"The turning point came when the mechanics of the storage of knowledge within the brain was worked out. Once that had been done, it became possible to devise Educational tapes that would modify the mechanics in such a way as to place within the mind a body of knowledge ready-made so to speak. But you know about *that*.

"Once that was done, trained men could be turned out by the thousands and millions, and we could begin what someone has since called the "Filling of the

Universe.'' There are now fifteen hundred inhabited planets in the Galaxy and there is no end in sight.

"Do you see all that is involved? Earth exports Education tapes for low-specialized professions and that keeps the Galactic culture unified. For instance, the Reading tapes insure a single language for all of us. Don't look so surprised, other languages are possible, and in the past were used. Hundreds of them.

"Earth also exports high-specialized professionals and keeps its own population at an endurable level. Since they are shipped out in a balanced sex ratio, they act as self-reproductive units and help increase the populations on the Outworlds where an increase is needed. Furthermore, tapes and men are paid for in material which we much need and on which our economy depends. *Now* do you understand why our Education is the best way?''

"Yes, sir.''

"Does it help you to understand, knowing that without it, interstellar colonization was impossible for fifteen hundred years?''

"Yes, sir.''

"Then you see the uses of history.'' The Historian smiled. "And now I wonder if you see why I'm interested in you?''

George snapped out of time and space back to reality. Ingenescu, apparently, didn't talk aimlessly. All this lecture had been a device to attack him from a new angle.

He said, once again withdrawn, hesitating, "Why?''

"Social Scientists work with societies and societies are made up of people.''

"All right.''

"But people aren't machines. The professionals in physical science work with machines. There is only a limited amount to know about a machine and the professionals know it all. Furthermore, all machines of a given sort are just about alike so that there is nothing to interest them in any given individual machine. But people, ah—— They are so complex and so different one from another that a Social Scientist never knows all there is to know or even a good part of what there is to know. To understand his own specialty, he must always be ready to study people; particularly unusual specimens.''

"Like me,'' said George tonelessly.

"I shouldn't call you a specimen, I suppose, but you are unusual. You're worth studying, and if you will allow me that privilege then, in return, I will help you if you are in trouble and if I can.''

There were pin wheels whirring in George's mind. All this talk about people and colonization made possible by Education. It was as though caked thought within him were being broken up and strewn about mercilessly.

He said, "Let me think,'' and clamped his hands over his ears.

He took them away and said to the Historian, "Will you do something for me, sir?''

"If I can,'' said the Historian amiably.

"And everything I say in this room is a privileged communication. You said so.''

"And I meant it.''

"Then get me an interview with an Outworld official, with—with a Novian.''

Ingenescu looked startled. "Well, now——''

"You can do it,'' said George earnestly. "You're an important official. I saw the policeman's look when you put that card in front of his eyes. If you refuse, I—I won't let you study me."

It sounded a silly threat in George's own ears, one without force. On Ingenescu, however, it seemed to have a strong effect.

He said, "That's an impossible condition. A Novian in Olympics month——"

"All right, then, get me a Novian on the phone and I'll make my own arrangements for an interview."

"Do you think you can?"

"I know I can. Wait and see."

Ingenescu stared at George thoughtfully and then reached for the visiphone.

George waited, half drunk with this new outlook on the whole problem and the sense of power it brought. It couldn't miss. It *couldn't* miss. He would be a Novian yet. He would leave Earth in triumph despite Antonelli and the whole crew of fools at the House for the (he almost laughed aloud) Feeble-minded.

George watched eagerly as the visiplate lit up. It would open up a window into a room of Novians, a window into a small patch of Novia transplanted to Earth. In twenty-four hours, he had accomplished that much.

There was a burst of laughter as the plate unmisted and sharpened, but for the moment no single head could be seen but rather the fast passing of the shadows of men and women, this way and that. A voice was heard, clear-worded over a background of babble. "Ingenescu? He wants me?"

Then there he was, staring out of the plate. A Novian. A genuine Novian. (George had not an atom of doubt. There was something completely Outworldly about him. Nothing that could be completely defined, or even momentarily mistaken.)

He was swarthy in complexion with a dark wave of hair combed rigidly back from his forehead. He wore a thin black mustache and a pointed beard, just as dark, that scarcely reached below the lower limit of his narrow chin, but the rest of his face was so smooth that it looked as though it had been depilated permanently.

He was smiling. "Ladislas, this goes too far. We fully expect to be spied on, within reason, during our stay on Earth, but mind reading is out of bounds."

"Mind reading, Honorable?"

"Confess! You knew I was going to call you this evening. You knew I was only waiting to finish this drink." His hand moved up into view and his eye peered through a small glass of a faintly violet liqueur. "I can't offer you one, I'm afraid."

George, out of range of Ingenescu's transmitter could not be seen by the Novian. He was relieved at that. He wanted time to compose himself and he needed it badly. It was as though he were made up exclusively of restless fingers, drumming, drumming——

But he was right. He hadn't miscalculated. Ingenescu *was* important. The Novian called him by his first name.

Good! Things worked well. What George had lost on Antonelli, he would make up, with advantage, on Ingenescu. And someday, when he was on his own at last, and could come back to Earth as powerful a Novian as this one who could negligently joke with Ingenescu's first name and be addressed as "Honorable" in turn—when he came back, he would settle with Antonelli. He had a year and a half to pay back and he——

He all but lost his balance on the brink of the enticing daydream and snapped back in sudden anxious realization that he was losing the thread of what was going on.

The Novian was saying, "——doesn't hold water. Novia has a civilization as complicated and advanced as Earth's. We're not Zeston, after all. It's ridiculous that we have to come here for individual technicians."

Ingenescu said soothingly, "Only for new models. There is never any certainty that new models will be needed. To buy the Educational tapes would cost you the same price as a thousand technicians and how do you know you would need that many?"

The Novian tossed off what remained of his drink and laughed. (It displeased George, somehow, that a Novian should be this frivolous. He wondered uneasily if perhaps the Novian ought not to have skipped that drink and even the one or two before that.)

The Novian said, "That's typical pious fraud, Ladislas. You know we can make use of all the late models we can get. I collected five Metallurgists this afternoon——"

"I know," said Ingenescu. "I was there."

"Watching me! Spying!" cried the Novian. "I'll tell you what it is. The new-model Metallurgists I got differed from the previous model only in knowing the use of Beeman Spectrographs. The tapes couldn't be modified that much, not that much" (he held up two fingers close together) "from last year's model. You introduce the new models only to *make* us buy and spend and come here hat in hand."

"We don't *make* you buy."

"No, but you sell late-model technicians to Landonum and so we have to keep pace. It's a merry-go-round you have us on, you pious Earthmen, but watch out, there may be an exit somewhere." There was a sharp edge to his laugh, and it ended sooner than it should have.

Ingenescu said, "In all honesty, I hope there is. Meanwhile, as to the purpose of my call——"

"That's right, *you* called. Oh, well, I've said my say and I suppose next year there'll be a new model of Metallurgist anyway for us to spend goods on, probably with a new gimmick for niobium assays and nothing else altered and the next year—— But go on, what is it you want?"

"I have a young man here to whom I wish you to speak."

"Oh?" The Novian looked not completely pleased with that. "Concerning what?"

"I can't say. He hasn't told me. For that matter he hasn't even told me his name and profession."

The Novian frowned. "Then why take up my time?"

"He seems quite confident that you will be interested in what he has to say."

"I dare say."

"And," said Ingenescu, "as a favor to me."

The Novian shrugged. "Put him on and tell him to make it short."

Ingenescu stepped aside and whispered to George, "Address him as 'Honorable.' "

George swallowed with difficulty. This was it.

George felt himself going moist with perspiration. The thought had come so recently, yet it was in him now so certainly. The beginnings of it had come when he had spoken to Trevelyan, then everything had fermented and billowed into shape while Ingenescu had prattled, and then the Novian's own remarks had seemed to nail it all into place.

George said, "Honorable, I've come to show you the exit from the merry-go-round." Deliberately, he adopted the Novian's own metaphor.

The Novian stared at him gravely. "What merry-go-round?"

"You yourself mentioned it, Honorable. The merry-go-round that Novia is on when you come to Earth to—to get technicians." (He couldn't keep his teeth from chattering; from excitement, not fear.)

The Novian said, "You're trying to say that you know a way by which we can avoid patronizing Earth's mental super-market. Is that it?"

"Yes, sir. You can control your own Educational system."

"Umm. Without tapes?"

"Y—yes, Honorable."

The Novian, without taking his eyes from George, called out, "Ingenescu, get into view."

The Historian moved to where he could be seen over George's shoulder.

The Novian said, "What is this? I don't seem to penetrate."

"I assure you solemnly," said Ingenescu, "that whatever this is it is being done on the young man's own initiative, Honorable. I have not inspired this. I have nothing to do with it."

"Well, then, what is the young man to you? Why do you call me on his behalf?"

Ingenescu said, "He is an object of study, Honorable. He has value to me and I humor him."

"What kind of value?"

"It's difficult to explain; a matter of my profession."

The Novian laughed shortly. "Well, to each his profession." He nodded to an invisible person or persons outside the plate range. "There's a young man here, a protégé of Ingenescu or some such thing, who will explain to us how to Educate without tapes." He snapped his fingers, and another glass of pale liqueur appeared in his hand. "Well, young man?"

The faces on the plate were multiple now. Men and women, both, crammed in for a view of George, their faces molded into various shades of amusement and curiosity.

George tried to look disdainful. They were all, in their own ways, Novians as well as the Earthman, "studying" him as though he were a bug on a pin. Ingenescu was sitting in a corner, now, watching him owl-eyed.

Fools, he thought tensely, one and all. But they would have to understand. He would *make* them understand.

He said, "I was at the Metallurgist Olympics this afternoon."

"You, too?" said the Novian blandly. "It seems all Earth was there."

"No, Honorable, but I was. I had a friend who competed and who made out very badly because you were using the Beeman machines. His education had included only the Henslers, apparently an older model. You said the modification involved was slight." George held up two fingers close together in conscious mimicry of the other's previous gesture. "And my friend had known some time in advance that knowledge of the Beeman machines would be required."

"And what does that signify?"

"It was my friend's lifelong ambition to qualify for Novia. He already knew the Henslers. He had to know the Beemans to qualify and he knew that. To learn about the Beemans would have taken just a few more facts, a bit more data, a small amount of practice perhaps. With a life's ambition riding the scale, he might have managed this——"

"And where would he have obtained a tape for the additional facts and data? Or has Education become a private matter for home study here on Earth?"

There was dutiful laughter from the faces in the background.

George said, "That's why he didn't learn, Honorable. He thought he needed a tape. He wouldn't even try without one, no matter what the prize. He refused to try without a tape."

"Refused, eh? Probably the type of fellow who would refuse to fly without a skimmer." More laughter and the Novian thawed into a smile and said, "The fellow is amusing. Go on. I'll give you another few moments."

George said tensely, "Don't think this is a joke. Tapes are actually bad. They teach too much; they're too painless. A man who learns that way doesn't know how to learn any other way. He's frozen into whatever position he's been taped. Now if a person *weren't* given tapes but were forced to learn by hand, so to speak, from the start; why, then he'd get the habit of learning, and continue to learn. Isn't that reasonable? Once he has the habit well developed he can be given just a small amount of tape-knowledge, perhaps, to fill in gaps or fix details. Then he can make further progress on his own. You can make Beeman Metallurgists out of your own Hensler Metallurgists in that way and not have to come to Earth for new models."

The Novian nodded and sipped at his drink. "And where does everyone get knowledge without tapes? From interstellar vacuum?"

"From books. By studying the instruments themselves. By *thinking*."

"Books? How does one understand books without Education?"

"Books are in words. Words can be understood for the most part. Specialized words can be explained by the technicians you already have."

"What about reading? Will you allow reading tapes?"

"Reading tapes are all right, I suppose, but there's no reason you can't learn to read the old way, too. At least in part."

The Novian said, "So that you can develop good habits from the start?"

"Yes, yes," George said gleefully. The man was beginning to understand.

"And what about mathematics?"

"That's the easiest of all, sir—Honorable. Mathematics is different from other technical subjects. It starts with certain simple principles and proceeds by steps. You can start with nothing and learn. It's practically designed for that. Then, once you know the proper types of mathematics, other technical books become quite understandable. Especially if you start with easy ones."

"Are there easy books?"

"Definitely. Even if there weren't, the technicians you now have can try to write easy books. Some of them might be able to put some of their knowledge into words and symbols."

"Good Lord," said the Novian to the men clustered about him. "The young devil has an answer for everything."

"I have. I have," shouted George. "Ask me."

"Have you tried learning from books yourself? Or is this just theory with you?"

George turned to look quickly at Ingenescu, but the Historian was passive. There was no sign of anything but gentle interest in his face.

George said, "I have."

"And do you find it works?"

"Yes, Honorable," said George eagerly. "Take me with you to Novia. I can set up a program and direct——"

"Wait, I have a few more questions. How long would it take, do you suppose, for you to become a Metallurgist capable of handling a Beeman machine, supposing you started from nothing and did not use Educational tapes?"

George hesitated. "Well—years, perhaps."

"Two years? Five? Ten?"

"I can't say, Honorable."

"Well, there's a vital question to which you have no answer, have you? Shall we say five years? Does that sound reasonable to you?"

"I suppose so."

"All right. We have a technician studying metallurgy according to this method of yours for five years. He's no good to us during that time, you'll admit, but he must be fed and housed and paid all that time."

"But——"

"Let me finish. Then when he's done and can use the Beeman, five years have passed. Don't you suppose we'll have modified Beemans then which he *won't* be able to use?"

"But by then he'll be expert on learning. He could learn the new details necessary in a matter of days."

"So you say. And suppose this friend of yours, for instance, had studied up on Beemans on his own and managed to learn it; would he be as expert in its use as a competitor who had learned it off the tapes?"

"Maybe not——" began George.

"Ah," said the Novian.

"Wait, let *me* finish. Even if he doesn't know something as well, it's the ability to learn further that's important. He may be able to think up things, new things that no tape-Educated man would. You'll have a reservoir of original thinkers——"

"In your studying," said the Novian, "have you thought up any new things?"

"No, but I'm just one man and I haven't studied long——"

"Yes. —— Well, ladies, gentlemen, have we been sufficiently amused?"

"Wait," cried George, in sudden panic. "I want to arrange a personal interview. There are things I can't explain over the visiphone. There are details——"

The Novian looked past George. "Ingenescu! I think I have done you your favor. Now, really, I have a heavy schedule tomorrow. Be well!"

The screen went blank.

George's hands shot out toward the screen, as though in a wild impulse to shake life back into it. He cried out, "He didn't believe me. He didn't believe me."

Ingenescu said, "No, George. Did you really think he would?"

George scarcely heard him. "But why not? It's all true. It's all so much to his advantage. No risk. I and a few men to work with—— A dozen men training for years would cost less than one technician. He was drunk! Drunk! He didn't understand.''

George looked about breathlessly. "How do I get to him? I've got to. This was wrong. Shouldn't have used the visiphone. I need time. Face to face. How do I——''

Ingenescu said, "He won't see you, George. And if he did, he wouldn't believe you.''

"He will, I tell you. When he isn't drinking. He——'' George turned squarely toward the Historian and his eyes widened. "Why do you call me George?''

"Isn't that your name? George Platen?''

"You know me?''

"All about you.''

George was motionless except for the breath pumping his chest wall up and down.

Ingenescu said, "I want to help you, George. I told you that. I've been studying you and I want to help you.''

George screamed, "I don't need help. I'm not feeble-minded. The whole world is, but I'm not.'' He whirled and dashed madly for the door.

He flung it open and two policemen roused themselves suddenly from their guard duty and seized him.

For all George's straining, he could feel the hypo-spray at the fleshy point just under the corner of his jaw, and that was it. The last thing he remembered was the face of Ingenescu, watching with gentle concern.

George opened his eyes to the whiteness of a ceiling. He remembered what had happened. He remembered it distantly as though it had happened to somebody else. He stared at the ceiling till the whiteness filled his eyes and washed his brain clean, leaving room, it seemed, for new thought and new ways of thinking.

He didn't know how long he lay there so, listening to the drift of his own thinking.

There was a voice in his ear. "Are you awake?''

And George heard his own moaning for the first time. Had he been moaning? He tried to turn his head.

The voice said, "Are you in pain, George?''

George whispered, "Funny. I was so anxious to leave Earth. I didn't understand.''

"Do you know where you are?''

"Back in the—the House.'' George managed to turn. The voice belonged to Omani.

George said, "It's funny I didn't understand.''

Omani smiled gently, "Sleep again——''

George slept.

And woke again. His mind was clear.

Omani sat at the bedside reading, but he put down the book as George's eyes opened.

George struggled to a sitting position. He said, "Hello.''

"Are you hungry?"

"You bet." He stared at Omani curiously. "I was followed when I left, wasn't I?"

Omani nodded. "You were under observation at all times. We were going to maneuver you to Antonelli and let you discharge your aggressions. We felt that to be the only way you could make progress. Your emotions were clogging your advance."

George said, with a trace of embarrassment, "I was all wrong about him."

"It doesn't matter now. When you stopped to stare at the Metallurgy notice board at the airport, one of our agents reported back the list of names. You and I had talked about your past sufficiently so that I caught the significance of Trevelyan's name there. You asked for directions to the Olympics; there was the possibility that this might result in the kind of crisis we were hoping for; we sent Ladislas Ingenescu to the hall to meet you and take over."

"He's an important man in the government, isn't he?"

"Yes, he is."

"And you had him take over. It makes me sound important."

"You *are* important, George."

A thick stew had arrived, steaming, fragrant. George grinned wolfishly and pushed his sheets back to free his arms. Omani helped arrange the bed-table. For a while, George ate silently.

Then George said, "I woke up here once before just for a short time."

Omani said, "I know. I was here."

"Yes, I remember. You know, everything was changed. It was as though I was too tired to feel emotion. I wasn't angry any more. I could just think. It was as though I had been drugged to wipe out emotion."

"You weren't," said Omani. "Just sedation. You had rested."

"Well, anyway, it was all clear to me, as though I had known it all the time but wouldn't listen to myself. I thought: What was it I had wanted Novia to let me do? I had wanted to go to Novia and take a batch of un-Educated youngsters and teach them out of books. I had wanted to establish a House for the Feeble-minded—like here—and Earth already has them—many of them."

Omani's white teeth gleamed as he smiled. "The Institute of Higher Studies is the correct name for places like this."

"Now I see it," said George, "so easily I am amazed at my blindness before. After all, who invents the new instrument models that require new-model technicians? Who invented the Beeman spectrographs, for instance? A man called Beeman, I suppose, but he couldn't have been tape-Educated or how could he have made the advance?"

"Exactly."

"Or who makes Educational tapes? Special tape-making technicians? Then who makes the tapes to train *them?* More advanced technicians? Then who makes the tapes— You see what I mean. Somewhere there has to be an end. Somewhere there must be men and women with capacity for original thought."

"Yes, George."

George leaned back, stared over Omani's head, and for a moment there was the return of something like restlessness to his eyes.

"Why wasn't I told all this at the beginning?"

"Oh, if we could," said Omani, "the trouble it would save us. We can analyze a mind, George, and say this one will make an adequate architect and that one a good woodworker. We know of no way of detecting the capacity for original, creative thought. It is too subtle a thing. We have some rule-of-thumb methods that mark out individuals who may possibly or potentially have such a talent.

"On Reading Day, such individuals are reported. You were, for instance. Roughly speaking, the number so reported comes to one in ten thousand. By the time Education Day arrives, these individuals are checked again, and nine out of ten of them turn out to have been false alarms. Those who remain are sent to places like this."

George said, "Well, what's wrong with telling people that one out of—of a hundred thousand will end at places like these? Then it won't be such a shock to those who do."

"And those who don't? The ninety-nine thousand nine hundred and ninety-nine that don't? We can't have all those people considering themselves failures. They aim at the professions and one way or another they all make it. Everyone can place after his or her name: Registered something-or-other. In one fashion or another every individual has his or her place in society and this is necessary."

"But we?" said George. "The one in ten thousand exception?"

"You can't be told. That's exactly it. It's the final test. Even after we've thinned out the possibilities on Education Day, nine out of ten of those who come here are not quite the material of creative genius, and there's no way we can distinguish those nine from the tenth that we want by any form of machinery. The tenth one must tell us himself."

"How?"

"We bring you here to a House for the Feeble-minded and the man who won't accept that is the man we want. It's a method that can be cruel, but it works. It won't do to say to a man, 'You can create. Do so.' It is much safer to wait for a man to say, 'I can create, and I will do so whether you wish it or not.' There are ten thousand men like you, George, who support the advancing technology of fifteen hundred worlds. We can't allow ourselves to miss one recruit to that number or waste our efforts on one member who doesn't measure up."

George pushed his empty plate out of the way and lifted a cup of coffee to his lips.

"What about the people here who don't—measure up?"

"They are taped eventually and become our Social Scientists. Ingenescu is one. I am a Registered Psychologist. We are second echelon, so to speak."

George finished his coffee. He said, "I still wonder about one thing?"

"What is that?"

George threw aside the sheet and stood up. "Why do they call them Olympics?"

SUCKER BAIT

— 1 —

THE SHIP Triple G. flashed silently out of the nothingness of hyperspace and into the allness of space-time. It emerged into the glitter of the great star cluster of Hercules.

It poised gingerly in space, surrounded by suns and suns and suns, each centering a gravitational field that wrenched at the little bubble of metal. But the ship's computers had done well and it had pin-pricked squarely into position. It was within a day's journey—ordinary space-drive journey—of the Lagrange System.

This face had varying significance to the different men aboard ship. To the crew, it was another day's work and another day's flight pay and then shore rest. The planet for which they were aiming was uninhabited, but shore rest could be a pleasant interlude even on an asteroid. They did not trouble themselves concerning a possible difference of opinion among the passengers.

The crew, in fact, were rather contemptuous of the passengers, and avoided them.

Eggheads!

And so they were, every one of them but one. Scientists, in politer terms—and a heterogeneous lot. Their nearest approach to a common emotion at that moment was a final anxiety for their instruments, a vague desire for a last check.

And perhaps just a small increase of tension and anxiety. It *was* an uninhabited planet. Each had expressed himself as firmly of that belief a number of times. Still, each man's thoughts are his own.

As for the one unusual man on board ship—not a crewman and not really a scientist—his strongest feeling was one of bone-weariness. He stirred to his feet weakly and fought off the last dregs of space-sickness. He was Mark Annuncio, and he had been in bed now for four days, feeding on almost nothing, while the ship wove in and out of the Universe, jumping its light-years of space.

But now he felt less certain of imminent death and he had to answer the summons of the Captain. In his inarticulate way, Mark resented that summons.

419

He was used to having his own way, seeing what he felt like seeing. Who was the Captain to——

The impulse kept returning to tell Dr. Sheffield about this and let it rest there. But Mark was curious, so he knew he would have to go.

It was his one great vice. Curiosity!

It also happened to be his profession and his mission in life.

— 2 —

CAPTAIN FOLLENBEE of the Triple G. was a hardheaded man. It was how he habitually thought of himself. He had made government-sponsored runs before. For one thing, they were profitable. The Confederacy didn't haggle. It meant a complete overhaul of his ship each time, replacement of defective parts, liberal terms for the crew. It was good business. Damned good business.

This run, of course, was a little different.

It wasn't so much the particular gang of passengers he had taken aboard. (He had expected temperament, tantrums, and unbearable foolishness but it turned out that eggheads were much like normal people.) It wasn't that half his ship had been torn down and rebuilt into what the contract called a "universal central-access laboratory."

Actually, and he hated the thought, it was "Junior"—the planet that lay ahead of them.

The crew didn't know, of course, but he, himself, hard head and all, was beginning to find the matter unpleasant.

But only beginning——

At the moment, he told himself, it was this Mark Annuncio, if that was the name, who was annoying him. He slapped the back of one hand against the palm of the other and thought angrily about it. His large, round face was ruddy with annoyance.

Insolence!

A boy of not more than twenty, with no position that he knew of among the passengers, to make a request like that.

What was behind it? That at least ought to be straightened out.

In his present mood, he would like to straighten it out by means of a jacket collar twisted in a fist and a rattle of teeth, but better not—better not——

After all, this was a curious kind of flight for the Confederacy of Worlds to sponsor, and a twenty-year-old, overcurious rubberneck might be an integral part of the strangeness. What was he on board for? There was this Dr. Sheffield, for instance, who seemed to have no job but to play nursemaid for the boy. Now why was that? Who was this Annuncio?

He had been space-sick for the entire trip, or was that just a device to keep to his cabin——

There was a light buzzing as the door signal sounded.

It would be the boy.

Easy now, thought the Captain. Easy now.

— 3 —

MARK ANNUNCIO entered the Captain's cabin and licked his lips in a futile attempt to get rid of the bitter taste in his mouth. He felt lightheaded and heavyhearted.

At the moment, he would have given up his Service status to be back on Earth.

He thought wishfully of his own familiar quarters; small but private; alone with his own kind. It was just a bed, desk, chair, and closet, but he had all of Central Library on free call. Here there was nothing. He had thought there would be a lot to learn on board ship. He had never been on board ship before. But he hadn't expected days and days of space-sickness.

He was so homesick he could cry, and he hated himself because he knew that his eyes were red and moist and that the Captain would see it. He hated himself because he wasn't large and wide; because he looked like a mouse.

In a word, that was it. He had mouse-brown hair with nothing but silken straightness to it; a narrow, receding chin, a small mouth, and a pointed nose. All he needed were five or six delicate vibrissae on each side of the nose to make the illusion complete. And he was below average in height.

And then he saw the star field in the Captain's observation port and the breath went out of him.

Stars!

Stars as he had never seen them.

Mark had never left the planet Earth before. (Dr. Sheffield told him that was why he was space-sick. Mark didn't believe him. He had read in fifty different books that space-sickness was psychogenic. Even Dr. Sheffield tried to fool him sometimes.)

He had never left Earth before, and he was used to Earth's sky. He was accustomed to viewing two thousand stars spread over half a celestial sphere, with only ten of the first magnitude.

But here they crowded madly. There were ten times the number in Earth's sky in that small square alone. And *bright!*

He fixed the star pattern greedily in his mind. It overwhelmed him. He knew the figures on the Hercules cluster, of course. It contained between one million and ten million stars (no exact census had been taken as yet), but figures are one thing and stars are another.

He wanted to count them. It was a sudden overwhelming desire. He was curious about the number. He wondered if they all had names; if there were astronomic data on all of them. Let's see . . .

He counted them in groups of hundreds. Two—three—he might have used the mental pattern alone, but he liked to watch the actual physical objects when they were so startlingly beautiful—six—seven——

The Captain's hearty voice splattered over him and brought him back to ship's interior.

"Mr. Annuncio. Glad to meet you."

Mark looked up, startled, resentful. Why was his count being interrupted? He said irritably, "The stars!" and pointed.

The Captain turned to stare. "What about them? What's wrong?"

Mark looked at the Captain's wide back and his overdeveloped posterior. He looked at the gray stubble that covered the Captain's head, at the two large hands with thick fingers that clasped one another in the small of the Captain's back and flapped rhythmically against the shiny plastex of his jacket.

Mark thought, What does *he* care about the stars? Does *he* care about their size and brightness and spectral classes?

His lower lip trembled. The Captain was just one of the noncompos. Everyone on ship was a noncompos. That's what they called them back in the Service. Noncompos. All of them. Couldn't cube fifteen without a computer.

Mark felt very lonely.

He let it go (no use trying to explain) and said, "The stars get so thick here. Like pea soup."

"All appearance, Mr. Annuncio." (The Captain pronounced the *c* in Mark's name like an *s* rather than a *ch* and the sound grated Mark's ear.) "Average distance between stars in the thickest cluster is over a light-year. Plenty of room, eh? Looks thick, though. Grant you that. If the light were out, they'd shine like a trillion Chisholm points in an oscillating force field."

But he didn't offer to put the lights out and Mark wasn't going to ask him to.

The Captain said, "Sit down, Mr. Annuncio. No use standing, eh? You smoke? Mind if I do? Sorry you couldn't be here this morning. Had an excellent view of Lagrange I and II at six space-hours. Red and green. Like traffic lights, eh? Missed you all trip. Space legs need strengthening, eh?"

He barked out his "eh's" in a high-pitched voice that Mark found devilishly irritating.

Mark said in a low voice, "I'm all right now."

The Captain seemed to find that unsatisfactory. He puffed at his cigar and stared down at Mark with eyebrows hunched down over his eyes. He said slowly, "Glad to see you now, anyway. Get acquainted a little. Shake hands. The *Triple G.*'s been on a good many government-chartered cruises. No trouble. Never had trouble. Wouldn't want trouble. You understand."

Mark didn't. He was tired of trying to. His eyes drifted back hungrily to the stars. The pattern had changed a little.

The Captain caught his eyes for a moment. He was frowning and his shoulders seemed to tremble at the edge of a shrug. He walked to the control panel, and like a gigantic eyelid, metal slithered across the studded observation port.

Mark jumped up in a fury, shrieking, "What's the idea? I'm counting them, you fool."

"*Counting—*" The Captain flushed, but maintained a quality of politeness in his voice. He said, "Sorry! Little matter of business we must discuss."

He stressed the word "business" lightly.

Mark knew what he meant. "There's nothing to discuss. I want to see the ship's log. I called you hours ago to tell you that. You're delaying me."

The Captain said, "Suppose you tell me why you want to see it, eh? Never been asked before. Where's your authority?"

Mark felt astonished. "I can look at anything I want to. I'm in Mnemonic Service."

The Captain puffed strongly at his cigar. (It was a special grade manufactured for use in space and on enclosed space objects. It had an oxidant included so that atmospheric oxygen was not consumed.)

He said cautiously, "That so? Never heard of it. What is it?"

Mark said indignantly, "It's the Mnemonic Service, that's all. It's my job to look at anything I want to and to ask anything I want to. And I've got the right to do it."

"Can't look at the log if I don't want you to."

"You've got no say in it, you—you *noncompos*."

The Captain's coolness evaporated. He threw his cigar down violently and stamped at it, then picked it up and poked it carefully into the ash vent.

"What the Galactic drift is this?" he demanded. "Who are you, anyway? Security agent? What's up? Let's have it straight. Right now."

"I've told you all I have to."

"Nothing to hide," said the Captain, "but I've got rights."

"Nothing to hide?" squeaked Mark. "Then why is this ship called the *Triple G.?*"

"That's its name."

"Go on. No such ship with an Earth registry. I knew that before I got on. I've been waiting to ask you."

The Captain blinked. He said, "Official name is *George G. Grundy. Triple G.* is what everyone calls it."

Mark laughed. "All right, then. And after I see the logbook, I want to talk to the crew. I have the right. You ask Dr. Sheffield."

"The crew, too, eh?" The Captain seethed. "Let's talk to Dr. Sheffield, and then let's keep you in quarters till we land. Sprout!"

He snatched at the intercom box.

— 4 —

THE SCIENTIFIC complement of the *Triple G.* were few in number for the job they had to do, and, as individuals, young. Not as young as Mark Annuncio, perhaps, who was in a class by himself, but even the oldest of them, Emmanuel George Cimon (astrophysicist), was not quite thirty-nine. And with his dark, unthinned hair and large, brilliant eyes, he looked still younger. To be sure, the optic brilliance was partly due to the wearing of contact lenses.

Cimon, who was perhaps overconscious of his relative age, and of the fact that he was the titular head of the expedition (a fact most of the others were inclined to ignore) usually affected an undramatic view of the mission. He ran the dotted tape through his fingers, then let it snake silently back into its spool.

"Run of the mill," he sighed, seating himself in the softest chair in the small passengers' lounge. "Nothing."

He looked at the latest color photographs of the Lagrange binary and was impervious to their beauty. Lagrange I, smaller and hotter than Earth's own sun, was a brilliant green blue, with a pearly green-yellow corona surrounding it like the gold setting of an emerald. It appeared to be the size of a lentil or of a ball bearing out of a Lenser ratchet. A short distance away (as distances go on a photograph) was Lagrange II. It appeared twice the size of Lagrange I, due to its position in space. (Actually, it was only four fifths the diameter of Lagrange I, half its volume, and two thirds its mass.) Its orange red, toward which the film was less sensitive, comparatively, than was the human retina, seemed dimmer than ever against the glory of its sister sun.

Surrounding both, undrowned by the near-by suns, as the result of the differentially polarized lens specifically used for the purpose, was the unbelievable brilliance of the Hercules cluster. It was diamond dust, scattered thickly, yellow, white, blue, and red.

"Nothing," said Cimon.

"Looks good to me," said the other man in the lounge. He was Groot Knoevenaagel (physician; short, plump, and known to man by no name other than Novee).

He went on to ask, "Where's Junior?" then bent over Cimon's shoulder, peering out of slightly myopic eyes.

Cimon looked up and shuddered. "Its name is not Junior. You can't see the planet, Troas, if *that's* what you mean, in this damned wilderness of stars. This picture is *Scientific Earthman* material. It isn't particularly useful."

"Oh, space and back!" Novee was disappointed.

"What difference is it to you, anyway?" demanded Cimon. "Suppose I said one of those dots was Troas. Any one of them. You wouldn't know the difference and what good would it do you?"

"Now wait, Cimon. Don't be so damned superior. It's legitimate sentiment. We'll be living on Junior for a while. For all we know, we'll be dying on it."

"There's no audience, Novee, no orchestra, no mikes, no trumpets, so why be dramatic? We won't be dying on it. If we do, it'll be our own fault, and probably as a result of overeating." He said it with the peculiar emphasis men of small appetite use when speaking to men of hearty appetite, as though a poor digestion were something that came only of rigid virtue and superior intellect.

"A thousand people did die," said Novee softly.

"Sure. About a billion men a day die all over the Galaxy."

"Not this way."

"Not what way?"

With an effort, Novee kept to his usual drawl. "No discussions except at official meetings. That was the decision."

"I'll have nothing to discuss," said Cimon gloomily. "They're just two ordinary stars. Damned if I know why I volunteered. I suppose it was just the chance of seeing an abnormally large Trojan system from close up. It was the thought of looking at a habitable planet with a double sun. I don't know why I should have thought there'd be anything amazing about it."

"Because you thought of a thousand dead men and women," said Novee, then went on hastily, "Listen, tell me something, will you? What's a Trojan planet, anyway?"

The physician bore the other's look of contempt for a moment, then said, "All right. All right. So I don't know. You don't know everything either. What do you know about ultrasonic incisions?"

Cimon said, "Nothing, and I think that's fine. It's my opinion that information outside a professional man's specialty is useless and a waste of psycho-potential. Sheffield's point of view leaves me cold."

"I still want to know. That is if you can explain it."

"I can explain it. As a matter of fact, it was mentioned in the original briefing, if you were listening. Most multiple stars, and that means one third of all stars, have planets of a sort. The trouble is that the planets are never habitable. If they're far enough away from the center of gravity of the stellar system to have a fairly circular orbit, they're cold enough to have helium oceans. If they're close enough to get heat, their orbit is so erratic that at least once in each revolution, they get close enough to one or another of the stars to melt iron.

"Here in the Lagrange System, however, we have an unusual case. The two stars, Lagrange I and Lagrange II, and the planet, Troas (along with its satellite, Ilium), are at the corners of an imaginary equilateral triangle. Got that? Such an arrangement happens to be a stable one, and for the sake of anything you like, don't ask me to tell you why. Just take it as my professional opinion."

Novee muttered under his breath, "I wouldn't dream of doubting it."

Cimon looked displeased and continued, "The system revolves as a unit. Troas is always a hundred million miles from each sun, and the suns are always a hundred million miles from one another."

Novee rubbed his ear and looked dissatisfied. "I know all that. I *was* listening at the briefing. But why is it a *Trojan* planet? Why *Trojan?*"

Cimon's thin lips compressed for a moment as though holding back a nasty word by force. He said, "We have an arrangement like that in the Solar System. The Sun, Jupiter, and a group of small asteroids form a stable equilateral triangle. It so happens that the asteroids had been given such names as Hector, Achilles, Ajax, and other heroes of the Trojan War, hence—— Or do I have to finish?"

"Is that all?" said Novee.

"Yes. Are you through bothering me?"

"Oh, boil your head."

Novee rose to leave the indignant astrophysicist but the door slid open a moment before his hand touched the activator and Boris Vernadsky (geochemist; dark eyebrows, wide mouth, broad face, and with an inveterate tendency to polka-dot shirts and magnetic clip-ons in red plastic) stepped in.

He was oblivious to Novee's flushed face and Cimon's frozen expression of distaste.

He said lightly, "Fellow scientists, if you listen very carefully, you will probably hear an explosion to beat the Milky Way from up yonder in Captain's quarters."

"What happened?" asked Novee.

"The Captain got hold of Annuncio, Sheffield's little pet wizard, and Sheffield went charging updeck, bleeding heavily at each eyeball."

Cimon, having listened so far, turned away, snorting.

Novee said, "Sheffield! The man can't get angry. I've never even heard him raise his voice."

"He did this time. When he found out the kid had left his cabin without telling him and that the Captain was bullyragging him—— Wow! Did you know he was up and about, Novee?"

"No, but I'm not surprised. Space-sickness is one of those things. When you have it, you think you're dying. In fact, you can hardly wait. Then, in two minutes it's gone and you feel all right. Weak, but all right. I told Mark this morning we'd be landing next day and I suppose it pulled him through. The thought of a planetary surface in clear prospect does wonders for space-sickness. We *are* landing soon, aren't we, Cimon?"

The astrophysicist made a peculiar sound that could have been interpreted as a grunt of assent. At least, Novee so interpreted it.

"Anyway," said Novee, "what happened?"

Vernadsky said, "Well, Sheffield's been bunking with me since the kid twirled on his toes and went over backward with space-sickness and he's sitting there at the desk with his damn charts and his fist computer chug-chugging away, when the room phone signals and it's the Captain. Well, it turns out he's got the boy with him and he wants to know what the blankety-blank and assorted dot and dash the government means by planting a spy on him. So Sheffield yells back at him that he'll stab him in the groin with a Collamore macro-leveling-tube if he's been fooling with the kid and off he goes, leaving the phone activated and the Captain frothing."

"You're making this up," said Novee. "Sheffield wouldn't say anything like that."

"Words to that effect."

Novee turned to Cimon. "You're heading our group. Why don't you do something about this?"

Cimon snarled, "In cases like this, I'm heading the group. My responsiblities always come on suddenly. Let them fight it out. Sheffield talks an excellent fight and the Captain never takes his hands out of the small of his back. Vernadsky's jitterbugging description doesn't mean there'll be physical violence."

"All right, but there's no point in having feuds of any kind in an expedition like ours."

"You mean our mission!" Vernadsky raised both hands in mock awe and rolled his eyes upward. "How I dread the time when we must find ourselves among the rags and bones of the first expedition."

And as though the picture brought to mind by that was not one that bore levity well after all, there was suddenly nothing to say. Even the back of Cimon's head, which was all that showed over the back of the easy chair, seemed a bit the stiffer for the thought.

— 5 —

OSWALD MAYER Sheffield (psychologist, thin as a string and as tall as a good length of it, and with a voice that could be used either for singing an operatic selection with surprising virtuosity or for making a point of argument, softly but with stinging accuracy) did not show the anger one would have expected from Vernadsky's account.

He was even smiling when he entered the Captain's cabin.

The Captain broke out mauvely as soon as he entered. "Look here, Sheffield——"

"One minute, Captain Follenbee," said Sheffield. "How are you, Mark?"

Mark's eyes fell and his words were muffled. "All right, Dr. Sheffield."

"I wasn't aware you'd gotten out of bed."

There wasn't the shade of reproach in his voice, but Mark grew apologetic. "I was feeling better, Dr. Sheffield, and I feel bad about not working. I haven't done anything in all the time I've been on the ship. So I put in a call to the Captain to ask to see the logbook and he had me come up here."

"All right. I'm sure he won't mind if you go back to your room now."

"Oh, won't I?" began the Captain.

Sheffield's mild eyes rose to meet the Captain. "I'm responsible for him, sir."

And somehow the Captain could think of nothing further to say.

Mark turned obediently and Sheffield watched him leave and waited till the door was well closed behind him.

Then he turned again to the Captain. "What's the bloody idea, Captain?"

The Captain's knees bent a little, then straightened and bent again with a sort of threatening rhythm. The invisible slap of his hands, clasped behind his back, could be heard distinctly. "That's my question. I'm Captain here, Sheffield."

"I know that."

"Know what it means, eh? This ship, in space, is a legally recognized planet. I'm absolute ruler. In space, what I say goes. Central Committee of the Confederacy can't say otherwise. I've got to maintain discipline, and no spy——"

"All right, and now let me tell *you* something, Captain. You're charted by the Bureau of Outer Provinces to carry a government-sponsored research expedition to the Lagrange System, to maintain it there as long as research necessity requires and the safety of the crew and vessel permits, and then to bring us home. You've signed that contract and you've assumed certain obligations, Captain or not. For instance, you can't tamper with our instruments and destroy their research usefulness."

"Who in space is doing that?" The Captain's voice was a blast of indignation.

Sheffield replied calmly, "You are. Hands off Mark Annuncio, Captain. Just as you've got to keep your hands off Cimon's monochrome and Vailleux's microptics, you've got to keep your hands off my Annuncio. And that means each one of your ten, four-striped fingers. Got it?"

The Captain's uniformed chest expanded. "I take no order on board my own ship. Your language is a breach of discipline, *Mister* Sheffield. Any more like that and it's cabin arrest. You *and* your Annuncio. Don't like it, then speak to Board of Review back on Earth. Till then, it's tongue behind teeth."

"Look, Captain, let me explain something. Mark is in the Mnemonic Service——"

"Sure, he said so. Nummonic Service. Nummonic Service. It's plain secret police as far as I'm concerned. Well, not on board *my* ship, eh?"

"Mnemonic Service," said Sheffield patiently. "*Em-en-ee-em-oh-en-eye-see* Service. You don't pronounce the first *em*. It's from a Greek word meaning memory."

The Captain's eyes narrowed. "He remembers things?"

"Correct, Captain. Look, in a way this is my fault. I should have briefed you on this. I would have, too, if the boy hadn't gotten so sick right after the take-off. It drove most other matters out of my mind. Besides, it didn't occur to me that he might be interested in the workings of the ship itself. Space knows why not. He should be interested in everything."

"He should, eh?" The Captain looked at the timepiece on the wall. "Brief me now, eh? But no fancy words. Not many of any other kind, either. Time limited."

"It won't take long, I assure you. Now you're a space-going man, Captain. How many inhabited worlds would you say there were in the Confederation?"

"Eighty thousand," said the Captain promptly.

"Eighty-three thousand two hundred," said Sheffield. "What do you suppose it takes to run a political organization that size?"

Again the Captain did not hesitate. "Computers," he said.

"All right. There's Earth, where half the population works for the government and does nothing but compute and there are computing subcenters on every other world. And even so data gets lost. Every world knows something no other world knows. Almost every man. Look at our little group. Vernadsky doesn't know any biology and I don't know enough chemistry to stay alive. There's not one of us can pilot the simplest space cruiser, except for Fawkes. So we work together, each one supplying the knowledge the others lack.

"Only there's a catch. Not one of us knows exactly which of our own data is meaningful to the other under a given set of circumstances. We can't sit and spout everything we know. So we guess, and sometimes we don't guess right. Two facts, A and B, can go together beautifully sometimes. So Person A, who knows Fact A, says to Person B, who knows Fact B, 'Why didn't you tell me this ten years ago?' and Person B answers, 'I didn't think it was important,' or, 'I thought everyone knew that.' "

The Captain said, "That's what computers are for."

Sheffield said, "Computers are limited, Captain. They have to be asked questions. What's more, the questions have to be the kind that can be put into a limited number of symbols. What's more, computers are very literal-minded. They answer exactly what you ask and not what you have in mind. Sometimes it never occurs to anyone to ask just the right question or feed the computer just the right symbols, and when that happens, the computer doesn't volunteer information.

"What we need, what all mankind needs, is a computer that is nonmechanical; a computer with imagination. There's one like that, Captain." The psychologist tapped his temple. "In everyone, Captain."

"Maybe," grunted the Captain, "but I'll stick to the usual, eh? Kind you punch a button."

"Are you sure? Machines don't have hunches. Did *you* ever have a hunch?"

"Is this on the point?" The Captain looked at the timepiece again.

Sheffield said, "Somewhere inside the human brain is a record of every datum that has impinged upon it. Very little of it is consciously remembered, but all of it's there, and a small association can bring an individual datum back without a person's knowing where it comes from. So you get a 'hunch' or a 'feeling.' Some people are better at it than others. And some can be trained. Some are almost perfect, like Mark Annuncio and a hundred like him. Someday, I hope, there'll be a billion like him, and we'll *really* have a Mnemonic Service.

"All their lives," Sheffield went on, "they do nothing but read, look, and listen. And train to do that better and more efficiently. It doesn't matter what data they collect. It doesn't have to have obvious sense or obvious significance. It doesn't matter if any man in the Service wants to spend a week going over the records of the space-polo teams of the Canopus Sector for the last century. *Any* datum may be useful someday. That's the fundamental axiom.

"Every once in a while one of the Service may correlate across a gap no machine could possibly manage. The machine would fail because no one machine is likely to possess those two pieces of thoroughly unconnected information, or else, if the machine does have them, no man would be insane enough to ask the right question. One good correlation out of the Service can pay for all the money appropriated for it in ten years or more.''

The Captain raised his broad hand. He looked troubled. He said, ''Wait a minute. Annuncio said no ship named *Triple G.* was under Earth registry. You mean he knows all registered ships by heart?''

''Probably,'' said Sheffield. ''He may have read through the Merchant-Ship Register. If he did, he knows all the names, tonnages, years of construction, ports of call, numbers of crews, and anything else the register would contain.''

''And he was counting stars.''

''Why not? It's a datum.''

''I'm damned.''

''Perhaps, Captain. But the point is that a man like Mark is different from other men. He's got a queer, distorted upbringing and a queer, distorted view of life. This is the first time he's been away from Service grounds since he entered them at the age of five. He's easily upset—and he can be ruined. That mustn't happen, and I'm in charge to see it doesn't. He's my instrument; a more valuable instrument than everything else on this entire ship baled into a neat little ball of plutonium wire. There are only a hundred like him in all the Milky Way.''

Captain Follenbee assumed an air of wounded dignity. ''All right, then. Logbook. Strictly confidential, eh?''

''Strictly. He talks only to me, and I talk to no one unless a correlation has been made.''

The Captain did not look as though that fell under his classification of the word ''strictly'' but he said, ''But no crew.'' He paused significantly. ''You know what I mean.''

Sheffield stepped to the door. ''Mark knows about that. The crew won't hear about it from him, believe me.''

And as he was about to leave, the Captain called out, ''Sheffield!''

''Yes?''

''What in space is a noncompos?''

Sheffield suppressed a smile. ''Did he call you that?''

''What is it?''

''Just short for *non compos mentis.* Everyone in the Service uses it for everyone not in the Service. You're one. I'm one. It's Latin for 'not of sound mind.' And you know, Captain—I think they're quite right.''

He stepped out the door quickly.

— 6 —

MARK ANNUNCIO went through ship's log in some fifteen seconds. He found it incomprehensible, but then most of the material he put into his mind was that. That was no trouble. Nor was the fact that it was dull. The disappointment was that it did not satisfy his curiosity, so he left it with a mixture of relief and displeasure.

He had then gone into the ship's library and worked his way through three dozen books as quickly as he could work the scanner. He had spent three years of his early teens learning how to read by total gestalt and he still recalled proudly that he had set a school record at the final examinations.

Finally he wandered into the laboratory sections of the ship and watched a bit here and a bit there. He asked no questions and he moved on when any of the men cast more than a casual glance at him.

He hated the insufferable way they looked at him, as though he were some sort of queer animal. He hated their air of knowledge, as though there were something of value in spending an entire brain on one tiny subject and remembering only a little of that.

Eventually, of course, he would *have* to ask them questions. It was his job, and even if it weren't, curiosity would drive him. He hoped, though, he could hold off till they had made planetary surface.

He found it pleasant that they were inside a stellar system. Soon he would see a new world with new suns—two of them—and a new moon. Four objects with brand-new information in each; immense storehouses of facts to be collected lovingly and sorted out.

It thrilled him just to think of the amorphous mountain of data waiting for him. He thought of his mind as a tremendous filing system with index, cross index, cross cross index. He thought of it as stretching indefinitely in all directions. Neat. Smooth. Well oiled. Perfect precision.

He thought of the dusty attic that the noncompos called minds and almost laughed. He could see it even talking to Dr. Sheffield, who was a nice fellow for a noncompos. He tried hard and sometimes he almost *understood*. The others, the men on board ship, their minds were lumberyards. Dusty lumberyards with splintery slats of wood tumbled every which way; and only whatever happened to be on top could be reached.

The poor fools! He could be sorry for them if they weren't so sloppy-nasty. If only they *knew* what they were like. If only they *realized*.

Whenever he could, Mark haunted the observation posts and watched the new worlds come closer.

They passed quite close to the satellite Ilium. (Cimon, the astrophysicist, was very meticulous about calling their planetary destination "Troas" and the satellite "Ilium," but everyone else aboard ship called them "Junior" and "Sister" respectively.) On the other side of the two suns, in the opposite Trojan position, were a group of asteroids. Cimon called them "Lagrange Epsilon" but everyone else called them "The Puppies."

Mark thought of all this with vague simultaneity at the moment the thought "Ilium" occurred to him. He was scarcely conscious of it, and let it pass as material of no immediate interest. Still more vague, and still further below his skin of mental consciousness were the dim stirrings of five hundred such homely misnomers of astronomical dignities of nomenclature. He had read about some, picked up others on subetheric programs, heard about still others in ordinary conversation, come across a few in news reports. The material might have been told him directly, or it might have been a carelessly overheard word. Even the substitution of *Triple G.* for *George G. Grundy* had its place in the shadowy file.

Sheffield had often questioned him about what went on in his mind—very gently, very cautiously.

"We want many more like you, Mark, for the Mnemonic Service. We need millions. Billions, eventually, if the race fills up the entire Galaxy, as it will someday. But where do we get them? Relying on inborn talent won't do. We all have that more or less. It's the training that counts, and unless we find out a little about what goes on, we won't know how to train.''

And urged by Sheffield, Mark had watched himself, listened to himself, turned his eyes inward and tried to become *aware*. He learned of the filing cases in his head. He watched them marshal past. He observed individual items pop up on call, always tremblingly ready. It was hard to explain, but he did his best.

His own confidence grew with it. The anxieties of his childhood, those first years in Service, grew less. He stopped waking in the middle of the night, perspiration dripping, screaming with fear that he would forget. And his headaches stopped.

He watched Ilium as it appeared in the viewport at closest approach. It was brighter than he could imagine a moon to be. (Figures for albedos of three hundred inhabited planets marched through his mind, neatly arrayed in decreasing order. It scarcely stirred the skin of his mind. He ignored them.)

The brightness he blinked at was concentrated in the vast, irregular patches that Cimon said (he overheard him, in weary response to another's question) had once been sea bottom. A fact popped into Mark's mind. The original report of Hidosheki Makoyama had given the composition of those bright salts as 78.6 per cent sodium chloride, 19.2 per cent magnesium carbonate, 1.4 per cent potassium sulf . . . The thought faded out. It wasn't necessary.

Ilium had an atmosphere. A total of about 100 mm. of mercury. (A little over an eighth of Earth's, ten times Mars', 0.254 that of Coralemon, 0.1376 that of Aurora.) Idly he let the decimals grow to more places. It was a form of exercise, but he grew bored. Instant arithmetic was fifth-grade stuff. Actually, he still had trouble with integrals and wondered if that was because he didn't know what an integral was. A half dozen definitions flashed by, but he had never had enough mathematics to understand the definitions, though he could quote them well enough.

At school, they had always said, ''Don't ever get too interested in any one thing or group of things. As soon as you do that, you begin selecting your facts and you must never do that. *Everything, anything* is important. As long as you have the facts on file, it doesn't matter whether you understand them or not.''

But the noncompos didn't think so. Arrogant minds with holes in them!

They were approaching Junior itself now. It was bright, too, but in a different way. It had icecaps north and south. (Textbooks of Earth's paleo-climatology drifted past and Mark made no move to stop them.) The icecaps were retreating. In a million years, Junior would have Earth's present climate. It was just about Earth's size and mass and it rotated in a period of thirty-six hours.

It might have been Earth's twin. What differences there were, according to Makoyama's reports, were to Junior's advantage. There was nothing on Junior to threaten mankind as far as was known. Nor would anyone imagine there possibly might be were it not for the fact that humanity's first colony on the planet had been wiped out to the last soul.

What was worse, the destruction had occurred in such a way that a study of all surviving information gave no reasonable clue whatever as to what had happened.

7

SHEFFIELD ENTERED Mark's cabin and joined the boy two hours before landing. He and Mark had orginally been assigned a room together. That had been an experiment. Mnemonics didn't like the company of noncompos. Even the best of them. In any case, the experiment had failed. Almost immediately after take-off, Mark's sweating face and pleading eyes made privacy absolutely essential for him.

Sheffield felt responsible. He felt responsible for everything about Mark whether it was actually his fault or not. He and men like himself had taken Mark and children like him and trained them into personal ruin. They had been force-grown. They had been bent and molded. They had been allowed no normal contact with normal children lest they develop normal mental habits. No Mnemonic had contracted a normal marriage, even within the group.

It made for a terrible guilt feeling on Sheffield's part.

Twenty years ago there had been a dozen lads trained at one school under the leadership of U Karaganda, as mad an Asiatic as had ever roused the snickers of a group of interviewing newsmen. Karaganda had committed suicide eventually, under some vague motivation, but other psychologists, Sheffield for one, of greater respectability and undoubtedly of lesser brilliance, had had time to join him and learn of him.

The school continued and others were established. One was even founded on Mars. It had an enrollment of five at the moment. At latest count, there were one hundred three living graduates with full honors (naturally, only a minority of those enrolled actually absorbed the entire course). Five years ago, the Terrestrial-planetary government (not to be confused with the Central Galactic Committee, based on Earth, and ruling the Galactic Confederation) allowed the establishment of the Mnemonic Service as a branch of the Department of the Interior.

It had already paid for itself many times over, but few people knew that. Nor did the Terrestrial government advertise the fact, or any other fact about the Mnemonics. It was a tender subject with them. It was an "experiment." They feared that failure might be politically expensive. The opposition (with difficulty prevented from making a campaign issue out of it as it was) spoke at the planetary conferences of "crackpotism" and "waste of the taxpayers' money." And the latter despite the existence of documentary proof of the precise opposite.

In the machine-centered civilization that filled the Galaxy, it was difficult to learn to appreciate the achievements of naked mind without a long apprenticeship.

Sheffield wondered how long.

But there was no use being depressed in Mark's company. Too much danger of contagion. He said instead, "You're looking fine, sport."

Mark seemed glad to see him. He said thoughtfully, "When we get back to Earth, Dr. Sheffield——"

He stopped, flushed slightly, and said, "I mean supposing we get back, I intend to get as many books and films as I can on folkways. I've hardly read anything on that subject. I was down in the ship's library and they had nothing."

"Why the interest?"

"It's the Captain. Didn't you say he told you that the crew were not to know we were visiting a world on which the first expedition had died?"

"Yes, of course. Well?"

"Because spacemen consider it bad luck to touch on a world like that, especially one that looks harmless? 'Sucker bait,' they call it."

"That's right."

"So the Captain *says*. It's just that I don't see how that can be true. I can think of seventeen habitable planets from which the first expeditions never returned and never established residence. And each one was later colonized and now is a member of the Confederation. Sarmatia is one of them, and it's a pretty big world now."

"There are planets of continuous disaster, too." Sheffield deliberately put that as a declarative statement.

(Never ask informational questions. That was one of the Rules of Karaganda. Mnemonic correlations weren't a matter of the conscious intelligence; they weren't volitional. As soon as a direct question was asked, the resultant correlations were plentiful but only such as any reasonably informed man might make. It was the unconscious mind that bridged the wide, unlikely gaps.)

Mark, as any Mnemonic would, fell into the trap. He said energetically, "No, I've never heard of one. Not where the planet was at all habitable. If the planet is solid ice, or complete desert, that's different. Junior isn't like that."

"No, it isn't," agreed Sheffield.

"Then why should the crew be afraid of it? I kept thinking about that all the time I was in bed. That's when I thought of looking at the log. I'd never actually seen one, so it would be a valuable thing to do in any case. And certainly, I thought, I would find the truth there."

"Uh-huh," said Sheffield.

"And, well—I may have been wrong. In the whole log, the purpose of the expedition was never mentioned. Now that wouldn't be so unless the purpose were secret. It was as if he were even keeping it from the other ship's officers. And the name of the ship *is* given as the *George G. Grundy*."

"It would be, of course," said Sheffield.

"I don't know. I suspected that business about *Triple G.*," said Mark darkly.

Sheffield said, "You seem disappointed that the Captain wasn't lying."

"Not disappointed. Relieved, I think. I thought—I thought——" He stopped, and looked acutely embarrassed, but Sheffield made no effort to rescue him. He was forced to continue. "I thought everyone might be lying to me, not just the Captain. Even *you* might, Dr. Sheffield. I thought you just didn't want me to talk to the crew for some reason."

Sheffield tried to smile and managed to succeed. The occupational disease of the Mnemonic Service was suspicion. They were isolated, these Mnemonics, and they were different. Cause and effect were obvious.

Sheffield said lightly, "I think you'll find in your reading on folkways that these superstitions are not necessarily based on logical analysis. A planet which has become notorious has evil expected of it. The good which happens is disregarded; the bad is cried up, advertised, and exaggerated. The thing snowballs."

He moved away from Mark. He busied himself with an inspection of the hydraulic chairs. They would be landing soon. He felt unnecessarily along the length of the broad webbing of the straps, keeping his back to the youngster. So protected, he said, almost in a whisper, "And, of course, what makes it worse is that Junior is so different."

(Easy now, easy. Don't push. He had tried that trick before this and——)

Mark was saying, "No, it isn't. Not a bit. The other expeditions that failed were different. That's true."

Sheffield kept his back turned. He waited.

Mark said, "The seventeen other expeditions that failed on planets that are now inhabited were all small exploring expeditions. In sixteen of the cases, the cause of death was shipwreck of one sort or another, and in the remaining case, Coma Minor that one was, the failure resulted from a surprise attack by indigenous life forms, not intelligent, of course. I have the details on all of them——"

(Sheffield couldn't forbear holding his breath. Mark *could* give the details on all of them. All the details. It was as easy for him to quote all the records on each expedition, word for word, as it was to say yes or no. And he might well choose to. A Mnemonic had no selectivity. It was one of the things that made ordinary companionship between Mnemonics and ordinary people impossible. Mnemonics were dreadful bores by the nature of things. Even Sheffield, who was trained and inured to listen to it all, and who had no intention of stopping Mark if he were really off on a talk jag, sighed softly.)

" —but what's the use," Mark continued, and Sheffield felt rescued from a horror. "They're just not in the same class with the Junior expedition. That consisted of an actual settlement of 789 men, 207 women, and fifteen children under the age of thirteen. In the course of the next year, 315 women, nine men, and two children were added by immigration. The settlement survived almost two years and the cause of death isn't known, except that from their report, it might be disease.

"Now *that* part is different. But Junior itself has nothing unusual about it, except—of course—— "

Mark paused as though the information were too unimportant to bother with and Sheffield almost yelled. He forced himself to say calmly, "*That* difference, of course."

Mark said, "We all know about that. It has two suns and the others only have one."

The psychologist could have cried his disappointment. Nothing!

But what was the use? Better luck next time. If you don't have patience with a Mnemonic, you might as well not have a Mnemonic.

He sat down in the hydraulic chair and buckled himself in tightly. Mark did likewise. (Sheffield would have liked to help, but they would have been injudicious.) He looked at his watch. They must be spiraling down even now.

Under his disappointment, Sheffield felt a stronger disturbance. Mark Annuncio had acted wrongly in following up his own hunch that the Captain and everybody else had been lying. Mnemonics had a tendency to believe that because their store of facts was great, it was complete. This, obviously, is a prime error. It is therefore necessary (thus spake Karaganda) for them to present their correlations to properly constituted authority and never to act upon it themselves.

Well, how significant was this error of Mark's? He was the first Mnemonic to be taken away from Service headquarters; the first to be separated from all of his kind; the first to be isolated among noncompos. What did that do to him? What would it continue to do to him? Would it be bad? If so, how to stop it?

To all of which questions, Dr. Oswald Mayer Sheffield knew no answer.

8

THE MEN at the controls were the lucky ones. They and, of course, Cimon, who, as astrophysicist and director of the expedition, joined them by special dispensation. The others of the crew had their separate duties, while the remaining scientific personnel preferred the relative comfort of their hydraulic seats during the spiral around and down to Junior.

It was while Junior was still far enough away to be seen as a whole that the scene was at its grandest.

North and south, a third of the way to the equator, lay the icecaps, still at the start of their millennial retreat. Since the *Triple G.* was spiraling on a north-south great circle (deliberately chosen for the sake of viewing the polar regions, as Cimon, at the cost of less than maximum safety, insisted), each cap in turn was laid out below them.

Each burned equally with sunlight, the consequence of Junior's untilted axis. And each cap was in sectors, cut like a pie with a rainbowed knife.

The sunward third of each was illuminated by both suns simultaneously into a brilliant white that slowly yellowed westward, and as slowly greened eastward. To the east of the white sector lay another, half as wide, which was reached by the light of Lagrange I only, and the snow there blazed a response of sapphire beauty. To the west, another half sector, exposed to Lagrange II alone, shone in the warm orange red of an Earthly sunset. The three colors graded into one another bandwise, and the similarity to a rainbow was increased thereby.

The final third was dark in contrast, but if one looked carefully enough, it, too, was in parts—unequal parts. The smaller portion was black indeed, but the larger portion had a faint milkiness about it.

Cimon muttered to himself, "Moonlight. Of course," then looked about hastily to see if he had been overheard. He did not like people to observe the actual process by which conclusions were brought to fruition in his mind. Rather they were to be presented to his students and listeners, to all about him in short, in a polished perfection that showed neither birth nor growth.

But there were only spacemen about and they did not hear him. Despite all their space-hardening, they were fixing whatever concentration they could spare from their duties and instruments upon the wonder before them.

The spiral curved, veered away from north-south to northeast-southwest, finally to the east-west, in which a safe landing was most feasible. The dull thunder of atmosphere carried into the pilot room, thin and shrill at first, but gathering body and volume as the minutes passed.

Until now, in the interests of scientific observation (and to the considerable uneasiness of the Captain) the spiral had been tight, deceleration slight, and the planetary circumnavigations numerous. As they bit into Junior's air covering, however, deceleration pitched high and the surface rose to meet them.

The icecaps vanished on either side and there began an equal alternation of land and water. A continent, mountainous on either seacoast and flat in between, like a soup plate with two ice-topped rims, flashed below at lengthening intervals. It spread halfway around Junior and the rest was water.

Most of the ocean at the moment was in the dark sector, and what was not lay in the red-orange light of Lagrange II. In the light of that sun, the waters were a dusky purple with a sprinkling of ruddy specks that thickened north and south. Icebergs!

The land was distributed at the moment between the red-orange half sector and the full white light. Only the eastern seacoast was in the blue green. The eastern mountain range was a startling sight, with its western slopes red and its eastern slopes green.

The ship was slowing rapidly now; the final trip over ocean was done. Next—landing!

— 9 —

THE FIRST steps were cautious enough. Slow enough, too. Cimon inspected his photochromes of Junior as taken from space with minute care. Under protest, he passed them among the others of the expedition, and more than a few groaned inwardly at the thought of having placed comfort before a chance to see the original of *that*.

Boris Vernadsky bent over his gas analyzer interminably, a symphony in loud clothes and soft grunts.

"We're about at sea level, I should judge," he said, "going by the value of g."

Then, because he was explaining himself to the rest of the group, he added negligently, "The gravitational constant, that is," which didn't help most of them.

He said, "The atmospheric pressure is just about eight hundred millimeters of mercury, which is about 5 per cent higher than on earth. And two hundred forty millimeters of that is oxygen as compared to only one hundred fifty on Earth. Not bad."

He seemed to be waiting for approval, but scientists found it best to comment as little as possible on data in another man's specialty.

He went on, "Nitrogen, of course. Dull, isn't it, the way nature repeats itself like a three-year-old who knows three lessons, period. Takes the fun away when it turns out that a water world always has an oxygen-nitrogen atmosphere. Makes the whole thing yawn-worthy."

"What else in the atmosphere?" asked Cimon irritably. "So far all we have is oxygen, nitrogen, and homely philosophy from kindly Uncle Boris."

Vernadsky hooked his arm over his seat and said, amiably enough, "What are you? Director or something?"

Cimon, to whom the directorship meant little more than the annoyance of preparing composite reports for the Bureau, flushed and said grimly, "What else in the atmosphere, Dr. Vernadsky?"

Vernadsky said, without looking at his notes, "Under 1 per cent and over a hundredth of 1 per cent: hydrogen, helium, and carbon dioxide in that order. Under a hundredth of 1 per cent and over a ten thousandth of 1 per cent: methane, argon, and neon in that order. Under a ten thousandth of 1 per cent and over a millionth of a per cent : radon, krypton, and xenon in that order.

"The figures aren't very informative. About all I can get out of them is that Junior is going to be a happy hunting ground for uranium, that it's low in potassium, and that it's no wonder it's such a lovely little double icecap of a world."

He did that deliberately, so that someone could ask him how he knew, and someone, with gratifying wonder, inevitably did.

Vernadsky smiled blandly and said, "Atmospheric radon is ten to a hundred times as high here as on Earth. So is helium. Both radon and helium are produced as by-products of the radioactive breakdown of uranium and thorium. Conclusion: Uranium and thorium minerals are ten to a hundred times as copious in Junior's crust as in Earth's.

"Argon, on the other hand, is over a hundred times as low as on Earth. Chances are Junior has none of the argon it originally started with. A planet of this type has only the argon which forms from the breakdown of K^{40}, one of the potassium isotopes. Low argon; low potassium. Simple, kids."

One of the assembled groups asked, "What about the icecaps?"

Cimon, who knew the answer to that, asked, before Vernadsky could answer the other, "What's the carbon dioxide content exactly?"

"Zero point zero one six em em," said Vernadsky.

Cimon nodded, and vouchsafed nothing more.

"Well?" asked the inquirer impatiently.

"Carbon dioxide is only about half what it is on Earth, and it's the carbon dioxide that gives the hothouse effect. It lets the short waves of sunlight pass through to the planet's surface, but doesn't allow the long waves of planetary heat to radiate off. When carbon dioxide concentration goes up as a result of volcanic action, the planet heats up a bit and you have a carboniferous age, with oceans high and land surface at a minimum. When carbon dioxide goes down as a result of the vegetation refusing to let a good thing alone, fattening up on the good old CO_2 and losing its head about it, temperature drops, ice forms, a vicious cycle of glaciation starts, and *voila*——"

"Anything else in the atmosphere?" asked Cimon.

"Water vapor and dust. I suppose there are a few million air-borne spores of various virulent diseases per cubic centimeter in addition to that." He said it lightly enough, but there was a stir in the room. More than one of the bystanders looked as though he were holding his breath.

Vernadsky shrugged and said, "Don't worry about it for now. My analyzer washes out dust and spores quite thoroughly. But then, that's not my angle. I suggest Rodriguez grow his damn cultures under glass right away. Good thick glass."

— 10 —

MARK ANNUNCIO wandered everywhere. His eyes shone as he listened, and he pressed himself forward to hear better. The group suffered him to do so with various degrees of reluctance, in accordance with individual personalities and temperaments. None spoke to him.

Sheffield stayed close to Mark. He scarcely spoke either. He bent all his effort on remaining in the background of Mark's consciousness. He wanted to refrain from giving Mark the feeling of being haunted by himself; give the boy the illusion of freedom instead. He wanted to seem to be there each time by accident only.

It was a most unsuccessful pretense, he felt, but what could he do? He *had* to keep the kid from getting into trouble.

— 11 —

MIGUEL ANTONIO Rodriguez y Lopez (microbiologist; small, tawny, with intensely black hair, which he wore rather long, and with a reputation, which he did nothing to discourage, of being a Latin in the grand style as far as the ladies were concerned) cultured the dust from Vernadsky's gas-analyzer trap with a combination of precision and respectful delicacy.

"Nothing," he said eventually. "What foolish growths I get look harmless."

It was suggested that Junior's bacteria need not necessarily look harmful; that toxins and metabolic processes could not be analyzed by eye, even by microscopic eye.

This was met with hot contempt, as almost an invasion of professional function. He said, with an eyebrow lifted, "One gets a feeling for these things. When one has seen as much of the microcosm as I have, one can sense danger— or lack of danger."

This was an outright lie, and Rodriguez proved it by carefully transferring samples of the various germ colonies into buffered, isotonic media and injecting hamsters with the concentrated result. They did not seem to mind.

Raw atmosphere was trapped in large jars and several specimens of minor animal life from Earth and other planets were allowed to disport themselves within. None of them seemed to mind either.

— 12 —

NEVILE FAWKES (botanist; a man who appreciated his own handsomeness by modeling his hair style after that shown on the traditional busts of Alexander the Great, but from whose appearance the presence of a nose far more aquiline than Alexander ever possessed noticeably detracted) was gone for two days, by Junior chronology, in one of the *Triple G.*'s atmospheric coasters. He could navigate one like a dream and was, in fact, the only man outside the crew who could navigate one at all, so he was the natural choice for the task. Fawkes did not seem noticeably overjoyed about that.

He returned, completely unharmed and unable to hide a grin of relief. He submitted to irradiation for the sake of sterilizing the exterior of his flexible air suit (designed to protect men from the deleterious effect of the outer environment, where no pressure differential existed; the strength and jointedness of a true space suit being obviously unnecessary within an atmosphere as thick as

Junior's). The coaster was subjected to a more extended irradiation and pinned down under a plastic coverall.

Fawkes flaunted color photographs in great number. The central valley of the continent was fertile almost beyond Earthly dreams. The rivers were mighty, the mountains rugged and snow-covered (with the usual pyrotechnic solar effects). Under Lagrange II alone, the vegetation looked vaguely repellent, seeming rather dark, like dried blood. Under Lagrange I, however, or under the suns together, the brilliant, flourishing green and the glisten of the numerous lakes (particularly north and south along the dead rims of the departing glaciers) brought an ache of homesickness to the hearts of many.

Fawkes said, "Look at these."

He had skimmed low to take a photochrome of a field of huge flowers dripping with scarlet. In the high ultra-violet radiation of Lagrange I, exposure times were of necessity extremely short, and despite the motion of the coaster, each blossom stood out as a sharp blotch of strident color.

"I swear," said Fawkes, "each one of those was six feet across."

They admired the flowers unrestrainedly.

Fawkes then said, "No intelligent life whatever, of course."

Sheffield looked up from the photographs with instant sharpness. Life and intelligence, after all, were by way of being his province. "How do you know?"

"Look for yourself," said the botanist. "There are the photos. No highways, no cities, no artificial waterways, no signs of anything man-made."

"No machine civilization," said Sheffield. "That's all."

"Even ape men would build shelters and use fire," said Fawkes, offended.

"The continent is ten times as large as Africa and you've been over it for two days. There's a lot you could miss."

"Not as much as you'd think," was the warm response. "I followed every sizable river up and down and looked over both seacoasts. Any settlements are bound to be there."

"In allowing seventy-two hours for two eight thousand-mile seacosts ten thousand miles apart, plus how many thousand miles of river, that had to be a pretty quick lookover."

Cimon interrupted, "What's this all about? *Homo sapiens* is the only intelligence ever discovered in the Galaxy through a hundred thousand and more explored planets. The chances of Troas possessing intelligence is virtually nil."

"Yes?" said Sheffield. "You could use the same argument to prove there's no intelligence on Earth."

"Makoyama," said Cimon, "in his report mentioned no intelligent life."

"And how much time did he have? It was a case of another quick feel through the haystack with one finger and a report of no needle."

"What the eternal Universe," said Rodriguez waspishly. "We argue like madmen. Call the hypothesis of indigenous intelligence unproven and let it go. We are not through investigating yet, I hope."

— 13 —

COPIES OF those first pictures of Junior's surface were added to what might be termed the open files. After a second trip, Fawkes returned in more somber mood and the meeting was correspondingly more subdued.

New photographs went from hand to hand and were then placed by Cimon himself in the special safe that nothing could open short of Cimon's own hands or an all-destroying nuclear blast.

Fawkes said, "The two largest rivers have a generally north-south course along the eastern edges of the western mountain range. The larger river comes down from the northern icecap, the smaller up from the southern one. Tributaries come in westward from the eastern range, interlacing the entire central plain. Apparently the central plain is tipped, the eastern edge being higher. It's what ought to be expected maybe. The eastern mountain range is the taller, broader, and more continuous of the two. I wasn't able to make actual measurements, but I wouldn't be surprised if they beat the Himalayas. In fact, they're a lot like the Wu Ch'ao range on Hesperus. You have to hit the stratosphere to get over them, and rugged—— Wow!

"Anyway" —he brought himself back to the immediate subject at hand with an effort— "the two main rivers join about a hundred miles south of the equator and pour through a gap in the western range. They make it to the ocean after that in just short of eighty miles.

"Where it hits the ocean is a natural spot for the planetary metropolis. The trade routes into the interior of the continent have to converge there so it would be the inevitable emporium for space trade. Even as far as surface trade is concerned, the continental east coast has to move goods across the ocean. Jumping the eastern range isn't worth the effort. Then, too, there are the islands we saw when we were landing.

"So right there is where I would have looked for the settlement even if we didn't have a record of the latitude and longitude. And those settlers had an eye for the future. It's where they set up shop."

Novee said in a low voice, "They thought they had an eye for the future, anyway. There isn't much left of them, is there?"

Fawkes tried to be philosophic about it. "It's been over a century. What do you expect? There's a lot more left of them than I honestly thought there would be. Their buildings were mostly prefab. They've tumbled and vegetation has forced its way over and through them. The fact that the climate of Junior is glacial is what's preserved it. The trees—or the objects that rather look like trees—are small and obviously very slow-growing.

"Even so, the clearing is gone. From the air, the only way you could tell there had once been a settlement in that spot was that the new growth had a slightly different color and—and, well, *texture*—than the surrounding forests."

He pointed at a particular photograph. "This is just a slag heap. Maybe it was machinery once. I think those are burial mounds."

Novee said, "Any actual remains? Bones?"

Fawks shook his head.

Novee said, "The last survivors didn't bury themselves, did they?"

Fawkes said, "Animals, I suppose." He walked away, his back to the group. "It was raining when I poked my way through. It went splat, splat on the flat leaves above me and the ground was soggy and spongy underneath. It was dark,

440

gloomy. There was a cold wind. The pictures I took don't get it across. I felt as though there were a thousand ghosts, waiting——''

The mood was contagious.

Cimon said savagely, "Stop that!"

In the background, Mark Annuncio's pointed nose fairly quivered with the intensity of his curiosity. He turned to Sheffield, who was at his side, and whispered, "Ghosts? No authentic case of seeing——''

Sheffield touched Mark's thin shoulder lightly. "Only a way of speaking, Mark. But don't feel badly that he doesn't mean it literally. You're watching the birth of a superstition, and that's something, isn't it?"

— 14 —

A SEMI-SULLEN Captain Follenbee sought out Cimon the evening after Fawkes' second return and said in his harumphy way, "Never do, Dr. Cimon. My men are unsettled. Very unsettled."

The port shields were open. Lagrange I was six hours gone, and Lagrange II's ruddy light, deepened to crimson in setting, flushed the Captain's face and tinged his short gray hair with red.

Cimon, whose attitude toward the crew in general and the Captain in particular was one of controlled impatience, said, "What is the trouble, Captain?"

"Been here two weeks, Earth time. Still no one leaves without suits. Always irradiate before you come back. Anything wrong with the air?"

"Not as far as we know."

"Why not breathe it then?"

"Captain, that's for me to decide."

The flush on the Captain's face became a real one. He said, "My papers say I don't have to stay if ship's safety is endangered. A frightened and mutinous crew is something I don't want."

"Can't you handle your own men?"

"Within reason."

"Well, what really bothers them? This is a new planet and we're being cautious. Can't they understand that?"

"Two weeks and still cautious. They think we're hiding something. And we are. You know that. Besides, surface leave is necessary. Crew's got to have it. Even if it's just on a bare rock a mile across. Gets them out of the ship. Away from the routine. Can't deny them that."

"Give me till tomorrow," said Cimon contemptuously.

— 15 —

THE SCIENTISTS gathered in the observatory the next day.

Cimon said, "Vernadsky tells me the data on air is still negative, and Rodriguez has discovered no air-borne pathogenic organism of any type."

There was a general air of dubiety over the last statement. Novee said, "The settlement died of disease. I'll swear to that."

"Maybe so," said Rodriguez at once, "but can you explain how? It's impossible. I tell you that and I tell you. See here. Almost all Earth-type planets give birth to life and that life is always protein in nature and always either cellular or virus in organization. But that's all. There the resemblance ends.

"You laymen think it's all the same; Earth or any planet. Germs are germs and viruses are viruses. I tell you you don't understand the infinite possibilities for variation in the protein molecule. Even on Earth, every species has its own diseases. Some may spread over several species but there isn't one single pathogenic life form of any type on Earth that can attack all other species.

"You think that a virus or a bacterium developing independently for a billion years on another planet with different amino acids, different enzyme systems, a different scheme of metabolism altogether is just going to happen to find *Homo sapiens* succulent like a lollipop. I tell you it is childishness."

Novee, his physician's soul badly pierced at having been lumped under the phrase, "You laymen," was not disposed to let it go that easily. "*Homo sapiens* brings its own germs with it wherever it goes, Rod. Who's to say the virus of the common cold didn't mutate under some planetary influence into something that was suddenly deadly? Or influenza. Things like that have happened even on Earth. The 2755 para-meas——"

"I know all about the 2755 para-measles epidemic," said Rodriguez, "and the 1918 influenza epidemic, and the Black Death, too. But when has it happened lately? Granted the settlement was a matter of a century and more ago—still that wasn't exactly pre-atomic times, either. They included doctors. They had supplies of antibiotics and for space' sake, they knew the techniques of antibody induction. They're simple enough. And there was the medical relief expedition, too."

Novee patted his round abdomen and said stubbornly, "The symptoms were those of a respiratory infection; dyspnea——"

"I know the list, but I tell you it wasn't a germ disease that got them. It couldn't be."

"What was it, then?"

"That's outside my professional competence. Talking from inside, I tell you it wasn't infection. Even mutant infection. It couldn't be. It *mathematically* couldn't be." He leaned heavily on the adverb.

There was a stir among his listeners as Mark Annuncio shoved his thin body forward into the space immediately before Rodriguez.

For the first time, he spoke at one of these gatherings.

"Mathematically?" he asked eagerly.

Sheffield followed after, his long body all elbows and knees as he made a path. He murmured "Sorry" half a dozen times.

Rodriguez, in an advanced stage of exasperation, thrust out his lower lip and said, "What do *you* want?"

Mark flinched. Less eagerly, he said, "You said you knew it wasn't infection mathematically. I was wondering how—mathematics . . ." He ran down.

Rodriguez said, "I have stated my professional opinion."

He said it formally, stiltedly, then turned away. No man questioned another's professional opinion unless he was of the same specialty. Otherwise the implication, clearly enough, was that the specialist's experience and knowledge was sufficiently dubious to be brought into question by an outsider.

Mark knew this, but then he was of the Mnemonic Service. He tapped Rodriguez's shoulder, while the others standing about listened in stunned fascination, and said, "I know it's your professional opinion, but still I'd like to have it explained."

He didn't mean to sound peremptory. He was just stating a fact.

Rodriguez whirled. "You'd like to have it explained? Who the eternal Universe are *you* to ask me questions?"

Mark was startled at the other's vehemence, but Sheffield had reached him now, and he gained courage. With it, anger. He disregarded Sheffield's quick whisper and said shrilly, "I'm Mark Annuncio of Mnemonic Service and I've asked you a question. I want your statement explained."

"It won't be explained. Sheffield, take this young nut out of here and tuck him into bed, will you? And keep him away from me after this. Damn young jackass." The last was a clearly heard aside.

Sheffield took Mark's wrist but it was wrenched out of his grasp. The young Mnemonic screamed, "You stupid noncompos. You—you moron. You forgettery on two feet. Sievemind. Let me *go*, Dr. Sheffield—— You're no expert. You don't remember anything you've learned, and you haven't learned much in the first place. You're not a specialist; none of you——"

"For space's sake," cried Cimon, "take the young idiot out of here, Sheffield."

Sheffield, his long cheeks burning, stooped and lifted Mark bodily into the air. Holding him close, he made his way out of the room.

Tears squeezed out of Mark's eyes, and just outside the door, he managed to speak with difficulty. "Let me down. I want to hear—I want to hear what they say."

Sheffield said, "Don't go back in. Please, Mark."

"I won't. Don't worry. But——"

He didn't finish the but.

— 16 —

INSIDE THE observatory room, Cimon, looking haggard, said, "All right. All right. Let's get back to the point. Come on, now. Quiet! I'm accepting Rodriguez's viewpoint. It's good enough for me and I don't suppose there's anyone else here who questions Rodriguez's professional opinion."

("Better not," muttered Rodriguez, his dark eyes hot with sustained fury.)

Cimon went on. "And since there's nothing to fear as far as infection is concerned, I'm telling Captain Follenbee that the crew may take surface leave without special protection against the atmosphere. Apparently the lack of surface leave is bad for morale. Are there any objections?"

There weren't any.

Cimon said, "I see no reason also why we can't pass on to the next stage of the investigation. I propose that we set up camp at the site of the original settlement. I appoint a committee of five to trek out there. Fawkes, since he can handle the coaster; Novee and Rodriguez to handle the biological data; Vernadsky and myself to take care of the chemistry and physics.

"The rest of you will, naturally, be apprised of all pertinent data in your own specialties, and will be expected to help in suggesting lines of attack, et cetera. Eventually, we may all be out there, but for the while only this small group. And until further notice, communication between ourselves and the main group on ship will be by radio only, since if the trouble, whatever it is, turns out to be localized at settlement site, five men are enough to lose."

Novee said, "The settlement lived on Junior several years before dying out. Over a year, anyway. It could be a long time before we are certain we're safe."

"We," said Cimon, "are not a settlement. We are a group of specialists who are looking for trouble. We'll find it if it's there to find, and when we do find it, we'll beat it. And it won't take us a couple of years, either. Now, are there any objections?"

There were none, and the meeting broke up.

— 17 —

MARK ANNUNCIO sat on his bunk, hands clasped about his knee, chin sunken and touching his chest. He was dry-eyed now, but his voice was heady with frustration.

"They're not taking me," he said. "They won't let me go with them."

Sheffield was in the chair opposite the boy, bathed in an agony of perplexity. He said, "They may take you later on."

"No," said Mark fiercely, "they won't. They hate me. Besides, I want to go now. I've never been on another planet before. There's so much to see and find out. They've got no right to hold me back if I want to go."

Sheffield shook his head. Mnemonics were so firmly trained into this belief that they *must* collect facts and that no one or nothing could or ought to stop them. Perhaps when they returned, he might recommend a certain degree of counterindoctrination. After all, Mnemonics had to live in the real world occasionally. More and more with each generation, perhaps, as they grew to play an increasing role in the Galaxy.

He tried an experiment. He said, "It may be dangerous, you know."

"I don't care. I've got to know. I've *got* to find out about this planet. Dr. Sheffield, you go to Dr. Cimon and tell him I'm going along."

"Now, Mark."

"If you don't, I will." He raised his small body from the bed in earnest of leaving that moment.

"Look, you're excited."

Mark's fists clenched. "It's not fair, Dr. Sheffield. I found this planet. It's *my* planet."

Sheffield's conscience hit him badly. What Mark said was true in a way. No one, except Mark, knew that better than Sheffield. And no one, again except Mark, knew the history of Junior better than Sheffield.

It was only in the last twenty years that, faced with the rising tide of population pressure in the older planets and the recession of the Galactic frontier from those same older planets, the Confederation of Worlds began exploring the Galaxy systematically. Before that, human expansion went on hit or miss. Men and women in search of new land and a better life followed rumor as to the existence of habitable planets or sent out amateur groups to find something promising.

A hundred ten years before, one such group found Junior. They didn't report their find officially because they didn't want a crowd of land speculators, promotion men, exploiters and general riffraff following. In the next months, some of the unattached men arranged to have women brought in, so the settlement must have flourished for a while.

It was a year later, when some had died and most or all the rest were sick and dying, that they beamed a cry of help to Pretoria, the nearest inhabited planet. The Pretorian government was in some sort of crisis at the time and relayed the message to the Sector government at Altmark. Pretoria then felt justified in forgetting the matter.

The Altmark government, acting in reflex fashion, sent out a medical ship to Junior. It dropped anti-sera and various other supplies. The ship did not land because the medical officer diagnosed the matter from a distance as influenza and minimized the danger. The medical supplies, his report said, would handle the matter perfectly. It was quite possible that the crew of the ship, fearing contagion, had prevented a landing, but nothing in the official report indicated that.

There was a final report from Junior three months later to the effect that only ten people were left alive and that they were dying. They begged for help. This report was forwarded to Earth itself along with the previous medical report. The Central government, however, was a maze in which reports regularly were forgotten unless someone had sufficient personal interest, and influence, to keep them alive. No one had much interest in a far-off, unknown planet with ten dying men and women on it.

Filed and forgotten—and for a century, no human foot was felt on Junior.

Then, with the new furor over Galactic exploration, hundreds of ships began darting through the empty vastness, probing here and there. Reports trickled in, then flooded in. Some came from Hidosheki Mikoyama, who passed through the Hercules cluster twice (dying in a crash landing the second time, with his tight and despairing voice coming over the subether in a final message: "Surface coming up fast now; ship walls frictioning into red he——" and no more.)

Last year the accumulation of reports, grown past any reasonable human handling, was fed into the overworked Washington computer on a priority so high that there was only a five-month wait. The operators checked out the data for planetary habitability and lo, Abou ben Junior led all the rest.

Sheffield remembered the wild hoorah over it. The stellar system was enthusiastically proclaimed to the Galaxy and the name Junior was thought up by a bright young man in the Bureau of Outer Provinces who felt the need for personal friendliness between man and world. Junior's virtues were magnified. Its fertility, its climate ("a New England perpetual spring"), and most of all, its vast future, were put across without any feeling of need for discretion. "For the next million years," propagandists declared, "Junior will grow richer. While other planets age, Junior will grow younger as the ice recedes and fresh soil is exposed. Always a new frontier; always untapped resources."

For a million years!

It was the Bureau's masterpiece. It was to be the tremendously successful start of a program of government-sponsored colonization. It was to be the beginning, at long last, of the scientific exploitation of the Galaxy for the good of humanity.

And then came Mark Annuncio, who heard much of all this and was as thrilled at the prospect as any Joe Earthman, but who one day thought of something he had seen while sniffing idly through the "dead matter" files of the Bureau of Outer Provinces. He had seen a medical report about a colony on a planet of a system whose description and position in space tallied with that of the Lagrange group.

Sheffield remembered the day Mark came to him with that news.

He also remembered the face of the Secretary for the Outer Provinces when the news was passed on to *him*. He saw the Secretary's square jaw slowly go slack and a look of infinite trouble come into his eyes.

The government was committed! It was going to ship millions of people to Junior. It was going to grant farmland and subsidize the first seed supplies, farm machinery, factories. Junior was going to be a paradise for numerous voters and a promise of more paradise for a myriad others.

If Junior turned out to be a killer planet for some reason or other, it would mean political suicide for all government figures concerned in the project. That meant some pretty big men, not least the Secretary for the Outer Provinces.

After days of checking and indecision, the Secretary had said to Sheffield, "It looks as though we've got to find out what happened and weave it into the propaganda somehow. Don't you think we could neutralize it that way?"

"If what happened isn't too horrible to neutralize."

"But it can't be, can it? I mean what can it be?" The man was miserably unhappy.

Sheffield shrugged.

The Secretary said, "See here. We can send a ship of specialists to the planet. Volunteers only and good reliable men, of course. We can give it the highest priority rating we can move, and Project Junior carries considerable weight, you know. We'll slow things up here, and hold on till they get back. That might work, don't you think?"

Sheffield wasn't sure, but he got the sudden dream of going on that expedition, of taking Mark with him. He could study a Mnemonic in an off-trail environment, and if Mark *should* be the means of working out the mystery——

From the beginning, a mystery was assumed. After all, people don't die of influenza. And the medical ship hadn't landed; they hadn't *really* observed what was going on. It was fortunate, indeed, that that medical man was now dead thirty-seven years, or he would be slated for court-martial now.

If Mark *should* help solve the matter, the Mnemonic Service would be enormously strengthened. The government had to be grateful.

But now——

Sheffield wondered if Cimon knew the story of how the matter of the first settlement had been brought to light. He was fairly certain that the rest of the crew did not. It was not something the Bureau would willingly speak about.

Nor would it be politic to use the story as a lever to pry concessions out of Cimon. If Mark's correction of Bureau "stupidity" (that would undoubtedly be the opposition's phrasing) were overpublicized, the Bureau would look bad. If they could be grateful, they could be vengeful, too. Retaliation against the Mnemonic Service would not be too petty a thing to expect.

Still——

Sheffield stood up with quick decision. "All right, Mark. I'll get you out to the settlement site. I'll get us both out there. Now you sit down and wait for me. Promise you'll try nothing on your own."

"All right," said Mark. He sat down on his bunk again.

— 18 —

"*WELL NOW*, Dr. Sheffield, what is it?" said Cimon. The astrophysicist sat at his desk, on which papers and film formed rigidly arranged heaps about a small Macfreed integrator, and watched Sheffield step over the threshold.

Sheffield sat carelessly down upon the tautly yanked top sheet of Cimon's bunk. He was aware of Cimon's annoyed glance in that direction and it did not worry him. In fact, he rather enjoyed it.

He said, "I have a quarrel with your choice of men to go to the expedition site. It looks as though you've picked two men for the physical sciences and three for the biological sciences. Right?"

"Yes."

"I suppose you think you've covered the ground like a Danielski ovospore at perihelion."

"Oh, space! Have you anything to suggest?"

"I would like to come along myself."

"Why?"

"You have no one to take care of the mental sciences."

"The *mental* sciences! Good Galaxy! Dr. Sheffield, five men are quite enough to risk. As a matter of fact, Doctor, you and your—uh—ward were assigned to the scientific personnel of this ship by order of the Bureau of Outer Provinces without any prior consultation of myself. I'll be frank. If I had been consulted, I would have advised against you. I don't see the function of mental science in an investigation such as this, which, after all, is purely physical. It is too bad that the Bureau wishes to experiment with Mnemonics on an occasion such as this. We can't afford scenes like that one with Rodriguez."

Sheffield decided that Cimon did not know of Mark's connection with the original decision to send out the expedition.

He sat upright, hands on knees, elbows cocked outward, and let a freezing formality settle over him. "So you wonder about the function of mental science in an investigation such as this, Dr. Cimon. Suppose I told you that the end of the first settlement might possibly be explained on a simple, psychological basis."

"It wouldn't impress me. A psychologist is a man who can explain anything and prove nothing." Cimon smirked like a man who had made an epigram and was proud of it.

Sheffield ignored it. He said, "Let me go into a little detail. In what way is Junior different from every one of the eighty-three thousand inhabited worlds?"

"Our information is as yet incomplete. I cannot say."

"Oh, cobber-vitals. You had the necessary information before you ever came here. Junior has two suns."

"Well, of course." But the astrophysicist allowed a trace of discomfiture to enter his expression.

"Colored suns, mind you. Colored suns. Do you know what that means? It means that a human being, yourself or myself, standing in the full glare of the two suns, would cast two shadows. One blue green, one red orange. The length of each would naturally vary with the time of day. Have you taken the trouble to verify the color distribution in those shadows? The what-do-you-call-'em—reflection spectrum?"

"I presume," said Cimon loftily, "they'd be about the same as the radiation spectra of the suns. What are you getting at?"

"You should check. Wouldn't the air absorb some wave lengths? And the vegetation? What's left? And take Junior's moon, Sister. I've been watching it in the last few nights. It's in colors, too, and the colors change position."

"Well, of course, damn it. It runs through its phases independently with each sun."

"You haven't checked its reflection spectrum, either, have you?"

"We have that somewhere. There are no points of interest about it. Of what interest is it to you, anyway?"

"My dear Dr. Cimon, it is a well-established psychological fact that combinations of red and green colors exert a deleterious effect on mental stability. We have a case here where the red-green chromopsychic picture (to use a technical term) is inescapable and is presented under circumstances which seem most unnatural to the human mind. It is quite possible that chromopsychosis could reach the fatal level by inducing hypertrophy of the trinitarian follicles, with consequent cerebric catatonia."

Cimon looked floored. He said, "I never heard of such a thing."

"Naturally not," said Sheffield (it was his turn to be lofty). "You are not a psychologist. Surely you are not questioning my professional opinion."

"No, of course not. But it's quite plain from the last reports of the expedition that they were dying of something that sounded like a respiratory disease."

"Correct, but Rodriguez denies that and you accepted his professional opinion."

"I didn't say it was a respiratory disease. I said it sounded like one. Where does your red-green chromothingumbob come in?"

Sheffield shook his head. "You laymen have your misconceptions. Granted that there is a physical effect, it still does not imply that there may not be a mental cause. The most convincing point about my theory is that red-green chromopsychosis has been recorded to exhibit itself first as a psychogenic respiratory infection. I take it you are not acquainted with psychogenics."

"No. It's out of my field."

"Well, yes. I should say so. Now my own calculations show me that under the heightened oxygen tension of this world, the psychogenic respiratory infection is both inevitable and particularly severe. For instance, you've observed the moon—Sister, I mean—in the last few nights."

"Yes, I have observed Ilium." Cimon did not forget Sister's official name even now.

"You watched it closely and over lengthy periods? Under magnification?"

"Yes." Cimon was growing uneasy.

"Ah," said Sheffield. "Now the moon colors in the last few nights have been particularly virulent. Surely you must be noticing just a small inflammation of the mucus membrane of the nose, a slight itching in the throat. Nothing painful yet, I imagine. Have you been coughing or sneezing? Is it a little hard to swallow?"

"I believe I——" Cimon swallowed, then drew in his breath sharply. He was testing.

Then he sprang to his feet, fists clenched and mouth working. "Great galaxy, Sheffield, you had no right to keep quiet about this. I can feel it now. What do I do, Sheffield? It's not incurable, is it? Damn it, Sheffield"—his voice went shrill—"why didn't you tell us this before?"

"Because," said Sheffield calmly, "there's not a word of truth in anything I've said. Not one word. There's no harm in colors. Sit down, Dr. Cimon. You're beginning to look foolish."

"You said," said Cimon, thoroughly confused, and in a voice that was beginning to strangle, "that it was your professional opinion that——"

"My professional opinion! Space and little comets, Cimon, what's so magic about a professional opinion? A man can be lying or he can just plain be ignorant, even about the final details of his own specialty. A professional can be wrong because he's ignorant of a neighboring specialty. He may be certain he's right and still be wrong.

"Look at you. You know all about what makes the Universe tick and I'm lost completely except that I know that a star is something that twinkles and a light-year is something that's long. And yet you'll swallow gibberish psychology that a freshman student of mentics would laugh his head off at. Don't you think, Cimon, it's time we worried less about professional opinion and more about over-all co-ordination?"

The color washed slowly out of Cimon's face. It turned waxy-pale. His lips trembled. He whispered, "You used professional status as a cloak to make a fool of me."

"That's about it," said Sheffield.

"I have never, *never*——" Cimon gasped and tried a new start. "I have never witnessed anything as cowardly and unethical."

"I was trying to make a point."

"Oh, you made it. You made it." Cimon was slowly recovering, his voice approaching normality. "You want me to take that boy of yours with us."

"That's right."

"No. No. Definitely no. It was no before you came in here and it's no a million times over now."

"What's your reason? I mean before I came in."

"He's psychotic. He can't be trusted with normal people."

Sheffield said grimly, "I'll thank you not to use the word, 'psychotic.' You are not competent to use it. If you're so precise in your feeling for professional ethics, remember to stay out of my specialty in my presence. Mark Annuncio is perfectly normal."

"After that scene with Rodriguez? Yes. Oh, yes."

"Mark had the right to ask his question. It was his job to do so and his duty. Rodriguez had no right to be boorish about it."

"I'll have to consider Rodriguez first, if you don't mind."

"Why? Mark Annuncio knows more than Rodriguez. For that matter, he knows more than you or I. Are you trying to bring back an intelligent report or to satisfy a petty vanity?"

"Your statements about what your boy knows do not impress me. I am quite aware he is an efficient parrot. He understands nothing, however. It is my duty to see to it that data is made available to him because the Bureau has ordered that. They did not consult me, but very well. I will co-operate that far. He will receive his data here in the ship."

Sheffield said, "Not adequate, Cimon. He should be on the spot. He may see things our precious specialists will not."

Cimon said freezingly, "Very likely. The answer, Sheffield, is no. There is no argument that can possibly persuade me." The astrophysicist's nose was pinched and white.

"Because I made a fool of you?"

"Because you violated the most fundamental obligation of a professional man. No respectable professional would ever use his specialty to prey on the innocence of a non-associate professional."

"So I made a fool of you."

Cimon turned away. "Please leave. There will be no further communication between us, outside the most necessary business, for the duration of the trip."

"If I go," said Sheffield, "the rest of the boys may get to hear about this."

Cimon started. "You're going to repeat our little affair?" A cold smile rested on his lips, then went its transient and contemptuous way. "You'll broadcast the dastard you were."

"Oh, I doubt they'll take it seriously. Everyone knows psychologists will have their little jokes. Besides, they'll be so busy laughing at you. You know—the very impressive Dr. Cimon scared into a sore throat and howling for mercy after a few mystic words of gibberish."

"Who'd believe you?" cried Cimon.

Sheffield lifted his right hand. Between thumb and forefinger was a small rectangular object, studded with a line of control toggles.

"Pocket recorder," he said. He touched one of the toggles and Cimon's voice was suddenly saying, "Well, now, Dr. Sheffield, what is it?"

It sounded pompous, peremptory, and even a little smug.

"Give me that!" Cimon hurled himself at the lanky psychologist.

Sheffield held him off. "Don't try force, Cimon. I was in amateur wrestling not too long ago. Look, I'll make a deal with you."

Cimon was still writhing toward him, dignity forgotten, panting his fury. Sheffield kept him at arm's length, backing slowly.

Sheffield said, "Let Mark and myself come along and no one will ever see or hear this."

Slowly Cimon simmered down. He gasped, "Will you let me have it, then?"

"After Mark and I are out at the settlement site."

"I'm to trust *you*." He seemed to take pains to make that as offensive as possible.

"Why not? You can certainly trust me to broadcast this if you *don't* agree. I'll play it off for Vernadsky first. He'll love it. You know his corny sense of humor."

Cimon said in a voice so low it could hardly be heard, "You and the boy can come along." Then vigorously, "But remember this, Sheffield. When we get back to Earth, I'll have you before the Central Committee of the G.A.A.S. That's a promise. You'll be de-professionalized."

Sheffield said, "I'm not afraid of the Galactic Association for the Advancement of Science." He let the syllables resound. "After all, what will you accuse me of? Are you going to play this recording before the Central Committee as evidence? Come, come, let's be friendly about this. You don't want to broadcast your own—uh—mistake before the primest stuffed shirts in eighty-three thousand worlds."

Smiling gently, he backed out the door.

But when he closed the door between himself and Cimon, his smile vanished. He hadn't liked to do this. Now that he had done it, he wondered if it were worth the enemy he had made.

— 19 —

SEVEN TENTS had sprung up near the site of the original settlement on Junior. Nevile Fawkes could see them all from the low ridge on which he stood. They had been there seven days now.

He looked up at the sky. The clouds were thick overhead and pregnant with rain. That pleased him. With both suns behind those clouds, the diffused light was gray white. It made things seem almost normal.

The wind was damp and a little raw, as though it were April in Vermont. Fawkes was a New Englander and he appreciated the resemblance. In four or five hours, Lagrange I would set and the clouds would turn ruddy while the landscape would become angrily dim. But Fawkes intended to be back in the tents by then.

So near the equator, yet so cool! Well, that would change with the millennia. As the glaciers retreated, the air would warm up and the soil would dry out. Jungles and deserts would make their appearance. The water level in the oceans would slowly creep higher, wiping out numberless islands. The two large rivers would become an inland sea, changing the configuration of Junior's one large continent; perhaps making several smaller ones out of it.

He wondered if settlement site would be drowned. Probably, he decided. Maybe that would take the curse off it.

He could understand why the Confederation were so damned anxious to solve the mystery of that first settlement. Even if it were a simple matter of disease, there would have to be proof. Otherwise, who would settle the world? The "sucker bait" superstition held for more than merely spacemen.

He, himself—— Well, his first visit to the settlement site hadn't been so bad, though he had been glad to leave the rain and the gloom. Returning was worse. It was difficult to sleep with the thought that a thousand mysterious deaths lay all about, separated from him only by that insubstantial thing time.

With medical coolness, Novee had dug up the moldering graves of a dozen of the ancient settlers. (Fawkes could not and did not look at the remains.) There had been only crumbling bones, Novee had said, out of which nothing could be made.

"There seem to be abnormalities of bone deposition," he said.

Then on questioning, he admitted that the effects might be entirely owing to a hundred years' exposure to damp soil.

Fawkes had constructed a fantasy that followed him even into his waking hours. It concerned an elusive race of intelligent beings dwelling underground, never being seen but haunting that first settlement a century back with a deadly perserverance.

He pictured a silent bacteriological warfare. He could see them in laboratories beneath the tree roots, culturing their molds and spores, waiting for one that could live on human beings. Perhaps they captured children to experiment upon.

And when they found what they were looking for, spores drifted silently out over the settlement in venomous clouds—

Fawkes knew all this to be fantasy. He had made it up in the wakeful nights out of no evidence but that of his quivering stomach. Yet alone in the forest, he whirled more than once in a sudden horror-filled conviction that bright eyes were staring out of the duskiness of a tree's Lagrange I shadow.

Fawkes' botanist's eye did not miss the vegetation he passed, absorbed as he was. He had deliberately struck out from camp in a new direction, but what he saw was what he had already seen. Junior's forests were neither thick nor tangled. They were scarcely a barrier to travel. The small trees (few were higher than ten feet, although their trunks were nearly as thick as the average Terrestrial tree) grew with considerable room between them.

Fawkes had constructed a rough scheme for arranging the plant life of Junior into some sort of taxonomic order. He was not unaware of the fact that he might be arranging for his own immortality.

There was the scarlet "bayonet tree," for instance. Its huge scarlet flowers attracted insect-like creatures that built small nests within it. Then (at what signal or what impulse Fawkes had not divined) all the flowers on some one given tree would grow a glistening white pistil over night. Each pistil stood two feet high, as though every bloom had been suddenly equipped with a bayonet.

By the next day, the flower had been fertilized and the petals closed shut— about pistil, insects, and all. The explorer, Makoyama, had named it the "bayonet tree," but Fawkes had made so bold as to rename it *Migrania Fawkesii*.

One thing the trees had in common. Their wood was incredibly tough. It would be the task of the biochemist to determine the physical state of the cellulose molecule and that of the biophysicist to determine how water could be transported through the wood's impervious texture. What Fawkes knew from experience was that the blossoms would break if pulled, that the stems would bend only with difficulty and break not at all. His pocketknife was blunted without so much as making a scratch.

The original settlers, in order to clear land, had obviously had to dig out the trees, roots and all.

Compared to Earth, the woods were almost free of animal life. That might be due to the glacial slaughter. Fawkes didn't know.

The insect-like creatures were all two winged. And those wings were feathery little fronds that beat noiselessly. None, apparently, were bloodsuckers.

The only major experience with animals that they had had was the sudden appearance of a large flying creature over the camp. It took high-speed photography to reveal the actual shape of the beast, for the specimen they observed, apparently overcome with curiosity, swooped low over the tents again and again at speeds too great for comfortable, naked-eye observation.

It was four-winged, the forward wings terminating in powerful claws, being membranous and nearly naked, serving the office of gliding planes. The hind pair, covered with a hairlike fuzz, beat rapidly.

Rodriguez suggested the name *Tetrapterus*.

Fawkes paused in his reminiscence to look at a variety of grass he had not seen before. It grew in a dense patch and each stem forked in three toward the top. He brought out his magnifying glass and felt one of the stems gingerly with his finger. Like other grasses on Junior, it——

It was here that he heard the rustle behind him—unmistakable. He listened for a moment, his own heartbeat drowning the sound, then whirled. A small manlike object dodged behind a tree.

Fawkes' breathing nearly stopped. He fumbled for the blaster he wore and his hand seemed to be moving through molasses.

Was his fantasy no fantasy at all? Was Junior inhabited after all?

Numbly Fawkes found himself behind another tree. He couldn't leave it at this. He knew that. He could not report to the rest: "I saw something alive. It might have been the answer to everything. But I was afraid and let it get away."

He would have to make some attempt.

There was a "chalice tree" just behind the tree that hid the creature. It was in bloom, the white and cream flowers lifted turgidly upward, waiting to catch the rain that would soon fall. There was the sharp tinkle of a breaking flower and cream slivers twisted and turned downward.

It wasn't imagination. Something *was* behind the tree.

Fawkes took a deep breath and dashed out, holding his blaster before him, nerving himself to shoot at the slightest sign of danger.

But a voice called out, "Don't. It's only I." A frightened but definitely human face looked out from behind the tree.

It was Mark Annuncio.

Fawkes stopped in mid-stride and stared. Finally, he managed to croak, "What are you doing here?"

Mark said, staring at the blaster in the other's hand, "I was following you."

"Why?"

"To see what you would do. I was interested in what you might find. I thought if you saw me, you would send me away."

Fawkes became conscious of the weapon he was still holding and put it away. It took three tries to get it into the holster.

The first fat drops of rain began to fall. Fawkes said harshly, "Don't say anything about this to the others."

He glared hostilely at the youngster and they walked back to camp separately and in silence.

— 20 —

A CENTRAL hall of prefab had been added to the seven tents now, and the group was together within it, sitting about the long table.

It was a great moment, but a rather subdued one. Vernadsky, who had cooked for himself in his college days, was in charge. He lifted the steaming stew off the short-wave heater and said, "Calories, anyone?"

He ladled the stuff lavishly.

"It smells very good," said Novee doubtfully.

He lifted a piece of meat with his fork. It was purplish and still felt tough despite internal heating. The shredded herbs that surrounded it seemed softer, but looked less edible.

"Well," said Vernadsky, "eat it. Put it in your mouth. I've tasted it and it's good."

He crammed his mouth and chewed. He kept on chewing. "Tough, but good."

Fawkes said gloomily, "It'll probably kill us."

"Nuts," said Vernadsky. "The rats have been living on it for two weeks."

"Two weeks isn't much," said Novee.

Rodriguez said, "Well, one bite won't kill. Say, it *is* good."

And it was. They all agreed eventually. So far, it seemed that whenever Junior's life could be eaten at all, it was good. The grains were almost impossible to grind into flour, but that done, a protein-high bread could be baked. There was some on the table now, dark and heavy. It wasn't bad, either.

Fawkes had studied the herb life on Junior and come to the conclusion that an acre of Junior's surface, properly seeded and watered, could support ten times the number of grazing animals that an acre of Earthly alfalfa could.

Sheffield had been impressed; had spoken of Junior as the granary of a hundred worlds, but Fawkes dismissed his own statements with a shrug.

He said, "Sucker bait."

About a week earlier, the party had been agitated by the sudden refusal of the hamsters and white rats to touch certain new herbs Fawkes had brought in. Mixing small quantities with regular rations had resulted in the death of those that fed on it.

Solution?

Not quite. Vernadsky came in a few hours later and said calmly, "Copper, lead, and mercury."

"What?" said Cimon.

"Those plants. They're high in heavy metals. Probably an evolutionary development to keep from being eaten."

"The first settlers——" began Cimon.

"No. That's impossible. Most of the plants are perfectly all right. Just these, and no person would eat them."

"How do you know?"

"The rats didn't."

"They're just rats."

It was what Vernadsky was waiting for. He said dramatically, "You may hail a modest martyr to science. I tasted the stuff."

"What?" yelled Novee.

"Just a lick. Don't worry. I'm the careful-type martyr. Anyway, the stuff is as bitter as strychnine. What do you expect? If a plant is going to fill itself with lead just to keep the animals off, what good does it do the plant to have the animal find out by dying after he's eaten it? A little bitter stuff in addition acts as a warning. The combination warning and punishment does the trick."

"Besides," said Novee, "it wasn't heavy metal poisoning that killed the settlers. The symptoms aren't right for it."

The rest knew the symptoms well enough. Some in lay terms and some in more technical language. Difficult and painful breathing that grew steadily worse. That's what it amounted to.

Fawkes put down his fork. "Look here, suppose this stuff contains some alkaloid that paralyzes the nerves that control the lung muscles."

"Rats have lung muscles," said Vernadsky. "It doesn't kill them."

"Maybe it's a cumulative thing."

"All right. All right. Any time your breathing gets painful, go back to ship rations and see if you improve. But no fair counting psychosomatics."

Sheffield grunted, "That's my job. Don't worry about it."

Fawkes drew a deep breath, then another. Glumly he put another piece of meat into his mouth.

At one corner of the table, Mark Annuncio, eating more slowly than the rest, thought of Norris Vinograd's monograph on "Taste and Smell." Vinograd had made a taste-smell classification based on enzyme inhibition patterns within the taste buds. Annuncio did not know what that meant exactly but he remembered the symbols, their values, and the descriptive definitions.

While he placed the taste of the stew to three subclassifications, he finished his helping. His jaws ached faintly because of the difficult chewing.

— 21 —

EVENING WAS approaching and Lagrange I was low in the sky. It had been a bright day, reasonably warm, and Boris Vernadsky felt pleased. He had made interesting measurements and his brilliantly colored sweater had showed fascinating changes from hour to hour as the suns' positions shifted.

Right now his shadow was a long red thing, with the lowest third of it gray, where the Lagrange II shadow coincided. He held out one arm and it cast two shadows. There was a smeared orange one some fifteen feet away and a denser blue one in the same direction but only five feet away. If he had time, he could work out a beautiful set of shadowgrams.

He was so pleased with the thought that he felt no resentment at seeing Mark Annuncio skirting his trail in the distance.

He put down his nucleometer and waved his hand. "Come here!"

The youngster approached diffidently. "Hello."

"Want something?"

"Just—just watching."

"Oh? Well, go ahead and watch. Do you know what I'm doing?"

Mark shook his head.

"This is a nucleometer," said Vernadsky. "You jab it into the ground like this. It's got a force-field generator at the top so it will penetrate any rock." He leaned on the nucleometer as he spoke, and it went two feet into the stony outcropping. "See?"

Mark's eyes shone, and Vernadsky felt pleased. The chemist said, "Along the sides of the uniped are microscopic atomic furnaces, each of which vaporizes about a million molecules or so in the surrounding rock and decomposes them into atoms. The atoms are then differentiated in terms of nuclear mass and charge and the results may be read off directly on the dials above. Do you follow all that?''

''I'm not sure. But it's a good thing to know.''

Vernadsky smiled and said, ''We end up with figures on the different elements in the crust. It's pretty much the same on all oxygen-water planets.''

Mark said seriously, ''The planet with the most silicon I know of is Lepta, with 32.765 per cent. Earth is only 24.862. That's by weight.''

Vernadsky's smile faded. He said dryly, ''You have the figures on all the planets, pal?''

''Oh no. I couldn't. I don't think they've all been surveyed. Bischon and Spenglow's *Handbook of Planetary Crusts* only lists figures for 21,854 planets. I know all those, of course.''

Vernadsky, with a definite feeling of deflation, said, ''Now Junior has a more even distribution of elements than is usually met up with. Oxygen is low. So far my average is a lousy 42.113. So is silicon, with 22.722. The heavy metals are ten to a hundred times as concentrated as on Earth. That's not just a local phenomenon, either, since Junior's over-all density is 5 per cent higher than Earth's.''

Vernadsky wasn't sure why he was telling the kid all this. Partly, he felt, because it was good to find someone who would listen. A man gets lonely and frustrated when there is no one of his own field to talk to.

He went on, beginning to relish the lecture. ''On the other hand, the lighter elements are also better distributed. The ocean solids aren't predominantly sodium chloride, as on Earth. Junior's oceans contain a respectable helping of magnesium salts. And take what they call the ''rare lights.'' Those are the elements lithium, beryllium, and boron. They're lighter than carbon, all of them, but they are of very rare occurrence on Earth, and in fact, on all planets. Junior, on the other hand, is quite rich in them. The three of them total almost four tenths of a per cent of the crust as compared to about four thousandths on Earth.''

Mark plucked at the other's sleeve. ''Do you have a list of figures on all the elements? May I see?''

''I suppose so.'' He took a folded piece of paper out of his hip pocket.

He grinned as Mark took the sheet and said, ''Don't publish those figures before I do.''

Mark glanced at them once and returned the paper.

''Are you through?'' asked Vernadsky in surprise.

''Oh yes,'' said Mark thoughtfully, ''I have it all.'' He turned on his heel and walked away with no word of parting.

The last glimmer of Lagrange I faded below the horizon.

Vernadsky gazed after Mark and shrugged. He plucked his nucleometer out of the ground, and followed after, walking back toward the tents.

— 22 —

SHEFFIELD WAS moderately pleased. Mark had been doing better than expected. To be sure, he scarcely talked but that was not very serious. At least, he showed interest and didn't sulk. And he threw no tantrums.

Vernadsky was even telling Sheffield that last evening Mark had spoken to him quite normally, without raised voices on either side, about planetary crust analyses. Vernadsky had laughed a bit about it, saying that Mark knew the crust analyses of twenty thousand planets and someday he'd have the boy repeat them all just to see how long it would take.

Mark, himself, had made no mention of the matter. In fact, he had spent the morning sitting in his tent. Sheffield had looked in, seen him on his cot, staring at his feet, and had left him to himself.

What he really needed at the moment, Sheffield felt, was a bright idea for himself. A really bright one.

So far, everything had come to nothing. A whole month of nothing. Rodriguez held fast against any infection. Vernadsky absolutely barred food poisoning. Novee shook his head with vehement negativeness at suggestions of disturbed metabolism. "Where's the evidence?" he kept saying.

What it amounted to was that every physical cause of death was eliminated on the strength of expert opinion. But men, women, and children had died. There must be a reason. Could it be psychological?

He had satirized the matter to Cimon for a purpose before they had come out here, but it was now time and more than time to be serious about it. Could the settlers have been driven to suicide? Why? Humanity had colonized tens of thousands of planets without its having seriously affected mental stability. In fact, the suicide rate, as well as the incidence of psychoses, was higher on Earth than anywhere else in the Galaxy.

Besides, the settlement had called frantically for medical help. They didn't want to die.

Personality disorders? Something peculiar to that one group? Enough to affect over a thousand people to the death? Unlikely. Besides, how could any evidence be uncovered? The settlement site had been ransacked for any films or records, even the most frivolous. Nothing. A century of dampness left nothing so fragile as purposeful records.

So he was working in a vacuum. He felt helpless. The others, at least, had data; something to chew on. He had nothing.

He found himself at Mark's tent again and looked inside automatically. It was empty. He looked about and spied Mark walking out of the camp and into the woods.

Sheffield cried out after him, "Mark! Wait for me!"

Mark stopped, made as though to go on, thought better of it, and let Sheffield's long legs consume the distance between them.

Sheffield said, "Where are you off to?" (Even after running, it was unnecessary to pant in Junior's rich atmosphere.)

Mark's eyes were sullen. "To the air-coaster."

"Oh?"

"I haven't had a chance to look at it."

"Why, of course you've had a chance," said Sheffield. "You were watching Fawkes like a hawk on the trip over."

Mark scowled. "Everyone was around. I want to see it for myself."

Sheffield felt disturbed. The kid was angry. He'd better tag along and try to find out what was wrong. He said, "Come to think of it, I'd like to see the coaster myself. You don't mind having me along, do you?"

Mark hesitated. Then he said, "We-ell. If you want to." It wasn't exactly a gracious invitation.

Sheffield said, "What are you carrying, Mark?"

"Tree branch. I cut it off with the buzz-field gun. I'm taking it with me just in case anyone wants to stop me." He swung it so that it whistled through the thick air.

"Why should anyone want to stop you, Mark? I'd throw it away. It's hard and heavy. You could hurt someone."

Mark was striding on. "I'm not throwing it away."

Sheffield pondered briefly, then decided against a quarrel at the moment. It would be better to get to the basic reason for this hostility first. "All right," he said.

The air-coaster lay in a clearing, its clear metal surface throwing back green high lights. (Lagrange II had not yet risen.)

Mark looked carefully about.

"There's no one in sight, Mark," said Sheffield.

They climbed aboard. It was a large coaster. It had carried seven men and the necessary supplies in only three trips.

Sheffield looked at its control panel with something quite close to awe. He said, "Imagine a botanist like Fawkes learning to run one of these things. It's so far outside his specialty."

"I can run one," said Mark suddenly.

Sheffield stared at him in surprise. "You can?"

"I watched Dr. Fawkes when we came. I know everything he did. And he has a repair manual for the coaster. I sneaked that out once and read it."

Sheffield said lightly, "Well, that's very nice. We have a spare navigator for an emergency, then."

He turned away from Mark then, so he never saw the tree limb as it came down on his head. He didn't hear Mark's troubled voice saying. "I'm sorry, Dr. Sheffield." He didn't even, properly speaking, feel the concussion that knocked him out.

— 23 —

IT WAS the jar of the coaster's landing, Sheffield later thought, that first brought consciousness back. It was a dim, aching sort of thing that had no understanding in it at first.

The sound of Mark's voice was floating up to him. That was his first sensation. Then as he tried to roll over and get a knee beneath him, he could feel his head throbbing.

For a while, Mark's voice was only a collection of sounds that meant nothing to him. Then they began to coalesce into words. Finally, when his eyes fluttered open and light entered stabbingly so that he had to close them again, he could make out sentences. He remained where he was, head hanging, one quivering knee holding him up.

Mark was saying in a breathless, high-pitched voice, " . . . a thousand people all dead. Just graves. And nobody knows why."

There was a rumble Sheffield couldn't make out. A hoarse, deep voice.

Then Mark again, "It's true. Why do you suppose all the scientists are aboard?"

Sheffield lifted achingly to his feet and rested against one wall. He put his hand to his head and it came away bloody. His hair was caked and matted with it. Groaning, he staggered toward the coaster's cabin door. He fumbled for the hook and yanked it inward.

The landing ramp had been lowered. For a moment, he stood there, swaying, afraid to trust his legs.

He had to take in everything by installments. Both suns were high in the sky and a thousand feet away the giant steel cylinder of the *Triple G.* reared its nose high above the runty trees that ringed it.

Mark was at the foot of the ramp, semi-circled by members of the crew. The crewmen were stripped to the waist and browned nearly black in the ultraviolet of Lagrange I. (Thanks only to the thick atmosphere and the heavy ozone coating in the upper reaches for keeping UV down to a livable range.)

The crewman directly before Mark was leaning on a baseball bat. Another tossed a ball in the air and caught it. Many of the rest were wearing gloves.

Funny, thought Sheffield erratically, Mark land right in the middle of a ball park.

Mark looked up and saw him. He screamed excitedly, "All right, ask him. Go ahead, ask him. Dr. Sheffield, wasn't there an expedition to this planet once and they all died mysteriously?"

Sheffield tried to say, "Mark, what are you doing?" He couldn't. When he opened his mouth, only a moan came out.

The crewman with the bat said, "Is this little gumboil telling the truth, mister?"

Sheffield held on to the railing with two perspiring hands. The crewman's face seemed to waver. The face had thick lips on it and small eyes buried under bristly eyebrows. It wavered very badly.

Then the ramp came up and whirled about his head. There was ground gripped in his hands suddenly and a cold ache on his cheekbone. He gave up the fight and let go of consciousness again.

— 24 —

HE CAME awake less painfully the second time. He was in bed now and two misty faces leaned over him. A long, thin object passed across his line of vision and a voice, just heard above the humming in his ears, said, "He'll come to now, Cimon."

Sheffield closed his eyes. Somehow he seemed to be aware of the fact that his skull was thoroughly bandaged.

He lay quietly for a minute, breathing deeply. When he opened his eyes again, the faces above him were clear. There was Novee's round face, a small, professionally serious line between his eyes that cleared away when Sheffield said, "Hello, Novee."

The other man was Cimon, jaws set and angry, yet with a look of something like satisfaction in his eyes.

Sheffield said, "Where are we?"

Cimon said coldly, "In space, Dr. Sheffield. Two days out in space."

"Two days out——" Sheffield's eyes widened.

Novee interposed. "You've had a bad concussion, nearly a fracture, Sheffield. Take it easy."

"Well, what hap—— Where's Mark? *Where's Mark?*"

"Easy. Easy now." Novee put a hand on each of Sheffield's shoulders and pressed him down.

Cimon said, "Your boy is in the brig. In case you want to know why, he deliberately caused mutiny on board ship, thus endangering the safety of five men. We were almost marooned at our temporary camp because the crew wanted to leave immediately. He persuaded them, the Captain did, to pick us up."

Sheffield remembered now, very vaguely. There was just that fuzzy memory of Mark and a man with a bat. Mark saying " . . . a thousand people all dead. . . ."

The psychologist hitched himself up on one elbow with a tremendous effort. "Listen, Cimon, I don't know why Mark did it, but let me talk to him. I'll find out."

Cimon said, "No need of that. It will all come out at the trial."

Sheffield tried to brush Novee's restraining arm to one side. "But why make it formal? Why involve the Bureau? We can settle this among ourselves."

"That's exactly what we intend to do. The Captain is empowered by the laws of space to preside over trials involving crimes and misdemeanors in deep space."

"The Captain. A trial here? On board ship? Cimon, don't let him do it. It will be murder."

"Not at all. It will be a fair and proper trial. I'm in full agreement with the Captain. Discipline demands a trial."

Novee said uneasily, "Look, Cimon, I wish you wouldn't. He's in no shape to take this."

"Too bad," said Cimon.

Sheffield said, "But you don't understand. I'm responsible for the boy."

"On the contrary, I do understand," said Cimon. "It's why we've been waiting for you to regain consciousness. You're standing trial with him."

"What!"

"You are generally responsible for his actions. Specifically, you were with him when he stole the air-coaster. The crew saw you at the coaster's cabin door while Mark was inciting mutiny."

"But he cracked my skull in order to take the coaster. Can't you see that's the act of a seriously disturbed mind? He can't be held responsible."

"We'll let the Captain decide, Sheffield. You stay with him, Novee." He turned to go.

Sheffield called on what strength he could muster. "Cimon," he shouted, "you're doing this to get back at me for the lesson in psychology I taught you. You're a narrow–petty——"

He fell back on his pillow, breathless.

Cimon, from the door, said, "And by the way, Sheffield, the penalty for inciting mutiny on board ship is death!"

— 25 —

WELL, IT was a *kind* of trial, Sheffield thought grimly. Nobody was following accurate legal procedure, but then, the psychologist felt certain, no one knew the accurate legal procedure, least of all the Captain.

They were using the large assembly room where, on ordinary cruises, the crew got together to watch subetheric broadcasts. At this time, the crew were rigidly excluded, though all the scientific personnel were present.

Captain Follenbee sat behind a desk just underneath the subetheric reception cube. Sheffield and Mark Annuncio sat by themselves at his left, faces toward him.

The Captain was not at ease. He alternated between informal exchanges with the various "witnesses" and sudden super-judicial blasts against whispering among the spectators.

Sheffield and Mark, having met one another in the "courtroom" for the first time since the flight of the air-coaster, shook hands solemnly on the former's initiative. Mark had hung back at first, looking up briefly at the crisscross of tape still present on the shaven patch on Sheffield's skull.

"I'm sorry, Dr. Sheffield. I'm very sorry."

"It's all right, Mark. How have they been treating you?"

"All right, I guess."

The Captain's voice boomed out, "No talking among the accused."

Sheffield retorted in a conversational tone, "Listen, Captain, we haven't had lawyers. We haven't had time to prepare a case."

"No lawyers necessary," said the Captain. "This isn't a court trial on Earth. Captain's investigation. Different thing. Just interested in facts, not legal fireworks. Proceedings can be reviewed back on Earth."

"And we can be dead by then," said Sheffield hotly.

"Let's get on with it," said the Captain, banging his desk with an aluminum T-wedge.

Cimon sat in the front row of the audience, smiling thinly. It was he whom Sheffield watched most uneasily.

The smile never varied as witnesses were called upon to state that they had been informed that the crew were on no account to be told of the true nature of the trip; that Sheffield and Mark had been present when told. A mycologist testified to a conversation he had had with Sheffield which indicated the latter to be well aware of the prohibition.

It was brought out that Mark had been sick for most of the trip out to Junior, that he had behaved erratically after they had landed on Junior.

"How do you explain all that?" asked the Captain.

From the audience, Cimon's calm voice suddenly sounded. "He was frightened. He was willing to do anything that would get him off the planet."

Sheffield sprang to his feet. "His remarks are out of order. He's not a witness."

The Captain banged his T-wedge and said, "Sit down!"

The trial went on. A crew member was called in to testify that Mark had informed them of the first expedition and that Sheffield had stood by while that was done.

Sheffield cried, "I want to cross-examine!"

The Captain said, "You'll get your chance later."

The crewman was shooed out.

Sheffield studied the audience. It seemed obvious that their sympathy was not entirely with the Captain. He was pyschologist enough to be able to wonder, even at this point, how many of them were secretly relieved at having left Junior and actually grateful to Mark for having precipitated the matter as he did. Then, too, the obvious kangaroo nature of the court didn't sit well with them. Vernadsky was frowning darkly while Novee stared at Cimon with obvious distaste.

It was Cimon who worried Sheffield. He, the psychologist felt, must have argued the Captain into this and it was he who might insist on the extreme penalty. Sheffield was bitterly regretful of having punctured the man's pathological vanity.

But what really puzzled Sheffield above all was Mark's attitude. He was showing no signs of space-sickness or of unease of any kind. He listened to everything closely but seemed moved by nothing. He acted as though nothing mundane concerned him at the moment; as though certain information he himself held made everything else of no account.

The Captain banged his T-wedge and said, "I guess we have it all. Facts all clear. No argument. We can finish this."

Sheffield jumped up again. "Hold on. Aren't we getting our turn?"

"Quiet," ordered the Captain.

"*You* keep quiet." Sheffield turned to the audience. "Listen, we haven't had a chance to defend ourselves. We haven't even had the right to cross-examine. Is that just?"

There was a murmur that buzzed up above the sound of the T-wedge.

Cimon said coldly, "What's there to defend?"

"Maybe nothing," shouted back Sheffield, "in which case what have you to lose by hearing us? Or are you afraid we have considerable to defend?"

Individual calls from the audience were sounding now. "Let him talk!"

Cimon shrugged. "Go ahead."

The Captain said sullenly, "What do you want to do?"

Sheffield said, "Act as my own lawyer and call Mark Annuncio as witness."

Mark stood up calmly enough. Sheffield turned his chair to face the audience and motioned him down again.

Sheffield decided there was no use in trying to imitate the courtroom dramas he had watched on the subether. Pompous questions on name and condition of past life would get nowhere. Better to be direct.

So he said, "Mark, did you know what would happen when you told the crew about the first expedition?"

"Yes, Dr. Sheffield."

"Why did you do it then?"

"Because it was important that we all get away from Junior without losing a minute. Telling the crew the truth was the fastest way of getting us off the planet.''

Sheffield could feel the bad impression that answer made on the audience, but he could only follow his instinct. That, and his psychologist's decision that only special knowledge could make Mark or any Mnemonic so calm in the face of adversity. After all, special knowledge was their business.

He said, ''Why was it important to leave Junior, Mark?''

Mark didn't flinch. He looked straight at the watching scientists. ''Because I know what killed the first expedition, and it was only a question of time before it killed us. In fact, it may be too late already. We may be dying now. We may, every one of us, be dead men.''

Sheffield let the murmur from the audience swell up and subside. Even the Captain seemed shocked into T-wedge immobility while Cimon's smile grew quite faint.

For the moment, Sheffield was less concerned with Mark's ''knowledge,'' whatever it was, than that he had acted independently on the basis of it. It had happened before. Mark had searched the ship's log on the basis of a theory of his own. Sheffield felt pure chagrin at not having probed that tendency to the uttermost then and there.

So his next question, asked in a grim enough voice, was, ''Why didn't you consult me about this, Mark?''

Mark faltered a trifle. ''You wouldn't have believed me. It's why I had to hit you to keep you from stopping me. None of them would have believed me. They all hated me.''

''What makes you think they hated you?''

''Well, you remember about Dr. Rodriguez.''

''That was quite a while ago. The others had no arguments with you.''

''I could tell the way Dr. Cimon looked at me. And Dr. Fawkes wanted to shoot me with a blaster.''

''What?'' Sheffield whirled, forgetting in his own turn any formality due the trial. ''Say, Fawkes, did you try to shoot him?''

Fawkes stood up, face crimson, as all turned to look at him. He said, ''I was out in the woods and he came sneaking up on me. I thought it was an animal and took precautions. When I saw it was he, I put the blaster away.''

Sheffield turned back to Mark. ''Is that right?''

Mark turned sullen again. ''Well—I asked Dr. Vernadsky to see some data he had collected and he told me not to publish it before he did. He tried to make out that I was dishonest.''

''For the love of Earth, I was only joking,'' came a yell from the audience.

Sheffield said hurriedly, ''Very well, Mark, you didn't trust us and you felt you had to take action on your own. Now, Mark, let's get to the point. What did you think killed the first settlers?''

Mark said, ''It might have killed the explorer, Makoyama, too, for all I know except that he died in a crash two months and three days after reporting on Junior, so we'll never know.''

''All right, but what is it you're talking about?''

A hush fell over everyone.

Mark looked about and said, ''The dust.''

There was general laughter, and Mark's cheeks flamed.

Sheffield said, ''What do you mean?''

"The dust! The dust in the air. It has beryllium in it. Ask Dr. Vernadsky."

Vernadsky stood up and pushed his way forward. "What's this?"

"Sure," said Mark. "It was in the data you showed me. Beryllium was very high in the crust, so it must be in the dust in the air as well."

Sheffield said, "What if beryllium is there? Let me ask the questions, Vernadsky. Please."

"Beryllium poisoning, that's what. If you breathe beryllium dust, non-healing granulomata, whatever they are, form in the lungs. Anyway, it gets hard to breathe and eventually you die."

A new voice, quite agitated, joined the melee. "What are you talking about? You're no physician." It was Novee.

"I know that," said Mark earnestly, "but I once read a very old book about poisons. It was so old it was printed on actual sheets of paper. The library had some and I went through them because it was such a novelty, you know."

"All right," said Novee. "What did you read? Can you tell me?"

Mark's chin lifted. "I can quote it. Word for word. 'A surprising variety of enzymatic reactions in the body are activated by any of a number of divalent metallic ions of similar ionic radius. Among these are magnesium, manganous, zinc, ferrous, cobaltous, and nickelous ions, as well as others. Against all of these, the beryllium ion, which has a similar charge and size, acts as an inhibitor. Beryllium therefore serves to derange a number of enzyme-catalyzed reactions. Since the lungs have, apparently, no way of excreting beryllium, diverse metabolic derangements causing serious illness and death can result from inhaling dust containing certain beryllium salts. Cases exist in which one known exposure has resulted in death. The onset of symptoms is insidious, being delayed sometimes for as long as three years after exposure. Prognosis is not good.' "

The Captain leaned forward in agitation. "What's all this, Novee? Is what he's saying making sense?"

Novee said, "I don't know if he's right or not, but there's nothing absurd in what he's saying."

Sheffield said sharply, "You mean you don't know if beryllium is poisonous or not."

"No, I don't," said Novee. "I've never read anything about it. No case has ever come up."

"Isn't beryllium used for anything?" Sheffield turned to Vernadsky. "Is it?"

Vernadsky said in vast surprise, "No, it isn't. Damn it, I can't think of a single use. I tell you what, though. In the early days of atomic power, it was used in the primitive uranium piles as a neutron decelerator, along with other things like paraffin and graphite. I'm almost sure of that."

"It isn't used now, though?" asked Sheffield.

"No."

An electronics man said quite suddenly, "I think beryllium-zinc coatings were used in the first fluorescent lights. I seem to recall a mention of that."

"No more, though?" asked Sheffield.

"No."

Sheffield said, "Well then, listen, all of you. In the first place, anything Mark quotes is accurate. That's what the book said. It's my opinion that beryllium is poisonous. In ordinary life, it doesn't matter because the beryllium content of the soil is so low. When man concentrates beryllium to use in nuclear piles or in fluorescent lights or even in alloys, he comes across the toxicity and looks for substitutes.

"He finds substitutes, forgets about beryllium, and eventually forgets about its toxicity. And then we come across an unusual beryllium-rich planet like Junior and we can't figure out what hits us."

Cimon didn't seem to be listening. He said in a low voice, "What does that mean, 'Prognosis is not good.' "

Novee said abstractedly, "It means that if you've got beryllium poisoning, you won't recover."

Cimon fell back in his chair, chewing his lip.

Novee said to Mark, "I suppose the symptoms of beryllium poisoning——"

Mark said at once, "I can give you the full list. I don't understand the words but——"

"Was one of them 'dyspnea'?"

"Yes."

Novee sighed and said, "I say that we get back to Earth as quickly as possible and get under medical investigation."

Cimon said weakly, "But if we won't recover, what use is it?"

Novee said, "Medical science has advanced since the days of books printed on paper. Besides, we may not have received the toxic dose. The first settlers survived for over a year of continuous exposure. We've had only a month, thanks to Mark Annuncio's quick and drastic action."

Fawkes, miserably unhappy, yelled, "For space's sake, Captain, get out of here and get this ship back to Earth."

It amounted to the end of the trial. Sheffield and Mark walked out among the first.

Cimon was the last to stir out of his chair, and when he did, it was with the listless gait of a man already dead in all but fact.

— 26 —

THE LAGRANGE System was only a star lost in the receding cluster.

Sheffield looked at that large patch of light and said, "So beautiful a planet." He sighed. "Well, let's hope we live. In any case, the government will watch out for beryllium-high planets in the future. There'll be no catching mankind with that particular variety of sucker bait any more."

Mark did not respond to that idealism. The trial was over; the excitement was gone. There were tears in his eyes. He could only think that he might die; and that if he did, there were so many things, so many, many things in the Universe that he would never learn.

THE UGLY LITTLE BOY

EDITH FELLOWES smoothed her working smock as she always did before opening the elaborately locked door and stepping across the invisible dividing line between the *is* and the *is not*. She carried her notebook and her pen although she no longer took notes except when she felt the absolute need for some report.

This time she also carried a suitcase. ("Games for the boy," she had said, smiling, to the guard—who had long since stopped even thinking of questioning her and who waved her on.)

And, as always, the ugly little boy knew that she had entered and came running to her, crying, "Miss Fellowes——Miss Fellowes——" in his soft, slurring way.

"Timmie," she said, and passed her hand over the shaggy, brown hair on his misshapen little head. "What's wrong?"

He said, "Will Jerry be back to play again? I'm sorry about what happened."

"Never mind that now, Timmie. Is that why you've been crying?"

He looked away. "Not just about that, Miss Fellowes. I dreamed again."

"The same dream?" Miss Fellowes' lips set. Of course, the Jerry affair would bring back the dream.

He nodded. His too large teeth showed as he tried to smile and the lips of his forward-thrusting mouth stretched wide. "When will I be big enough to go out there, Miss Fellowes?"

"Soon," she said softly, feeling her heart break. "Soon."

Miss Fellowes let him take her hand and enjoyed the warm touch of the thick dry skin of his palm. He led her through the three rooms that made up the whole of Stasis Section One—comfortable enough, yes, but an eternal prison for the ugly little boy all the seven (was it seven?) years of his life.

He led her to the one window, looking out onto a scrubby woodland section of the world of *is* (now hidden by night), where a fence and painted instructions allowed no men to wander without permission.

He pressed his nose against the window. "Out there, Miss Fellowes?"

"Better places. Nicer places," she said sadly as she looked at his poor little imprisoned face outlined in profile against the window. The forehead retreated flatly and his hair lay down in tufts upon it. The back of his skull bulged and seemed to make the head overheavy so that it sagged and bent forward, forcing the whole body into a stoop. Already, bony ridges were beginning to bulge the skin above his eyes. His wide mouth thrust forward more prominently than did his wide and flattened nose and he had no chin to speak of, only a jawbone that curved smoothly down and back. He was small for his years and his stumpy legs were bowed.

He was a very ugly little boy and Edith Fellowes loved him dearly.

Her own face was behind his line of vision, so she allowed her lips the luxury of a tremor.

They would *not* kill him. She would do anything to prevent it. Anything. She opened the suitcase and began taking out the clothes it contained.

Edith Fellowes had crossed the threshold of Stasis, Inc. for the first time just a little over three years before. She hadn't, at that time, the slightest idea as to what Stasis meant or what the place did. No one did then, except those who worked there. In fact, it was only the day after she arrived that the news broke upon the world.

At the time, it was just that they had advertised for a woman with knowledge of physiology, experience with clinical chemistry, and a love for children. Edith Fellowes had been a nurse in a maternity ward and believed she fulfilled those qualifications.

Gerald Hoskins, whose name plate on the desk included a Ph.D. after the name, scratched his cheek with his thumb and looked at her steadily.

Miss Fellowes automatically stiffened and felt her face (with its slightly asymmetric nose and its a-trifle-too-heavy eyebrows) twitch.

He's no dreamboat himself, she thought resentfully. He's getting fat and bald and he's got a sullen mouth. But the salary mentioned had been considerably higher than she had expected, so she waited.

Hoskins said, "Now do you really love children?"

"I wouldn't say I did if I didn't."

"Or do you just love pretty children? Nice chubby children with cute little button-noses and gurgly ways?"

Miss Fellowes said, "Children are children, Dr. Hoskins, and the ones that aren't pretty are just the ones who may happen to need help the most."

"Then suppose we take you on——"

"You mean you're offering me the job now?"

He smiled briefly, and for a moment, his broad face had an absentminded charm about it. He said, "I make quick decisions. So far the offer is tentative, however. I may make as quick a decision to let you go. Are you ready to take the chance?"

Miss Fellowes clutched at her purse and calculated just as swiftly as she could, then ignored calculations and followed impulse. "All right."

"Fine. We're going to form the Stasis tonight and I think you had better be there to take over at once. That will be at 8 P.M. and I'd appreciate it if you could be here at 7:30."

"But what——"

"Fine. Fine. That will be all now." On signal, a smiling secretary came in to usher her out.

Miss Fellowes stared back at Dr. Hoskins' closed door for a moment. What was Stasis? What had this large barn of a building—with its badged employees, its makeshift corridors, and its unmistakable air of engineering—to do with children?

She wondered if she should go back that evening or stay away and teach that arrogant man a lesson. But she knew she would be back if only out of sheer frustration. She would have to find out about the children.

She came back at 7:30 and did not have to announce herself. One after another, men and women seemed to know her and to know her function. She found herself all but placed on skids as she was moved inward.

Dr. Hoskins was there, but he only looked at her distantly and murmured, "Miss Fellowes."

He did not even suggest that she take a seat, but she drew one calmly up to the railing and sat down.

They were on a balcony, looking down into a large pit, filled with instruments that looked like a cross between the control panel of a spaceship and the working face of a computer. On one side were partitions that seemed to make up an unceilinged apartment, a giant dollhouse into the rooms of which she could look from above.

She could see an electronic cooker and a freeze-space unit in one room and a washroom arrangement off another. And surely the object she made out in another room could only be part of a bed, a small bed.

Hoskins was speaking to another man and, with Miss Fellowes, they made up the total occupancy of the balcony. Hoskins did not offer to introduce the other man, and Miss Fellowes eyed him surreptitiously. He was thin and quite fine-looking in a middle-aged way. He had a small mustache and keen eyes that seemed to busy themselves with everything.

He was saying, "I won't pretend for one moment that I understand all this, Dr. Hoskins; I mean, except as a layman, a reasonably intelligent layman, may be expected to understand it. Still, if there's one part I understand less than another, it's this matter of selectivity. You can only reach out so far; that seems sensible; things get dimmer the further you go; it takes more energy. But then, you can only reach out so near. That's the puzzling part."

"I can make it seem less paradoxical, Deveney, if you will allow me to use an analogy."

(Miss Fellowes placed the new man the moment she heard his name, and despite herself was impressed. This was obviously Candide Deveney, the science writer of the Telenews, who was notoriously at the scene of every major scientific break-through. She even recognized his face as one she saw on the news-plate when the landing on Mars had been announced. ——So Dr. Hoskins must have something important here.)

"By all means use an analogy," said Deveney ruefully, "if you think it will help."

"Well, then, you can't read a book with ordinary-sized print if it is held six feet from your eyes, but you can read it if you hold it one foot from your eyes. So far, the closer the better. If you bring the book to within one inch of your eyes, however, you've lost it again. There is such a thing as being too close, you see."

"Hmm," said Deveney.

"Or take another example. Your right shoulder is about thirty inches from the tip of your right forefinger and you can place your right forefinger on your right shoulder. Your right elbow is only half the distance from the tip of your right forefinger; it should by all ordinary logic be easier to reach, and yet you cannot place your right finger on your right elbow. Again, there is such a thing as being too close.''

Deveney said, ''May I use these analogies in my story?''

''Well, of course. Only too glad. I've been waiting long enough for someone like you to have a story. I'll give you anything else you want. It is time, finally, that we want the world looking over our shoulder. They'll see something.''

(Miss Fellowes found herself admiring his calm certainty despite herself. There was strength there.)

Deveney said, ''How far out will you reach?''

''Forty thousand years.''

Miss Fellowes drew in her breath sharply.

Years?

There was tension in the air. The men at the controls scarcely moved. One man at a microphone spoke into it in a soft monotone, in short phrases that made no sense to Miss Fellowes.

Deveney, leaning over the balcony railing with an intent stare, said, ''Will we see anything, Dr. Hoskins?''

''What? No. Nothing till the job is done. We detect indirectly, something on the principle of radar, except that we use mesons rather than radiation. Mesons reach backward under the proper conditions. Some are reflected and we must analyze the reflections.''

''That sounds difficult.''

Hoskins smiled again, briefly as always. ''It is the end product of fifty years of research; forty years of it before I entered the field. ——Yes, it's difficult.''

The man at the microphone raised one hand.

Hoskins said, ''We've had the fix on one particular moment in time for weeks; breaking it, remaking it after calculating our own movements in time; making certain that we could handle time-flow with sufficient precision. This must work now.''

But his forehead glistened.

Edith Fellowes found herself out of her seat and at the balcony railing, but there was nothing to see.

The man at the microphone said quietly, ''Now.''

There was a space of silence sufficient for one breath and then the sound of a terrified little boy's scream from the dollhouse rooms. Terror! Piercing terror!

Miss Fellowes' head twisted in the direction of the cry. A child was involved. She had forgotten.

And Hoskins' fist pounded on the railing and he said in a tight voice, trembling with triumph, *''Did* it.''

Miss Fellowes was urged down the short, spiral flight of steps by the hard press of Hoskins' palm between her shoulder blades. He did not speak to her.

The men who had been at the controls were standing about now, smiling, smoking, watching the three as they entered on the main floor. A very soft buzz sounded from the direction of the dollhouse.

Hoskins said to Deveney, "It's perfectly safe to enter Stasis. I've done it a thousand times. There's a queer sensation which is momentary and means nothing."

He stepped through an open door in mute demonstration, and Deveney, smiling stiffly and drawing an obviously deep breath, followed him.

Hoskins said, "Miss Fellowes! Please!" He crooked his forefinger impatiently.

Miss Fellowes nodded and stepped stiffly through. It was as though a ripple went through her, an internal tickle.

But once inside all seemed normal. There was the smell of the fresh wood of the dollhouse and—of—of soil somehow.

There was silence now, no voice at least, but there was the dry shuffling of feet, a scrabbling as of a hand over wood—then a low moan.

"Where is it?" asked Miss Fellowes in distress. Didn't these fool men *care?*

The boy was in the bedroom; at least the room with the bed in it.

It was standing naked, with its small, dirt-smeared chest heaving raggedly. A bushel of dirt and coarse grass spread over the floor at his bare brown feet. The smell of soil came from it and a touch of something fetid.

Hoskins followed her horrified glance and said with annoyance, "You can't pluck a boy cleanly out of time, Miss Fellowes. We had to take some of the surroundings with it for safety. Or would you have preferred to have it arrive here minus a leg or with only half a head?"

"*Please!*" said Miss Fellowes, in an agony of revulsion. "Are we just to stand here? The poor child is frightened. And it's *filthy.*"

She was quite correct. It was smeared with encrusted dirt and grease and had a scratch on its thigh that looked red and sore.

As Hoskins approached him, the boy, who seemed to be something over three years in age, hunched low and backed away rapidly. He lifted his upper lip and snarled in a hissing fashion like a cat. With a rapid gesture, Hoskins seized both the child's arms and lifted him, writhing and screaming, from the floor.

Miss Fellowes said, "Hold him, now. He needs a warm bath first. He needs to be cleaned. Have you the equipment? If so, have it brought here, and I'll need to have help in handling him just at first. Then, too, for heaven's sake, have all this trash and filth removed."

She was giving the orders now and she felt perfectly good about that. And because now she was an efficient nurse, rather than a confused spectator, she looked at the child with a clinical eye—and hesitated for one shocked moment. She saw past the dirt and shrieking, past the thrashing of limbs and useless twisting. She saw the boy himself.

It was the ugliest little boy she had ever seen. It was horribly ugly from misshapen head to bandy legs.

She got the boy cleaned with three men helping her and with others milling about in their efforts to clean the room. She worked in silence and with a sense of outrage, annoyed by the continued strugglings and outcries of the boy and by the undignified drenchings of soapy water to which she was subjected.

Dr. Hoskins had hinted that the child would not be pretty, but that was far from stating that it would be repulsively deformed. And there was a stench about the boy that soap and water was only alleviating little by little.

She had the strong desire to thrust the boy, soaped as he was, into Hoskins' arms and walk out; but there was the pride of profession. She had accepted an assignment after all. And there would be the look in his eyes. A cold look that would read: Only pretty children, Miss Fellowes?

He was standing apart from them, watching coolly from a distance with a half-smile on his face when he caught her eyes, as though amused at her outrage.

She decided she would wait a while before quitting. To do so now would only demean her.

Then, when the boy was a bearable pink and smelled of scented soap, she felt better anyway. His cries changed to whimpers of exhaustion as he watched carefully, eyes moving in quick frightened suspicion from one to another of those in the room. His cleanness accentuated his thin nakedness as he shivered with cold after his bath.

Miss Fellowes said sharply, "Bring me a nightgown for the child!"

A nightgown appeared at once. It was as though everything were ready and yet nothing were ready unless she gave orders; as though they were deliberately leaving this in her charge without help, to test her.

The newsman, Deveney, approached and said, "I'll hold him, Miss. You won't get it on yourself."

"Thank you," said Miss Fellowes. And it was a battle indeed, but the nightgown went on, and when the boy made as though to rip it off, she slapped his hand sharply.

The boy reddened, but did not cry. He stared at her and the splayed fingers of one hand moved slowly across the flannel of the nightgown, feeling the strangeness of it.

Miss Fellowes thought desperately: Well, what next?

Everyone seemed in suspended animation, waiting for her—even the ugly little boy.

Miss Fellowes said sharply, "Have you provided food? Milk?"

They had. A mobile unit was wheeled in, with its refrigeration compartment containing three quarts of milk, with a warming unit and a supply of fortifications in the form of vitamin drops, copper-cobalt-iron syrup and others she had no time to be concerned with. There was a variety of canned self-warming junior foods.

She used milk, simply milk, to begin with. The radar unit heated the milk to a set temperature in a matter of ten seconds and clicked off, and she put some in a saucer. She had a certainty about the boy's savagery. He wouldn't know how to handle a cup.

Miss Fellowes nodded and said to the boy, "Drink. Drink." She made a gesture as though to raise the milk to her mouth. The boy's eyes followed but he made no move.

Suddenly, the nurse resorted to direct measures. She seized the boy's upper arm in one hand and dipped the other in the milk. She dashed the milk across his lips, so that it dripped down cheeks and receding chin.

For a moment, the child uttered a high-pitched cry, then his tongue moved over his wetted lips. Miss Fellowes stepped back.

The boy approached the saucer, bent toward it, then looked up and behind sharply as though expecting a crouching enemy; bent again and licked at the milk eagerly, like a cat. He made a slurping noise. He did not use his hands to lift the saucer.

Miss Fellowes allowed a bit of the revulsion she felt show on her face. She couldn't help it.

Deveney caught that, perhaps. He said, "Does the nurse know, Dr. Hoskins?"

"Know what?" demanded Miss Fellowes.

Deveney hesitated, but Hoskins (again that look of detached amusement on his face) said, "Well, tell her."

Deveney addressed Miss Fellowes. "You may not suspect it, Miss, but you happen to be the first civilized woman in history ever to be taking care of a Neanderthal youngster."

She turned on Hoskins with a kind of controlled ferocity. "You might have told me, Doctor."

"Why? What difference does it make?"

"You said a child."

"Isn't that a child? Have you ever had a puppy or kitten, Miss Fellowes? Are those closer to the human? If that were a baby chimpanzee, would you be repelled? You're a nurse, Miss Fellowes. Your record places you in a maternity ward for three years. Have you ever refused to take care of a deformed infant?"

Miss Fellowes felt her case slipping away. She said, with much less decision, "You might have told me."

"And you would have refused the position? Well, do you refuse it now?" He gazed at her coolly, while Deveney watched from the other side of the room, and the Neanderthal child, having finished the milk and licked the plate, looked up at her with a wet face and wide, longing eyes.

The boy pointed to the milk and suddenly burst out in a short series of sounds repeated over and over, sounds made up of gutturals and elaborate tongue-clickings.

Miss Fellowes said, in surprise, "Why, he talks."

"Of course," said Hoskins. "Homo neanderthalensis is not a truly separate species, but rather a subspecies of Homo sapiens. Why shouldn't he talk? He's probably asking for more milk."

Automatically, Miss Fellowes reached for the bottle of milk, but Hoskins seized her wrist. "Now, Miss Fellowes, before we go any further, are you staying on the job?"

Miss Fellowes shook free in annoyance. "Won't you feed him if I don't? I'll stay with him—for a while."

She poured the milk.

Hoskins said, "We are going to leave you with the boy, Miss Fellowes. This is the only door to Stasis Number One and it is elaborately locked and guarded. I'll want you to learn the details of the lock which will, of course, be keyed to your fingerprints as they are already keyed to mine. The spaces overhead" (he looked upward to the open ceilings of the dollhouse) "are also guarded and we will be warned if anything untoward takes place in here."

Miss Fellowes said indignantly, "You mean I'll be under view." She thought suddenly of her own survey of the room interiors from the balcony.

"No, no," said Hoskins seriously, "your privacy will be respected completely. The view will consist of electronic symbolism only, which only a computer will deal with. Now you will stay with him tonight, Miss Fellowes, and every night until further notice. You will be relieved during the day according to some schedule you will find convenient. We will allow you to arrange that."

Miss Fellowes looked about the dollhouse with a puzzled expression. "But why all this, Dr. Hoskins? Is the boy dangerous?"

"It's a matter of energy, Miss Fellowes. He must never be allowed to leave these rooms. Never. Not for an instant. Not for any reason. Not to save his life. Not even to save *your* life, Miss Fellowes. Is that clear?"

Miss Fellowes raised her chin. "I understand the orders, Dr. Hoskins, and the nursing profession is accustomed to placing its duties ahead of self-preservation."

"Good. You can always signal if you need anyone." And the two men left.

Miss Fellowes turned to the boy. He was watching her and there was still milk in the saucer. Laboriously, she tried to show him how to lift the saucer and place it to his lips. He resisted, but let her touch him without crying out.

Always, his frightened eyes were on her, watching, watching for the one false move. She found herself soothing him, trying to move her hand very slowly toward his hair, letting him see it every inch of the way, see there was no harm in it.

And she succeeded in stroking his hair for an instant.

She said, "I'm going to have to show you how to use the bathroom. Do you think you can learn?"

She spoke quietly, kindly, knowing he would not understand the words but hoping he would respond to the calmness of the tone.

The boy launched into a clicking phrase again.

She said, "May I take your hand?"

She held out hers and the boy looked at it. She left it outstretched and waited. The boy's own hand crept forward toward hers.

"That's right," she said.

It approached within an inch of hers and then the boy's courage failed him. He snatched it back.

"Well," said Miss Fellowes calmly, "we'll try again later. Would you like to sit down here?" She patted the mattress of the bed.

The hours passed slowly and the progress was minute. She did not succeed either with bathroom or with the bed. In fact, after the child had given unmistakable signs of sleepiness he lay down on the bare ground and then, with a quick movement, rolled beneath the bed.

She bent to look at him and his eyes gleamed out at her as he tongue-clicked at her.

"All right," she said, "if you feel safer there, you sleep there."

She closed the door to the bedroom and retired to the cot that had been placed for her use in the largest room. At her insistence, a make-shift canopy had been stretched over it. She thought: Those stupid men will have to place a mirror in this room and a larger chest of drawers and a separate washroom if they expect me to spend nights here.

It was difficult to sleep. She found herself straining to hear possible sounds in the next room. He couldn't get out, could he? The walls were sheer and impossibly high but suppose the child could climb like a monkey? Well, Hoskins said there were observational devices watching through the ceiling.

Suddenly she thought: Can he be dangerous? Physically dangerous?

Surely, Hoskins couldn't have meant that. Surely, he would not have left her here alone, if——

She tried to laugh at herself. He was only a three- or four-year-old child. Still, she had not succeeded in cutting his nails. If he should attack her with nails and teeth while she slept——

Her breath came quickly. Oh, ridiculous, and yet——

She listened with painful attentiveness, and this time she heard the sound. The boy was crying.

Not shrieking in fear or anger; not yelling or screaming. It was crying softly, and the cry was the heartbroken sobbing of a lonely, lonely child.

For the first time, Miss Fellowes thought with a pang: Poor thing!

Of course, it was a child; what did the shape of its head matter? It was a child that had been orphaned as no child had ever been orphaned before. Not only its mother and father were gone, but all its species. Snatched callously out of time, it was now the only creature of its kind in the world. The last. The only.

She felt pity for it strengthen, and with it shame at her own callousness. Tucking her own nightgown carefully about her calves (incongruously, she thought: Tomorrow I'll have to bring in a bathrobe) she got out of bed and went into the boy's room.

"Little boy," she called in a whisper. "Little boy."

She was about to reach under the bed, but she thought of a possible bite and did not. Instead, she turned on the night light and moved the bed.

The poor thing was huddled in the corner, knees up against his chin, looking up at her with blurred and apprehensive eyes.

In the dim light, she was not aware of his repulsiveness.

"Poor boy," she said, "poor boy." She felt him stiffen as she stroked his hair, then relax. "Poor boy. May I hold you?"

She sat down on the floor next to him and slowly and rhythmically stroked his hair, his cheek, his arm. Softly, she began to sing a slow and gentle song.

He lifted his head at that, staring at her mouth in the dimness, as though wondering at the sound.

She maneuvered him closer while he listened to her. Slowly, she pressed gently against the side of his head, until it rested on her shoulder. She put her arm under his thighs and with a smooth and unhurried motion lifted him into her lap.

She continued singing, the same simple verse over and over, while she rocked back and forth, back and forth.

He stopped crying, and after a while the smooth burr of his breathing showed he was asleep.

With infinite care, she pushed his bed back against the wall and laid him down. She covered him and stared down. His face looked so peaceful and little-boy as he slept. It didn't matter so much that it was so ugly. Really.

She began to tiptoe out, then thought: If he wakes up?

She came back, battled irresolutely with herself, then sighed and slowly got into bed with the child.

It was too small for her. She was cramped and uneasy at the lack of canopy, but the child's hand crept into hers and, somehow, she fell asleep in that position.

She awoke with a start and a wild impulse to scream. The latter she just managed to suppress into a gurgle. The boy was looking at her, wide-eyed. It took her a long moment to remember getting into bed with him, and now, slowly, without unfixing her eyes from his, she stretched one leg carefully and let it touch the floor, then the other one.

She cast a quick and apprehensive glance toward the open ceiling, then tensed her muscles for quick disengagement.

But at that moment, the boy's stubby fingers reached out and touched her lips. He said something.

She shrank at the touch. He was terribly ugly in the light of day.

The boy spoke again. He opened his own mouth and gestured with his hand as though something were coming out.

Miss Fellowes guessed at the meaning and said tremulously, "Do you want me to sing?"

The boy said nothing but stared at her mouth.

In a voice slightly off key with tension, Miss Fellowes began the little song she had sung the night before and the ugly little boy smiled. He swayed clumsily in rough time to the music and made a little gurgly sound that might have been the beginnings of a laugh.

Miss Fellowes sighed inwardly. Music hath charms to soothe the savage beast. It might help——

She said, "You wait. Let me get myself fixed up. It will just take a minute. Then I'll make breakfast for you."

She worked rapidly, conscious of the lack of ceiling at all times. The boy remained in bed, watching her when she was in view. She smiled at him at those times and waved. At the end, he waved back, and she found herself being charmed by that.

Finally, she said, "Would you like oatmeal with milk?" It took a moment to prepare, and then she beckoned to him.

Whether he understood the gesture or followed the aroma, Miss Fellowes did not know, but he got out of bed.

She tried to show him how to use a spoon but he shrank away from it in fright. (Time enough, she thought.) She compromised on insisting that he lift the bowl in his hands. He did it clumsily enough and it was incredibly messy but most of it did get into him.

She tried the drinking milk in a glass this time, and the little boy whined when he found the opening too small for him to get his face into conveniently. She held his hand, forcing it around the glass, making him tip it, forcing his mouth to the rim.

Again a mess but again most went into him, and she was used to messes.

The washroom, to her surprise and relief, was a less frustrating matter. He understood what it was she expected him to do.

She found herself patting his head, saying, "Good boy. Smart boy."

And to Miss Fellowes' exceeding pleasure, the boy smiled at that.

She thought: When he smiles, he's quite bearable. Really.

Later in the day, the gentlemen of the press arrived.

She held the boy in her arms and he clung to her wildly while across the open door they set cameras to work. The commotion frightened the boy and he began to cry, but it was ten minutes before Miss Fellowes was allowed to retreat and put the boy in the next room.

She emerged again, flushed with indignation, walked out of the apartment (for the first time in eighteen hours) and closed the door behind her. "I think you've had enough. It will take me a while to quiet him. Go away."

"Sure, sure," said the gentleman from the *Times-Herald*. "But is that really a Neanderthal or is this some kind of gag?"

"I assure you," said Hoskins' voice, suddenly, from the background, "that this is no gag. The child is authentic Homo neanderthalensis."

"Is it a boy or a girl?"

"Boy," said Miss Fellowes briefly.

"Ape-boy," said the gentleman from the *News*. "That's what we've got here. Ape-boy. How does he act, Nurse?"

"He acts exactly like a little boy," snapped Miss Fellowes, annoyed into the defensive, "and he is not an ape-boy. His name is—is Timothy, Timmie—and he is perfectly normal in his behavior."

She had chosen the name Timothy at a venture. It was the first that had occurred to her.

"Timmie the Ape-boy," said the gentleman from the *News* and, as it turned out, Timmie the Ape-boy was the name under which the child became known to the world.

The gentleman from the *Globe* turned to Hoskins and said, "Doc, what do you expect to do with the ape-boy?"

Hoskins shrugged. "My original plan was completed when I proved it possible to bring him here. However, the anthropologists will be very interested, I imagine, and the physiologists. We have here, after all, a creature which is at the edge of being human. We should learn a great deal about ourselves and our ancestry from him."

"How long will you keep him?"

"Until such time as we need the space more than we need him. Quite a while, perhaps."

The gentleman from the *News* said, "Can you bring it out into the open so we can set up sub-etheric equipment and put on a real show?"

"I'm sorry, but the child cannot be removed from Stasis."

"Exactly what is Stasis?"

"Ah." Hoskins permitted himself one of his short smiles. "That would take a great deal of explanation, gentlemen. In Stasis, time as we know it doesn't exist. Those rooms are inside an invisible bubble that is not exactly part of our Universe. That is why the child could be plucked out of time as it was."

"Well, wait now," said the gentleman from the *News* discontentedly, "what are you giving us? The nurse goes into the room and out of it."

"And so can any of you," said Hoskins matter-of-factly. "You would be moving parallel to the lines of temporal force and no great energy gain or loss would be involved. The child, however, was taken from the far past. It moved across the lines and gained temporal potential. To move it into the Universe and into our own time would absorb enough energy to burn out every line in the place and probably blank out all power in the city of Washington. We had to store trash brought with him on the premises and will have to remove it little by little.''

The newsmen were writing down sentences busily as Hoskins spoke to them. They did not understand and they were sure their readers would not, but it sounded scientific and that was what counted.

The gentleman from the *Times-Herald* said, ''Would you be available for an all-circuit interview tonight?''

''I think so,'' said Hoskins, at once, and they all moved off.

Miss Fellowes looked after them. She understood all this about Stasis and temporal force as little as the newsmen but she managed to get this much. Timmie's imprisonment (she found herself suddenly thinking of the little boy as Timmie) was a real one and not one imposed by the arbitrary fiat of Hoskins. Apparently, it was impossible to let him out of Stasis at all, ever.

Poor child. Poor child.

She was suddenly aware of his crying and she hastened in to console him.

Miss Fellowes did not have a chance to see Hoskins on the all-circuit hookup, and though his interview was beamed to every part of the world and even to the outpost on the Moon, it did not penetrate the apartment in which Miss Fellowes and the ugly little boy lived.

But he was down the next morning, radiant and joyful.

Miss Fellowes said, ''Did the interview go well?''

''Extremely. And how is—Timmie?''

Miss Fellowes found herself pleased at the use of the name. ''Doing quite well. Now come out here, Timmie, the nice gentleman will not hurt you.''

But Timmie stayed in the other room, with a lock of his matted hair showing behind the barrier of the door and, occasionally, the corner of an eye.

''Actually,'' said Miss Fellowes, ''he is settling down amazingly. He is quite intelligent.''

''Are you surprised?''

She hesitated just a moment, then said, ''Yes, I am. I suppose I thought he was an ape-boy.''

''Well, ape-boy or not, he's done a great deal for us. He's put Stasis, Inc. on the map. We're in, Miss Fellowes, we're in.'' It was as though he had to express his triumph to someone, even if only to Miss Fellowes.

''Oh?'' She let him talk.

He put his hands in his pockets and said, ''We've been working on a shoestring for ten years, scrounging funds a penny at a time wherever we could. We had to shoot the works on one big show. It was everything, or nothing. And when I say the works, I mean it. This attempt to bring in a Neanderthal took every cent we could borrow or steal, and some of it *was* stolen—funds for other projects, used for this one without permission. If that experiment hadn't succeeded, I'd have been through.''

Miss Fellows said abruptly, ''Is that why there are no ceilings?''

''Eh?'' Hoskins looked up.

"Was there no money for ceilings?"

"Oh. Well, that wasn't the only reason. We didn't really know in advance how old the Neanderthal might be exactly. We can detect only dimly in time, and he might have been large and savage. It was possible we might have had to deal with him from a distance, like a caged animal."

"But since that hasn't turned out to be so, I suppose you can build a ceiling now."

"Now, yes. We have plenty of money, now. Funds have been promised from every source. This is all wonderful, Miss Fellowes." His broad face gleamed with a smile that lasted and when he left, even his back seemed to be smiling.

Miss Fellowes thought: He's quite a nice man when he's off guard and forgets about being scientific.

She wondered for an idle moment if he was married, then dismissed the thought in self-embarrassment.

"Timmie," she called. "Come here, Timmie."

In the months that passed, Miss Fellowes felt herself grow to be an integral part of Stasis, Inc. She was given a small office of her own with her name on the door, an office quite close to the dollhouse (as she never stopped calling Timmie's Stasis bubble). She was given a substantial raise. The dollhouse was covered by a ceiling; its furnishings were elaborated and improved; a second washroom was added—and even so, she gained an apartment of her own on the institute grounds and, on occasion, did not stay with Timmie during the night. An intercom was set up between the dollhouse and her apartment and Timmie learned how to use it.

Miss Fellowes got used to Timmie. She even grew less conscious of his ugliness. One day she found herself staring at an ordinary boy in the street and finding something bulgy and unattractive in his high domed forehead and jutting chin. She had to shake herself to break the spell.

It was more pleasant to grow used to Hoskins' occasional visits. It was obvious he welcomed escape from his increasingly harried role as head of Stasis, Inc., and that he took a sentimental interest in the child who had started it all, but it seemed to Miss Fellowes that he also enjoyed talking to her.

(She had learned some facts about Hoskins, too. He had invented the method of analyzing the reflection of the past-penetrating mesonic beam; he had invented the method of establishing Stasis; his coldness was only an effort to hide a kindly nature; and, oh yes, he *was* married.)

What Miss Fellowes could *not* get used to was the fact that she was engaged in a scientific experiment. Despite all she could do, she found herself getting personally involved to the point of quarreling with the physiologists.

On one occasion, Hoskins came down and found her in the midst of a hot urge to kill. They had no right; they had no *right*——Even if he *was* a Neanderthal, he still wasn't an animal.

She was staring after them in a blind fury; staring out the open door and listening to Timmie's sobbing, when she noticed Hoskins standing before her. He might have been there for minutes.

He said, "May I come in?"

She nodded curtly, then hurried to Timmie, who clung to her, curling his little bandy legs—still thin, so thin—about her.

Hoskins watched, then said gravely, "He seems quite unhappy."

Miss Fellowes said, "I don't blame him. They're at him every day now with their blood samples and their probings. They keep him on synthetic diets that I wouldn't feed a pig."

"It's the sort of thing they can't try on a human, you know."

"And they can't try it on Timmie, either. Dr. Hoskins, I insist. You told me it was Timmie's coming that put Stasis, Inc. on the map. If you have any gratitude for that at all, you've *got* to keep them away from the poor thing at least until he's old enough to understand a little more. After he's had a bad session with them, he has nightmares, he can't sleep. Now I warn you," (she reached a sudden peak of fury) "I'm not letting them in here any more."

(She realized that she had screamed that, but she couldn't help it.)

She said more quietly, "I know he's Neanderthal but there's a great deal we don't appreciate about Neanderthals. I've read up on them. They had a culture of their own. Some of the greatest human inventions arose in Neanderthal times. The domestication of animals, for instance; the wheel; various techniques in grinding stone. They even had spiritual yearnings. They buried their dead and buried possessions with the body, showing they believed in a life after death. It amounts to the fact that they invented religion. Doesn't that mean Timmie has a right to human treatment?"

She patted the little boy gently on his buttocks and sent him off into his playroom. As the door was opened, Hoskins smiled briefly at the display of toys that could be seen.

Miss Fellowes said defensively, "The poor child deserves his toys. It's all he has and he earns them with what he goes through."

"No, no. No objections, I assure you. I was just thinking how you've changed since the first day, when you were quite angry I had foisted a Neanderthal on you."

Miss Fellowes said in a low voice, "I suppose I didn't——" and faded off.

Hoskins changed the subject, "How old would you say he is, Miss Fellowes?"

She said, "I can't say, since we don't know how Neanderthals develop. In size, he'd only be three but Neanderthals are smaller generally and with all the tampering they do with him, he probably isn't growing. The way he's learning English, though, I'd say he was well over four."

"Really? I haven't noticed anything about learning English in the reports."

"He won't speak to anyone but me. For now, anyway. He's terribly afraid of others, and no wonder. But he can ask for an article of food; he can indicate any need practically; and he understands almost anything I say. Of course," (she watched him shrewdly, trying to estimate if this was the time), "his development may not continue."

"Why not?"

"Any child needs stimulation and this one lives a life of solitary confinement. I do what I can, but I'm not with him all the time and I'm not all he needs. What I mean, Dr. Hoskins, is that he needs another boy to play with."

Hoskins nodded slowly. "Unfortunately, there's only one of him, isn't there? Poor child."

Miss Fellowes warmed to him at once. She said, "You do like Timmie, don't you?" It was so nice to have someone else feel like that.

"Oh, yes," said Hoskins, and with his guard down, she could see the weariness in his eyes.

Miss Fellowes dropped her plans to push the matter at once. She said, with real concern, "You look worn out, Dr. Hoskins."

"Do I, Miss Fellowes? I'll have to practice looking more lifelike then."

"I suppose Stasis, Inc. is very busy and that keeps you very busy."

Hoskins shrugged. "You suppose right. It's a matter of animal, vegetable, and mineral in equal parts, Miss Fellowes. But then, I suppose you haven't ever seen our displays."

"Actually, I haven't. But it's not because I'm not interested. It's just that I've been so busy."

"Well, you're not all that busy right now," he said with impulsive decision. "I'll call for you tomorrow at eleven and give you a personal tour. How's that?"

She smiled happily. "I'd love it."

He nodded and smiled in his turn and left.

Miss Fellowes hummed at intervals for the rest of the day. Really— to think so was ridiculous, of course—but really, it was almost like—like making a date.

He was quite on time the next day, smiling and pleasant. She had replaced her nurse's uniform with a dress. One of conservative cut, to be sure, but she hadn't felt so feminine in years.

He complimented her on her appearance with staid formality and she accepted with equally formal grace. It was really a perfect prelude, she thought. And then the additional thought came, prelude to what?

She shut that off by hastening to say good-bye to Timmie and to assure him she would be back soon. She made sure he knew all about what and where lunch was.

Hoskins took her into the new wing, into which she had never yet gone. It still had the odor of newness about it and the sound of construction, softly heard, was indication enough that it was still being extended.

"Animal, vegetable, and mineral," said Hoskins, as he had the day before. "Animal right there; our most spectacular exhibits."

The space was divided into many rooms, each a separate Stasis bubble. Hoskins brought her to the view-glass of one and she looked in. What she saw impressed her first as a scaled, tailed chicken. Skittering on two thin legs it ran from wall to wall with its delicate birdlike head, surmounted by a bony keel like the comb of a rooster, looking this way and that. The paws on its small forelimbs clenched and unclenched constantly.

Hoskins said, "It's our dinosaur. We've had it for months. I don't know when we'll be able to let go of it."

"Dinosaur?"

"Did you expect a giant?"

She dimpled. "One does, I suppose. I know some of them are small."

"A small one is all we aimed for, believe me. Generally, it's under investigation, but this seems to be an open hour. Some interesting things have been discovered. For instance, it is not entirely cold-blooded. It has an imperfect method of maintaining internal temperatures higher than that of its environment. Unfortunately, it's a male. Ever since we brought it in we've been trying to get a fix on another that may be female, but we've had no luck yet."

"Why female?"

He looked at her quizzically. "So that we might have a fighting chance to obtain fertile eggs, and baby dinosaurs."

"Of course."

He led her to the trilobite section. "That's Professor Dwayne of Washington University," he said. "He's a nuclear chemist. If I recall correctly, he's taking an isotope ratio on the oxygen of the water."

"Why?"

"It's primeval water; at least half a billion years old. The isotope ratio gives the temperature of the ocean at that time. He himself happens to ignore the trilobites, but others are chiefly concerned in dissecting them. They're the lucky ones because all they need are scalpels and microscopes. Dwayne has to set up a mass spectrograph each time he conducts an experiment."

"Why's that? Can't he——"

"No, he can't. He can't take anything out of the room as far as can be helped."

There were samples of primordial plant life too and chunks of rock formations. Those were the vegetable and mineral. And every specimen had its investigator. It was like a museum; a museum brought to life and serving as a superactive center of research.

"And you have to supervise all of this, Dr. Hoskins?"

"Only indirectly, Miss Fellowes. I have subordinates, thank heaven. My own interest is entirely in the theoretical aspects of the matter: the nature of Time, the technique of mesonic intertemporal detection and so on. I would exchange all this for a method of detecting objects closer in Time than ten thousand years ago. If we could get into historical times——"

He was interrupted by a commotion at one of the distant booths, a thin voice raised querulously. He frowned, muttered hastily, "Excuse me," and hastened off.

Miss Fellowes followed as best she could without actually running.

An elderly man, thinly-bearded and red-faced, was saying, "I had vital aspects of my investigations to complete. Don't you understand that?"

A uniformed technician with the interwoven SI monogram (for Stasis, Inc.) on his lab coat, said, "Dr. Hoskins, it was arranged with Professor Ademewski at the beginning that the specimen could only remain here two weeks."

"I did not know then how long my investigations would take. I'm not a prophet," said Ademewski heatedly.

Dr. Hoskins said, "You understand, Professor, we have limited space; we must keep specimens rotating. That piece of chalcopyrite must go back; there are men waiting for the next specimen."

"Why can't I have it for myself, then? Let me take it out of there."

"You know you can't have it."

"A piece of chalcopyrite; a miserable five-kilogram piece? Why not?"

"We can't afford the energy expense!" said Hoskins brusquely. "You know that."

The technician interrupted. "The point is, Dr. Hoskins, that he tried to remove the rock against the rules and I almost punctured Stasis while he was in there, not knowing he was in there."

There was a short silence and Dr. Hoskins turned on the investigator with a cold formality. "Is that so, Professor?"

Professor Ademewski coughed. "I saw no harm——"

Hoskins reached up to a hand-pull dangling just within reach, outside the specimen room in question. He pulled it.

Miss Fellowes, who had been peering in, looking at the totally undistinguished sample of rock that occasioned the dispute, drew in her breath sharply as its existence flickered out. The room was empty.

Hoskins said, "Professor, your permit to investigate matters in Stasis will be permanently voided. I am sorry."

"But wait——"

"I am sorry. You have violated one of the stringent rules."

"I will appeal to the International Association——"

"Appeal away. In a case like this, you will find I can't be overruled."

He turned away deliberately, leaving the professor still protesting and said to Miss Fellowes (his face still white with anger), "Would you care to have lunch with me, Miss Fellowes?"

He took her into the small administration alcove of the cafeteria. He greeted others and introduced Miss Fellowes with complete ease, although she herself felt painfully self-conscious.

What must they think, she thought, and tried desperately to appear business-like.

She said, "Do you have that kind of trouble often, Dr. Hoskins? I mean like that you just had with the professor?" She took her fork in hand and began eating.

"No," said Hoskins forcefully. "That was the first time. Of course I'm always having to argue men out of removing specimens but this is the first time one actually tried to *do* it."

"I remember you once talked about the energy it would consume."

"That's right. Of course, we've tried to take it into account. Accidents will happen and so we've got special power sources designed to stand the drain of accidental removal from Stasis, but that doesn't mean we want to see a year's supply of energy gone in half a second—or can afford to without having our plans of expansion delayed for years. Besides, imagine the professor's being in the room while Stasis was about to be punctured."

"What would have happened to him if it had been?"

"Well, we've experimented with inanimate objects and with mice and they've disappeared. Presumably they've traveled back in time; carried along, so to speak, by the pull of the object simultaneously snapping back into its natural time. For that reason, we have to anchor objects within Stasis that we don't want to move and that's a complicated procedure. The professor would not have been anchored and he would have gone back to the Pliocene at the moment when we abstracted the rock—plus, of course, the two weeks it had remained here in the present."

"How dreadful it would have been."

"Not on account of the professor, I assure you. If he were fool enough to do what he did, it would serve him right. But imagine the effect it would have on the public if the fact came out. All people would need is to become aware of the dangers involved and funds could be choked off like that." He snapped his fingers and played moodily with his food.

Miss Fellowes said, "Couldn't you get him back? The way you got the rock in the first place?"

"No, because once an object is returned, the original fix is lost unless we deliberately plan to retain it and there was no reason to do that in this case. There never is. Finding the professor again would mean relocating a specific fix and that would be like dropping a line into the oceanic abyss for the purpose of dredging up a particular fish. My God, when I think of the precautions we take to prevent accidents, it makes me mad. We have every individual Stasis unit set up with its own puncturing device—we have to, since each unit has its separate fix and must be collapsible independently. The point is, though, none of the puncturing devices is ever activated until the last minute. And then we deliberately make activation impossible except by the pull of a rope carefully led outside the Stasis. The pull is a gross mechanical motion that requires a strong effort, not something that is likely to be done accidentally.''

Miss Fellowes said, ''But doesn't it—change history to move something in and out of Time?''

Hoskins shrugged. ''Theoretically, yes; actually, except in unusual cases, no. We move objects out of Stasis all the time. Air molecules. Bacteria. Dust. About 10 per cent of our energy consumption goes to make up micro-losses of that nature. But moving even large objects in Time sets up changes that damp out. Take that chalcopyrite from the Pliocene. Because of its absence for two weeks some insect didn't find the shelter it might have found and is killed. That could initiate a whole series of changes, but the mathematics of Stasis indicates that this is a converging series. The amount of change diminishes with time and then things are as before.''

''You mean, reality heals itself?''

''In a manner of speaking. Abstract a human from Time or send one back, and you make a larger wound. If the individual is an ordinary one, that wound still heals itself. Of course, there are a great many people who write to us each day and want us to bring Abraham Lincoln into the present, or Mohammed, or Lenin. *That* can't be done, of course. Even if we could find them, the change in reality in moving one of the history molders would be too great to be healed. There are ways of calculating when a change is likely to be too great and we avoid even approaching that limit.''

Miss Fellowes said, ''Then, Timmie——''

''No, he presents no problem in that direction. Reality is safe. But——'' He gave her a quick, sharp glance, then went on, ''But never mind. Yesterday you said Timmie needed companionship.''

''Yes,'' Miss Fellowes smiled her delight. ''I didn't think you paid that any attention.''

''Of course I did. I'm fond of the child. I appreciate your feelings for him and I was concerned enough to want to explain to you. Now I have; you've seen what we do; you've gotten some insight into the difficulties involved; so you know why, with the best will in the world, we can't supply companionship for Timmie.''

''You can't?'' said Miss Fellowes, with sudden dismay.

''But I've just explained. We couldn't possibly expect to find another Neanderthal his age without incredible luck, and if we could, it wouldn't be fair to multiply risks by having another human being in Stasis.''

Miss Fellowes put down her spoon and said energetically, ''But, Dr. Hoskins, that is not at all what I meant. I don't want you to bring another Neanderthal into the present. I know that's impossible. But it isn't impossible to bring another child to play with Timmie.''

Hoskins stared at her in concern. "A *human* child?"

"*Another* child," said Miss Fellowes, completely hostile now. "Timmie is human."

"I couldn't dream of such a thing."

"Why not? Why couldn't you? What is wrong with the notion? You pulled that child out of Time and made him an eternal prisoner. Don't you owe him something? Dr. Hoskins, if there is any man who, in this world, is that child's father in every sense but the biological, it is you. Why can't you do this little thing for him?"

Hoskins said, "His *father?*" He rose, somewhat unsteadily, to his feet. "Miss Fellowes, I think I'll take you back now, if you don't mind."

They returned to the dollhouse in a complete silence that neither broke.

It was a long time after that before she saw Hoskins again, except for an occasional glimpse in passing. She was sorry about that at times; then, at other times, when Timmie was more than usually woebegone or when he spent silent hours at the window with its prospect of little more than nothing, she thought, fiercely: Stupid man.

Timmie's speech grew better and more precise each day. It never entirely lost a certain soft, slurriness that Miss Fellowes found rather endearing. In times of excitement, he fell back into tongue-clicking but those times were becoming fewer. He must be forgetting the days before he came into the present—except for dreams.

As he grew older, the physiologists grew less interested and the psychologists more so. Miss Fellowes was not sure that she did not like the new group even less than the first. The needles were gone; the injections and withdrawals of fluid; the special diets. But now Timmie was made to overcome barriers to reach food and water. He had to lift panels, move bars, reach for cords. And the mild electric shocks made him cry and drove Miss Fellowes to distraction.

She did not wish to appeal to Hoskins; she did not wish to have to go to him; for each time she thought of him, she thought of his face over the luncheon table that last time. Her eyes moistened and she thought: Stupid, *stupid* man.

And then one day Hoskins' voice sounded unexpectedly, calling into the dollhouse, "Miss Fellowes."

She came out coldy, smoothing her nurse's uniform, then stopped in confusion at finding herself in the presence of a pale woman, slender and of middle height. The woman's fair hair and complexion gave her an appearance of fragility. Standing behind her and clutching at her skirt was a round-faced, large-eyed child of four.

Hoskins said, "Dear, this is Miss Fellowes, the nurse in charge of the boy. Miss Fellowes, this is my wife."

(Was this his wife? She was not as Miss Fellowes had imagined her to be. But then, why not? A man like Hoskins would choose a weak thing to be his foil. If that was what he wanted——)

She forced a matter-of-fact greeting. "Good afternoon, Mrs. Hoskins. Is this your—your little boy?"

(*That* was a surprise. She had thought of Hoskins as a husband, but not as a father, except, of course—— She suddenly caught Hoskins' grave eyes and flushed.)

Hoskins said, "Yes, this is my boy, Jerry. Say hello to Miss Fellowes, Jerry."

(Had he stressed the word "this" just a bit? Was he saying *this* was his son and not——)

Jerry receded a bit further into the folds of the maternal skirt and muttered his hello. Mrs. Hoskins' eyes were searching over Miss Fellowes' shoulders, peering into the room, looking for something.

Hoskins said, "Well, let's go in. Come, dear. There's a trifling discomfort at the threshold, but it passes."

Miss Fellowes said, "Do you want Jerry to come in, too?"

"Of course. He is to be Timmie's playmate. You said that Timmie needed a playmate. Or have you forgotten?"

"But——" She looked at him with a colossal, surprised wonder. *"Your* boy?"

He said peevishly, "Well, who's boy, then? Isn't this what you want? Come in, dear. Come on in."

Mrs. Hoskins lifted Jerry into her arms with a distinct effort and, hesitantly, stepped over the threshold. Jerry squirmed as she did so, disliking the sensation.

Mrs. Hoskins said in a thin voice, "Is the creature here? I don't see him."

Miss Fellowes called, "Timmie. Come out."

Timmie peered around the edge of the door, staring up at the little boy who was visiting him. The muscles in Mrs. Hoskins' arms tensed visibly.

She said to her husband, "Gerald, are you sure it's safe?"

Miss Fellowes said at once, "If you mean is Timmie safe, why, of course he is. He's a gentle little boy."

"But he's a sa—savage."

(The ape-boy stories in the newspapers!) Miss Fellowes said emphatically, "He is not a savage. He is just as quiet and reasonable as you can possibly expect a five-and-a-half-year-old to be. It is very generous of you, Mrs. Hoskins, to agree to allow your boy to play with Timmie but please have no fears about it."

Mrs. Hoskins said with mild heat, "I'm not sure that I agree."

"We've had it out, dear," said Hoskins. "Let's not bring up the matter for new argument. Put Jerry down."

Mrs. Hoskins did so and the boy backed against her, staring at the pair of eyes which were staring back at him from the next room.

"Come here, Timmie," said Miss Fellowes. "Don't be afraid."

Slowly, Timmie stepped into the room. Hoskins bent to disengage Jerry's fingers from his mother's skirt. "Step back, dear. Give the children a chance."

The youngsters faced one another. Although the younger, Jerry was nevertheless an inch taller, and in the presence of his straightness and his high-held, well-proportioned head, Timmie's grotesqueries were suddenly almost as pronounced as they had been in the first days.

Miss Fellowes' lips quivered.

It was the little Neanderthal who spoke first, in childish treble. "What's your name?" And Timmie thrust his face suddenly forward as though to inspect the other's features more closely.

Startled, Jerry responded with a vigorous shove that sent Timmie tumbling. Both began crying loudly and Mrs. Hoskins snatched up her child, while Miss Fellowes, flushed with repressed anger, lifted Timmie and comforted him.

Mrs. Hoskins said, "They just instinctively don't like one another."

"No more instinctively," said her husband wearily, "than any two children dislike each other. Now put Jerry down and let him get used to the situation. In fact, we had better leave. Miss Fellowes can bring Jerry to my office after a while and I'll have him taken home.''

The two children spent the next hour very aware of each other. Jerry cried for his mother, struck out at Miss Fellowes and, finally, allowed himself to be comforted with a lollipop. Timmie sucked at another, and at the end of an hour, Miss Fellowes had them playing with the same set of blocks, though at opposite ends of the room.

She found herself almost maudlinly grateful to Hoskins when she brought Jerry to him.

She searched for ways to thank him but his very formality was a rebuff. Perhaps he could not forgive her for making him feel like a cruel father. Perhaps the bringing of his own child was an attempt, after all, to prove himself both a kind father to Timmie and, also, not his father at all. Both at the same time!

So all she could say was, ''Thank you. Thank you very much.''

And all he could say was, ''It's all right. Don't mention it.''

It became a settled routine. Twice a week, Jerry was brought in for an hour's play, later extended to two hours' play. The children learned each other's names and ways and played together.

And yet, after the first rush of gratitude, Miss Fellowes found herself disliking Jerry. He was larger and heavier and in all things dominant, forcing Timmie into a completely secondary role. All that reconciled her to the situation was the fact that, despite difficulties, Timmie looked forward with more and more delight to the periodic appearances of his playfellow.

It was all he had, she mourned to herself.

And once, as she watched them, she thought: Hoskins' two children, one by his wife and one by Stasis.

While she herself——

Heavens, she thought, putting her fists to her temples and feeling ashamed: I'm jealous!

''Miss Fellowes,'' said Timmie (carefully, she had never allowed him to call her anything else) ''when will I go to school?''

She looked down at those eager brown eyes turned up to hers and passed her hand softly through his thick, curly hair. It was the most disheveled portion of his appearance, for she cut his hair herself while he sat restlessly under the scissors. She did not ask for professional help, for the very clumsiness of the cut served to mask the retreating fore part of the skull and the bulging hinder part.

She said, ''Where did you hear about school?''

''Jerry goes to school. Kin-der-gar-ten.'' He said it carefully. ''There are lots of places he goes. Outside. When can I go outside, Miss Fellowes?''

A small pain centered in Miss Fellowes' heart. Of course, she saw, there would be no way of avoiding the inevitability of Timmie's hearing more and more of the outer world he could never enter.

She said, with an attempt at gaiety, ''Why, whatever would you do in kindergarten, Timmie?''

''Jerry says they play games, they have picture tapes. He says there are lots of children. He says—he says——" A thought, then a triumphant upholding of both small hands with the fingers splayed apart. "He says this many."

Miss Fellowes said, "Would you like picture tapes? I can get you picture tapes. Very nice ones. And music tapes, too."

So that Timmie was temporarily comforted.

He pored over the picture tapes in Jerry's absence and Miss Fellowes read to him out of ordinary books by the hours.

There was so much to explain in even the simplest story, so much that was outside the perspective of his three rooms. Timmie took to having his dreams more often now that the outside was being introduced to him.

They were always the same, about the outside. He tried haltingly to describe them to Miss Fellowes. In his dreams, he was outside, an empty outside, but very large, with children and queer indescribable objects half-digested in his thought out of bookish descriptions half-understood, or out of distant Neanderthal memories half-recalled.

But the children and objects ignored him and though he was in the world, he was never part of it, but was as alone as though he were in his own room—and would wake up crying.

Miss Fellowes tried to laugh at the dreams, but there were nights in her own apartment when she cried, too.

One day, as Miss Fellowes read, Timmie put his hand under her chin and lifted it gently so that her eyes left the book and met his.

He said, "How do you know what to say, Miss Fellowes?"

She said, "You see these marks? They tell me what to say. These marks make words."

He stared at them long and curiously, taking the book out of her hands. "Some of these marks are the same."

She laughed with pleasure at this sign of his shrewdness and said, "So they are. Would you like to have me show you how to make the marks?"

"All right. That would be a nice game."

It did not occur to her that he could learn to read. Up to the very moment that he read a book to her, it did not occur to her that he could learn to read.

Then, weeks later, the enormity of what had been done struck her. Timmie sat in her lap, following word by word the printing in a child's book, reading to her. He was reading to her!

She struggled to her feet in amazement and said, "Now Timmie, I'll be back later. I want to see Dr. Hoskins."

Excited nearly to frenzy, it seemed to her she might have an answer to Timmie's unhappiness. If Timmie could not leave to enter the world, the world must be brought into those three rooms to Timmie—the whole world in books and film and sound. He must be educated to his full capacity. So much the world owed him.

She found Hoskins in a mood that was oddly analogous to her own; a kind of triumph and glory. His offices were unusually busy, and for a moment, she thought she would not get to see him, as she stood abashed in the anteroom.

But he saw her, and a smile spread over his broad face. "Miss Fellowes, come here."

He spoke rapidly into the intercom, then shut it off. "Have you heard? No, of course, you couldn't have. We've done it. We've actually done it. We have intertemporal detection at close range."

"You mean," she tried to detatch her thought from her own good news for a moment, "that you can get a person from historical times into the present?"

"That's just what I mean. We have a fix on a fourteenth-century individual right now. Imagine. *Imagine!* If you could only know how glad I'll be to shift from the eternal concentration on the Mesozoic, replace the paleontologists with the historians—— But there's something you wish to say to me, eh? Well, go ahead; go ahead. You find me in a good mood. Anything you want you can have."

Miss Fellowes smiled. "I'm glad. Because I wonder if we might not establish a system of instruction for Timmie?"

"Instruction? In what?"

"Well, in everything. A school. So that he might learn."

"But *can* he learn?"

"Certainly, he *is* learning. He can read. I've taught him so much myself."

Hoskins sat there, seeming suddenly depressed. "I don't know, Miss Fellowes."

She said, "You just said that anything I wanted——"

"I know and I should not have. You see, Miss Fellowes, I'm sure you must realize that we cannot maintain the Timmie experiment forever."

She stared at him with sudden horror, not really understanding what he had said. How did he mean "cannot maintain"? With an agonizing flash of recollection, she recalled Professor Ademewski and his mineral specimen that was taken away after two weeks. She said, "But you're talking about a boy. Not about a rock——"

Dr. Hoskins said uneasily, "Even a boy can't be given undue importance, Miss Fellowes. Now that we expect individuals out of historical time, we will need Stasis space, all we can get."

She didn't grasp it. "But you can't. Timmie—Timmie——"

"Now, Miss Fellowes, please don't upset yourself. Timmie won't go right away; perhaps not for months. Meanwhile we'll do what we can."

She was still staring at him.

"Let me get you something, Miss Fellowes."

"No," she whispered. "I don't need anything." She arose in a kind of nightmare and left.

Timmie, she thought, you will *not* die. You will *not* die.

It was all very well to hold tensely to the thought that Timmie must not die, but how was that to be arranged? In the first weeks, Miss Fellowes clung only to the hope that the attempt to bring forward a man from the fourteenth century would fail completely. Hoskins' theories might be wrong or his practice defective. Then things could go on as before.

Certainly, that was not the hope of the rest of the world and, irrationally, Miss

Fellowes hated the world for it. "Project Middle Ages" reached a climax of white-hot publicity. The press and the public had hungered for something like this. Stasis, Inc. had lacked the necessary sensation for a long time now. A new rock or another ancient fish failed to stir them. But *this* was *it*.

A historical human; an adult speaking a known language; someone who could open a new page of history to the scholar.

Zero-time was coming and this time it was not a question of three onlookers from a balcony. This time there would be a world-wide audience. This time the technicians of Stasis, Inc. would play their role before nearly all of mankind.

Miss Fellowes was herself all but savage with waiting. When young Jerry Hoskins showed up for his scheduled playtime with Timmie, she scarcely recognized him. He was not the one she was waiting for.

(The secretary who brought him left hurriedly after the barest nod for Miss Fellowes. She was rushing for a good place from which to watch the climax of Project Middle Ages. And so ought Miss Fellowes with far better reason, she thought bitterly, if only that stupid girl would arrive.)

Jerry Hoskins sidled toward her, embarrassed. "Miss Fellowes?" He took the reproduction of a news-strip out of his pocket.

"Yes? What is it, Jerry?"

"Is this a picture of Timmie?"

Miss Fellowes stared at him, then snatched the strip from Jerry's hand. The excitement of Project Middle Ages had brought about a pale revival of interest in Timmie on the part of the press.

Jerry watched her narrowly, then said, "It says Timmie is an ape-boy. What does that mean?"

Miss Fellowes caught the youngster's wrist and repressed the impulse to shake him. "Never say that, Jerry. Never, do you understand? It is a nasty word and you mustn't use it."

Jerry struggled out of her grip, frightened.

Miss Fellowes tore up the news-strip with a vicious twist of the wrist. "Now go inside and play with Timmie. He's got a new book to show you."

And then, finally, the girl appeared. Miss Fellowes did not know her. None of the usual stand-ins she had used when business took her elsewhere was available now, not with Project Middle Ages at climax, but Hoskins' secretary had promised to find *someone* and this must be the girl.

Miss Fellowes tried to keep querulousness out of her voice. "Are you the girl assigned to Stasis Section One?"

"Yes, I'm Mandy Terris. You're Miss Fellowes, aren't you?"

"That's right."

"I'm sorry I'm late. There's just so much excitement."

"I know. Now I want you——"

Mandy said, "You'll be watching, I suppose." Her thin, vacuously pretty face filled with envy.

"Never mind that. Now I want you to come inside and meet Timmie and Jerry. They will be playing for the next two hours so they'll be giving you no trouble. They've got milk handy and plenty of toys. In fact, it will be better if you leave them alone as much as possible. Now I'll show you where everything is located and ——"

"Is it Timmie that's the ape-b——"

"Timmie is the Stasis subject," said Miss Fellowes firmly.

"I mean, he's the one who's not supposed to get out, is that right?"

"Yes. Now, come in. There isn't much time."

And when she finally left, Mandy Terris called after her shrilly, "I hope you get a good seat and, golly, I sure hope it works."

Miss Fellowes did not trust herself to make a reasonable response. She hurried on without looking back.

But the delay meant she did *not* get a good seat. She got no nearer than the wall-viewing-plate in the assembly hall. Bitterly, she regretted that. If she could have been on the spot; if she could somehow have reached out for some sensitive portion of the instrumentations; if she were in some way able to wreck the experiment——

She found the strength to beat down her madness. Simple destruction would have done no good. They would have rebuilt and reconstructed and made the effort again. And she would never be allowed to return to Timmie.

Nothing would help. Nothing but that the experiment itself fail; that it break down irretrievably.

So she waited through the countdown, watching every move on the giant screen, scanning the faces of the technicians as the focus shifted from one to the other, watching for the look of worry and uncertainty that would mark something going unexpectedly wrong; watching, watching——

There was no such look. The count reached zero, and very quietly, very unassumingly, the experiment succeeded!

In the new Stasis that had been established there stood a bearded, stoop-shouldered peasant of indeterminate age, in ragged dirty clothing and wooden shoes, staring in dull horror at the sudden mad change that had flung itself over him.

And while the world went mad with jubilation, Miss Fellowes stood frozen in sorrow, jostled and pushed, all but trampled; surrounded by triumph while bowed down with defeat.

And when the loud-speaker called her name with strident force, it sounded three times before she responded.

"Miss Fellowes. Miss Fellowes. You are wanted in Stasis Section One immediately. Miss Fellowes. Miss Fell——"

"Let me through!" she cried breathlessly, while the loud-speaker continued its repetitions without pause. She forced her way through the crowds with wild energy, beating at it, striking out with closed fists, flailing, moving toward the door in a nightmare slowness.

Mandy Terris was in tears. "I don't know how it happened. I just went down to the edge of the corridor to watch a pocket-viewing-plate they had put up. Just for a minute. And then before I could move or do anything——" She cried out in sudden accusation, "You said they would make no trouble; you *said* to leave them alone——"

Miss Fellowes, disheveled and trembling uncontrollably, glared at her. "Where's Timmie?"

A nurse was swabbing the arm of a wailing Jerry with disinfectant and another was preparing an anti-tetanus shot. There was blood on Jerry's clothes.

"He bit me, Miss Fellowes," Jerry cried in rage. "He *bit* me."

But Miss Fellowes didn't even see him.

"What did you do with Timmie?" she cried out.

"I locked him in the bathroom," said Mandy. "I just threw the little monster in there and locked him in."

Miss Fellowes ran into the dollhouse. She fumbled at the bathroom door. It took an eternity to get it open and to find the ugly little boy cowering in the corner.

"Don't whip me, Miss Fellowes," he whispered. His eyes were red. His lips were quivering. "I didn't mean to do it."

"Oh, Timmie, who told you about whips?" She caught him to her, hugging him wildly.

He said tremulously, "She said, with a long rope. She said you would hit me and hit me."

"You won't be. She was wicked to say so. But what happened? What happened?"

"He called me an ape-boy. He said I wasn't a real boy. He said I was an animal." Timmie dissolved in a flood of tears. "He said he wasn't going to play with a monkey anymore. I said I wasn't a monkey; I *wasn't* a monkey. He said I was all funny-looking. He said I was horrible ugly. He kept saying and saying and I bit him."

They were both crying now. Miss Fellowes sobbed, "But it isn't true. You know that, Timmie. You're a real boy. You're a dear real boy and the best boy in the world. And no one, *no* one will ever take you away from me."

It was easy to make up her mind, now; easy to know what to do. Only it had to be done quickly. Hoskins wouldn't wait much longer, with his own son mangled——

No, it would have to be done this night, *this* night; with the place four-fifths asleep and the remaining fifth intellectually drunk over Project Middle Ages.

It would be an unusual time for her to return but not an unheard of one. The guard knew her well and would not dream of questioning her. He would think nothing of her carrying a suitcase. She rehearsed the noncommittal phrase, "Games for the boy," and the calm smile.

Why shouldn't he believe that?

He did. When she entered the dollhouse again, Timmie was still awake, and she maintained a desperate normality to avoid frightening him. She talked about his dreams with him and listened to him ask wistfully after Jerry.

There would be few to see her afterward, none to question the bundle she would be carrying. Timmie would be very quiet and then it would be a *fait accompli*. It would be done and what would be the use of trying to undo it. They would leave her be. They would leave them both be.

She opened the suitcase, took out the overcoat, the woolen cap with the ear-flaps and the rest.

Timmie said, with the beginning of alarm, "Why are you putting all these clothes on me, Miss Fellowes?"

She said, "I am going to take you outside, Timmie. To where your dreams are."

"My dreams?" His face twisted in sudden yearning, yet fear was there, too.

"You won't be afraid. You'll be with me. You won't be afraid if you're with me, will you, Timmie?"

"No, Miss Fellowes." He buried his little misshapen head against her side, and under her enclosing arm she could feel his small heart thud.

It was midnight and she lifted him into her arms. She disconnected the alarm and opened the door softly.

And she screamed, for facing her across the open door was Hoskins!

There were two men with him and he stared at her, as astonished as she.

Miss Fellowes recovered first by a second and made a quick attempt to push past him; but even with the second's delay he had time. He caught her roughly and hurled her back against a chest of drawers. He waved the men in and confronted her, blocking the door.

"I didn't expect this. Are you completely insane?"

She had managed to interpose her shoulder so that it, rather than Timmie, had struck the chest. She said pleadingly, "What harm can it do if I take him, Dr. Hoskins? You can't put energy loss ahead of a human life?"

Firmly, Hoskins took Timmie out of her arms. "An energy loss this size would mean millions of dollars lost out of the pockets of investors. It would mean a terrible setback for Stasis, Inc. It would mean eventual publicity about a sentimental nurse destroying all that for the sake of an ape-boy."

"*Ape-boy!*" said Miss Fellowes, in helpless fury.

"That's what the reporters would call him," said Hoskins.

One of the men emerged now, looping a nylon rope through eyelets along the upper portion of the wall.

Miss Fellowes remembered the rope that Hoskins had pulled outside the room containing Professor Ademewski's rock specimen so long ago.

She cried out, "No!"

But Hoskins put Timmie down and gently removed the overcoat he was wearing. "You stay here, Timmie. Nothing will happen to you. We're just going outside for a moment. All right?"

Timmie, white and wordless, managed to nod.

Hoskins steered Miss Fellowes out of the dollhouse ahead of himself. For the moment, Miss Fellowes was beyond resistence. Dully, she noticed the hand-pull being adjusted outside the dollhouse.

"I'm sorry, Miss Fellowes," said Hoskins. "I would have spared you this. I planned it for the night so that you would know only when it was over."

She said in a weary whisper, "Because your son was hurt. Because he tormented this child into striking out at him."

"No. Believe me. I understand about the incident today and I know it was Jerry's fault. But the story has leaked out. It would have to with the press surrounding us on this day of all days. I can't risk having a distorted story about negligence and savage Neanderthalers, so-called, distract from the success of Project Middle Ages. Timmie has to go soon anyway; he might as well go now and give the sensationalists as small a peg as possible on which to hang their trash."

"It's not like sending a rock back. You'll be killing a human being."

"Not killing. There'll be no sensation. He'll simply be a Neanderthal boy in a Neanderthal world. He will no longer be a prisoner and alien. He will have a chance at a free life."

"What chance? He's only seven years old, used to being taken care of, fed, clothed, sheltered. He will be alone. His tribe may not be at the point where he left them now that four years have passed. And if they were, they would not recognize him. He will have to take care of himself. How will he know how?"

Hoskins shook his head in hopeless negative. "Lord, Miss Fellowes, do you think we haven't thought of that? Do you think we would have brought in a child if it weren't that it was the first successful fix of a human or near-human we made and that we did not dare to take the chance of unfixing him and finding another fix as good? Why do you suppose we kept Timmie as long as we did, if it were not for our reluctance to send a child back into the past. It's just"—his voice took on a desperate urgency—"that we can wait no longer. Timmie stands in the way of expansion! Timmie is a source of possible bad publicity; we are on the threshold of great things, and I'm sorry, Miss Fellowes, but we can't let Timmie block us. We cannot. We cannot. I'm sorry, Miss Fellowes."

"Well, then," said Miss Fellowes sadly. "Let me say good-bye. Give me five minutes to say good-bye. Spare me that much."

Hoskins hesitated. "Go ahead."

Timmie ran to her. For the last time he ran to her and for the last time Miss Fellowes clasped him in her arms.

For a moment, she hugged him blindly. She caught at a chair with the toe of one foot, moved it against the wall, sat down.

"Don't be afraid, Timmie."

"I'm not afraid if you're here, Miss Fellowes. Is that man mad at me, the man out there?"

"No, he isn't. He just doesn't understand about us. Timmie, do you know what a mother is?"

"Like Jerry's mother?"

"Did he tell you about his mother?"

"Sometimes. I think maybe a mother is a lady who takes care of you and who's very nice to you and who does good things."

"That's right. Have you ever wanted a mother, Timmie?"

Timmie pulled his head away from her so that he could look into her face. Slowly, he put his hand to her cheek and hair and stroked her, as long, long ago she had stroked him. He said, "Aren't you my mother?"

"Oh, Timmie."

"Are you angry because I asked?"

"No. Of course not."

"Because I know your name is Miss Fellowes, but—but sometimes, I call you 'Mother' inside. Is that all right?"

"Yes. Yes. It's all right. And I won't leave you any more and nothing will hurt you. I'll be with you to care for you always. Call me Mother, so I can hear you."

"Mother," said Timmie contentedly, leaning his cheek against hers.

She rose, and, still holding him, stepped up on the chair. The sudden beginning of a shout from outside went unheard and, with her free hand, she yanked with all her weight at the cord where it hung suspended between two eyelets.

And Stasis was punctured and the room was empty.

YOUTH

— 1 —

THERE WAS a spatter of pebbles against the window and the youngster stirred in his sleep. Another, and he was awake.

He sat up stiffly in bed. Seconds passed while he interpreted his strange surroundings. He wasn't in his own home, of course. This was out in the country. It was colder than it should be and there was green at the window.

"Slim!"

The call was a hoarse, urgent whisper, and the youngster bounded to the open window.

Slim wasn't his real name, but the new friend he had met the day before had needed only one look at his slight figure to say, "You're Slim." He added, "I'm Red."

Red wasn't his real name, either, but its appropriateness was obvious. They were friends instantly with the quick, unquestioning friendship of young ones not yet quite in adolescence, before even the first stains of adulthood began to make their appearance.

Slim cried, "Hi, Red!" and waved cheerfully, still blinking the sleep out of himself.

Red kept to his croaking whisper, "Quiet! You want to wake somebody?"

Slim noticed all at once that the sun scarcely topped the low hills in the east, that the shadows were long and soft, and that the grass was wet.

Slim said more softly, "What's the matter?"

Red only waved for him to come out.

Slim dressed quickly, gladly confining his morning wash to the momentary sprinkle of a little lukewarm water. He let the air dry the exposed portions of his body as he ran out, while bare skin grew wet against the dewy grass.

Red said, "You've got to be quiet. If Mom wakes up or Dad or your dad or even any of the hands, then it'll be 'Come on in or you'll catch your death of cold tramping bare in the dew.' "

He mimicked voice and tone faithfully, so that Slim laughed and thought that there had never been so funny a fellow as Red.

497

Slim said eagerly, "Do you come out here every day like this, Red? Real early? It's like the whole world is just yours, isn't it, Red? No one else around, and all like that." He felt proud at being allowed entrance into this private world.

Red stared at him sidelong. He said carelessly, "I've been up for hours. Didn't you hear it last night?"

"Hear what?"

"Thunder."

"Was there a thunderstorm?" Slim was startled. He never slept through a thunderstorm.

"I guess not. But there was thunder. I heard it, and then I went to the window and it wasn't raining. It was all stars and the sky was just getting sort of almost gray. You know what I mean?"

Slim had never seen it so, but he nodded.

"So I just thought I'd go out," said Red.

They walked along the grassy side of the concrete road that split the panorama right down the middle all the way down to where it vanished among the hills. The road was so old that Red's father couldn't tell Red when it had been built. It didn't have a crack or a rough spot in it.

Red said, "Can you keep a secret?"

"Sure, Red. What kind of a secret?"

"Just a secret. Maybe I'll tell you and maybe I won't. I don't know yet." Red broke a long, supple stem from a fern they passed, methodically stripped it of its leaflets, and swung what was left whip-fashion. For a moment, he was on a wild charger, which reared and champed under his iron control. Then he got tired, tossed the whip aside, and stowed the charger away in a corner of his imagination for future use.

He said, "There'll be a circus around."

Slim said, "That's no secret. I knew that. My dad told me even before we came here——"

"That's not the secret. Fine secret! Ever see a circus?"

"Oh, sure. You bet."

"Like it?"

"Say, there isn't anything I like better."

Red was watching out of the corner of his eyes again. "Ever think you would like to be with a circus? I mean, for good?"

Slim considered. "I guess not. I think I'll be an astronomer like my dad. I think he wants me to be."

"Huh! Astronomer!" said Red.

Slim felt the doors of the new, private world closing on him and astronomy became a thing of dead stars.

He said placatingly, "A circus *would* be more fun."

"You're just saying that."

"No, I'm not. I mean it."

Red grew argumentative. "Suppose you had a chance to join the circus right now. What would you do?"

"I—I——"

"See!" Red affected scornful laughter.

Slim was stung. "I'd join up."

"Go on."

"Try me."

Red whirled at him, strange and intense. "You mean that? You want to go in with me?"

"What do you mean?" Slim stepped back a bit.

"I got something that can get us into the circus. Maybe someday we can even have a circus of our own. We could be the biggest circus fellows in the world. That's if you want to go in with me. Otherwise—— Well, I guess I can do it on my own. I just thought, Let's give good old Slim a chance."

The world was strange and glamorous, and Slim said, "Sure thing, Red. I'm in! What is it, huh, Red? Tell me what it is."

"Figure it out. What's the most important thing in circuses?"

Slim thought desperately. He wanted to give the right answer. Finally he said, "Acrobats?"

"Holy smokes! I wouldn't go five steps to look at acrobats."

"I don't know then."

"Animals, that's what! What's the best side show? Where are the biggest crowds? Even in the main rings the best acts are animal acts."

"Do you think so?"

"Everyone thinks so. You ask anyone. Anyway, I found animals this morning. Two of them."

"And you've got them?"

"Sure. That's the secret. Are you telling?"

"Of course not."

"Okay. I've got them in the barn. Do you want to see them?"

They were almost at the barn; its huge open door black. Too black. They had been heading there all the time. Slim stopped in his tracks.

He tried to make his words casual. "Are they big?"

"Would I fool with them if they were big? They can't hurt you. They're only about so long. I've got them in a cage."

They were in the barn now and Slim saw the large cage suspended from a hook in the roof. It was covered with stiff canvas.

Red said, "We used to have some bird there or something. Anyway, they can't get away from there. Come on, let's go up to the loft."

They clambered up the wooden stairs and Red hooked the cage toward them.

Slim pointed and said, "There's sort of a hole in the canvas."

Red frowned. "How'd that get there?" He lifted the canvas, looked in, and said with relief, "They're still there."

"The canvas looks burned," worried Slim.

"You want to look or don't you?"

Slim nodded slowly. He wasn't sure he wanted to, after all. They might be——

But the canvas had been jerked off and there they were. Two of them, the way Red said. They were small and sort of disgusting-looking. The animals moved quickly as the canvas lifted and were on the side toward the youngsters. Red poked a cautious finger at them.

"Watch out," said Slim in agony.

"They don't hurt you," said Red. "Ever see anything like them?"

"No."

"Can't you see how a circus would jump at a chance to have these?"

"Maybe they're too small for a circus."

Red looked annoyed. He let go the cage which swung back and forth pendulum-fashion. "You're just backing out."

"No, I'm not. It's just——"

"They're not too small, don't worry. Right now, I've only got one worry."

"What's that?"

"Well, I've got to keep them till the circus comes, don't I? I've got to figure out what to feed them meanwhile."

The cage swung and the little trapped creatures clung to its bars, gesturing at the youngsters with queer, quick motions—almost as though they were intelligent.

— 2 —

THE ASTRONOMER entered the dining room with decorum. He felt very much the guest.

He said, "Where are the youngsters? My son isn't in his room."

The Industrialist smiled. "They've been out for hours. However, breakfast was forced into them by the women some time ago, so there is nothing to worry about. Youth, Doctor, youth!"

"Youth!" The word seemed to depress the Astronomer.

They ate breakfast in silence. The Industrialist said once, "You really think they'll come. The day looks so—*normal.*"

The Astronomer said, "They'll come."

That was all.

Afterward the Industrialist said, "You'll pardon me. I can't conceive your playing so elaborate a hoax. You really spoke to them?"

"As I speak to you. At least, in a sense. They can project thoughts."

"I gathered that must be so from your letter. How, I wonder."

"I could not say. I asked them and, of course, they were vague. Or perhaps it was just that I could not understand. It involves a projector for the focusing of thought and, even more than that, conscious attention on the part of both projector and receptor. It was quite a while before I realized they were trying to think at me. Such thought projectors may be part of the science they will give us."

"Perhaps," said the Industrialist. "Yet think of the changes it would bring to society. A thought projector!"

"Why not? Change would be good for us."

"I don't think so."

"It is only in old age that change is unwelcome," said the Astronomer, "and races can be old as well as individuals."

The Industrialist pointed out the window. "You see that road. It was built Beforethewars. I don't know exactly when. It is as good now as the day it was built. We couldn't possibly duplicate it now. The race was young when that was built, eh?"

"Then? Yes! At least they weren't afraid of new things."

"No. I wish they had been. Where is the society of Beforethewars? Destroyed, Doctor! What good were youth and new things? We are better off now. The world is peaceful and jogs along. The race goes nowhere but after all, there is nowhere to go. *They* proved that. The men who built the road. I will speak with your visitors as I agreed, if they come. But I think I will only ask them to go.''

"The race is not going nowhere," said the Astronomer earnestly. "It is going toward final destruction. My university has a smaller student body each year. Fewer books are written. Less work is done. An old man sleeps in the sun and his days are peaceful and unchanging, but each day finds him nearer death all the same."

"Well, well," said the Industrialist.

"No, don't dismiss it. Listen. Before I wrote you, I investigated your position in the planetary economy."

"And you found me solvent?" interrupted the Industrialist, smiling.

"Why, yes. Oh, I see, you are joking. And yet—perhaps the joke is not far off. You are less solvent than your father and he was less solvent than his father. Perhaps your son will no longer be solvent. It becomes too troublesome for the planet to support even the industries that still exist, though they are toothpicks to the oak trees of Beforethewars. We will be back to village economy, and then to what? The caves?''

"And the infusion of fresh technological knowledge will be the changing of all that?''

"Not just the new knowledge. Rather the whole effect of change, of a broadening of horizons. Look, sir, I chose you to approach in this matter not only because you were rich and influential with government officials, but because you had an unusual reputation, for these days, of daring to break with tradition. Our people will resist change and you would know how to handle them, how to see to it that—that——''

"That the youth of the race is revived?"

"Yes."

"With its atomic bombs?"

"The atomic bombs," returned the Astronomer, "need not be the end of civilization. These visitors of mine had their atomic bomb, or whatever their equivalent was on their own worlds, and survived it, because they didn't give up. Don't you see? It wasn't the bomb that defeated us, but our own shell shock. This may be the last chance to reverse the process.''

"Tell me," said the Industrialist, "what do these friends from space want in return?"

The Astronomer hesitated. He said, "I will be truthful with you. They come from a denser planet. Ours is richer in the lighter atoms."

"They want magnesium? Aluminum?"

"No, sir. Carbon and hydrogen. They want coal and oil."

"Really?"

The Astronomer said quickly, "You are going to ask why creatures who have mastered space travel, and therefore atomic power, would want coal and oil. I can't answer that."

The Industrialist smiled. "But I can. This is the best evidence yet of the truth of your story. Superficially, atomic power would seem to preclude the use of coal and oil. However, quite apart from the energy gained by their combustion, they remain, and always will remain, the basic raw material for all organic chemistry. Plastics, dyes, pharmaceuticals, solvents. Industry could not exist without them, even in an atomic age. Still, if coal and oil are the low price for which they would sell us the troubles and tortures of racial youth, my answer is that the commodity would be dear if offered gratis.''

The Astronomer sighed and said, ''There are the boys!''

They were visible through the open window, standing together in the grassy field and lost in animated conversation. The Industrialist's son pointed imperiously and the Astronomer's son nodded and made off at a run toward the house.

The Industrialist said, ''There is the youth you speak of. Our race has as much of it as it ever had.''

''Yes, but we age them quickly and pour them into the mold.''

Slim scuttled into the room, the door banging behind him.

The Astronomer said in mild disapproval, ''What's this?''

Slim looked up in surprise and came to a halt. ''I beg your pardon. I didn't know anyone was here. I am sorry to have interrupted.'' His enunciation was almost painfully precise.

The Industrialist said, ''It's all right, youngster.''

But the Astronomer said, ''Even if you had been entering an empty room, son, there would be no cause for slamming a door.''

''Nonsense,'' insisted the Industrialist. ''The youngster has done no harm. You simply scold him for being young. You, with your views!''

He said to Slim, ''Come here, lad.''

Slim advanced slowly.

''How do you like the country, eh?''

''Very much, sir, thank you.''

''My son has been showing you about the place, has he?''

''Yes, sir. Red—I mean——''

''No, no. Call him Red. I call him that myself. Now tell me, what are you two up to, eh?''

Slim looked away. ''Why—just exploring, sir.''

The Industrialist turned to the Astronomer. ''There you are, youthful curiosity and adventure lust. The race has not yet lost it.''

Slim said, ''Sir?''

''Yes, lad.''

The youngster took a long time in getting on with it. He said, ''Red sent me in for something good to eat, but I don't exactly know what he meant. I didn't like to say so.''

''Why, just ask Cook. She'll have something good for young'uns to eat.''

''Oh no, sir. I mean for animals.''

''For animals?''

''Yes, sir. What do animals eat?''

The Astronomer said, ''I am afraid my son is city-bred.''

''Well,'' said the Industrialist, ''there's no harm in that. What kind of an animal, lad?''

''A small one, sir.''

''Then try grass or leaves, and if they don't want that, nuts or berries would probably do the trick.''

''Thank you, sir.'' Slim ran out again, closing the door gently behind him.

The Astronomer said, ''Do you suppose they've trapped an animal alive?'' He was obviously perturbed.

''That's common enough. There's no shooting on my estate and it's tame country, full of rodents and small creatures. Red is always coming home with pets of one sort or another. They rarely maintain his interest for long.''

He looked at the wall clock. ''Your friends should have been here by now, shouldn't they?''

— 3 —

THE SWAYING had come to a halt and it was dark. The Explorer was not comfortable in the alien air. It felt as thick as soup and he had to breath shallowly. Even so——

He reached out in a sudden need for company. The Merchant was warm to the touch. His breathing was rough, he moved in an occasional spasm, and was obviously asleep. The Explorer hesitated and decided not to wake him. It would serve no real purpose.

There would be no rescue, of course. That was the penalty paid for the high profits which unrestrained competition could lead to. The Merchant who opened a new planet could have a ten-year monopoly of its trade, which he might hug to himself or, more likely, rent out to all comers at a stiff price. It followed that planets were searched for in secrecy and preferably away from the usual trade routes. In a case such as theirs then, there was little or no chance that another ship would come within range of their subetherics except for the most improbable of coincidences. Even if they were in their ship, that is, rather than in this—this—*cage*.

The Explorer grasped the thick bars. Even if they blasted those away, as they could, they would be stuck too high in open air for leaping.

It was too bad. They had landed twice before in the scout ship. They had established contact with the natives, who were grotesquely huge, but mild and unaggressive. It was obvious that they had once owned a flourishing technology, but hadn't faced up to the consequences of such a technology. It would have been a wonderful market.

And it was a tremendous world. The Merchant, especially, had been taken aback. He had known the figures that expressed the planet's diameter, but from a distance of two light-seconds, he had stood at the visiplate and muttered, ''Unbelievable!''

''Oh, there are larger worlds,'' the Explorer said. It wouldn't do for an Explorer to be too easily impressed.

''Inhabited?''

''Well, no.''

''Why, you could drop your planet into that large ocean and drown it.''

The Explorer smiled. It was a gentle dig at his Arcturian homeland, which was smaller than most planets. He said, ''Not quite.''

The Merchant followed along the line of his thoughts. ''And the inhabitants are large in proportion to their world?'' He sounded as though the news struck him less favorably now.

''Nearly ten times our height.''

''Are you sure they are friendly?''

"That is hard to say. Friendship between alien intelligences is an imponderable. They are not dangerous, I think. We've come across other groups that could not maintain equilibrium after the atomic war stage and you know the results. Introversion. Retreat. Gradual decadence and increasing gentleness."

"Even if they are such monsters?"

"The principle remains."

It was about then that the Explorer felt the heavy throbbing of the engines. He frowned and said, "We are descending a bit too quickly."

There had been some speculation on the dangers of landing several hours before. The planetary target was a huge one for an oxygen-water world. Though it lacked the size of the uninhabitable hydrogen-ammonia planets and its low density made its surface gravity fairly normal, its gravitational forces fell off, but slowly with distance. In short, its gravitational potential was high and the ship's calculator was a run-of-the-mill model not designed to plot landing trajectories at that potential range. That meant the Pilot would have to use manual controls.

It would have been wiser to install a more high-powered model, but that would have meant a trip to some outpost of civilization; lost time; perhaps a lost secret. The Merchant demanded an immediate landing.

The Merchant felt it necessary to defend his position now. He said angrily to the Explorer, "Don't you think the Pilot knows his job? He landed you safely twice before."

Yes, thought the Explorer, in a scout ship, not in this unmaneuverable freighter. Aloud, he said nothing.

He kept his eye on the visiplate. They were descending too quickly. There was no room for doubt. Much too quickly.

The Merchant said peevishly, "Why do you keep silence?"

"Well then, if you wish me to speak, I would suggest that you strap on your floater and help me prepare the ejector."

The Pilot fought a noble fight. He was no beginner. The atmosphere, abnormally high and thick in the gravitational potential of this world, whipped and burned about the ship, but to the very last, it looked as though he might bring it under control despite that.

He even maintained course, following the extrapolated line to the point on the northern continent toward which they were headed. Under other circumstances, with a shade more luck, the story eventually would have been told and retold as a heroic and masterly reversal of a lost situation. But within sight of victory, tired body and tired nerves clamped a control bar with a shade too much pressure. The ship, which had almost leveled off, dipped down again.

There was no room to retrieve the final error. There was only a mile left to fall. The Pilot remained at his post to the actual landing, his only thought that of breaking the force of the crash, of maintaining the spaceworthiness of the vessel. He did not survive. With the ship bucking madly in a soupy atmosphere, few ejectors could be mobilized and only one of them in time.

When afterward the Explorer lifted out of unconsciousness and rose to his feet, he had the definite feeling that but for himself and the Merchant, there were no survivors. And perhaps that was an overcalculation. His floater had burned out while still sufficiently distant from surface to have the fall stun him. The Merchant might have had less luck, even, than that.

He was surrounded by a world of thick, ropy stalks of grass, and in the distance were trees that reminded him vaguely of similar structures on his native

Arcturian world except that their lowest branches were high above what he would consider normal treetops.

He called, his voice sounding basso in the thick air, and the Merchant answered. The Explorer made his way toward him, thrusting violently at the coarse stalks that barred his path.

"Are you hurt?" he asked.

The Merchant grimaced, "I've sprained something. It hurts to walk."

The Explorer probed gently. "I don't think anything is broken. You'll have to walk despite the pain."

"Can't we rest first?"

"It's important to try to find the ship. If it is spaceworthy or if it can be repaired, we may live. Otherwise, we won't."

"Just a few minutes. Let me catch my breath."

The Explorer was glad enough for those few minutes. The Merchant's eyes were already closed. He allowed his to do the same.

He heard the trampling and his eyes snapped open. "Never sleep on a strange planet," he told himself futilely.

The Merchant was awake too and his steady screaming was a rumble of terror.

The Explorer called, "It's only a native of this planet. It won't harm you."

But even as he spoke, the giant had swooped down, and in a moment, they were in its grasp, being lifted closer to its monstrous ugliness.

The Merchant struggled violently and, of course, quite futilely. "Can't you talk to it?" he yelled.

The Explorer could only shake his head. "I can't reach it with the projector. It won't be listening."

"Then blast it. Blast it down."

"We can't do that." The phrase "you fool" had almost been added. The Explorer struggled to keep his self-control. They were swallowing space as the monster moved purposefully away.

"Why not?" cried the Merchant. "You can reach your blaster. I see it in plain sight. Don't be afraid of falling."

"It's simpler than that. If this monster is killed, you'll never trade with this planet. You'll never even leave it. You probably won't live the day out."

"Why? Why?"

"Because this is one of the young of the species. You should know what happens when a trader kills a native young, even accidentally. What's more, if this is the target point, then we are on the estate of a powerful native. This might be one of his brood."

That was how they entered their present prison. They had carefully burned away a portion of the thick, stiff covering and it was obvious that the height from which they were suspended was a killing one.

Now, once again, the prison cage shuddered and lifted in an upward arc. The Merchant rolled to the lower rim and startled awake. The cover lifted and light flooded in. As was the case the time before, there were two specimens of the young. They were not very different in appearance from adults of the species, reflected the Explorer, though, of course, they were considerably smaller.

A handful of reedy green stalks was stuffed between the bars. Its odor was not unpleasant but it carried clods of soil at its ends.

The Merchant drew away and said huskily, "What are they doing?"

The Explorer said, "Trying to feed us, I should judge. At least, this seems to be the native equivalent of grass."

The cover was replaced and they were set swinging again, alone with their fodder.

— 4 —

SLIM STARTED at the sound of footsteps and brightened when it turned out to be only Red.

He said, "No one's around. I had my eye peeled, you bet."

Red said, "Ssh. Look. You take this stuff and stick it in the cage. I've got to scoot back to the house."

"What is it?" Slim reached reluctantly.

"Ground meat. Holy smokes, haven't you ever seen ground meat? That's what you should've got when I sent you to the house instead of coming back with that stupid grass."

Slim was hurt. "How'd I know they don't eat grass? Besides, ground meat doesn't come loose like that. It comes in cellophane and it isn't that color."

"Sure—in the city. Out here we grind our own and it's always this color till it's cooked."

"You mean it isn't cooked?" Slim drew away quickly.

Red looked disgusted. "Do you think animals eat *cooked* food? Come on, take it. It won't hurt you. I tell you there isn't much time."

"Why? What's doing back at the house?"

"I don't know. Dad and your father are walking around. I think maybe they're looking for me. Maybe the cook told them I took the meat. Anyway, we don't want them coming here after me."

"Didn't you ask the cook before you took this stuff?"

"Who? That crab? Shouldn't wonder if she only let me have a drink of water because Dad makes her. Come on. Take it."

Slim took the large glob of meat though his skin crawled at the touch. He turned toward the barn and Red sped away in the direction from which he had come.

Red slowed when he approached the two adults, took a few deep breaths to bring himself back to normal, and then carefully and nonchalantly sauntered past. (They were walking in the general direction of the barn, he noticed, but not dead on.)

He said, "Hi, Dad. Hello, sir."

The Industrialist said, "Just a moment, Red. I have a question to ask you."

Red turned a carefully blank face to his father. "Yes, Dad?"

"Mother tells me you were out early this morning."

"Not real early, Dad. Just a little before breakfast."

"She said you told her it was because you had been awakened during the night."

Red waited before answering. Should he have told Mom that?

Then he said, "Yes, sir."

"What was it that awakened you?"

Red saw no harm in it. He said, "I don't know, Dad. It sounded like thunder, sort of, and like a collision, sort of."

"Could you tell where it came from?"

"It *sounded* like it was out by the hill." That was truthful, and useful as well, since the direction was almost opposite that in which the barn lay.

The Industrialist looked at his guest. "I suppose it would do no harm to walk toward the hill."

The Astronomer said, "I am ready."

Red watched them walk away, and when he turned, he saw Slim peering cautiously out from among the briers of a hedge.

Red waved at him. "Come on."

Slim stepped out and approached. "Did they say anything about the meat?"

"No. I guess they don't know about that. They went down to the hill."

"What for?"

"Search me. They kept asking about the noise I heard. Listen, did the animals eat the meat?"

"Well," said Slim cautiously, "they were sort of *looking* at it and smelling it or something."

"Okay," Red said, "I guess they'll eat it. Holy smokes, they've got to eat *something*. Let's walk along toward the hill and see what Dad and your father are going to do."

"What about the animals?"

"They'll be all right. A fellow can't spend all his time on them. Did you give them water?"

"Sure. They drank that."

"See. Come on. We'll look at them after lunch. I tell you what. We'll bring them fruit. Anything'll eat fruit."

Together they trotted up the rise, Red, as usual, in the lead.

— 5 —

THE ASTRONOMER said, "You think the noise was their ship landing?"

"Don't you think it could be?"

"If it were, they may all be dead."

"Perhaps not." The Industrialist frowned.

"If they have landed and are still alive, where are they?"

"Think about that for a while." He was still frowning.

The Astronomer said, "I don't understand you."

"They may not be friendly."

"Oh no. I've spoken with them. They've——"

"You've spoken with them. Call that reconnaissance. What would their next step be? Invasion?"

"But they only have one ship, sir."

"You know that only because they say so. They might have a fleet."

"I've told you about their size. They——"

"Their size would not matter if they have hand weapons that may well be superior to our artillery."

"That is not what I meant."

"I had this partly in mind from the first." The Industrialist went on. "It is for that reason I agreed to see them after I received your letter. Not to agree to an unsettling and impossible trade, but to judge their real purposes. I did not count on their evading the meeting."

He sighed and added, "I suppose it isn't our fault. You are right in one thing, at any rate. The world has been at peace too long. We are losing a healthy sense of suspicion."

The Astronomer's mild voice rose to an unusual pitch and he said, "I *will* speak. I tell you that there is no reason to suppose they can possibly be hostile. They are small, yes, but that is only important because it is a reflection of the fact that their native worlds are small. Our world has what is for them a normal gravity, but because of our much higher gravitational potential, our atmosphere is too dense to support them comfortably over sustained periods. For a similar reason, the use of the world as a base for interstellar travel, except for trade in certain items, is uneconomical. And there are important differences in chemistry of life due to the basic differences in soils. They couldn't eat our food or we theirs."

"Surely all this can be overcome. They can bring their own food, build domed stations of lowered air pressure, devise specially designed ships."

"They can. And how glibly you can describe feats that are easy to a race in its youth. It is simply that they don't have to do any of that. There are millions of worlds suitable for them in the Galaxy. They don't need this one which isn't."

"How do you know? All this is their information again."

"This I was able to check independently. I am an astronomer, after all."

"That is true. Let me hear what you have to say then while we walk."

"Then, sir, consider that for a long time our astronomers have believed that two general classes of planetary bodies existed. First, the planets which formed at differences far enough from their stellar nuclei to become cool enough to capture hydrogen. These would be large planets rich in hydrogen, ammonia, and methane. We have examples of these in the giant outer planets. The second class would include those planets formed so near the stellar center that the high temperature would make it impossible to capture much hydrogen. These would be smaller planets, comparatively poorer in hydrogen and richer in oxygen. We know that type very well since we live on one. Ours is the only solar system we know in detail, however, and it has been reasonable for us to assume that these were the *only* two planetary classes."

"I take it then that there is another."

"Yes. There is a super-dense class, still smaller, poorer in hydrogen than the inner planets of the solar system. The ratio of occurrence of hydrogen-ammonia planets and these super-dense water-oxygen worlds of theirs over the entire Galaxy—and remember that they have actually conducted a survey of significant sample volumes of the Galaxy, which we, without interstellar travel, cannot do—is about three to one. This leaves them several million super-dense worlds for exploration and colonization."

The Industrialist looked at the blue sky and the green-crowned trees among which they were making their way. He said, "And worlds like ours?"

The Astronomer said softly, "Ours is the first solar system they have found which contains them. Apparently the development of our solar system was unique and did not follow the ordinary rules."

The Industrialist considered that. "What it amounts to is that these creatures from space are asteroid dwellers."

"No, no. The asteroids are something else again. They occur, I was told, in one out of eight stellar systems, but they're completely different from what we've been discussing."

"And how does your being an astronomer change the fact that you are still only quoting their unsupported statements?"

"But they did not restrict themselves to bald items of information. They presented me with a theory of stellar evolution which I had to accept and which is more nearly valid than anything our own astronomy has ever been able to devise, if we except possible lost theories dating from Beforethewars. Mind you, their theory had a rigidly mathematical development and it predicted just such a galaxy as they describe. So you see, they have all the worlds they wish. They are not land-hungry. Certainly not for our land."

"Reason would say so, if what you say is true. But creatures may be intelligent and not reasonable. Our forefathers were presumably intelligent, yet they were certainly not reasonable. Was it reasonable to destroy almost all their tremendous civilization in atomic warfare over causes our historians can no longer accurately determine?" The Industrialist brooded over it. "From the dropping of the first atom bomb over the Eastern Islands of the Sun—I forget the ancient name—there was only one end in sight, and in plain sight. Yet events were allowed to proceed to that end."

He looked up, said briskly, "Well, where are we? I wonder if we are not on a fool's errand after all."

But the Astronomer was a little in advance and his voice came thickly. "No fool's errand, sir. Look there."

— 6 —

RED AND Slim had trailed their elders with the experience of youth, aided by the absorption and anxiety of their fathers. Their view of the final object of the search was somewhat obscured by the underbrush behind which they remained.

Red said, "Holy smokes. Look at that. It's all shiny silver or something."

But it was Slim who was really excited. He caught at the other. "I know what this is. It's a spaceship. That must be why my father came here. He's one of the biggest astronomers in the world and your father would have to call him if a spaceship landed on his estate."

"What are you talking about? Dad didn't even know that thing was there. He only came here because I told him I heard the thunder from here. Besides, there isn't any such thing as a spaceship."

"Sure, there is. Look at it. See those round things. They're ports. And you can see the rocket tubes."

"How do you know so much?"

Slim was flushed. He said, "I read about them. My father has books about them. Old books. From Beforethewars."

"Huh. Now I know you're making it up. Books from Beforethewars!"

"My father *has* to have them. He teaches at the University. It's his job."

His voice had risen and Red had to pull at him. "You want them to hear us?" he whispered indignantly.

"Well, it is, too, a spaceship."

"Look here, Slim, you mean that's a ship from another world."

"It's *got* to be. Look at my father going round and round it. He wouldn't be so interested if it was anything else."

"Other worlds! Where are there other worlds?"

"Everywhere. How about the planets? They're worlds just like ours, some of them. And other stars probably have planets. There's probably zillions of planets."

Red felt outweighed and outnumbered. He muttered, "You're crazy!"

"All right, then. I'll show you."

"Hey! Where are you going?"

"Down there. I'm going to ask my father. I suppose you'll believe it if *he* tells you. I suppose you'll believe a Professor of Astronomy knows what——"

He had scrambled upright.

Red said, "Hey. You don't want them to see us. We're not supposed to be here. Do you want them to start asking questions and find out about our animals?"

"I don't care. You said I was crazy."

"Snitcher! You promised you wouldn't tell."

"I'm *not* going to tell. But if they find out themselves, it's your fault for starting an argument and saying I was crazy."

"I take it back then," grumbled Red.

"Well, all right. You better."

In a way, Slim was disappointed. He wanted to see the spaceship at closer quarters. Still, he could not break his vow of secrecy even in spirit without at least the excuse of personal insult.

Red said, "It's awfully small for a spaceship."

"Sure, because it's probably a scout ship."

"I'll bet Dad couldn't even get into the old thing."

So much Slim realized to be true. It was a weak point in his argument and he made no answer.

Red rose to his feet; an elaborate attitude of boredom all about him. "Well, I guess we better be going. There's business to do and I can't spend all day here looking at some old spaceship or whatever it is. We've got to take care of the animals if we're going to be circus folks. That's the first rule with circus folks. They've got to take care of the animals. And," he finished virtuously, "that's what I aim to do, anyway."

Slim said, "What for, Red? They've got plenty of meat. Let's watch."

"There's no fun in watching. Besides Dad and your father are going away and I guess it's about lunch time."

Red became argumentative. "Look, Slim, we can't start acting suspicious or they're going to start investigating. Holy smokes, don't you ever read any detective stories? When you're trying to work a big deal without being caught, it's practically the main thing to keep on acting just like always. Then they don't suspect anything. That's the first law————''

"Oh, all right."

Slim rose resentfully. At the moment, the circus appeared to him a rather tawdry and shoddy substitute for the glories of astronomy, and he wondered how he had come to fall in with Red's silly scheme.

Down the slope they went, Slim, as usual, in the rear.

— 7 —

THE INDUSTRIALIST said, "It's the workmanship that gets me. I never saw such construction."

"What good is it now?" said the Astronomer bitterly. "There's nothing left. There'll be no second landing. This ship detected life on our planet through accident. Other exploring parties would come no closer than necessary to establish the fact that no super-dense worlds existed in our solar system."

"Well, there's no quarreling with a crash landing."

"The ship hardly seems damaged. If only some had survived, the ship might have been repaired."

"If they had survived, there would be no trade in any case. They're too different. Too disturbing. In any case—it's over."

They entered the house and the Industrialist greeted his wife calmly. "Lunch about ready, dear?"

"I'm afraid not. You see——" She looked hesitantly at the Astronomer.

"Is anything wrong?" asked the Industrialist. "Why not tell me? I'm sure our guest won't mind a little family discussion."

"Pray don't pay any attention whatever to me," muttered the Astronomer. He moved miserably to the other end of the living room.

The woman said in low, hurried tones, "Really, dear, Cook's that upset. I've been soothing her for hours and honestly I don't know why Red should have done it."

"Done what?" The Industrialist was more amused than otherwise. It had taken the united efforts of himself and his son months to argue his wife into using the name "Red" rather than the perfectly ridiculous (viewed youngster-fashion) name which was his real one.

She said, "He's taken most of the chopped meat."

"He's eaten it?"

"Well, I hope not. It was raw."

"Then what would he want it for?"

"I haven't the slightest idea. I haven't seen him since breakfast. Meanwhile Cook's just furious. She caught him vanishing out the kitchen door and there was the bowl of chopped meat just about empty and she was going to use it for lunch. Well, you know Cook. She had to change the lunch menu and that means she won't be worth living with for a week. You'll just have to speak to Red, dear, and make him promise not to do things in the kitchen any more. And it wouldn't hurt to have him apologize to Cook.''

"Oh, come. She works for us. If we don't complain about a change in lunch menu, why should she?"

"Because she's the one who has double work made for her, and she's talking about quitting. Good cooks aren't easy to get. Do you remember the one before her?"

It was a strong argument.

The Industrialist looked about vaguely. He said, "I suppose you're right. He isn't here, I suppose. When he comes in, I'll talk to him."

"You'd better start. Here he comes."

Red walked into the house and said cheerfully, "Time for lunch, I guess." He looked from one parent to the other in quick speculation at their fixed stares and said, "Got to clean up first, though," and made for the other door.

The Industrialist said, "One moment, son."

"Sir?"

"Where's your little friend?"

Red said carelessly, "He's around somewhere. We were just sort of walking and I looked around and he wasn't there." This was perfectly true, and Red felt on safe ground. "I told him it was lunch time. I said, 'I suppose it's about lunch time.' I said, 'We got to be getting back to the house.' And he said, 'Yes.' And I just went on, and then when I was about at the creek, I looked around and——''

The Astronomer interrupted the voluble story, looking up from a magazine he had been sightlessly rummaging through. "I wouldn't worry about my youngster. He is quite self-reliant. Don't wait lunch for him."

"Lunch isn't ready in any case, Doctor." The Industrialist turned once more to his son. "And talking about that, son, the reason for it is that something happened to the ingredients. Do you have anything to say?"

"Sir?"

"I hate to feel that I have to explain myself more fully. Why did you take the chopped meat?"

"The chopped meat?"

"The chopped meat." He waited patiently.

Red said, "Well, I was sort of——''

"Hungry?" prompted his father. "For raw meat?"

"No, sir. I just sort of needed it."

"For what exactly?"

Red looked miserable and remained silent.

The Astronomer broke in again. "If you don't mind my putting in a few words—you'll remember that just after breakfast, my son came in to ask what animals ate."

"Oh, you're right. How stupid of me to forget. Look here, Red, did you take it for an animal pet you've got?"

Red recovered indignant breath. He said, "You mean Slim came in here and said I had an animal? He came in here and said that? He said I had an animal?"

"No, he didn't. He simply asked what animals ate. That's all. Now if he promised he wouldn't tell on you, he didn't. It's your own foolishness in trying to take something without permission that gave you away. That happened to be stealing. Now have you an animal? I ask you a direct question."

"Yes, sir." It was a whisper so low as hardly to be heard.

"All right, you'll have to get rid of it. Do you understand?"

Red's mother intervened. "Do you mean to say you're keeping a meat-eating animal, Red? It might bite you and give you blood poison."

"They're only small ones," quavered Red. "They hardly budge if you touch them."

"They? How many do you have?"

"Two."

"Where are they?"

The Industrialist touched her arm. "Don't chivvy the child any further," he said in a low voice. "If he says he'll get rid of them, he will, and that's punishment enough."

He dismissed the matter from his mind.

— 8 —

LUNCH WAS half over when Slim dashed into the dining room. For a moment, he stood abashed, and then he said in what was almost hysteria, "I've got to speak to Red. I've got to say something."

Red looked up in fright, but the Astronomer said, "I don't think, son, you're being very polite. You've kept lunch waiting."

"I'm sorry, Father."

"Oh, don't rate the lad," said the Industrialist's wife. "He can speak to Red if he wants to, and there was no damage done to the lunch."

"I've got to speak to Red alone," Slim insisted.

"Now that's enough," said the Astronomer with a kind of gentleness that was obviously manufactured for the benefit of strangers and which had beneath it an easily recognized edge. "Take your seat."

Slim did so, but he ate only when someone looked directly upon him. Even then he was not very successful.

Red caught his eyes. He made soundless words, "Did the animals get loose?"

Slim shook his head slightly. He whispered, "No, it's——"

The Astronomer looked at him hard and Slim faltered to a stop.

With lunch over, Red slipped out of the room, with a microscopic motion at Slim to follow.

They walked in silence to the creek.

Then Red turned fiercely upon his companion. "Look here, what's the idea of telling my dad we were feeding animals?"

Slim said, "I didn't. I asked what you feed animals. That's not the same as saying we were doing it. Besides, it's something else, Red."

But Red had not used up his grievances. "And where did you go, anyway? I thought you were coming to the house. They acted like it was my fault you weren't there."

"But I'm trying to tell you about that, if you'd only shut *up* a second and let me talk. You don't give a fellow a chance."

"Well, go on and tell me if you've got so much to say."

"I'm *trying* to. I went back to the spaceship. The folks weren't there any more and I wanted to see what it was like."

"It isn't a spaceship," said Red sullenly. He had nothing to lose.

"It is, too. I looked inside. You could look through the ports and I looked inside and they were *dead*." He looked sick. "They were dead."

"*Who* were dead?"

Slim screeched, "Animals! Like *our* animals! Only they *aren't* animals. They're people things from other planets."

For a moment, Red might have been turned to stone. It didn't occur to him to disbelieve Slim at this point. Slim looked too genuinely the bearer of just such tidings. He said finally, "Oh, my."

"Well, what are we going to do? Golly, will we get a whopping if they find out!" He was shivering.

"We better turn them loose," said Red.

"They'll tell on us."

"They can't talk our language. Not if they're from another planet."

"Yes, they can. Because I remember my father talking about some stuff like that to my mother when he didn't know I was in the room. He was talking about visitors who could talk with the mind. Telepathery or something. I thought he was making it up."

"Well, holy smokes. I mean—holy smokes." Red looked up. "I tell you. My dad said to get rid of them. Let's sort of bury them somewhere or throw them in the creek."

"He *told* you to do that?"

"He made me say I had animals and then he said, 'Get rid of them.' I got to do what he says. Holy smokes, he's my dad."

Some of the panic left Slim's heart. It was a thoroughly legalistic way out. "Well, let's do it right now then, before they find out. Oh, golly, if they find out, will we be in trouble!"

They broke into a run toward the barn, unspeakable visions in their minds.

— 9 —

IT WAS different, looking at them as though they were "people." As animals, they had been interesting; as "people," horrible. Their eyes, which were neutral little objects before, now seemed to watch them with active malevolence.

"They're making noises," said Slim in a whisper.

"I guess they're talking or something," said Red. Funny that those noises which they had heard before had not had significance earlier. He was making no move toward them. Neither was Slim.

The canvas was off but they were just watching. The ground meat, Slim noticed, hadn't been touched.

Slim said, "Aren't you going to do something?"

"Aren't you?"

"You found them."

"It's your turn now."

"No, it isn't. You found them. It's your fault, the whole thing. I was just watching."

"You joined in, Slim. You know you did."

"I don't care. You found them and that's what I'll say when they come here looking for us."

Red said, "All right for you." But the thought of the consequences inspired him anyway, and he reached for the cage door.

Slim said, "Wait!"

Red was glad to. He said, "Now what's biting you?"

"One of them's got something on him that looks like it might be iron or something."

"Where?"

"Right there. I saw it before but I thought it was just part of him. But if he's 'people,' maybe it's a disintegrator gun."

"What's that?"

"I read about it in the books from Beforethewars. Mostly people with spaceships have disintegrator guns. They point them at you and you get disintegratored."

"They didn't point it at us till now," pointed out Red with his heart not quite in it.

"I don't care. I'm not hanging around here and getting disintegratored. I'm getting my father."

"Cowardy-cat. Yellow cowardy-cat."

"I don't care. You can call all the names you want, but if you bother them now, you'll get disintegratored. You wait and see, and it'll be all your fault."

He made for the narrow spiral stairs that led to the main floor of the barn, stopped at its head, then backed away.

Red's mother was moving up, panting a little with the exertion and smiling a tight smile for the benefit of Slim in his capacity as guest.

"Red! You, Red! Are you up there? Now don't try to hide. I know this is where you're keeping them. Cook saw where you ran with the meat."

Red quavered, "Hello, Ma!"

"Now show me those nasty animals. I'm going to see to it that you get rid of them right away."

It was over! And despite the imminent corporal punishment, Red felt something like a load fall from him. At least the decision was out of his hands.

"Right there, Ma. I didn't do anything to them, Ma. I didn't know. They just looked like little animals and I thought you'd let me keep them, Ma. I wouldn't have taken the meat only they wouldn't eat grass or leaves and we couldn't find good nuts or berries and Cook never lets me have anything or I would have asked her and I didn't know it was for lunch and——"

He was speaking on the sheer momentum of terror and did not realize that his mother did not hear him but, with eyes frozen and popping at the cage, was screaming in thin, piercing tones.

THE ASTRONOMER was saying, "A quiet burial is all we can do. There is no point in any publicity now," when they heard the screams.

She had not entirely recovered by the time she reached them, running and running. It was minutes before her husband could extract sense from her.

She was saying finally, "I tell you they're in the barn. I don't know what they are. No, no——"

She barred the Industrialist's quick movement in that direction. She said, "Don't *you* go. Send one of the hands with a shotgun. I tell you I never saw anything like it. Little horrible beasts with—with—— I can't describe it. To think that Red was touching them and trying to feed them. He was *holding* them, and feeding them meat."

Red began, "I only——"

And Slim said, "It wasn't——"

The Industrialist said quickly, "Now you boys have done enough harm today. March! Into the house! And not a word; not one word! I'm not interested in anything you have to say. After this is all over, I'll hear you out and as for you, Red, I'll see that you're properly punished."

He turned to his wife, "Now whatever the animals are, we'll have them killed." He added quietly once the youngsters were out of hearing, "Come, come. The children aren't hurt, and after all, they haven't done anything really terrible. They've just found a new pet."

The Astronomer spoke with difficulty. "Pardon me, ma'am, but can you describe these animals?"

She shook her head. She was quite beyond words.

"Can you just tell me if they——"

"I'm sorry," said the Industrialist apologetically, "but I think I had better take care of her. Will you excuse me?"

"A moment. Please. One moment. She said she had never seen such animals before. Surely it is not usual to find animals that are completely unique on an estate such as this."

"I'm sorry. Let's not discuss that now."

"Except that unique animals might have landed during the night."

The Industrialist stepped away from his wife. "What are you implying?"

"I think we had better go to the barn, sir!"

The Industrialist stared a moment, turned, and suddenly and quite uncharacteristically began running. The Astronomer followed and the woman's wail rose unheeded behind them.

THE INDUSTRIALIST stared, looked at the Astronomer, turned to stare again.

"Those?"

"Those," said the Astronomer. "I have no doubt we appear as strange and repulsive to them."

"What do they say?"

"Why, that they are uncomfortable and tired and even a little sick, but that they are not seriously damaged, and that the youngsters treated them well."

"Treated them well! Scooping them up, keeping them in a cage, giving them grass and raw meat to eat? Tell me how to speak to them."

"It may take a little time. Think *at* them. Try to listen. It will come to you, but perhaps not right away."

The Industrialist tried. He grimaced with the effort of it, thinking over and over again, The youngsters were ignorant of your identity.

And the thought was suddenly in his mind, We were quite aware of it and because we knew they meant well by us according to their own view of the matter, we did not attempt to attack them.

Attack them? thought the Industrialist, and said it aloud in his concentration.

Why, yes, came the answering thought. We are armed.

One of the revolting little creatures in the cage lifted a metal object and there was a sudden hole in the top of the cage and another in the roof of the barn, each hole rimmed with charred wood.

We hope, the creatures thought, it will not be too difficult to make repairs.

The Industrialist found it impossible to organize himself to the point of directed thought. He turned to the Astronomer. "And with that weapon in their possession, they let themselves be handled and caged? I don't understand it."

But the calm thought came, We would not harm the young of an intelligent species.

— 12 —

IT WAS twilight. The Industrialist had entirely missed the evening meal and remained unaware of the fact.

He said, "Do you really think the ship will fly?"

"If they say so," said the Astronomer, "I'm sure it will. They'll be back, I hope, before too long."

"And when they do," said the Industrialist energetically, "I will keep my part of the agreement. What is more I will move sky and earth to have the world accept them. I was entirely wrong, Doctor. Creatures that would refuse to harm children under such provocation as they received are admirable. But you know— I almost hate to say this——"

"Say what?"

"The kids. Yours and mine. I'm almost proud of them. Imagine seizing these creatures, feeding them or trying to, and keeping them hidden. The amazing gall of it. Red told me it was his idea to get a job in a circus on the strength of them. Imagine!"

The Astronomer said, "Youth!"

— 13 —

THE MERCHANT said, "Will we be taking off soon?"

"Half an hour," said the Explorer.

It was going to be a lonely trip back. All the remaining seventeen of the crew were dead and their ashes were to be left on a strange planet. Back they would go with a limping ship and the burden of the controls entirely on himself.

The Merchant said, "It was a good business stroke, not harming the young ones. We will get very good terms; *very* good terms."

The Explorer thought, Business!

The Merchant said, "They've lined up to see us off. All of them. You don't think they're too close, do you? It would be bad to burn any of them with the rocket blast at this stage of the game."

"They're safe."

"Horrible-looking things, aren't they?"

"Pleasant enough, inside. Their thoughts are perfectly friendly."

"You wouldn't believe it of them. That immature one, the one that first picked us up——"

"They call him Red."

"That's a queer name for a monster. Makes me laugh. He actually feels *bad* that we're leaving. Only I can't make out exactly why. The nearest I can come to it is something about a lost opportunity with some organization or other that I can't quite interpret."

"A circus," said the Explorer briefly.

"What? Why, the impertinent monstrosity."

"Why not? What would you have done if you had found *him* wandering on *your* native world; found him sleeping on a field on Earth, red tentacles, six legs, pseudopods and all?"

— 14 —

RED WATCHED the ship leave. His red tentacles, which gave him his nickname, quivered their regret at lost opportunity to the very last, and the eyes at their tips filled with drifting yellowish crystals that were the equivalent of Earthly tears.

THE END
OF ETERNITY

A NOVEL

TECHNICIAN

— 1 —

ANDREW HARLAN stepped into the kettle. Its sides were perfectly round and it fit snugly inside a vertical shaft composed of widely spaced rods that shimmered into an unseeable haze six feet above Harlan's head. Harlan set the controls and moved the smoothly working starting lever.

The kettle did not move.

Harlan did not expect it to. He expected no movement; neither up nor down, left nor right, forth nor back. Yet the spaces between the rods had melted into a gray blankness which was solid to the touch, though nonetheless immaterial for all that. And there *was* the little stir in his stomach, the faint (psychosomatic?) touch of dizziness, that told him that all the kettle contained, including himself, was rushing upwhen through Eternity.

He had boarded the kettle in the 575th Century, the base of operations assigned him two years earlier. At the time the 575th had been the farthest upwhen he had ever traveled. Now he was moving upwhen to the 2456th Century.

Under ordinary circumstances he might have felt a little lost at the prospect. His native Century was in the far downwhen, the 95th Century, to be exact. The 95th was a Century stiffly restrictive of atomic power, faintly rustic, fond of natural wood as a structural material, exporters of certain types of distilled potables to nearly everywhen and importers of clover seed. Although Harlan had not been in the 95th since he entered special training and became a Cub at the age of fifteen, there was always that feeling of loss when one moved outwhen from "home." At the 2456th he would be nearly two hundred forty millennia from his birthwhen and that is a sizable distance even for a hardened Eternal.

Under ordinary circumstances all this would be so.

But right now Harlan was in poor mood to think of anything but the fact that his documents were heavy in his pocket and tense, a little confused.

It was his hands acting by themselves that brought the kettle to the proper halt at the proper Century.

Strange that a Technician should feel tense or nervous about anything. What was it that Educator Yarrow had once said:

"Above all, a Technician must be dispassionate. The Reality Change he initiates may affect the lives of as many as fifty billion people. A million or more of these may be so drastically affected as to be considered new individuals. Under these conditions, an emotional make-up is a distinct handicap.''

Harlan put the memory of his teacher's dry voice out of his mind with an almost savage shake of his head. In those days he had never imagined that he himself would have the peculiar talent for that very position. But emotion had come upon him after all. Not for fifty billion people. What in Time did he care for fifty billion people? There was just one. One person.

He became aware that the kettle was stationary and with the merest pause to pull his thoughts together, put himself into the cold, impersonal frame of mind a Technician must have, he stepped out. The kettle he left, of course, was not the same as the one he had boarded, in the sense that it was not composed of the same atoms. He did not worry about that any more than any Eternal would. To concern oneself with the *mystique* of Time-travel, rather than with the simple fact of it, was the mark of the Cub and newcomer to Eternity.

He paused again at the infinitely thin curtain of non-Space and non-Time which separated him from Eternity in one way and from ordinary Time in another.

This would be a completely new section of Eternity for him. He knew about it in a rough way, of course, having checked upon it in the *Temporal Handbook*. Still, there was no substitute for actual appearance and he steeled himself for the initial shock of adjustment.

He adjusted the controls, a simple matter in passing into Eternity (and a very complicated one in passing into Time, a type of passage which was correspondingly less frequent). He stepped through the curtain and found himself squinting at the brilliance. Automatically he threw up his hand to shield his eyes.

Only one man faced him. At first Harlan could see him only blurrily.

The man said, ''I am Sociologist Kantor Voy. I imagine you are Technician Harlan.''

Harlan nodded and said, ''Father Time! Isn't this sort of ornamentation adjustable?''

Voy looked about and said tolerantly, ''You mean the molecular films?''

''I certainly do,'' said Harlan. The *Handbook* had mentioned them, but had said nothing of *such* an insane riot of light reflection.

Harlan felt his annoyance to be quite reasonable. The 2456th Century was matter-oriented, as most Centuries were, so he had a right to expect a basic compatibility from the very beginning. It would have none of the utter confusion (for anyone born matter-oriented) of the energy vortices of the 300's, or the field dynamics of the 600's. In the 2456th, to the average Eternal's comfort, matter was used for everything from walls to tacks.

To be sure, there was matter and matter. A member of an energy-oriented Century might not realize that. To him all matter might seem minor variations on the theme that was gross, heavy, and barbaric. To matter-oriented Harlan, however, there was wood, metal (subdivisions, heavy and light), plastic, silicates, concrete, leather, and so on.

But matter consisting entirely of mirrors!

That was his first impression of the 2456th. Every surface reflected and glinted light. Everywhere was the illusion of complete smoothness; the effect of a molecular film. And in the ever-repeated reflection of himself, of Sociologist Voy, of everything he could see, in scraps and wholes, in all angles, there was confusion. Garish confusion and nausea!

"I'm sorry," said Voy, "it's the custom of the Century, and the Section assigned to it finds it good practice to adopt the customs where practical. You get used to it after a time."

Voy walked rapidly upon the moving feet of another Voy, upside down beneath the floor, who matched him stride for stride. He reached to move a hair-contact indicator down a spiral scale to point of origin.

The reflections died; extraneous light faded. Harlan felt his world settle.

"If you'll come with me now," said Voy.

Harlan followed through empty corridors that, Harlan knew, must moments ago have been a riot of made light and reflection, up a ramp, through an anteroom, into an office.

In all the short journey no human being had been visible. Harlan was so used to that, took it so for granted, that he would have been surprised, almost shocked, if a glimpse of a human figure hurrying away had caught his eyes. No doubt the news had spread that a Technician was coming through. Even Voy kept his distance and when, accidentally, Harlan's hand had brushed Voy's sleeve, Voy shrank away with a visible start.

Harlan was faintly surprised at the touch of bitterness he felt at this. He had thought the shell he had grown about his soul was thicker, more efficiently insensitive than that. If he was wrong, if his shell had worn thinner, there could only be one reason for that.

Noÿs!

Sociologist Kantor Voy leaned forward toward the Technician in what seemed a friendly enough fashion, but Harlan noted automatically that they were seated on opposite sides of the long axis of a fairly large table.

Voy said, "I am pleased to have a Technician of your reputation interest himself in our little problem here."

"Yes," said Harlan with the cold impersonality people would expect of him. "It has its points of interest." (Was he impersonal enough? Surely his real motives must be apparent, his guilt be spelled out in beads of sweat on his forehead.)

He removed from an inner pocket the foiled summary of the projected Reality Change. It was the very copy which had been sent to the Allwhen Council a month earlier. Through his relationship with Senior Computer Twissell (*the* Twissell, himself) Harlan had had little trouble in getting his hands on it.

Before unrolling the foil, letting it peel off onto the table top where it would be held by a soft paramagnetic field, Harlan paused a split moment.

The molecular film that covered the table was subdued but was not zero. The motion of his arm fixed his eye and for an instant the reflection of his own face seemed to stare somberly up at him from the table top. He was thirty-two, but he looked older. He needed no one to tell him that. It might be partly his long face and dark eyebrows over darker eyes that gave him the lowering expression and cold glare associated with the caricature of the Technician in the minds of all Eternals. It might be just his own realization that he was a Technician.

But then he flicked the foil out across the table and turned to the matter at hand.

"I am not a Sociologist, sir."

Voy smiled. "That sounds formidable. When one begins by expressing lack of competence in a given field, it usually implies that a flat opinion in that field will follow almost immediately.''

"No," said Harlan, "not an opinion. Just a request. I wonder if you won't look over this summary and see if you haven't made a small mistake somewhere here.''

Voy looked instantly grave. "I hope not," he said.

Harlan kept one arm across the back of his chair, the other in his lap. He must let neither hand drum restless fingers. He must not bite his lips. He must not show his feelings in any way.

Ever since the whole orientation of his life had so changed itself, he had been watching the summaries of projected Reality Changes as they passed through the grinding administrative gears of the Allwhen Council. As Senior Computer Twissell's personally assigned Technician, he could arrange that by a slight bending of professional ethics. Particularly with Twissell's attention caught ever more tightly in his own overwhelming project. (Harlan's nostrils flared. He knew *now* a little of the nature of that project.)

Harlan had had no assurance that he would ever find what he was looking for in a reasonable time. When he had first glanced over projected Reality Change 2456-2781, Serial Number V-5, he was half inclined to believe his reasoning powers were warped by wishing. For a full day he had checked and rechecked equations and relationships in a rattling uncertainty, mixed with growing excitement and a bitter gratitude that he had been taught at least elementary psychomathematics.

Now Voy went over those same puncture patterns with a half-puzzled, half-worried eye.

He said, "It seems to me; I say, it *seems* to me that this is all perfectly in order.''

Harlan said, "I refer you particularly to the matter of the courtship characteristics of the society of the current Reality of this Century. That's sociology and your responsibility, I believe. It's why I arranged to see *you* when I arrived, rather than someone else.''

Voy was now frowning. He was still polite, but with an icy touch now. He said, "The Observers assigned to our Section are highly competent. I have every certainty that those assigned to this project have given accurate data. Have you evidence to the contrary?''

"Not at all, Sociologist Voy. I accept their data. It is the development of the data I question. Do you not have an alternate tensor-complex at this point, if the courtship data is taken properly into consideration?''

Voy stared, and then a look of relief washed over him visibly. "Of course, Technician, of course, but it resolves itself into an identity. There is a loop of small dimensions with no tributaries on either side. I hope you'll forgive me for using picturesque language rather than precise mathematical expressions.''

"I appreciate it," said Harlan dryly. "I am no more a Computer than a Sociologist.''

"Very good, then. The alternate tensor-complex you refer to, or the forking of the road, as we might say, is nonsignificant. The forks join up again and it is a single road. There was not even any need to mention it in our recommendations.''

"If you say so, sir, I will defer to your better judgment. However, there is still the matter of the M.N.C.''

The Sociologist winced at the initials as Harlan knew he would. M.N.C.—Minimum Necessary Change. There the Technician was master. A Sociologist might consider himself above criticism by lesser beings in anything involving the mathematical analysis of the infinite possible Realities in Time, but in matters of M.N.C. the Technician stood supreme.

Mechanical computing would not do. The largest Computaplex ever built, manned by the cleverest and most experienced Senior Computer ever born, could do no better than to indicate the ranges in which the M.N.C. might be found. It was then the Technician, glancing over the data, who decided on an exact point within that range. A good Technician was rarely wrong. A top Technician was never wrong.

Harlan was never wrong.

"Now the M.N.C. recommended," said Harlan (he spoke coolly, evenly, pronouncing the Standard Intertemporal Language in precise syllables), "by your Section involves induction of an accident in space and the immediate death by fairly horrible means of a dozen or more men."

"Unavoidable," said Voy, shrugging.

"On the other hand," said Harlan, "I suggest that the M.N.C. can be reduced to the mere displacement of a container from one shelf to another. Here!" His long finger pointed. His white, well-cared-for index nail made the faintest mark along one set of perforations.

Voy considered matters with a painful but silent intensity.

Harlan said, "Doesn't that alter the situation with regard to your unconsidered fork? Doesn't it take advantage of the fork of lesser probability, changing it to a near-certainty, and does that not then lead to——"

"—to virtually the M.D.R." whispered Voy.

"To *exactly* the Maximum Desired Response," said Harlan.

Voy looked up, his dark face struggling somewhere between chagrin and anger. Harlan noted absently that there was a space between the man's large upper incisors which gave him a rabbity look quite at odds with the restrained force of his words.

Voy said, "I suppose I will be hearing from the Allwhen Council?"

"I don't think so. As far as I know, the Allwhen Council does not know of this. At least, the projected Reality Change was passed over to me without comment." He did not explain the word "passed," nor did Voy question it.

"*You* discovered this error, then?"

"Yes."

"And you did not report it to the Allwhen Council?"

"No, I did not."

Relief first, then a hardening of countenance. "Why not?"

"Very few people could have avoided this error. I felt I could correct it before damage was done. I have done so. Why go any further?"

"Well—thank you, Technician Harlan. You have been a friend. The Section's error which, as you say, was practically unavoidable, would have looked unjustifiably bad in the record."

He went on after a moment's pause. "Of course, in view of the alterations in personality to be induced by this Reality Change, the death of a few men as preliminary is of little importance."

Harlan thought, detachedly: He doesn't sound really grateful. He probably resents it. If he stops to think, he'll resent it even more, this being saved a downstroke in rating by a Technician. If I were a Sociologist, he would shake my hand, but he won't shake the hand of a Technician. He defends condemning a dozen people to asphyxiation, but he won't touch a Technician.

And because waiting to let resentment grow would be fatal, Harlan said without waiting, "I hope your gratitude will extend to having your Section perform a slight chore for me."

"A chore?"

"A matter of Life-Plotting. I have the data necessary here with me. I have also the data for a suggested Reality Change in the 482nd. I want to know the effect of the Change on the probability-pattern of a certain individual."

"I am not quite sure," said the Sociologist slowly, "that I understand you. Surely you have the facilities for doing this in your own Section?"

"I have. Nevertheless, what I am engaged in is a personal research which I don't wish to appear in the records just yet. It would be difficult to have this carried out in my own Section without——" He gestured an uncertain conclusion to the unfinished sentence.

Voy said, "Then you want this done *not* through official channels."

"I want it done confidentially. I want a confidential answer."

"Well, now, that's very irregular. I can't agree to it."

Harlan frowned. "No more irregular than my failure to report your error to the Allwhen Council. You raised no objection to that. If we're going to be strictly regular in one case, we must be as strict and as regular in the other. You follow me, I think?"

The look on Voy's face was proof positive of that. He held out his hand. "May I see the documents?"

Harlan relaxed a bit. The main hurdle had been passed. He watched eagerly as the Sociologist's head bent over the foils he had brought.

Only once did the Sociologist speak. "By Time, this is a small Reality Change."

Harlan seized his opportunity and improvised. "It is. Too small, I think. It's what the argument is about. It's below critical difference, and I've picked an individual as a test case. Naturally, it would be undiplomatic to use our own Section's facilities until I was certain of being right."

Voy was unresponsive and Harlan stopped. No use running this past the point of safety.

Voy stood up. "I'll pass this along to one of my Life-Plotters. We'll keep this private. You understand, though, that this is not to be taken as establishing a precedent."

"Of course not."

"And if you don't mind, I'd like to watch the Reality Change take place. I trust you will honor us by conducting the M.N.C. personally."

Harlan nodded. "I will take full responsibility."

Two of the screens in the viewing chamber were in operation when they entered. The engineers had focused them already to the exact co-ordinates in Space and Time and then had left. Harlan and Voy were alone in the glittering room. (The molecular film arrangement was perceptible and even a bit more than perceptible, but Harlan was looking at the screens.)

THE END OF ETERNITY

Both views were motionless. They might have been scenes of the dead, since they pictured mathematical instants of Time.

One view was in sharp, natural color; the engine room of what Harlan knew to be an experimental space-ship. A door was closing, and a glistening shoe of a red, semi-transparent material was just visible through the space that remained. It did not move. Nothing moved. If the picture could have been made sharp enough to picture the dust motes in the air, *they* would not have moved.

Voy said, "For two hours and thirty-six minutes after the viewed instant, that engine room will remain empty. In the current Reality, that is."

"I know," murmured Harlan. He was putting on his gloves and already his quick eyes were memorizing the position of the critical container on its shelf, measuring the steps to it, estimating the best position into which to transfer it. He cast one quick look at the other screen.

If the engine-room, being in the range described as "present" with respect to that Section of Eternity in which they now stood, was clear and in natural color, the other scene, being some twenty-five Centuries in the "future," carried the blue luster all views of the "future" must.

It was a space-port. A deep blue sky, blue-tinged buildings of naked metal on blue-green ground. A blue cylinder of odd design, bulge-bottomed, stood in the foreground. Two others like it were in the background. All three pointed cleft noses upward, the cleavage biting deeply into the vitals of the ship.

Harlan frowned. "They're queer ones."

"Electro-gravitic," said Voy. "The 2481st is the only Century to develop electro-gravitic space-travel. No propellants, no nucleonics. It's an aesthetically pleasing device. It's a pity we must Change away from it. A pity." His eyes fixed themselves on Harlan with distinct disapproval.

Harlan's lips compressed. Disapproval of course! Why not? He was the Technician.

To be sure, it had been some Observer who had brought in the details of drug addiction. It had been some Statistician who had demonstrated that recent Changes had increased the addiction rate until now it was the highest in all the current Reality of man. Some Sociologist, probably Voy himself, had interpreted that into the psychiatric profile of a society. Finally, some Computer had worked out the Reality Change necessary to decrease addiction to a safe level and found that, as a side effect, electro-gravitic space-travel must suffer. A dozen, a hundred men of every rating in Eternity had had a hand in this.

But then, at the end, a Technician such as himself must step in. Following the directions all the others had combined to give him, he must be the one to initiate the actual Reality Change. And then, all the others would stare in haughty accusation at him. Their stares would say: *You,* not we, have destroyed this beautiful thing.

And for that, they would condemn and avoid him. They would shift their own guilt to his shoulders and scorn him.

Harlan said harshly, "Ships aren't what count. We're concerned with those things."

The "things" were people, dwarfed by the space-ship, as Earth and Earth's society is always dwarfed by the physical dimensions of space-flight.

They were little puppets in clusters, these people. Their tiny arms and legs were in raised, artificial-looking positions, caught in the frozen instant of Time.

Voy shrugged.

Harlan was adjusting the small field-generator about his left wrist. "Let's get this job done."

"One minute. I want to get in touch with the Life-Plotter and find out how long his job for you will take. I want to get that job done, too."

His hands worked cleverly at a little movable contact and his ear listened astutely to the pattern of clicks that came back. (Another characteristic of this Section of Eternity, thought Harlan—sound codes in clicks. Clever, but affected, like the molecular films.)

"He says it won't take more than three hours," said Voy at length. "Also, by the way, he admires the name of the person involved. Noÿs Lambent. It is a female, isn't it?"

There was a dryness in Harlan's throat. "Yes."

Voy's lips curled into a slow smile. "Sounds interesting. I'd like to meet her, sight unseen. Haven't had any women in this Section for months."

Harlan didn't trust himself to answer. He stared a moment at the Sociologist and turned abruptly.

If there was a flaw in Eternity, it involved women. He had known the flaw for what it was from almost his first entrance into Eternity, but he felt it personally only that day he had first met Noÿs. From that moment it had been an easy path to this one, in which he stood false to his oath as an Eternal and to everything in which he had believed.

For what?

For Noÿs.

And he was not ashamed. It was that which really rocked him. He was not ashamed. He felt no guilt for the crescendo of crimes he had committed, to which this latest addition of the unethical use of confidential Life-Plotting could rank only as a peccadillo.

He would do worse than his worst if he had to.

For the first time the specific and express thought came to him. And though he pushed it away in horror, he knew that, having once come, it would return.

The thought was simply this: That he would ruin Eternity, if he had to.

The worst of it was that he knew he had the power to do it.

OBSERVER

— 2 —

HARLAN STOOD at the gateway to Time and thought of himself in new ways. It had been very simple once. There were such things as ideals, or at least catchwords, to live by and for. Every stage of an Eternal's life had a reason. How did "Basic Principles" start?

"The life of an Eternal may be divided into four parts . . ."

It all worked out neatly, yet it had all changed for him, and what was broken could not be made whole again.

Yet he had gone faithfully through each of the four parts of an Eternal's life. First, there was the period of fifteen years in which he was not an Eternal at all, but only an inhabitant of Time. Only a human being out of Time, a Timer, could become an Eternal; no one could be born into the position.

At the age of fifteen he was chosen by a careful process of elimination and winnowing, the nature of which he had no conception of at the time. He was taken beyond the veil of Eternity after a last agonized farewell to his family. (Even then it was made clear to him that whatever else happened he would not return. The true reason for that he was not to learn till long afterward.)

Once within Eternity, he spent ten years in school as a Cub, and then graduated to enter his third period as Observer. It was only after that that he became a Specialist and a true Eternal. The fourth and last part of the Eternal's life: Timer, Cub, Observer and Specialist.

He, Harlan, had gone through it all so neatly. He might say, successfully.

He could remember, so clearly, the moment that Cubhood was done, the moment they became independent members of Eternity, the moment when, even though un-Specialized, they still rated the legal title of "Eternal."

He could remember it. School done, Cubhood over, he was standing with the five who completed training with him, hands clasped in the small of his back, legs a trifle apart, eyes front, listening.

Educator Yarrow was at a desk talking to them. Harlan could remember Yarrow well: a small, intense man, with ruddy hair in disarray, freckled forearms, and a look of loss in his eyes. (It wasn't uncommon, this look of loss in the eyes of an Eternal—the loss of home and roots, the unadmitted and unadmittable longing for the one Century he could never see.)

Harlan could not remember Yarrow's exact words, of course, but the substance of it remained sharp.

Yarrow said, in substance, "You will be Observers now. It isn't a highly regarded position. Specialists look upon it as a boy's job. Maybe you Eternals" (he deliberately paused after that word to give each man a chance to straighten his back and brighten at the glory of it) "think so too. If so, you are fools who don't deserve to be Observers.

"The Computers would have no Computing to do, Life-Plotters no lives to Plot, Sociologists no societies to profile; none of the Specialists would have anything to do, if it weren't for the Observer. I know you've heard this said before, but I want you to be very firm and clear in your mind about it.

"It will be you youngsters who will go out into Time, under the most strenuous conditions, to bring back facts. Cold, objective facts uncolored by your own opinions and likings, you understand. Facts accurate enough to be fed into Computing machines. Facts definite enough to make the social equations stand up. Facts honest enough to form a basis for Reality Changes.

"And remember this, too. Your period as Observer is not something to get through with as quickly and as unobtrusively as possible. It is as an Observer that you will make your mark. Not what you did in school, but what you will do as an Observer will determine your Specialty and how high you will rise in it. This will be your post-graduate course, Eternals, and failure in it, even small failure, will put you into Maintenance no matter how brilliant your potentialities now seem. That is all."

He shook hands with each of them, and Harlan, grave, dedicated, proud in his belief that the privileges of being an Eternal contained its greatest privilege in the assumption of responsibility for the happiness of all the human beings who were or ever would be within the reach of Eternity, was deep in self-awe.

Harlan's first assignments were small and under close direction, but he sharpened his ability on the honing strap of experience in a dozen Centuries through a dozen Reality Changes.

In his fifth year as Observer he was given a Senior's rating in the field and assigned to the 482nd. For the first time he would be working unsupervised, and knowledge of that fact robbed him of some of his self-assurance when he first reported to the Computer in charge of the Section.

That was Assistant Computer Hobbe Finge, whose pursed, suspicious mouth and frowning eyes seemed ludicrous in such a face as his. He had a round button of a nose, two larger buttons of cheeks. He needed only a touch of red and a fringe of white hair to be converted into the picture of the Primitive myth of St. Nicholas.

(—or Santa Claus or Kriss Kringle. Harlan knew all three names. He doubted if one Eternal out of a hundred thousand had heard of any one of them. Harlan took a secret, shamefaced pride in this sort of arcane knowledge. From his earliest days in school he had ridden the hobbyhorse of Primitive history, and Educator Yarrow had encouraged it. Harlan had grown actually fond of those odd, perverted Centuries that lay, not only before the beginning of Eternity in the 27th, but even before the invention of the Temporal Field, itself, in the 24th. He had used old books and periodicals in his studies. He had even traveled far downwhen to the earliest Centuries of Eternity, when he could get permission, to consult better sources. For over fifteen years he had managed to collect a remarkable library of his own, almost all in print-on-paper. There was a volume by a man called H. G. Wells, another by a man named W. Shakespeare, some tattered histories. Best of all there was a complete set of bound volumes of a Primitive news weekly that took up inordinate space but that he could not, out of sentiment, bear to reduce to micro-film.

Occasionally he would lose himself in a world where life was life and death, death; where a man made his decisions irrevocably; where evil could not be prevented, nor good promoted, and the Battle of Waterloo, having been lost, was really lost for good and all. There was even a scrap of poetry he treasured which stated that a moving finger having once written could never be lured back to unwrite.

And then it was difficult, almost a shock, to return his thoughts to Eternity, and to a universe where Reality was something flexible and evanescent, something men such as himself could hold in the palms of their hands and shake into better shape.)

The illusion of St. Nicholas shattered when Hobbe Finge spoke to him in a brisk, matter-of-fact way. "You can start in tomorrow with a routine screening of current Reality. I want it good, thorough, and to the point. There will be no slackness permitted. Your first spatio-temporal chart will be ready for you tomorrow morning. Got it?"

"Yes, Computer," said Harlan. He decided as early as that that he and Assistant Computer Hobbe Finge would not get along, and he regretted it.

The next morning Harlan got his chart in intricately punched patterns as they emerged from the Computaplex. He used a pocket decoder to translate them into Standard Intertemporal in his anxiety to make not even the smallest mistake at the very beginning. Of course, he had reached the stage where he could read the perforations direct.

The chart told him where and when in the world of the 482nd Century he might go and where he might not; what he could do and what he could not; what he must avoid at all costs. His presence must impinge only upon those places and times where it would not endanger Reality.

The 482nd was not a comfortable Century for him. It was not like his own austere and conformist homewhen. It was an era without ethics or principles, as he was accustomed to think of such. It was hedonistic, materialistic, more than a little matriarchal. It was the only era (he checked this in the records in the most painstaking way) in which ectogenic birth flourished and, at its peak, 40 per cent of its women gave eventual birth by merely contributing a fertilized ovum to the ovaria. Marriage was made and unmade by mutual consent and was not recognized legally as anything more than a personal agreement without binding force. Union for the sake of childbearing was, of course, carefully differentiated from the social functions of marriage and was arranged on purely eugenic principles.

In a hundred ways Harlan thought the society sick and therefore hungered for a Reality Change. More than once it occurred to him that his own presence in the Century, as a man not of that time, could fork its history. If his disturbing presence could only be made disturbing enough at some key point, a different branch of possibility would become real, a branch in which millions of pleasure-seeking women would find themselves transformed into true, pure-hearted mothers. They would be in another Reality with all the memories that belonged with it, unable to tell, dream, or fancy that they had ever been anything else.

Unfortunately, to do that, he would have to step outside the bounds of the spatio-temporal chart and that was unthinkable. Even if it weren't, to step outside the bounds at random could change Reality in many possible ways. It could be made worse. Only careful analysis and Computing could properly pin-point the nature of a Reality change.

Outwardly, whatever his private opinions, Harlan remained an Observer, and the ideal Observer was merely a set of sense-perceptive nerve patches attached to a report-writing mechanism. Between perception and report there must be no intervention of emotion.

Harlan's reports were perfection itself in that respect.

Assistant Computer Finge called him in after his second weekly report.

"I congratulate you, Observer," he said in a voice without warmth, "on the organization and clarity of your reports. But what do you really think?"

Harlan sought refuge in an expression as blank as though chipped painstakingly out of native 95th Century wood. He said, "I have no thoughts of my own in the matter."

"Oh, come. You're from the 95th and we both know what that means. Surely this Century disturbs you."

Harlan shrugged. "Does anything in my reports lead you to think that I am disturbed?"

It was near to impudence and the drumming of Finge's blunt nails upon his desk showed it. Finge said, "Answer my question."

Harlan said, "Sociologically, many facets of the Century represent an extreme. The last three Reality Changes in the aboutwhen have accentuated that. Eventually, I suppose the matter should be rectified. Extremes are never healthy.''

"Then you took the trouble to check the past Realities of the Century."

"As an Observer, I must check all pertinent facts."

It was a standoff. Harlan, of course, did have the right and the duty to check those facts. Finge must know that. Every Century was continually being shaken by Reality Changes. No Observations, however painstaking, could ever stand for long without rechecking. It was standard procedure in Eternity to have every Century in a chronic state of being Observed. And to Observe properly, you must be able to present, not only the facts of the current Reality, but also of their relationship to those of previous Realities.

Yet it seemed obvious to Harlan that this was not merely unpleasantness on Finge's part, this probing of the Observer's opinions. Finge seemed definitely hostile.

At another time Finge said to Harlan (having invaded the latter's small office to bring the news), "Your reports are creating a very favorable impression with the Allwhen Council."

Harlan paused, uncertain, then mumbled, "Thank you."

"All agree that you show an uncommon degree of penetration."

"I do my best."

Finge asked suddenly, "Have you ever met Senior Computer Twissell?"

"Computer Twissell?" Harlan's eyes widened. "No, sir. Why do you ask?"

"He seems particularly interested in your reports." Finge's round cheeks drew downward sulkily and he changed the subject. "To me it seems that you have worked out a philosophy of your own, a viewpoint of history."

Temptation tugged hard at Harlan. Vanity and caution battled and the former won. "I've studied Primitive history, sir."

"*Primitive* history? At school?"

"Not exactly, Computer. On my own. It's my—hobby. It's like watching history standing still, frozen! It can be studied in detail whereas the Centuries of Eternity are always changing." He warmed up a trifle at the thought of it. "It's as though we were to take a series of stills from a book-film and study each painstakingly. We would see a great deal we would miss if we just scanned the film as it went past. I think that helps me a great deal with my work."

Finge stared at him in amazement, widened his eyes a little, and left with no further remark.

Occasionally, thereafter, he brought up the subject of Primitive history and accepted Harlan's reluctant comments with no decisive expression on his own plump face.

Harlan was not sure whether to regret the whole matter or to regard it as a possible way of speeding his own advancement.

He decided on the first alternative when, passing him one day in Corridor A, Finge said abruptly and in the hearing of others, "Great Time, Harlan, don't you *ever* smile?"

The thought came, shockingly, to Harlan that Finge hated him. His own feeling for Finge approached something like detestation thereafter.

Three months of raking through the 482nd had exhausted most of its worth-while meat and when Harlan received a sudden call to Finge's office, he was not surprised. He was expecting a change in assignment. His final summary had been prepared days before. The 482nd was anxious to export more cellulose-base textiles to Centuries which were deforested, such as the 1174th, but were unwilling to accept smoked fish in return. A long list of such items was contained in due order and with due analysis.

He took the draft of the summary with him.

But no mention of the 482nd was made. Instead Finge introduced him to a withered and wrinkled little man, with sparse white hair and a gnomelike face that throughout the interview was stamped with a perpetual smile. It varied between extremes of anxiety and joviality but never quite disappeared. Between two of his yellow-stained fingers lay a burning cigarette.

It was the first cigarette Harlan had ever seen, otherwise he would have paid more attention to the man, less to the smoking cylinder, and been better prepared for Finge's introduction.

Finge said, "Senior Computer Twissell, this is Observer Andrew Harlan."

Harlan's eyes shifted in shock from the little man's cigarette to his face.

Senior Computer Twissell said in a high-pitched voice, "How do you do? So this is the young man who writes those excellent reports?"

Harlan found no voice. Laban Twissell was a legend, a living myth. Laban Twissell was a man he should have recognized at once. He was the outstanding Computer in Eternity, which was another way of saying he was the most eminent Eternal alive. He was the dean of the Allwhen Council. He had directed more Reality Changes than any man in the history of Eternity. He was——He had——

Harlan's mind failed him altogether. He nodded his head with a doltish grin and said nothing.

Twissell put his cigarette to his lips, puffed quickly, and took it away. "Leave us, Finge. I want to talk to the boy."

Finge rose, murmured something, and left.

Twissell said, "You seem nervous, boy. There is nothing to be nervous about."

But meeting Twissell like that was a shock. It is always disconcerting to find that someone you have thought of as a giant is actually less than five and a half feet tall. Could the brain of a genius actually fit behind the retreating, bald-smooth forehead? Was it sharp intelligence or only good humor that beamed out of the little eyes that screwed up into a thousand wrinkles.

Harlan didn't know what to think. The cigarette seemed to obscure what small scrabble of intelligence he could collect. He flinched visibly as a puff of smoke reached him.

Twissell's eyes narrowed as though he were trying to peer through the smoke haze and he said in horribly accented tenth-millenial dialect, "Will you petter feel if I in your yourself dialect should speech, poy?"

Harlan, brought to the sudden brink of hysterical laughter, said carefully, "I speak Standard Intertemporal quite well, sir." He said it in the Intertemporal he and all other Eternals in his presence had used ever since his first months in Eternity.

"Nonsense," said Twissell imperiously. "I do not bother of Intertemporal. My speech of ten-millenial is over than perfect."

Harlan guessed that it had been some forty years since Twissell had had to make use of localwhen dialects.

But having made his point to his own satisfaction, apparently, he shifted to
Intertemporal and remained there. He said, "I would offer you a cigarette, but
I am certain you don't smoke. Smoking is approved of hardly anywhen in
history. In fact, good cigarettes are made only in the 72nd and mine have to be
specially imported from there. I give you that hint in case you ever become a
smoker. It is all very sad. Last week, I was stuck in the 123rd for two days. No
smoking. I mean, even in the Section of Eternity devoted to the 123rd. The
Eternals there have picked up the *mores*. If I lit a cigarette it would have been like
the sky collapsing. Sometimes I think I should like to calculate one great Reality
Change and wipe out all the no-smoking taboos in all the Centuries, except that
any Reality Change like that would make for wars in the 58th or a slave society
in the 1000th. Always something."

Harlan was first confused, then anxious. Surely these rattling irrelevancies
must be hiding something.

His throat felt a little constricted. He said, "May I ask why you've arranged
to see me, sir?"

"I like your reports, boy."

There was a veiled glimmer of joy in Harlan's eyes, but he did not smile.
"Thank you, sir."

"It has a touch of the artist. You are intuitive. You feel strongly. I think I
know your proper position in Eternity and I have come to offer it to you."

Harlan thought: I can't believe this.

He held all triumph out of his voice. "You do me great honor, sir," he said.

Whereupon Senior Computer Twissell, having come to the end of his
cigarette, produced another in his left hand by some unnoted feat of legerdemain
and lit it. He said between puffs, "For Time's sake, boy, you talk as though you
rehearsed lines. Great honor, bah. Piffle. Trash. Say what you feel in plain
language. You're glad, hey?"

"Yes, sir," said Harlan cautiously.

"All right. You should be. How would you like to be a Technician?"

"A Technician!" cried Harlan, leaping from his seat.

"Sit down. Sit down. You seem surprised."

"I hadn't expected to be a Technician, Computer Twissell."

"No," said Twissell dryly, "somehow no one ever does. They expect
anything but that. Yet Technicians are hard to find, and are always in demand.
Not a Section in Eternity has what it considers enough."

"I don't think I'm suited."

"You mean you're not suited to take a job with trouble in it. By Time, if you
are devoted to Eternity, as I believe you are, you won't mind that. So the fools
will avoid you and you will feel ostracized. You will grow used to that. And you
will have the satisfaction of knowing you are needed, and needed badly. By
me."

"By you, sir? By you particularly?"

"Yes." An element of shrewdness entered the old man's smile. "You are not
to be just a Technician. You will be my personal Technician. You will have
special status. How does that sound now?"

Harlan said, "I don't know, sir. I may not qualify."

Twissell shook his head firmly. "I need you. I need just you. Your reports
assure me you have what I need up here." He tapped his forehead quickly with

a ridge-nailed forefinger. "Your record as Cub is good; the Sections for which you have Observed reported favorably. Finally, Finge's report was most suitable of all."

Harlan was honestly startled. "Computer Finge's report was favorable?"

"You didn't expect that?"

"I—don't know."

"Well, boy, I didn't say it was favorable. I said it was suitable. As a matter of fact, Finge's report was *not* favorable. He recommended that you be removed from all duties connected with Reality Changes. He suggested it wasn't safe to keep you anywhere but in Maintenance."

Harlan reddened. "What were his reasons for saying so, sir?"

"It seems you have a hobby, boy. You are interested in Primitive history, eh?" He gestured expansively with his cigarette and Harlan, forgetting in his anger to control his breathing, inhaled a cloud of smoke and coughed helplessly.

Twissell regarded the young Observer's coughing spell benignly and said, "Isn't that so?"

Harlan began, "Computer Finge had no right——"

"Now, now. I told you what was in the report because it hinges on the purpose I need you most for. Actually, the report was confidential and you are to forget I told you what was in it. Permanently, boy."

"But what's wrong with being interested in Primitive history?"

"Finge thinks your interest in it shows a strong Wish-to-Time. You understand me, boy?"

Harlan did. It was impossible to avoid picking up psychiatric lingo. That phrase above all. Every member of Eternity was supposed to have a strong drive, the stronger for being officially suppressed in all its manifestations, to return, not necessarily to his own Time, but at least to some one definite Time; to become part of a Century, rather than to remain a wanderer through them all. Of course in most Eternals the drive remained safely hidden in the unconscious.

"I don't think that's the case," said Harlan.

"Nor I. In fact, I think your hobby is interesting and valuable. As I said, it's why I want you. I want you to teach a Cub I shall bring to you all you know and all you can learn about Primitive history. In between, you will also be my personal Technician. You'll start in a few days. Is that agreeable?"

Agreeable? To have official permission to learn all he could about the days before Eternity? To be personally associated with the greatest Eternal of them all? Even the nasty fact of Technician's status seemed bearable under those conditions.

His caution, however, did not entirely fail him. He said, "If it's necessary for the good of Eternity, sir——"

"For the *good* of Eternity?" cried the gnomish Computer in sudden excitement. He threw his cigarette butt from him with such energy that it hit the far wall and bounced off in a shower of sparks. "I need you for the *existence* of Eternity."

CUB

— 3 —

HARLAN HAD been in the 575th for weeks before he met Brinsley Sheridan Cooper. He had time to grow used to his new quarters and to the antisepsis of glass and porcelain. He learned to wear the Technician's mark with only moderate shrinking and to refrain from making things worse by standing so that the insigne was hidden against a wall or was covered by the interposition of some object he was carrying.

Others smiled disdainfully when that was done and turned colder as though they suspected an attempt to invade their friendship on false pretenses.

Senior Computer Twissell brought him problems daily. Harlan studied them and wrote his analyses in drafts that were four times rewritten, the last version being handed in reluctantly even so.

Twissell would appraise them and nod and say, "Good, good." Then his cold blue eyes would dart quickly at Harlan and his smile would narrow a bit as he said, "I'll test this guess on the Computaplex."

He always called the analysis a "guess." He never told Harlan the result of the Computaplex check, and Harlan dared not ask. He was despondent over the fact that he was never asked to put any of his own analyses into action. Did that mean that the Computaplex was *not* checking him, that he had been choosing the wrong item for the induction of a Reality Change, that he did not have the knack of seeing the Minimum Necessary Change in an indicated range? (It was not until later that he grew sufficiently sophisticated to have the phrase come rolling off his tongue as M.N.C.)

One day Twissell came in with an abashed individual who seemed scarcely to dare raise his eyes to meet Harlan's.

Twissell said, "Technician Harlan, this is Cub B. S. Cooper."

Automatically Harlan said, "Hello," weighed the man's appearance, and was unimpressed. The fellow was on the shortish side, with dark hair parted in the middle. His chin was narrow, his eyes an indefinite light brown, his ears a little large, and his fingernails bitten.

Twissell said, "This is the boy to whom you will be teaching Primitive history."

"Great Time," said Harlan with suddenly increased interest. *"Hello!"* He had almost forgotten.

Twissell said, "Arrange a schedule with him that will suit you, Harlan. If you can manage two afternoons a week, I think that would be fine. Use your own method of teaching him. I'll leave that to you. If you should need book-films or old documents, tell me, and if they exist in Eternity or in any part of Time that can be reached, we'll get them. Eh, boy?"

He plucked a lit cigarette out of nowhere (as it always seemed) and the air reeked with smoke. Harlan coughed and from the twisting of the Cub's mouth it was quite obvious that the latter would have done the same had he dared.

After Twissell left, Harlan said, "Well, sit down"—he hesitated a moment, then added determinedly—"Son. Sit down, son. My office isn't much, but it's yours whenever we're together."

Harlan was almost flooded with eagerness. This project was *his!* Primitive history was something that was all his own.

The Cub raised his eyes (for the first time, really) and said stumblingly, "You *are* a Technician."

A considerable part of Harlan's excitement and warmth died. "What of it?"

"Nothing," said the Cub. "I just——"

"You heard Computer Twissell address me as Technician, didn't you?"

"Yes, sir."

"Did you think it was a slip of the tongue? Something too bad to be true?"

"No, sir."

"What's wrong with your speech?" Harlan asked brutally, and even as he did so, he felt shame nudge him.

Cooper blushed painfully. "I'm not very good at Standard Intertemporal."

"Why not? How long have you been a Cub?"

"Less than one year, sir."

"One year? How old are you, for Time's sake?"

"Twenty-four physioyears, sir."

Harlan stared. "Are you trying to tell me that they took you into Eternity at twenty-three?"

"Yes, sir."

Harlan sat down and rubbed his hands together. That just wasn't done. Fifteen to sixteen was the age of entrance into Eternity. What was this? A new kind of testing of himself on the part of Twissell?

He said, "Sit down and let's get started. Your name in full and your homewhen."

The Cub stammered, "Brinsley Sheridan Cooper of the 78th, sir."

Harlan almost softened. That was close. It was only seventeen Centuries downwhen from his own homewhen. Almost a Temporal neighbor.

He said, "Are you interested in Primitive history?"

"Computer Twissell asked me to learn. I don't know much about it."

"What else are you learning?"

"Mathematics. Temporal engineering. I'm just getting the fundamentals so far. Back in the 78th, I was a Speedy-vac repairman."

There was no point in asking the nature of a Speedy-vac. It might be a suction cleaner, a computing machine, a type of spray painter. Anything. Harlan wasn't particularly interested.

He said, "Do you know anything about history? Any kind of history?"

"I studied European history."

"Your particular political unit, I take it."

"I was born in Europe. Yes. Mostly, of course, they taught us modern history. After the revolutions of '54; 7554, that is."

"All right. First thing you do is to forget it. It doesn't mean anything. The history they try to teach Timers changes with every Reality Change. Not that they realize that. In each Reality, their history is the only history. That's what's so different about Primitive history. That's the beauty of it. No matter what any of us does, it exists precisely as it has always existed. Columbus and Washington, Mussolini and Hereford, they all exist."

Cooper smiled feebly. He brushed his little finger across his upper lip and for the first time Harlan noticed a trace of bristle there as though the Cub were cultivating a mustache.

Cooper said, "I can't quite—get used to it, all the time I've been here."

"Get used to what?"

"Being five hundred Centuries away from homewhen."

"I'm nearly that myself. I'm 95th."

"That's another thing. You're older than I am and yet I'm seventeen Centuries older than you in another way. I can be your great-great-great-and-so-on-grandfather."

"What's the difference? Suppose you are?"

"Well, it takes getting used to." There was a trace of rebellion in the Cub's voice.

"It does for all of us," said Harlan callously, and began talking about the Primitives. By the time three hours had passed, he was deep in an explanation concerning the reasons why there were Centuries before the 1st Century.

("But isn't the 1st Century *first?*" Cooper had asked plaintively.)

Harlan ended by giving the Cub a book, not a good one, really, but one that would serve as a beginning. "I'll get you better stuff as we go along," he said.

By the end of a week Cooper's mustache had become a pronounced dark bristle that made him look ten years older and accentuated the narrowness of his chin. On the whole, Harlan decided, it would not be an improvement, that mustache.

Cooper said, "I've finished your book."

"What did you think of it?"

"In a way—" There was a long pause. Cooper began over again. "Parts of the later Primitive was something like the 78th. It made me think of home, you know. Twice, I dreamed about my wife."

Harlan exploded. "Your *wife?*"

"I was married before I came here."

"Great Time! Did they bring your wife across too?"

Cooper shook his head. "I don't even know if she's been Changed in the last year. If she has, I suppose she's not really my wife now."

Harlan recovered. Of course, if the Cub were twenty-three years old when he was taken into Eternity, it was quite possible that he might have been married. One thing unprecedented led to another.

What was going on? Once modifications were introduced into the rules, it wouldn't be a long step to the point where everything would decline into a mass of incoherency. Eternity was too finely balanced an arrangement to endure modification.

It was his anger on behalf of Eternity, perhaps, that put an unintended harshness into Harlan's next words. "I hope you're not planning on going back to the 78th to check on her."

The Cub lifted his head and his eyes were firm and steady. "No."

Harlan shifted uneasily. "Good. You have no family. Nothing. You're an Eternal and don't ever think of anyone you knew in Time."

Cooper's lips thinned, and his accent stood out sharply in his quick words. "You're speaking like a Technician."

Harlan's fists clenched along the sides of his desk. He said hoarsely, "What do you imply? I'm a Technician so I make the Changes? So I defend them and demand that you accept them? Look, kid, you haven't been here a year; you can't speak Intertemporal; you're all misgeared on Time and Reality, but you think you know all about Technicians and how to kick them in the teeth.''

"I'm sorry," said Cooper quickly; "I didn't mean to offend you."

"No, no, who offends a Technician? You just hear everyone else talking, is that it? They say, 'Cold as a Technician's heart,' don't they? They say, 'A trillion personalities changed—just a Technician's yawn.' Maybe a few other things. What's the answer, Mr. Cooper? Does it make you feel sophisticated to join in? It makes you a big man? A big wheel in Eternity?''

"I said I'm sorry."

"All right. I just want you to know I've been a Technician for less than a month and I personally have never induced a Reality Change. Now let's get on with business.''

Senior Computer Twissell called Andrew Harlan to his office the next day. He said, "How would you like to go on an M.N.C., boy?"

It was almost too apposite. All that morning Harlan had been regretting his cowardly disclaimer of personal involvement in the Technician's work; his childish cry of: I haven't done anything wrong yet, so don't blame me.

It amounted to an admission that there *was* something wrong about a Technician's work, and that he himself was blameless only because he was too new at the game to have had time to be a criminal.

He welcomed the chance to kill that excuse now. It would be almost a penance. He could say to Cooper: Yes, because of something I have done, this many millions of people are new personalities, but it was necessary and I am proud to have been the cause.

So Harlan said joyfully, "I'm ready, sir."

"Good. Good. You'll be glad to know, boy," (a puff, and the cigarette tip glowed brilliantly) "that every one of your analyses checked out with high-order accuracy.''

"Thank you, sir." (They were analyses now, thought Harlan, not guesses.)

"You've got a talent. Quite a touch, boy. I look for great things. And we can begin with this one, 223rd. Your statement that a jammed vehicle clutch would supply the necessary fork without undesirable side effects is perfectly correct. Will you jam it?''

"Yes, sir."

That was Harlan's true initiation into Technicianhood. After that he was more than just a man with a rose-red badge. He had handled Reality. He had tampered with a mechanism during a quick few minutes taken out of the 223rd and, as a result, a young man did not reach a lecture on mechanics he had meant to attend. He never went in for solar engineering, consequently, and a perfectly simple device was delayed in its development a crucial ten years. A war in the 224th, amazingly enough, was moved out of Reality as a result.

Wasn't *that* good? What if personalities were changed? The new personalities were as human as the old and as deserving of life. If some lives were shortened, more were lengthened and made happier. A great work of literature, a monument of Man's intellect and feeling, was never written in the new Reality, but several copies were preserved in Eternity's libraries, were they not? And new creative works had come into existence, had they not?

Yet that night Harlan spent hours in a hot agony of wakefulness, and when he finally drowsed groggily, he did something he hadn't done in years.

He dreamed of his mother.

Despite the weakness of such a beginning a physioyear was sufficient to make Harlan known throughout Eternity as "Twissell's Technician," and with more than a trace of ill-humor as "The Wonder Boy" and "The Never-Wrong."

His contact with Cooper became almost comfortable. They never grew completely friendly. (If Cooper could have brought himself to make advances, Harlan might not have known how to respond.) Nevertheless they worked well together, and Cooper's interest in Primitive history grew to the point where it nearly rivaled Harlan's.

One day Harlan said to Cooper, "Look, Cooper, would you mind coming in tomorrow instead? I've got to get up to the 3000's sometime this week to check on an Observation and the man I want to see is free this afternoon."

Cooper's eyes lit up hungrily, "Why can't I come?"

"Do you want to?"

"Sure. I've never been in a kettle except when they brought me here from the 78th and I didn't know what was happening at the time."

Harlan was accustomed to using the kettle in Shaft C, which was, by unwritten custom, reserved for Technicians along its entire immeasurable length through the Centuries. Cooper showed no embarrassment at being led there. He stepped into the kettle without hesitation and took his seat on the curved molding that completely circled it.

When Harlan, however, had activated the Field, and kicked the kettle into upwhen motion, Cooper's face screwed into an almost comic expression of surprise.

"I don't feel a thing," he said. "Is anything wrong?"

"Nothing's wrong. You're not feeling anything because you're not really moving. You're being kicked along the temporal extension of the kettle. In fact," Harlan said, growing didactic, "at the moment, you and I aren't matter, really, in spite of appearances. A hundred men could be using this same kettle, moving (if you can call it that) at various velocities in either Time-direction, passing through one another and so on. The laws of the ordinary universe just don't apply to the kettle shafts!"

Cooper's mouth quirked a bit and Harlan thought uneasily: The kid's taking temporal engineering and knows more about this than I do. Why don't I shut up and stop making a fool of myself?

He retreated into silence, and stared somberly at Cooper. The younger man's mustache had been full-grown for months. It drooped, framing his mouth in what Eternals called Mallansohn hairline, because the only photograph known to be authentic of the Temporal Field inventor (and that a poor one and out of focus) showed him with just such a mustache. For that reason it maintained a certain popularity among Eternals even though it did few of them justice.

Cooper's eyes were fixed on the shifting numbers that marked the passing of the Centuries with respect to themselves. He said, "How far upwhen does the kettle shaft go?"

"Haven't they taught you that?"

"They've hardly mentioned the kettles."

Harlan shrugged. "There's no end to Eternity. The shaft goes on forever."

"How far upwhen have you gone?"

"This will be the uppest. Dr. Twissell has been up to the 50,000's."

"Great Time!" whispered Cooper.

"That's still nothing. Some Eternals have been up past the 150,000th Century."

"What's *that* like?"

"Like nothing at all," said Harlan morosely. "Lots of life but none of it human. Man is gone."

"Dead? Wiped out?"

"I don't know that anyone exactly knows."

"Can't something be done to change that?"

"Well, from the 70,000's on—" began Harlan, then ended abruptly. "Oh, to Time with it. Change the subject."

If there was one subject about which Eternals were almost superstitious, it was the "Hidden Centuries," the time between the 70,000th and the 150,000th. It was a subject that was rarely mentioned. It was only Harlan's close association with Twissell that accounted for his own small knowledge of the era. What it amounted to was that Eternals couldn't pass into Time in all those thousands of Centuries.

The doors between Eternity and Time were impenetrable. Why? No one knew.

Harlan imagined, from some casual remarks of Twissell's, that attempts had been made to Change the Reality in the Centuries just downwhen from the 70,000th, but without adequate Observation beyond the 70,000th not much could be done.

Twissell had laughed a bit one time and said, "We'll get through someday. Meanwhile, 70,000 Centuries is quite enough to take care of."

It did not sound wholly convincing.

"What happens to Eternity after the 150,000th?" asked Cooper.

Harlan sighed. The subject, apparently, was not to be changed. "Nothing," he said. "The Sections are there but there are no Eternals in it anywhere after the 70,000th. The Sections keep on going for millions of Centuries till all life is gone and past that, too, till the sun becomes a nova, and past that, too. There isn't any end to Eternity. That's why it's called Eternity."

"The sun *does* become a nova, then?"

"It certainly does. Eternity couldn't exist if that weren't so. Nova Sol is our power supply. Listen, do you know how much power is required to set up a Temporal Field? Mallansohn's first Field was two seconds from extreme downwhen to extreme upwhen and big enough to hold not more than a match head and that took a nuclear power plant's complete output for one day. It took nearly a hundred years to set up a hair-thin Temporal Field far enough upwhen to be able to tap the radiant power of the nova so that a field could be built big enough to hold a man."

Cooper sighed. "I wish they would get to the point where they stopped making me learn equations and field mechanics and start telling me some of the interesting stuff. Now if I had lived in Mallansohn's time—"

"You would have learned nothing. He lived in the 24th, but Eternity didn't start till late in the 27th. Inventing the Field isn't the same as constructing Eternity, you know, and the rest of the 24th didn't have the slightest inkling of what Mallansohn's invention signified."

"He was ahead of his generation, then?"

"Very much so. He not only invented the Temporal Field, but he described the basic relationships that made Eternity possible and predicted almost every aspect of it except for the Reality Change. Quite closely, too—but I think we're pulling to a halt, Cooper. After you."

They stepped out.

Harlan had never seen Senior Computer Laban Twissell angry before. People always said that he was incapable of any emotion, that he was an unsouled fixture of Eternity to the point where he had forgotten the exact number of his homewhen Century. People said that at an early age his heart had atrophied and that a hand computer similar to the model he carried always in his trouser pocket had taken its place.

Twissell did nothing to deny these rumors. In fact most people guessed that he believed them himself.

So even while Harlan bent before the force of the angry blast that struck him, he had room in his mind to be amazed at the fact that Twissell could display anger. He wondered if Twissell would be mortified in some calmer aftermath to realize that his hand-computer heart had betrayed him by exposing itself as only a poor thing of muscle and valves subject to the twists of emotion.

Twissell said, in part, his old voice creaking, "Father Time, boy, are you on the Allwhen Council? Do you give the orders around here? Do you tell me what to do or do I tell you what to do? Are you making arrangements for all kettle trips now?"

He interrupted himself with occasional exclamations of "Answer me," then continued pouring more questions into the boiling interrogative cauldron.

He said finally, "If you ever get above yourself this way again, I'll have you on plumbing repair and for good. Do you understand me?"

Harlan, pale with his own gathering embarrassment, said, "I was never told that Cub Cooper was not to be taken on the kettle."

The explanation did not act as an emollient. "What kind of an excuse is a double negative, boy? You were never told not to get him drunk. You were never told not to shave him bald. You were never told not to skewer him with a fine-edged Tav curve. Father Time, boy, what *were* you told to do with him?"

"I was told to teach him Primitive history."

"Then do so. Do nothing more than that." Twissell dropped his cigarette and ground it savagely underfoot as though it were the face of a lifelong enemy.

"I'd like to point out, Computer," said Harlan, "that many Centuries under the current Reality somewhat resemble specific eras of Primitive history in one or more respects. It had been my intention to take him out to those Times, under careful spatio-temporal charting, of course, as a form of field trip."

"What? Listen, you chucklehead, don't you ever intend to ask my permission for *anything?* That's out. Just teach him Primitive history. No field trips. No laboratory experiments, either. Next you'll be changing Reality just to show him how."

Harlan licked his dry lips with a dry tongue, muttered a resentful acquiescence, and, eventually, was allowed to leave.

It took weeks for his hurt feelings to heal over somewhat.

COMPUTER

— 4 —

HARLAN HAD been two years a Technician when he reentered the 482nd for the first time since leaving with Twissell. He found it almost unrecognizable.

It had not changed. He had.

Two years of Technicianhood had meant a number of things. In one sense it had increased his feeling of stability. He had no longer to learn a new language, get used to new styles of clothing and new ways of life with every new Observation project. On the other hand, it had resulted in a withdrawal on his own part. He had almost forgotten now the camaraderie that united all the rest of the Specialists in Eternity.

Most of all, he had developed the feeling of the *power* of being a Technician. He held the fate of millions in his finger tips, and if one must walk lonely because of it, one could also walk proudly.

So he could stare coldly at the Communications man behind the entry desk of the 482nd and announce himself in clipped syllables: "Andrew Harlan, Technician, reporting to Computer Finge for temporary assignment to the 482nd," disregarding the quick glance from the middle-aged man he faced.

It was what some people called the "Technician glance," a quick, involuntary sidelong peek at the rose-red shoulder emblem of the Technician, then an elaborate attempt not to look at it again.

Harlan stared at the other's shoulder emblem. It was not the yellow of the Computer, the green of the Life-Plotter, the blue of the Sociologist, or the white of the Observer. It was not the Specialist's solid color at all. It was simply a blue bar on white. The man was Communications, a subbranch of Maintenance, not a Specialist at all.

And *he* gave the "Technician glance" too.

Harlan said a little sadly, "Well?"

Communications said quickly, "I'm ringing Computer Finge, sir."

Harlan remembered the 482nd as solid and massive, but now it seemed almost squalid.

Harlan had grown used to the glass and porcelain of the 575th, to its fetish of cleanliness. He had grown accustomed to a world of whiteness and clarity, broken by sparse patches of light pastel.

The heavy plaster swirls of the 482nd, its splashy pigments, its areas of painted metal were almost repulsive.

Even Finge seemed different, less than life-size, somewhat. Two years earlier, to Observer Harlan, Finge's every gesture had seemed sinister and powerful.

Now, from the lofty and isolated heights of Technicianhood, the man seemed pathetic and lost. Harlan watched him as he leafed through a sheaf of foils and got ready to look up, with the air of someone who is beginning to think he has made his visitor wait the duly required amount of time.

Finge was from an energy-centered Century in the 600's. Twissell had told him that and it explained a good deal. Finge's flashes of ill-temper could easily be the result of the natural insecurity of a heavy man used to the firmness of field-forces and unhappy to be dealing with nothing more than flimsy matter. His tiptoeing walk (Harlan remembered Finge's catlike tread well; often he would look up from his desk, see Finge standing there staring at him, his approach having been unheard) was no longer something sly and sneaking, but rather the fearful and reluctant tread of one who lives in the constant, if unconscious, fear that the flooring would break under his weight.

Harlan thought, with a pleasant condescension: The man is poorly adjusted to the Section. Reassignment is probably the only thing that would help him.

Finge said, "Greetings, Technician Harlan."

"Greetings, Computer," said Harlan.

Finge said, "It seems that in the two years since—"

"Two physioyears," said Harlan.

Finge looked up in surprise. "Two physioyears, of course."

In Eternity there was no Time as one ordinarily thought of Time in the universe outside, but men's bodies grew older and that was the unavoidable measure of Time even in the absence of meaningful physical phenomena. Physiologically Time passed, and in a physioyear within Eternity a man grew as much older as he would have in an ordinary year in Time.

Yet even the most pedantic Eternal remembered the distinction only rarely. It was too convenient to say, "See you tomorrow," or "I missed you yesterday," or "I will see you next week," as though there were a tomorrow or a yesterday or a last week in any but a physiological sense. And the instincts of humanity were catered to by having the activities of Eternity tailored to an arbitrary twenty-four "physiohour" day, with a solemn assumption of day and night, today and tomorrow.

Finge said, "In the two *physioyears* since you left, a crisis has gradually gathered about the 482nd. A rather peculiar one. A delicate one. Almost unprecedented. We need accurate Observation now as we never have needed it before."

"And you want me to Observe?"

"Yes. In a way, it's a waste of talent to ask a Technician to do a job of Observation, but your previous Observations, for clarity and insight, were perfect. We need that again. Now I'll just sketch in a few details. . . ."

What those details were Harlan was not to find out just then. Finge spoke, but the door opened, and Harlan did not hear him.

He stared at the person who entered.

It was not that Harlan had never seen a girl in Eternity before. Never was too strong a word. Rarely, yes, but not never.

But a girl such as *this!* And in *Eternity!*

Harlan had seen many women in his passages through Time, but in Time they were only objects to him, like walls and balls, barrows and harrows, kittens and mittens. They were facts to be Observed.

In Eternity a girl was a different matter. And one like *this!*

She was dressed in the style of the upper classes of the 482nd, which meant transparent sheathing and not very much else above the waist, and flimsy, knee-length trousers below. The latter, while opaque enough, hinted delicately at gluteal curves.

Her hair was glossily dark and shoulder length, her lips redly penciled thin above and full below in an exaggerated pout. Her upper eyelids and her ear lobes were tinted a pale rose and the rest of her youthful (almost girlish) face was a startlingly milky white. Jeweled pendants descended forward from mid-shoulder to tinkle now this side, now that of the graceful breasts to which they drew attention.

She took her seat at a desk in the corner of Finge's office, lifting her eyelashes only once to sweep her dark glance across Harlan's face.

When Harlan heard Finge's voice again, the Computer was saying, "You'll get all this in an official report and meanwhile you can have your old office and sleeping quarters."

Harlan found himself outside Finge's office without quite remembering the details of his leaving. Presumably he had walked out.

The emotion within him that was easiest to recognize was anger. *By Time,* Finge ought not to be allowed to do this. It was bad for morale. It made a mockery—

He stopped himself, unclenched his fist, unclamped his jaw. Let's see, now! His footsteps sounded sharply in his own ear as he strode firmly toward the Communications man behind the desk.

Communications looked up, without quite meeting his eye, and said cautiously, "Yes, sir."

Harlan said, "There's a woman at a desk in Computer Finge's office. Is she new here?"

He had meant to ask it casually. He had meant to make it a bored, indifferent question. It rang out, instead, like a pair of cymbals clashing.

But it roused Communications. The look in his eye became something that made all men kin. It even embraced the Technician, drew him in as a fellow. Communications said, "You mean the babe? Wow! Isn't she built like a force-field latrine, though?"

Harlan stammered a bit. "Just answer my question."

Communications stared and some of his steam evaporated. He said, "She's new. She's a Timer."

"What's her job?"

A slow smile crept over Communications' face and grew into a leer. "She's supposed to be the boss's secretary. Her name is Noÿs Lambent."

"All right." Harlan turned on his heel and left.

Harlan's first Observation trip into the 482nd came the next day, but it lasted for thirty minutes only. It was obviously only an orientation trip, intended to get him into the feel of things. He entered it for an hour and a half the next day and not at all on the third.

He occupied his time in working his way through his original reports, relearning his own knowledge, brushing up on the language system of the time, accustoming himself to the local costumes again.

One Reality Change had hit the 482nd, but it was very minor. A political clique that had been In was now Out, but there seemed no change in the society otherwise.

Without quite realizing it he slipped into the habit of searching his old reports for information on the aristocracy. Surely he had made Observations.

He had, but they were impersonal, from a distance. His data concerned them as a class, not as individuals.

Of course his spatio-temporal charts had never demanded or even permitted him to observe the aristocracy from within. What the reasons for that might have been was beyond the purview of an Observer. He was impatient with himself at feeling curiosity concerning that now.

During those three days he had caught glimpses of the girl, Noÿs Lambent, four times. At first he had been aware only of her clothes and her ornaments.

Now he noticed that she was five feet six in height, half a head shorter than himself, yet slim enough and with a carriage erect and graceful enough to give an impression of height. She was older than she first seemed, approaching thirty perhaps, certainly over twenty-five.

She was quiet and reserved, smiled at him once when he passed her in the corridor, then lowered her eyes. Harlan drew aside to avoid touching her, then walked on feeling angry.

By the close of the third day Harlan was beginning to feel that his duty as an Eternal left him only one course of action. Doubtless her position was a comfortable one for herself. Doubtless Finge was within the letter of the law. Yet Finge's indiscretion in the matter, his carelessness certainly went against the spirit of the law, and something should be done about it.

Harlan decided that, after all, there wasn't a man in Eternity he disliked quite as much as Finge. The excuses he had found for the man only a few days before vanished.

On the morning of the fourth day Harlan asked for and received permission to see Finge privately. He walked in with a determined step and, to his own surprise, made his point instantly. "Computer Finge, I suggest that Miss Lambent be returned to Time."

Finge's eyes narrowed. He nodded toward a chair, placed clasped hands under his soft, round chin, and showed some of his teeth. "Well, sit down. Sit down. You find Miss Lambent incompetent? Unsuitable?"

"As to her incompetence and unsuitability, Computer, I cannot say. It depends on the uses to which she is put, and I have put her to none. But you must realize that she is bad for the morale of this Section."

Finge stared at him distantly as though his Computer's mind were weighing abstractions beyond the reach of an ordinary Eternal. "In what way is she hurting morale, Technician?"

"There's no real necessity for you to ask," said Harlan, his anger deepening. "Her costume is exhibitionistic. Her—"

"Wait, wait. Now wait a while, Harlan. You've been an Observer in this era. You know her clothes are standard costume for the 482nd."

"In her own surroundings, in her own cultural milieu, I would have no fault to find, though I'll say right now that her costume is extreme even for the 482nd. You'll allow me to be the judge of that. Here in Eternity, a person such as she is certainly out of place."

Finge nodded his head slowly. He actually seemed to be enjoying himself. Harlan stiffened.

Finge said, "She is here for a deliberate purpose. She is performing an essential function. It is only temporary. Try to endure her meanwhile."

Harlan's jaw quivered. He had protested and was being fobbed off. To hell with caution. He would speak his mind. He said, "I can imagine what the woman's 'essential function' is. To keep her so openly will not be allowed to pass."

He turned stiffly, walked to the door. Finge's voice stopped him.

"Technician," Finge said. "Your relationship with Twissell may have given you a distorted notion about your own importance. Correct that! And meanwhile tell me, Technician, have you ever had a" (he hesitated, seeming to pick among words) "girl friend?"

With painstaking and insulting accuracy, back still turned, Harlan quoted: "In the interest of avoiding emotional entanglements with Time, an Eternal may not marry. In the interest of avoiding emotional entanglements with family, an Eternal may not have children.''

The Computer said gravely, ''I didn't ask about marriage, or children.''

Harlan quoted further: ''Temporary liaisons may be made with Timers only after application with the Central Charting Board of the Allwhen Council for an appropriate Life-Plot of the Timer concerned. Liaisons may be conducted thereafter only according to the requirements of specific spatio-temporal charting.''

''Quite true. Have you ever applied for temporary liaison, Technician?''

''No, Computer.''

''Do you intend to?''

''No, Computer.''

''Perhaps you ought to. It would give you a greater breadth of view. You would become less concerned about the details of a woman's costume, less disturbed about her possible personal relations with other Eternals.''

Harlan left, speechless with rage.

He found it almost impossible to perform his near-daily trek into the 482nd (the longest continuous period remaining something under two hours).

He was upset, and he knew why. Finge! Finge, and his coarse advice concerning liaisons with Timers.

Liaisons existed. Everyone knew that. Eternity had always been aware of the necessity for compromising with human appetites (to Harlan the phrase carried a quivery repulsion), but the restrictions involved in choosing mistresses made the compromise anything but lax, anything but generous. And those who were lucky enough to qualify for such an arrangement were expected to be most discreet about it, out of common decency and consideration for the majority.

Among the lower classes of Eternals, particularly among Maintenance, there were always the rumors (half hopeful, half resentful) of women imported on a more or less permanent basis for the obvious reasons. Always rumor pointed to the Computers and Life-Plotters as the benefiting groups. They and only they could decide which women could be abstracted from Time without danger of significant Reality Change.

Less sensational (and therefore less tongue-worthy) were the stories concerning the Timer employees that every Section engaged temporarily (when spatio-temporal analysis permitted) to perform the tedious tasks of cooking, cleaning, and heavy labor.

But a Timer, and *such* a Timer, employed as ''secretary,'' could only mean that Finge was thumbing his nose at the ideals that made Eternity what it was.

Regardless of the facts of life to which the practical men of Eternity made a perfunctory obeisance it remained true that the ideal Eternal was a dedicated man living for the mission he had to perform, for the betterment of Reality and the improvement of the sum of human happiness. Harlan liked to think that Eternity was like the monasteries of Primitive times.

He dreamed that night that he spoke to Twissell about the matter, and that Twissell, the ideal Eternal, shared his horror. He dreamed of a broken Finge, stripped of rank. He dreamed of himself with the yellow Computer's insigne, instituting a new regime in the 482nd, ordering Finge grandly to a new position in Maintenance. Twissell sat next to him, smiling with admiration, as he drew up a new organizational chart, neat, orderly, consistent, and asked Noÿs Lambent to distribute copies.

But Noÿs Lambent was nude, and Harlan woke up, trembling and ashamed.

He met the girl in a corridor one day and stood aside, eyes averted, to let her pass.

But she remained standing, looking at him, until he had to look up and meet her eyes. She was all color and life and Harlan was conscious of a faint perfume about her.

She said, "You're Technician Harlan, aren't you?"

His impulse was to snub her, to force his way past, but, after all, he told himself, all this wasn't her fault. Besides, to move past her now would mean touching her.

So he nodded briefly. "Yes."

"I'm told you're quite an expert on our Time."

"I have been in it."

"I would love to talk to you about it someday."

"I am busy. I wouldn't have time."

"But Mr. Harlan, surely you could *find* time someday."

She smiled at him.

Harlan said in a desperate whisper, "Will you pass, please? Or will you stand aside to let me pass? Please!"

She moved by with a slow swing of her hips that brought blood tingling to his embarrassed cheeks.

He was angry at her for embarrassing him, angry at himself for being embarrassed, and angry, most of all, for some obscure reason, at Finge.

Finge called him in at the end of two weeks. On his desk was a sheet of perforated flimsy the length and intricacy of which told Harlan at once that this concerned no half-hour excursion into Time.

Finge said, "Would you sit down, Harlan, and scan this thing right now? No, not by eye. Use the machine."

Harlan lifted indifferent eyebrows, and inserted the sheet carefully between the lips of the scanner on Finge's desk. Slowly it passed into the intestines of the machine and, as it did so, the perforation pattern was translated into words that appeared on the cloudy-white rectangle that was the visual attachment.

Somewhere about midpoint, Harlan's hand shot out and disconnected the scanner. He yanked the flimsy out with a force that tore its tough cellulite structure.

Finge said calmly, "I have another copy."

But Harlan was holding the remnants between thumb and forefinger as though it might explode. "Computer Finge, there is some mistake. Surely I am not to be expected to use the home of this woman as base for a near-week stay in Time."

The Computer pursed his lips. "Why not, if the spatio-temporal requirements are such. If there is a personal problem involved between yourself and Miss Lam—"

"No personal problem at all," interposed Harlan hotly.

"Some kind of problem, certainly. In the circumstances, I will go as far as to explain certain aspects of the Observational problem. This is not to be taken as a precedent, of course."

Harlan sat motionless. He was thinking hard and fast. Ordinarily professional pride would have forced Harlan to disdain explanation. An Observer, or Technician, for that matter, did his job without question. And ordinarily a Computer would never dream of offering explanation.

Here, however, was something unusual. Harlan had complained concerning the girl, the so-called secretary. Finge was afraid the complaint might go further. ("The guilty fleeth when no man pursueth," thought Harlan with grim satisfaction and tried to remember where he had read that phrase.)

Finge's strategy was obvious, therefore. By stationing Harlan in the woman's dwelling place he would be ready to make counteraccusations if matters went far enough. Harlan's value as a witness against him would be destroyed.

And, of course, he would have to have some specious explanation for placing Harlan in such a place, and this would be it. Harlan listened with barely hidden contempt.

Finge said, "As you know, the various Centuries are aware of the existence of Eternity. They know that we supervise intertemporal trade. They consider that to be our chief function, which is good. They have a dim knowledge that we are also here to prevent catastrophe from striking mankind. That is more a superstition than anything else, but it is more or less correct, and good, too. We supply the generations with a mass father image and a certain feeling of security. You see all that, don't you?"

Harlan thought: Does the man think I'm still a Cub?

But he nodded briefly.

Finge went on. "There are some things, however, they must not know. Prime among them, of course, is the manner in which we alter Reality when necessary. The insecurity such knowledge would arouse would be most harmful. It is always necessary to breed out of Reality any factors that might lead to such knowledge and we have never been troubled with it.

"However, there are always other undesirable beliefs about Eternity which spring up from time to time in one Century or another. Usually, the dangerous beliefs are those which concentrate particularly in the ruling classes of an era; the classes that have most contact with us and, at the same time, carry the important weight of what is called public opinion."

Finge paused as though he expected Harlan to offer some comment or ask some question. Harlan did neither.

Finge continued. "Ever since the Reality Change 433-486, Serial Number F-2, which took place about a year—a physioyear ago, there has been evidence of the bringing into Reality of such an undesirable belief. I have come to certain conclusions about the nature of that belief and have presented them to the Allwhen Council. The Council is reluctant to accept them since they depend upon the realization of an alternate in the Computing Pattern of an extremely low probability.

"Before acting on my recommendation, they insist on confirmation by direct Observation. It's a most delicate job, which is why I recalled you, and why Computer Twissell allowed you to be recalled. Another thing I did was to locate a member of the current aristocracy, who thought it would be thrilling or exciting to work in Eternity. I placed her in this office and kept her under close observation to see if she were suitable for our purpose—"

Harlan thought: Close observation! Yes!

Again his anger focused itself on Finge rather than upon the woman.

Finge was still speaking. "By all standards, she is suitable. We will now return her to her Time. Using her dwelling as a base, you will be able to study the social life of her circle. Do you understand now the reason I had the girl here and the reason I want you in her house?"

Harlan said with an almost open irony, "I understand quite well, I assure you."

"Then you will accept this mission."

Harlan left with the fire of battle burning inside his chest. Finge was *not* going to outsmart him. He was *not* going to make a fool of him.

Surely it was that fire of battle, the determination to outwit Finge, that caused him to experience an eagerness, almost an exhilaration, at the thought of this next excursion into the 482nd.

Surely it was nothing else.

TIMER
— 5 —

NOŸS LAMBENT'S estate was fairly isolated, yet within easy reach of one of the larger cities of the Century. Harlan knew that city well; he knew it better than any of its inhabitants could. In his exploratory Observations into this Reality he had visited every quarter of the city and every decade within the purview of the Section.

He knew the city both in Space and Time. He could piece it together, view it as an organism, living and growing, with its catastrophes and recoveries, its gaieties and troubles. Now he was in a given week of Time in that city, in a moment of suspended animation of its slow life of steel and concrete.

More than that, his preliminary explorations had centered themselves more and more closely about the "perioeci," the inhabitants who were the most important of the city, yet who lived outside the city, in room and relative isolation.

The 482nd was one of the many Centuries in which wealth was unevenly distributed. The Sociologists had an equation for the phenomenon (which Harlan had seen in print, but which he understood only vaguely). It worked itself out for any given Century to three relationships, and for the 482nd those relationships stood near the limits of what could be permitted. Sociologists shook their heads over it and Harlan had heard one say at one time that any further deterioration with new Reality Changes would require "the closest Observation."

Yet there was this to be said for unfavorable relationships in the wealth-distribution equation. It meant the existence of a leisure class and the development of an attractive way of life which, at its best, encouraged culture and grace. As long as the other end of the scale was not too badly off, as long as the leisure classes did not entirely forget their responsibilities while enjoying their privileges, as long as their culture took no obviously unhealthy turn, there was always the tendency in Eternity to forgive the departure from the ideal wealth-distribution pattern and to search for other, less attractive maladjustments.

Against his will Harlan began to understand this. Ordinarily his overnight stays in Time involved hotels in the poorer sections, where a man might easily stay anonymous, where strangers were ignored, where one presence more or less was nothing and therefore did not cause the fabric of Reality to do more than tremble. When even that was unsafe, where there was a good chance that the trembling might pass the critical point and bring down a significant part of the card house of Reality, it was not unusual to have to sleep under a particular hedge in the countryside.

And it was usual to survey various hedges to see which would be least disturbed by farmers, tramps, even stray dogs, during the night.

But now Harlan, at the other end of the scale, slept in a bed with a surface of field-permeated matter, a peculiar welding of matter and energy that entered only the highest economic levels of this society. Throughout Time it was less common than pure matter but more common than pure energy. In any case it molded itself to his body as he lay down, firm when he lay still, yielding when he moved or turned.

Reluctantly he confessed the attraction of such things, and he accepted the wisdom which caused each Section of Eternity to live on the *median* scale of its Century rather than at its most comfortable level. In that way it could maintain contact with the problems and "feel" of the Century, without succumbing to too close an indentification with a sociological extreme.

It is easy, thought Harlan, that first evening, to live with aristocrats.

And just before he fell asleep, he thought of Noÿs.

He dreamed he was on the Allwhen Council, fingers clasped austerely before him. He was looking down on a small, a very small, Finge, listening in terror to the sentence that was casting him out of Eternity to perpetual Observation of one of the unknown Centuries of the far, far upwhen. The somber words of exile were coming from Harlan's own mouth, and immediately to his right sat Noÿs Lambent.

He hadn't noticed her at first, but his eyes kept sliding to his right, and his words faltered.

Did no one else see her? The rest of the members of the Council looked steadily forward, except for Twissell. He turned to smile at Harlan, looking through the girl as though she weren't there.

Harlan wanted to order her away, but words were no longer coming out of his mouth. He tried to beat at the girl, but his arm moved sluggishly and she did not move. Her flesh was cold.

Finge was laughing—louder—louder——

—and it was Noÿs Lambent laughing.

Harlan opened his eyes to bright sunlight and stared at the girl in horror for a moment before he remembered where she was and where he was.

She said, "You were moaning and beating the pillow. Were you having a bad dream?"

Harlan did not answer.

She said, "Your bath is ready. So are your clothes. I've arranged to have you join the gathering tonight. It felt queer to step back into my ordinary life after being in Eternity so long."

Harlan felt acutely disturbed at her easy flow of words. He said, "You didn't tell them who I was, I hope."

"Of *course* not."

Of *course* not! Finge would have taken care of that little matter by having her lightly psychoed under narcosis, if he felt that necessary. He might not have thought it necessary, however. After all, he had given her "close observation."

The thought annoyed him. He said, "I'd prefer to be left to myself as much as possible."

She looked at him uncertainly a moment or two and left.

Harlan went through the morning ritual of washing and dressing glumly. He had no great hopes of an exciting evening. He would have to say as little as possible, do as little as possible, be a part of the wall as much as possible. His true function was that of a pair of ears and pair of eyes. Connecting those senses with the final report was his mind, which, ideally, had no other function.

Ordinarily it did not disturb him that, as an Observer, he did not know what he was looking for. An Observer, he had been taught as a Cub, must not have preconceived notions as to what data is desired or what conclusions are expected. The knowledge, it was said, would automatically distort his view, however conscientious he tried to be.

But under the circumstances ignorance was irritating. Harlan suspected strongly that there was nothing to look for, that he was playing Finge's game in some way. Between that and Noÿs . . .

He stared savagely at the image of himself cast in three-dimensional accuracy two feet in front of him by the Reflector. The clinging garments of the 482nd, seamless and bright in coloring, made him, he thought, look ridiculous.

Noÿs Lambent came running to him just after he had finished a solitary breakfast brought to him by a Mekkano.

She said breathlessly, "It's June, Technician Harlan."

He said harshly, "Do not use the title here. What if it is June?"

"But it was February when I joined"—she paused doubtfully—"*that* place, and that was only a month ago."

Harlan frowned. "What year is it now?"

"Oh, it's the right year."

"Are you sure?"

"I'm quite positive. Has there been a mistake?" She had a disturbing habit of standing quite close to him as they talked and her slight lisp (a trait of the Century rather than of herself personally) gave her the sound of a young and rather helpless child. Harlan was not fooled by that. He drew away.

"No mistake. You've been put here because it's more suitable. Actually, in Time, you have been here all along."

"But how could I?" She looked more frightened still. "I don't remember anything about it. Are there two me's?"

Harlan was far more irritated than the cause warranted. How could he explain to her the existence of micro-changes induced by every interference with Time which could alter individual lives without appreciable effect on the Century as a whole. Even Eternals sometimes forgot the difference between micro-changes (small "c") and Changes (large "C") which significantly altered Reality.

He said, "Eternity knows what it's doing. Don't ask questions." He said it proudly, as though he, himself, were a Senior Computer and had personally decided that June was the proper moment in time and that the micro-change induced by skipping three months could not develop into a Change.

She said, "But then I've lost three months of my life."

He sighed. "Your movements through Time have nothing to do with your physiological age."

"Well, have I or haven't I?"

"Have or haven't what?"

"Lost three months."

"By Time, woman, I'm telling you as plainly as I can. You haven't lost any time out of your life. You can't lose any."

She stepped backward at his shout and then, suddenly, giggled. She said, "You have the funniest accent. Especially when you get angry."

He frowned at her retreating back. What accent? He spoke fifty-millennial as well as anyone in the Section. Better probably.

Stupid girl!

He found himself back at the Reflector staring at his image, which stared back at him, vertical furrows deep between its eyes.

He smoothed them out and thought: I'm not handsome. My eyes are too small and my ears stick out and my chin is too big.

He had never particularly thought about the matter before, but now it occurred to him, quite suddenly, that it would be pleasant to be handsome.

Late at night Harlan added his notes to the conversations he had gathered, while it was all fresh in his mind.

As always in such cases he made use of a molecular recorder of 55th century manufacture. In shape it was a featureless thin cylinder about four inches long by half an inch in diameter. It was colored a deep but noncommittal brown. It could be easily held in cuff, pocket, or lining, depending on the style of clothing, or, for that matter, suspended from belt, button, or wristband.

However held, wherever kept, it had the capacity of recording some twenty million words on each of three molecular energy levels. With one end of the cylinder connected to a transliterator, resonating efficiently with Harlan's earpiece, and the other end connected field-wise to the small mike at his lips, Harlan could listen and speak simultaneously.

Every sound made during the hours of the "gathering" repeated itself now in his ear, and as he listened, he spoke words that recorded themselves on a second level, coordinate with but different from the primary level on which the gathering had been recorded. On this second level he described his own impressions, he ascribed significance, pointed out correlations. Eventually, when he made use of the molecular recorder to write a report, he would have, not simply a sound-for-sound recording, but an annotated reconstruction.

Noÿs Lambent entered. She did *not* signal her entrance in any way.

Annoyed, Harlan removed lip-piece and earpiece, clipped them to the molecular recorder, placed the whole into its kit, and clasped that shut.

"Why do you act so angry with me?" asked Noÿs. Her arms and shoulders were bare and her long legs shimmered in faintly luminescent foamite.

He said, "I am not angry. I have no feeling for you at all." At the moment he felt the statement to be rigidly true.

She said, "Are you still working? Surely, you must be tired."

"I can't work if you're here," he replied peevishly.

"You *are* angry with me. You did not say a word to me all evening."

"I said as little as I could to anybody. I wasn't there to speak." He waited for her to leave.

But she said, "I brought you another drink. You seemed to enjoy one at the gathering and one isn't enough. Especially if you're going to be working."

He noticed the small Mekkano behind her, gliding in on a smooth force-field.

He had eaten sparingly that evening, picking lightly at dishes concerning which he had reported in full in past Observations but which (except for fact-searching nibbles) he had thus far refrained from eating. Against his will, he had liked them. Against his will, he had enjoyed the foaming, light green, peppermint-flavored drink (not quite alcoholic, something else, rather) that was currently fashionable. It had not existed in the Century two physioyears earlier, prior to the latest Reality Change.

He took the second drink from the Mekkano with an austere nod of thanks to Noÿs.

Now why had a Reality Change which had had virtually no physical effect on the Century brought a new drink into existence? Well, he wasn't a Computer, so there was no use asking himself that question. Besides, even the most detailed possible Computations could never eliminate all uncertainty, all random effects. If that weren't so, there would be no need for Observers.

They were alone together in the house, Noÿs and himself. Mekkanos were at the height of their popularity these two decades past and would remain so for nearly a decade more in this Reality, so there were no human servants about.

Of course, with the female of the species as economically independent as the male, and able to attain motherhood, if she so wished, without the necessities of physical childbearing, there could be nothing "improper" in their being together alone in the eyes of the 482nd, at least.

Yet Harlan felt compromised.

The girl was stretched out on her elbow on a sofa opposite. Its patterned covering sank beneath her as though avid to embrace her. She had kicked off the transparent shoes she had been wearing and her toes curled and uncurled within the flexible foamite, like the soft paws of a luxuriant cat.

She shook her head and whatever it was that had kept her hair arranged upward away from her ears in intricate intertwinings was suddenly loosened. The hair tumbled about her neck and her bare shoulders became more creamily lovely at the contrast with the black hair.

She murmured, "How old are you?"

That he certainly should not have answered. It was a personal question and the answer was none of her business. What he should have said at that point with polite firmness was: May I be left to my work? Instead what he heard himself saying was, "Thirty-two years." He meant physioyears, of course.

She said, "I'm younger than you. I'm twenty-seven. But I suppose I won't always look younger than you. I suppose you'll be like this when I'm an old

woman. What made you decide to be thirty-two? Can you change if you wish?
Wouldn't you want to be younger?''

"What are you talking about?" Harlan rubbed his forehead to clear his mind.
She said softly, "You live forever. You're an Eternal."
Was it a question or a statement?
He said, "You're mad. We grow old and die like anyone else."
She said, "You can tell me." Her voice was low and cajoling. The
fifty-millennial language, which he had always thought harsh and unpleasant,
seemed euphonious after all. Or was it merely that a full stomach and the scented
air had dulled his ears?

She said, "You can see all Times, visit all places. I so wanted to work in
Eternity. I waited the longest time for them to let me. I thought maybe they'd
make me an Eternal, and then I found there were only men there. Some of them
wouldn't even talk to me because I was a woman. *You* wouldn't talk to me."

"We're all busy," mumbled Harlan, fighting to keep off something that could
only be described as a numb content. "I was very busy."

"But why aren't there more women Eternals?"

Harlan couldn't trust himself to speak. What could he say? That members of
Eternity were chosen with infinite care since two conditions had to be met. First,
they must be equipped for the job; second, their withdrawal from Time must
have no deleterious effect upon Reality.

Reality! That was the word he must not mention under any circumstances. He
felt the spinning sensation in his head grow stronger and he closed his eyes for
a moment to stop it.

How many excellent prospects had been left untouched in Time because their
removal into Eternity would have meant the non-birth of children, the non-death
of women and men, non-marriage, non-happenings, non-circumstance that
would have twisted Reality in directions the Allwhen Council could not permit.

Could he tell her any of this? Of course not. Could he tell her that women
almost never qualified for Eternity because, for some reason he did not
understand (Computers might, but he himself certainly did not), their abstraction
from Time was from ten to a hundred times as likely to distort Reality as was the
abstraction of a man.

(All the thoughts jumbled together in his head, lost and whirling, joined to one
another in a free association that produced odd, almost grotesque, but not
entirely unpleasant, results. Noÿs was closer to him now, smiling.)

He heard her voice like a drifting wind. "Oh, you Eternals. You are so
secretive. You won't share at all. Make me an Eternal."

Her voice was a sound now that didn't coalesce into separate words, just a
delicately modulated sound that insinuated itself into his mind.

He wanted, he longed to tell her: There's no fun in Eternity, lady. We work!
We work to plot out all the details of everywhen from the beginning of Eternity
to where Earth is empty, and we try to plot out all the infinite possibilities of all
the might-have-beens and pick out a might-have-been that is better than what is
and decide where in Time we can make a tiny little change to twist the is to the
might-be and we have a new is and look for a new might-be, forever, and
forever, and that is how it has been since Vikkor Mallansohn discovered the
Temporal Field in the 24th, way back in the Primitive 24th and then it was
possible to start Eternity in the 27th, the mysterious Mallansohn whom no man

knows and who started Eternity, really, and the new might-be, forever and forever and forever and . . .

He shook his head, but the whirligig of thought went on and on in stranger and more jagged breaks and leaps until it jumped into a sudden flash of illumination that persisted for a brilliant second, then died.

That moment steadied him. He grasped for it, but it was gone.

The peppermint drink?

Noÿs was still closer, her face not quite clear in his gaze. He could feel her hair against his cheek, the warm, light pressure of her breath. He ought to draw away, but—strangely, strangely—he found he did not want to.

"If I were made an Eternal . . ." she breathed, almost in his ear, though the words were scarcely heard above the beating of his heart. Her lips were moist and parted. "Wouldn't you like to?"

He did not know what she meant, but suddenly he didn't care. He seemed in flames. He put out his arms clumsily, gropingly. She did not resist, but melted and coalesced with him.

It all happened dreamily, as though it were happening to someone else.

It wasn't nearly as repulsive as he had always imagined it must be. It came as a shock to him, a revelation, that it wasn't repulsive at all.

Even afterward, when she leaned against him with her eyes all soft and smiling a little, he found he had to reach out and stroke her damp hair with slow and trembling delight.

She was entirely different in his eyes now. She was not a woman, not an individual at all. She was suddenly an aspect of himself. She was, in a strange and unexpected way, a part of himself.

The spatio-temporal chart said nothing of this, yet Harlan felt no guilt. It was only the thought of Finge that aroused strong emotion in Harlan's breast. And that wasn't guilt. Not at all.

It was satisfaction, even triumph!

In bed Harlan could not sleep. The lightheadedness had worn off now, but there was still the unusual fact that for the first time in his adult life a grown woman shared his bed.

He could hear her soft breathing and in the ultra-dim glow to which the internal light of the walls and ceiling had been reduced he could see her body as the merest shadow next to his.

He had only to move his hand to feel the warmth and softness of her flesh, and he dared not do that, lest he wake her out of whatever dreaming she might have. It was as though she were dreaming for the two of them, dreaming herself and himself and all that had happened, and as though her waking would drive it all from existence.

It was a thought that seemed a piece of those other queer, unusual thoughts he had experienced just before . . .

Those had been strange thoughts, coming to him at a moment between sense and nonsense. He tried to recapture them and could not. Yet suddenly it was very important that he recapture them. For although he could not remember the details, he could remember that, for just an instant, he had understood something.

He was not certain what that something was, but there had been the unearthly clarity of the half-asleep, when more than mortal eye and mind seems suddenly to come to life.

His anxiety grew. Why couldn't he remember? So much had been in his grasp.

For the moment even the sleeping girl beside him receded into the hinterland of his thoughts.

He thought: If I follow the thread . . . I was thinking of Reality and Eternity . . . yes, and Mallansohn and the Cub!

He stopped there. Why the Cub? Why Cooper? He *hadn't* thought of him.

But if he hadn't, then why should he think of Brinsley Sheridan Cooper now?

He frowned! What was the truth that connected all this? What was it he was trying to find? What made him so sure there *was* something to find?

Harlan felt chilled, for with these questions a distant glow of that earlier illumination seemed to break upon the horizons of his mind and he almost knew.

He held his breath, did not press for it. Let it come.

Let it come.

And in the quite of that night, a night already so uniquely significant in his life, an explanation and interpretation of events came to him that at any saner, more normal time he would not have entertained for a moment.

He let the thought bud and flower, let it grow until he could see it explain a hundred odd points that otherwise simply remained—odd.

He would have to investigate this, check this, back in Eternity, but in his heart he was already convinced that he knew a terrible secret he was not meant to know.

A secret that embraced all Eternity!

LIFE-PLOTTER
— 6 —

A MONTH of physiotime had passed since that night in the 482nd, when he grew acquainted with many things. Now, if one calculated by ordinary time, he was nearly 2000 Centuries in Noÿs Lambent's future, attempting by a mixture of bribery and cajolery to learn what lay in store for her in a new Reality.

It was worse than unethical, but he was past caring. In the physiomonth just gone he had, in his own eyes, become a criminal. There was no way of glossing over that fact. He would be no more a criminal by compounding his crime and he had a great deal to gain by doing so.

Now, as part of his felonious maneuvering (he made no effort to choose a milder phrase) he stood at the barrier before the 2456th. Entry into Time was much more complicated than mere passage between Eternity and the kettle shafts. In order to enter Time the co-ordinates fixing the desired region on Earth's surface had painstakingly to be adjusted and the desired moment of Time pin-pointed within the Century. Yet despite inner tension Harlan handled the controls with the ease and quick confidence of a man with much experience and a great talent.

Harlan found himself in the engine room he had seen first on the viewing screen within Eternity. At this physiomoment Sociologist Voy would be sitting safely before that screen watching for the Technician's Touch that was to come.

Harlan felt no hurry. The room would remain empty for the next 156 minutes. To be sure, the spatio-temporal chart allowed him only 110 minutes, leaving the remaining 46 as the customary 40 per cent "margin." Margin was there in case of necessity, but a Technician was not expected to have to use it. A "margin-eater" did not remain a Specialist long.

Harlan, however, expected to use no more than 2 minutes of the 110. Wearing his wrist-borne field generator so that he was surrounded by an aura of physiotime (an effluvium, so to speak, of Eternity) and therefore protected from any of the effects of Reality Change, he took one step toward the wall, lifted a small container from its position on a shelf, and placed it in a carefully adjusted spot on the shelf below.

Having done that, he re-entered Eternity in a way that seemed as prosaic to himself as passage through any door might be. Had there been a Timer watching, it would have seemed to him that Harlan had simply disappeared.

The small container stayed where he put it. It played no immediate role in world history. A man's hand, hours later, reached for it but did not find it. A search revealed it half an hour later still, but in the interim a force-field had blanked out and a man's temper had been lost. A decision which would have remained unmade in the previous Reality was now made in anger. A meeting did not take place; a man who would have died lived a year longer, under other circumstances; another who would have lived died somewhat sooner.

The ripples spread wider, reaching their maximum in the 2481st, which was twenty-five Centuries upwhen from the Touch. The intensity of the Reality Change declined thereafter. Theorists pointed out that nowhere to the infinite upwhen from the Touch the Change had become too small to detect by the finest Computing, and that was the practical limit.

Of course no human being in Time could ever possibly be aware of any Reality Change having taken place. Mind changed as well as matter and only Eternals could stand outside it all and see the change.

Sociologist Voy was staring at the bluish scene in the 2481st, where earlier there had been all the activity of a busy space-port. He barely looked up when Harlan entered. He barely mumbled something that might have been a greeting.

A change had indeed blasted the space-port. Its shininess was gone; what buildings there stood were not the grand creations they had been. A space-ship rusted. There were no people. There was no motion.

Harlan allowed himself a small smile that flickered for a moment, then vanished. It was M.D.R. all right. Maximum Desired Response. And it had happened at once. The Change did not necessarily take place at the precise moment of the Technician's Touch. If the calculations that went into the Touch were sloppy, hours or days might elapse before the Change actually took place (counting, of course, by physiotime). It was only when all degrees of freedom vanished that the Change took place. While there was even a mathematical chance for alternate actions, the Change did *not* take place.

It was Harlan's pride that when *he* calculated an M.N.C., when it was *his* hand that contrived the Touch, the degrees of freedom vanished at once, and the Change took place instantly.

Voy said softly, "It had been very beautiful."

The phrase grated Harlan's ears, seeming to detract from the beauty of his own performance. "I wouldn't regret," he said, "having space-travel bred out of Reality altogether."

"No?" said Voy.

"What good is it? It never lasts more than a millennium or two. People get tired. They come back home and the colonies die out. Then after another four or five millennia, or forty or fifty, they try again and it fails again. It is a waste of human ingenuity and effort."

Voy said dryly, "You're quite a philosopher."

Harlan flushed. He thought: What's the use in talking to any of them? He said, angrily, with a sharp change of subject, "What about the Life-Plotter?"

"What about him?"

"Would you check with the man? He ought to have made some progress by now."

The Sociologist let a look of disapproval drift across his face, as though to say: You're the impatient one, aren't you? Aloud he said, "Come with me and let's see."

The name plate on the office door said Neron Feruque, which struck Harlan's eye and mind because of its faint similarity to a pair of rulers in the Mediterranean area during Primitive times. (His weekly discourses with Cooper had sharpened his own preoccupation with the Primitive almost feverishly.)

The man, however, resembled neither ruler, as Harlan recalled it. He was almost cadaverously lean, with skin stretched tightly over a high-bridged nose. His fingers were long and his wrists knobby. As he caressed his small Summator, he looked like Death weighing a soul in the balance.

Harlan found himself staring at the Summator hungrily. It was the heart and blood of Life-Plotting, the skin and bones, sinew, muscle, and all else. Feed into it the required data of a personal history, and the equations of the Reality Change; do that and it would chuckle away in obscene merriment for any length of time from a minute to a day, and then spit out the possible companion lives for the person involved (under the new Reality), each neatly ticketed with a probability value.

Sociologist Voy introduced Harlan. Feruque, having stared in open annoyance at the Technician's insigne, nodded his head and let the matter go.

Harlan said, "Is the young lady's Life-Plot complete yet?"

"It is not. I'll let you know when it is." He was one of those who carried contempt for the Technician to the point of open rudeness.

Voy said, "Take it easy, Life-Plotter."

Feruque had eyebrows which were light almost to invisibility. It heightened the resemblance of his face to a skull. His eyes rolled in what should have been empty sockets as he said, "Killed the space-ships?"

Voy nodded. "Cut it down a Century."

Feruque's lips twisted softly and formed a word.

Harlan folded his arms and stared at the Life-Plotter, who looked away in eventual discomfiture.

Harlan thought: He *knows* it's his guilt too.

Feruque said to Voy, "Listen, as long as you're here, what in Time am I going to do about the anti-cancer serum requests? We're not the only Century with anti-cancer. Why do we get all the applications?''

"All the other Centuries are just as crowded. You know that.''

"Then they've got to stop sending in applications altogether.''

"How do we go about making them?''

"Easy. Let the Allwhen Council stop receiving them.''

"I have no pull with the Allwhen Council.''

"You have pull with the old man.''

Harlan listened to the conversation dully, without real interest. At least it served to keep his mind on inconsequentials and away from the chuckling Summator. The "old man,'' he knew, would be the Computer in charge of the Section.

"I've talked to the old man,'' said the Sociologist, "and he's talked to the Council.''

"Nuts. He's just sent through a routine tape-strip. He has to fight for this. It's a matter of basic policy.''

"The Allwhen Council isn't in the mood these days to consider changes in basic policy. You know the rumors going round.''

"Oh, sure. They're busy on a big deal. Whenever there's dodging to do, the word gets round that Council's busy on some big deal.''

(If Harlan could have found the heart for it, he would have smiled at that point.)

Feruque brooded a few moments, and then burst out, "What most people don't understand is that anti-cancer serum isn't a matter of tree seedlings or field motors. I know that every sprig of spruce has to be watched for adverse effects on Reality, but anti-cancer always involves a human life and that's a hundred times as complicated.

"Consider! Think how many people a year die of cancer in each Century that doesn't have anti-cancer serums of one sort or another. You can imagine how many of the patients want to die. So the Timer governments in every Century are forever forwarding applications to Eternity to 'please, pretty please ship them seventy-five thousand ampules of serum on behalf of the men critically stricken who are absolutely vital to the cultures, enclosed see biographical data.' ''

Voy nodded rapidly, "I know. I know.''

But Feruque was not to be denied his bitterness. "So you read the biographical data and it's every man a hero. Every man an insupportable loss to his world. So you work it through. You see what would happen to Reality if each man lived, and for Time's sake, if different *combinations* of men lived.

"In the last month, I've done 572 cancer requests. Seventeen, count them, seventeen Life-Plots came out to involve no undesirable Reality Changes. Mind you, there wasn't one case of a possible *desirable* Reality Change, but the Council says neutral cases get the serum. Humanity, you know. So exactly seventeen people in assorted Centuries get cured this month.

"And what happens? Are the Centuries happy? Not on your life. One man gets cured and a dozen, same country, same Time, don't. Everyone says, Why *that* one? Maybe the guys we didn't treat are better characters, maybe they're rosy-cheeked philanthropists beloved by all, while the one man we cure kicks his aged mother all around the block whenever he can spare the time from beating his kids. They don't know about Reality Changes and we can't tell them.

"We're just making trouble for ourselves, Voy, unless the Allwhen Council decides to screen all applications and approve only those which result in a desirable Reality Change. That's all. Either curing them does some good for humanity, or else it's out. Never mind this business of saying: 'Well, it does no harm.' "

The Sociologist had been listening with a look of mild pain on his face, and now he said, "If it were *you* with cancer . . ."

"That's a stupid remark, Voy. Is that what we base decisions on? In that case there'd never be a Reality Change. Some poor sucker always gets it in the neck, doesn't he? Suppose you were that sucker, hey?

"And another thing. Just remember that every time we make a Reality Change it's harder to find a good next one. Every physioyear, the chance that a random Change is likely to be for the worse increases. That means the proportion of guys we can cure gets smaller anyway. It's always going to get smaller. Someday, we'll be able to cure only one guy a physioyear, even counting the neutral cases. Remember that."

Harlan lost even the faintest interest. This was the type of griping that went with the business. The Psychologists and Sociologists, in their rare introvertive studies of Eternity, called it identification. Men identified themselves with the Century with which they were associated professionally. Its battles, all too often, became their own battles.

Eternity fought the devil of identification as best it could. No man could be assigned to any Section within two Centuries of his homewhen, to make identification harder. Preference was given to Centuries with cultures markedly different from that of their homewhen. (Harlan thought of Finge and the 482nd.) What was more, their assignments were shifted as often as their reactions grew suspect. (Harlan wouldn't give a 50th Century grafenpiece for Feruque's chances of retaining this assignment longer than another physioyear at the outside.)

And still men identified out of a silly yearning for a home in Time (the Time-wish; everyone knew about it). For some reason this was particularly true in Centuries with space-travel. It was something that should be investigated and would be but for Eternity's chronic reluctance to turn its eyes inward.

A month earlier Harlan might have despised Feruque as a blustering sentimentalist, a petulant oaf who eased the pain of watching the electro-gravitics lose intensity in a new Reality by railing against those of other Centuries who wanted anti-cancer serum.

He might have reported him. It would have been his duty to do so. The man's reactions obviously could no longer be trusted.

He could not do so, now. He even found sympathy for the man. His own crime was so much greater.

How easy it was to slip back to thoughts of Noÿs.

Eventually he had fallen asleep that night, and he awoke in daylight, with brightness shining through translucent walls all about until it was as though he had awakened on a cloud in a misty morning sky.

Noÿs was laughing down at him. "*Goodness,* it was hard to wake you."

Harlan's first reflexive action was a scrabble for bedclothes that weren't there. Then memory arrived and he stared at her hollowly, his face burning red. How should he feel about this?

But then something else occurred to him and he shot to a sitting position. "It isn't past one, is it? Father Time!"

"It's only eleven. You've got breakfast waiting and lots of time."

"Thanks," he mumbled.

"The shower controls are all set and your clothes are all ready."

What could he say? "Thanks," he mumbled.

He avoided her eyes during the meal. She sat opposite him, not eating, her chin buried in the palm of one hand, her dark hair combed thickly to one side and her eyelashes preternaturally long.

She followed every gesture he made while he kept his eyes lowered and searched for the bitter shame he knew he ought to feel.

She said, "Where will you be going at one?"

"Aeroball game," he muttered, "I have the ticket."

"That's the rubber game. And I missed the whole season because of just skipping the time, you know. Who'll win the game, Andrew?"

He felt oddly weak at the sound of his first name. He shook his head curtly and tried to look austere. (It used to have been so easy.)

"But surely you know. You've inspected this whole period, haven't you?"

Properly speaking, he ought to maintain a flat and cold negative, but weakly he explained, "There was a lot of Space and Time to cover. I wouldn't know little precise things like game scores."

"Oh, you just don't want to tell me."

Harlan said nothing to that. He inserted the pene-prong into the small, juicy fruit and lifted it, whole, to his lips.

After a moment Noÿs said, "Did you see what happened in this neighborhood before you came?"

"No details, N—noÿs." (He forced her name past his lips.)

The girl said softly, "Didn't you see us? Didn't you know all along that——"

Harlan stammered, "No, no, I couldn't see myself. I'm not in Rea—— I'm not here till I come. I can't explain." He was doubly flustered. First, that she should speak of it. Second, that he had almost been trapped into saying, "Reality," of all the words the most forbidden in conversations with Timers.

She lifted her eyebrows and her eyes grew round and a little amazed. "Are you ashamed?"

"What we did was not proper."

"Why not?" And in the 482nd her question was perfectly innocent. "Aren't Eternals allowed to?" There was almost a joking cast to that question as though she were asking if Eternals weren't allowed to eat.

"Don't use the word," said Harlan. "As a matter of fact, we're not, in a way."

"Well, then, don't tell them. I won't."

And she walked about the table and sat down on his lap, pushing the small table out of the way with a smooth and flowing motion of her hip.

Momentarily he stiffened, lifted his hands in a gesture that might have been intended to hold her off. It didn't succeed.

She bent and kissed him on his lips, and nothing seemed shameful any more. Nothing that involved Noÿs and himself.

He wasn't sure when first he began to do something that an Observer, ethically, had no right to do. That is, he began to speculate on the nature of the problem involving the current Reality and of the Reality Change that would be planned.

It was not the loose morals of the Century, not ectogenesis, not matriarchy, that disturbed Eternity. All of that was as it was in the previous Reality and the Allwhen Council had viewed it with equanimity then. Finge had said it was something very subtle.

The Change then would have to be very subtle and it would have to involve the group he was Observing. So much seemed obvious.

It would involve the aristocracy, the well-to-do, the upper classes, the beneficiaries of the system.

What bothered him was that it would most certainly involve Noÿs.

He got through the remaining three days called for in his chart in a gathering cloud that dampened even his joy of Noÿs's company.

She said to him, "What happened? For a while, you seemed all different from the way you were in Eter—in that place. You weren't stiff at all. Now, you seem concerned. Is it because you have to go back?"

Harlan said, "Partly."

"Do you have to?"

"I have to."

"Well, who would care if you were late?"

Harlan almost smiled at that. "They wouldn't like me to be late," he said, yet thought longingly just the same of the two-day margin allowed for in his chart.

She adjusted the controls of a musical instrument that played soft and complicated strains out of its own creative bowels by striking notes and chords in a random manner: the randomness weighted in favor of pleasant combinations by intricate mathematical formulae. The music could no more repeat itself than could snowflakes, and could no more fail of beauty.

Through the hypnosis of sound Harlan gazed at Noÿs and his thoughts wound tightly about her. What would she be in the new dispensation? A fishwife, a factory girl, the mother of six, fat, ugly, diseased? Whatever she was, she would not remember Harlan. He would have been no part of her life in a new Reality. And whatever she would be then, she would not be Noÿs.

He did not simply love a *girl*. (Strangely, he used the word "love" in his own thoughts for the first time and did not even pause long enough to stare at the strange thing and wonder at it.) He loved a complex of factors; her choice of clothes, her walk, her manner of speech, her tricks of expression. A quarter century of life and experience in a given Reality had gone into the manufacture of all that. She had not been his Noÿs in the previous Reality of a physioyear earlier. She would not be his Noÿs in the next Reality.

The new Noÿs might, conceivably, be better in some ways, but he knew one thing very definitely. He wanted this Noÿs here, the one he saw at this moment, the one of this Reality. If she had faults, he wanted those faults, too.

What could he do?

Several things occurred to him, all illegal. One of them was to learn the nature of the Change and find out definitely how it would affect Noÿs. One could not, after all, be certain that . . .

* * *

A dead silence wrenched Harlan out of his reverie. He was in the Life-Plotter's office once more. Sociologist Voy was watching him out of the corner of his eye. Feruque's death's-head was lowering at him.

And the silence was piercing.

It took a moment for the significance to penetrate. Just a moment. The Summator had ceased its inner clucking.

Harlan jumped up. "You have the answer, Life-Plotter."

Feruque looked down at the flimsies in his hand. "Yeah. Sure. Sort of funny."

"May I have it?" Harlan held out his hand. It was trembling visibly.

"There's nothing to see. That's what's funny."

"What do you mean—nothing?" Harlan stared at Feruque with eyes that suddenly smarted till there was only a tall, thin blur where Feruque stood.

The Life-Plotter's matter-of-fact voice sounded thin. "The dame doesn't exist in the new Reality. No personality shift. She's just out, that's all. Gone. I ran the alternatives down to Probability 0.0001. She doesn't make it anywhere. In fact"—and he reached up to rub his cheek with long, spare fingers—"with the combination of factors you handed me I don't quite see how she fit in the old Reality."

Harlan hardly heard. "But—but the Change was such a small one."

"I know. A funny combination of factors. Here, you want the flimsies?"

Harlan's hand closed over them, unfeeling. Noÿs gone? Noÿs nonexistent? How could that be?

He felt a hand on his shoulder and Voy's voice clashed on his ear. "Are you ill, Technician?" The hand drew away as though it already regretted its careless contact with a Technician's body.

Harlan swallowed and with an effort composed his features. "I'm quite well. Would you take me to the kettle?"

He *must not* show his feelings. He must act as though this were what he represented it to be, a mere academic investigation. He must disguise the fact that with Noÿs's nonexistence in the new Reality he was almost physically overwhelmed by a flood of pure elation, unbearable joy.

PRELUDE TO CRIME

— 7 —

HARLAN STEPPED into the kettle at the 2456th and looked backward to make certain that the barrier that separated the shaft from Eternity was truly flawless; that Sociologist Voy was not watching. In these last weeks it had grown to be a habit with him, an automatic twitch, there was always the quick backward glance across the shoulder to make sure no one was behind him in the kettle shafts.

And then, though already in the 2456th, it was for *up*when that Harlan set the kettle controls. He watched the numbers on the temporometer rise. Though they moved with blurry quickness, there would be considerable time for thought.

How the Life-Plotter's finding changed matters! How the very nature of his crime had changed!

And it had all hinged on Finge. The phrase caught at him with its ridiculous rhyme and its heavy beat circled dizzyingly inside his skull: It hinged on Finge. It hinged on Finge. . . .

Harlan had avoided any personal contact with Finge on his return to Eternity after those days with Noÿs in the 482nd. As Eternity closed in about him, so did guilt. A broken oath of office, which seemed nothing in the 482nd, was enormous in Eternity.

He had sent in his report by impersonal air-chute and took himself off to personal quarters. He needed to think this out, gain time to consider and grow accustomed to the new orientation within himself.

Finge did not permit it. He was in communication with Harlan less than an hour after the report had been coded for proper direction and inserted into the chute.

The Computer's image stared out of the vision plate. His voice said, "I expected you to be in your office."

Harlan said, "I delivered the report, sir. It doesn't matter where I wait for a new assignment."

"Yes?" Finge scanned the roll of foil he held in his hands, holding it up, squint-eyed, and peering at its perforation pattern.

"It is scarcely complete," he went on. "May I visit your rooms?"

Harlan hesitated a moment. The man was his superior and to refuse the self-invitation at this moment would have a flavor of insubordination. It would advertise his guilt, it seemed, and his raw, painful conscience dared not permit that.

"You will be welcome, Computer," he said stiffly.

Finge's sleek softness introduced a jarring element of epicureanism into Harlan's angular quarters. The 95th, Harlan's homewhen, tended toward the Spartan in house furnishings and Harlan had never completely lost his taste for the style. The tubular metal chairs had been surfaced with a dull veneer that had been artificially grained into the appearance of wood (though not very successfully). In one corner of the room was a small piece of furniture that represented an even wider departure from the customs of the times.

It caught Finge's eye almost at once.

The Computer put a pudgy finger on it, as though to test its texture. "What is this material?"

"Wood, sir," said Harlan.

"The real thing? Actual wood? Amazing! You use wood in your homewhen, I believe?"

"We do."

"I see. There's nothing in the rules against this, Technician"—he dusted the finger with which he had touched the object against the side seam of his trouser leg—"but I don't know that it's advisable to allow the culture of the homewhen to affect one. The true Eternal adopts whatever culture he is surrounded by. I doubt, for instance, if I have eaten out of an energic utensil more than twice in five years." He sighed. "And yet to allow food to touch matter has always seemed unclean. But I don't give in. I don't give in."

His eyes returned to the wooden object, but now he held both hands behind his back, and said, "What is it? What is its purpose?"

"It's a bookcase," said Harlan. He had the impulse to ask Finge how he felt now that his hands rested firmly upon the small of his back. Would he not consider it cleaner to have his clothes and his own body constructed of pure and undefiled energy fields?

Finge's eyebrows lifted. "A bookcase. Then those objects resting upon the shelves are books. Is that right?"

"Yes, sir."

"Authentic specimens?"

"Entirely, Computer. I picked them up in the 24th. The few I have here date from the 20th. If—if you intend to look at them, I wish you'd be careful. The pages have been restored and impregnated, but they're not foil. They take careful handling."

"I won't touch them. I have no intention of touching them. Original 20th Century dust is on them, I imagine. Actual books!" He laughed. "Pages of cellulose, too? You implied that."

Harlan nodded. "Cellulose modified by the impregnation treatment for longer life. Yes." He opened his mouth for a deep breath, forcing himself to remain calm. It was ridiculous to identify himself with these books, to feel a slur upon them to be a slur upon himself.

"I dare say," said Finge, still on the subject, "that the whole content of those books could be placed on two meters of film and stored in a finger's end. What do the books contain?"

Harlan said, "They are bound volumes of a news magazine of the 20th."

"You read that?"

Harlan said proudly, "These are a few volumes of the complete collection I have. No library in Eternity can duplicate it."

"Yes, your hobby. I remember now you once told me about your interest in the Primitive. I'm amazed your Educator ever allowed you to grow interested in such a thing. A complete waste of energy."

Harlan's lips thinned. The man, he decided, was deliberately trying to irritate him out of possession of calm reasoning faculties. If so, he must not be allowed to succeed.

Harlan said flatly, "I think you've come to see me about my report."

"Yes, I have." The Computer looked about, selected a chair, and sat down gingerly. "It is not complete, as I said over the communicator."

"In what way, sir?" (Calm! Calm!)

Finge broke into a nervous twitch of a smile. "What happened that you didn't mention, Harlan?"

"Nothing, sir." And though he said it firmly, he stood there, hangdog.

"Come, Technician. You spent several periods of time in the society of the young lady. Or you did if you followed the spatio-temporal chart. You did follow it, I suppose?"

Harlan's guilt riddled him to the point where he could not even rise to the bait of this open assault upon his professional competence.

He could only say, "I followed it."

"And what happened? You include nothing of the private interludes with the woman."

"Nothing of importance happened," said Harlan, drylipped.

"That is ridiculous. At your time of life and with your experience, I don't have to tell you that it is not for an Observer to judge what is important and what is not."

Finge's eyes were keenly upon Harlan. They were harder and more eager than quite befitted his soft line of questioning.

Harlan noted that well and was not fooled by Finge's gentle voice, yet the habit of duty tugged at him. An Observer must report *everything*. An Observer was merely a sense-perceptive pseudopod thrust out by Eternity into Time. It tested its surroundings and was drawn back. In the fulfillment of his function an Observer had no individuality of his own; he was not really a man.

Almost automatically Harlan began his narration of the events he had left out of his report. He did it with the trained memory of the Observer, reciting the conversations with word-for-word accuracy, reconstructing the tone of voice and cast of countenance. He did it lovingly, for in the telling he lived it again, and almost forgot, in the process, that a combination of Finge's probing and his own healing sense of duty was driving him into an admission of guilt.

It was only as he approached the end result of that first long conversation that he faltered and the shell of his Observer's objectivity showed cracks.

He was saved from further details by the hand that Finge suddenly raised and by the Computer's sharp, edgy voice. "Thank you. It is enough. You were about to say that you made love to the woman."

Harlan grew angry. What Finge said was the literal truth, but Finge's tone of voice made it sound lewd, coarse, and, worse than that, commonplace. Whatever else it was, or might be, it was not commonplace.

Harlan had an explanation for Finge's attitude, for his anxious cross-examination, for his breaking off the verbal report at the moment he did. Finge was jealous! That much Harlan would have sworn was obvious. Harlan had succeeded in taking away a girl that Finge had meant to have.

Harlan felt the triumph in that and found it sweet. For the first time in his life he knew an aim that meant more to him than the frigid fulfillment of Eternity. He was going to keep Finge jealous, because Noÿs Lambent was to be permanently his.

In this mood of sudden exaltation he plunged into the request that originally he had planned to present only after a wait of a discreet four or five days.

He said, "It is my intention to apply for permission to form a liaison with a Timed individual."

Finge seemed to snap out of a reverie. "With Noÿs Lambent, I presume."

"Yes, sir. As Computer in charge of the Section, it will have to go through you. . . ."

Harlan wanted it to go through Finge. Make him suffer. If he wanted the girl himself, let him say so and Harlan could insist on allowing Noÿs to make her choice. He almost smiled at that. He hoped it would come to that. It would be the final triumph.

Ordinarily, of course, a Technician could not hope to push through such a matter in the face of a Computer's desires, but Harlan was sure he could count on Twissell's backing, and Finge had a long way to go before he could buck Twissell.

Finge, however, seemed tranquil. "It would seem," he said, "that you have already taken illegal possession of the girl."

Harlan flushed and was moved to a feeble defense. "The spatio-temporal chart insisted on our remaining alone together. Since nothing of what happened was specifically forbidden, I feel no guilt."

Which was a lie, and from Finge's half-amused expression one could feel that he knew it to be a lie.

He said, "There will be a Reality Change."

Harlan said, "If so, I will amend my application to request liaison with Miss Lambent in the new Reality."

"I don't think that would be wise. How can you be sure in advance? In the new Reality, she may be married, she may be deformed. In fact I can tell you this. In the new Reality, she will not want you. She will *not* want you."

Harlan quivered. "You know nothing about it."

"Oh? You think this great love of yours is a matter of soul-to-soul contact? That it will survive all external changes? Have you been reading novels out of Time?"

Harlan was goaded into indiscretion. "For one thing, I don't believe you."

Finge said coldly, "I beg pardon."

"You're lying." Harlan didn't care what he said now. "You're jealous. It's all it amounts to. You're jealous. You had your own plans for Noÿs but she chose me."

Finge said, "Do you realize——"

"I realize a great deal. I'm no fool. I may not be a Computer, but neither am I an ignoramus. You say she won't want me in the new Reality. How do you know? You don't even know yet what the new Reality will be. You don't know if there must be a new Reality at all. You just received my report. It must be analyzed before a Reality Change can be computed, let alone submitted for approval. So when you affect to know the nature of the Change, you are lying."

There were a number of ways in which Finge might have made response. Harlan's heated mind was aware of many. He did not try to choose among them. Finge might stalk out in affected dudgeon; he might call in a member of Security and have Harlan taken into custody for insubordination; he might shout back, yelling as angrily as Harlan; he might put in an immediate call to Twissell, lodging a formal complaint; he might—he might . . .

Finge did none of this.

He said gently, "Sit down, Harlan. Let's talk about this."

And because that response was completely unexpected, Harlan's jaw sagged and he sat down in confusion. His resolution faltered. What was this?

"You remember, of course," said Finge, "that I told you that our problem with the 482nd involved an undesirable attitude on the part of the Timers of the current Reality toward Eternity. You do remember that, don't you?" He spoke with the mild urging of a schoolmaster toward a somewhat backward student, yet Harlan thought he could detect a kind of hard glitter in his eye.

Harlan said, "Of course."

"You remember, too, that I told you that the Allwhen Council was reluctant to accept my analysis of the situation without specific confirming Observations. Doesn't that imply to you that I had already Computed the necessary Reality Change?"

"But my own Observations represent the confirmation, don't they?"

"They do."

"And it would take time to analyze them properly."

"Nonsense. Your report means nothing. The confirmation lay in what you told me orally moments ago."

"I don't understand you."

"Look, Harlan, let me tell you what is wrong with the 482nd. Among the upper classes of this Century, particularly among the women, there has grown up the notion that Eternals are really Eternal, literally so; that they live forever. . . . Great Time, man, Noÿs Lambent told you as much. You repeated her statements to me not twenty minutes ago."

Harlan stared blankly at Finge. He was remembering Noÿs's soft, caressing voice as she leaned toward him and caught at his eyes with her own lovely, dark glance: *You live forever. You're an Eternal.*

Finge went on, "Now a belief like that is bad, but, in itself, not too bad. It can lead to inconveniences, increase difficulties for the Section, but Computation would show that only in a minority of cases would Change be necessary. Still, if a Change *is* desirable, isn't it obvious to you that the inhabitants of the Century who must, above all, change maximally with the Change, be those who are subject to the superstition. In other words, the female aristocracy. Noÿs."

"It may be, but I'll take my chance," said Harlan.

"You have no chance at all. Do you think your fascinations and charm persuaded the soft aristocrat to fall into the arms of an unimportant Technician? Come, Harlan, be realistic about this."

Harlan's lips grew stubborn. He said nothing.

Finge said, "Can't you guess the additional superstition which these people have added to their belief in the actual eternal life of the Eternals? Great Time, Harlan! Most of the women believe that intimacy with an Eternal will enable a mortal woman (as they think of themselves) to live forever!"

Harlan swayed. He could hear Noÿs's voice again so clearly: *If I were made an Eternal . . .*

And then her kisses.

Finge went on. "The existence of such a superstition was hard to believe, Harlan. It was unprecedented. It lay within the region of random error so that a search through the Computations for the previous Change yielded no information respecting it one way or the other. The Allwhen Council wanted firm evidence, direct substantiation. I chose Miss Lambent as a good example of her class. I chose you as the other subject——"

Harlan struggled to his feet. "You chose *me?* As a *subject?*"

"I'm sorry," said Finge stiffly, "but it was necessary. You made a very good subject."

Harlan stared at him.

Finge had the grace to squirm a bit under that wordless stare. He said, "Don't you see? No, you still don't. Look, Harlan, you're a cold-fish product of Eternity. You won't look at a woman. You consider women and all that concerns them unethical. No, there's a better word. You consider them *sinful.* That attitude shows all over you, and to any woman you'd have all the sex appeal of a month-dead mackerel. Yet here we have a woman, a beautiful pampered product of a hedonistic culture, who ardently seduces you on your first evening together, virtually begging for your embrace. Don't you understand that that is ridiculous, impossible, unless—well, unless it is the confirmation we were looking for."

Harlan struggled for words. "You say she sold herself——"

"Why that expression? There is no shame attached to sex in this Century. The only strange thing is that she chose you as partner, and *that* she did for the sake of eternal life. It's plain."

And Harlan, arms raised, hands claw-bent, with no rational thought in his mind, or any irrational one other than to choke and throttle Finge, sprang forward.

Finge stepped back hastily. He brought out a blaster with a quick, trembling gesture. "Don't touch me! Back!"

Harlan had just enough sanity to halt his rush. His hair was matted. His shirt was stained with perspiration. His breath whistled through pinched white nostrils.

Finge said shakily, "I know you very well, you see, and I thought your reaction might be violent. Now I'll shoot if I have to."

Harlan said, "Get out."

"I will. But first you'll listen. For attacking a Computer, you can be declassified, but we'll let that go. You will understand, however, that I did not lie. The Noÿs Lambent of the new Reality, whatever else may be or not be, will lack this superstition. The whole purpose of the Change will be to wipe out the superstition. And without it, Harlan"—his voice was almost a snarl—"how could a woman like Noÿs want a man like you?"

The pudgy Computer backed toward the door of Harlan's personal quarters, blaster still leveled.

He paused to say, with a sort of grim gaiety, "Of course, if you had her now, Harlan, if you had her now, you could enjoy her. You could keep your liaison and make it formal. That is, if you had her now. But the Change will come soon, Harlan, and after that, you will not have her. What a pity, the now does not last, even in Eternity, eh, Harlan?"

Harlan no longer looked at him. Finge had won after all and was leaving in clear and leering possession of the field. Harlan stared unseeingly at his own toes, and when he looked up Finge was gone—whether five seconds earlier or fifteen minutes Harlan could not have said.

Hours had passed nightmarishly and Harlan felt trapped in the prison of his mind. All that Finge had said was so true, so transparently true. Harlan's Observer mind could look back upon the relationship of himself and Noÿs, that short, unusual relationship, and it took on a different texture.

It wasn't a case of instant infatuation. How could he have believed it was? Infatuation for a man like himself?

Of course not. Tears stung his eyes and he felt ashamed. How obvious it was that the affair was a case of cool calculation. The girl had certain undeniable physical assets and no ethical principles to keep her from using them. So she used them and that had nothing to do with Andrew Harlan as a person. He simply represented her distorted view of Eternity and what it meant.

Automatically Harlan's long fingers caressed the volumes in his small bookshelf. He took one out and, unseeingly, opened it.

The print blurred. The faded colors of the illustrations were ugly, meaningless blotches.

Why had Finge troubled to tell him all this? In the strictest sense he ought not to have. An Observer, or anyone acting as Observer, ought never to know the ends attained by his Observation. It removed him by so much from the ideal position of the objective non-human tool.

It was to crush him, of course; to take a mean and jealous revenge!

Harlan fingered the open page of the magazine. He found himself staring at a duplication, in startling red, of a ground vehicle, similar to vehicles characteristic of the 45th, 182nd, 590th, and 984th Centuries, as well as of late Primitive times. It was a very common sort of affair with an internal-combustion motor. In the Primitive era natural petroleum fractions were the source of power and natural rubber cushioned the wheels. That was true of none of the later Centuries, of course.

Harlan had pointed that out to Cooper. He had made quite a point of it, and now his mind, as though longing to turn away from the unhappy present, drifted back to that moment. Sharp, irrelevant images filled the ache within Harlan.

"These advertisements," he had said, "tell us more of Primitive times than the so-called news articles in the same magazine. The news articles assume a basic knowledge of the world it deals with. It uses terms it feels no necessity of explaining. What is a 'golf ball,' for instance?"

Cooper had professed his ignorance readily.

Harlan went on in the didactic tone he could scarcely avoid on occasions such as this. "We could deduce that it was a small pellet of some sort from the nature of the casual mentions it receives. We know that it is used in a game, if only because it is mentioned in an item under the heading 'Sport.' We can even make further deductions that it is hit by a long rod of some sort and the object of the game is to drive the ball into a hole in the ground. But why bother with deduction and reasoning? Observe this advertisement! The object of it is only to induce readers to buy the ball, but in so doing we are presented with an excellent close-range portrait of one, with a section cut into it to show its construction."

Cooper, coming from an era in which advertisement was not as wildly proliferative as it was in the later Centuries of Primitive times, found all this difficult to appreciate. He said, "Isn't it rather disgusting the way these people blow their own horn? Who would be fool enough to believe a person's boastings about his own products? Would he admit defects? Is he likely to stop at any exaggeration?"

Harlan, whose homewhen was middling fruitful in advertisement, raised tolerant eyebrows and merely said, "You'll have to accept that. It's their way and we never quarrel with the ways of any culture as long as it does not seriously harm mankind as a whole."

But now Harlan's mind snapped back to his present situation and he was back in the present, staring at the loudmouthed, brassy advertisements in the news magazine. He asked himself in sudden excitement: Were the thoughts he had just experienced really irrelevant? Or was he tortuously finding a way out of the blackness and back to Noÿs?

Advertisement! A device for forcing the unwilling into line. Did it matter to a ground-vehicle manufacturer whether a given individual felt an original or spontaneous desire for his product? If the prospect (that was the word) could be artificially persuaded or cajoled into feeling that desire and acting upon it, would that not be just as well?

Then what did it matter if Noÿs loved him out of passion or out of calculation? Let them but be together long enough and she would grow to love him. He would *make* her love him and, in the end, love and not its motivation was what counted. He wished now he had read some of the novels out of Time that Finge had mentioned scornfully.

Harlan's fists clenched at a sudden thought. If Noÿs had come to *him*, to *Harlan*, for immortality, it could only mean that she had not yet fulfilled the requirement for that gift. She could have made love to no Eternal previously. That meant that her relationship to Finge had been nothing more than that of secretary and employer. Otherwise what need would she have had for Harlan?

Yet Finge surely must have tried—must have attempted . . . (Harlan could not complete the thought even in the secrecy of his own mind.) Finge could have proved the superstition's existence on his own person. Surely he could not have missed the thought with Noÿs an ever-present temptation. Then she must have refused him.

He had had to use Harlan and Harlan had succeeded. It was for that reason that Finge had been driven into the jealous revenge of torturing Harlan with the knowledge that Noÿs's motivation had been a practical one, and that he could never have her.

Yet Noÿs had refused Finge even with eternal life at stake and *had* accepted Harlan. She had that much of a choice and she had made it in Harlan's favor. So it wasn't calculation entirely. Emotion played a part.

Harlan's thoughts were wild and jumbled, and grew more heated with every moment.

He *must* have her, and *now*. Before any Reality Change. What was it Finge had said to him, jeering: *The now does not last, even in Eternity.*

Doesn't it, though? Doesn't it?

Harlan had known exactly what he must do. Finge's angry taunting had goaded him into a frame of mind where he was ready for crime and Finge's final sneer had, at least, inspired him with the nature of the deed he must commit.

He had not wasted a moment after that. It was with excitement and even joy that he left his quarters, at all but a run, to commit a major crime against Eternity.

CRIME
— 8 —

NO ONE had questioned him. No one had stopped him.

There was that advantage, anyway, in the social isolation of a Technician. He went via the kettle channels to a door to Time and set its controls. There was the chance, of course, that someone would happen along on a legitimate errand and wonder why the door was in use. He hesitated, and then decided to stamp his seal on the marker. A sealed door would draw little attention. An unsealed door in active use would be a nine-day wonder.

Of course, it might be Finge who stumbled upon the door. He would have to chance that.

Noÿs was still standing as he had left her. Wretched hours (physiohours) had passed since Harlan had left the 482nd for a lonely Eternity, but he returned now to the same Time, within a matter of seconds, that he had left. Not a hair on Noÿs's head had stirred.

She looked startled. "Did you forget something, Andrew?"

Harlan stared at her hungrily, but made no move to touch her. He remembered Finge's words, and he dared not risk a repulse. He said stiffly, "You've got to do as I say."

She said, "But is something wrong, then? You just left. You just this minute left."

"Don't worry," said Harlan. It was all he could do to keep from taking her hand, from trying to soothe her. Instead he spoke harshly. It was as though some demon were forcing him to do all the wrong things. Why had he come back at the first available moment? He was only disturbing her by his almost instantaneous return after leaving.

(He knew the answer to that, really. He had a two-day margin of grace allowed by the spatio-temporal chart. The earlier portions of that period of grace were safer and yielded least chance of discovery. It was a natural tendency to crowd it as far downwhen as he could. A foolish risk, too, though. He might easily have miscalculated and entered Time before he had left it physiohours earlier. What then? It was one of the first rules he had learned as an Observer: One person occupying two points in the same Time of the same Reality runs a risk of meeting himself.

Somehow that was something to be avoided. Why? Harlan knew he didn't want to meet himself. He didn't want to be staring into the eyes of another and earlier [or later] Harlan. Beyond that it would be a paradox, and what was it Twissell was fond of saying? "There are no paradoxes in Time, but only because Time deliberately avoids paradoxes.")

All the time Harlan thought dizzily of all this Noÿs stared at him with large, luminous eyes.

Then she came to him and put cool hands on either burning cheek and said softly, "You're in trouble."

To Harlan her glance seemed kindly, loving. Yet how could that be? She had what she wanted. What else was there? He seized her wrists and said huskily, "Will you come with me? Now? Without asking any questions? Doing exactly as I say?"

"Must I?" she asked.

"You must, Noÿs. It's very important."

"Then I'll come." She said it matter-of-factly, as though such a request came to her each day and was always accepted.

At the lip of the kettle Noÿs hesitated a moment, then stepped in.

Harlan said, "We're going upwhen, Noÿs."

"That means the future, doesn't it?"

The kettle was already faintly humming as she entered it and she was scarcely seated when Harlan unobtrusively moved the contact at his elbow.

She showed no signs of nausea at the beginnings of that indescribable sensation of "motion" through Time. He was afraid she might.

She sat there quietly, so beautiful and so at ease that he ached, looking at her, and gave not the particle of a damn that, by bringing a Timer, unauthorized, into Eternity, he had committed a felony.

She said, "Does that dial show the numbers of the years, Andrew?"

"The Centuries."

"You mean we're a thousand years in the future? Already?"

"That's right."

"It doesn't feel like it."

"I know."

She looked about. "But how are we moving?"

"I don't know, Noÿs."

"You *don't?*"

"There are many things about Eternity that are hard to understand."

The numbers on the temporometer *marched.* Faster and faster they moved till they were a blur. With his elbow Harlan had nudged the speed stick to high. The power drain might cause some surprise in the power plants, but he doubed it. No one had been waiting for him in Eternity when he returned with Noÿs and that was nine tenths the battle. Now it was only necessary to get her to a safe place.

Again Harlan looked at her. "Eternals don't know everything."

"And I'm not an Eternal," she murmured. "I know so little."

Harlan's pulse quickened. *Still* not an Eternal? But Finge said . . .

Leave it at that, he pleaded with himself. Leave it at that. She's coming with you. She smiles at you. What more do you want?

But he spoke anyway. He said, "You think an Eternal lives forever, don't you?"

"Well, they call them Eternals, you know, and everyone says they do." She smiled at him brightly. "But they don't, do they?"

"You don't think so, then?"

"After I was in Eternity a while, I didn't. People didn't talk as though they lived forever, and there were old men there."

"Yet you told me I lived forever—that night."

She moved closer to him along the seat, still smiling. "I thought: who knows?"

He said, without being quite able to keep the strain out of his voice, "How does a Timer go about becoming an Eternal?"

Her smile vanished and was it his imagination or was there a trace of heightened color in her cheek. She said, "Why do you ask that?"

"To find out."

"It's silly," she said. "I'd rather not talk about it." She stared down at her graceful fingers, edged with nails that glittered colorlessly in the muted light of the kettle shaft. Harlan thought abstractedly and quite apropos of nothing that at an evening gathering, with a touch of mild ultraviolet in the wall illumination, those nails would glow a soft apple-green or a brooding crimson, depending on the angle she held her hands. A clever girl, one like Noÿs, could produce half a dozen shades out of them, and make it seem as though the colors were reflecting her moods. Blue for innocence, bright yellow for laughter, violet for sorrow, and scarlet for passion.

He said, "Why did you make love to me?"

She shook her hair back and looked at him out of a pale, grave face. She said, "If you must know, part of the reason was the theory that a girl can become an Eternal that way. I wouldn't mind living forever."

"I thought you said you didn't believe that."

"I didn't, but it couldn't hurt a girl to take the chance. Especially——"

He was staring at her sternly, finding refuge from hurt and disappointment in a frozen look of disapproval from the heights of the morality of his homewhen. "Well?"

"Especially since I wanted to, anyway."

"Wanted to make love to me?"

"Yes."

"Why me?"

"Because I liked you. Because I thought you were funny."

"Funny!"

"Well, odd, if you like that better. You always worked so hard not to look at me, but you always looked at me anyway. You tried to hate me and I could see you wanted me. I was sorry for you a little, I think."

"What were you sorry about?" He felt his cheeks burning.

"That you should have such trouble about wanting me. It's such a simple thing. You just ask a girl. It's so easy to be friendly. Why suffer?"

Harlan nodded. The morality of the 482nd! "Just ask a girl," he muttered. "So simple. Nothing more necessary."

"The girl has to be willing, of course. Mostly she is, if she's not otherwise engaged. Why not? It's simple enough."

It was Harlan's turn to drop his eyes. Of course, it was simple enough. And nothing wrong with it, either. Not in the 482nd. Who in Eternity should know this better? He would be a fool, an utter and unspeakable fool, to ask her now about earlier affairs. He might as well ask a girl of his own homewhen if she had ever eaten in the presence of a man and how dared she?

Instead he said humbly, "And what do you think of me now?"

"That you are very nice," she said softly, "and that if you ever relaxed—— Won't you smile?"

"There's nothing to smile about, Noÿs."

"Please. I want to see if your cheeks can crease right. Let's see." She put her fingers to the corners of his mouth and pressed them backward. He jerked his head back in surprise and couldn't avoid smiling.

"See. Your cheeks didn't even crack. You're almost handsome. With enough practice—standing in front of a mirror and smiling and getting a twinkle in your eye—I'll bet you could be really handsome."

But the smile, fragile enough to begin with, vanished.

Noÿs said, "We *are* in trouble, aren't we?"

"Yes, we are, Noÿs. Great trouble."

"Because of what we did? You and I? That evening?"

"Not really."

"That was my fault, you know. I'll tell them so, if you wish."

"Never," said Harlan with energy. "Don't take on any fault in this. You've done nothing, *nothing,* to be guilty for. It's something else."

Noÿs looked uneasily at the temporometer. "Where are we? I can't even see the numbers."

"When are we?" Harlan corrected her automatically. He slowed the velocity and the Centuries came into view.

Her beautiful eyes widened and the lashes stood out against the whiteness of her skin. "Is that *right?"*

Harlan looked at the indicator casually. It was in the 72,000's. "I'm sure it is."

"But where are we going?"

"To *when* are we going. To the far upwhen," he said, grimly. "Good and far. Where they won't find you."

And in silence they watched the numbers mount. In silence Harlan told himself over and over that the girl was innocent of Finge's charge. She had owned up frankly to its partial truth and she had admitted, just as frankly, the presence of a more personal attraction.

He looked up, then, as Noÿs shifted position. She had moved to his side of the kettle and, with a resolute gesture, brought the kettle to a halt at a most uncomfortable temporal deceleration.

Harlan gulped and closed his eyes to let the nausea pass. He said, "What's the matter?"

She looked ashen and for a moment made no reply. Then she said, "I don't want to go any further. The numbers are so high."

The temporometer read: 111,394.

He said, "Far enough."

Then he held out his hand gravely, "Come, Noÿs. This will be your home for a while."

They wandered through the corridors like children, hand in hand. The lights along the mainways were on, and the darkened rooms blazed at the touch of a contact. The air was fresh and had a liveliness about it which, without sensible draft, yet indicated the presence of ventilation.

Noÿs whispered, "Is there no one here?"

"No one," said Harlan. He tried to say it firmly and loudly. He wanted to break the spell of being in a "Hidden Century," but he said it in only a whisper after all.

He did not even know how to refer to anything so far upwhen. To call it the one-one-one-three-ninety-fourth was ridiculous. One would have to say simply and indefinitely, "The hundred thousands."

It was a foolish problem to be concerned with, but now that the exaltation of actual flight was done with, he found himself alone in a region of Eternity where no human footsteps had wandered and he did not like it. He was ashamed, doubly ashamed since Noÿs was witness, at the fact that the faint chill within him was the faint chill of a faint fear.

Noÿs said, "It's so clean. There's no dust."

"Self-cleaning," said Harlan. With an effort that seemed to tear at his vocal cords he raised his voice to near-normal level. "But no one's here, upwhen or downwhen for thousands and thousands of Centuries."

Noÿs seemed to accept that. "And everything is fixed up so? We passed food stores and a viewing-film library. Did you see that?"

"I saw that. Oh, it's fully equipped. They're all fully equipped. Every Section."

"But why, if no one ever comes here?"

"It's logical," said Harlan. Talking about it took away some of the eeriness. Saying out loud what he already knew in the abstract would pin-point the matter, bring it down to the level of the prosaic. He said, "Early in the history of Eternity, one of the Centuries in the 300's came up with a mass duplicator. Do you know what I mean? By setting up a resonating field, energy could be converted to matter with subatomic particles taking up precisely the same pattern of positions, within the uncertainty requirements, as those in the model being used. The result is an exact copy.

"We in Eternity commandeered the instrument for our own purposes. At that time, there were only about six or seven hundred Sections built up. We had plans for expansion, of course. 'Ten new Sections a physioyear' was one of the slogans of the time. The mass duplicator made that all unnecessary. We built one new Section complete with food, power supply, water supply, all the best automatic features; set up the machine and duplicated the Section once each Century all along Eternity. I don't know how long they kept it going—millions of Centuries, probably."

"All like this, Andrew?"

"All exactly like this. And as Eternity expands, we just fill in, adapting the construction to whatever fashion turns out to be current in the Century. The only troubles come when we hit an energy-centered Century. We—we haven't reached this Section yet." (No use telling her that the Eternals couldn't penetrate into Time here in the Hidden Centuries. What difference did that make?)

He glanced at her and she seemed troubled. He said hastily, "There's no waste involved in building the Sections. It took energy, nothing more, and with the nova to draw on——"

She interrupted. "No. I just don't remember."

"Remember what?"

"You said the duplicator was invented in the 300's. We don't have it in the 482nd. I don't remember viewing anything about it in history."

Harlan grew thoughtful. Although she was within two inches of being as tall as himself, he suddenly felt giant-size by comparison. She was a child, an infant, and he was a demigod of Eternity who must teach her and lead her carefully to the truth.

He said, "Noÿs, dear, let's find a place to sit down and—and I'll have to explain something."

The concept of a variable Reality, a Reality that was not fixed and eternal and immutable was not one that could be faced casually by anyone.

In the dead of the sleep period, sometimes, Harlan would remember the early days of his Cubhood and recall the wrenching attempts to divorce himself from his Century and from Time.

It took six months for the average Cub to learn all the truth, to discover that he could never go home again in a very literal way. It wasn't Eternity's law, alone, that stopped him, but the frigid fact that home as he knew it might very well no longer exist, might, in a sense, never have existed.

It affected Cubs differently. Harlan remembered Bonky Latourette's face turning white and gaunt the day Instructor Yarrow had finally made it unmistakably clear about Reality.

None of the Cubs ate that night. They huddled together in search of a kind of psychic warmth, all except Latourette, who had disappeared. There was a lot of false laughter and miserably poor joking.

Someone said with a voice that was tremulous and uncertain, "I suppose I never had a mother. If I go back into the 95th, they'd say: 'Who are you? We don't know you. We don't have any records of you. You don't exist.' "

They smiled weakly and nodded their heads, lonely boys with nothing left but Eternity.

They found Latourette at bedtime, sleeping deeply and breathing shallowly. There was the slight reddening of a spray injection in the hollow of his left elbow and fortunately that was noted too.

Yarrow was called and for a while it looked as though one Cub would be out of the course, but he was brought around eventually. A week later he was back in his seat. Yet the mark of that evil night was on his personality for as long as Harlan knew him thereafter.

And now Harlan had to explain Reality to Noÿs Lambent, a girl not much older than those Cubs, and explain it at once and in full. He had to. There was no choice about that. She must learn exactly what faced them and exactly what she would have to do.

He told her. They ate canned meats, chilled fruits, and milk at a long conference table designed to hold twelve, and there he told her.

He did it as gently as possible, but he scarcely found need for gentleness. She snapped quickly at every concept and before he was half though it was borne in upon him, to his great amazement, that she wasn't reacting badly. She wasn't afraid. She showed no sense of loss. She only seemed angry.

The anger reached her face and turned it a glowing pink while her dark eyes seemed somehow the darker for it.

"But that's criminal," she said. "Who are the Eternals to do this?"

"It's done for humanity's good," said Harlan. Of course, she couldn't really understand that. He felt sorry for the Time-bound thinking of a Timer.

"Is it? I suppose that's how the mass duplicator was wiped out."

"We have copies still. Don't worry about that. We've preserved it."

"*You've* preserved it. But what about us? We of the 482nd might have had it." She gestured with little movements of two clenched fists.

"It wouldn't have done you good. Look, don't get excited, dear, and listen." With an almost convulsive gesture (he would have to learn how to touch her naturally, without making the movement seem a sheepish invitation to a repulse) he took her hands in his and held them tightly.

For a moment she tried to free them, and then she relaxed. She even laughed a bit. "Oh, go ahead, silly, and don't look so solemn. I'm not blaming you."

"You mustn't blame anyone. There is no blame necessary. We do what must be done. That mass duplicator is a classic case. I studied it in school. When you duplicate mass, you can duplicate persons, too. The problems that arise are very complicated."

"Isn't it up to the society to solve its own problems?"

"It is, but we studied that society throughout Time and it doesn't solve the problem satisfactorily. Remember that its failure to do so affects not only itself but all its descendant societies. In fact, there is no satisfactory solution to the mass-duplicator problem. It's one of those things like atomic wars and dreamies that just can't be allowed. Developments are never satisfactory."

"What makes you so sure?"

"We have our Computing machines, Noÿs; Computaplexes far more accurate than any ever developed in any single Reality. These Compute the possible Realities and grade the desirabilities of each over a summation of thousands and thousands of variables."

"Machines!" She said it with scorn.

Harlan frowned, then relented hastily. "Now don't be like that. Naturally, you resent learning that life is not as solid as you thought. You and the world you lived in might have been only a probability shadow a year ago, but what's the difference? You have all your memories, whether they're of probability shadows or not, haven't you? You remember your childhood and your parents, don't you?"

"Of course."

"Then it's just as if you lived it, isn't it? Isn't it? I mean, whether you did or not?"

"I don't know. I'll have to think about it. What if tomorrow it's a dream world again, or a shadow, or whatever you call it?"

"Then there would be a new Reality and a new you with new memories. It would be just as though nothing had happened, except that the sum of human happiness would have been increased again."

"I don't find that satisfying, somehow."

"Besides," said Harlan hastily, "nothing will happen to you now. There *will* be a new Reality but you're in Eternity. You won't be changed."

"But you say it makes no difference," said Noÿs gloomily. "Why go to all the trouble?"

With sudden ardor Harlan said, "Because I want you as you are. Exactly as you are. I don't want you changed. Not in any way."

He came within a hair of blurting out the truth, that without the advantage of the superstition about Eternals and eternal life she would never have inclined toward him.

She said, looking about with a slight frown, "Will I have to stay here forever, then? It would be—lonely."

"No, no. Don't think of it," he said wildly, gripping her hands so tight that she winced. "I'll find out what you will be in the new Reality of the 482nd, and you'll go back in disguise, so to speak. I'll take care of you. I'll apply for permission for formal liaison and see to it that you remain safely through future Changes. I'm a Technician and a good one and I know about Changes." He added grimly, "And I know a few other things as well," and stopped there.

Noÿs said, "Is all this allowed? I mean, can you take people into Eternity and keep them from changing? It doesn't sound right, somehow, from the things you've told me."

For a moment Harlan felt shrunken and cold in the large emptiness of the thousands of Centuries that surrounded him upwhen and down. For a moment he felt cut off even from the Eternity that was his only home and only faith, doubly cast out from Time and Eternity; and only the woman for whom he had forsaken it all left at his side.

He said, and he meant it deeply, "No, it is a crime. It is a very great crime, and I am bitterly ashamed. But I would do it again, if I had to, and any number of times, if I had to."

"For me, Andrew? For me?"

He did not raise his eyes to hers. "No, Noÿs, for myself. I could not bear to lose you."

She said, "And if we are caught . . .?"

Harlan knew the answer to that. He knew the answer since that moment of insight in bed in the 482nd, with Noÿs sleeping at his side. But, even yet, he dared not think of the wild truth.

He said, "I am not afraid of anyone. I have ways of protecting myself. They don't imagine how much I know."

INTERLUDE
— 9 —

IT WAS, looking back at it, an idyllic period that followed.

A hundred things took place in those physioweeks, and all confused itself inextricably in Harlan's memory, later, making the period seem to have lasted much longer than it did. The one idyllic thing about it was, of course, the hours he could spend with Noÿs, and that cast a glow over everything else.

Item One: At the 482nd he slowly packed his personal effects; his clothing and films, most of all his beloved and tenderly handled news-magazine volumes out of the Primitive. Anxiously he supervised their return to his permanent station in the 575th.

Finge was at his elbow as the last of it was lifted into the freight kettle by Maintenance men.

Finge said, choosing his words with unerring triteness, "Leaving us, I see." His smile was broad, but his lips were carefully held together so that only the barest trace of teeth showed. He kept his hands clasped behind his back and his pudgy body teetered forward on the balls of his feet.

Harlan did not look at his superior. He muttered a monotoned "Yes, sir."

Finge said, "I will report to Senior Computer Twissell concerning the entirely satisfactory manner in which you performed your Observational duties in the 482nd."

Harlan could not bring himself to utter even a sullen word of thanks. He remained silent.

Finge went on, in a suddenly much lower voice, "I will not report, for the present, your recent attempt at violence against me." And although his smile remained and his glance remained mild, there was a relish of cruel satisfaction about him.

Harlan looked up sharply and said, "As you wish, Computer."

Item Two: He re-established himself at the 575th.

He met Twissell almost at once. He found himself happy to see that little body, topped by that lined and gnomelike face. He was even happy to see the white cylinder nestling smokily between two stained fingers and being lifted rapidly toward Twissell's lips.

Harlan said, "Computer."

Twissell, emerging from his office, looked for a moment unseeingly and unrecognizingly at Harlan. His face was haggard and his eyes squinted with weariness.

He said, "Ah, Technician Harlan. You are done with your work on the 482nd?"

"Yes, sir."

Twissell's comment was strange. He looked at his watch, which, like any watch in Eternity, was geared to physiotime, giving the day number as well as the time of day, and said, "On the nose, my boy, on the nose. Wonderful. Wonderful."

Harlan felt his heart give a small bound. When he had last seen Twissell he would not have been able to make sense of that remark. Now he thought he did. Twissell was tired, or he would not have spoken so close to the core of things, perhaps. Or the Computer might have felt the remark to be so cryptic as to feel safe despite its closeness to the core.

Harlan said, speaking as casually as he could to avoid letting it seem that his remark had any conception at all with what Twissell had just said, "How's my Cub?"

"Fine, fine," said Twissell, with only half his mind, apparently, on his words. He took a quick puff at the shortening tube of tobacco, indulged in a quick nod of dismissal, and hurried off.

Item Three: the Cub.

He seemed older. There seemed to be a greater feeling of maturity to him as he held out his hand and said, "Glad to see you back, Harlan."

Or was it merely that, where earlier Harlan had been conscious of Cooper only as a pupil, he now seemed more than a Cub. He now seemed a gigantic instrument in the hands of the Eternals. Naturally he could not help but attain a new stature in Harlan's eyes.

Harlan tried not to show that. They were in Harlan's own quarters, and the Technician basked in the creamy porcelain surfaces about him, glad to be out of the ornate splash of the 482nd. Try as he might to associate the wild baroque of the 482nd with Noÿs, he only succeeded in associating it with Finge. With Noÿs he associated a pink, satiny twilight and, strangely, the bare austerity of the Sections of the Hidden Centuries.

He spoke hastily, almost as though he were anxious to hide his dangerous thoughts. "Well, Cooper, what have they been doing with you while I was away?"

Cooper laughed, brushed his drooping mustache self-consciously with one finger and said, "More math. Always math."

"Yes? Pretty advanced stuff by now, I guess."

"Pretty advanced."

"How's it coming?"

"So far its bearable. It comes pretty easy, you know. I like it. But now they're really loading it on."

Harlan nodded and felt a certain satisfaction. He said, "Temporal Field matrices and all that?"

But Cooper, his color a little high, turned toward the stacked volumes in the bookshelves, and said, "Let's get back to the Primitives. I've got some questions."

"About what?"

"City life in the 23rd. Los Angeles, especially."

"Why Los Angeles?"

"It's an interesting city. Don't you think so?"

"It is, but let's hit it in the 21st, then. It was at its peak in the 21st."

"Oh, let's try the 23rd."

Harlan said, "Well, why not?"

His face was impassive, but if the impassiveness could have been peeled off, there would have been a grimness about him. His grand, intuitional guess was more than a guess. Everything was checking neatly.

Item Four: research. Twofold research.

For himself, first. Each day, with ferreting eyes, he went through the reports on Twissell's desk. The reports concerned the various Reality Changes being scheduled or suggested. Copies went to Twissell routinely since he was a member of the Allwhen Council, and Harlan knew he would not miss one. He looked first for the coming Change in the 482nd. Secondly he looked for other Changes, any other Changes, that might have a flaw, an imperfection, some deviation from maximum excellence that might be visible to his own trained and talented Technician's eyes.

In the strictest sense of the word the reports were not for his study, but Twissell was rarely in his office these days, and no one else saw fit to interfere with Twissell's personal Technician.

That was one part of his research. The other took place in the 575th Section branch of the library.

For the first time he ventured out of those portions of the library which, ordinarily, monopolized his attention. In the past he had haunted the section on Primitive history (very poor indeed, so that most of his references and source materials had to be derived from the far downwhen of the 3rd millennium, as was only natural, of course). To an even greater extent he had ransacked the shelves devoted to Reality Change, its theory, technique, and history; an excellent collection (best in Eternity outside the Central branch itself, thanks to Twissell) of which he had made himself full master.

Now he wandered curiously among the other film-racks. For the first time he Observed (in the capital-O sense) the racks devoted to the 575th itself; its geographies, which varied little from Reality to Reality, its histories, which varied more, and its sociologies, which varied still more. These were not the books or reports written about the Century by Observing and Computing Eternals (with those he was familiar), but by the Timers themselves.

There were the works of literature of the 575th and these stirred memories of tremendous arguments he had heard of concerning the values of alternate Changes. Would this masterpiece be altered or not? If so, how? How did past Changes affect works of art?

For that matter, could there ever be general agreement about art? Could it ever be reduced to quantitative terms amenable to mechanical evaluation by the Computing machines?

A Computer named August Sennor was Twissell's chief opponent in these matters. Harlan, stirred by Twissell's feverish denunciations of the man and his views, had read some of Sennor's papers and found them startling.

Sennor asked publicly and, to Harlan, disconcertingly, whether a new Reality might not contain a personality within itself analogous to that of a man who had been withdrawn into Eternity in a previous Reality. He analyzed then the possibility of an Eternal meeting his analogue in Time, either with or without knowing it, and speculated on the results in each case. (That came fairly close to one of Eternity's most potent fears, and Harlan shivered and hastened uneasily through the discussion.) And, of course, he discussed at length the fate of literature and art in various types and classifications of Reality Changes.

But Twissell would have none of the last. "If the values of art can't be computed," he would shout at Harlan, "then what's the use of arguing about it?"

And Twissell's views, Harlan knew, were shared by the large majority of the Allwhen Council.

Yet now Harlan stood at the shelves devoted to the novels of Eric Linkollew, usually described as the outstanding writer of the 575th, and wondered. He counted fifteen different "Complete Works" collections, each, undoubtedly, taken out of a different Reality. Each was somewhat different, he was sure. One set was noticeably smaller than all the others, for instance. A hundred Sociologists, he imagined, must have written analyses of the differences between the sets in terms of the sociological background of each Reality, and earned status thereby.

Harlan passed on to the wing of the library which was devoted to the devices and instrumentation of the various 575th's. Many of these last, Harlan knew, had been eliminated in Time and remained intact, as a product of human ingenuity, only in Eternity. Man had to be protected from his own too flourishing technical mind. That more than anything else. Not a physioyear passed but that somewhere in Time nuclear technology veered too close to the dangerous and had to be steered away.

He returned to the library proper and to the shelves on mathematics and mathematical histories. His fingers skimmed across individual titles, and after some thought he took half a dozen from the shelves and signed them out.

Item five: Noÿs.

That was the really important part of the interlude, and all the idyllic part.

In his off-hours, when Cooper was gone, when he might ordinarily have been eating in solitude, reading in solitude, sleeping in solitude, waiting in solitude for the next day—he took to the kettles.

With all his heart he was grateful for the Technician's position in society. He was thankful, as he had never dreamed he could be, for the manner in which he was avoided.

No one questioned his right to be in a kettle, nor cared whether he aimed it upwhen or down. No curious eyes followed him, no willing hands offered to help him, no chattering mouths discussed it with him.

He could go where and when he pleased.

Noÿs said, "You've changed, Andrew. Heavens, you've changed."

He looked at her and smiled. "In what way, Noÿs?"

"You're smiling, aren't you? That's one of the ways. Don't you ever look in a mirror and see yourself smiling?"

"I'm afraid to. I'd say: 'I can't be that happy. I'm sick. I'm delirious. I'm confined to an asylum, living in daydreams, and unaware of it.' "

Noÿs leaned close to pinch him. "Feel anything?"

He drew her head toward him, felt bathed in her soft, black hair.

When they separated, she said breathlessly, "You've changed there, too. You've become very good at it."

"I've got a good teacher," began Harlan, and stopped abruptly, fearing that would imply displeasure at the thought of the many who might have had the making of such a good teacher.

But her laugh seemed untroubled by such a thought. They had eaten and she looked silky-smooth and warmly soft in the clothing he had brought her.

She followed his eyes and fingered the skirt gently, lifting it loose from its soft embrace of her thigh. She said, "I wish you wouldn't, Andrew. I really wish you wouldn't."

"There's no danger," he said carelessly.

"There *is* danger. Now don't be foolish. I can get along with what's here, until—until you make arrangements."

"Why shouldn't you have your own clothes and doodads?"

"Because they're not worth your going to my house in Time and being caught. And what if they make the Change while you're there?"

He evaded that uneasily. "It won't catch me." Then, brightening, "Besides my wrist generator keeps me in physiotime so that a Change can't affect me, you see."

Noÿs sighed. "I don't see. I don't think I'll ever understand it all."

"There's nothing to it." And Harlan explained and explained with great animation and Noÿs listened with sparkling eyes that never quite revealed whether she was entirely interested, or amused, or, perhaps, a little of both.

It was a great addition to Harlan's life. There was someone to talk to, someone with whom to discuss his life, his deeds, and thoughts. It was as though she were a portion of himself, but a portion sufficiently separate to require speech in communication rather than thought. She was a portion sufficiently separate to be able to answer unpredictably out of independent thought processes. Strange, Harlan thought, how one might Observe a social phenomenon such as matrimony and yet miss so vital a truth about it. Could he have predicted in advance, for instance, that it would be the passionate interludes that he would later least often associate with the idyl?

She snuggled into the crook of his arm and said, "How is your mathematics coming along?"

Harlan said, "Want to look at a piece of it?"

"Don't tell me you carry it around with you?"

"Why not? The kettle trip takes time. No use wasting it, you know."

He disengaged himself, took a small viewer from his pocket, inserted the film, and smiled fondly as she put it to her eyes.

She returned the viewer to him with a shake of her head. "I never saw so many squiggles. I wish I could read your Standard Intertemporal."

"Actually," said Harlan, "most of the squiggles you mention aren't Intertemporal really, just mathematical notation."

"You understand it, though, don't you?"

Harlan hated to do anything to disillusion the frank admiration in her eyes, but he was forced to say, "Not as much as I'd like to. Still, I have been picking up enough math to get what I want. I don't have to understand everything to be able to see a hole in a wall big enough to push a freight kettle through."

He tossed the viewer into the air, caught it with a flick of his hand, and put it on a small end-table.

Noÿs's eyes followed it hungrily and sudden insight flashed on Harlan.

He said, "Father Time! You can't read Intertemporal at that."

"No. Of course not."

"Then the Section library here is useless to you. I never thought of that. You ought to have your own films from the 482nd."

She said quickly, "No. I don't want any."

He said, "You'll have them."

"Honestly, I don't want them. It's silly to risk——"

"You'll have them!" he said.

For the last time he stood at the immaterial boundary separating Eternity from Noÿs's house in the 482nd. He had intended the time before to be the last time. The Change was nearly upon them now, a fact he had not told Noÿs out of the decent respect he would have had for anyone's feelings, let alone those of his love.

Yet it wasn't a difficult decision to make, this one additional trip. Partly it was bravado, to shine before Noÿs, bring her the book-films from out the lion's mouth; partly it was a hot desire (what was the Primitive phrase?) "to singe the beard of the King of Spain," if he might refer to the smooth-cheeked Finge so.

Then, too, he would have the chance once again of savoring the weirdly attractive atmosphere about a doomed house.

He had felt it before, when entering it carefully during the period of grace allowed by the spatio-temporal charts. He had felt it as he wandered through its rooms, collecting clothing, small *objets d'art,* strange containers, and instruments from Noÿs's vanity table.

There was the somber silence of a doomed Reality that was past merely the physical absence of noise. There was no way for Harlan to predict its analogue in a new Reality. It might be a small suburban cottage or a tenement in a city street. It might be zero with untamed scrubland replacing the parklike terrain on which it now stood. It might, conceivably, be almost unchanged. And (Harlan touched on this thought gingerly) it might be inhabited by the analogue of Noÿs or, of course, it might not.

To Harlan the house was already a ghost, a premature specter that had begun its hauntings before it had actually died. And because the house, as it was, meant a great deal to him, he found he resented its passing and mourned it.

Once, only, in five trips had there been any sound to break the stillness during his prowlings. He was in the pantry, then, thankful that the technology of that Reality and Century had made servants unfashionable and removed a problem. He had, he recalled, chosen among the cans of prepared foods, and was just deciding that he had enough for one trip, and that Noÿs would be pleased indeed to intersperse the hearty but uncolorful basic diet provided in the empty Section with some of her own dietary. He even laughed aloud to think that not long before he had thought her diet decadent.

It was in the middle of the laugh that he heard a distinct clapping noise. He froze!

The sound had come from somewhere behind him, and in the startled moment during which he had not moved the lesser danger that it was a housebreaker occurred to him first and the greater danger of its being an investigating Eternal occurred second.

It *couldn't* be a housebreaker. The entire period of the spatio-temporal chart, grace period and all, had been painstakingly cleared and chosen out of other similar periods of Time because of the lack of complicating factors. On the other hand, he had introduced a micro-change (perhaps not so micro at that) by abstracting Noÿs.

Heart pounding, he forced himself to turn. It seemed to him that the door behind him had just closed, moving the last millimeter required to bring it flush with the wall.

He repressed the impulse to open that door, to search the house. With Noÿs's delicacies in tow he returned to Eternity and waited two full days for repercussions before venturing into the far upwhen. There were none and eventually he forgot the incident.

But now, as he adjusted the controls to enter Time this one last time, he thought of it again. Or perhaps it was the thought of the Change, nearly upon him now, that preyed on him. Looking back on the moment later, he felt that it was one or the other that caused him to misadjust the controls. He could think of no other excuse.

The misadjustment was not immediately apparent. It pinpointed the proper room and Harlan stepped directly into Noÿs's library.

He had become enough of a decadent himself, now, to be not altogether repelled by the workmanship that went into the design of the film-cases. The lettering of the titles blended in with the intricate filigree until they were attractive but nearly unreadable. It was a triumph of aesthetics over utility.

Harlan took a few from the shelves at random and was surprised. The title of one was *Social and Economic History of our Times*.

Somehow it was a side of Noÿs to which he had given little thought. She was certainly not stupid and yet it never occurred to him that she might be interested in weighty things. He had the impulse to scan a bit of the *Social and Economic History,* but fought it down. He would find it in the Section library of the 482nd, if he ever wanted it. Finge had undoubtedly rifled the libraries of this Reality for Eternity's records months earlier.

He put that film to one side, ran through the rest, selected the fiction and some of what seemed light non-fiction. Those and two pocket viewers. He stowed them carefully into a knapsack.

It was at that point that, once more, he heard a sound in the house. There was no mistake this time. It was not a short sound of indeterminate origin. It was a laugh, a man's laugh. He was *not* alone in the house.

He was unaware that he had dropped the knapsack. For one dizzy second he could think only that he was trapped!

TRAPPED!

— 10 —

ALL AT once it had seemed inevitable. It was the rawest dramatic irony. He had entered Time one last time, tweaked Finge's nose one last time, brought the pitcher to the well one last time. It had to be then that he was caught.

Was it Finge who laughed?

Who else would track him down, lie in wait, stay a room away, and burst into mirth?

Well, then, was all lost? And because in that sickening moment he was sure all was lost it did not occur to him to run again or to attempt flight into Eternity once more. He would face Finge.

He would kill him, if necessary.

Harlan stepped to the door from behind which the laugh had sounded, stepped to it with the soft, firm step of the premeditated murderer. He flicked loose the automatic door signal and opened it by hand. Two inches. Three. It moved without sound.

The man in the next room had his back turned. The figure seemed too tall to be Finge and that fact penetrated Harlan's simmering mind and kept him from advancing further.

Then, as though the paralysis that seemed to hold both men in rigor was slowly lifting, the other turned, inch by inch.

Harlan never witnessed the completion of that turn. The other's profile had not yet come into view when Harlan, holding back a sudden gust of terror with a last fragment of moral strength, flung himself back out the door. Its mechanism, not Harlan, closed it soundlessly.

Harlan fell back blindly. He could breathe only by struggling violently with the atmosphere, fighting air in and pushing it out, while his heart beat madly as though in an effort to escape his body.

Finge, Twissell, all the Council together could not have disconcerted him so much. It was the fear of nothing physical that had unmanned him. Rather it was an almost instinctive loathing for the nature of the accident that had befallen him.

He gathered the stack of book-films to himself in a formless lump and managed, after two futile tries, to re-establish the door to Eternity. He stepped through, his legs operating mechanically. Somehow he made his way to the 575th, and then to personal quarters. His Technicianhood, newly valued, newly appreciated, saved him once again. The few Eternals he met turned automatically to one side and looked steadfastly over his head as they did so.

That was fortunate, for he lacked any ability to smooth his face out of the death's-head grimace he felt he was wearing, or any power to put the blood back into it. But they didn't look, and he thanked Time and Eternity and whatever blind thing wove Destiny for that.

He had not truly recognized the other man in Noÿs's house by his appearance, yet he knew his identity with a dreadful certainty.

The first time Harlan had heard a noise in the house he, Harlan, had been laughing and the sound that interrupted his laugh was of something weighty dropping in the next room. The second time someone had laughed in the next room and he, Harlan, had dropped a knapsack of book-films. The first time he,

Harlan, had turned and caught sight of a door closing. The second time he, Harlan, closed a door as a stranger turned.

He had met himself!

In the same Time and nearly in the same place he and his earlier self by several physiodays had nearly stood face to face. He had misadjusted the controls, set it for an instant in Time which he had already used and he, Harlan, had seen him, Harlan.

He had gone about his work with the shadow of horror upon him for days thereafter. He cursed himself for a coward, but that did not help.

Indeed from that moment matters took a downward trend. He could put his finger on the Great Divide. The key moment was the instant in which he had adjusted the door controls for his entry into the 482nd for one last time and somehow had adjusted it wrongly. Since then things went badly, badly.

The Reality Change in the 482nd went through during that period of despondency and accentuated it. In the past two weeks he had picked up three proposed Reality Changes which contained minor flaws, and now he chose among them, yet could do nothing to move himself to action.

He chose Reality Change 2456-2781, V-5 for a number of reasons. Of the three, it was farthest upwhen, the most distant. The error was minute, but was significant in terms of human life. It needed, then, only a quick trip to the 2456th to find out the nature of Noÿs's analogue in the new Reality, by use of a little blackmailing pressure.

But the unmanning of his recent experience betrayed him. It seemed to him no longer a simple thing, this gentle application of threatened exposure. And once he found the nature of Noÿs's analogue, what then? Put Noÿs in her place as charwoman, seamstress, laborer, or whatever. Certainly. But what, then, was to be done with the analogue herself? With any husband the analogue might have? Family? Children?

He had thought of none of this earlier. He had avoided the thought. "Sufficient unto the day . . ."

But now he could think of nothing else.

So he lay skulking in his room, hating himself, when Twissell called him, his tired voice questioning and a little puzzled.

"Harlan, are you ill? Cooper tells me you've skipped several discussion periods."

Harlan tried to smooth the trouble out of his face. "No, Computer Twissell. I'm a little tired."

"Well, that's forgivable, at any rate, boy." And then the smile on his face came about as close as it ever did to vanishing entirely. "Have you heard that the 482nd has been Changed?"

"Yes," said Harlan shortly.

"Finge called me," said Twissell, "and asked that you be told that the Change was entirely successful."

Harlan shrugged, then grew aware of Twissell's eyes staring out of the Communiplate and hard upon him. He grew uneasy and said, "Yes, Computer?"

"Nothing," said Twissell, and perhaps it was the cloak of age weighing down upon his shoulders, but his voice was unaccountably sad. "I thought you were about to speak."

"No," said Harlan. "I had nothing to say."

"Well, then, I'll see you tomorrow at opening in the Computing Room, boy. I have a great deal to say."

"Yes, sir," said Harlan. He stared for long minutes at the plate after it went dark.

That had almost sounded like a threat. Finge had called Twissell, had he? What had he said that Twissell did not report?

But an outside threat was what he needed. Battling a sickness of the spirit was like standing in a quicksand and beating it with a stick. Battling Finge was another thing altogether. Harlan had remembered the weapon at his disposal and for the first time in days felt a fraction of self-confidence return.

It was as though a door had closed and another had opened. Harlan grew as feverishly active as previously he had been catatonic. He traveled to the 2456th and bludgeoned Sociologist Voy to his own exact will.

He did it perfectly. He got the information he sought.

And more than he sought. Much more.

Confidence is rewarded, apparently. There was a homewhen proverb that went: "Grip the nettle firmly and it will become a stick with which to beat your enemy."

In short, Noÿs had no analogue in the new Reality. No analogue at all. She could take her position in the new society in the most inconspicuous and convenient manner possible, or she could stay in Eternity. There could be no reason to deny him liaison except for the highly theoretical fact that he had broken the law—and he knew very well how to counter that argument.

So he went racing upwhen to tell Noÿs the great news, to bathe in undreamed-of success after a few days horrible with apparent failure.

And at this moment the kettle came to a halt.

It did not slow; it simply halted. If the motion had been one along any of the three dimensions of space, a halt that sudden would have smashed the kettle, brought its metal to a dull red heat, turned Harlan into a thing of broken bone and wet, crushed flesh.

As it was, it merely doubled him with nausea and cracked him with inner pain.

When he could see, he fumbled to the temporometer and stared at it with fuzzy vision. It read 100,000.

Somehow that frightened him. It was too round a number.

He turned feverishly to the controls. What had gone wrong?

That frightened him too, for he could see nothing wrong. Nothing had tripped the drive-lever. It remained firmly geared into the upwhen drive. There was no short circuit. All the indicator dials were in the black safety range. There was no power failure. The tiny needle that marked the steady consumption of meg-megcoulombs of power calmly insisted that power was being consumed at the usual rate.

What, then, had stopped the kettle?

Slowly, and with considerable reluctance, Harlan touched the drive-lever, curled his hand about it. He pushed it to neutral, and the needle on the power gauge declined to zero.

He twisted the drive-lever back in the other direction. Up went the power gauge again, and this time the temporometer flicked downwhen along the line of Centuries.

Downwhen—downwhen—99,983—99,972—99,959—

Again Harlan shifted the lever. Upwhen again. Slowly. Very slowly.

Then 99,985—99,993—99,997—99,998—99,999—100,000—

Smash! Nothing past 100,000. The power of Nova Sol was silently being consumed, at an incredible rate, to no purpose.

He went downwhen again, farther. He roared upwhen. Smash!

His teeth were clenched, his lips drawn back, his breath rasping. He felt like a prisoner hurling himself bloodily against the bars of a prison.

When he stopped, a dozen smashes later, the kettle rested firmly at 100,000. Thus far, and no farther.

He would change kettles! (But there was not much hope in that thought.)

In the empty silence of the 100,000th Century, Andrew Harlan stepped out of one kettle and chose another kettle shaft at random.

A minute later, with the drive-lever in his hand, he stared at the marking of 100,000 and knew that here, too, he could not pass.

He raged! Now! At this time! When things so unexpectedly had broken in his favor, to come to so sudden a disaster. The curse of that moment of misjudgment in entering the 482nd was still on him.

Savagely he spun the lever downwhen, pressing it hard at maximum and keeping it there. At least in one way he was free now, free to do anything he wanted. With Noÿs cut off behind a barrier and out of his reach, what more could they do to him? What more had he to fear?

He carried himself to the 575th and sprang from the kettle with a reckless disregard for his surroundings that he had never felt before. He made his way to the Section library, speaking to no one, regarding no one. He took what he wanted without glancing about to see if he were observed. What did he care?

Back to the kettle and downwhen again. He knew exactly what he would do. He looked at the large clock as he passed, measuring off Standard Physiotime, numbering the days and marking off the three coequal work shifts to the physioday. Finge would be at his private quarters now, and that was so much the better.

Harlan felt as though he were running a temperature when he arrived at the 482nd. His mouth was dry and cottony. His chest hurt. But he felt the hard shape of the weapon under his shirt as he held it firmly against his side with one elbow and that was the only sensation that counted.

Assistant Computer Hobbe Finge looked up at Harlan, and the surprise in his eyes slowly gave way to concern.

Harlan watched him silently for a while, letting the concern grow and waiting for it to change to fear. He circled slowly, getting between Finge and the Communiplate.

Finge was partly undressed, bare to the waist. His chest was sparsely haired, his breasts puffy and almost womanish. His tubby abdomen lapped over his waistband.

He looks undignified, thought Harlan with satisfaction, undignified and unsavory. So much the better.

He put his right hand inside his shirt and closed it firmly on the grip of his weapon.

Harlan said, "No one saw me, Finge, so don't look toward the door. No one's coming here. You've got to realize, Finge, that you're dealing with a Technician. Do you know what that means?"

His voice was hollow. He felt angry that fear wasn't entering Finge's eyes, only concern. Finge even reached for his shirt and, without a word, began to put it on.

Harlan went on, "Do you know the privilege of being a Technician, Finge? You've never been one, so you can't appreciate it. It means no one watches where you go or what you do. They all look the other way and work so hard at not seeing you that they really succeed at it. I could, for instance, go to the Section library, Finge, and help myself to any curious thing while the librarian busily concerns himself with his records and sees nothing. I can walk down the residential corridors of the 482nd and anyone passing turns out of my way and will swear later on he saw no one. It's that automatic. So you see, I can do what I want to do, go where I want to go. I can walk into the private apartments of the Assistant Computer of a Section and force him to tell the truth at weapon point and there'll be no one to stop me."

Finge spoke for the first time. "What are you holding?"

"A weapon," said Harlan, and brought it out. "Do you recognize it?" Its muzzle flared slightly and ended in a smooth metallic bulge.

"If you kill me . . ." began Finge.

"I won't kill you," said Harlan. "At a recent meeting you had a blaster. This is not a blaster. It is an invention of one of the past Realities of the 575th. Perhaps you are not acquainted with it. It was bred out of Reality. Too nasty. It can kill, but at low power it activates the pain centers of the nerve system and paralyzes as well. It is called, or was called, a neuronic whip. It works. This one is fully charged. I tested it on a finger." He held up his left hand with its stiffened little finger. "It was very unpleasant."

Finge stirred restlessly. "What is all this about, for Time's sake?"

"There is some sort of a block across the kettle shafts at the 100,000th. I want it removed."

"A block across the shafts?"

"Let's not work away at being surprised. Yesterday you spoke to Twissell. Today there is the block. I want to know what you said to Twissell. I want to know what's been done and what will be done. By Time, Computer, if you don't tell me, I'll use the whip. Try me, if you doubt my word."

"Now listen"—Finge's words slurred a bit and the first edge of fear made its appearance, and also a kind of desperate anger—"if you want the truth, it's this. We know about you and Noÿs."

Harlan's eyes flickered. "What about myself and Noÿs?"

Finge said, "Did you think you were getting away with anything?" The Computer kept his eyes fixed on the neuronic whip and his forehead was beginning to glisten. "By Time, with the emotion you showed after your period of Observation, with what you did during the period of Observation, did you think we wouldn't observe *you*? I would deserve to be broken as Computer if I had missed that. We know you brought Noÿs into Eternity. We knew it from the first. You wanted the truth. There it is."

At that moment Harlan despised his own stupidity. "You knew?"

"Yes. We knew you had brought her to the Hidden Centuries. We knew every time you entered the 482nd to supply her with appropriate luxuries; playing the fool, with your Eternal's Oath completely forgotten."

"Then why didn't you stop me?" Harlan was tasting the very dregs of his own humiliation.

"Do you still want the truth?" Finge flashed back, and seemed to gain courage in proportion as Harlan sank into frustration.

"Go on."

"Then let me tell you that I didn't consider you a proper Eternal from the start. A flashy Observer, perhaps, and a Technician who went through the motions. But no Eternal. When I brought you here on this last job, it was to prove as much to Twissell, who values you for some obscure reason. I wasn't just testing the society in the person of the girl, Noÿs. I was testing you, too, and you failed as I thought you would fail. Now put away that weapon, that whip, whatever it is, and get out of here."

"And you came to my personal quarters once," said Harlan breathlessly, working hard to keep his dignity and feeling it slip from him as though his mind and spirit were as stiff and unfeeling as the whiplashed little finger on his left hand, "to goad me into doing what I did."

"Yes, of course. If you want the phrase exactly, I tempted you. I told you the exact truth, that you could keep Noÿs only in the then-present Reality. You chose to act, not as an Eternal, but as a sniveler. I expected you to."

"I would do it again now," said Harlan gruffly, "and since it's all known, you can see I have nothing to lose." He thrust his whip outward toward Finge's plump waistline and spoke through pale lips and clenched teeth. "What has happened to Noÿs?"

"I have no idea."

"Don't tell me that. What has happened to Noÿs?"

"I tell you I don't know."

Harlan's fist tightened on the whip; his voice was low. "Your leg first. This will hurt."

"For Time's sake, listen. Wait!"

"All right. What has happened to her?"

"No, listen. So far it's just a breach of discipline. Reality wasn't affected. I made checks on that. Loss of rating is all you'll get. If you kill me, though, or hurt me with intent to kill, you've attacked a superior. There's the death penalty for that."

Harlan smiled at the futility of the threat. In the face of what had already happened death would offer a way out that in finality and simplicity had no equal.

Finge obviously misunderstood the reasons for the smile. He said hurriedly, "Don't think there's no death penalty in Eternity because you've never come across one. We know of them; we Computers. What's more, executions have taken place, too. It's simple. In any Reality, there are numbers of fatal accidents in which bodies are not recovered. Rockets explode in mid-air, aeroliners sink in mid-ocean or crash to powder in mountains. A murderer can be put on one of those vessels minutes, or seconds, before the fatal results. Is this worth that to you?"

Harlan stirred and said, "If you're stalling for rescue, it won't work. Let me tell you this: I'm not afraid of punishment. Furthermore, I intend to have Noÿs.

I want her now. She does not exist in the current Reality. She has no analogue. There is no reason why we cannot establish formal liaison.''

"It is against regulations for a Technician——''

"We will let the Allwhen Council decide,'' said Harlan, and his pride broke through at last. "I am not afraid of an adverse decision, either, any more than I am afraid of killing you. I am no ordinary Technician.''

"Because you are Twissell's Technician?'' and there was a strange look on Finge's round, sweating face that might have been hatred or triumph or part of each.

Harlan said, "For reasons much more important than that. And now . . .'' With grim determination he touched finger to the weapon's activator.

Finge screamed, "Then go to the Council. The Allwhen Council; *they* know. If you are that important——'' He ended, gasping.

For a moment Harlan's finger hovered irresolutely. "What?''

"Do you think I would take unilateral action in a case like this? I reported this whole incident to the Council, timing it with the Reality Change. Here! Here are the duplicates.''

"Hold on, don't move.''

But Finge disregarded that order. With a speed as from the spur of a possessing fiend Finge was at his files. The finger of one hand located the code combination of the record he wanted, the fingers of the other punched it into the file. A silvery tongue of tape slithered out of the desk, its pattern of dots just visible to the naked eye.

"Do you want it sounded?'' asked Finge, and without waiting threaded it into the sounder.

Harlan listened, frozen. It was clear enough. Finge had reported in full. He had detailed every motion of Harlan's in the kettle shafts. He hadn't missed one that Harlan could remember up to the point of making the report.

Finge shouted when the report was done, "Now, then, go to the Council. I've put no block in Time. I wouldn't know how. And don't think they're unconcerned about the matter. You said I spoke to Twissell yesterday. You're right. But I didn't call him; he called me. So go; ask Twissell. Tell them what an important Technician you are. And if you want to shoot me first; shoot and to Time with you.''

Harlan could not miss the actual exultation in the Computer's voice. At that moment he obviously felt enough the victor to believe that even a neuronic whipping would leave him on the profit side of the ledger.

Why? Was the breaking of Harlan so dear to his heart? Was his jealousy over Noÿs so all-consuming a passion?

Harlan did scarcely more than formulate the questions in his mind, and then the whole matter, Finge and all, seemed suddenly meaningless to him.

He pocketed his weapon, whirled out the door, and toward the nearest kettle shaft.

It was the Council, then, or Twissell, at the very least. He was afraid of none of them, nor of all put together.

With each passing day of the last unbelievable month he had grown more convinced of his own indispensability. The Council, even the Allwhen Council itself, would have no choice but to come to terms when it was a choice of bartering one girl for the existence of all of Eternity.

IT WAS with a dull surprise that Technician Andrew Harlan, on bursting into the 575th, found himself in the night shift. The passing of the physiohours had gone unnoticed during his wild streaks along the kettle shafts. He stared hollowly at the dimmed corridors, the occasional evidence of the thinned-out night force at work.

But in the continued grip of his rage Harlan did not pause long to watch uselessly. He turned toward personal quarters. He would find Twissell's room on Computer Level as he had found Finge's and he had as little fear of being noticed or stopped.

The neuronic whip was still hard against his elbow as he stopped before Twissell's door (the name plate upon it advertising the fact in clear, inlaid lettering).

Harlan activated the door signal brashly on the buzzer level. He shorted the contact with a damp palm and let the sound become continuous. He could hear it dimly.

A step sounded lightly behind him and he ignored it in the sure knowledge that the man, whoever he was, would ignore him. (Oh, rose-red Technician's patch!)

But the sound of steps halted and a voice said, "Technician Harlan?"

Harlan whirled. It was a Junior Computer, relatively new to the Section. Harlan raged inwardly. This was not quite the 482nd. Here he was not merely a Technician, he was Twissell's Technician, and the younger Computers, in their anxiety to ingratiate themselves with the great Twissell, would extend a minimum civility to his Technician.

The Computer said, "Do you wish to see Senior Computer Twissell?"

Harlan fidgeted and said, "Yes, sir." (The fool! What did he think anyone would be standing signaling at a man's door for? To catch a kettle?)

"I'm afraid you can't," said the Computer.

"This is important enough to wake him," said Harlan.

"Maybe so," said the other, "but he's outwhen. He's not in the 575th."

"Exactly when is he, then?" asked Harlan impatiently.

The Computer's glance became a supercilious stare. "I wouldn't know."

Harlan said, "But I have an important appointment first thing in the morning."

"You have," said the Computer, and Harlan was at a loss to account for his obvious amusement at the thought.

The Computer went on, even smiling now, "You're a little early, aren't you?"

"But I must see him."

"I'm sure he'll be here in the morning." The smile broadened.

"But——"

The Computer passed by Harlan, carefully avoiding any contact, even of garments.

Harlan's fists clenched and unclenched. He stared helplessly after the Computer and then, simply because there was nothing else to do, he walked slowly, and without full consciousness of his surroundings, back to his own room.

* * *

Harlan slept fitfully. He told himself he needed sleep. He tried to relax by main force, and, of course, failed. His sleep period was a succession of futile thought.

First of all, there was Noÿs.

They would not dare harm her, he thought feverishly. They could not send her back to Time without first calculating the effect on Reality and that would take days, probably weeks. As an alternative, they might do to her what Finge had threatened for him; place her in the path of an untraceable accident.

He did not take that into serious consideration. There was no necessity for drastic action such as that. They would not risk Harlan's displeasure by doing it. (In the quiet of a darkened sleeping room, and in that phase of half sleep where things often grew queerly disproportionate in thought, Harlan found nothing grotesque in his sure opinion that the Allwhen Council would not dare risk a Technician's displeasure.)

Of course, there were uses to which a woman in captivity might be put. A beautiful woman from a hedonistic Reality . . .

Resolutely Harlan put the thought away as often as it returned. It was at once more likely and more unthinkable than death, and he would have none of it.

He thought of Twissell.

The old man was out of the 575th. Where was he during hours when he should have been asleep? An old man needs his sleep. Harlan was sure of the answer. There were Council consultations going on. About Harlan. About Noÿs. About what to do with an indispensable Technician one dared not touch.

Harlan's lips drew back. If Finge reported Harlan's assault of that evening, it would not affect their considerations in the least. His crimes could scarcely be worsened by it. His indispensability would certainly not be lessened.

And Harlan was by no means certain that Finge *would* report him. To admit having been forced to cringe before a Technician would put an Assistant Computer in a ridiculous light, and Finge might not choose to do so.

Harlan thought of Technicians as a group, which, of late, he had done rarely. His own somewhat anomalous position as Twissell's man and as half an Educator had kept him too far apart from other Technicians. But Technicians lacked solidarity anyway. Why should that be?

Did he have to go through the 575th and the 482nd rarely seeing or speaking to another Technician? Did they have to avoid even one another? Did they have to act as though they accepted the status into which the superstition of others forced them?

In his mind he had already forced the capitulation of the Council as far as Noÿs was concerned, and now he was making further demands. The Technicians were to be allowed an organization of their own, regular meetings—more friendship— better treatment from the others.

His final thought of himself was as a heroic social revolutionary, with Noÿs at his side, when he sank finally into a dreamless sleep. . . .

The door signal awoke him. It whispered at him with hoarse impatience. He collected his thoughts to the point of being able to look at the small clock beside his bed and groaned inwardly.

Father Time! After all that he had overslept.

He managed to reach the proper button from bed and the view-square high on the door grew transparent. He did not recognize the face, but it carried authority whoever it was.

He opened the door and the man, wearing the orange patch of Administration, stepped in.

"Technician Andrew Harlan?"

"Yes, Administrator? You have business with me?"

The Administrator seemed in no wise discommoded at the sharp belligerence of the question. He said, "You have an appointment with Senior Computer Twissell?"

"Well?"

"I am here to inform you that you are late."

Harlan stared at him. "What's this all about? You're not from the 575th, are you?"

"The 222nd is my station," said the other frigidly. "Assistant Administrator Arbut Lemm. I'm in charge of the arrangements and I'm trying to avoid undue excitement by by-passing official notification over the Communiplate."

"What arrangements? What excitement? What's it all about? Listen, I've had conferences with Twissell before. He's my superior. There's no excitement involved."

A look of surprise passed momentarily over the studious lack of expression the Administrator had so far kept on his face. "You haven't been informed?"

"About what?"

"Why, that a subcommittee of the Allwhen Council is holding session here at the 575th. This place, I am told, has been alive with the news for hours."

"And they want to see me?" As soon as he asked that, Harlan thought: Of course they want to see me. What else could the session be about but me?

And he understood the amusement of the Junior Computer last night outside Twissell's room. The Computer knew of the projected committee meeting and it amused him to think that a Technician could possibly expect to see Twissell at a time like that. Very amusing, thought Harlan bitterly.

The Administrator said, "I have my orders. I know nothing more." Then, still surprised, "You've heard nothing of this?"

"Technicians," said Harlan sarcastically, "lead sheltered lives."

Five besides Twissell! Senior Computers all, none less than thirty-five years an Eternal.

Six weeks earlier Harlan would have been overwhelmed by the honor of sitting at lunch with such a group, tongue-tied by the combination of responsibility and power they represented. They would have seemed twice life-size to him.

But now they were antagonists of his, worse still, judges. He had no time to be impressed. He had to plan his strategy.

They might not know that he was aware they had Noÿs. They could not know unless Finge told them of his last meeting with Harlan. In the clear light of day, however, he was more than ever convinced that Finge was not the man to broadcast publicly the fact that he had been browbeaten and insulted by a Technician.

It seemed advisable, then, for Harlan to nurse this possible advantage for the time being, to let *them* make the first move, say the first sentence that would join actual combat.

They seemed in no hurry. They stared at him placidly over an abstemious lunch as though he were an interesting specimen spread-eagled against a plane of force by mild repulsors. In desperation Harlan stared back.

He knew all of them by reputation and by trimensional reproduction in the physiomonthly orientation films. The films co-ordinated developments throughout the various Sections of Eternity and were required viewing for all Eternals with rating from Observer up.

August Sennor, the bald one (not even eyebrows or eyelashes), of course attracted Harlan most. First, because of the odd appearance of those dark, staring eyes against bare eyelids and forehead was remarkably greater in person than it had ever seemed in trimension. Second, because of his knowledge of past collisions of view between Sennor and Twissell. Finally, because Sennor did not confine himself to watching Harlan. He shot questions at him in a sharp voice.

For the most part his questions were unanswerable, such as: "How did you first come to be interested in Primitive times, young man?" "Do you find the study rewarding, young man?"

Finally, he seemed to settle himself in his seat. He pushed his plate casually onto the disposal chute and clasped his thick fingers lightly before him. (There was no hair on the back of the hands, Harlan noticed.)

Sennor said, "There is something I have always wanted to know. Perhaps you can help me."

Harlan thought: All right, now, this is it.

Aloud he said, "If I can, sir."

"Some of us here in Eternity—I won't say all, or even enough" (and he cast a quick glance at Twissell's tired face, while the others drew closer to listen) "but some, at any rate—are interested in the philosophy of Time. Perhaps you know what I mean."

"The paradoxes of Time-travel, sir?"

"Well, if you want to put it melodramatically, yes. But that's not all, of course. There is the question of the true nature of Reality, the question of the conservation of mass-energy during Reality Change and so on. Now we in Eternity are influenced in our consideration of such things by knowing the facts of Time-travel. Your creatures of the Primitive era, however, knew nothing of Time-travel. What were *their* views on the matter?"

Twissell's whisper carried the length of the table. "Cobwebs!"

But Sennor ignored that. He said, "Would you answer my question, Technician?"

Harlan said, "The Primitives gave virtually no thought to Time-travel, Computer."

"Did not consider it possible, eh?"

"I believe that's right."

"Did not even speculate?"

"Well, as to that," said Harlan uncertainly, "I believe there were speculations of sorts in some types of escape literature. I am not well acquainted with these, but I believe a recurrent theme was that of the man who returned in Time to kill his own grandfather as a child."

Sennor seemed delighted. "Wonderful! Wonderful! After all, that is at least an expression of the basic paradox of Time-travel, if we assume an indeviant Reality, eh? Now your Primitives, I'll venture to state, never assumed anything *but* an indeviant Reality. Am I right?"

Harlan waited to answer. He did not see where the conversation was aiming or what Sennor's deeper purposes were, and it unnerved him. He said, "I don't know enough to answer you with certainty, sir. I believe there may have been speculations as to alternate paths of time or planes of existence. I don't know."

Sennor thrust out a lower lip. "I'm sure you're wrong. You may have been misled by reading your own knowledge into various ambiguities you may have come across. No, without actual experience of Time-travel, the philosophic intricacies of Reality would be quite beyond the human mind. For instance, why does Reality possess inertia? We all know that it does. Any alteration in its flow must reach a certain magnitude before a Change, a true Change, is effected. Even then, Reality has a tendency to flow back to its original position.

"For instance, suppose a Change here in the 575th. Reality will change with increasing effects to perhaps the 600th. It will change, but with continually lesser effects to perhaps the 650th. Thereafter, Reality will be unchanged. We all know this is so, but do any of us know why it is so? Intuitive reasoning would suggest that any Reality Change would increase its effects without limit as the Centuries pass, yet that is not so.

"Take another point. Technician Harlan, I'm told, is excellent at selecting the exact Minimum Change Required for any situation. I'll wager he cannot explain how he arrives at his own choice.

"Consider how helpless the Primitives must be. They worry about a man killing his own grandfather because they do not understand the truth about Reality. Take a more likely and a more easily analyzed case and let's consider the man who in his travels through time meets himself——"

Harlan said sharply, "What about a man who meets himself?"

The fact that Harlan interrupted a Computer was a breach of manners in itself. His tone of voice worsened the breach to a scandalous extent, and all eyes turned reproachfully on the Technician.

Sennor harumphed, but spoke in the trained tone of one determined to be polite despite nearly insuperable difficulties. He said, continuing his broken sentence and thus avoiding the appearance of answering directly the unmannerly question addressed to him, "And the four subdivisions into which such an act can fall. Call the man earlier in physiotime, A, and the one later, B, Subdivision one, A and B may not see one another, or do anything that will significantly affect one another. In that case, they have not really met and we may dismiss this case as trivial.

"Or B, the later individual, may see A while A does not see B. Here, too, no serious consequences need be expected. B, seeing A, sees him in a position and engaged in activity of which he already has knowledge. Nothing new is involved.

"The third and fourth possibilities are that A sees B, while B does not see A, and that A and B see one another. In each possibility, the serious point is that A has seen B; the man at an earlier stage in his physiological existence sees himself at a later stage. Observe that he has learned he will be alive at the apparent age of B. He knows he will live long enough to perform the action he has witnessed. Now a man in knowing his own future in even the slightest detail can act on that knowledge and therefore changes his future. It follows that Reality must be changed to the extent of not allowing A and B to meet or, at the very least, of preventing A from seeing B. Then, since nothing in a Reality made un-Real can be detected, A never has met B. Similarly, in every apparent paradox of Time-travel, Reality always changes to avoid the paradox and we come to the conclusion that there are no paradoxes in Time-travel and that there can be none.''

Sennor looked well pleased with himself and his exposition, but Twissell rose to his feet.

Twissell said, ''I believe, gentlemen, that time presses.''

Far more suddenly than Harlan would have thought the lunch was over. Five of the subcommittee members filed out, nodding at him, with the air of those whose curiosity, mild at best, had been assuaged. Only Sennor held out a hand and added a gruff ''Good day, young man'' to the nod.

With mixed feelings Harlan watched them go. What had been the purpose of the luncheon? Most of all, why the reference to men meeting themselves? They had made no mention of Noÿs. Were they there, then, only to study him? Survey him from top to bottom and leave him to Twissell's judging?

Twissell returned to the table, empty now of food and cutlery. He was alone with Harlan now, and almost as though to symbolize that, he wielded a new cigarette between his fingers.

He said, ''And now to work, Harlan. We have a great deal to do.''

But Harlan would not, could not, wait longer. He said flatly, ''Before we do anything, I have something to say.''

Twissell looked surprised. The skin of his face puckered up about his faded eyes, and he tamped at the ash end of his cigarette thoughtfully.

He said, ''By all means, speak if you wish, but first, sit down, sit down, boy.''

Technician Andrew Harlan did not sit down. He strode up and back the length of the table, biting off his sentences hard to keep them from boiling and bubbling into incoherence. Senior Computer Laban Twissell's age-yellowed pippin of a head turned back and forth as he followed the other's nervous stride.

Harlan said, ''For weeks now I've been going through films on the history of mathematics. Books from several Realities of the 575th. The Realities don't matter much. Mathematics doesn't change. The order of its development doesn't change either. No matter how else the Realities shifted, mathematical history stayed about the same. The mathematicians changed; different ones switched discoveries, but the end results——— Anyway, I pounded a lot of it into my head. How does that strike you?''

Twissell frowned and said, ''A queer occupation for a Technician?''

''But I'm not just a Technician,'' said Harlan. ''You know that.''

''Go on,'' said Twissell and he looked at the timepiece he wore. The fingers that held his cigarette played with it with unwonted nervousness.

Harlan said, ''There was a man named Vikkor Mallansohn who lived in the 24th Century. That was part of the Primitive era, you know. The thing he is known best for is the fact that he first successfully built a Temporal Field. That means, of course, that he invented Eternity, since Eternity is only tremendous Temporal Field shortcircuiting ordinary Time and free of limitations of ordinary Time.''

''You were taught this as a Cub, boy.''

''But I was not taught that Vikkor Mallansohn could not possibly have invented the Temporal Field in the 24th Century. Nor could anyone have. The mathematical basis for it didn't exist. The fundamental Lefebvre equations did not exist; nor could they exist until the researches of Jan Verdeer in the 27th Century.''

If there was one sign by which Senior Computer Twissell could indicate complete astonishment, it was that of dropping his cigarette. He dropped it now. Even his smile was gone.

He said, ''Were you taught the Lefebvre equations, boy?''

''No. And I don't say I understand them. But they're necessary for the Temporal Field. I've learned that. And they weren't discovered till the 27th. I know that, too.''

Twissell bent to pick up his cigarette and regarded it dubiously. ''What if Mallansohn had stumbled on the Temporal Field without being aware of the mathematical justification? What if it were simply an empirical discovery? There have been many such.''

''I've thought of that. But after the Field was invented, it took three centuries to work out its implications and at the end of that time there was no one way in which Mallansohn's Field could be improved on. That could not be coincidence. In a hundred ways, Mallansohn's design showed that he must have used the Lefebvre equations. If he knew them or had developed them without Verdeer's work, which is impossible, why didn't he say so?''

Twissell said, ''You insist on talking like a mathematician. Who told you all this?''

''I've been viewing films.''

''No more?''

''And thinking.''

''Without advanced mathematical training? I've watched you closely for years, boy, and would not have guessed that particular talent of yours. Go on.''

''Eternity could never have been established without Mallansohn's discovery of the Temporal Field. Mallansohn could never have accomplished this without a knowledge of mathematics that existed only in his future. That's number one. Meanwhile, here in Eternity at this moment, there is a Cub who was selected as an Eternal against all the rules, since he was overage and married, to boot. You are educating him in mathematics and in Primitive sociology. That's number two.''

''Well?''

''I say that it is your intention to send him back into Time somehow, back past the downwhen terminus of Eternity, back to the 24th. It is your intention to have the Cub, Cooper, teach the Lefebvre equations to Mallansohn. You see, then,'' Harlan added with tense passion, ''that my own position as expert in the Primitive and my knowledge of that position entitles me to special treatment. *Very* special treatment.''

''Father Time!'' muttered Twissell.

''It's true, isn't it? We come full circle, *with my help*. Without it . . .'' He let the sentence hang.

''You come so close to the truth,'' said Twissell. ''Yet I could swear there was nothing to indicate——'' He fell into a study in which neither Harlan nor the outside world seemed to play a part.

Harlan said quickly. ''Only close to the truth? It *is* the truth.'' He could not tell why he was so certain of the essentials of what he said, even quite apart from the fact that he so desperately wanted it to be so.

Twissell said, "No, no, not the exact truth. The Cub, Cooper, is not going back to the 24th to teach Mallansohn anything."

"I don't believe you."

"But you must. You must see the importance of this. I want your co-operation through what is left of the project. You see, Harlan, the situation is more full circle than you imagine. Much more so, boy. Cub Brinsley Sheridan Cooper *is* Vikkor Mallansohn!"

THE BEGINNING OF ETERNITY

— 12 —

HARLAN WOULD not have thought that Twissell could have said anything at that moment that could have surprised him. He was wrong.

He said, "Mallansohn, He——"

Twissell, having smoked his cigarette to a stub, produced another and said, "Yes, Mallansohn. Do you want a quick summary of Mallansohn's life? Here it is. He was born in the 78th, spent some time in Eternity, and died in the 24th."

Twissell's small hand placed itself lightly on Harlan's elbow and his gnomish face broke into a wrinkled extension of his usual smile. "But come, boy, physiotime passes even for us and we are not completely masters of ourselves this day. Won't you come with me to my office?"

He led the way and Harlan followed, not entirely aware of the opening doors and the moving ramps.

He was relating the new information to his own problem and plan of action. With the passing of the first moment of disorientation his resolution returned. After all, how did this change things except to make his own importance to Eternity still more crucial, his value higher, his demands more sure to be met, Noÿs more certain to be bartered back to him.

Noÿs!

Father Time, they must not harm her! She seemed the only real part of his life. All Eternity beside was only a filmy fantasy, and not a worth-while one, either.

When he found himself in Computer Twissell's office, he could not clearly recall how it had come about that he had passed from the dining area here. Though he looked about and tried to make the office grow real by sheer force of the mass of its contents, it still seemed but another part of a dream that had outlived its usefulness.

Twissell's office was a clean, long room of porcelain asepsis. One wall of the office was crowded from floor to ceiling and wall to distant wall with the computing micro-units which, together, made up the largest privately operated Computaplex in Eternity and, indeed, one of the largest altogether. The opposite wall was crammed with reference films. Between the two what was left of the room was scarcely more than a corridor, broken by a desk, two chairs, recording and projecting equipment, and an unusual object the like of which Harlan was not familiar with and which did not reveal its use until Twissell flicked the remnants of a cigarette into it.

It flashed noiselessly and Twissell, in his usual prestidigitational fashion, held another in his hands.

Harlan thought: To the point, now.

He began, a trifle too loudly, a bit too truculently, "There is a girl in the 482nd——"

Twissell frowned, waved one hand quickly as though brushing an unpleasant matter hastily to one side. "I know, I know. She will not be disturbed, nor you. All will be well. I will see to it."

"Do you mean——"

"I tell you I know the story. If the matter has troubled you, it need trouble you no more."

Harlan stared at the old man, stupefied. Was this all? Though he had thought intently of the immensity of his power, he had not expected so clear a demonstration.

But Twissell was talking again.

"Let me tell you a story," he began, with almost the tone he would have used in addressing a newly inducted Cub. "I had not thought this would be necessary, and perhaps it still isn't, but your own researches and insight deserve it."

He stared at Harlan quizzically and said, "You know, I still can't quite believe that you worked this out on your own," then went on:

"The man most of Eternity knows as Vikkor Mallansohn left the record of his life behind him after he died. It was not quite a diary, not quite a biography. It was more of a guide, bequeathed to the Eternals he knew would someday exist. It was enclosed in a volume of Time-stasis which could be opened only by the Computers of Eternity, and which therefore remained untouched for three Centuries after his death, until Eternity was established and Senior Computer Henry Wadsman, the first of the great Eternals, opened it. The document has been passed along in strictest security since, along a line of Senior Computers ending with myself. It is referred to as the Mallansohn memoir.

"The memoir tells the story of a man named Brinsley Sheridan Cooper, born in the 78th, inducted as a Cub into Eternity at the age of twenty-three, having been married for a little over a year, but having been, as yet, childless.

"Having entered Eternity, Cooper was trained in mathematics by a Computer named Laban Twissell and in Primitive sociology by a Technician named Andrew Harlan. After a thorough grounding in both disciplines, and in such matters as temporal engineering as well, he was sent back to the 24th to teach certain necessary techniques to a Primitive scientist named Vikkor Mallansohn.

"Once having reached the 24th, he embarked first on a slow process of adjusting himself to the society. In this he benefited a great deal from the training of Technician Harlan and the detailed advice of Computer Twissell, who seemed to have an uncanny insight into some of the problems he was to face.

"After the passage of two years, Cooper located one Vikkor Mallansohn, an eccentric recluse in the California backwoods, relationless and friendless but gifted with a daring and unconventional mind. Cooper made friends slowly, acclimated the man to the thought of having met a traveler from the future still more slowly, and set about teaching the man the mathematics he must know.

"With the passage of time, Cooper adopted the other's habits, learned to shift for himself with the help of a clumsy Diesel-oil electric generator and with wired electrical appliances which freed them of dependence on power beams.

"But progress was slow and Cooper found himself something less than a marvelous teacher. Mallansohn grew morose and unco-operative and then one day died, quite suddenly, in a fall down a canyon of the wild, mountainous country in which they lived. Cooper, after weeks of despair, with the ruin of his life-work and, presumably, of all Eternity, staring him in the eye, decided on a desperate expedient. He did not report Mallansohn's death. Instead, he slowly took to building, out of the materials at hand, a Temporal Field.

"The details do not matter. He succeeded after mountains of drudgery and improvisation and took the generator to the California Institute of Technology, just as years before he had expected the real Mallansohn to do.

"You know the story from your own studies. You know of the disbelief and rebuffs he first met, his period under observation, his escape and the near-loss of his generator, the help he received from the man at the lunch counter whose name he never learned, but who is now one of Eternity's heroes, and of the final demonstration for Professor Zimbalist, in which a white mouse moved backward and forward in Time. I won't bore you with any of that.

"Cooper used the name of Vikkor Mallansohn in all this because it gave him a background and made him an authentic product of the 24th. The body of the real Mallansohn was never recovered.

"In the remainder of his life, he cherished his generator and co-operated with the Institute scientists in duplicating it. He dared do no more than that. He could not teach them the Lefebvre equations without outlining three Centuries of mathematical development that was to come. He could not, dared not, hint at his true origin. He dared not do more than the real Vikkor Mallansohn had, to his knowledge, done.

"The men who worked with him were frustrated to find a man who could perform so brilliantly and yet was unable to explain the whys of his performance. And he himself was frustrated too, because he foresaw, without in any way being able to quicken, the work that would lead, step by step, to the classic experiments of Jan Verdeer, and how from that the great Antoine Lefebvre would construct the basic equations of Reality. And how, after that, Eternity would be constructed.

"It was only toward the end of his long life that Cooper, staring into a Pacific sunset (he describes the scene in some detail in his memoir) came to the great realization that he was Vikkor Mallansohn; he was not a substitute but the man himself. The name might not be his, but the man history called Mallansohn was really Brinsley Sheridan Cooper.

"Fired with that thought, and with all that implied, anxious that the process of establishing Eternity be somehow quickened, improved, and made more secure, he wrote his memoir and placed it in a tube of Time-stasis in the living room of his house.

"And so the circle was closed. Cooper-Mallansohn's intentions in writing the memoir were, of course, disregarded. Cooper must go through his life exactly as he had gone through it. Primitive Reality allows of no changes. At this moment in physiotime, the Cooper you know is unaware of what lies ahead of him. He believes he is only to instruct Mallansohn and to return. He will continue to believe so until the years teach him differently and he sits down to write his memoir.

"The intention of the circle in Time is to establish the knowledge of Time-travel and of the nature of Reality, to build Eternity, ahead of its natural Time. Left to itself, mankind would not have learned the truth about Time before their technological advances in other directions had made racial suicide inevitable."

Harlan listened intently, caught up in the vision of a mighty circle in Time, closed upon itself, and traversing Eternity in part of its course. He came as close to forgetting Noÿs, for the moment, as he ever could.

He asked, "Then you knew all along everything you were to do, everything I was to do, everything I *have* done."

Twissell, who seemed lost in his own telling of the tale, his eyes peering through a haze of bluish tobacco smoke, came slowly to life. His old, wise eyes fixed themselves on Harlan and he said reproachfully, "No, of course not. There was a lapse of decades of physiotime between Cooper's stay in Eternity and the moment when he wrote his memoir. He could remember only so much, and only what he himself had witnessed. You should realize that."

Twissell sighed and he drew a gnarled finger through a line of updrafting smoke, breaking it into little turbulent swirls. "It worked itself out. First, I was found and brought to Eternity. When, in the fullness of physiotime, I became a Senior Computer, I was given the memoir and placed in charge. I had been described as in charge, so I was placed in charge. Again in the fullness of physiotime, you appeared in the changing of a Reality (we had watched your earlier analogues carefully), and then Cooper.

"I filled in the details by using my common sense and the services of the Computaplex. How carefully, for instance, we instructed Educator Yarrow in his part while betraying none of the significant truth. How carefully, in his turn, he stimulated your interest in the Primitive.

"How carefully we had had to keep Cooper from learning anything he did not prove he had learned by reference in the memoir." Twissell smiled sadly. "Sennor amuses himself with matters such as this. He calls it the reversal of cause and effect. Knowing the effect, one adjusts the cause. Fortunately, I am not the cobweb spinner Sennor is.

"I was pleased, boy, to find you so excellent an Observer and Technician. The memoir had not mentioned that since Cooper had no opportunity to observe your work or evaluate it. This suited me. I could use you in a more ordinary task that would make your essential one less noticeable. Even your recent stay with Computer Finge fitted in. Cooper mentioned a period of your absence during which his mathematical studies were so sharpened that he longed for your return. Once, though, you frightened me."

Harlan said, at once, "You mean the time I took Cooper along the kettle ways."

"How do you come to guess that?" demanded Twissell.

"It was the one time you were really angry with me. I suppose now it went against something in the Mallansohn memoir."

"Not quite. It was just that the memoir did not speak of the kettles. It seemed to me that to avoid mention of such an outstanding aspect of Eternity meant he had little experience with it. It was my intention therefore to keep him away from the kettles as much as possible. The fact that you had taken him upwhen in one disturbed me greatly, but nothing happened afterward. Things continued as they should, so all is well.''

The old Computer rubbed one hand slowly over the other, staring at the young Technician with a look compounded of surprise and curiosity. ''And all along you've been guessing this. It simply astonishes me. I would have sworn that even a fully trained Computer could not have made the proper deductions, given only the information you had. For a Technician to do it is uncanny.'' He leaned forward, tapped Harlan's knee lightly. ''The Mallansohn memoir says nothing about your life after Cooper's leaving, of course.''

''I understand, sir,'' said Harlan.

''We will be free then, in a manner of speaking, to do as we please with it. You show a surprising talent that must not be wasted. I think you are meant for something more than a Technician. I promise nothing now, but I presume that you realize that Computership is a distinct possibility.''

It was easy for Harlan to keep his dark face expressionless. He had had years of practice for that.

He thought: An additional bribe.

But nothing must be left to conjecture. His guesses, wild and unsupported at the start, arrived at by a freak of insight in the course of a very unusual and stimulating night, had become reasonable as the result of directed library research. They had become certainties now that Twissell had told him the story. Yet in one way at least there had been a deviation. Cooper was Mallansohn.

That had simply improved his position, but, wrong in one respect, he might be wrong in another. He must leave nothing to chance, then. Have it out! Make certain!

He said levelly, almost casually, ''The responsibility is great for me, also, now that I know the truth.''

''Yes, indeed?''

''How fragile is the situation? Suppose something unexpected were to happen and I were to miss a day when I ought to have been teaching Cooper something vital.''

''I don't understand you.''

(Was it Harlan's imagination, or had a spark of alarm sprung to life in those old, tired eyes?)

''I mean, can the circle break? Let me put it this way. If an unexpected blow on the head puts me out of action at a time when the memoir distinctly states I am well and active, is the whole scheme disrupted? Or suppose, for some reason, I deliberately choose not to follow the memoir. What then?''

''But what puts all this in your mind?''

''It seems a logical thought. It seems to me that by a careless or willful action, I could break the circle, and well, what? Destroy Eternity? It seems so. If it *is* so,'' Harlan added composedly, ''I ought to be told so that I may be careful to do nothing unfitting. Though I imagine it would take a rather unusual circumstance to drive me to such a thing.''

Twissell laughed, but the laughter rang false and empty in Harlan's ear. ''This is all purely academic, my boy. Nothing of this will happen since it hasn't happened. The full circle will not break.''

''It might,'' said Harlan. ''The girl of the 482nd——''

''Is safe,'' said Twissell. He rose impatiently. ''There's no end to this kind of talk and I have quite enough of logic-chopping from the rest of the subcommittee in charge of the project. Meanwhile, I have yet to tell *you* what I originally called you here to hear and physiotime is still passing. Will you come with me?''

Harlan was satisfied. The situation was clear and his power unmistakable. Twissell knew that Harlan could say, at will: ''I will no longer have anything to do with Cooper.'' Twissell knew Harlan could at any moment destroy Eternity by giving Cooper significant information concerning the memoir.

Harlan had known enough to do this yesterday. Twissell had thought to overwhelm him with the knowledge of the importance of his task, but if the Computer had thought to force Harlan into line in that way, he was mistaken.

Harlan had made his threat very clear with respect to Noÿs's safety, and Twissell's expression as he had barked, ''Is safe,'' showed he realized the nature of the threat.

Harlan rose and followed Twissell.

Harlan had never been in the room they now entered. It was large and looked as though walls had been knocked down for its sake. It had been entered through a narrow corridor which had been blocked off by a force-screen that did not go down until after a pause sufficient for Twissell's face to be scanned thoroughly by automatic machinery.

The largest part of the room was filled by a sphere that reached nearly to the ceiling. A door was open, showing four small steps leading to a well-lit platform within.

Voices sounded from inside and even as Harlan watched, legs appeared in the opening and descended the steps. A man emerged and another pair of legs appeared behind him. It was Sennor of the Allwhen Council and behind him was another of the group at the breakfast table.

Twissell did not look pleased at this. His voice, however, was restrained. ''Is the subcommittee still here?''

''Only we two,'' said Sennor casually, ''Rice and myself. A beautiful instrument we have here. It has the level of complexity of a spaceship.''

Rice was a paunchy man with the perplexed look of one who is accustomed to being right yet finds himself unaccountably on the losing side of an argument. He rubbed his bulbous nose and said, ''Sennor's mind is running on space-travel lately.''

Sennor's bald head glistened in the light. ''It's a neat point Twissell,'' he said. ''I put it to you. Is space-travel a positive factor or a negative factor in the calculus of Reality?''

''The question is meaningless,'' said Twissell impatiently. ''What type of space-travel in what society under what circumstances?''

''Oh, come. Surely there's something to be said concerning space-travel in the abstract.''

''Only that it is self-limiting, that it exhausts itself and dies out.''

''Then it is useless,'' said Sennor with satisfaction, ''and therefore it is a negative factor. My view entirely.''

''If you please,'' said Twissell, ''Cooper will be here soon. We will need the floor clear.''

''By all means.'' Sennor hooked an arm under that of Rice and led him away. His voice declaimed clearly as they departed. ''Periodically, my dear Rice, all the mental effort of mankind is concentrated on space-travel, which is doomed to a frustrated end by the nature of things. I would set up the matrices except that I am certain this is obvious to you. With minds concentrated on space, there is neglect of the proper development of things earthly. I am preparing a thesis now for submission to the Council recommending that Realities be changed to eliminate all space-travel eras as a matter of course."

Rice's treble sounded. "But you can't be that drastic. Space-travel is a valuable safety-valve in some civilizations. Take Reality 54 of the 290th, which I happen to recall offhand. Now there——"

The voices cut off and Twissell said, "A strange man, Sennor. Intellectually, he's worth two of any of the rest of us, but his worth is lost in leapfrog enthusiasms."

Harlan said, "Do you suppose he can be right? About space-travel, I mean."

"I doubt it. We'd have a better chance of judging if Sennor would actually submit the thesis he mentioned. But he won't. He'll have a new enthusiasm before he's finished and drop the old. But never mind——" He brought the flat of his hand against the sphere so that it rang resoundingly, then brought his hand back so that he could remove a cigarette from his lip. He said, "Can you guess what this is, Technician?"

Harlan said, "It looks like an outsize kettle with a top."

"Exactly. You're right. You've got it. Come on inside."

Harlan followed Twissell into the sphere. It was large enough to hold four or five men, but the interior was absolutely featureless. The floor was smooth, the curved wall was broken by two windows. That was all.

"No controls?" asked Harlan.

"Remote controls," said Twissell. He ran his hand over the smoothness of the wall and said, "Double walls. The entire interwall volume is given over to a self-contained Temporal Field. This instrument is a kettle that is not restricted to the kettle shafts but can pass beyond the downwhen terminus of Eternity. Its design and construction were made possible by valuable hints in the Mallansohn memoir. Come with me."

The control room was a cut-off corner of the large room. Harlan stepped in and stared somberly at immense bus bars.

Twissell said, "Can you hear me, boy?"

Harlan started and looked about. He had not been aware that Twissell had not followed him inside. He stepped automatically to the window and Twissell waved to him. Harlan said, "I can hear you, sir. Do you want me outside?"

"Not at all. You are locked in."

Harlan sprang to the door and his stomach turned into a series of cold, wet knots. Twissell was correct and what in Time was going on?

Twissell said, "You will be relieved to know, boy, that your responsibility is over. You were worried about that responsibility; you asked searching questions about it; and I think I know what you meant. This should not be your responsibility. It is mine alone. Unfortunately, we must have you in the control room, since it is stated that you were there and handled the controls. It is stated in the Mallansohn memoir. Cooper will see you through the window and that will take care of that.

"Furthermore, I will ask you to make the final contact according to instructions I will give you. If you feel that that, too, is too great a responsibility, you may relax. Another contact in parallel with yours is in charge of another man. If, for any reason, you are unable to operate the contact, he will do so.

Furthermore, I will cut off radio transmission from within the control room. You will be able to hear us but not to speak to us. You need not fear, therefore, that some involuntary exclamation from you will break the circle.''

Harlan stared helplessly out the window.

Twissell went on, "Cooper will be here in moments and his trip to the Primitive will take place within two physiohours. After that, boy, the project will be over and you and I will be free.''

Harlan was plunging chokingly through the vortex of a waking nightmare. Had Twissell tricked him? Had everything he had done been designed only to get Harlan quietly into a locked control room? Having learned that Harlan knew his own importance, had he improvised with diabolical cleverness, keeping him engaged in conversation, drugging his emotions with words, leading him here, leading him there, until the time was ripe for locking him in?

That quick and easy surrender over Noÿs. She won't be hurt, Twissell had said. All will be well.

How could he have believed that! If they were not going to harm her, or touch her, why the temporal barrier across the kettleways at the 100,000th? That alone should have given Twissell completely away.

But because he (fool!) wanted to believe, he allowed himself to be led through those last physiohours blindly, placed inside a locked room where he was no longer needed, even to close the final contact.

In one stroke he had been robbed of his essentiality. The trumps in his hand had been neatly maneuvered into deuces and Noÿs was out of his reach forever. What punishment might lie in wait for him did not concern him. Noÿs was out of his reach forever.

It had never occurred to him that the project would be so close to its end. That, of course, was what had really made his defeat possible.

Twissell's voice sounded dimly. "You'll be cut off now, boy.''

Harlan was alone, helpless, useless. . . .

BEYOND THE DOWN-WHEN TERMINUS
— 13 —

BRINSLEY COOPER entered. Excitement flushed his thin face and made it almost youthful, despite the heavy Mallansohn mustache that draped its upper lip.

(Harlan could see him through the window, hear him clearly over the room's radio. He thought bitterly: A Mallansohn mustache! Of course!)

Cooper strode toward Twissell. "They wouldn't let me in till now, Computer.''

"Very right,'' said Twissell. "They had their instructions.''

"Now's the time, though? I'll be heading out?"

"Almost the time."

"And I'll be coming back? I'll be seeing Eternity again?" Despite the straightness Cooper gave his back, there was an edge of uncertainty in his voice.

(Within the control room Harlan brought his clenched hands bitterly to the reinforced glass of the window, longing to break through somehow, to shout: "Stop it! Meet my terms, or I'll—" What was the use?)

Cooper looked about the room, apparently unaware that Twissell had refrained from answering his question. His glance fell on Harlan at the control-room window.

He waved his hand excitedly. "Technician Harlan! Come on out. I want to shake your hand before I go."

Twissell interposed. "Not now, boy, not now. He's at the controls."

Cooper said, "Oh? You know, he doesn't look well."

Twissell said, "I've been telling him the true nature of the project. I'm afraid that's enough to make anyone nervous."

Cooper said, "Great Time, yes! I've known about it for weeks now and I'm not used to it yet." There was a trace of near-hysteria in his laugh. "I still haven't got it through my thick head that it is really my show. I—I'm a little scared."

"I scarcely blame you for that."

"It's my stomach, mostly, you know. It's the least happy part of me."

Twissell said, "Well, it's very natural and it will pass. Meanwhile, your time of departure on Standard Intertemporal has been set and there is still a certain amount of orientation to be gone through. For instance, you haven't actually seen the kettle you will use."

In the two hours that passed Harlan heard it all, whether they were in sight or not. Twissell lectured Cooper in an oddly stilted manner, and Harlan knew the reason. Cooper was being informed of just those things that he was to mention in Mallansohn's memoir.

(Full circle. Full circle. And no way for Harlan to break that circle in one, last defiant Samson-smash of the temple—round and round the circle goes; round and round it goes.)

"Ordinary kettles," he heard Twissell say, "are both pushed and pulled, if we can use such terms in the case of Intertemporal forces. In traveling from Century X to Century Y within Eternity there is a fully powered initial point and a fully powered final point.

"What we have here is a kettle with a powered initial point but an unpowered destination point. It can only be pushed, not pulled. For that reason, it must utilize energies at a level whole orders of magnitude higher than those used by ordinary kettles. Special power-transfer units have had to be laid down along the kettleways to siphon in sufficient concentrations of energy from Nova Sol.

"This special kettle, its controls and power supply, are a composite structure. For physiodecades, the passing Realities have been combed for special alloys and special techniques. The 13th Reality of the 222nd was the key. It developed the Temporal Pressor and without that, this kettle could not have been built. The 13th Reality of the 222nd."

He pronounced that with elaborate distinctness.

(Harlan thought: Remember that, Cooper! Remember the 13th Reality of the 222nd so you can put it into the Mallansohn memoir so that the Eternals will know where to look so they will know what to tell you so you can put it. . . . Round and round the circle goes. . . .)

Twissell said, "The kettle has not been tested past the downwhen terminus, of course, but it has taken numerous trips within Eternity. We are convinced there will be no bad effects."

"There can't be, can there?" said Cooper. "I mean I did get there or Mallansohn could not have succeeded in building the field and he *did* succeed."

Twissell said, "Exactly. You will find yourself in a protected and isolated spot in the sparsely populated southwestern area of the United States of Amellika——"

"America," corrected Cooper.

"America, then. The Century will be the 24th; or, to put it to nearest hundredth, the 23.17th. I suppose we can even call it the year 2317, if we wish. The kettle, as you saw, is large, much larger than necessary for you. It is being filled now with food, water, and the means of shelter and defense. You will have detailed instructions that will, of course, be meaningless to anyone but you. I must impress upon you now that your first task will be to make certain that none of the indigenous inhabitants discovers you before you are ready for them. You will have force-diggers with which you will be able to burrow well into a mountain to form a cache. You will have to remove the contents of the kettle rapidly. They will be stacked so as to facilitate that."

(Harlan thought: Repeat! Repeat! He must have been told all this before, but repeat what must go into the memoir. Round and round . . .)

Twissell said, "You will have to unload in fifteen minutes. After that, the kettle will return automatically to starting point, carrying with it all tools that are too advanced for the Century. You will have a list of those. After the kettle returns, you will be on your own."

Cooper said, "Must the kettle return so quickly?"

Twissell said, "A quick return increases the probabilities of success."

(Harlan thought: The kettle *must* return in fifteen minutes because it *did* return in fifteen minutes. Round and . . .)

Twissell hurried on. "We cannot attempt to counterfeit their medium of exchange of any of their negotiable scrip. You will have gold in the form of small nuggets. You will be able to explain its possession according to your detailed instructions. You will have native clothing to wear or at least clothing that will pass for native."

"Right," said Cooper.

"Now, remember. Move slowly. Take weeks, if necessary. Work your way into the era, spiritually. Technician Harlan's instructions are a good basis but they are not enough. You will have a wireless receiver built on the principles of the 24th which will enable you to come abreast of the current events and, more important, learn the proper pronunciation and intonation of the language of the times. Do that thoroughly. I'm sure that Harlan's knowledge of English is excellent, but nothing can substitute for native pronunciation on the spot."

Cooper said, "What if I don't end up in the right spot? I mean, not in the 23.17?"

"Check on that very carefully, of course. But it will be right. It will be right."

(Harlan thought: It will be right because it was right. Round . . .)

Cooper must have looked unconvinced, though, for Twissell said, "The accuracy of focus was carefully worked out. I intended to explain our methods and now is a good time. For one thing, it will help Harlan understand the controls.''

(Suddenly Harlan turned away from the windows and fixed his gaze on the controls. A corner of the curtain of despair lifted. What if——)

Twissell still lectured Cooper with the anxious overprecise tone of the schoolteacher, and with part of his mind Harlan still listened.

Twissell said, "Obviously a serious problem was that of determining how far into the Primitive an object is sent after the application of a given energy thrust. The most direct method would have been to send a man into the downwhen via this kettle using carefully graduated thrust levels. To do that, however, would have meant a certain lapse of time in each case while the man determined the Century to its nearest hundredth through astronomical observation or by obtaining appropriate information over the wireless. That would be slow and also dangerous since the man might well be discovered by the native inhabitants with probably catastrophic effects on our project.

"What we did then instead was this: We sent back a known mass of the radioactive isotope, niobium-94, which decays by beta-particle emission to the stable isotope, molybdenum-94. The process has a half-life of almost exactly 500 Centuries. The original radiation intensity of the mass was known. That intensity decreases with time according to the simple relationship involved in first-order kinetics, and, of course, the intensity can be measured with great precision.

"When the kettle reaches its destination in Primitive times, the ampule containing the isotope is discharged into the mountainside and the kettle then returns to Eternity. At the moment in physiotime that the ampule is discharged, it simultaneously appears at all future Times growing progressively older. At the place of discharge in the 575th (in actual Time and not in Eternity) a Technician detects the ampule by its radiation and retrieves it.

"The radiation intensity is measured, the time it has remained in the mountainside is then known, the Century to which the kettle traveled is also known to two decimal places. Dozens of ampules were then sent back at various thrust levels and a calibration curve set up. The curve was a check against ampules sent not all the way into the Primitive but into the early Centuries of Eternity where direct observations could also be made.

"Naturally, there were failures. The first few ampules were lost until we learned to allow for the not too major geological changes between the late Primitive and the 575th. Then, three of the ampules later on never showed up in the 575th. Presumably, something went wrong with the discharge mechanism and they were buried too deeply in the mountain for detection. We stopped our experiments when the level of radiation grew so high that we feared that some of the Primitive inhabitants might detect and wonder what radioactive artifacts might be doing in the region. But we had enough for our purposes and we are certain we can send back a man to any hundredth of a Century of the Primitive that is desired.

"You follow all this, Cooper, don't you?"

Cooper said, "Perfectly, Computer Twissell. I have seen the calibration curve without understanding the purpose at the time. It is quite clear now."

But Harlan was exceedingly interested now. He stared at the measured arc marked off in centuries. The shining arc was porcelain on metal and the fine lines divided it into Centuries, Decicenturies, and Centicenturies. Silvery metal gleamed thinly through the porcelain-penetrating lines, marking them clearly. The figures were as finely done and, bending close, Harlan could make out the Centuries from 17 to 27. The hairline was fixed at the 23.17th Century mark.

He had seen similar time-gauges and almost automatically he reached to the pressure-control lever. It did not respond to his grasp. The hairline remained in place.

He nearly jumped when Twissell's voice suddenly addressed him.

"Technician Harlan!"

He cried, "Yes, Computer," then remembered that he could not be heard. He stepped to the window and nodded.

Twissell said, almost as though chiming in with Harlan's thoughts, "The time-gauge is set for a thrust back to the 23.17th. That requires no adjustment. Your only task is to pour energy through at the proper moment in physiotime. There is a chronometer to the right of the gauge. Nod if you see it."

Harlan nodded.

"It will reach zero-point backward. At the minus-fifteen-second point, align the contact points. It's simple. You see how?"

Harlan nodded again.

Twissell went on, "Synchronization is not vital. You can do it at minus fourteen or thirteen or even minus five seconds, but please make every effort to stay this side of minus ten for safety's sake. Once you've closed contact, a synchronized force-gear will do the rest and make certain that the final energy thrust will occur precisely at time zero. Understood?"

Harlan nodded still again. He understood more than Twissell said. If he himself did not align the points by minus ten, it would be taken care of from without.

Harlan thought grimly: There'll be no need for outsiders.

Twissell said, "We have thirty physiominutes left. Cooper and I will leave to check on the supplies."

They left. The door closed behind them, and Harlan was left alone with the thrust control, the time (already moving slowly backward toward zero)—and a resolute knowledge of what must be done.

Harlan turned away from the window. He put his hand inside his pocket and half withdrew the neuronic whip it still contained. Through all this he had kept the whip. His hand shook a little.

An earlier thought recurred: a Samson-smash of the temple!

A corner of his mind wondered sickly: How many Eternals have ever heard of Samson? How many know how he died?

There were only twenty-five minutes left. He was not certain how long the operation would take. He was not really certain it would work at all.

But what choice had he? His damp fingers almost dropped the weapon before he succeeded in unhinging the butt.

He worked rapidly and in complete absorption. Of all the aspects of what he planned, the possibility of his own passage into nonexistence occupied his mind the least and bothered him not at all.

*   *   *

At minus one minute Harlan was standing at the controls.

Detachedly he thought: The last minute of life?

Nothing in the room was visible to him but the backward sweep of the red hairline that marked the passing seconds.

Minus thirty seconds.

He thought: It will not hurt. It is not death.

He tried to think only of Noÿs.

Minus fifteen seconds.

Noÿs!

Harlan's left hand moved a switch down toward contact. Not hastily!

Minus twelve seconds.

Contact!

The force-gear would take over now. Thrust would come at zero time. And that left Harlan one last manipulation. The Samson-smash!

His right hand moved. He did not look at his right hand.

Minus five seconds.

Noÿs!

His right hand mo—ZERO—ved again, spasmodically. He did not look at it. Was this nonexistence?

Not yet. Nonexistence not yet.

Harlan stared out the window. He did not move. Time passed and he was unaware of its passage.

The room was empty. Where the giant, enclosed kettle had been was nothing. Metal blocks that had served as its base sat emptily, lifting their huge strength against air.

Twissell, strangely small and dwarfed in the room that had become a waiting cavern, was the only thing that moved as he tramped edgily this way and that.

Harlan's eyes followed him for a moment and then left him.

Then, without any sound or stir, the kettle was back in the spot it had left. Its passage across the hairline from time past to time present did not as much as disturb a molecule of air.

Twissell was hidden from Harlan's eyes by the bulk of the kettle, but then he rounded it, came into view. He was running.

A flick of his hand was enough to activate the mechanism that opened the door of the control room. He hurtled inside, shouting with an almost lyrical excitement. "It's done. It's done. We've closed the circle." He had breath to say no more.

Harlan made no answer.

Twissell stared out the window, his hands flat against the glass. Harlan noted the blotches of age upon them and the way in which they trembled. It was as though his mind no longer had the ability or the strength to filter the important from the inconsequential, but were selecting observational material in a purely random manner.

Wearily he thought: What does it matter? What does anything matter now?

Twissell said (Harlan heard him dimly), "I'll tell you now that I've been more anxious than I cared to admit. Sennor used to say once that this whole thing was impossible. He insisted something must happen to stop it—— What's the matter?"

He had turned at Harlan's odd grunt.

Harlan shook his head, managed a choked "Nothing."

Twissell left it at that and turned away. It was doubtful whether he spoke to Harlan or to the air. It was as though he were allowing years of pent-up anxieties to escape in words.

"Sennor," he said, "was the doubter. We reasoned with him and argued. We used mathematics and presented the results of generations of research that had preceded us in the physiotime of Eternity. He put it all to one side and presented his case by quoting the man-meets-himself paradox. You heard him talk about it. It's his favorite.

"We knew our own future, Sennor said. I, Twissell, knew, for instance, that I would survive, despite the fact that I would be quite old, until Cooper made his trip past the downwhen terminus. I knew other details of my future, the things I would do.

"Impossible, he would say. Reality must change to correct your knowledge, even if it meant the circle would never close and Eternity never established.

"Why he argued so, I don't know. Perhaps he honestly believed it, perhaps it was an intellectual game with him, perhaps it was just the desire to shock the rest of us with an unpopular viewpoint. In any case, the project proceeded and some of the memoir began to be fulfilled. We located Cooper, for instance, in the Century and Reality that the memoir gave us. Sennor's case was exploded by that alone, but it didn't bother him. By that time, he had grown interested in something else.

"And yet, and yet"—he laughed gently, with more than a trace of embarrassment, and let his cigarette, unnoticed, burn down nearly to his fingers—"you know I was never quite easy in my mind. Something *might* happen. The Reality in which Eternity was established *might* change in some way in order to prevent what Sennor called a paradox. It would have to change to one in which Eternity would not exist. Sometimes, in the dark of a sleeping period, when I couldn't sleep, I could almost persuade myself that that was indeed so—and now it's all over and I laugh at myself as a senile fool."

Harlan said in a low voice, "Computer Sennor was right."

Twissell whirled. "What?"

"The project failed." Harlan's mind was coming out of the shadows (why, and into what, he was not sure). "The circle is not complete."

"What are you talking about?" Twissell's old hands fell on Harlan's shoulders with surprising strength. "You're ill, boy. The strain."

"Not ill. Sick of everything. You. Me. Not ill. The gauge. See for yourself."

"The gauge?" The hairline on the gauge stood at the 27th Century, hard against the right-hand extreme. "What happened?" The joy was gone from his face. Horror replaced it.

Harlan grew matter-of-fact. "I melted the locking mechanism, freed the thrust control."

"How could you——"

"I had a neuronic whip, I broke it open and used its micropile energy source in one flash, like a torch. There's what's left of it." He kicked at a small heap of metal fragments in one corner.

Twissell wasn't taking it in. "In the 27th? You mean Cooper's in the 27th——"

"I don't know where he is," said Harlan dully. "I shifted the thrust control downwhen, further down than the 24th. I don't know where. I didn't look. Then I brought it back. I still didn't look."

Twissell stared at him, his face a pale, unhealthy yellowish color, his lower lip trembling.

"I don't know where he is now," said Harlan. "He's lost in the Primitive. The circle is broken. I thought everything would end when I made the stroke. At zero time. That's silly. We've got to wait. There'll be a moment in physiotime when Cooper will realize he's in the wrong Century, when he'll do something against the memoir, when he——" He broke off, then broke into a forced and creaky laughter. "What's the difference? It's only a delay till Cooper makes the final break in the circle. There's no way of stopping it. Minutes, hours, days. What's the difference? When the delay is done, there will be no more Eternity. Do you hear me? It will be the end of Eternity."

THE EARLIER CRIME

— 14 —

"*WHY? WHY?*"

Twissell looked helplessly from the gauge to the Technician, his eyes mirroring the puzzled frustration in his voice.

Harlan lifted his head. He had only one word to say. "Noÿs!"

Twissell said, "The woman you took into Eternity?"

Harlan smiled bitterly, said nothing.

Twissell said, "What has she to do with this? Great Time, I don't understand, boy."

"What is there to understand?" Harlan burned with sorrow. "Why do you pretend ignorance? I had a woman. I was happy and so was she. We harmed no one. She did not exist in the new Reality. What difference would it have made to anyone?"

Twissell tried vainly to interrupt.

Harlan shouted. "But there are rules in Eternity, aren't there? I know them all. Liaisons require permission; liaisons require computations; liaisons require status; liaisons are tricky things. What were you planning for Noÿs when all this was over? A seat in a crashing rocket? Or a more comfortable position as community mistress for worthy Computers? You won't make any plans *now*, I think."

He ended in a kind of despair and Twissell moved quickly to the Communiplate. Its function as a transmitter had obviously been restored.

The Computer shouted into it till he aroused an answer. Then he said, "This is Twissell. No one is to be allowed in here. No one. No one. Do you understand? . . . Then see to it. It goes for members of the Allwhen Council. It goes for them particularly."

He turned back to Harlan, saying abstractedly, "They'll do it because I'm old and senior member of the Council and because they think I'm cranky and queer. They give in to me because I'm cranky and queer." For a moment he fell into a ruminative silence. Then he said, "Do you think I'm queer?" and his face turned swiftly up to Harlan's like that of a seamed monkey.

Harlan thought: Great Time, the man's mad. The shock has driven him mad.

He took a step backward, automatically aghast at being trapped with a madman. Then he steadied. The man, be he ever so mad, was feeble, and even madness would end soon.

Soon? Why not at once? What delayed the end of Eternity?

Twissell said (he had no cigarette in his fingers; his hand made no move to take one) in a quiet insinuating voice, "You haven't answered me. *Do* you think I'm queer? I suppose you do. Too queer to talk to. If you had thought of me as a friend instead of as a crotchety old man, whimsical and unpredictable, you would have spoken openly to me of your doubts. You would have taken no such action as you did."

Harlan frowned. The man thought *Harlan* was mad. That was it!

He said angrily, "My action was the right one. I'm quite sane."

Twissell said, "I told you the girl was in no danger, you know."

"I was a fool to believe that even for a while. I was a fool to believe the Council would be just to a Technician."

"Who told you the Council knew of any of this?"

"Finge knew of it and sent in a report concerning it to the Council."

"And how do you know that?"

"I got it out of Finge at the point of a neuronic whip. The business end of a whip abolishes comparative status."

"The same whip that did this?" Twissell pointed to the gauge with its blob of molten metal perched wryly above the face of the dial.

"Yes."

"A busy whip." Then, sharply, "Do you know why Finge took it to the Council instead of handling the matter himself?"

"Because he hated me and wanted to make certain I lost all status. He wanted Noÿs."

Twissell said, "You're naïve! If he had wanted the girl, he could easily have arranged liaison. A Technician would not have been in the way. The man hated *me*, boy." (Still no cigarette. He looked odd without one and the stained finger he laid on his chest as he spoke the last pronoun looked almost indecently bare.)

"You?"

"There's such a thing, boy, as Council politics. Not every Computer is appointed to the Council. Finge wanted an appointment. Finge is ambitious and wanted it badly. I blocked it because I thought him emotionally unstable. Time, I never fully appreciated how right I was. . . . Look, boy. He knew you were a protégé of mine. He had seen me take you out of a job as an Observer and make you a master Technician. He saw you working for me steadily. How better could he get back at me and destroy my influence? If he could prove my pet Technician guilty of a terrible crime against Eternity, it would reflect on me. It might force my resignation from the Allwhen Council, and who do you suppose would then be a logical successor?"

His empty hands moved to his lips and when nothing happened, he looked at the space between finger and thumb blankly.

Harlan thought: He's not as calm as he's trying to sound. He can't be. But why does he talk all this nonsense *now?* With Eternity ending?

Then in agony: But why doesn't it *end* then? Now!

Twissell said, "When I allowed you to go to Finge just recently, I more than half suspected danger. But Mallansohn's memoir *said* you were away the last month and no other natural reason for your absence offered itself. Fortunately, Finge underplayed his hand."

"In what way?" asked Harlan wearily. He didn't really care, but Twissell talked and talked and it was easier to take part than to try to shut the sound out of his ears.

Twissell said, "Finge labeled his report: '*In re* unprofessional conduct of Technician Andrew Harlan.' He was being the faithful Eternal, you see, being cool, impartial, unexcited. He was leaving it to the Council to rage and throw itself at me. Unfortunately for himself, he did not know of your real importance. He did not realize that any report concerning you would be instantly referred to me, unless its supreme importance were made perfectly clear on the very face of things."

"You never spoke to me of this?"

"How could I? I was afraid to do anything that would disturb you with the crisis of the project at hand. I gave you every opportunity to bring your problem to me."

Every opportunity? Harlan's mouth twisted in disbelief, but then he thought of Twissell's weary face on the Communiplate asking him if he had nothing to say to him. That was yesterday. Only yesterday.

Harlan shook his head, but turned his face away now.

Twissell said softly, "I realized at once that he had deliberately goaded you into your—rash action."

Harlan looked up. "You know that?"

"Does that surprise you? I knew Finge was after my neck. I've known it for a long time. I am an old man, boy. I know these things. But there are ways in which doubtful Computers can be checked upon. There are some protective devices, culled out of Time, that are not placed in the museums. There are some that are known to the Council alone."

Harlan thought bitterly of the time-block at the 100,000th.

"From the report and from what I knew independently, it was easy to deduce what must have happened."

Harlan asked suddenly, "I suppose Finge suspected you of spying?"

"He might have. I wouldn't be surprised."

Harlan thought back to his first days with Finge when Twissell first showed his abnormal interest in the young Observer. Finge had known nothing of the Mallansohn project, and he had been interested in Twissell's interference. "Have you ever met Senior Computer Twissell?" he had once asked and, thinking back, Harlan could recall the exact tone of sharp uneasiness in the man's voice. As early as that Finge must have suspected Harlan of being Twissell's finger-man. His enmity and hate must have begun that early.

Twissell was speaking, "So if you had come to me——"

"Come to *you?*" cried Harlan. "What of the Council?"

"Of the entire Council, only I know."

"You never told them?" Harlan tried to be mocking.

"I never did."

Harlan felt feverish. His clothes were choking him. Was this nightmare to go on forever. Foolish, irrelevant chatter! *For what? Why?*

Why didn't Eternity end? Why didn't the clean peace of non-Reality reach out for them? *Great Time, what was wrong?*

Twissell said, "Don't you believe me?"

Harlan shouted, "Why should I? They came to look at me, didn't they? At that breakfast? Why should they have done that if they didn't know of the report? They came to look at the queer phenomenon who had broken the laws of Eternity but who couldn't be touched for one more day. One more day and then the project would be over. They came to gloat for the tomorrow they were expecting."

"My boy, there was nothing of that. They wanted to see you only because they were human. Councilmen are human too. They could not witness the final kettle drive because the Mallansohn memoir did not place them at the scene. They could not interview Cooper since the memoir made no mention of that either. Yet they wanted something. Father Time, boy, don't you see they would want something? You were as close as they could get, so they brought you close and stared at you."

"I don't believe you."

"It's the truth."

Harlan said, "Is it? And while we ate, Councilman Sennor talked of a man meeting himself. He obviously knew about my illegal trips to the 482nd and my nearly meeting myself. It was his way of poking fun at me, enjoying himself cutely at my expense."

Twissell said, "Sennor? You worried about Sennor? Do you know the pathetic figure he is? His homewhen is the 803rd, one of the few cultures in which the human body is deliberately disfigured to meet the aesthetic requirements of the time. It is rendered hairless at adolescence.

"Do you know what that means in the continuity of man? Surely you do. A disfigurement sets men apart from their ancestors and descendants. Men of the 803rd are poor risks as Eternals; they are too different from the rest of us. Few are chosen. Sennor is the only one of his Century ever to sit on the Council.

"Don't you see how that affects him? Surely you understand what insecurity means. Did it ever occur to you that a Councilman could be insecure? Sennor has to listen to discussions involving the eradication of his Reality for the very characteristic that makes him so conspicuous among us. And eradicating it would leave him one of a very few in all the generation to be disfigured as he is. Someday it will happen.

"He finds refuge in philosophy. He overcompensates by taking the lead in conversation, by deliberately airing unpopular or unaccepted viewpoints. His man-meeting-himself paradox is a case in point. I told you that he used it to predict disaster for the project and it was we, the Councilmen, that he was attempting to annoy, not you. It had nothing to do with you. Nothing!"

Twissell had grown heated. In the long emotion of his words he seemed to forget where he was and the crisis that faced them, for he slipped back into the quick-gestured, uneasily motioned gnome that Harlan knew so well. He even slipped a cigarette from his sleeve pouch and had all but frictioned it into combustion.

But then he stopped, wheeled, and looked at Harlan again, reaching back through all his own words to what Harlan had last said, as though until that moment, he had not heard them properly.

He said, "What do you mean, you almost met yourself?"

Harlan told him briefly and went on, "You didn't know that?"

"No."

There were a few moments of silence that were as welcome to the feverish Harlan as water would have been.

Twissell said, "Is that it? What if you *had* met yourself?"

"I didn't."

Twissell ignored that. "There is always room for random variation. With an infinite number of Realities there can be no such thing as determinism. Suppose that in the Mallansohn Reality, in the previous turn of the cycle——"

"The circle goes on forever?" asked Harlan with what wonder he could still find in himself.

"Do you think only twice? Do you think two is a magic number? It's a matter of infinite turns of the circle in finite physiotime. Just as you can draw a pencil round and round the circumference of a circle infinitely yet enclose a finite area. In previous turns of the cycle, you had not met yourself. This one time, the statistical uncertainty of things made it possible for you to meet yourself. Reality had to change to prevent the meeting and in the new Reality, you did not send Cooper back to the 24th but——"

Harlan cried, "What's all the talk about? What are you getting at? It's all done. Everything. Let me alone now! *Let me alone!*"

"I want you to know you've done wrong. I want you to realize you did the wrong thing."

"I didn't. And even if I did, *it's done.*"

"But it is *not* done. Listen just a little while longer." Twissell was wheedling, almost crooning with an agonized gentleness. "You will have your girl. I promised that. I still promise it. She will not be harmed. You will not be harmed. I promise you this. It is my personal guarantee."

Harlan stared at him wide-eyed. "But it's too late. What's the use?"

"It is *not* too late. Things are *not* irreparable. With your help, we can succeed yet. I must have your help. You must realize that you did wrong. I am trying to explain this to you. You must want to undo what you have done."

Harlan licked his dry lips with a dry tongue and thought: he *is* mad. His mind can't accept the truth—or, does the Council know more?

Did it? Did it? Could it reverse the verdict of the Changes?

Could they halt Time or reverse it?

He said, "You locked me in the control room, kept me helpless, you thought, till it was all over."

"You said you were afraid something might go wrong with you; that you might not be able to carry on with your part."

"That was meant to be a threat."

"I took it literally. Forgive me. I must have your help."

It came to that. Harlan's help must be had. Was he mad? Was Harlan mad? Did madness have meaning? Or anything at all, for that matter?

The Council needed his help. For that help they would promise him anything. Noÿs. Computership. What would they not promise him? And when his help was done with, what would he get? He would not be fooled a second time.

"No!"

"You'll have Noÿs."

"You mean the Council will be willing to break the laws of Eternity once the danger is safely gone? I don't believe it." How could the danger safely be passed, a sane scrap of his mind demanded. What was this all about?

"The Council will never know."

"Would *you* be willing to break the laws? You're the ideal Eternal. With the danger gone, you would obey the law. You couldn't act otherwise."

Twissell reddened blotchily, high on each cheekbone. From the old face all shrewdness and strength drained away. There was left only a strange sorrow.

"I will keep my word to you and break the law," said Twissell, "for a reason you don't imagine. I don't know how much time is left us before Eternity disappears. It could be hours; it could be months. But I have spent so much time in the hope of bringing you to reason that I will spend a little more. Will you listen to me? Please?"

Harlan hesitated. Then, out of a conviction of the uselessness of all things as much as out of anything else, said wearily, "Go on."

I have heard (began Twissell) that I was born old, that I cut my teeth on a Micro-Computaplex, that I keep my hand computer in a special pocket of my pajamas when I sleep, that my brain is made up of little force-relays in endless parallel hookups and that each corpuscle of my blood is a microscopic spatio-temporal chart floating in computer oil.

All these stories come to me eventually, and I think I must be a little proud of them. Maybe I go around believing them a bit. It's a foolish thing for an old man to do, but it makes life a little easier.

Does that surprise you? That I must find a way to make life easier? I, Senior Computer Twissell, senior member of the Allwhen Council?

Maybe that's why I smoke. Ever think of that? I have to have a reason, you know. Eternity is essentially an unsmoking society, and most of Time is, too. I've thought of that often. I sometimes think it's a rebellion against Eternity. Something to take the place of a greater rebellion that failed . . .

No, it's all right. A tear or two won't hurt me, and it isn't pretense, believe me. It's just that I haven't thought about this for a long time. It isn't pleasant.

It involved a woman, of course, as your affair did. That's not coincidence. It's almost inevitable, if you stop to think of it. An Eternal, who must sell the normal satisfactions of family life for a handful of perforations on foil, is ripe for infection. That's one of the reasons Eternity must take the precautions it does. And, apparently, that's also why Eternals are so ingenious in evading the precautions once in a while.

I remember my woman. It's foolish of me to do so, perhaps. I can't remember anything else about that physiotime. My old colleagues are only names in the record books; the Changes I supervised—all but one—are only items in the Computaplex memory pools. I remember her, though, very well. Perhaps you can understand that.

I had had a long-standing request for liaison in the books; and after I achieved status as a Junior Computer, she was assigned to me. She was a girl of this very Century, the 575th. I didn't see her until after the assignment, of course. She was intelligent and kind. Not beautiful or even pretty, but then, even when young (yes, I was young, never mind the myths) I was not noted for my own looks. We were well suited to one another by temperament, she and I, and if I were a Timed man, I would have been proud to have her as my wife. I told her that many times. I believe it pleased her. I know it was the truth. Not all Eternals, who must take their women as and how Computing permits, are that fortunate.

In that particular Reality, she was to die young, of course, and none of her analogues was available for liaison. At first, I took that philosophically. After all, it was her short lifetime which made it possible for her to live with me without deleteriously affecting Reality.

I am ashamed of that now, of the fact that I was glad she had a short time to live. Just at first, that is. Just at first.

I visited her as often as spatio-temporal charting allowed. I squeezed every minute out of it, giving up meals and sleep when necessary, shifting my labor load shamelessly whenever I could. Her amiability passed the heights of my expectations, and I was in love. I put it bluntly. My experience of love is very small, and understanding it through Observation in Time is a shaky matter. As far as my understanding went, however, I was in love.

What began as the satisfaction of an emotional and physical need became a great deal more. Her imminent death stopped being a convenience and became a calamity. I Life-Plotted her. I didn't go to the Life-Plotting departments, either. I did it myself. That surprises you, I imagine. It was a misdemeanor, but it was nothing compared to the crimes I committed later.

Yes, I, Laban Twissell, Senior Computer Twissell.

Three separate times, a point in physiotime came and passed, during which some simple action of my own might have altered her personal Reality. Naturally, I knew that no such personally motivated Change could possibly be authorized by the Council. Still, I began to feel personally responsible for her death. That was part of my motivation later on, you see.

She became pregnant. I took no action, though I should have. I had worked her Life-Plot, modified to include her relationship with me, and I knew pregnancy to be a high-probability consequence. As you may or may not know, Timed women are occasionally made pregnant by Eternals despite precautions. It is not unheard of. Still, since no Eternal may have a child, such pregnancies as do occur are ended painlessly and safely. There are many methods.

My Life-Plotting had indicated she would die before delivery, so I took no precautions. She was happy in her pregnancy and I wanted her to remain so. So I only watched and tried to smile when she told me she could feel life stirring within her.

But then something happened. She gave birth prematurely——

I don't wonder you look that way. I had a child. A real child of my own. You'll find no other Eternal, perhaps, who can say that. That was more than a misdemeanor. That was a serious felony, but it was still nothing.

I hadn't expected it. Birth and its problems were an aspect of life with which I had had little experience.

I went back to the Life-Plot in panic and found the living child, in an alternate solution to a low-probability forklet I had overlooked. A professional Life-Plotter would not have overlooked it and I had done wrong to trust my own abilities that far.

But what could I do now?

I couldn't kill the child. The mother had two weeks to live. Let the child live with her till then, I thought. Two weeks of happiness is not an exorbitant gift to ask.

The mother died, as foreseen, and in the manner foreseen. I sat in her room, for all the time permitted by the spatio-temporal chart, aching with a sorrow all the keener for my having waited for death, in full knowledge, for over a year. In my arms, I held my son and hers.

—Yes, I let it live. Why do you cry out so? Are *you* going to condemn me?

You cannot know what it means to hold a little atom of your own life in your arms. I may have a Computaplex for nerves and spatio-temporal charts for a bloodstream, but I do know.

I let it live. I committed that crime, too. I put it in the charge of an appropriate organization and returned when I could (in strict temporal sequence, held even with physiotime) to make necessary payments and to watch the boy grow.

Two years went by that way. Periodically, I checked the boy's Life-Plot (I was used to breaking that particular rule, by now) and was pleased to find that there were no signs of deleterious effects on the then-current Reality at probability levels over 0.0001. The boy learned to walk and mispronounced a few words. He was not taught to call me "daddy." Whatever speculations the Timed people of the child-care institution might have made concerning me I don't know. They took their money and said nothing.

Then, when the two years had passed, the necessities of a Change that included the 575th at one wing was brought up before the Allwhen Council. I, having been lately promoted to Assistant Computer, was placed in charge. It was the first Change ever left to my sole supervision.

I was proud, of course, but also apprehensive. My son was an intruder in the Reality. He could scarcely be expected to have analogues. Thought of his passage into nonexistence saddened me.

I worked at the Change and I flatter myself even yet that I did a flawless job. My first one. But I succumbed to a temptation. I succumbed to it all the more easily because it was becoming an old story now for me. I was a hardened criminal, a habitué of crime. I worked out a new Life-Plot for my son under the new Reality, certain of what I would find.

But then for twenty-four hours, without eating or sleeping, I sat in my office, striving with the completed Life-Plot, tearing at it in a despairing effort to find an error.

There was no error.

The next day, holding back my solution to the Change, I worked out a spatio-temporal chart, using rough methods of approximation (after all, the Reality was not to last long) and entered Time at a point more than thirty years upwhen from the birth of my child.

He was thirty-four years old, as old as I myself. I introduced myself as a distant relation, making use of my knowledge of his mother's family, to do so. He had no knowledge of his father, no memory of my visits to him in his infancy.

He was an aeronautical engineer. The 575th was expert in half a dozen varieties of air travel (as it still is in the current Reality), and my son was a happy and successful member of his society. He was married to an ardently enamored girl, but would have no children. Nor would the girl have married at all in the Reality in which my son had not existed. I had known that from the beginning. I had known there would be no deleterious affect on Reality. Otherwise, I might not have found it in my heart to let the boy live. I am not *completely* abandoned.

I spent the day with my son. I spoke to him formally, smiled politely, took my leave coolly when the spatio-temporal chart dictated. But underneath all that, I watched and absorbed every action, filling myself with him, and trying to live one day at least out of a Reality that the next day (by physiotime) would no longer have existed.

How I longed to visit my wife one last time, too, during that portion of Time in which she lived, but I had used every second that had been available to me. I dared not even enter Time to see her, unseen.

I returned to Eternity and spent one last horrible night wrestling futilely against what must be. The next morning I handed in my computations together with my recommendations for Change.

Twissell's voice had lowered to a whisper and now it stopped. He sat there with his shoulders bent, his eyes fixed on the floor between his knees, and his fingers twisting slowly into and out of a knotted clasp.

Harlan, waiting vainly for another sentence out of the old man, cleared his throat. He found himself pitying the man, pitying him despite the many crimes he had committed. He said, "And that's all?"

Twissell whispered, "No, the worst—the worst—— An analogue of my son did exist. In the new Reality, he existed—as a paraplegic from the age of four. Forty-two years in bed, under circumstances that barred me from arranging to have the nerve-regenerating techniques of the 900's applied to his case, or even for arranging to have his life ended painlessly.

"That new Reality still exists. My son is still out there in the appropriate portion of the Century. *I* did that to him. It was my mind and my Computaplex that discovered this new life for him, and my word that ordered the Change. I had committed a number of crimes for his sake and for his mother's, but that one last deed, though strictly in accordance with my oath as an Eternal, has always seemed to me to be my great crime, *the* crime."

There was nothing to say, and Harlan said nothing.

Twissell said, "But you see now why I understand your case, why I will be willing to let you have your girl. It would not harm Eternity and, in a way, it would be expiation for my crime."

And Harlan believed. All in one change of mind, he believed!

Harlan sank to his knees and lifted his clenched fists to his temples. He bent his head and rocked slowly as savage despair beat through him.

He had thrown Eternity away, and lost Noÿs—when, except for his Samson-smash, he might have saved one and kept the other.

SEARCH THROUGH
THE PRIMITIVE

— 15 —

TWISSELL WAS shaking Harlan's shoulders. The old man's voice urgently called his name.

"Harlan! Harlan! For Time's sake, man."

Harlan emerged only slowly from the slough. "What are we to do?"

"Certainly not *this*. Not despair. To begin with, listen to me. Forget your Technician's view of Eternity and look at it through a Computer's eyes. The view is more sophisticated. When you alter something in Time and create a Reality Change, the Change may take place at once. Why should that be?"

Harlan said shakily, "Because your alteration has made the Change inevitable?"

"Has it? You could go back and reverse your alteration, couldn't you?"

"I suppose so. I never did, though. Or anyone that I heard of."

"Right. There is no intention of reversing an alteration, so it goes through as planned. But here we have something else. An unintentional alteration. You sent Cooper into the wrong Century and now I firmly intend to reverse that alteration and bring Cooper back here."

"For Time's sake, how?"

"I'm not sure yet, but there *must* be a way. If there were no way, the alteration would be irreversible; Change would come at once. But Change has not come. We are still in the Reality of the Mallansohn memoir. That means the alteration is reversible and *will* be reversed."

"What?" Harlan's nightmare was expanding and swirling, growing murkier and more engulfing.

"There must be some way of knitting the circle in Time together again and our ability to find the way to do it must be a high-probability affair. As long as our Reality exists, we can be certain that the solution remains high-probability. If at any moment, you or I make the wrong decision, if the probability of healing the circle falls below some crucial magnitude, Eternity disappears. Do you understand?"

Harlan was not sure that he did. He wasn't trying very hard. Slowly he got to his feet and stumbled his way into a chair.

"You mean we can get Cooper back——"

"And send him to the right place, yes. Catch him at the moment he leaves the kettle and he may end up in his proper place in the 24th no more than a few physiohours older; physiodays, at the most. It would be an alteration, of course, but undoubtedly not enough of one. Reality would be rocked, boy, but not upset."

"But how do we get him?"

"We know there's a way, or Eternity wouldn't be existing at this moment. As to what that way is, that is why I need you, why I've fought to get you back on my side. You're the expert on the Primitive. Tell me."

"I can't," groaned Harlan.

"You can," insisted Twissell.

There was suddenly no trace of age or weariness in the old man's voice. His eyes were ablaze with the light of combat and he wielded his cigarette like a lance. Even to Harlan's regret-drugged senses the man seemed to be enjoying himself, actually enjoying himself, now that battle had been joined.

"We can reconstruct the event," said Twissell. "Here is the thrust control. You're standing at it, waiting for the signal. It comes. You make contact and at the same time squeeze the power thrust in the downwhen direction. How far?"

"I don't know, I tell you. I don't know."

"*You* don't know, but your muscles do. Stand there and take the control in your hand. Get hold of yourself. Take them, boy. You're waiting for the signal. You're hating me. You're hating the Council. You're hating Eternity. You're wearying your heart out for Noÿs. Put yourself back at that moment. Feel what you felt then. Now I'll set the clock in motion again. I'll give you one minute, boy, to remember your emotions and force them back into your thalamus. Then, at the approach of zero, let your right hand jerk the control as it had done before. Then take your hand away! Don't move it back again. Are you ready?"

"I don't think I can do it."

"You don't think—— Father Time, you have no choice. Is there another way you can get back your girl?"

There wasn't. Harlan forced himself back to the controls, and as he did so emotion flooded back. He did not have to call on it. Repeating the physical movements brought them back. The red hairline on the clock started moving.

Detachedly he thought: The last minute of life?

Minus thirty seconds.

He thought: It will not hurt. It is not death.

He tried to think only of Noÿs.

Minus fifteen seconds.

Noÿs!

Harlan's left hand moved a switch down toward contact.

Minus twelve seconds.

Contact!

His right hand moved.

Minus five seconds.

Noÿs!

His right hand mo—ZERO—ved spasmodically.

He jumped away, panting.

Twissell came forward, peering at the dial. "Twentieth Century," he said. "Nineteen point three eight, to be exact."

Harlan choked out, "I don't know. I tried to feel the same, but it was different. I knew what I was doing and that made it different."

Twissell said, "I know, I know. Maybe it's all wrong. Call it a first approximation." He paused a moment in mental calculation, took a pocket computer half out of its container and thrust it back without consulting it. "To Time with the decimal points. Say the probability is 0.99 that you sent him back to the second quarter of the 20th. Somewhere between 19.25 and 19.50. All right?"

"I don't know."

"Well, now, look. If I make a firm decision to concentrate on that part of the Primitive to the exclusion of all else and if I am wrong, the chances are that I will have lost my chance to keep the circle in time closed and Eternity will disappear. The decision itself will be the crucial point, the Minimum Necessary Change, the

M.N.C., to bring about the Change. I now make the decision. I decide, definitely——''

Harlan looked about cautiously, as though Reality had grown so fragile that a sudden head movement might shatter it.

Harlan said, ''I'm thoroughly conscious of Eternity.'' (Twissell's normality had infected him to the point where his voice sounded firm in his own ears.)

''Then Eternity still exists,'' said Twissell in a blunt, matter-of-fact manner, ''and we have made the right decision. Now there's nothing more to do here for the while. Let's get to my office and we can let the subcommittee of the Council swarm over this place, if that will make them any happier. As far as they are concerned, the project has ended successfully. If it doesn't, they'll never know. Nor we.''

Twissell studied his cigarette and said, ''The question that now confronts us is this: What will Cooper do when he finds himself in the wrong Century?''

''I don't know.''

''One thing is obvious. He's a bright lad, intelligent, imaginative, wouldn't you say?''

''Well, he's Mallansohn.''

''Exactly. And he wondered if he would end up wrong. One of his last questions was: What if I don't end up in the right spot? Do you remember?''

''Well?'' Harlan had no idea where this was leading.

''So he is mentally prepared for being displaced in Time. He will do something. Try to reach us. Try to leave traces for us. Remember, for part of his life he was an Eternal. That's an important thing.'' Twissell blew a smoke ring, hooked it with a finger, and watched it curl about and break up. ''He's used to the notion of communications across Time. He is not likely to surrender to the thought of being marooned in Time. He'll know that we're looking for him.''

Harlan said, ''Without kettles and with no Eternity in the 20th, how would he go about communicating with us?''

''With *you*, Technician, with *you*. Use the singular. You're our expert on the Primitive. You taught Cooper about the Primitive. You're the one he would expect to be capable of finding his traces.''

''*What* traces, Computer?''

Twissell's shrewd old face stared up at Harlan, its lines crinkling. ''It was intended to leave Cooper in the Primitive. He is without the protection of an enclosing shield of physiotime. His entire life is woven into the fabric of Time and will remain so until you and I reverse the alteration. Likewise woven into the fabric of Time is any artifact, sign, or message he may have left for us. Surely there must be particular sources you used in studying the 20th Century. Documents, archives, films, artifacts, reference works. I mean primary sources, dating from the Time itself.''

''Yes.''

''And he studied them with you?''

''Yes.''

''And is there any particular reference that was your favorite, one that he knew you were intimately acquainted with, so that you would recognize in it some reference to himself?''

"I see what you're driving at, of course," said Harlan. He grew thoughtful.

"Well?" asked Twissell with an edge of impatience.

Harlan said, "My news magazines, almost surely. News magazines were a phenomenon of the early 20's. The one of which I have nearly a complete set dates from early in the 20th and continues well into the 22nd."

"Good. Now is there any way, do you suppose, in which Cooper could make use of that news magazine to carry a message? Remember, he'd know you'd be reading the periodical, that you'd be acquainted with it, that you'd know your way about in it."

"I don't know," Harlan shook his head. "The magazine affected an artificial style. It was selective rather than inclusive and quite unpredictable. It would be difficult or even impossible to rely on its printing something you would plan to have it print. Cooper couldn't very well create news and be sure of its appearance. Even if Cooper managed to get a position on its editorial staff, which is very unlikely, he couldn't be certain that his exact wording would pass the various editors. I don't see it, Computer."

Twissell said, "For Time's sake, think! Concentrate on that news magazine. You're in the 20th and you're Cooper with his education and background. You taught the boy, Harlan. You molded his thinking. Now what would he do? How would he go about placing something in the magazine; something with the exact wording he wants?"

Harlan's eyes widened. "An advertisement!"

"What?"

"An advertisement. A paid notice which they would be compelled to print exactly as requested. Cooper and I discussed them occasionally."

"Ah, yes. They have that sort of thing in the 186th," said Twissell.

"Not like the 20th. The 20th is peak in that respect. The cultural milieu——"

"Considering the advertisement now," interposed Twissell hastily, "what kind would it be?"

"I wish I knew."

Twissell stared at the lighted end of his cigarette as though seeking inspiration. "He can't say anything directly. He can't say: 'Cooper of the 78th, stranded in the 20th and calling Eternity——' "

"How can you be sure?"

"Impossible! To give the 20th information we know they did not have would be as damaging to the Mallansohn circle as would wrong action on our part. We're still here, so in his whole lifetime in the current Reality of the Primitive he's done no harm of that sort."

"Besides which," said Harlan, retreating from the contemplation of the circular reasoning which seemed to bother Twissell so little, "the news magazine is not likely to agree to publish anything which seems mad to it or which it cannot understand. It would suspect fraud or some form of illegality and would not wish to be implicated. So Cooper couldn't use Standard Intertemporal for his message."

"It would have to be something subtle," said Twissell. "He would have to use indirection. He would have to place an advertisement that would seem perfectly normal to the men of the Primitive. Perfectly normal! And yet something that is obvious to us, once we knew what we were searching for. Very obvious. Obvious at a glance because it would have to be found among uncounted individual items. How *big* do you suppose it would be, Harlan? Are those advertisements expensive?''

"Quite expensive, I believe.''

"And Cooper would have to hoard his money. Besides which, to avoid the wrong kind of attention, it would have to be small, anyway. Guess, Harlan. How large?''

Harlan spread his hands. "Half a column?''

"Column?''

"They were printed magazines, you know. On paper. With print arranged in columns.''

"Oh yes. I can't seem to separate literature and film somehow. . . . Well, we have a first approximation of another sort now. We must look for a half-column advertisement which will, practically at a glance, give evidence that the man who placed it came from another Century (in the upwhen direction, of course) and yet which is so normal an advertisement that no man of that Century would see anything suspicious in it.''

Harlan said, "What if I don't find it?''

"You will. Eternity exists, doesn't it. As long as it does, we're on the right track. Tell me, can you recall such an advertisement in your work with Cooper? Anything which struck you, even momentarily, as odd, queer, unusual, subtly wrong.''

"No.''

"I don't want an answer so quickly. Take five minutes and think.''

"No point. At the time I was going over the news magazines with Cooper, he hadn't been in the 20th.''

"Please, boy. Use your head. Sending Cooper to the 20th has introduced an alteration. There's no Change; it isn't an irreversible alteration. But there have been some changes with a small 'c,' or micro-changes, as it is usually referred to in Computation. At the instant Cooper was sent to the 20th, the advertisement appeared in the appropriate issue of the magazine. Your own Reality has micro-changed in the sense that you may have looked at the page with that advertisement on it rather than one without that advertisement as you did in the previous Reality. Do you understand?''

Harlan was again bewildered, almost as much at the ease with which Twissell picked his way through the jungle of temporal logic, as at the "paradoxes" of Time. He shook his head, "I remember nothing of the sort.''

"Well, then, where do you keep the files of that periodical?''

"I had a special library built on Level Two, using the Cooper priority.''

"Good enough,'' said Twissell. "Let's go there. *Now!*''

Harlan watched Twissell stare curiously at the old, bound volumes in the library and then take one down. They were so old that the fragile paper had to be preserved by special methods and they creaked under Twissell's insufficiently gentle handling.

Harlan winced. In better times he would have ordered Twissell away from the books, Senior Computer though he was.

The old man peered through the crinkling pages and silently mouthed the archaic words. "This is the English the linguists are always talking about, isn't it?'' he asked, tapping a page.

"Yes. English," muttered Harlan.

Twissell put the volume back. "Heavy and clumsy."

Harlan shrugged. To be sure, most of the Centuries of Eternity were film eras. A respectable minority were molecular-recording eras. Still, print and paper were not unheard of.

He said, "Books don't require the investment in technology that films do."

Twissell rubbed his chin. "Quite. Shall we get started?"

He took another volume down from the shelf, opening it at random and staring at the page with odd intentness.

Harlan thought: Does the man think he's going to hit the solution by a lucky stab?

The thought might have been correct, for Twissell, meeting Harlan's appraising eyes, reddened and put the book back.

Harlan took the first volume of the 19.25th Centicentury and began turning the pages regularly. Only his right hand and his eyes moved. The rest of his body remained at rigid attention.

At what seemed aeonic intervals to himself Harlan rose, grunting, for a new volume. On those occasions there would be the coffee break or the sandwich break or the other breaks.

Harlan said heavily, "It's useless your staying."

Twissell said, "Do I bother you?"

"No."

"Then I'll stay," muttered Twissell. Throughout he wandered occasionally to the bookshelves, staring helplessly at the bindings. The sparks of his furious cigarettes burned his finger ends at times, but he disregarded them.

A physioday ended.

Sleep was poor and sparse. Midmorning, between two volumes, Twissell lingered over his last sip of coffee and said, "I wonder sometimes why I didn't throw up my Computership after the matter of my—— You know."

Harlan nodded.

"I felt like it," the old man went on. "I felt like it. For physiomonths, I hoped desperately that no Changes would come my way. I got morbid about it. I began to wonder if Changes were right. Funny, the tricks emotions will play on you.

"*You* know Primitive history, Harlan. You know what it was like. Its Reality flowed blindly along the line of maximum probability. If that maximum probability involved a pandemic, or ten Centuries of slave economy, a breakdown of technology, or even a—a—let's see, what's really bad—even an atomic war if one had been possible then, why, by Time, it *happened*. There was nothing to stop it.

"But where Eternity exists, that's been stopped. Upwhen from the 28th, things like that don't happen. Father Time, we've lifted our Reality to a level of well-being far beyond anything Primitive times could imagine; to a level which, but for the interference of Eternity, would have been very low probability indeed."

Harlan thought in shame: What's he trying to do? Get me to work harder? I'm doing my best.

Twissell said, "If we miss our chance now, Eternity disappears, probably through all of physiotime. And in one vast Change all Reality reverts to maximum probability with, I am positive, atomic warfare and the end of man.''

Harlan said, ''I'd better get on to the next volume.''

At the next break Twissell said helplessly, ''There's so much to do. Isn't there a faster way?''

Harlan said, ''Name it. To me it seems that I must look at every single page. And look at every part of it, too. How can I do it faster?''

Methodically he turned the pages.

''Eventually,'' said Harlan, ''the print starts blurring and that means it's time for sleep.''

A second physioday ended.

At 10:22 A.M., Standard Physiotime, of the third physioday of the search Harlan stared at a page in quiet wonder and said, ''This is it!''

Twissell didn't absorb the statement. He said, ''What?''

Harlan looked up, his face twisted with astonishment. ''You know, I didn't believe it. By Time, I never really believed it, even while you were working out all that rigmarole about news magazines and advertisements.''

Twissell had absorbed it now. *''You've found it!''*

He leaped at the volume Harlan was holding, clutching at it with shaking fingers.

Harlan held it out of reach and slammed the volume shut. ''Just a moment. *You* won't find it, even if I showed you the page.''

''What are you doing?'' shrieked Twissell. ''You've lost it.''

''It's not lost. I know where it is. But first——''

''First what?''

Harlan said, ''There's one point remaining, Computer Twissell. You say I can have Noÿs. Bring her to me, then. Let me see her.''

Twissell stared at Harlan, his thin white hair in disarray. ''Are you joking?''

''No,'' said Harlan sharply. ''I'm not joking. You assured me that you would make arrangements—— Are *you* joking? Noÿs and I would be together. You promised that.''

''Yes, I did. That part's settled.''

''Then produce her alive, well, and untouched.''

''But I don't understand you. I don't have her. No one has. She's still in the far upwhen, where Finge reported her to be. No one has touched her. Great Time, I told you she was safe.''

Harlan stared at the old man and grew tense. He said, chokingly, ''You're playing with words. All right, she's in the far upwhen, but what good is that to me? Take down the barrier at the 100,000th—''

''The what?''

''The barrier. The kettle won't pass it.''

''You never said anything of this,'' said Twissell wildly.

''I haven't?'' said Harlan with sharp surprise. Hadn't he? He had thought of it often enough. Had he never said a word about it? He couldn't recall, at that. But then he hardened.

He said, ''All right, I tell you *now*. Take it down.''

"But the thing is impossible. A barrier against the kettle? A temporal barrier?"

"Are you telling me you didn't put one up?"

"I didn't. By Time, I swear it."

"Then—then——" Harlan felt himself grow pale. "Then the Council did it. They know of all this and they've taken action independently of you and—and by all of Time and Reality, they can whistle for their ad and for Cooper, for Mallansohn and all of Eternity. They'll have none of it. None of it."

"Wait. Wait." Twissell yanked despairingly at Harlan's elbow. "Keep hold of yourself. Think, boy, think. The Council put up no barrier."

"It's there."

"But they can't have put up such a barrier. No one could have. It's theoretically impossible."

"You don't know it all. It's there."

"I know more than anyone else on the Council and such a thing is impossible."

"But it's there."

"But if it is——"

And Harlan grew sufficiently aware of his surroundings to realize that there was a kind of abject fear in Twissell's eyes; a fear that had not been there even when he first learned of Cooper's misdirection and of the impending end of Eternity.

THE HIDDEN CENTURIES
— 16 —

ANDREW HARLAN watched the men at work with abstracted eyes. They ignored him politely because he was a Technician. Ordinarily he would have ignored them somewhat less politely because they were Maintenance men. But now he watched them and, in his misery, he even caught himself envying them.

They were service personnel from the Department of Intertemporal Transportation, in dun-gray uniforms with shoulder patches showing a red, double-headed arrow against a black background. They used intricate force-field equipment to test the kettle motors and the degrees of hyper-freedom along the kettleways. They had, Harlan imagined, little theoretical knowledge of temporal engineering, but it was obvious that they had a vast practical knowledge of the subject.

Harlan had not learned much concerning Maintenance when he was a Cub. Or, to put it more accurately, he had not really wished to learn. Cubs who did not make the grade were put into Maintenance. The "unspecialized profession" (as the euphemism had it) was the hallmark of failure and the average Cub automatically avoided the subject.

Yet now, as he watched the Maintenance men at work, they seemed to Harlan to be quietly, tensionlessly efficient, reasonably happy.

Why not? They outnumbered the Specialists, the "true Eternals," ten to one. They had a society of their own, residential levels devoted to them, pleasures of their own. Their labor was fixed at so many hours per physioday and there was no social pressure in their case to make them relate their spare-time activity to their profession. They had time, as Specialists did not, to devote to the literature and film dramatizations culled out of the various Realities.

It was they, after all, who probably had the better-rounded personalities. It was the Specialist's life which was harried and affected, artificial in comparison with the sweet and simple life in Maintenance.

Maintenance was the foundation of Eternity. Strange that such an obvious fact had not struck him earlier. They supervised the importation of food and water from Time, the disposal of waste, the functioning of the power plants. They kept all the machinery of Eternity running smoothly. If every Specialist were to die of a stroke on the spot, Maintenance could keep Eternity going indefinitely. Yet were Maintenance to disappear, the Specialists would have to abandon Eternity in days or die miserably.

Did Maintenance men resent the loss of their homewhens, or their womanless, childless lives? Was security from poverty, disease, and Reality Change sufficient compensation? Were their views ever consulted on any matter of importance? Harlan felt some of the fire of the social reformer within him.

Senior Computer Twissell broke Harlan's train of thought by bustling in at a half run, looking even more haunted than he had an hour before, when he had left, with Maintenance already at work.

Harlan thought: How does he keep it up? He's an old man.

Twissell glanced about him with birdlike brightness as the men automatically straightened up to respectful attention.

He said, "What about the kettleways?"

One of the men responded, "Nothing wrong, sir. The ways are clear, the fields mesh."

"You've checked everything?"

"Yes, sir. As far upwhen as the Department's stations go."

Twissell said, "Then go."

There was no mistaking the brusque insistence of the dismissal. They bowed respectfully, turned, and hastened out briskly.

Twissell and Harlan were alone in the kettleways.

Twissell turned to him. "You'll stay here. Please."

Harlan shook his head. "I must go."

Twissell said, "Surely you understand. If anything happens to me, you still know how to find Cooper. If anything happens to you, what can I or any Eternal or any combination of Eternals do alone?"

Harlan shook his head again.

Twissell put a cigarette between his lips. He said, "Sennor is suspicious. He's called me several times in the last two physiodays. Why am I in seclusion, he wants to know. When he finds out I've ordered a complete overhaul of the kettleway machinery . . . I must go now, Harlan. I can't delay."

"I don't want delay. I'm ready."

"You insist on going?"

"If there's no barrier, there'll be no danger. Even if there is, I've been there already and come back. What are you afraid of, Computer?"

"I don't want to risk anything I don't have to."

"Then use your logic, Computer. Make the decision that I'm to go with you. If Eternity still exists after that, then it means that the circle can still be closed. It means we'll survive. If it's a wrong decision, then Eternity will pass into nonexistence, but it will anyway if I don't go, because without Noÿs, I'll make no move to get Cooper. I swear it."

Twissell said, "I'll bring her back to you."

"If it is so simple and safe, there will be no harm if I come along."

Twissell was in an obvious torture of hesitation. He said gruffly, "Well, then, come!"

And Eternity survived.

Twissell's haunted look did not disappear once they were within the kettle. He stared at the skimming figures of the temporometer. Even the scaler gauge, which measured in units of Kilocenturies, and which the men had adjusted for this particular purpose, was clicking at minute intervals.

He said, "You should not have come."

Harlan shrugged. "Why not?"

"It disturbs me. No sensible reason. Call it a long-standing superstition of mine. It makes me restless." He clasped his hands together, holding them tightly.

Harlan said, "I don't understand you."

Twissell seemed eager to talk, as though to exorcise some mental demon. He said, "Maybe you'll appreciate this, at that. You're the expert on the Primitive. How long did man exist in the Primitive?"

Harlan said, "Ten thousand Centuries. Fifteen thousand, maybe."

"Yes. Beginning as a kind of primitive apelike creature and ending as Homo sapiens. Right?"

"It's common knowledge. Yes."

"Then it must be common knowledge that evolution proceeds at a fairly rapid pace. Fifteen thousand Centuries from ape to Homo sapiens."

"Well?"

"Well, I'm from a Century in the 30,000's——"

(Harlan could not help starting. He had never known Twissell's homewhen or known of anyone who did.)

"I'm from a Century in the 30,000's," Twissell said again, "and you're from the 95th. The time between our homewhens is twice the total length of time of man's existence in the Primitive, yet what change is there between us? I was born with four fewer teeth than you, and without an appendix. The physiological differences about end with that. Our metabolism is almost the same. The major difference is that your body can synthesize the steroid nucleus and my body can't, so that I require cholesterol in my diet and you don't. I was able to breed with a woman of the 575th. That's how undifferentiated with time the species is."

Harlan was unimpressed. He had never questioned the basic identity of man throughout the Centuries. It was one of those things you lived with and took for granted. He said, "There have been cases of species living unchanged through millions of Centuries."

"Not many, though. And it remains a fact that the cessation of human evolution seems to coincide with the development of Eternity. Just coincidence?

It's not a question which is considered, except by a few here and there like Sennor, and I've never been a Sennor. I didn't believe speculation was proper. If something couldn't be checked by a Computaplex, it had no business taking up the time of a Computer. And yet, in my younger days, I sometimes thought——"

"Of what?" Harlan thought: Well, it's something to listen to, anyway.

"I sometimes thought about Eternity as it was when it was first established. It stretched over just a few Centuries in the 30's and 40's, and its function was mostly trade. It interested itself in the reforestation of denuded areas, shipping topsoil back and forth, fresh water, fine chemicals. Those were simple days.

"But then we discovered Reality Changes. Senior Computer Henry Wadsman, in the dramatic manner with which we are all acquainted, prevented a war by removing the safety brake of a Congressman's ground vehicle. After that, more and more, Eternity shifted its center of gravity from trade to Reality Change. Why?"

Harlan said, "The obvious reason. Betterment of humanity."

"Yes. Yes. In normal times, I think so too. But I'm talking of my nightmare. What if there were another reason, an unexpressed one, an unconscious one. A man who can travel into the indefinite future may meet men as far advanced over himself as he himself is over an ape. Why not?"

"Maybe. But men are men——"

"—even in the 70,000th. Yes, I know. And have our Reality Changes had something to do with it? We bred out the unusual. Even Sennor's homewhen with its hairless creatures is under continual question and that's harmless enough. Perhaps in all honesty, in all sincerity, we've prevented human evolution because we don't *want* to meet the supermen."

Still no spark was struck. Harlan said, "Then it's done. What does it matter?"

"But what if the superman exists just the same, further upwhen than we can reach? We control only to the 70,000th. Beyond that are the Hidden Centuries! Why are they hidden? Because evolved man does not want to deal with us and bars us from his time? Why do we allow them to remain hidden? Because we don't want to deal with them and, having failed to enter in our first attempt, we refuse even to make additional attempts? I don't say it's our conscious reason, but conscious or unconscious, it's a reason."

"Grant everything," said Harlan sullenly. "They're out of our reach and we're out of theirs. Live and let live."

Twissell seemed struck by the phrase. "Live and let live. But we don't. We make Changes. The Changes extend only through a few Centuries before temporal inertia causes its effects to die out. You remember Sennor brought that up as one of the unanswered problems of Time at our breakfast. What he might have said was that it's all a matter of statistics. Some Changes affect more Centuries than others. Theoretically, any number of Centuries can be affected by the proper Change; a hundred Centuries, a thousand, a hundred thousand. Evolved man of the Hidden Centuries may know that. Suppose he is disturbed by the possibility that someday a Change may reach him clear to the 200,000th."

"It's useless to worry about such things," said Harlan with the air of a man who had much greater worries.

"But suppose," went on Twissell in a whisper, "they were calm enough as long as we left the Sections of the Hidden Centuries empty. It meant we weren't aggressing. Suppose this truce, or whatever you wish to call it, were broken, and someone appeared to have established permanent residence upwhen from the 70,000th. Suppose they thought it might mean the first of a serious invasion? They can bar us from their Time, so their science is that far advanced beyond ours. Suppose they may further do what seems impossible to us and throw a barrier across the kettleways, cutting us off——''

And now Harlan was on his feet, in full horror, *"They* have Noÿs?''

"I don't know. It's speculation. Maybe there is no barrier. Maybe there was something wrong with your ket——''

"There was a barrier!'' yelled Harlan. "What other explanation is there? Why didn't you tell me this before.''

"I don't believe it,'' groaned Twissell. "I still don't. I shouldn't have said a word of this foolish dreaming. My own fears—the question of Cooper— everything—— But wait, just a few minutes.''

He pointed at the temporometer. The scaler indicated them to be between the 95,000th and 96,000th Centuries.

Twissell's hand on the controls slowed the kettle. The 99,000th was passed. The scaler's motions stopped. The individual Centuries could be read.

99,726—99,727—99,728—

"What will we do?'' muttered Harlan.

Twissell shook his head in a gesture that spoke eloquently of patience and hope, but perhaps also of helplessness.

99,851—99,852—99,853—

Harlan steeled himself for the shock of the barrier and thought desperately: Would preserving Eternity be the only means of finding time to fight back at the creatures of the Hidden Centuries? How else recover Noÿs? Dash back, back to the 575th and work like fury to—

99,938—99,939—99,940—

Harlan held his breath. Twissell slowed the kettle further, let it creep. It responded perfectly to the controls.

99,984—99,985—99,986—

"Now, now, now,'' said Harlan in a whisper, unaware that he had made any sound at all.

99,998—99,999—100,000—100,001—100,002—

The numbers mounted and the two men watched them continue to mount in paralytic silence.

Then Twissell cried, "There *is* no barrier.''

And Harlan answered, "There was! There was!'' Then, in agony, "Maybe they've got her, and need a barrier no longer.''

111,394th!

Harlan leaped from the kettle, and raised his voice. "Noÿs! Noÿs!''

The echoes bounced off the walls of the empty Section in hollow syncopation.

Twissell, climbing out more sedately, called after the younger man, "Wait, Harlan——''

That was useless. Harlan, at a run, was hurtling along the corridors toward that portion of the Section they had made a kind of home.

He thought vaguely of the possibility of meeting one of Twissell's "evolved men" and momentarily his skin prickled, but then that was drowned in his urgent need to find Noÿs.

"Noÿs!"

And all at once, so quickly that she was in his arms before he was sure he had seen her at all, she was there with him, and her arms were around him and clutching him and her cheek was against his shoulder and her dark hair was soft against his chin.

"Andrew?" she said, her voice muffled by the pressure of his body. "Where were you? It's been days and I was getting frightened."

Harlan held her out at arm's length, staring at her with a kind of hungry solemnity. "Are you all right?"

"I'm all right. I thought something might have happened to you. I thought——" She broke off, terror springing into her eyes and gasped, "Andrew!"

Harlan whirled.

It was only Twissell, panting.

Noÿs must have gained confidence from Harlan's expression. She said more quietly, "Do you know him, Andrew? Is it all right?"

Harlan said, "It's all right. This is my superior, Senior Computer Laban Twissell. He knows of you."

"A Senior Computer?" Noÿs shrank away.

Twissell advanced slowly. "I will help you, my child. I will help you both. The Technician has my promise, if he would only believe it."

"My apologies, Computer," said Harlan stiffly, and not yet entirely repentant.

"Forgiven," said Twissell. He held out his hand, took the girl's reluctant one. "Tell me, girl, has it been well with you here?"

"I've been worried."

"There's been no one here, since Harlan last left you."

"N—no, sir."

"No one at all? Nothing?"

She shook her head. Her dark eyes sought Harlan's. "Why do you ask?"

"Nothing, girl. A foolish nightmare. Come, we will take you back to the 575th."

On the kettle back Andrew Harlan sank, by degrees, into a troubled and deepening silence. He did not look up when the 100,000th was passed in the downwhen direction and Twissell had snorted an obvious sigh of relief as though he had half expected to be trapped on the upwhen side.

He scarcely moved when Noÿs' hand stole into his, and the manner in which he returned the pressure of her fingers was almost mechanical.

Noÿs slept in another room and now Twissell's restlessness reached a peak of devouring intensity.

"The advertisement, boy! You have your woman. My part of the agreement is done."

Silently, still abstracted, Harlan turned the pages of the volume on the desk. He found his page.

"It's simple enough," he said, "but it's in English. I'll read it to you and then translate it."

It was a small advertisement in the upper left-hand corner of a page numbered 30. Against an irregular line drawing as background were the unadorned words, in block letters:

ALL THE
TALK
OF THE
MARKET

Underneath, in smaller letters, it said: "Investments News-Letter, P. O. Box 14, Denver, Colorado."

Twissell listened painstakingly to Harlan's translation and was obviously disappointed. He said, "What is the market? What do they mean by that?"

"The stock market," said Harlan impatiently. "A system by which private capital was invested in business. But that's not the point at all. Don't you see the line drawing against which the advertisement is set?"

"Yes. The mushroom cloud of an A-bomb blast. An attention getter. What about it?"

Harlan exploded. "Great Time, Computer, what's wrong with you? Look at the date of the magazine issue."

He pointed to the top heading, just to the left of the page number. It read March 28, 1932.

Harlan said, "That scarcely needs translation. The numbers are about those of Standard Intertemporal and you see it's the 19.32nd Century. Don't you know that at that time no human being who had ever lived had seen the mushroom cloud? No one could possibly reproduce it so accurately, except——"

"Now, wait. It's just a line pattern," said Twissell, trying to retain his equilibrium. "It might resemble the mushroom cloud only coincidentally."

"Might it? Will you look at the wording again?" Harlan's fingers punched out the short lines: "All the—Talk—Of the—Market. The initials spell out ATOM, which is English for atom. Is that coincidence, too? Not a chance.

"Don't you see, Computer, how this advertisement fits the conditions you yourself set up? It caught my eye instantly. Cooper knew it would out of sheer anachronism. At the same time, it has no meaning other than its face value, no meaning at all, for any man of the 19.32nd.

"So it must be Cooper. That's his message. We have the date to the nearest week of a Centicentury. We have his mailing address. It is only necessary to go after him and I'm the only one with enough knowledge of the Primitive to manage that."

"And you'll go?" Twissell's face was ablaze with relief and happiness.

"I'll go—on one condition."

Twissell frowned in a sudden reversal of emotion. "Again conditions?"

"The same condition. I'm not adding new ones. Noÿs must be safe. She must come with me. I will not leave her behind."

"You *still* don't trust me? In what way have I failed you? What can there be that still disturbs you?"

"One thing, Computer," said Harlan solemnly. "One thing still. There *was* a barrier across the 100,000th. Why? That is what still disturbs me."

THE CLOSING CIRCLE
— 17 —

IT DID not stop disturbing him. It was a matter that grew in mind as the days of preparation sped by. It interposed itself between him and Twissell; then between him and Noÿs. When the day of departure came, he was only distantly aware of the fact.

It was all he could do to rouse a shadow of interest when Twissell returned from a session with the Council subcommittee. He said, "How did it go?"

Twissell said wearily, "It wasn't exactly the most pleasant conversation I've ever had."

Harlan was almost willing to let it go at that, but he broke his moment's silence with a muttered "I suppose you said nothing about——"

"No, no," was the testy response. "I said nothing about the girl or about your part in the misdirection of Cooper. It was an unfortunate error, a mechanical failure. I took full responsibility."

Harlan's conscience, burdened as it was, could find room for a twinge. He said, "That won't affect you well."

"What can they do? They must wait for the correction to be made before they can touch me. If we fail, we're all beyond help or harm. If we succeed, success itself will probably protect me. And if it doesn't——" The old man shrugged. "I plan to retire from active participation in Eternity's affairs thereafter anyway." But he fumbled his cigarette and disposed of it before it was half burned away.

He sighed. "I would rather not have brought them into this at all, but there would have been no way, otherwise, of using the special kettle for further trips past the downwhen terminus."

Harlan turned away. His thoughts moved around and about the same channels that had been occupied to the increasing exclusion of all else for days. He heard Twissell's further remark dimly, but it was only at its repetition that he said with a start, "Pardon me?"

"I say, is your woman ready, boy? Does she understand what she's to do?"

"She's ready. I've told her everything."

"How did she take it?"

"What? . . . Oh, yes, uh, as I expected her to. She's not afraid."

"It's less than three physiohours now."

"I know."

That was all for the moment, and Harlan was left alone with his thoughts and a sickening realization of what he must do.

With the kettle loading done and the controls adjusted Harlan and Noÿs appeared in a final change of costume, approximating that of an unurbanized area of the early 20th.

Noÿs had modified Harlan's suggestion for her wardrobe, according to some instinctive feeling she claimed women had when it came to matters of clothing and aesthetics. She chose thoughtfully from pictures in the advertisements of the appropriated volumes of the news magazine and had minutely scrutinized items imported from a dozen different Centuries.

Occasionally she would say to Harlan, "What do you think?"

He would shrug. "If it's instinctive knowledge, I'll leave it to you."

"That's a bad sign, Andrew," she said, with a lightness that did not quite ring true. "You're too pliable. What's the matter, anyway? You're just not yourself. You haven't been for days."

"I'm all right," Harlan said in a monotone.

Twissell's first sight of them in the role of natives of the 20th elicited a feeble attempt at jocularity. "Father Time," he said, "what ugly costumes in the Primitive, and yet how it fails to hide your beauty, my—my dear."

Noÿs smiled warmly at him, and Harlan, standing there impassively silent, was forced to admit that Twissell's rust-choked vein of gallantry had something of truth in it. Noÿs's clothing encompassed her without accentuating her as clothing should. Her make-up was confined to unimaginative dabs of color on lips and cheeks and an ugly rearrangement of the eyebrow line. Her lovely hair (this had been the worst of it) had been cut ruthlessly. Yet she was beautiful.

Harlan himself was already growing accustomed to his own uncomfortable belt, the tightness of fit under armpits and in the crotch and the mousy lack of color about his rough-textured clothing. Wearing strange costumes to suit a Century was an old story to him.

Twissell was saying, "Now what I really wanted to do was to install hand controls inside the kettle, as we discussed, but there isn't any way, apparently. The engineers simply must have a source of power large enough to handle temporal displacement and that isn't available outside Eternity. Temporal tension while occupying the Primitive is all that can be managed. However, we have a return lever."

He led them into the kettle, picking his way among the piled supplies, and pointed out the obtruding finger of metal that now marred the smooth inner wall of the kettle.

"It amounts to the installation of a simple switch," he said. "Instead of returning automatically to Eternity, the kettle will remain in the Primitive indefinitely. Once the lever is plunged home, however, you will return. There will then be the matter of the second and, I hope, final trip——"

"A second trip?" asked Noÿs at once.

Harlan said, "I haven't explained that. Look, this first trip is intended merely to fix the time of Cooper's arrival precisely. We don't know how long a Time-lapse exists between his arrival and the placing of the advertisement. We'll reach him by the post-office box, and learn, if possible, the exact minute of his arrival, or as close as we can, anyway. We can then return to that moment plus fifteen minutes to allow for the kettle to have left Cooper——"

Twissell interposed, "Couldn't have the kettle in the same place at the same time in two different physiotimes, you know," and tried to smile.

Noÿs seemed to absorb it. "I see," she said, not too definitely.

Twissell said to Noÿs, "Picking up Cooper at the time of his arrival will reverse all micro-changes. The A-bomb advertisement will disappear again and Cooper will know only that the kettle, having disappeared as we told him it would, had unexpectedly appeared again. He will not know that he was in the wrong Century and he will not be told. We will tell him that there was some vital instruction we had forgotten to give him (we'll have to manufacture some) and we can only hope that he will regard the matter as so unimportant that he won't mention being sent back twice when he writes his memoir."

Noÿs lifted her plucked eyebrows. "It's very complicated."

"Yes. Unfortunately." He rubbed his hands together and looked at the others as though nursing an inner doubt. Then he straightened, produced a fresh cigarette, and even managed a certain jauntiness as he said, "And now, boy, good luck." Twissell touched hands briefly with Harlan, nodded to Noÿs, and stepped out of the kettle.

"Are we leaving now?" asked Noÿs of Harlan when they were alone.

"In a few minutes," said Harlan.

He glanced sideways at Noÿs. She was looking up at him, smiling, unfrightened. Momentarily his own spirits responded to that. But that was emotion, not reason, he counseled himself, instinct, not thought. He looked away.

The trip was nothing, or almost nothing; no different from an ordinary kettle ride. Midway there was a kind of internal jar that might have been the downwhen terminus and might have been purely psychosomatic. It was barely noticeable.

And then they were in the Primitive and they stepped into a craggy, lonely world brightened by the splendor of an afternoon sun. There was a soft wind with a chilly edge to it and, most of all, silence.

The bare rocks were tumbled and mighty, colored into dull rainbows by compounds of iron, copper, and chromium. The grandeur of the manless and all but lifeless surroundings dwarfed and shriveled Harlan. Eternity, which did not belong to the world of matter, had no sun and none but imported air. His memories of his own homewhen were dim. His Observations in the various Centuries had dealt with men and their cities. He had never experienced *this*.

Noÿs touched his elbow.

"Andrew! I'm cold."

He turned to her with a start.

She said, "Hadn't we better set up the Radiant?"

He said, "Yes. In Cooper's cavern."

"Do you know where it is?"

"It's right here," he said shortly.

He had no doubt of that. The memoir had located it and first Cooper, now he, had been pin-pointed back to it.

He had not doubted precision pin-pointing in Time-travel since his Cubhood days. He remembered himself then, facing Educator Yarrow seriously, saying, "But Earth moves about the Sun, and the Sun moves about the Galactic Center and the Galaxy moves too. If you start from some point on Earth, and move downwhen a hundred years, you'll be in empty space, because it will take a hundred years for Earth to reach that point." (Those were the days when he still referred to a Century as a "hundred years.")

And Educator Yarrow had snapped back, "You don't separate Time from space. Moving through Time, you share Earth's motions. Or do you believe that a bird flying through the air whiffs out into space because the Earth is hurrying around the Sun at eighteen miles a second and vanishes from under the creature?"

Arguing from analogy is risky, but Harlan obtained more rigorous proof in later days and, now, after a scarcely precedented trip into the Primitive, he could turn confidently and feel no surprise at finding the opening precisely where he had been told it would be.

He moved the camouflage of loose rubble and rock to one side and entered.

He probed the darkness within, using the white beam of his flash almost like a scalpel. He scoured the walls, ceiling, floor, every inch.

Noÿs, remaining close behind him, whispered, "What are you looking for?"

He said, "Something. Anything."

He found his something, anything, at the very rear of the cave in the shape of a flattish stone covering greenish sheets like a paperweight.

Harlan threw the stone aside and flipped the sheets past one thumb.

"What are they?" asked Noÿs.

"Bank notes. Medium of exchange. Money."

"Did you know they were there?"

"I knew nothing. I just hoped."

It was only a matter of using Twissell's reverse logic, of calculating cause from effect. Eternity existed, so Cooper must be making correct decisions too. In assuming the advertisement would pull Harlan into the correct Time, the cave was an obvious additional means of communication.

Yet this was almost better than he had dared hope. More than once during the preparations for his trip into the Primitive, Harlan had thought that making his way into a town with nothing but bullion in his possession would result in suspicion and delay.

Cooper had managed, to be sure, but Cooper had had time. Harlan hefted the sheaf of bills. And he must have used time to accumulate this much. He had done well, the youngster, marvelously well.

And the circle was closing!

The supplies had been moved into the cave, in the increasingly ruddy glow of the westering sun. The kettle had been covered by a diffuse reflecting film which would hide it from any but the closest of prying eyes, and Harlan had a blaster to take care of those, if need be. The Radiant was set up in the cave and the flash was wedged into a crevice, so that they had heat and light.

Outside it was a chill March night.

Noÿs stared thoughtfully into the smooth paraboloid interior of the Radiant as it slowly rotated. She said, "Andrew, what are your plans?"

"Tomorrow morning," he said, "I'll leave for the nearest town. I know where it is—or should be." (He changed it back to "is" in his mind. There would be no trouble. Twissell's logic again.)

"I'll come with you, won't I?"

He shook his head. "You can't speak the language, for one thing, and the trip will be difficult enough for one to negotiate."

Noÿs looked strangely archaic in her short hair and the sudden anger in her eyes made Harlan look away uneasily.

She said, "I'm no fool, Andrew. You scarcely speak to me. You don't look at me. What is it? Is your homewhen morality taking hold? Do you feel you have betrayed Eternity and are you blaming me for that? Do you feel I have corrupted you? What is it?"

He said, "You don't know what I feel."

She said, "Then describe it. You might as well. You'll never have a chance as good as this one. Do you feel love? For me? You couldn't or you wouldn't be using me as a scapegoat. Why did you bring me here? Tell me. Why not have left me in Eternity since you have no use for me here and since it seems you can hardly bear the sight of me?"

Harlan muttered, "There's danger."

"Oh, come now."

"It's more than danger. It's a nightmare. Computer Twissell's nightmare," said Harlan. "It was during our last panicky flash upwhen into the Hidden Centuries that he told me of thoughts he had had concerning those Centuries. He speculated on the possibility of evolved varieties of man, new species, supermen perhaps, hiding in the far upwhen, cutting themselves off from our interference, plotting to end our tamperings with Reality. He thought it was they who built the barrier across the 100,000th. Then we found you, and Computer Twissell abandoned his nightmare. He decided there had never been a barrier. He returned to the more immediate problem of salvaging Eternity.

"But I, you see, had been infected by his nightmare. I had experienced the barrier, so I knew it existed. No Eternal had built it, for Twissell said such a thing was theoretically impossible. Maybe Eternity's theories didn't go far enough. The barrier was there. Someone had built it. Or something.

"Of course," he went on thoughtfully, "Twissell was wrong in some ways. He felt that man *must* evolve, but that's not so. Paleontology is not one of the sciences that interest Eternals, but it interested the late Primitives, so I picked up a bit of it myself. I know this much: species evolve only to meet the pressures of new environments. In a stable environment, a species may remain unchanged for millions of Centuries. Primitive man evolved rapidly because his environment was a harsh and changing one. Once, however, mankind learned to create his own environment, he created a pleasant and stable one, so he just naturally stopped evolving."

"I don't know what you're talking about," said Noÿs, sounding not the least mollified, "and you're not saying anything about us, which is what I want to talk about."

Harlan managed to remain outwardly unmoved. He said, "Now why the barrier at the 100,000th? What purpose did it serve? You weren't harmed. What other meaning could it have? I asked myself: What happened because of its presence that would not have happened had it been absent?"

He paused, looking at his clumsy and heavy boots of natural leather. It occurred to him that he could add to his comfort by removing them for the night, but not now, not now . . .

He said, "There was only one answer to that question. The existence of that barrier sent me raving back downwhen to get a neuronic whip, to assault Finge. It fired me to the thought of risking Eternity to get you back and smashing Eternity when I thought I had failed. Do you see?"

Noÿs stared at him with a mixture of horror and disbelief. "Do you mean the people in the upwhen wanted you to do all that? They planned it?"

"*Yes.* Don't look at me like that. *Yes!* And don't you see how it makes everything different? As long as I acted on my own, for reasons of my own, I'll take all the consequences, material and spiritual. But to be *fooled* into it, to be *tricked* into it, by people handling and manipulating my emotions as though I were a Computaplex on which it was only necessary to insert the properly perforated foils—"

Harlan realized suddenly that he was shouting and stopped abruptly. He let a few moments pass, then said, "That is impossible to take. I've got to undo what I was marionetted into doing. And when I undo it, I will be able to rest again."

And he would—perhaps. He could feel the coming of an impersonal triumph, dissociated from the personal tragedy which lay behind and ahead. The circle was closing!

Noÿs's hand reached out uncertainly as though to take his own rigid, unyielding one.

Harlan drew away, avoided her sympathy. He said, "It had all been arranged. My meeting with you. Everything. My emotional make-up had been analyzed. Obviously. Action and response. Push this button and the man will do that. Push that button and he will do this."

Harlan was speaking with difficulty, out of the depths of shame. He shook his head, trying to shake the horror of it away as a dog would water, then went on. "One thing I didn't understand at first. How did I come to guess that Cooper was to be sent back into the Primitive? It was a most unlikely thing to guess. I had no basis. Twissell didn't understand it. More than once he wondered how I could have done it with so little understanding of mathematics.

"Yet I had. The first time was that—that night. You were asleep, but I wasn't. I had the feeling then that there was something I must remember; some remark, some thought, *something* that I had caught sight of in the excitement and exhilaration of the evening. When I thought long, the whole significance of Cooper sprang into my mind, and along with it the thought entered my mind that I was in a position to destroy Eternity. Later I checked through histories of mathematics, but it was unnecessary really. I already knew. I was certain of it. How? How?"

Noÿs stared at him intently. She didn't try to touch him now. "Do you mean the men of the Hidden Centuries arranged that, too? They put it all in your mind, then maneuvered you properly?"

"Yes. Yes. Nor are they done. There is still work for them to do. The circle may be closing, but it is not yet closed."

"How can they do anything now? They're not here with us."

"No?" He said the word in so hollow a voice that Noÿs paled.

"Invisible superthings?" she whispered.

"Not superthings. Not invisible. I told you man would not evolve while he controlled his own environment. The people of the Hidden Centuries are Homo sapiens. Ordinary people."

"Then they're certainly not here."

Harlan said sadly, "You're here, Noÿs."

"Yes. And you. And no one else."

"You and I," agreed Harlan. "No one else. A woman of the Hidden Centuries and I . . . Don't act any more, Noÿs. Please."

She stared at him with horror. "What are you saying, Andrew?"

"What I must say. What were *you* saying that evening, when you gave me the peppermint drink? You were talking to me. Your soft voice—soft words . . . I heard nothing, not consciously, but I remember your delicate voice whispering. About what? The downwhen journey of Cooper; the Samson-smash of Eternity. Am I right?"

Noÿs said, "I don't even know what Samson-smash means."

"You can guess very accurately, Noÿs. Tell me, when did you enter the 482nd? Whom did you replace? Or did you just—squeeze in. I had your Life-Plot worked out by an expert in the 2456th. In the new Reality, you had no existence at all. No analogue. Strange for such a small Change, but not impossible. And then the Life-Plotter said one thing which I heard with my ears but not with my mind. Strange that I should remember it. Perhaps even then, something clanged in my mind, but I was too full of—you to listen. He said: *'with the combination of factors you handed me, I don't quite see how she fit in the old Reality.'*

"He was right. You didn't fit in. You were an invader from the far upwhen, manipulating me and Finge, too, to suit yourself."

Noÿs said urgently, "Andrew——"

"It all fit in, if I had the eyes to look. A book-film in your house entitled *Social and Economic History*. It surprised me when first I saw it. You needed it, didn't you, to teach you how best to be a woman of the Century. Another item. Our first trip into the Hidden Centuries, remember? *You* stopped the kettle at the 111,394th. You stopped it with finesse, without fumbling. Where did you learn to control a kettle? If you were what you seemed to be, that would have been your first trip in a kettle. Why the 111,394th, anyway? Was it your homewhen?"

She said softly, "Why did you bring me to the Primitive, Andrew?"

He shouted suddenly, "To protect Eternity. I could not tell what damage you might do there. Here, you are helpless, because I know you. Admit that all I say is true! Admit it!"

He rose in a paroxysm of wrath, arm upraised. She did not flinch. She was utterly calm. She might have been modeled out of warm, beautiful wax. Harlan did not complete his motion.

He said, "Admit it!"

She said, "Are you so uncertain, after all your deductions? What will it matter to you whether I admit it or not?"

Harlan felt the wildness mount. "Admit it, anyway, so that I need feel no pain at all. None at all."

"Pain?"

"Because I have a blaster, Noÿs, and it is my intention to kill you."

THE BEGINNING
OF INFINITY

— 18 —

THERE WAS a crawling uncertainty inside Harlan, an irresolution that was consuming him. He had the blaster in his hand. It was aimed at Noÿs.

But why did she say nothing? Why did she persist in this impassive attitude?

How could he kill her?

How could he not kill her?

He said hoarsely, "Well?"

She moved, but it was only to clasp her hands loosely in her lap, to look more relaxed, more aloof. When she spoke her voice seemed scarcely that of a human being. Facing the muzzle of a blaster, it yet gained assurance and took on an almost mystic quality of impersonal strength.

She said, "You cannot wish to kill me only in order to protect Eternity. If that were your desire, you could stun me, tie me firmly, pin me within this cave and then take to your travels in the dawn. Or you might have asked Computer Twissell to keep me in solitary confinement during your absence in the Primitive. Or you might take me with you at dawn, lose me in the wastes. If it is only killing that will satisfy you, it is only because you think that I have betrayed you, that I have tricked you into love first in order that I might trick you into treason later. This is murder out of wounded pride and not at all the just retribution you tell yourself it is."

Harlan squirmed. "Are you from the Hidden Centuries? Tell me."

Noÿs said, "I am. Will you now blast?"

Harlan's finger trembled on the blaster's contact point. Yet he hesitated. Something irrational within him could still plead her case and point up the remnants of his own futile love and longing. Was she desperate at his rejection of her? Was she deliberately courting death by lying? Was she indulging in foolish heroics born of despair at his doubts of her?

No!

The book-films of the sickly-sweet literary tradition of the 289th might have it so, but not a girl like Noÿs. She was not one to meet her death at the hands of a false lover with the joyful masochism of a broken, bleeding lily.

Then was she scornfully denying his ability to kill her for any reason whatever? Was she confidently relying on the attraction she knew she had for him even now, certain that it would immobilize him, freeze him in weakness and shame.

That hit too closely. His finger clamped a bit harder on the contact.

Noÿs spoke again. "You're waiting. Does that mean you expect me to enter a brief for the defense?"

"What defense?" Harlan tried to make that scornful, yet he welcomed the diversion. It could postpone the moment when he must look down upon her blasted body, upon whatever remnants of bloody flesh might remain, and know that what had been done to his beautiful Noÿs had been done by his own hand.

He found excuses for his delay. He thought feverishly: Let her talk. Let her tell what she can about the Hidden Centuries. So much better protection for Eternity.

It put a front of firm policy on his action and for the moment he could look at her with as calm a face, almost, as she looked at him.

Noÿs might have read his mind. She said, "Do you want to know about the Hidden Centuries? If that will be a defense, it is easily done. Would you like to know, for instance, why Earth is empty of mankind after the 150,000th? Would you be interested?"

Harlan wasn't going to plead for knowledge, nor was he going to buy knowledge. He had the blaster. He was very intent on no show of weakness.

He said, "Talk!" and flushed at the little smile which was her first response to his exclamation.

She said, "At a moment in physiotime before Eternity had reached very far upwhen, before it had reached even the 10,000th, we of our Century—and you're right, it was the 111,394th—learned of Eternity's existence. We, too, had Time-travel, you see, but it was based on a completely different set of postulates than yours, and we preferred to view Time, rather than shifting mass. Furthermore, we dealt with our past only, our downwhen.

"We discovered Eternity indirectly. First, we developed the calculus of

Realities and tested our own Reality through it. We were amazed to find we lived in a Reality of rather low probability. It was a serious question. Why such an improbable Reality? . . . You seem abstracted, Andrew! Are you interested at all?''

Harlan heard her say his name with all the intimate tenderness she had used in weeks past. It should grate on him now, anger him with its cynical faithlessness. And yet it didn't.

He said desperately, "Go on and get it over with, woman."

He tried to balance the warmth of her "Andrew" with the chill anger of his "woman" and yet she only smiled again, pallidly.

She said, "We searched back through time and came across the growing Eternity. It seemed obvious to us almost at once that there had been at one point in physiotime (a conception we have also, but under another name) another Reality. The other Reality, the one of maximum probability we call the Basic State. The Basic State had encompassed us once, or had encompassed our analogues, at least. At the time we could not say what the nature of the Basic State was. We could not possibly know.

"We did know, however, that some Change initiated by Eternity in the far downwhen had managed, through the workings of statistical chance, to alter the Basic State all the way up to our Century and beyond. We set about determining the nature of the Basic State, intending to undo the evil, if evil it was. First we set up the quarantine area you call the Hidden Centuries, isolating the Eternals on the downwhen side of the 70,000th. This armor of isolation would protect us from all but a vanishingly small percentage of the Changes being made. It wasn't absolute security but it gave us time.

"We next did something our culture and ethics did not ordinarily allow us to do. We investigated our own future, our upwhen. We learned the destiny of man in the Reality that actually existed in order that we might compare it eventually with Basic State. Somewhere past the 125,000th, mankind solved the secret of the interstellar drive. They learned how to manage the Jump through hyperspace. Finally, mankind could reach the stars."

Harlan was listening in growing absorption to her measured words. How much truth was there in all this? How much was a calculated attempt to deceive him? He tried to break the spell by speaking, by breaking the smooth flow of her sentences. He said:

"And once they could reach the stars, they did so and left the Earth. Some of us have guessed that."

"Then some of you have guessed wrong. Man *tried* to leave Earth. Unfortunately, however, we are not alone in the Galaxy. There are other stars with other planets, you know. There are even other intelligences. None, in this Galaxy at least, are as ancient as mankind, but in the 125,000 Centuries man remained on Earth, younger minds caught up and passed us, developed the interstellar drive, and colonized the Galaxy.

"When we moved out into space, the signs were up. *Occupied! No Trespassing! Clear Out!* Mankind drew back its exploratory feelers, remained at home. But now he knew Earth for what it was: a prison surrounded by an infinity of freedom . . . And mankind died out!"

Harlan said, "Just died out. Nonsense."

"They didn't *just* die out. It took thousands of Centuries. There were ups and downs but, on the whole, there was a loss of purpose, a sense of futility, a feeling of hopelessness that could not be overcome. Eventually there was one last decline of the birth rate and finally, extinction. Your Eternity did that.''

Harlan could defend Eternity now, the more intensely and extravagantly for having so shortly before attacked it so keenly. He said, "Let us at the Hidden Centuries and we will correct that. We have not failed yet to achieve the greatest good in those Centuries we could reach.''

"The greatest good?'' asked Noÿs in a detached tone that seemed to make a mockery of the phrase. "What is that? Your machines tell you. Your Computaplexes. But who adjusts the machines and tells them what to weigh in the balance? The machines do not solve problems with greater insight than men do, only faster. Only faster! Then what is it the Eternals consider good? I'll tell you. Safety and security. Moderation. Nothing in excess. No risks without overwhelming certainty of an adequate return.''

Harlan swallowed. With sudden force he remembered Twissell's words in the kettle while talking about the evolved men of the Hidden Centuries. He said: *"We bred out the unusual.''*

And wasn't it so?

"Well,'' said Noÿs, "you seem to be thinking. Think of this, then. In the Reality that now exists, why is it that man is continually attempting space-travel and continually failing? Surely each space-travel era must know of previous failures. Why try again, then?''

Harlan said, "I haven't studied the matter.'' But he thought uneasily of the colonies on Mars, established again and again, always failing. He thought of the odd attraction that space-flight always had, even for Eternals. He could hear Sociologist Kantor Voy of the 2456th, sighing at the loss of electro-gravitic spaceflight in one Century, and saying longingly: *"It had been very beautiful.''* And Life-Plotter Neron Feruque, who had sworn bitterly at its passing and had launched into a fit of railing at Eternity's handling of anti-cancer serums to ease his spirit.

Was there such a thing as an instinctive yearning on the part of intelligent beings to expand outward, to reach the stars, to leave the prison of gravity behind? Was it that which forced man to develop interplanetary travel dozens of times, forced him to travel over and over again to the dead worlds of a solar system in which only Earth was livable? Was it the eventual failure, the knowledge that one must return to the home prison, that brought about the maladjustments that Eternity was forever fighting. Harlan thought of the drug addiction in those same futile Centuries of the electrogravitics.

Noÿs said, "In ironing out the disasters of Reality, Eternity rules out the triumphs as well. It is in meeting the great tests that mankind can most successfully rise to great heights. Out of danger and restless insecurity comes the force that pushes mankind to newer and loftier conquests. Can you understand that? Can you understand that in averting the pitfalls and miseries that beset man, Eternity prevents men from finding their own bitter and better solutions, the real solutions that come from conquering difficulty, not avoiding it.''

Harlan began woodenly, "The greatest good of the greatest number——''

Noÿs cut in. "Suppose Eternity had never been established?''

"Well?''

"I'll tell you what would have happened. The energies that went into temporal engineering would have gone into nucleonics instead. Eternity would not have come but the interstellar drive would. Man would have reached the stars more than a hundred thousand Centuries before he did in this current Reality. The stars would then have been untenanted and mankind would have established itself throughout the Galaxy. *We* would have been first.''

''And what would have been gained?'' asked Harlan doggedly. ''Would we be happier?''

''Whom do you mean by 'we'? Man would not be a world but a million worlds, a billion worlds. We would have the infinite in our grasp. Each world would have its own stretch of the Centuries, each its own values, a chance to seek happiness after ways of its own in an environment of its own. There are many happinesses, many goods, infinite variety. . . . *That* is the Basic State of mankind.''

''You're guessing,'' said Harlan, and he was angry at himself for feeling attraction for the picture she had conjured. ''How can you tell what would have happened?''

Noÿs said, ''You smile at the ignorance of the Timers who know only one Reality. We smile at the ignorance of the Eternals who think there are many Realities but that only one exists at a time.''

''What does that gibberish mean?''

''We don't calculate alternate Realities. We view them. We see them in their state of non-Reality.''

''A kind of ghostly never-never land where the might-have-beens play with the ifs.''

''Without the sarcasm, yes.''

''And how do you do that?''

Noÿs paused, then said, ''How can I explain that, Andrew? I have been educated to know certain things without really understanding all about them, just as you have. Can you explain the workings of a Computaplex? Yet you know it exists and works.''

Harlan flushed. ''Well, then?''

Noÿs said, ''We learned to view Realities and we found Basic State to be as I have described. We found, too, the Change that had destroyed Basic State. It was not any Change that Eternity had initiated; it was the establishment of Eternity itself—the mere fact of its existence. Any system like Eternity, which allows men to choose their own future, will end by choosing safety and mediocrity, and in such a Reality the stars are out of reach. The mere existence of Eternity at once wiped out the Galactic Empire. To restore it, Eternity must be done away with.

''The number of Realities is infinite. The number of any subclass of Realities is also infinite. For instance, the number of Realities containing Eternity is infinite; the number in which Eternity does not exist is infinite; the number in which Eternity does exist but is abolished is also infinite. But my people chose from among the infinite a group that involved me.

''I had nothing to do with that. They educated me for my job as Twissell and yourself educated Cooper for his job. But the number of Realities in which I was the agent in destroying Eternity was also infinite. I was offered a choice among five Realities that seemed least complex. I chose this one, the one involving you, the only Reality system involving you.''

Harlan said, ''Why did you choose it?''

Noÿs looked away. ''Because I loved you, you see. I loved you long before I met you.''

Harlan was shaken. She said it with such depths of sincerity. He thought, sickly: She's an actress——

He said, "That's rather ridiculous."

"Is it? I studied the Realities at my disposal. I studied the Reality in which I went back to the 482nd, met first Finge, then you. The one in which you came to me and loved me, in which you took me into Eternity and the far upwhen of my own Century, in which you misdirected Cooper, and in which you and I, together, returned to the Primitive. We lived in the Primitive for the rest of our days. I saw our lives together and they were happy and I loved you. So it's not ridiculous at all. I chose this alternative so that our love might be true."

Harlan said, "All this is false. It's false. How can you expect me to believe you?" He stopped, then said suddenly, "Wait! You say you knew all this in advance? All that would happen?"

"Yes."

"Then you're obviously lying. You would have known that I would have you here at blaster point. You would have known you would fail. What is your answer to that?"

She sighed lightly. "I told you there are an infinite number of any subclass of Realities. No matter how finely we focus on a given Reality it always represents an infinite number of very similar Realities. There are fuzzy spots. The finer we focus, the less fuzzy, but perfect sharpness cannot be obtained. The less fuzzy, the lower the probability of chance variation spoiling the result, but the probability is never absolutely zero. One fuzzy spot spoiled things."

"Which?"

"You were to have come back to the far upwhen after the barrier at the 100,000th had been lowered and you did. But you were to have come back alone. It is for that reason that I was momentarily so startled at seeing Computer Twissell with you."

Again Harlan was troubled. How she made things fit in!

Noÿs said, "I would have been even more startled, had I realized the significance of that alteration in full. Had you come alone, you would have brought me back to the Primitive as you did. Then, for love of humanity, for love of me, you would have left Cooper untouched. Your circle would have been broken, Eternity ended, our life together here safe.

"But you came with Twissell, a chance variation. While coming, he talked to you of his thoughts about the Hidden Centuries and started you on a train of deductions that ended with your doubting *my* good faith. It ended with a blaster between us. . . . And now, Andrew, that's the story. You may blast me. There is nothing to stop you."

Harlan's hand ached from its spastic grip on the blaster. He shifted it dizzily to the other hand. Was there no flaw in her story? Where was the resolution he was to have gained from knowing certainly that she was a creature of the Hidden Centuries? He was more than ever tearing at himself in conflict, and dawn was approaching.

He said, "Why two efforts to end Eternity? Why couldn't Eternity have ended once and for all when I sent Cooper back to the 20th? Things would have ended then and there would not have been this agony of uncertainty."

"Because," said Noÿs, "ending this Eternity is not enough. We must reduce the probability of establishing any form of Eternity to as near zero as we can manage. So there is one thing we must do here in the Primitive. A small Change, a little thing. You know what a Minimum Necessary Change is like. It is only a letter to a peninsula called Italy here in the 20th. It is now the 19.32nd. In a few Centicenturies, provided I send the letter, a man of Italy will begin experimenting with the neutronic bombardment of uranium.''

Harlan found himself horrified. ''You will alter Primitive history?''

''Yes. It is our intention. In the new Reality, the final Reality, the first nuclear explosion will take place not in the 30th Century but in the 19.45th.''

''But do you know the danger? Can you possibly estimate the danger?''

''We know the danger. We have viewed the sheaf of resulting Realities. There is a probability, not a certainty, of course, that Earth will end with a largely radioactive crust, but before that——''

''You mean there can be compensation for that?''

''A Galactic Empire. An actual intensification of the Basic State.''

''Yet you accuse the Eternals of interfering——''

''We accuse them of interfering many times to keep mankind safely at home and in prison. We interefere, once, *once,* to turn him prematurely to nucleonics so that he might never, *never,* establish an Eternity.''

''No,'' said Harlan desperately. ''There must be an Eternity.''

''If you choose. It is yours to choose. If you wish to have psychopaths dictate the future of man——''

''*Psychopaths!*'' exploded Harlan.

''Aren't they? You know them. Think!''

Harlan stared at her in outraged horror, yet he could not help thinking. He thought of Cubs learning the truth about Reality and Cub Latourette trying to kill himself as a result. Latourette had survived to become an Eternal with what scars on his personality none could say, yet helping to decide on alternate Realities.

He thought of the caste system in Eternity, of the abnormal life that turned guilt feelings into anger and hatred against Technicians. He thought of Computers, struggling against themselves, of Finge intriguing against Twissell and Twissell spying on Finge. He thought of Sennor, fighting his bald head by fighting all the Eternals.

He thought of himself.

Then he thought of Twissell, the great Twissell, also breaking the laws of Eternity.

It was as though he had always known Eternity to be all this. Why else should he have been so willing to destroy it? Yet he had never admitted it to himself fully; he had never looked it clearly in the face, until, suddenly, now.

And he saw Eternity with great clarity as a sink of deepening psychoses, a writhing pit of abnormal motivation, a mass of desperate lives torn brutally out of context.

He looked blankly at Noÿs.

She said softly, ''Do you see? Come to the mouth of the cave with me, Andrew.''

He followed her, hypnotized, appalled at the completeness with which he had gained a new viewpoint. His blaster fell away from the line connecting it and Noÿs's heart for the first time.

* * *

The pale streakings of dawn grayed the sky, and the bulking kettle just outside the cave was an oppressive shadow against the pallor. Its outlines were dulled and blurred by the film thrown over it.

Noÿs said, "This is Earth. Not the eternal and only home of mankind, but only a starting point of an infinite adventure. All you need do is make the decision. It is yours to make. You and I and the contents of this cave will be protected by a physiotime field against the Change. Cooper will disappear along with his advertisement; Eternity will go and the Reality of my Century, but *we* will remain to have children and grandchildren, and mankind will remain to reach the stars."

He turned to look at her, and she was smiling at him. It was Noÿs as she had been, and his own heart beating as it had used to.

He wasn't even aware that he had made his decision until the grayness suddenly invaded all the sky as the hulk of the kettle disappeared from against it.

With that disappearance, he knew, even as Noÿs moved slowly into his arms, came the end, the final end of Eternity.

—And the beginning of Infinity.